LIE TO ME

CHLOE COX

Copyright © 2013 Chloe Cox

All rights reserved.

ISBN: 1493670417
ISBN-13: 978-1493670413

DEDICATION

To anyone who ever gave me a book.

CONTENTS

Acknoweldgements

chapter 1	1
chapter 2	14
chapter 3	26
chapter 4	44
chapter 5	57
chapter 6	66
chapter 7	79
chapter 8	96
chapter 9	102
chapter 10	118
chapter 11	131
chapter 12	156
chapter 13	171
chapter 14	187
chapter 15	202
chapter 16	213
chapter 17	229
chapter 18	245
chapter 19	261
chapter 20	270

| chapter 21 | 279 |
| epilogue | 289 |

ACKNOWLEDGMENTS

A giant, enormous thank you to my family, because, well, they put up with me when I'm writing. I honestly don't know how you do it, but I'm very lucky that you do. I love you.

Another giant thank you to Alicia and Danielle, for also putting up with me when I'm writing and when I'm losing my mind because of it. You are both amazing friends, and I know exactly how lucky I am to have you both in my life.

A big thank you to Liz at Sinfully Sexy Book Reviews for all her hard work and hand holding while we set up that blog tour, and also for just being generally awesome and fun to email with at all hours of the night. And finally, thank you Ann Marie, for that last minute beta read!

And finally, a big thank you to the real life Shantha, for being an amazing person.

I am very grateful to all of you.

1

HARLOW

So here's the thing: most people don't think. And I'm not saying that's a bad thing—far from it. But it's true. Most people, like the small group of commuters emerging out from under an awning about a block ahead of me, all huddled together in the rain waiting for the B39 bus to roll to a stop; I'd bet not one of them is thinking about how easy it would be for the bus driver's foot to slip and hit the gas instead of the brake. Jump the curb, skid in the rain, ruin a few lives.

I hate that I even thought it. I'm running as fast as I can to catch the Death Bus, and this is what I think about? No wonder most people don't live this way.

Because why would you, if you didn't have to? Why would you think about how fragile you are, about how little connects you to this physical world, and to the people in it that you love? How it can all just shatter in a moment. I mean, this is some emo crap right here, and it annoys even me. It's just that I'm stuck with it. Believe me, I wouldn't think like this if life hadn't interfered and turned me into the kind of person who can't help it.

I try to be the old me whenever I can.

It's not usually this bad. Usually I've got a handle on it. I mean, I have to: I've got my brother, Dill. The little man is almost eleven and does not need my craziness making his life any weirder. He's already got enough of that going on. So no one needs to know how often I check that the front door is locked, or how I have a living will just in case, or how many times a day I ask myself 'what if?'—least of all Dill, who is already convinced that his big sister / guardian / general meddler is more than a little embarrassing.

But today? Today, while I'm trying to navigate through the rain on the Lower East Side, looking for a second bartending job just in case Shantha's place back in Brooklyn really does get swallowed up in the latest real estate development deal, I get a phone call. Already I was kind of stressed because my custody of Dill is always a tenuous thing, and suddenly becoming unemployed would *not* endear me to the family court, and then the universe—that asshole again—is like, nope, you are not stressed out enough, here, let me make your phone ring.

It was my neighbor, Maria. She watches Dill for me. She was just calling to tell me that Mr. Wolfe had come by to see me.

"Mr. Wolfe?"

"Yes," she whispered.

"Oh Jesus, Maria, is he still there?"

"Yes!" she said again. "In the living room, with Dill. He's waiting for you. They're playing Dill's game."

Fantastic. So I found out that Dill is hanging out with Mr. Wolfe, showing him the latest version of the computer game that Dill's been working on. Like hanging out with Mr. Wolfe is a normal thing. Like that couldn't possibly end badly.

Strictly speaking, there is nothing about Mr. Wolfe that should be frightening. And there isn't. Kind of. Except that there are a few things I know about Mr. Wolfe that I am not supposed to know, and the man is one of those old time neighborhood fixtures who has money even though nobody knows exactly what he does for a living, and who, somehow, everybody knows. And who everybody owes.

Including me.

I was already anxious to get home. Now I'm just wishing I had the ability to teleport, rather than have to fight through the rain and the crush of commuters and the sea of yellow cabs rushing together in the tight, old streets of the Lower East Side.

The other thing about Mr. Wolfe is that he makes me think about those things that I know that I'm not supposed to know. And thus he makes me think about the man who told them to me.

Marcus Roma.

When I met Marcus, he was Mr. Wolfe's godson, and yet he is so much more than that. Thinking about Marcus makes it very, very difficult to be my old, happy self. Because Marcus is the man who made me into that old self, who lifted me up from the worst thing that had ever happened to me—right before he ruined me.

I shake it off, like I'm trying to shake off the rain under my crappy umbrella. The bus is stuck in traffic just shy of the stop now, and if the light turns I'll make it, no problem at all. There are enough people waiting that there'll be a line, so I'll have enough time, even if it means standing out in the rain some more. I'm already soaked anyway. Converse and skinny jeans are not the most waterproof combination in the world.

I weave between the stalled traffic, silently grateful for the delivery truck that just decided to stop in the middle of the street, and jog toward the rapidly forming line to get on the bus. Thirty minutes and I'll be home. Thirty minutes until I absolutely have to think about Mr. Wolfe and how I'm sure he's going to demand that I sell my parents' house to the developers, along with the half of the neighborhood that already has sold out, and how I'm going to have to tell him no, even though I owe Mr. Wolfe everything. Just, everything.

I mean, I owe him Dill.

So screw that misery. I've got thirty minutes. I decide to try to be my old self for those thirty minutes. To try to be the best version of me, before I got my heart broken twice over, before I lost everything, twice; it's the person I want to be for Dill. Happy, silly, joyful.

I look around rather grimly for sources of joy, and this alone makes me laugh, because way to force it, right? Joy through grim determination—sounds legit. The weird thing is that this is a game I invented. I invented it, and I taught it to Marcus Roma, when we first met. And then when I forgot how to find joy in the world after the accident, he taught it back to me all over again. But that is ancient history, and I am trying very hard not to have a brain full of Marcus Roma or Mr. Wolfe right now.

In the end I don't have to look very far, because right ahead of me in line for the bus is a mom and her little girl. The girl is maybe three, four? Decked out in a pink raincoat with yellow flowers on it and matching pink rain boots, and she is just having a ball. Like, seriously going to town on those puddles while the line for the bus inches ever forward, dancing around and laughing every time the water splashes up on her pink boots. She's trying to see how much she can get it to splash, and cackling madly every time she gets it a little higher.

I grin like a loon and time it just right, jumping into the big puddle between us just as she lands, giving her an epic splash. She just stands there, frozen, for a second, looking up at me with big eyes, and then she squeals and claps her hands.

Ok, so that is joy. I will take a lesson from a little kid any day of the week.

Now I'm laughing, too, and even her tired looking mom has cracked a smile. The little girl takes me to school again by tilting her head, squinting up at the sky, and sticking her little tongue out to catch some rain drops. Technically this probably isn't a good idea, what with rainwater actually being kind of gross and all, but whatever. It's an awesome idea. I decide to join her.

Like a proper grown up (which is kind of laughable, really), I tilt my cheap umbrella to the side and put my head back and my arms out, as if I can catch more rain drops this way. Together we spin a little, slow motion dervishes moving up the line toward the B39 bus, and I can feel that old sense of gratitude flowing through me. Yes, the universe is an asshole, and everything can shatter in a moment, but there's also kids laughing and catching raindrops on your tongue. Sometimes it evens out. I decide that I'll take Dill out to play in the rain, if he feels like going, just as soon as we get rid of Mr. Wolfe.

It's then that a gust of wind catches my umbrella and rips it out of my hand. I snap my head up, worried it could hit the little girl. She's clear of it and it's fine, but it's just instinct to chase after it. That must be what it is. I mean, it's a cheap umbrella, and when it rains you can find guys selling those same cheap umbrellas for like five dollars on every other corner in Manhattan, and even the busier corners in the outer boroughs. So it's just stupid instinct, not rational thought, that makes me leave my place in line and chase after it.

Somebody's already got it.

Somebody's already picked it up.

A man in a dark raincoat and a hat, a tall man, broad shouldered, a man I feel like I know even before he straightens up and looks at me—through me—with those pale gray and green eyes.

Marcus Roma.

I stop. Just stand there, in the rain, blinking. It can't be real. It can't be him. It's been five years since he dropped out of my life with no warning, no real explanation, five years since he just left. He's different now, different enough that it can't be a dream, a hallucination. His black hair is longer, peeking out from under the brim of that hat, the scruff on his jaw darker. Rougher. His skin is the same golden bronze, his eyes still light like beacons. Like a hypnotist's trick. He seems taller, but I know that doesn't make sense. Maybe it's the suit. In a million years I never would have put Marcus Roma in a suit. Even with that fighter's body underneath it.

God, he looks amazing.

"Harlow," he says. He chokes on my name.

That breaks the spell.

This is real. This is the man who broke me. This is the man who kept me going during the darkest time of my life and then disappeared.

This is the man who made me.

And I hate him.

I force myself to move, to jump back. I can already feel the pull of him on me and I know, I know that I am weak and that if I stay here I will get sucked back in. And inevitably I will be destroyed. And I can't. I can't afford to be weak anymore. I can't afford to indulge in what-ifs, to even take a turn to yell at the man who broke my heart like nothing, like no one else ever could have broken it. Because I have Dill now. It's not just about me.

Marcus steps forward, says my name again. I turn, see the bus ahead of me, the last person in line stepping up into it, and I just run. I don't think, I don't speak, I just sprint.

I was always fast off the block.

I hear him shouting my name and I run away from it as fast as I can, like it's a deadly siren's call, like it represents a black pit of emotional fuckery from which I just know I will never emerge. I barely got out five years ago, when he left, and I definitely wasn't the same afterwards. I can't do it again.

I just barely make the bus, jumping on and catching a side eye from the bus driver as he pulls the lever to close the doors. The finality of that sound — that distinctive whoosh of a bus door closing behind me — is the most comforting thing I've heard in a long time.

I stand there, swaying, digging for my Metrocard as the bus finally begins to pull away from the curb. The light ahead on Delancey Street is green, and beyond that is the long expanse of the Williamsburg Bridge. My heart is thudding against my ribcage, each beat threatening to crack the thin veneer of stability I have erected around me and let it all out: all the tears, the heartbreak, the grief. The loneliness. The lust. I just manage to swipe my Metrocard, catching myself on the handrail as the bus lurches ahead, when I hear it.

Marcus pounding on the bus door.

I don't know why, but I turn to watch him. Everybody else thinks he's just a guy who missed the bus in the rain, who knows he can't catch a cab when the weather's like this, who's pissed he's going to have to wait to get across the bridge.

But I know he's chasing me.

That Marcus Roma, for once, is the one chasing me.

Now, from inside this bus, from the other side of what might as well be an impenetrable barrier, I can look at him. I can look at him run after me, a look of desperation on his face that I've only ever seen once or twice, and only when he didn't know how to help me. Marcus Roma raw is too much for me to handle right now. Maybe ever again. No one else has ever seen through me like Marcus, no one else has ever stripped me of all pretense. It was always intoxicating. It was always a rush.

It always made me so very, very vulnerable. Once it made me strong, too. Now?

Now it would just make it all that easier to fall.

But would it? And here is where I really start to drive myself crazy, in the seconds when I'm watching Marcus run in the rain, falling farther behind the bus with every step. Because now that I'm not standing in front of him, exposed to those eyes, I'm thinking, Maybe this is actually what I need.

Maybe I need to yell at him. Maybe an explanation would end it. Maybe it would exorcise the ghost of Marcus Roma from my life once and for all and I could move on.

Or maybe this is just my body making rationalizations for what it wants. Which is Marcus.

It's shocking to me, after everything I've been through, to feel this way again, to feel actual physical need. But the sight of Marcus does it. Five years, and I've never forgotten the feel of his hands on my body.

My throat tightens up and my mouth goes dry. We're on the bridge. Marcus is far behind us. The rain slams into the big, broad windshield of the bus as we speed toward Brooklyn, and I'm thinking about how I just ran. I never used to run. That's not what I do. I'm a fighter.

Marcus taught me that.

I fought my way through after my parents died in the accident, with Marcus's help. I fought for Dill. I fought for myself. And I just ran from Marcus, because I wasn't sure I could fight…

What?

I'm kidding myself. I know what. I know what I felt for him, what I never stopped feeling, even after he was gone: no man has ever made me feel like that. Like he could turn me molten with just a look. Like I could drown in him, like I wanted to drown in him. Like I loved him so much that everything else faded away, like I could live on that feeling alone, burning bright and beautiful in the dark of my wounded heart.

I've thought about what it felt like to have Marcus Roma touch me so many times. What it was like to have him inside me. Even after he abandoned me without any explanation, even after he broke me, even after he did all that knowing exactly what it would do to me, he's still the only man I've ever dreamed of. I tried with other men for a while, and every time I was painfully aware of how much they were not Marcus.

Fuck him for that. Seriously.

I'm angry and overwhelmed and I'm feeling way too many things in a short period of time, like all the joy, rage, loss, grief, and lust of those years is condensed into this one moment on a public bus, speeding across the Williamsburg Bridge, and I just can't shut down my brain. I can't stop myself from asking what if? What if I don't see him again? What if he just doesn't care to try again? What if this is it?

What if this is the last time I see him, and I've run away?

Great. I get to add shame to the mix of emo crap I've got brewing inside me. I feel like I'm going to be sick. Apparently it's noticeable, because a guy sitting up front actually gets up and offers me his seat. You have to be very pregnant or very old or, apparently, very much on the verge of totally losing your shit in public to get that offer.

I say thanks, but no thanks. I grip the handrail harder. I need to feel myself grounded to the physical earth, not resting on a seat, mind free to wander and think about all the what-ifs. About how, if I'm truly honest, for that one second when I locked eyes with him, I felt like I did back in the old days. Like I wasn't alone in the world. Like I was safe. Just because he could see me and I could see him.

And if there's one thing I still need, almost more than I need my next breath, it's to feel like I'm not alone in the world.

Except that I am, and I have been, since Marcus left. Maybe when Dill is older I won't feel like that, but right now I'm all Dill has, and I have to stay strong and sane. Which means no chasing after the man who made me this way, or letting him chase after me, or indulging in any of that hopeful bullshit that is sure to get my heart broken all over again.

So it's done. He's gone. Probably he won't try to contact me or anything, because it was just a chance encounter, and now it's over. That is a very good thing.

So why am I hyperventilating? Why is my palm sliding down the handrail, slick with sweat?

Why do I feel nauseous when I think, *It's over*.

People are still looking at me. I'm soaking wet, my blonde hair plastered to my head, my leather jacket beaded with rain. I can feel that my lips are blue. The bus is slowing down, running into traffic on the other end of the bridge, and I think this is good. This will give me some time to get myself together, to get my head right before I have to go home and see Mr. Wolfe.

And then it hits me. Mr. Wolfe. Marcus.

Both back in town at the same time.

That can't be a coincidence.

I think that, and relief blossoms in me. Because Marcus isn't here for me. It's not about me; it never was. Marcus left to go work for Mr. Wolfe, and he's still working for him, and that's why he's here. So even if I'd decided that getting some kind of closure, or an explanation, or whatever was a good idea, it's not like I'd get it. I just dodged a major, major bullet, because I can't ever be in a position where I want more from Marcus than he wants from me.

This is what I tell myself while the bus lurches toward the other end of the bridge. This was a lucky escape. Good job, running away.

I have to tell myself this over and over and over again.

So by the time the bus slows to a stop in Williamsburg, I've calmed down slightly. Figuring out that Marcus still doesn't give a crap is somehow liberating, I guess because it's a familiar kind of pain. Like, this I know how to deal with, if only because I've had a lot of practice. It was just the shock of seeing him that put me off balance. I'm over it now.

I'm totally, totally over it.

I climb down the stairs, out of the bus, almost expecting to see, like, sunshine and bluebirds and whatever else — that's how liberating that thought feels. Marcus is across the river, on a different island entirely, and out of my life, and if I can just avoid him from here on out, I will only have the real estate developers and Mr. Wolfe to deal with.

So, no worse than things were when I got up this morning.

I'm expecting the clouds to part and the sun to shine, but obviously it's still raining. That's ok, too. I let it wash over me, imagining the relief I've convinced myself I'm supposed to feel, trying to let it flow through me all over again before I walk home in the rain, umbrella-less.

I close my eyes, turn my face up to the sky.

When I open them again, I see Marcus.

Standing tall, breathing hard, his black hair wet with rain. Hat gone. Coat open, white dress shirt soaked through, his pecs and abs contracting with every strained breath. Pale gray green eyes on fire.

"Harlow," he chokes out.

He's still holding my umbrella.

He ran. He chased me across the bridge. He beat a bus, across the bridge.

To catch me.

He's panting still, out of breath, and now it's like he's stolen mine, too. He takes another step toward me and this time I can't look away. His eyes have me. It's the same, the same as it always was, only different, now, too: more. There's all those years, all those shared memories flying between us, swirling around in an invisible field that I know we both feel, all those things that we know about each other that no one else will ever really, truly know, no matter how much we might want to tell them, because they weren't there. It was just us. Just Marcus and me.

And those eyes, seeing through me.

And now there's what's different about it, too. What's changed. How I can't ignore the man he's become. Jesus God, no one could ignore that. Can he see through that, too? Can he see me watch his body move, watch how he brushes that black hair out of his eyes, how the rain is caught on those long eyelashes? How when he licks his lips, moving toward me, I'm transfixed?

The thing between us is alive, I swear to God. All that history, all those memories, and now this, this unique awareness of the physical man in front of me, and the way my traitorous body responds: it's a living thing, whipping between us, drawing us closer, something blind and stupid, fierce and feral. It's choking me, making it hard to see straight, to remember all the reasons I have to be afraid for my heart. All I can see is that strong jaw, those huge shoulders, that tie dancing in the wind, water dripping down his face while he looks at me with those beautiful, sad eyes…

No single human being has ever hurt me the way Marcus Roma has, and now he's back. And I don't want him to leave. And that will be my downfall.

If I let it.

"What are you doing?" I whisper. It's all I can think to say. I don't understand any of this. Why is here? What does he want from me?

"You ran," he says. Like that's an explanation.

"I can't," I say. I don't know what to call what's happening, or what might happen, but with every step he takes toward me, I know.

"I can't," I say again.

Marcus's face screws up like he's in actual pain. "Please, Harlow," he says. "Just talk to me."

He puts his hand out. Such a simple thing, and yet it means everything. I stare at it for I don't know how long, not trusting myself to look him in the eyes again. The worst part of this is that I want to take it so badly. I want…whatever I can get.

And that is pathetic.

If it weren't for Dill, I'd throw myself at his mercy all over again. My heart is pounding, my blood rushing in my ears, my body and soul screaming for some kind of release from the last five years of torture. From five years of not knowing why. From five years of thinking he just didn't care enough, of thinking that I was just that easy to throw away. Five years of suffering.

And I'd do it all over again, if it weren't for my responsibilities.

"I don't talk to ghosts," I say, and walk away.

I walk away, but I don't escape. Not even a little bit. I feel his eyes on me the whole time. I feel him, with me. And all the way home, the only thing I can think is: What does Marcus Roma want from me?

After all this time, what does he want?

2

MARCUS

The first time I ever saw Harlow Chase, she got me with those eyes. Not even the eyes, but the way she was looking at me with them. Like she saw right through my bullshit.

Harlow was different. I was hooked from the moment I saw her. And I was done for the moment she saw me.

Both times.

Let me back up. Now, today, it's about seven years, give or take, from that first time that I saw Harlow Chase. I feel old, even though I'm only twenty-four. I've seen a lot in the five years since I left Brooklyn to go work for Alex.

I don't call him Mr. Wolfe anymore. I don't call him Godfather.

I don't call him anything unless I have to.

But he still calls me. And it was one of those phone calls that put me here, on the Lower East Side, watching Harlow Chase in the rain. I've been following her all day. She has no idea. I picked her up back in the old neighborhood, seeing she still lives in her parents' old house, finally getting that inheritance she had coming. That was how it was supposed to happen and I made damn sure that it did, because there was no way in hell I was going to let her go it entirely alone, even if I couldn't be there. But I wasn't there when she got the keys. Or when she moved in.

There were a lot of things I wasn't there for. I'm not there now, as far as Harlow's concerned. And I know I don't deserve to be.

Some decisions haunt you, even if it was the only decision you could make at the time.

I followed her all the way to Manhattan, crisscrossing all over the island below Fourteenth Street, hitting up every damn bar, even the sketchy ones I hated to watch her walk into. She was putting resumes out, or whatever it is bartenders do. Worried her place back in Brooklyn will close.

She's right to be worried.

Because I'm supposed to be here as Alex's fixer. That's what I do, I fix problems. Find a solution, even if it's not always pretty, or legal.

Only this time the problem is Harlow Chase and her refusal to sell that house she inherited so that Alex and his partners can move ahead with another development of luxury condos. Alex knows all about my history with Harlow. Hell, Alex Wolfe is part of that history. So I know he thinks that this is a test, in more ways than one. Alex has been grooming me as an heir to his business, right up there with his proper kids, and now he thinks he's testing my loyalty.

Alex Wolfe, or Harlow Chase. My future, or my past.

Alex thinks he know which one is which. He has no idea. And I have to keep it that way if I'm going to protect Harlow from Alex Wolfe.

All of that's in the background the whole time I'm watching her, the tension ratcheting up with every passing second. But the longer I stay on her tail, the more single-minded I become. She's always had that effect on me, she's always made the world simple. I see her and nothing else.

Five years without her made me dead inside, and now it's like feeling is slowly coming back. Every second I watch her, it hurts more.

I wonder how she spends her time now when she's not working. If she still trains at the gym. What she does for fun.

Who she does for fun.

That thought makes me growl, balls my fists up good, like some dipshit just threatened me. It's stupid and I know it. And I have no right to it. Of course she's been with other men. She's a grown woman living her life, and I'm not in it.

And I can tell myself that all damn day, and it doesn't do jack shit to change the way it makes me crazy.

I have checked up on her over the years—I'm not a complete asshole. Used to pay a guy, a private investigator, to check in every now and again, make sure she was doing ok. She always was. Creepy? Maybe. But I don't apologize for what I am anymore.

What I did do, though, was make sure those reports didn't tell me about any other guys, because of what I know I would do. I'm a man, after all. If she was dating, engaged, married, could I stay away like I had to, for Harlow's sake?

Hell no.

So I tried to be good. But a report on a desk from some jerk in a bad suit who watches people all day long isn't the same thing as seeing it for yourself. It isn't the details. It isn't watching her face as she walks from bar to bar in this weather, seeing faint circles under her eyes from lack of sleep, her lips almost starting to turn blue the way they always did when she got cold. It isn't seeing the way she still hunts for happy moments in the middle of a shitty day like this, dancing with a little girl in a rain puddle, trying to cheer herself up, and in the process cheering up everyone around her.

I see that, and it all starts to come back. She's never really been out of my mind, and there isn't a day that goes by that I don't spend most of it thinking about her, but nothing compares to seeing her in real life. I see the way Harlow laughs, sticking her tongue out, catching raindrops, and there's a twinge in my gut, like my body remembers already, screaming at my mind to let it go, let it all come rushing back. But I can't. I fucking can't. Harlow was always the strong one. I'm the guy who'd cave under the weight of remembering all that happiness that I used to have and do something stupid, something that would screw everything up, just because I can't stand being without her one more minute.

And I'm the guy who's still dumb enough to get closer, because I can't fucking help it.

I'm not thinking about my job as I walk towards her. I'm not thinking about my plan. I'm not thinking about anything but Harlow as I stoop to get her umbrella.

And then she meets my eyes, and I'm done.

Here's what I see, all at once: I see her pain, I see her anger, and I meet it with my own. I know there's no way she can hate me as much as I hate myself. I see the nakedness of it, the fearlessness of it, the way she was always unafraid to feel the worst things life had to offer.

And for one split second, I see that she misses me. And that's it. That's what undoes everything. That one sliver of a second chance, shining softly in front of me, and everything inside me reaches for it.

And then she runs.

Harlow Chase runs.

I'm so surprised by it that I don't even move immediately; I just stand there, stupid. And by the time it clicks, she's jumping on that bus and the doors are closing, and I'm just thinking: No. This is Harlow. And Harlow doesn't run away from anything.

I don't even chase after her because I want something from her. I chase after her because I want to give her the chance to do it differently. Slap me in the face, kick me in the balls, tell me the hard truth—any of that would be better than this, this thing that scares me more than anything, this thing that makes me think she has no more fight in her.

It's all wrong.

I've done more bad things than I like to think about, working for Alex, and the very worst thing I ever did was leave Harlow the way I did. But for some reason none of it clicks fully into place until I see the consequences of all those things right in front of me. Until I see Harlow running away, as if she weren't the strongest woman in the world, as if she had anything to fear. And right then it sets a fire inside me: I have to make it right. I have to do it *now*. No more fucking waiting, no more planning. I have to make her whole.

I have to make us both whole.

And now I'm running. I'm pounding on the door of that goddamn bus, thinking about that look, that moment where she forgot to hate me the way I deserve to be hated and was just happy to see me. Thinking about what she used to look like when I made her happy. When I made her come.

Five years away from Harlow and working for Alex Wolfe has turned me into a ruthless son of a bitch. I will do anything to get what I want. And this ruthless son of a bitch wants Harlow Chase.

Fuck this bus. Fuck this bridge. Fuck me, too, because I'm still running, sprinting past the joggers in their reflective jerseys plodding through the rain, dodging a dude on a bike, and now it's just me and the open walkway on the bridge, no other people. Just me and the bus I'm going to catch.

Legs pumping. Lungs burning. Hands shaking, I'm working so hard, pushing through, further into the pain, as far as I can go, because as that bus gets farther and farther away I know: this is how I should feel. The pain feels good, it feels right, like I should feel this every goddamn moment of every goddamn day, a reminder of the pain I've caused her.

I run harder.

I think about the first time that I saw Harlow, and I run harder.

***

All the other days that I spent at Pop's Gym, they blur together, the way that kind of thing does. One workout isn't so different from another; one day of training 'til you throw up is basically the same as any other.

Except for the day she showed up.

All the girls in my high school, the pretty ones, the ones who looked old enough to do the things the fighters at my gym wanted to do with them, they'd all show up after school and hang out right outside with those jeans on while we sweated in the sun. You'd get heat stroke and a boner.

I was used to it. Kind of a perk of the boxing thing. I'd had most of those girls already, would have them again when I wanted, wasn't interested in much more. I was always honest about it. But the older guys at Pop's Gym? They'd been *around*. And I'd see those girls trying to look older than they were, but still thinking about writing a dude's name on their school notebook with hearts around it and shit, and it was just like watching a train wreck in slow motion. Like throwing Bambi in with some wolves.

So I'd warn 'em once, then stay the hell away. Not my business. Generally I just put my head down and hit the bag harder, knowing I had to push myself, had to get great. I had an exhibition match coming up against Manny Dolan, this guy who was about to go pro. And I wanted it. I wanted it so bad, I'd bite my cheek while I worked until I tasted blood. I was sure my dad would have to come to this one; the whole damn gym was talking about it. And I wasn't going to lose.

So the fact that I looked up and paid attention to anybody else at all was practically a miracle. I was training day and night, sweat stinging my eyes, gut churning, thinking about nothing else but winning that fight in front of my father, not giving a crap about all the flirtatious bullshit going on around me, all that jailbait trouble. And then the bell went off, I looked up, and there she was.

Blonde girl, skinny, kinda young. Like an awkward colt, not fully grown, but not a girl, either. Definitely not a girl. Grown enough to get the attention of the fighters, young enough for it to piss me off. She didn't stand like a girl, though, unsure of herself or how to hold her body. She stood like she owned the ground she was standing on. Sun glaring off that pale skin, eyes narrowed, hair shining. And she wasn't there looking for a man's attention, either. She was watching us work like she was trying to figure out how it was done.

I don't know. I've thought about it many times since then. Why I went over there on that day. What it was about her. I think I just had to know more.

And then I got up close, and she hit me with those eyes.

I don't know how to describe it. It wasn't all sexual, even then. I'll admit that was part of it. But there was something so nakedly unashamed about how she looked at me, those baby blues taking everything in, and not reacting like anyone else did. Not reacting to who she thought I was, like those other girls at school, talking to me like they were desperate to get with me, or the guys in the gym, giving me shit until I proved myself. Or my father, pretending not to see me at all.

It made me want to know her. And it made me want to protect her.

Then I got an even better look at how beautiful she was, and how young, and I thought about all the other fighters in the gym looking at her, making cracks, and I got mad.

"What are you doing here?" I asked her. I didn't even introduce myself, just got right into it. She looked up at me like I was nuts.

The bell rang. I was missing a round on the bag. I never missed rounds.

"What does it look like I'm doing?" she said.

"These aren't nice guys," I said to her.

"So? I'm not here for them."

She was tough. I liked it.

"You sure?" I asked. "Your friends are."

She kind of screwed up her lip, looked over at Rosa and a girl called Katya, the girls who ran their crew over at Lafayette High. Now that I was looking a little bit closer I could see she was with them, but maybe not one of them. I don't know—female drama was always complicated.

"Well, I was curious," the girl said. "I think boxing's cool. I'm not looking for a date or anything."

"They don't know that," I told her, looking back at the guys working the bags.

She bristled, maybe because she knew I was right.

"I've got a swift kick to the 'nads for them if they need convincing," she said.

I laughed. "I'm Marcus."

"Harlow," she said, and she smiled at me for the first time, and I swear to God the whole world got brighter. My lips smiled back all on their own, creaking on the way, because I didn't do a whole lot of that back then.

"Why are you really here?" I asked her. "You want to fight?"

She was quiet a moment. Then she shrugged and said, "Yes."

Man, I was almost kidding. I don't even know why I said it. Pops was old school, not the kind of guy to let a female fighter in his gym. I'd never thought about it much before, but thinking about it now, I didn't like it. I wanted this girl at the gym.

She was looking at me, too, like she didn't know if she could ask.

"You want me to talk to Pops for you?" I said.

"You would do that?"

She smiled shyly at me, and I tried to ignore how it made me feel—good, like I had done something worthwhile. Man, all I'd done was ask a question. I shook my head, tore off the velcro strap of my gloves with my teeth, let my hands air out.

"Don't get excited," I told her. "Pops is old."

"So?" she asked.

"So I've never seen a woman in this gym, ever," I said.

"Then there's got to be a first," she said, looked me in the eye, and laughed a crooked little laugh. Her eyes were twinkling, I swear. One moment she's young and scared, pretending to be tough, and then the next she does something like that, laugh up at me like she can't wait to cause trouble, and it's like she knows far more of the world than she lets on. First too young, because two years can be a long ass time when you're in high school, then too damn beautiful. All the time seeing through me.

That was my first hit of Harlow. That was the first time I saw how beautiful she really was. And I didn't know what I was feeling, but no way in hell I was going to let any other man get at her. No way I was going to let anyone else mess with her. I was fucking mesmerized.

I liked the idea of her learning how to defend herself, I'll tell you that.

"Yeah, I'll talk to Pops," I said. "Come on."

It was my fault, no doubt, opening the gate and leading her through the parking lot and in through the open double doors of the gym, feeling all of those male eyes on her and just having to take it. If I did it again, fully grown and knowing what's what, I'd have knocked every single one of those guys the fuck out.

But like an idiot who still believed in the men he looked up to, I actually thought Pops would help her.

"No," Pops said, looking at me like I was crazy, shaking his head. "No, no good."

Normally you didn't argue with Pops. His gym, his rules, his way. But it was almost like I couldn't believe he'd heard right, that's how wrong he was.

"Just give her a chance," I said, looking down at Harlow. "You work hard, right? You don't slack off."

"I always work hard," she said. But her voice was softer.

"No," Pops said, angry now, the way he got when a fighter broke his diet or didn't show any heart. He was shaking his head back and forth, coming out from behind the front desk, waving his arms to get us to go back outside. "What kind of girl wants to fight? Don't bring this in here, no, no good," he said again.

Looking at me like *he* was the one who was disappointed.

And Pops didn't even look at Harlow. Treated her like she was invisible, not even worth talking to. I looked down at Harlow and I recognized the expression on her face, and that's when I realized I got it. That's how I would have looked if he'd shut the door in my face when I'd come to the gym. Pissed off and hurt and disappointed and, above all that, humiliated. Cut down.

That's how I felt around my dad all the damn time.

So it's what she did next that sold me.

Right in the middle of that disappointment and hurt, she crossed her eyes and stuck her tongue out at Pops's back as he walked away.

Now, I know it sounds stupid. It was stupid, yeah. And it sounds juvenile, but it wasn't. It wasn't a serious response to a serious thing, it was like…man, I don't know how to tell it. It was like she took this unfair bullshit and treated it with the seriousness it deserved, which was none at all. Like she took that humiliation you feel when someone treats you like less than what you are and disarmed it with just a silly face.

That's not something I knew how to do. She taught it to me. I didn't know it then, but I think that's when I started to fall in love with her.

And then she looked at me and smiled as we walked back out, still trying to hide that disappointment. She said, "He's never heard of feminism?"

I wasn't the most educated guy in the world, but I at least knew enough to laugh at that idea.

"Maybe I should go back and burn my bra," she said.

I stopped and held the gate open for her, and, I admit it, I looked down. Maybe she wasn't grown into her limbs, long arms, long legs, and all that, but damn she was grown into that chest. Jesus.

"I'm not gonna let you do that," I said gruffly.

She smirked up at me. "Maybe I should go back and burn *his* bra."

For the second time that day, I smiled wide and laughed. Pops had let himself go and had grown himself some man-titties, as the other fighters called them—but never to his face.

Then she got real serious. Softly she said, "Thank you."

Right then, my heart cracked open a little bit, and she got in. She got right in. And I opened my mouth and said, "I could train you. You come in the mornings, no one else is here but me, I could train you. Just don't tell anyone."

And she said yes.

***

That's what I'm thinking about as I run across that bridge in the rain, my eyes locked on the back of that bus like a goddamned heat-seeking missile, refusing to lose her again, even if it's only temporary. This is where I draw the line of screwing up, of losing Harlow, and that's why I'm running. And I'm thinking about the first time she cracked open my heart, and then the last time, which was just a few minutes ago, when she danced in the rain with a little girl and then looked at me like she missed me. After how I left her, after what I've done and what I've failed to do, she still feels for me. My heart is broken open and filling with happiness, or the memory of happiness, for the first time in five long years. My rotten, withered, crusted over heart is warm again, and it feels good. And I know I don't deserve it, but I don't care: I want more.

I yell out into the rain, glad to feel the burn in my legs and my lungs, dare my body to fail me, and run harder. I will catch her. I will.

And when I do, she gives me the greatest gift she can in that moment: She shows me she's still got that fight. Harlow looking me in the eye, telling me she doesn't talk to ghosts? I'm happier than I've been in months. Years.

Untilt I get the text from Mr. Alex Wolfe, professional ruthless bastard: "Take care of Harlow Chase. I don't need to spell out the alternative."

3

HARLOW

Leaving Marcus on that rainy street corner is harder than it should be. Every step farther away from him feels like pushing against a current, like the whole world is screaming at me to go back, to finish this. To get some answers. I still can't think straight; my mind just a jumble, my body aching to turn back. I have to fight the whole way.

The worst part is that it's physical. Being near him, thinking about him? It's awakened something. It's awakened memories, physical memories, and now it's all I can do to keep walking forward away from him, with the ghost of his touch all over me. Remembering what he smelled like. What he tasted like.

It kind of shocks me—I thought this part of my life was over. And why should this be the thing that stands out? Why don't I think about the nights I couldn't sleep from crying, wondering why he'd left? Or hell, why not even think about the good times, the times he was there for me emotionally? I know why, though. It's because it's too hard to bring those memories up. They're too big. They'll swallow me whole.

I cannot deal with Marcus on an emotional level.

But on a physical level?

I've never felt like this before. Ever.

I feel like I'm burning up, grateful for the rain, something, anything to cool me off as I force one foot in front of the other. My core is liquid heat, my body aware of every sensation, every touch of cold water, every brush of harsh fabric, all of it charged with the knowledge that Marcus Roma is nearby.

It is beyond inappropriate. I'm relieved, in a sick, sad way, to know I can feel these things again, but really? Now?

I mean, honestly. I'm trudging back through the rain, past the new condo developments with their glass walls and trust fund hipsters, past the developments still in construction, past the few old houses left between them like lonely baby teeth just waiting to be replaced, and I'm doing all this on my way to what is likely to be a very important meeting with Alex Wolfe.

I cannot be turned on right now. Never mind the fact that it's kind of twisted, considering. I have to handle this.

Alex Wolfe gave me Dill. Whatever else he did, he gave me Dill. I have to treat this with the respect it deserves.

At least, that's what I think happened. I was probably more surprised than anybody when Judge McPhereson awarded me full custody. I'd expected to have to keep petitioning the court, building my credibility over time or something, but nope. First time. Custody of my little brother. The one thing I wanted more than anything in the world, and I was still technically a teenager. And there was Mr. Wolfe, whom I'd spoken to what—once, twice? When he'd come by to see Marcus, before Marcus left me to go work for him. Alex Wolfe, the guy I associated with Marcus leaving me, sitting right there in the front row of Dill's custody hearing, smiling.

Smiling.

And then, when it was over, and I couldn't believe what had just happened, Alex Wolfe looked right at me and winked. I went up to him, dumbfounded. All he said was, "Do a good job."

I knew it was him. Knew he'd somehow fixed it so that I got Dill. I didn't ask any questions, didn't want to know how he'd done it, didn't want to jinx it—but I never knew why he helped me, either. I still don't. I only know that it's because of him that I have what's left of my family back.

Kind of a big debt, right?

I never saw Mr. Wofle around much after that. Rumor is he has real estate and construction concerns nationwide now, working as a consultant on other things, a finger in many pies. Except that now he's back, convincing his old neighborhood to sell out to a developer. Maria already told me—Mr. Wolfe had gotten three families to sign on the dotted line in only a few weeks.

And now I'm going to have to tell him no. The man who gave me my brother back finally wants something from me, and I'm going to have to say no.

I'm thinking about this as I finally approach the small two-story house my parents left me when they died. When the developers started coming around, trying to buy up property, I'd put a great big "NOT FOR SALE, SUCKERS" sign in the front yard. Now I'm thinking that that was the first thing Mr. Wolfe saw.

Well, at least I won't have to break the news to him myself.

I take a deep breath, try to shake off as much of the rain as possible, and open the front door.

Maria comes rushing forward to meet me in the hall, her whole body moving in seemingly different directions under a dress layered with her favorite apron. I can hear voices coming from the living room, one of them Dill's, the other deeper—bigger, somehow. Mr. Wolfe. And the sounds of

Dill's latest video game, sounds that I made for him. I write the music for his games.

It's a silly thing to be thinking about, but it bothers me, that Dill's playing that game—our game, sort of, though really it's Dill's—with Alex Wolfe. I have to shake that off, too.

"You're soaking wet!" Maria says to me, helping me take off my leather jacket. "What happened to your umbrella?"

"It broke," I lie. Maria makes a clucking noise, looking up and down at my wet jeans, soaked through shoes, wet hair. She hasn't had enough people to mother since her kids moved away. I think maybe that's why she takes such good care of Dill and me, always volunteering to watch my brother, always bringing over leftovers, coming over to make cookies when she knows I'm working late. I don't need the help as much anymore, but I'd be lying if I didn't say Maria had saved us in the beginning, when I had no idea what I was doing.

People in this neighborhood look out for each other. It's what makes it worth saving. I learned that the day my parents died.

"He say anything?" I ask her.

"No, no," she says, shaking her head. Maria wrings her hands, like she always does when she doesn't have something to do or someone to take care of, and I know she's anxious.

"Ok, I'll talk to him," I say, slipping my shoes off, at least, so I won't squelch all over the floor.

"I'll make cookies with Dill," she says. I nod, and she's relieved. You would think it was her house, she's so nervous.

I walk into the living room in my bare feet and wet clothes, running my hand through my hair, trying to be as presentable as possible. Dill and Mr. Wolfe look up at the same time, both of them hunched over the computer by the desk, the one piece of high tech gadgetry we have in the house. Dill laughs when he sees me, and Mr. Wolfe smiles.

"You look like the creature from the black lagoon," Dill says.

"Har, har," I say, and look down to see that I am dripping on the floor.

"Harlow, it's good to see you," Mr. Wolfe says. "I just came by to talk. Why don't you go change, and—"

"No," I say, cutting him off. "Dill, go help Maria with the cookies. Mr. Wolfe and I have to talk."

There's an awkward silence, even from Dill. Mr. Wolfe is not a man who you cut off in conversation, or whom you contradict lightly. He has a definite presence. He stands up and I can see the full height of the man, tall and broad with an athlete's build and a big shock of silver hair. And gray eyes. Cold gray eyes. He seems to fill the room.

And he looks right at me.

I shiver. The truth is I don't want to go change into warm, dry clothes, because then it will be like Mr. Wolfe is here to stay a while. Like he won't leave until he's convinced me to do what he wants if I give him even the slightest opening.

The only other person I've ever met who's that persistent just chased me across a bridge.

"Dill, go help Maria," I repeat.

I will say this for my bratty, brainiac little brother: The little man knows when things get serious, and he lets me do my thing. Probably comes from those years of being hyper aware around bitchy Aunt Jill, after our parents died and Jill had temporary custody, years I wish I could take back. Dill clears out without further protest, letting Maria fuss over him the way she does, and gives me one worried little look as he passes by.

That's it. That's the look that breaks my heart and hardens it all at the same time. I never want Dill to have to worry like this, ever again.

But what really messes with my head is the way that Alex Wolfe, Marcus's godfather, chucks my little brother on the side of the head as he walks past. Affectionately. Familiarly. In a fatherly way.

And Dill leans into it, smiling.

And I think about who else Alex Wolfe has been a father to.

***

I should be clear. Watching Alex Wolfe behave that way with Dill messes with me on many levels, but the thing that stands out the most is the way it makes me think about Marcus. And I guess it's possible that just about anything would make me think about Marcus right now, but most things probably wouldn't be as scary as this one.

It makes me think about Marcus and fathers, mine and his both, and the morning my dad caught me sneaking out.

You wouldn't think it would be easy for a fifteen-year-old girl to get up at the ass crack of dawn to go train at a boxing gym, but it turns out it is actually incredibly easy to do if that fifteen-year-old girl knows she gets to train with Marcus Roma. Or at least that's how it worked for me. And believe me, I have never been a morning person. But my alarm would go off at four thirty and I would practically shoot out of bed, full of energy and actually smiling.

It would have been creepy if there'd been anyone around to see it. But I normally left for school before my parents were up, since the high school got an early start and my parents both worked in creative fields where everyone rolled into the office sometime after ten, and I had, um, elected *not* to tell them that the school lothario had volunteered to teach me to box in the mornings. Alone. Just the two of us. In a gym.

I can't imagine why I didn't share that particular piece of information.

Obviously I was rocking a massive crush on Marcus. I mean, I was aware of it. It kind of annoyed me, in a way, because it felt very schoolgirlish. And I was, technically, a schoolgirl, but I also very much wanted to be older, wiser. More mature.

The girls Marcus went out with, for example: they seemed way mature, at the time. They acted like they were, anyway, going out clubbing on weekends, getting wasted, and I was too young to always spot the difference. And they had sex. There were those who had sex and those who didn't. It was like a divided country, and Marcus and those other girls were on the other side of the wall.

Basically I felt hopelessly inadequate, but I wanted him to like me. Not just want me, though I wanted that, too. I wanted him to...I don't know. Approve.

So I worked my ass off. And I did my best to ignore my silly schoolgirl crush. I decided that if I was going to have a crush on Marcus Roma, it was going to be for real reasons. Like, that we had the same thoughts about literature or something, I had no idea. But definitely not just because he was gorgeous, and not just because every other girl in school wanted him, and not just because it would make me feel special to have him look at me that way.

Real reasons.

Later, after the accident, after everything that happened, that felt a whole lot like tempting fate.

Anyhow, Marcus Roma really got to me, even before the accident, and I know because of what happened the morning I got caught sneaking out in the morning by my dad.

My dad was *not* amused. He didn't entirely believe me at first. Who sneaks out to go to the gym, right? I had to show him all my workout stuff to convince him, and even then he still looked suspicious.

"Who is this Marcus?" he demanded, pushing his glasses up the bridge of his nose, the way he did when he wanted me to know he was serious. He was still in his bathrobe and the cow slippers I'd bought him for Christmas.

"He's a friend, Dad," I said. I probably rolled my eyes at him obnoxiously. One of those things I wish I could take back.

"A friend who gets up to meet you in secret at the crack of dawn?" my dad said. "A male friend?"

"It is not like that."

"Then tell me what it's like, Harlow."

Dad used his stern voice, which I remember thinking was funny at the time, because his curly hair was still sticking out all over the place from sleeping on it weird.

God, it's strange, the things you miss after someone's gone.

Anyway, I tried to tell him about it, but I didn't have a good explanation of why I wanted to learn how to fight, at least not one I was able to articulate at the time. I think I said, "It makes me feel good about myself."

I just didn't specify in what *way* it made me feel good about myself.

And I had to explain that we had to train in secret, because Pops didn't believe girls should fight. And though Dad couldn't help but give Marcus points for that, he still insisted that he was coming to the gym with me to meet "this Marcus person."

"What?" I said.

"Let me just get some real pants on," Dad said, and shuffled off.

I could have died. I mean, I was pretty sure I was going to just wilt from embarrassment, in that way you can only be embarrassed by your dad when you're fifteen, and he's insisting on meeting the guy you have a huge crush on.

I think about these things now, and how I had no idea how lucky I was.

Marcus knew, though.

He was waiting for me by the gate, the way he always was. He'd asked if he should meet me at my house so he could walk me over when it was still dark out, but I'd told him no because I didn't want to explain stuff to my parents. Guess the cat was out of the bag now. I could see Marcus shift his position, push off the gate, and stand up straight, and then he was walking toward us, tall and big and looking so much like a full grown *man* that I could actually feel my father getting freaked out.

Marcus didn't hesitate. He put his hand out to my dad like it was no big thing and said, "Hello, Mr. Chase. I'm Marcus Roma. You here to see what Lo's been up to?"

Marcus was the first person to call me Lo. That threw my Dad for bit, too.

"Yes, I am," my dad said. "I don't appreciate my daughter sneaking out like this."

Marcus looked at me. I didn't know what to say.

"I apologize, sir," Marcus said, carefully. "We only have to meet like this because the owner of this gym is…old fashioned."

"I told him," I said.

"Would you like to stay and watch us?" Marcus asked. "Lo, why don't you go warm up and I can answer questions, if that works for you, Mr. Chase?"

I stared at Marcus. He seemed so adult, so in control. I had never felt so young and immature compared to him, and now…

I felt even more infatuated with him, and even stupider for it. He was so obviously beyond me.

I was glad to go lose myself in a warm up, working too hard too quickly and feeling nauseous for it, and not caring even a little bit. I jumped rope until my calves started to burn, and then started my shadow boxing, getting my shoulders loose, trying to focus on anything other than the conversation my father was having with Marcus just out of earshot.

The next time I looked over there, Marcus was showing my dad some basic boxing moves, the two of them talking together like old friends.

It was the weirdest feeling. If there was a Parental Embarrassment Olympics, I would have medaled that morning. Gold medal in cringing, right here.

I mean, what was my dad saying about me? I just remember being so sure that whatever headway I'd made into being a cool girl, a friend even, someone maybe on Marcus's maturity level, it was probably all ruined now. I felt like such a child that my dad had come, that Marcus had to convince my parents that everything was cool. By the time I was done with my warm up, I was actually pissed off.

Which worked out, because Marcus set the timer on the bell, put on the mitts, and said, "Come on, Lo, combinations, let's go!"

So my dad watched Marcus call out punches to me and watched me nail every single one, hitting those mitts as hard as I could, driving Marcus around the floor of the gym, working off all that humiliation. The bell went off after that first round and I looked over at my dad, who was shaking his head and smiling a little.

"Wow, Harlow," he said. "Wow."

I was sweating, out of breath, feeling weird about my worlds colliding like this.

"Dad, the bell's going to go off again in a minute," I said. Impatient with him. I just wanted him out of there.

"Ok, ok," Dad said, putting his hands up. "I'll leave you to it. I don't want to mess up your work out. Marcus, thank you, and I'll take you up on that offer. Harlow, have fun. You're still grounded for a week, so come home right after school." Dad smiled at me. "C'mon, you know you have to tell us these things. See you tonight, sweetheart."

I am loath to admit this, but that right there? That moment, when my Dad told me I was grounded, right in front of Marcus? I probably would have told my father that I hated him if Marcus hadn't been there. Because I was young, and lucky, and sheltered, and immature.

And because it made me feel even more child like in front of Marcus.

I worked so hard that morning. I overdid it. And when Marcus told me to cool it, I didn't listen, kept pushing as hard as I could, running toward that burning feeling as fast as I could because it was better than the humiliation.

Which is how I ended up with a wicked cramp in my calf.

I collapsed to the ground, completely and utterly shocked that something could actually hurt that bad. Marcus was right there, right away, taking my shoes off and pushing my foot back, stretching the muscle out. He talked to me in low, calm tones, telling me to try to relax as much as possible.

"These suck, but it will be ok," he said, his fingers working into my leg. "Just breathe, ok? Breathe with me, Lo."

Pretty soon there was just the sound of us breathing together, and Marcus's hands on my leg, his fingers kneading and rubbing. Once the pain subsided I pulled my leg back, instinctively embarrassed, knowing I was starting to get turned on. But Marcus grabbed my leg, kept me in place.

"You have your water bottle?" he asked.

I nodded, not trusting myself to speak.

"Drink up," he said. "You're too tight. Stay right here."

He got up and I watched him walk away, too dumbfounded to even drink my water properly. Every fiber of my being wished that whatever was going to happen next involved more of his hands on my body. When he came back with a banana, my reaction was probably less than enthused.

Marcus smiled. "It's got potassium. Eat it. And drink up." Then he sat down in front of me, his legs on either side of me, and said, "Now gimme your legs."

Right there, in that moment, I swear the clouds parted, angels sang, and I promised about a million unreasonable things to God. Marcus took first one leg, then the other, and pulled them on either side of his lap. Then he began to massage my muscles, carefully at first, slowly, his eyes narrowed in concentration.

I was in some kind of heaven.

He only had to touch my calves, gently, softly, searchingly, and I honestly think I was halfway there. At the time I didn't have a lot of experience with sex. Just some fumbling make out sessions, and once I let Jared Kozwolski try to go down on me, which was an awkward disaster that no one was happy with. But I had made myself orgasm plenty of times. I knew what it felt like.

I just didn't know I could get so close from such a simple touch.

I leaned back on my hands and watched him with my mouth open, trying to keep my breathing slow and regular, so it wouldn't give me away. Marcus worked his thumbs on me in slow circles, probing my calves, calming them. Now that I was no longer worried about my calf seizing up, now that we'd settled into this, whatever it was that was happening, all I had to concentrate on was his touch. The skin-to-skin contact, the feel of the pads of his fingers on my legs, the sheer strength of his huge hands…

Even thinking about it now makes me feel…soft.

I was quiet, maybe for the first time ever, just letting it happen. Watching him. What I remember most was how intense he was, his eyes focused and his lips slightly downturned, like he wasn't thinking about anything else on the planet except my body and me. And his hands explored me the same way, feeling me out, figuring out what my body needed. No words, just touch. Totally in tune in a way that was beyond words. And it was the most intimate I'd ever been with anyone.

And I forgot, momentarily, that he was just supposed to be massaging out a cramp. It was so much more than that to me.

I think it was for him, too. We both forgot ourselves in that moment. His hands kept working up my leg, to my quads, my thigh. Oh God, his hands on my thigh. Even the memory…

I will remember this until the day I die. Such a little thing, but it felt like fire. Marcus looked up at me, locked his beautiful pale eyes with mine, and I was rooted in place. His fingertips grazed the delicate skin on my inner thigh as he shifted his grip, and the sensation shot straight to my core, pushing the pressure up over what I could handle. Overwhelming me. I dug my fingers into the floor mat and gasped audibly, my lower abs contracting in that distinctive way.

I was *so* mortified.

There was literally nothing else it could be. I was sure I'd just given away what I was feeling, and that made me acutely aware of how inappropriate it was, how almost skeevy it was, to be totally turned on by something that was supposed to be innocent. I yanked my leg away from him, drawing it up close to me, and then just stayed there, awkward and off balance, trying not to breathe too hard.

Marcus was silent a moment.

Finally he said, "Lo, why are you mad?"

I think he was trying to figure out if I was mad at him, if I thought he'd been trying to molest me or whatever. But that didn't occur to me until later. I was mad, and I guess that was obvious in my expression, but not at him—I was mad at myself for being so pathetic, for being humiliated yet again, for wanting something I couldn't have.

But I couldn't say any of that, so of course I blamed it on my poor dad.

"He didn't have to humiliate me," I said bitterly. I put my leg back down, still resting on Marcus's, greedy for the contact, and leaned forward so I could stare at the small diamond of floor mat between us.

"What are you talking about?" he asked.

"My dad." I sighed, like I was sorry to even have to explain it. "Grounding me? I mean, honestly."

"You're mad at your dad for this morning?"

He sounded genuinely confused. And in retrospect, I understand why. At the time? Not so much.

"Yeah," I said, like it was obvious. "He was a freaking jerk."

"Look at me," Marcus commanded.

Believe me, I've never obeyed anyone so quickly in my entire life. And when I looked up? Those eyes. Staring right into mine. Serious. Intense.

Everything still.

"Don't say that," Marcus said. "I don't know, maybe he is a jerk sometimes. But not for this morning. He cares about you. He came down here because he was worried. And he didn't have to be, you could've told him what you were doing. But you didn't. And now you're mad at him for caring enough about what happens to you to be worried."

His eyes never left mine. He was serious, yes, but more than that—it was like he was looking for something in me. Like this mattered to him, like it was important that I understand what he was saying. And that's when I had one of those little epiphanies, the kind I remember from growing up, when I would suddenly understand where someone else was coming from.

Marcus needed to see that I understood, because it would be like understanding him. His reaction was all out of proportion to my calling my dad a jerk, and it was because Marcus knew what I didn't, in a very real way: not all fathers care for their children. Not all dads get worried. Not all of them show up.

Marcus knew that already.

I thought about how I'd never heard anything about Marcus's dad. Or his mom, even. He never talked about them, not even in passing. And I thought about how weird that was for a seventeen year old. How much could I reveal about my life without reference to my family? Barely anything.

Right then, I got that about him. He was alone. Maybe he lived in the same house, but physical proximity only goes so far. That's why he spent all his time in a gym. I had so much more than he did, and I didn't even know it.

"I'm sorry," I said softly. "You're right."

His expression relaxed, and he grinned at me, squeezing my knees with those big hands. "Good," he said.

I don't remember the rest of that work out. I do remember that after that things changed for me. Our mornings together weren't just about the giddiness of this new, gorgeous guy, of being around someone who made me feel more alive, more deliciously conscious of my body just by being nearby, who made me glad to learn how to use that body. That was all still there, constantly, making every moment with Marcus charged with newly formed, raw desire. But now there was this added depth to all of it. Like when he looked at me and seemed to see through me, I knew now that I wasn't just imagining it. His loneliness gave him insight, and he made me look at things in a new way.

Marcus was the first person who, when he told me how lucky I was, I believed him.

As time went by, I learned I was right about his family. I didn't get the details until later, but I don't think the details really mattered. Sometimes I wondered if I'd be as good a person as Marcus if I'd grown up without my parents loving me. I honestly don't think I would. Marcus made himself. He decided what kind of man he would be all on his own. I don't know if I would have been strong enough for that.

After all, when my turn came to be alone, I had Marcus. Right up until I didn't.

***

All of these thoughts about Marcus and fathers, and what it might mean to suddenly have someone in your life to be that father figure when you'd never had one before, come rushing through my head as I watch Mr. Wolfe with my little brother. Because Mr. Wolfe was the one who stepped in when Marcus's own neglectful dad died about two years after my own parents died. You could ask where Mr. Wolfe was before Mr. Roma died, but that's a complicated question. As far as Marcus was concerned, he had no one. His dad hated him and his mother was ashamed of him.

And then, soon after Mr. Roma's funeral, Mr. Wolfe showed up, and a little while after that, Marcus left to go work for Mr. Wolfe. And watching Mr. Wolfe with Dill, I can see it. I can see Mr. Wolfe stepping in, showing Marcus what it might be like to have a father, to have a family.

I'd even felt it myself for that one moment inside the courtroom when Mr. Wolfe smiled at me. That feeling that someone is looking out for you, that someone is on your side? It's powerful.

And that's why, standing soaking wet in my living room, watching Mr. Wolfe chuck my little brother on the side of the head in that familiar way, I'm scared shitless. Because it suddenly occurs to me that maybe Mr. Wolfe offered something I never could: the chance to have a family. And the thought that he might come after Dill like that fills my body with dread.

Which, I'll be honest: not the best way to start a tough conversation.

Mr. Wolfe almost seems to sense his advantage. As soon as Dill and Maria leave for the kitchen, Dill looking scared in that way I hate to see, Mr. Wolfe gives me that same knowing smile I remember from the custody hearing.

"Harlow," he says, still smiling, standing in my living room with his arms open, like he's welcoming me to my own home. It's unnerving. "It's been a long time."

"Yup," I say. "You're here about the development, aren't you?"

I was never good at playing it cool. Give me the option, and I jump right in. I'd rather know what I'm fighting against than have to do all that guesswork. Maybe part of it is because I feel so guilty, knowing I have to go up against Mr. Wolfe.

My hair drips on the floor some more, and Mr. Wolfe lets the silence grow into something vaguely ominous.

"You know I am," he says finally. "Why haven't you taken the offer, Harlow?"

"You know why I haven't, Mr. Wolfe," I say.

Mr. Wolfe looks down at me, his hand brushing aside his suit jacket to find the pocket of his chinos, and he frowns. Like he's trying to pull that fatherly thing on me. It's kind of working, too.

"I assure you, Harlow, I do not," he says. "Why don't you explain it to me."

I hear my teeth grinding in my head. This is harder than I thought it would be.

"Dill has a home here, Mr. Wolfe," I say. "He has friends at school, and neighbors who look out for him. You know why. You know how all these people helped me after my parents died. How you helped me. How they help with Dill now. Dill has a family here. I can't take him away from that just for a payday on our parents' house."

It sounds simple. It's not. It's so much deeper than that, I don't even know how to express it.

"Harlow," Mr. Wolfe says, his eyebrows up, his head shaking, but his eyes cold. Like a parody of fatherly advice. "That's a bad decision."

And that, right there, is where I start to get angry.

I welcome it. The feeling of being ready to fight, rising up in me, balling my fists, putting my chin out. This is familiar. This, I know how to do. I can fight for my little brother.

"My brother *will* have a normal childhood," I say through clenched teeth. "I know I owe you everything, Mr. Wolfe, and I wish there was something else you wanted, because I can't give you this. Dill has a family here. He's going to keep it."

"Will he?" Mr. Wolfe asked, taking out his phone. He sends off a text or something and then looks back at me, truly surprised that I don't know what he's talking about. "So many have already left. It's inevitable, Harlow."

I don't have an answer to that. It won't be inevitable if I can help it.

Mr. Wolfe shakes his head again, sadly this time, and walks to the hall to get his coat. He looks back at me as he's shrugging his expensive trenchcoat over his broad shoulders and says, "It's a very good offer, Harlow. With that money you could take care of Dill for the rest of his life."

"Money isn't everything."

"But it's very close." He has one hand on the front door now, and I am just wishing for him to use it. Just get out. Don't make me have to deal with this.

And then something occurs to me.

"How do you know how much they're offering me?" I ask him. "You're one of the investors, aren't you?"

Mr. Wolfe laughs, a silvery, hollow sound. He says, "I'm asking you to consider, Harlow, that's all. While the offer is still on the table."

"I told you I can't. And I'm sorry, I really, really am," I say, and my voice almost catches, because it's true. "But I will always do what is best for Dill."

He looks at me sadly for a moment. Then he says, "I know you will, Harlow. That's why I stood up for you. Now I'm trying to do what's best for you."

Mr. Wolfe opens the door, and I can see a black town car outside, waiting for him. It's almost stopped raining now. As he steps out on the porch, I realize I might not see him again, and I just blurt it out. I feel like an idiot, but I just blurt it out.

"Why is Marcus back?" I ask.

Mr. Wolfe smiles over his shoulder. "Sign the papers, Harlow. You never know what might happen to an old house like this."

4

MARCUS

The first time Harlow said, "Lie to me," she was joking, but I did it anyway.

I like to think about that first time, when I made my girl laugh, rather than all the times that came after it, when she asked me to lie to her to keep her from crying. But I'm thinking about *all* those times she asked me to lie to her as I'm walking around Williamsburg, into Greenpoint, slowly circling in on the bar where Harlow works now. I can't help it. You return to visit the past and find it all different, you end up going through every single one of your memories like the last change left in your pocket just to make sure you're remembering it right.

So my head is full of Harlow. I don't really mind.

That first time she told me to lie to her, she'd sent me a text at like five in the morning, telling me she couldn't come by to train that morning. I'll be honest, I was paranoid. It was after her father had been by the gym to check me out, and I thought I'd handled that, you know? And hell, I was already on my way over to her house to pick her up like we'd agreed after that, just to walk her over to the gym, make sure she got there safe.

It didn't even occur to me not to go to her house. Not until I was there, seeing the windows all lit up, way too early in the morning for that. I knocked on the door, and only after that did I think that wait, maybe something was really wrong. The idea that something might be really wrong with Lo?

That made me knock harder.

So that was when I met Mrs. Chase.

She looked like Harlow, or would have if she'd slept more in the last few days and didn't have a little boy in her arms. Actually, she looked like hell.

Turns out Mr. Chase was on a business trip, some kind of advertising thing, and first the little guy, Dill, and then Harlow had gotten some kind of bug. Mrs. Chase looked like she was about to lose her mind.

"What, Marcus?" she said. "What?"

I had to try not to laugh, because it sounded like she was just pleading with the universe, just begging it not to throw anything else at her.

"Need any help?" I asked.

Mrs. Chase blinked a few times. Then she said, "Yes," and pulled me inside.

So I fixed their garbage disposal. Ran the trash out. Did whatever. All that took like twenty minutes while Mrs. Chase was taking care of Dill, and when I was done she looked at me like I was an angel.

Come on. You know I liked that. The parents thinking I'm Superman? Not too bad.

I should probably say, at this point, that I had not yet admitted to myself that I had feelings for Harlow. I mean, yeah, I had sexual feelings for her. That was a given, with that body and that face. But in my eyes she was still too young, at least in experience—I'd already figured out she was smarter than me, but smart doesn't get you everything. So it was more like I cared about her, but I was looking out for her. Like she was in the minors, looking to move up to the majors.

That's kind of a lie, though. I don't know what I was waiting on, exactly, maybe just reassurance that I wouldn't screw it up and hurt her. Because the truth was, I got a lot of pussy, but not a whole lot of relationships. Or maybe I was just afraid. Or maybe my instincts were just that good. No matter what the real reasons behind my decision to hold off, I still saw her as mine, regardless. Not that I told her that.

So maybe I was always kind of a bastard.

Anyway, twenty minutes of doing chores for Mrs. Chase and I was walking upstairs to check in on Harlow. I would have been there anyway if she'd told me she was sick. I smiled, thinking maybe she knew that. She had to know I was going to come check up on her if she sent me a text like that with no explanation.

You know what I remember most about the Chase home before the accident? All the pictures. They had all these family pictures all over the walls, and on the wall of the staircase, so they were at eye level all the way up. Happy family type pictures, all smiling and teasing each other. Walking up that staircase was like taking a tour of the kind of life I'd heard about but never saw for myself.

Harlow's room was near the stairs, and I thought how Mrs. Chase would be able to hear me if she came back out. I cleared my throat and said, "Lo, you up?"

That was a thin door. I heard her make a sound, like a kind of squeak. Never heard her do that before, so I laughed and said, "I'm coming in."

I opened the door and her room was still mostly dark, just a lamp on by the side of her bed. And her bed was just a lumpy mess. My girl was hiding under the damn covers.

"What are you doing?" I asked, still smiling, walking over to her bed.

"Hiding."

The idea was crazy to me. Have you ever seen someone's face when they're hitting the bag so hard you know they're going to throw up when the round is over? I'd seen her like that.

"You kidding?" I said, sitting down on the edge of her bed. My weight moved the lump under the blankets, she was so little. "Why?"

"I look like something that lives under a bridge."

I laughed. "No, you don't."

"Well, I feel like something that lives under a bridge."

I grabbed hold of the blanket with my left hand and gave it a little tug, felt the give on it, and pulled it down over her head. Down to her waist.

Man, she was wearing nothing but a tank top that I could see, all ruffled up under the covers, leaning back against those pillows with her hair all messed up.

Jesus Christ.

Even with her tired eyes and pale skin, for a second—just a second—she looked like what I suddenly knew she'd look like after sex. Do I even need to say what that did to me? It would have brought me to my knees if I wasn't already sitting down, and it was nothing compared to the real thing.

But that was later. That was after everything changed. That was the best night of my life, the night Harlow and I first made love.

But before then, in her room, just seeing her all mussed up in a tank top, no bra? I don't know if she knew what was going through my mind. She thought she looked terrible, I thought she was gorgeous. But she let me look. She let me look, and she looked so damn happy to see me. We were both just quiet for a moment while I stared at her.

Then she smiled a little and said, "Lie to me."

"You look like something that lives under a bridge," I said.

Harlow opened her eyes wide, her mouth open, trying not to smile too much, and threw one of those pillows at me.

"You said lie!" I laughed at her.

"So we're lying to each other now?"

I shrugged. "Special circumstances, when you need lying to, sure."

Harlow narrowed her eyes and gave me one of those wicked grins. "Ok. You're going to lose your fight," she said.

If she'd jabbed me then, I swear to God she could have knocked me over. Then I started to laugh my ass off.

Harlow had seen how hard I'd been training for that fight with Manny Dolan, and because of that she was maybe the only one who knew how important it was to me, even if I hadn't said it outright. I always liked that, that she let it alone unless I wanted to bring it up. But I knew she knew how important it was, that it was live or die to me, and she took this thing I was worried about and made it harmless. Made it funny.

She was fucking amazing.

I threw the pillow back and said, "Pops says it's fine now, and you should come by the gym. Says girls can fight."

"Yeah? My parents *hate* you."

"I didn't want to tell you this, Lo, but you're gonna fail the SATs," I said.

Harlow laughed until she started to cough, but that one actually made me think. Because the truth was that Harlow was going to ace that test, and she was going to go to any college she wanted to. I was the one who was going to stick around, maybe get a job with my godfather. And I hadn't thought much about that. How, in less than two years, she'd be gone.

It didn't feel so good, I'll be honest. But knowing what I know now? I wish to God I could have traded the future she got for one where she got to take that test like a normal girl, go to college like a normal girl, get all the normal things, even if she was doing it thousands of miles away from me.

Hell, I would have followed her. She's got something on me, always has. All these years away and I still feel tethered to her, like what kept my blood pumping all this time was that she was out there, existing somewhere in the world. And the closer I get to her now, the more alive I feel. Like I'm just waking up.

Feels dangerous, somehow.

And I know why her words keep echoing around inside my head as I walk around the old neighborhood, trying to find anything, anything at all that I recognize. I keep seeing crazy condos and hipster bars and white guys my age dressed up to look like Kanye but looking instead like characters from a Dr. Seuss book or something, and I just keep hearing her say: *Lie to me. Lie to me, Marcus.*

Yeah, I know what that's about. You don't have to be a shrink to figure that one out. I ended up lying to Harlow a bunch when she needed me to, and now I'm circling in, walking in orbit around where I know Harlow Chase to be at this very moment, because I have to go do it again. I have to lie to her in order to save her.

Should be easier this time around, right?

***

I walk into the bar where she works, The Alley, and I swear to God it's another world. All those Dr. Seuss looking guys I saw out on the street are actually in here, in this bar, drinking whiskey and laughing too loudly at each other's jokes. There's a stage. There's a woman on the stage, and she's doing burlesque or something.

Man, if you had told me five years ago what would happen to the neighborhood, I'd have tried to get you to put money on it and then I would have laughed and called you a chump.

But they all seem to be having fun, so to each his own. It is different than I remember, that's all.

I wander for a while, my whole body tense, knowing she's close. And then there, behind the bar: Harlow.

Jesus.

So. Fucking. Beautiful.

My world goes from black and white to color, from dead and dull to alive and intense. It's almost too much, like my entire nervous system clicks on at once, every nerve firing at maximum capacity, telling me to get the hell over there and claim her. Because she is mine, she was always meant to be mine, and I'll be hers even when she hates me.

I kept it under control these past five years just by being away from her, but now that I've seen her, it's done. There's no going back. She's all I can think about. All I breathe. All I want. And there's nothing left in me I care about except what I can be for her.

I forget all about my job. I forget all about how dangerous Alex Wolfe will be if he doesn't get what he wants. I forget about everything except what I need to do for Harlow.

Fuck, I want her.

My muscles are coiled up tight with the effort of holding back, because the truth is I know I have to earn it. That's fine. That's as it should be. I'm not afraid of hard work. But my blood burns me and my bones feel like they'll crack under the pressure, because everything in my primal being knows where I should be right now. And it's not watching her from far away.

I should have been here all along.

And instead I have to watch her frown down at her phone, have to watch her face fall in that faint blue light, fall in that way I haven't seen in years. And then some asshole in a skull cap is right on top of her at the bar, hollering at her, hassling her, trying to flirt like he doesn't see or doesn't care that she obviously just got some very bad news.

What is wrong with people?

I don't consciously walk over to the bar. It's like I'm there instantaneously, grabbing Skull Cap's arm, pulling him back and away from her. He tries to yank his arm free and it makes me smile.

"Hey, what's your problem?" he asks me.

I stare down at him, rolling my shoulders, feeling the weight of all that muscle I spent years earning.

"Go. Somewhere. Else," I say.

He looks like he maybe thinks about arguing, but not for very long. He looks into my chest, his eye level, then slowly looks up. Then he mumbles something that sounds like an apology and disappears back into the crowd.

I'm a big guy.

I straighten my tie and turn, finally, to Harlow. She's staring at me with her mouth open, having no idea how beautiful she is even when she's annoyed.

"Are you kidding me?" she says.

I grin at her. "Me? Have you seen the people in this bar? Or out on the street? Tell me they're not trying to be funny."

Harlow's suppresses a smile. "I wondered if you'd have a stroke, checking out the new neighbors."

"I thought I might've, and that's why I was seeing a bunch of glow in the dark Muppets walking around."

These new hipster guys, they seem to like neon colors. But you know what? That got a laugh. Harlow Chase forgot to hate me long enough to laugh.

But then she remembers.

"What are you doing here?" she says, her tone hard again, sharp. Like a weapon.

I don't flinch. "I'm here to see you."

"Well, get out."

"No."

We stare at each other across the bar, Harlow raising her chin up the way she does, the blue glow from her phone illuminating her face, giving her away. She's upset. I look right back at her, steadily, and I don't know what happens; maybe she can see what I'm feeling in my face, that I just want to fix it, to help, that it's still me, it's still her Marcus.

There's that same thing that happened back by the bridge, that same way the air changed, the sound changed, like the world slid sideways and snapped back into place, where it should have been all along. Me and her. Together. I want to reach out and touch her but I hold myself back, just savor the feel of this thing between us.

"What's wrong, Lo?" I ask her.

"Besides the fact that you won't get out of my bar?" she says. "None of your business."

"We can disagree about that," I say, leaning over the bar. The closer I get to her, the stronger I feel, and I think about hopping over, picking her up, burying my face in her neck. Goddamn. "But I can still help."

She works her jaw, and I can tell she's grinding her teeth. "I don't want your help," she finally says.

"You need it, though."

"How the hell would you know?"

I study her for another second, give her a look, like come on, you know the answer to that. "You don't look like that unless you need help," I tell her. "Because you hate needing help."

She's stung that I know this, that I can still read her face. And I have to admit it isn't fair.

"Fuck you," she says softly.

I glare at her. "Are you going to tell me, or do I have to stand here until you cave?"

Harlow looks at me, her lips pursed, and then she sighs. She knows I really will just stand here until she tells me. She used to call me her pit bull, I was so stubborn. Still am.

And she's still smarter than me. Knows when to pick her battles.

"The septic tank at the house is apparently busted," she says, her tone flat. "Septic tanks are also apparently expensive."

And she turns to wipe down a part of the bar that's already clean, not wanting to have to look me in the eye any longer, as though the conversation is over, which tells me all I need to know.

"You don't have the money?" I ask.

She stops, freezes, like that hurt her. Then she looks back at me, standing up as tall and straight as she can, so I can see how she's kept her body up, her skin luminescent in the low light. I feel like an asshole for noticing, but I think most men would. Then again, most men are assholes.

"I have the money," she says, and she's gone full ice queen.

"But?" I say.

"But I was going to spend it on something else," she spits out. "You know, like people do with money."

"What were you going to spend it on?"

"Jesus Christ, Marcus, can't you just leave me alone?"

"I should tell you, Lo, that's the one thing I'll never do again," I say.

She stops.

Those big blue eyes lock on me while the rest of her just…stops. I can tell she's holding her breath. Waiting. Not sure of what to say, what to think, what to feel. She blinks and it looks like there's water in her eyes, and I know I got through to her, said the thing she wanted me to say, and maybe also the thing she never wanted to hear. Maybe it will always be this way with us now, the thing you love and the thing you hate all wrapped up in one.

So there's that moment when she's just looking at me raw and exposed, and believe me when I say it takes all my strength not to jump over that bar and take her in my arms. Just to hold her. Just to feel her skin against mine. Just to say I'm sorry in the one moment in time when she might actually believe me.

But then it's over just as soon as it came on, and Lo is pissed. She's mad that I can still get to her like that, that I can still pierce her defenses, all the way through to the parts of her she keeps hidden away. And she's right, it wasn't fair.

But love isn't fair.

"Go to hell," she says.

"Already there," I shoot back.

She laughs bitterly and turns to get a rack of glasses out of a Hobart machine, steam billowing out, swallowing up her face and giving her a little break. I can see the muscles in her arms flex as she lifts the rack and sets it on the bar, not looking at me, like she's just going to go on with her shift.

"I'm not going anywhere, Lo," I say. "And I know you're not gonna call the bouncers on me."

"Yeah?" she says, looking up. "How do you know?"

"Because I do. I know you."

Harlow slams the door to the Hobart closed and she's even more mad because I'm right again. She would never ask someone else to take care of her problem. That, and part of her doesn't really want me to leave.

I can see that part fighting to get out.

"Just tell me, Lo," I say. "I can help."

Harlow spins back around, her face all twisted up, tears in her eyes. "Fine, you unbelievable asshole. It's Dill," she says. "The money was for Dill, Marcus. For this special genius programming camp he got into so he can finish the video game he's been making. I saved up all year. And now instead he's going to get indoor plumbing. Hooray for me."

When I see how upset she is, I know immediately that I'm going to take care of it. The only question is how I'm going to convince her to let me do it. She won't take my money. Under no circumstances will she just take my money and give nothing in return; it's not how she's wired. And that pride, that toughness would rear up all over again. The idea that she owed me anything at all would keep her up nights.

Even worse, I can't tell her the truth about what I think might have happened to her septic system, or she'd really go ballistic. I wouldn't blame her, either. But that's why I came here, right?

To lie to her in order to help her.

It's just that now I have the opportunity to get something out of it, too.

"I'll pay for it," I say.

She rolls her eyes.

"You didn't let me finish," I smile. "I'll pay for it, on one condition."

There. Now she's taking me seriously. She's looking at me like she's about three seconds away from jumping me, but there's that shine in her eyes, too. She understands this kind of game. Maybe even misses it. When fighting, arguing, becomes like a dance.

"What?" she says.

"You see me every day until Dill comes back from his camp," I say. "Not for five minutes or anything like that, either. All day, as much as you're off. Every day."

Harlow stares at me. She laughs a little, shaking her head.

"Unbelievable," she says.

"Nah," I say. "You knew I'd do something like that."

She nods. I'm right. I can see she hates it. And I know she hates even more that maybe she kind of wanted me to say something like that.

Then Harlow comes right up close to the bar, so there's only this thin plank of wood separating us, and she leans right over it, and I have to try damn hard not to look at her perfect breasts pressed up against the bar.

She looks me dead in the eye and says, "Marcus, do you really think there's even the tiniest chance I'll ever forgive you? That I'll ever, ever trust you again?"

"Yes, I do," I say, and dig my fingers into the wood in front of me. God, I want her. I want to be her everything. "Do you?"

She says nothing. Just chews her lip, and watches me.

I lean closer, and rest my hand on hers, the first time I've touched her in five years. She feels warm and magnetic, my hand more alive than any other part of my body, my fingers tingling. I put everything I have into it when I say, "So then lie to me, Lo."

She doesn't move her hand.

She almost looks like she's going to cry.

And then we're interrupted, some woman coming in behind Harlow, penciled on eyebrows raised to the sky, saying, "Harlow, everything ok?"

Harlow snatches her hand back like she needs to keep it safe, rubbing the skin where I touched her. "It's cool, Shantha. Just someone I used to know."

That was for my benefit. Yeah. That's ok. I'll be someone she knows again. I nod at this woman called Shantha, who's looking at me like I might be a criminal, and reach over to grab some napkins. I write my phone number down in big black letters, because I know Harlow deleted my number a long time ago, and give it back to her, folded up.

"Think about it, Lo," I say, knowing she won't be able to resist in the end. Even if she didn't need house repairs, even if it weren't for the way she needs to be the best mother Dill never had, she wouldn't be able to resist the opportunity to make me pay, to make me tell her the one thing I can't tell her—why I left. She's going to torture me, especially when she finds out I won't tell her. I'll deserve all of it.

I hold onto the napkin one second too long, making her look back up at me, just so I can say this: "I'm not going anywhere."

When I walk out of there, it's with the knowledge that I'm walking on the razor's edge. Alex Wolfe and everything he's capable of on one side. The love of my life on the other.

5

HARLOW

I only lasted about half an hour after Marcus left before Shantha sent me home from the bar.

"You're useless." She smiled at me.

"I'm sorry, I just—"

"Go home, get some sleep. Or call that unbelievable hunk of man and don't get some sleep, whatever works."

I had to try to force a smile. Shantha saw through it. But she didn't pry, because Shantha's always looking out for me, just hugged me and sent me on my way.

Which is why I'm home early with nothing to do but think about Marcus's offer.

And think about Marcus himself.

Seeing him up close, talking to him—it feels like I've been drugged. My head is swimming in memories of Marcus, in sensations of Marcus, and it's outrageously unfair because what I should be thinking about is how I'm supposed to provide for Dill. And about how I'm evidently failing at that.

I made myself a promise when I got custody: I would not touch our inheritance except for medical emergencies or similar, because otherwise it would be gone way too soon, and it's not like I had a lot of career prospects at the time. I still don't. You make decent money bartending at some places, but one, I don't work at those places, and two, I don't pick up enough shifts, since I want to be home when Dill is at least some of the time.

So we get by, and my life is made immeasurably easier knowing we have a cushion in case disaster strikes again, but I will not break those rules. I will not.

I'd be lying if I said I wasn't thinking about it, though, before Marcus's offer.

Marcus. I thought I almost caught his scent when he leaned across the bar to get close to me. It made my heart stop.

I shake my head and pry the bottle cap off a beer, expertly hitting the garbage can on the other side of the kitchen. Dill's asleep, has been for a few hours. The house is quiet. I kick off my shoes, take a swig of my beer, and head to the master bath.

I never moved into my parents' master bedroom when I took possession of the house. Just couldn't do it. So I'm still in my old room, and Dill's in his. That doesn't mean I don't take advantage, from time to time, of the swank bathroom my mom insisted on having put in. I mean, my mother would kill me if she thought I was letting all that marble go to waste.

I run the water and strip, saving the rest of my cold beer for when I'm submerged in the hot water, and the brief chill on my bare skin reminds me of what I felt when he put his hand on mine.

Damn it. I can't even be naked without thinking about Marcus.

I still can't believe my physical reaction to him. It's somehow more intense than it was years ago, if that's even possible—and I was sure it wasn't possible, because of what happened after he left during what I refer to as my Dark Period. I'm frankly astonished. It's like my sexuality has been partially defined by Marcus Roma, and now I need him to…I just *need* him.

It fucking *sucks*. Why does it have to be him?

Because he's going to leave again. I don't care what he says to me in a bar when he's trying to be charming. And he's still the guy who left and broke my heart, and he still hasn't offered a damn explanation.

And I'm still going to take him up on his offer.

I sigh, admitting the truth. What choice do I have? Dill needs to go to camp, and I need answers and closure. And I need to make him suffer. The only real question is whether I'll be able to resist Marcus Roma and end up on top in the end.

"On top" was not a helpful phrase.

I sink back into the water and try to think of whether I've ever been able to resist Marcus. Not just the man himself, but his influence. It's a question I've thought about before, when trying to get over him. If my parents hadn't gotten into that car to go on their first getaway weekend in years and gotten run off the road by a drunk, would he have been the same force in my life?

I always think about the one day I went back to the gym after school with Katya and Rosa to watch the fighters after Marcus and I started training. It was after we'd gotten kind of close, Marcus coming to check on me when I as sick, stuff like that.

Anyway, we showed up, hung around the gate, trying to pretend we weren't looking and being looked at. Same as always.

Marcus didn't make any pretense about anything. The second he saw me there, leaning against the fence with the other girls, he ripped off his gloves and walked right over, ignoring everyone else, his gray-green eyes boring into me. He unlatched the gate, came outside, grabbed me by the elbow, and walked me down the block while the other girls watched in hushed, jealous silence.

"What do you think you're doing?" he said. He was almost angry. It was the first time I'd seen him register any kind of strong emotion at all.

"What do you mean, what am I doing?" I asked. "I'm, you know, whatever. Hanging out. What people do."

"With them?" he said, tilting his head towards the girls by the gate.

"Yeah. So?"

I was already defensive, because, truth be told? It was kind of lame. I was definitely kind of bored, even if watching Marcus work out had its merits.

"You know what they're here for?" he said.

I thought about his question. On the one hand, it was obvious. They were here to flirt, to be seen. But what was the harm in that? Who cared?

Marcus answered for me, pointing at them. "They're here because they don't have anything better to do than hope someone wants to fuck them. That's all they're here for."

I didn't say anything. He was right. And when he said it out loud like that it was impossible to deny how dumb it was.

Marcus leaned in closer, his hand still on my elbow. I could feel his hot breath on me, and I stopped breathing.

"You know how these guys talk about them?" Marcus said.

"I don't care," I said, defiant, almost glad to have something to argue. "Those guys are assholes."

"Yeah, they are," Marcus said. "And I don't want them being assholes to you."

I was speechless.

Marcus wasn't.

He looked at me, hard. Right in the eyes.

"I don't want them talking about you like that," he said, his hand hot on my arm, his voice gruff. "I don't want them thinking about you like that. I don't want them thinking you're an easy fuck because you don't have anything better to do than come around and walk the damn street in front of them after school. You're better than that, Lo. You can do damn near anything. What the hell are you doing here?"

Oh God, I was so overwhelmed by him. First time I felt like I was drowning in him, right there, on the hot sidewalk, in front of everybody. I scrabbled for purchase, for my next breath, for anything that would keep me from just melting in front of him.

"Then tell them I'm not an easy fuck," I said, and pulled away. I put my chin up and walked right back over to Rosa and Katya, determined to hang around for a while just to piss Marcus off. Just to show him he couldn't tell me what to do.

Because while his macho thing made me feel good, it also made me want to fight him, just to prove a point. And yet, standing out there in the hot sun, watching those girls flirt with new eyes? Man, did he have a point of his own. It did look like none of us had our own interests, like all we could think to do was hang out and watch a bunch of guys, hoping they liked us.

So for a while I watched Marcus pound the bag like I'd never seen, knowing I was the one who'd pissed him off. I didn't totally mind that, watching him sweat, his muscles roiling, churning in the glare of the sun. But then I started to feel stupid, standing out there like that, proving him right.

And eventually I asked this girl Lisa, the quietest one, if she wanted to go see a movie or something.

Which was how I started to make a new group of friends. I mean, never mind that they all of those friends kind of faded away later, after the accident, because they just couldn't handle it; the point is that I made the choice. And it's how I decided I wanted to be more than a woman who defined herself by what men wanted her, even if I was too stubborn to admit it at the time. All because Marcus annoyed me into it with his macho protective crap.

I didn't understand how much that meant at the time. So yeah, it's kind of funny that I used to think that maybe if it wasn't for the accident, if my parents hadn't died, maybe I could have avoided Marcus. Maybe he just would have been the boy who taught me how to box and nothing more. If not for that one stupid accident, if not for the one day my life was wrecked beyond all repair, maybe it all would have turned out differently.

But probably not, and it's this memory that tells me that. Marcus helped to shape who I was even before my world ended. He was always destined to ruin me. Fate just helped him to do it quicker.

***

So I'm thinking about all this in the bath while I'm pretending to debate my options, because it's a lot easier to think about harmless high school drama than it is to think about what came later, when the shit really hit the fan. I still can't go there. That's fine. I don't particularly want to.

But I'm in the hot water, naked, with the awareness of Marcus sliding over my skin like a living thing. He moves differently now. I noticed in the bar. Just a subtle difference, like he's grown into himself, more relaxed about being an apex predator type. Supple. Confident. Leonine.

It was sexy as hell when he pulled that guy off the bar. I have my own cavewoman instincts.

I can't help but think about the other things Marcus taught me. But so many of those are walled off in the garden of Things I Can't Bear To Think About, buried deep next to a grief that I don't want to dig up, so that as my mind sifts through all my memories of Marcus in search of something that will help me to understand what I feel, what I want, I come back to the first night we had sex.

Sometimes this memory is in the walled-off garden, too. Sometimes I can't bear to remember what I've lost.

Would it be different now? Of course it would. It would have to be. I was so nervous, wound so tight, even though I wasn't quite scared, because it was Marcus. And he was so huge above me, so overwhelming, and that was the final time I felt like I drowned in him, his shoulders blotting out the light, his arms cradling me on either side. He was so gentle, stretching me softly, treating me like I might break even as he stoked a fever in me that drove me nearly insane with wanting him.

Oh God, the intensity of that. Wanting him so badly, all at once, in a rush, like I just couldn't wait anymore. And he made me wait. Later, I learned that I liked it when he took control, even when he was rough.

It is so weird to be thinking about this. Part of me is horrified. I know what rough actually means now; I know how scary it can get in the real world, and it's turned me off men and relationships. Until now.

I can't help it.

My hand moves south, over my stomach, down between my legs, almost of its own accord. I'm not even totally conscious of it; it's just something that feels right, the more I think about him. But the Marcus in my mind isn't the Marcus I remember from that first time; he's different, darker. Rougher.

My mind shies away now every time I flash on the tenderness of that first night. I don't want tenderness from him anymore. Or I can't bear it. It hurts too much to imagine him touching me softly.

I want him hard.

And when I come, splashing water on the clean marble floors, I realize I'm crying. Because I do want him. Because I do need something from him, no matter how much that frightens me. I need those answers. I need that closure.

And Marcus helped make me into the kind of person who takes control of their life. I'm not just someone who watches on the sidelines. I take charge.

I get up from the bath, soaking the floor in water, not caring even a little bit, and walk over to where I put my phone on the vanity. I put Marcus's number in it, just in case. I don't hesitate. I send a simple text: "You have a deal."

And only then do I realize that I've stopped breathing again. I suck in a huge gulp of air and promise myself that I will get answers. I will learn why he left like that, why he hurt me.

And that will make it better. After that, I'll be able to move on.

Thinking about this starts to make me crazy, as it inevitably does when I think about people I've lost or could lose, and I pad quickly down the hall on wet feet so I can pull some sweatpants and a t-shirt on. I don't even bother to towel off my hair before I'm tiptoeing to Dill's room.

I know it's not fair, but I won't be able to sleep until I see that he's safe.

Which he is, of course. The sliver of light from where I've cracked the door open falls right on his bed, and he's curled up on his side, sleeping soundly. Or he is until I sneak into his room—I can see the shift in his shoulders, the change in breathing, and I know I've woken him up. I feel like a jerk, but it's not like I can stop myself once the anxiety takes hold. I will be up all night, paralyzed with fear, unless I check up on him.

He's kind of gotten used to it a little bit. Something else I feel bad about.

"You can't sleep?" he murmurs into his pillow.

My heart breaks a little bit. Dill shouldn't have to worry about me. I walk over to him, no longer worrying about the sound I make, and bend down to kiss him on the forehead.

He makes a face without opening his eyes, registering little boy disgust at any of that mushy stuff, and so I reach down to give him the world's gentlest noogie on the top of his head.

"Just getting my noogies in before you go away to camp," I whisper.

He smiles sleepily, excited by programming camp even when he's half-asleep. "'S not for two days."

"You'll be gone for six weeks. I've got a lot of noogies to make up for," I say. "Go back to sleep, little man."

I close Dill's door on my way out so I don't keep him awake, because I'm worried I'll be up for a while. I've taken a massive gamble with that text. Because if I don't end up on top? If I don't find the answers I think I need, if I don't get the closure I want? Then what? I can't afford to go back to that place Marcus put me in the first time he broke my heart. I can't do that to Dill.

Marcus leveled me with just one phrase, back at the bar. "Lie to me." What's he going to do with six weeks?

6

MARCUS

I'm standing on an unnamed corner on Kent Avenue, a place that used to be just abandoned warehouses and is now all expensive lofts, watching a bunch of little rich kids get ready to board the bus to go to their computer camp. I'm waiting for Harlow and Dill and the first day of the deal we made. I don't know if Dill will remember me. I doubt it. I don't know if Harlow will be able to look at me without wanting to punch me in the face. I doubt that, too.

The last time I felt like this, this out of whack, this out of my element, was the morning I walked to Harlow's house to beg her forgiveness and found a cop car rolling up the drive, bearing bad news.

Let me explain.

That fight I had against Manny Dolan, the guy who was going pro? The one I trained day and night for, the one I was sure I was going to win in front of my asshole father, the fight that would make my dad finally say he was proud of me?

My old man didn't show up.

Now, in retrospect, I understand the how and why of this. But I still don't get the sheer cold-bloodedness of the man, the cowardice of choosing simply not to show. In one sense, I was crushed. In another, deeper way, I wasn't surprised at all.

You know who did show up? Harlow. And she brought her entire family. For real, all the Chases, cheering me on in a damn blood sport. Imagine that? My head was twisted, I'll tell you that.

I fought hard.

And the thing is, I won.

I was not supposed to win.

I won't lie, I wasn't feeling good going into that fight. It had been childish to expect that my dad's interest in boxing would overcome his lifelong disinterest in me, and it had been stupid to fixate on that, but I had done both of those things, and realizing my folks didn't show was a giant mindfuck five minutes before the bell. It knocked my focus.

But I followed Pops out into that high school gym with the ring set up in the middle of what was usually a basketball court, people filling the bleachers on one side, sitting in folding chairs on all the others, yelling and drinking out of paper bags, and I heard one voice above all the others. Screaming my name.

Yeah, Harlow, screaming my name. You better believe I heard that.

My head snapped around and my eyes locked in on her like I didn't know how to see anything else. She was smiling, but it wasn't an innocent smile. More like fierce.

She was beautiful.

I felt every hour I'd spent with her, training. Every time she'd innocently touched me, not knowing how much I wanted her, even though I thought I wasn't supposed to. Every time I'd gotten her to smile like that. I don't know how to describe what happened after that. It was the adrenaline rush you get before a fight, but taken to another level. My heart hit my chest in loud, strong beats, and my blood echoed with that strength, rushing through my veins with a pressure I could feel, and I felt like King fucking Kong. I wanted that fight. I wanted to crush Manny Dolan and anyone else who got in my way. I would have fought every fighter in that gym if Harlow asked me to, and I would have won every belt, just to have something to give her at the end of the night.

That's when I knew I was going to win. Nothing else could happen with her there. I told myself I was fighting for her and everything clicked into place. The air got sharper, the man in front of me moved slower, my punches got stronger. Maybe it was because I didn't have much to start with, maybe it was just because of who she was, but that was when I knew that she was my world. My everything.

So I knocked Manny Dolan out cold.

I did kinda mess up Manny's career, set him back at least a year. And Alex Wolfe—or Mr. Wolfe, as I called him at the time, even though the man was my godfather—came back into the girls' locker room to let me know it.

The fight was in our own high school gym, if you can believe it. They'd given me the girls' locker room, which, I won't lie—I had been in there before, only under different circumstances. Usually those circumstances involved a girl, and left me feeling a lot better than I did this time. Never with a cut above my eye and my body aching and my heart pumping from knowing I had kicked some serious ass out there in front of Lo and her family. I'd done someone proud, even if it wasn't my own father, or, apparently, Alex Wolfe.

"You have no idea what kind of headache this makes for me, Marcus," I remember him saying.

"Sorry." I'd smiled.

It was just about then, as I was unwrapping my hands and looking for an icepack to put on my face, that Harlow had come through and Alex excused himself, not wanting anyone to hear what he had to say. Let me be clear: Harlow came in by herself. Just me and Harlow, in the locker room, after I'd just pounded another man into jelly. And Harlow wearing one of those summer time tank tops that kills every man in sight.

I don't know what it is about a fight that puts you in a certain frame of mind. Maybe the testosterone. But I was very, very aware of the way she smelled and the shirt she was wearing and how alone we were.

Keep in mind, she wasn't mine. Not yet.

"Hey," she said, with this big grin on her face.

I didn't have much experience being self-conscious then, and I still don't now. But I remember that moment, when I became aware of the fact that I'd just won this fight, but there was no one in the locker room celebrating with me. For the first time I felt the need to explain and I couldn't. Instead I just told the truth.

"My folks didn't show," I said.

Harlow looked at me for a long moment. Then she took the ice pack from my hands and held it to my cheek and said, "I did."

Yeah. I will remember that until the day I die.

Maybe I was too young to know what to do with a gift like that, I don't know. But after a little while I smiled back at her to let her know things weren't serious and said, "Why you grinning like that? You like to see me get hit?"

"No," she said, rolling her eyes at me while I undid my boots. "But you know what the odds were, right? You weren't even supposed to last all ten rounds, let alone knock him out."

"So?"

She gave me that wicked smile I loved. "So I told my dad to bet on you with Mr. Wolfe."

That's when I started laughing. Alex Wolfe ran book on this fight with the odds against me? No wonder he was so pissed. He took a bath.

"You did?"

"Of course I did," she said, switching the ice to my other cheek. "And now my dad says we're taking you out for ice cream."

"Ice cream?" I laughed some more. "Like I'm five?"

I thought I might have caught Harlow looking at my arms right about then. Quietly, she said, "Let's just let him think that for now, ok?"

Yeah, I didn't imagine that. We sat there a moment, quiet together. I let my eyes fall on those perfect breasts, and after a second I was aware that we were breathing together, feeling the rise and fall, the same rhythm. There was a single drop of sweat on her chest, about to fall between her beasts, and I wanted to push her back on that bench and lick it off. But when I looked up Harlow just looked earnest, baby blues wide open and totally unaware of the thoughts going through my head.

"Ice cream, huh?" I finally said.

"Ice cream. I love my dad, but he's a cheapskate. Maybe next time you let Mike Tyson bite your ear off, you'll get a steak dinner."

I grinned back at her. "I could pay for college that way, maybe. Invest wisely, you know?"

"One ear at a time," she said, and bopped me on the head with the melting ice.

Seems stupid, but what came later was even better. Her parents? Man, they were all over me, her dad talking about the fight like he knew anything about boxing, her mom fretting, getting all worried, making me promise up and down that Harlow was never going to get in a ring like that, making me promise that I wouldn't do it again, either.

I mostly looked at Harlow.

"You didn't tell me you wanted to compete," I said.

"That's because I don't. I don't actually like the idea of getting hit in the head," she said. Then she threw her maraschino cherry at me. "I like being smarter than you."

Her dad laughed, and I asked him, "She like this with you?"

Like I knew all of them. Like we were close. It felt easy, comfortable. And then Dill started to wake up, and her parents were going home, but they were ok with leaving their daughter with me for a little while. And as her dad got up, he shook my hand and said, "Call me Paul. And thank you for teaching my daughter how to protect herself."

Man to man. Looking me in the eye.

One of the proudest moments of my life.

Which, looking back on it, is probably why I screwed up so badly right after that.

In my defense, my attraction to Harlow had been sneaking up on me. All the time, in little increments, getting stronger. It wasn't just the way she looked—although, damn, the way she looked—and it wasn't just the way she smelled or the way she carried herself. It was the way she looked at the world. It was a way I wanted to look at the world. I liked who I was when I was with her, and I was becoming that man more and more, and I liked that.

So it was getting harder and harder to ignore how much I wanted her and how well we fit together, but I knew she didn't have much experience. I knew I'd be her first. And for some reason I didn't feel right about it.

No, I'm lying. It wasn't just some reason. Straight up? I didn't think I was good enough for her. I thought I would mess it up. Thought I would hurt her. That we'd take that plunge and she'd discover who I really was, and then I'd lose her. And again it doesn't take a psychiatrist to see why; I was aware even then that my parents messed me up. I knew my parents didn't think much about me. I just didn't think they were wrong. Not that I would have said that at the time. I would have talked about how she was younger than me, too inexperienced, all that. Just excuses.

Sometimes I wonder what might have been different if I'd made a move after that fight instead of doing what I did, which was go off and screw another girl at the first party I could find. If I'd had the guts to make a move on Harlow, knowing her parents liked me, knowing that it was the real thing, maybe I wouldn't have known how to handle it. Maybe I would have screwed it up, and her parents would have stayed home that weekend from their couple's retreat or whatever it was, and never would have been in that car accident.

Who knows?

Instead this is what I remember: walking around the neighborhood with Harlow. Putting my arm around her. Feeling her warmth against me, how she fit perfectly under my arm. How good she smelled. How good I felt just being close to her. Holding her outside on her porch after midnight, knowing she needed to go inside and not wanting it to end.

Kissing her on the damn cheek, like an idiot, thinking I was doing the right thing.

And then going to my buddy Chino's house, getting fucking wasted, and nailing Rosa in Chino's bed. It was even worse than that, though, because I was so stupid about it. I was all over Rosa in front of everybody, making it real obvious, so it got back to Harlow at the speed of light, basically. And then I was in trouble. "Trouble" didn't quite cover it. She wasn't talking to me.

She wouldn't come down to train the morning after that, either. And because I knew I was wrong, I got mad about it and acted like she was overreacting or something. So I went to the gym without her and worked out. By the time I was done I had worked through all that stupidity and was well aware of just how badly I'd messed up, both by screwing Rosa and by pretending Harlow didn't have a reason to be upset about it. So, all sweaty and sorry, I practically ran back over there to apologize, to beg her to forgive me. I didn't have much of a plan after that. I don't know if I would have told her we had to wait or what, but it turned out not to matter.

I knocked on the door and got nothing. She was still mad. Fine. I would just stay there until she decided to hear me out. She was there alone, her parents away for the weekend, Dill was with Maria; I could hang out on that porch all damn day. And the way it happened, you wouldn't believe it if you saw it in a movie or something. Harlow finally came downstairs and opened the door, and I could tell she'd been crying. Seeing that was like getting kicked in the balls. I'd made her cry.

I don't even know what I said, exactly. I said I was sorry about a million times, I know I admitted I was wrong, that I was done sleeping around like that, that I didn't know what we were, but I knew that what I did hurt her. I remember saying that. I remember saying, "It was wrong and dumb because it hurt you, and I swear to God, Lo, I would take the hurt on myself if I could."

I said that, and it was like God said, oh yeah? Try this.

Because it was at that point that I noticed her eyes weren't on mine anymore. She was watching something behind me. So I turned around, and that's when I saw the cop car and two police officers walking up the steps, both of them with sad, sad looks on their faces.

This is all just to say that the moment I realized I loved Harlow Chase was the moment that her world ended. The moment I realized I would do anything for her, I was asked to. I had no idea what the fuck I was doing—I couldn't even get loving her right, and now I needed to figure out how to help her deal with the worst thing that had ever happened to her. I had never felt that lost, and I had never felt so determined to step up.

I don't remember the actual words. I know the cop said them several times. I know it took me a while to get it—the Chases flipped their car, dead on impact. But I don't remember the exact words.

I do remember the exact moment Harlow understood what they meant. Her face...cracked. And something inside of her escaped, something left, seeped out and floated away. She fell against the door before I could catch her and I just remember that she didn't look like she was all there. Like part of her was gone. And that was when I was sure, really sure, that seeing her in pain hurt me, too. It hurt me physically to see that on her face, to see how much she hurt. I felt it right in my chest, this ache, this hole, this thing I didn't know how to fill. So I just gathered her in my arms and held her as close as I could.

The police had to stay until social services decided what to do with Harlow and Dill, so they were still there when she finally came to and just...exploded. She just started punching things, anything, walls, the bannister, whatever she could. She threw anything she could get her hands on. She screamed. They were going to call the paramedics, take her to a fucking hospital, so I just swallowed her back up in my arms and let her beat on me until she dropped from exhaustion. Even then, I didn't let go. I didn't know how to.

That's mostly what I remember: Harlow. The details of the rest are hazy. I do know the whole neighborhood came out, everyone trying to figure out what to do. There was an aunt somewhere, but the aunt didn't have a good relationship with them, and she wouldn't be there right away. So the neighborhood came through, mostly Maria Ruiz, who lived next door, doing all the organizing, making sure Harlow got put in with a foster family nearby, volunteering to take care of Dill until the aunt got there. Everyone staring at Harlow like she was a bomb waiting to go off, and me not wanting to let her go. Mr. Mankowski, the guy who would be her foster father, I remember him coming forward carefully, like either of us might go off at any moment, and I just explained that I was coming with them, and he said that was fine in a real calm voice.

I slept on the Mankowskis' couch that night, waiting until everyone was asleep to go sneak into the room they'd put Harlow in. She wasn't sleeping. Or maybe she was crying in her sleep—it was hard to tell. But I just lay down next to her, not knowing what else to do, and then she took my hand and squeezed as hard as she could. I stayed until her grip softened and her breathing calmed down, and eventually I found my way back home. Only when I got there, I knew it wasn't where I was supposed to be. Not anymore.

I think that was the exact moment I grew up: when I decided to be good enough because someone I loved needed me to.

I spent a lot of nights with Harlow after that, sneaking in and out, just letting her hold on to me.

Shit, just thinking about this is hard. I can't even imagine how much harder it is for Harlow. Because no matter what I did, no matter how hard I tried, I could never make it better for her. I could never figure out how to take that pain and make it fully mine. That was hers forever.

And I'm thinking about that now while I wait for her and Dill, while I keep seeing them out of the corner of my eye only to realize that it's wishful thinking again, because this is the first time in my life I've felt like I did when I saw Harlow's heart break that day. Because I have no fucking idea how to fix what I've broken.

But I have to figure it out. I have to find a way to make it up to her, and I have to do it without telling her why I left. Because if I tell her—if she finds out—she'll pick a fight that she'll lose, and she'll put herself in Alex Wolfe's crosshairs. Harlow Chase will always choose to go down swinging, and this time she'll lose everything she has all over again.

That is not going to happen.

I will move mountains, I will go to prison, I will do anything before I let that happen again.

And as Harlow rounds the corner with Dill right behind her, I'm reminded why. She's fucking perfection. I don't know what anyone else sees and I don't care. I see the best woman I've ever known, her blonde hair tied up in a loose knot, a few loose strands dancing around her face, her eyes bright and big, her lips just as soft as I remembered. It's a gray day, like it might rain, everybody else looks miserable. She glows.

She *moves*. I don't know why, but the way she moves, like she's aware of every single motion of her body, her curves, her limbs, her hips—it drives me insane. It's like she dances without knowing it.

I exhale and curl my hands. It's like getting smacked in the face with just how amazing she is, how no woman can ever live up to her, so I stand there, immovable, trying to roll with the blow.

No chance. No way to roll with it. Full impact, every time.

And then her eyes meet mine and the world around us grinds to a stop. I don't know why it's different now, but it is. Maybe it's because now we've known each other, physically. Maybe it's because we've both had five years to think about every moment, every memory, every desire, and now it's all finally spilling out. Maybe it's just because now we're ready for each other. But this thing between us, this thing that happens when I look at her and know she's looking back at me the same way, this thing is powerful. I feel the shift and I swear to God the air around her shimmers, and the crackling of the heat between us raises the hairs on the back of my neck.

It's not gentle, like it used to be. It's raw. Primal. Animal.

I can tell she'd leave marks across my back. I can tell I'd make her scream.

Goddamn, she almost snarls at me. I stride over, carving a path in the sea of kids and parents, making straight for them.

It's good that Dill is here to bring us both back down to earth.

"Lo?" he says, and tugs at her sleeve. I look down at him briefly, but I can only keep my eyes off of Harlow for so long.

I breathe deeply and try to be a better man.

"Lo, they're boarding," Dill says. He looks at me, I guess finally picking up on the fact that there's something going on here, and I can see that look of puzzlement, of almost-recognition.

"Hi, Dill," I say.

That snaps Harlow out of it. "Don't," she warns.

I can't help it. I don't know why. Something in me is possessive as hell over both of them.

"Does he know he got that from me?" I ask. "Calling you Lo?"

"You're Marcus, aren't you?" Dill says, and now both Harlow and I snap out of it and look at Dill like he's got two heads. Or maybe just one really smart head.

"Yeah," I say, wondering what the hell that means to Dill. What does he know? Screw it. I put my hand out. "Nice to meet you again, Dill."

Dill shakes my hand solemnly.

"Be nice to my sister," he says.

Damn. I'm in trouble now. I look up at Harlow, and yup, she is pissed. Well, the damage is done. I might as well roll with this if I can.

"I promise," I say just as solemnly. I mean it, too.

"Ok, good," Dill says, as if that's settled now. "Lo, I really have to go now. They're all getting on the bus, choosing seats, and what if I have to sit by myself? I don't—"

"Dill, relax," Harlow says, and the anger in her face fades, replaced by affection. She bends at the knees and meets her little brother face to face. "Promise me you'll try to relax. You'll have fun, right?"

Dill takes a deep breath and blows out it with big cheeks, like a blowfish. Looks like he's just as much of a stress case as Harlow is.

"I promise. Can I go now?"

Harlow gives him one last hug, embarrassing the kid, and then shoves him off in the direction of the bus. "Go! Have fun! Send me a text as soon as you get there!" she calls after him. Dill ignores her, like a kid who can take that kind of love for granted is supposed to.

I am so damn proud of Harlow.

Oh, Christ, I am so proud of her. And at the same time I don't ever want to think of her having to do this alone.

Damn.

The bus driver honks his horn, and all the parents scatter out of the way, waving furiously. Harlow is just one of them, waving at Dill, trying to pretend she's not feeling anxious and worried and probably just plain emotional, watching him go away to camp for the summer.

And then the bus is gone, and Harlow's gaze sweeps back around and finds mine. The thing between us now is thicker, heavier, bearing the weight of all those years. Everything I've done.

It's angrier.

"I just want you to know one thing," she says, and I feel her voice crack against my skin, driving in deep. I want her so bad it hurts.

"What?" I say.

She's breathing different. Faster. So am I.

"I only agreed to this for one reason," she says, her eyes holding mine. "Because I want a goddamn explanation. I deserve an explanation. I am going to get it, and then I am going to be done with you, Marcus."

I lick my lips, looking at hers. Everything she said made sense except for that last part. It was such a transparent lie. Even she knows it.

"That's understandable," I say. "But it's not going to happen."

Her eyes flash. It occurs to me that though I taught Harlow how to fight in the physical sense, I've never been on the other side of it. I've never been her adversary. Until now.

The messed up thing is that I want to tell her. I want to tell her why I left, why I couldn't help her the first night Dill came home, why she had to go through all of this without me. And I can't, or Alex Wolfe will come after her.

I'm actually curious about what will happen next when we're interrupted by the last person in the world I want to see.

Brison Wolfe.

7

HARLOW

I'm just about to lay into Marcus for telling me I'm not going to get the answers I need—I mean, like hell I'm not, that is the whole point of this ridiculous arrangement—when his face darkens and he pulls me close to him.

It's so sudden I don't know exactly how to react. I haven't been this close to him in years. I haven't felt the heat of him, the hardness of him, the maleness of him. It all overwhelms and bypasses the higher functions of my brain, going straight for my core, and igniting my more animal urges.

"What the hell are you doing here?" Marcus barks.

I blink. It's only then that I recover enough to look back, to just behind where I'd been standing. There's a man there, tall and gorgeous, like Marcus, and with light gray eyes, but fair-haired. There's a similarity there.

Maybe it's just the shared look of arrogance. I shake Marcus off, annoyed at myself for my moment of weakness, and look between these two men. There's suddenly a whole lot of tension in the air. And this new man is looking at me, not at Marcus, his eyes appraising.

I shiver and rethink my decision to step away from Marcus.

"Just checking out the neighborhood, seeing what it has to offer," the man says. "Just like you."

I look up to see the muscle on the side of Marcus's jaw tense, but he doesn't say anything. I feel like I'm about to see a fight.

"Excuse me," I say. "And you are?"

"This is Mr. Wolfe's son," Marcus says, biting off those words as though he hates the taste of them in his mouth. He hasn't taken his eyes off this other man—Mr. Wolfe's son, apparently, who I did not know about—but he's moved closer, so that I stand somewhat back, behind him.

Well. Alex Wolfe's son. That explains it.

The man laughs. "'Mr. Wolfe's son?' That's cold, Marcus, even for you." Gray Eyes smiles brilliantly at me and puts his hand out. "I'm Brison Wolfe."

I'm not normally rude, but I don't want to shake his hand. I feel like there's something more going on here than I know, even beyond Marcus's involvement with the Wolfe family, and I don't like it. I don't like being ignorant, I don't like being out of control. I don't like feeling crowded by Wolfe men when they're trying to get me to do something. I just look at Brison's hand until he puts it down with a shrug.

"Maybe that's why you look familiar," I say. "Did you grow up here?"

"They lived out on Long Island," Marcus says. "Nice big house."

The change in Marcus's voice gets my attention. It sounds strained, pulled tight and taut, right on the breaking point. I look up at his face like I expect to be able to read him the way I used to, and I'm only reminded of how much time has passed between us when I don't know immediately what's going on his mind. It's the weirdest kind of near-déjà vu, and it unsettles me. Because the thing is, I can read Marcus's emotions plain as day, just like I always could. He's furious, and he's protective—of me.

But I don't know why. I have no idea what he's reacting to, what's going on his life, what kind of history he has with this Brison. At least not the specifics of it. And this is getting weird. Maybe it's natural that Brison Wolfe would be in the area, helping his father out while Alex Wolfe is apparently working with the developers to make sure everything goes through smoothly. But Marcus works for Alex Wolfe, too. It's not like they're on different sides of the issue.

And then I suddenly remember that I am on the other side of the issue, and both of these men are here messing up my neighborhood and my life. That Marcus is not my friend, and that whatever macho pissing contest is going on between Marcus and Brison has nothing to do with me.

And I know this—I know this, even if I have to remind myself of it—because Marcus chose to go work for Alex Wolfe. He chose to leave me the way he did, and he did it like it was the easiest thing in the world.

So I watch Marcus practically snarl at Brison, like Brison is invading his territory or something, and I kind of can't believe it. I'm not Marcus's territory.

In fact, I can't trust him at all.

Right?

"Jesus," I mutter. Neither of them seem to notice.

And I'm trying not to notice Marcus like he is now, his shoulders back, his arms tense, his back stretching his leather jacket to its limit. Getting all primitive and possessive, putting himself between another man and me, his moods mercurial and mystifying. I want to tell him he's a jerk and then beg him to fuck me.

What is wrong with me?

"Ok, well," Brison says, shaking his head, "this has been awkward, so Marcus, thank you for that. Harlow, I hope to see you around the neighborhood."

"You stay away from her," Marcus growls, and I have to do a double take.

I'm not even thinking about how ridiculous the whole thing is anymore. Or why Marcus feels the need to turn full caveman. I'm not thinking about anything but how much I want him, because it all just hit me in a frightening, dysfunctional rush. It washes over me like a tide, heat pooling between my legs, my skin prickling with electric awareness, my knees feeling weak from the pressure of it, and not for the first time I feel like I'm overcome by him. Only it's not him, this time, not in the same way — I don't feel close to him in the same way that I did back then. But I want all of him. I want this darkness that I see.

It's overwhelming.

It's more than that. It's debilitating. I have to fight it.

I stop and close my eyes, and the first thing that comes back to me is a memory I can't handle right now — right after my parents died, Marcus comforting me, holding me while I dissolved in his arms. My mind quickly shies away, and the memory fades into the darkness like some rare and terrible fish, flashing away into the depths. What I'm left with, though, is something helpful. I'm left thinking about how Marcus's training helped me through that.

Marcus taught me how to push through the pain. How when you hit that wall you need to push *into* the pain, let it become you, until you break through to the next level and get your much-needed reward of endorphins. And so that was how we approached the grief, too. It was weird — I don't know if it's like this for everyone, but for me grief was almost like getting a stomach bug. You'd think you were ok — or what passed for ok — and then it would hit you in this sudden wave of sickness and despair, and you'd be in utter hell until the wave would pass. I pushed through that pain the same way I pushed through the body pain at the end of a round, letting it wash over and through me, and the wave would eventually subside, leaving me exhausted but relatively free.

Fighting it like that makes it less terrifying. It makes you feel like you're in control of what happens to you, of the choices you make. I asked Marcus about it once, after one horrible workout, when I was just flattened, lying on the concrete floor of Pops's gym.

"Why do we do this to ourselves?" I panted. "It's not normal."

I remember the sound of his laugh, echoing in the empty gym. "We're not normal," he said. "I need it. Need to find that space, when you're just about to give up…"

"But you keep going," I finished for him.

"You decide who you're going to be," he'd said.

It was clearly something he'd thought about before.

I could read into that all day if I wanted to. But the main thing was that we were alike. We understood each other. And it was because he understood me that he could teach me. And it was because he could teach me that I survived what happened later.

And since it was Marcus who taught me about love and lust, too, now I'm wondering if the same technique will work here. If I can just push through these waves of intense attraction, of wanting him so badly I can practically feel myself vibrate with need, of wanting him to just shut up about everything, stop trying to tell me lies or make it up to me, and just do what I want. Give me something that will make it all stop.

I don't want to hear him. I don't want to have to forgive him. I just want to get over him, and for that I feel like I need him. It's like an itch I need to scratch. And I know that I can't.

I touch his hand.

I see the sensation of that touch travel through his body, I see it ripple up his arm, his shoulder, his neck, until he's turning to look at me, his expression softening, his eyes wide and burning.

Just touching him leaves me unable to breathe.

"Let's leave," I say. "Please, let's go."

Marcus swallows, his Adam's apple dipping up and down. "Yes," he says, his voice hoarse.

He grabs my hand, dwarfing it in size, and pulls me alongside him as he starts to walk down the street, away from Brison Wolfe.

"I'll be in touch!" Brison shouts after us.

I can't help but wonder what that's about.

***

We're past Driggs Avenue now, walking toward Bedford Avenue, and I remember myself enough to pull my hand from his. I sever contact, and it's like it shocks both of us—we stop our brisk pace, Marcus looking at me, confused. It's a strange moment. Like a spell has been broken.

We stare at each other for way too long. I'm the first one to try to cover it up.

"Are you going to tell me what that was about?" I ask.

"No," he says. His voice is deep. I feel another wave coming on. Damn it.

"Marcus," I say, taking a step back. "I wasn't kidding before. I need an explanation from you."

He looks pained. He opens and closes his hands. Finally, he says, "It's not that simple."

I'm getting pissed.

"Yes, actually, it's exactly that simple. People do it all the time. They explain things. In fact, you should have done it before you left."

"No," he says, running a hand through his dark hair. "I just shouldn't have left. At least not the way I did."

"What the hell does that mean?" I say, throwing my hands up.

Marcus glares at me, irritated. "Sometimes things are complicated, Harlow! Will you just…Christ, Lo, look at me."

Marcus grabs my hand before I can pull it back and the spell is activated. Whatever it is, it's infuriating. Some kind of sense memory of this man, of everything he did for me, of the way he used to hold me, invades my mind and colors my perception of the present. I'm not just feeling Marcus's hand around mine today, and I'm not just seeing him standing in front of me, begging me to listen. I'm feeling and seeing all the times Marcus Roma has mattered to me.

It's a lot.

I look. And I listen. And I am mesmerized by those eyes.

"Harlow, will you at least believe one thing?" he says, and draws me closer. His thumb is pressing into the palm of my hand, moving in small circles, and his voice is urgent with need. "Will you please believe that I will do my damn best for you?"

I am transfixed, and for a second I'm falling for it. Completely. Because I want to believe that Marcus Roma will give me what I need, in every possible way. I want to believe that this feeling will leave me one day, that I'll be free of both loving and hating him, that I won't crave his touch like this. That I'll be able to forget the things he put me through, the things that happened to me, after he left. That I'll move on.

I really need to believe that.

"Fine," I choke back. I take my hand from his, needing a clear head. "But that won't be good enough, Marcus."

"Ok," he says with a grin. "I'll work on getting good enough."

Where have I heard that before? I look at him quizzically, but he just smiles that newly enigmatic smile, and resumes walking toward busy Bedford Avenue.

I have freaking whiplash.

"So what do we have planned for today?" he asks.

"Wait a minute," I say. "How did Brison Wolfe know me by sight?"

Marcus's expression hardens. I would regret bringing it up, except for the fact that I just realized that even though I didn't introduce myself to Brison he knew my name, and it creeps me out.

"That's a good question, Lo," Marcus says. "I would have to say it has something to do with the way you're holding out on that offer for your house."

I stop. "What exactly do you do for Alex Wolfe?"

Marcus exhales. "I'm a fixer."

"Is that what it sounds like? You fix problems?"

"Yes."

"Problems like me?"

"It's complicated."

"So you want me to sell my house?" I demand. I'm so enraged by this idea I don't even know where to start. I mean, I knew he worked for Alex Wolfe, and I have to assume Wolfe has money in this development deal, otherwise he wouldn't care about it one way or the other. But some part of me kind of thought that Marcus would rebel against the whole thing somehow.

I also expect Marcus to be mad about this accusation. He's not. He just looks at me with a kind of sad expression.

"Yeah, I want you to sell, Lo."

"Well, I'm not going to."

"But you will, Lo," he says. "I just want it to be your choice when you do."

I start. It hadn't even occurred to me that I might fight and lose. Fighting is what I do. It's what we do, Marcus and I. And he doesn't think I can win.

I don't have anything to say to that. Mostly because it makes me feel alone in a whole new way.

"You asked what we were doing today?" I say, starting to walk toward Shantha's bar. "Today we are figuring out how to stop this development so that everybody stops bothering me about my house. Or I am, anyway. You are tagging along."

Out of the corner of my eye I see Marcus shaking his head, but he's walking beside me now, coming with me. The more we walk in silence, the angrier I get. How dare he think I'm going to have to sell my house? He has no right. He hasn't been here. He has no idea how important it is to Dill and me.

It's only a few blocks to The Alley, and by the time we get there I am steaming, partially because it's easier to be angry than to have to constantly fight my very complicated feelings about Marcus. I practically slam into the door of The Alley, refusing to look at him as he stands behind me.

Shantha opens the door with her incredulous face on. "There a reason you're banging on my door before we open, honey?" she asks.

"Yeah," I say. "I have an idea I want to bounce off of you."

Shantha opens the door in the full light of day and I look nervously back at Marcus to see how he'll react. I figured in the bar the other night it was dark, and Marcus was mostly focused on me. But now he's looking right at Shantha and I'm wondering if he can tell. I'm wondering if it will matter if he can tell. I wonder if getting over him will be easier on me if he turns out to be really awful to my best friend just because she happens to be transgender. I mean, you never know. People have reactions.

Marcus just waves.

"What about him?" Shantha asks, smiling at me way too suggestively. She recognizes Marcus from the other night, though she doesn't know who he is. Yet. "You been bouncing ideas off him?"

I can hear Marcus stifle a laugh.

He wouldn't laugh if he knew how much Shantha wanted me to start dating again. Or if he knew the reason why she thinks I don't.

"Not like that," I say with perhaps a bit too much vehemence. "I will explain inside."

"Sure. You want a drink, honey?" Shantha says to Marcus, and shows him inside.

I hate that I hear Marcus apologize to Shantha for me. Like I'm the jerk in this situation. And I hate that, for the first time in years, walking into this bar has triggered my anxiety. I hate that I have to sit down, and fight off a sudden panic attack while Shantha chats with Marcus at the bar.

There's a reason for that.

This is the place where I met Shantha, more than four years ago. We got very close very quickly, for very bad reasons. We met because Shantha was the one who saved me.

It's not something I like to talk about for obvious reasons. And for the most part, I don't spend a lot of time thinking about it. I think I have done a good job at dealing with it, even if I haven't really wanted to date much—I mean, there are a lot of reasons that I haven't been interested in relationships. But Marcus being here, in this place…it's messing with me.

After I realized Marcus wasn't coming back, or maybe just to spite him, I don't fucking know why I did it, but for a little while, I hooked up with guys kind of randomly. I made a few poor decisions, right before I got my life together for Dill. Sometimes I think I was just looking for someone, anyone, to fill Marcus's place, but when I put it like that it's so obviously laughable, isn't it? As though anyone could ever take Marcus's place.

So maybe I was just trying to dull the pain. Maybe I just had to keep doing things that confirmed that I was, in fact, just as worthless as Marcus made me feel when he left. I don't know.

Anyway. I got involved with some questionable guys. And one really bad one.

I think, all things considered, I was actually lucky. I mean, in an ideal world, no woman should have to be afraid that a man will force her to do something she doesn't want to do just because he can, because she's drunk, because there's no one else around. But we don't live in an ideal world.

His name was Dylan.

I'd met up with him a few times at bars, gotten drunk. I hadn't gone home with him—and I wasn't going to—because he didn't do it for me, but he was just awful enough, just angry enough, with his unwashed hipster hair and this sneer he always had going, like one of those guys who'd been uncool his whole life and then moved to New York and got a new wardrobe but never got rid of the chip on his shoulder, that I think he scratched that self-destructive itch. That place where the wound Marcus had left me with had started to scab over, where it somehow felt satisfying to scratch at it, to make myself feel worthless all over again—Dylan was perfect for that.

I mean, I wasn't kidding: these were some seriously poor decisions. Marcus messed me up pretty badly. Almost worse, in some ways, than my parents dying, because that at least wasn't personal. That was just life screwing me and my family over. Marcus? Marcus left *me*. It was as personal as you could get.

I really, really, really did not handle it well. So, besides being constantly drunk, there were guys like Dylan. Not too many, thank God, before Dylan himself scared me into getting myself together, but it's not a period of my life I like to think about. I mean, I think sex is awesome, generally, but I have a problem with sleeping around out of self-loathing, you know?

I'm ashamed of it. I'm ashamed that I was that weak.

And even though I know it's not my fault, I'm ashamed of what happened.

So one night I met up with Dylan at The Alley, just after Shantha had bought it and had everything redone. I was getting pretty drunk, I guess, on lots of shots of whiskey—a liquor I can't stand now—and I remember being kind of mean to Dylan, and I remember him getting aggressive back, just because I wasn't being flirtatious. It must have seemed so fucked up to anyone who was watching—and thank God Shantha was watching.

Because when I got up to go to the bathroom, Dylan followed me.

I really don't like to think about it, but I will be damned if I'm afraid to remember. I'm not going to let him have that power over me.

I didn't hear him come in.

I saw him in the mirror, and it was this moment of confusion, like, is this right? Can this be right? And then there was just the shock of his hands suddenly on me.

There was the smell of his whiskey breath as he forced me up against the wall. There was the way twisted my wrist until I cried out in pain. There were the things he said, how he called me a bitch and a slut as he fumbled with my jeans. He was *angry*. I remember that, most of all, how angry and hateful he was. I remember how he wanted to rape me because he was angry with me.

And I remember not being able to fight him off.

I remember thinking, *I can't believe this is happening. This is really happening.*

I remember begging.

I remember how my mind started to drift away, like it was separate from my body, like whatever part of me could escape was determined to do so. I remember going slack at one point, after struggling so hard that I sprained my left wrist, that there were bruises all over me. I just went slack. Like if I stopped it would somehow cancel everything out. Like somehow if I wasn't fighting, this wasn't really happening.

I still don't understand that. I still can't think about that without...I don't even know. It makes me feel ashamed, yeah, but also frightened and confused, because I just cannot understand what my own body did. I was always a fighter. I was supposed to be a *fighter*.

And I remember Shantha pounding on the door. She told me I screamed, but I don't know. I just remember she unlocked the door—the bastard had locked the bathroom door—and busted in full of rage. Dylan let go of me like I was suddenly hot to the touch, like that would change what he had tried to do, and in a rush the world came back to me. My mind came back and my body hurt and I went from being dead inside to terrified and *angry*. I immediately started crying out of pure, incandescent rage.

Shantha tried to hold him, screaming about calling the police, but Dylan shoved her into the sink and ran. That was the last I ever saw of him. The last thing I wanted to do was get the police involved; I didn't trust them, and I wanted to get Dill, and above all, I just wanted to forget about it. And after that? It's somewhat of a blur. Mostly I remember Shantha, taking care of me, doing all the right things. I remember shaking, like, watching my hand shake uncontrollably while I said that I was ok.

So Shantha and I met in kind of a weird way. I mean, underage girl in bar gets drunk and then someone tries to rape her—not ideal from the proprietor's point of view. But the thing about Shantha is that she can see through almost anyone's defenses. She has this almost unerring ability to see when people are in need. I think it comes from all those years she spent in the closet, hiding herself—she got good at recognizing when anyone hid their hurt. She saw right through me, that's for sure.

And she offered me a job. Like, to keep me out of trouble. To try to be a good influence on my life. She helped out with Dill when I finally got custody. In a very real way, Shantha stepped in and saved me, all over again.

So, when I come here, now, *that* is what I've trained myself to think about. I think about Shantha coming into my life, I think about Shantha showing me just endless patience and compassion, I think about this being the first place I learned how to have fun again, because of her. I don't think about that night. I don't think about Dylan, even though I still won't use that bathroom.

And even though this is one of the reasons I don't really date. It was already hard enough for me to feel safe in the world after Marcus left, and then Dylan happened. I haven't felt truly safe since.

And I haven't really been able to feel that way about a guy since Marcus, anyway, even though I've tried. I haven't even wanted anyone until Marcus came back, because the only man I've ever really wanted is him. Which is why I'm so off balance, and Shantha is so excited to see me with a guy, and why I'm inevitably thinking about the night some asshole tried to rape me.

That's why Marcus being here messes me up so much. It's like two worlds colliding all over again. Marcus reminds me of how bad things got after he left, and of what almost happened here. And while I don't blame him for it, but I can't help feeling angry.

Or maybe I'm just looking for reasons to be mad at him. More reasons, I mean.

My head is all over the place right now.

"So what's your idea?" Marcus says walking back over to me. He flips a chair off of one of the tables and straddling it in one smooth motion.

I stare at him.

"You think I'm going to tell you?" I say.

"Come on, I won't spill," he says, grinning. "I promise."

He thinks I'm teasing. Somehow that's more insulting than an actual insult, like he doesn't take me or my feelings seriously. I take all that anger I've been stewing on the whole walk over here—or maybe I take all five years' worth—and hone it down into one phrase.

"And what exactly is a promise from you worth, Marcus?"

I swear I can feel the temperature in the room drop. Shantha backs off without a word, finding something to do in the office with the door cracked open. Marcus meets my eyes, unflinching. He's taken his jacket off, and now he folds those thick, corded arms over the back of the chair and leans forward, his expression serious.

"Lie to me, Lo, and tell me it's a lot," he says.

The second time. That's the second time he's said that to me. Knowing what it means. Knowing why I used to ask him to do that. There's a crackling feeling around me while I stare at him, like the charge between us just doubled and it's inexorably drawing me to him, even while I'm furious with him. That phrase did what it was supposed to: it reminded me of us, of everything, of the intimacy we will always have. Of those private moments I shared with him that I can never take back. Of how I want to tell him about the bad things that happened to me when he wasn't here, how I want him to comfort me.

It reminds me that I love him and makes me hate him even more.

"Stop saying that," I whisper. "You don't get to say that to me anymore."

Marcus stands up suddenly, toppling the chair. He doesn't come closer, though I can see him struggling. Part of me wants him to come closer.

"The hell I don't," he says.

"It's so shitty of you," I say. "Why would you do that? Why would you make me think about all that? Why would you make me think about how I used to need you? Is it just to humiliate me?"

"No," he says, angry. "It's because maybe now I need something from you."

We both seem surprised at that.

Marcus Roma, needing something from me?

His mind works faster than mine, gets there before I figure out how pissed off I am. He says, "Wait, Lo. I'm not saying you owe me anything. I'm saying I need you. There's a difference."

That shuts me up. And melts me.

I mean, actually melts me. I lean on a table for support, unable to take my eyes off him, feeling my knees turn to jelly. Five years ago this wouldn't have been such an affecting statement. Five years ago I helped Marcus after his own father died, when we were already so close that we hardly had to speak to communicate, when I took it for granted that we needed each other. But then he left, and he left without telling me. Without saying goodbye.

This whole time I've been thinking how could someone who did that have loved me? How could someone who threw me away have ever needed me?

And here he is, the only man I've ever dreamed about, this gorgeous, perfect man, the only person who stood by me through the worst days of my life, telling me he needs me. And I can't take my eyes from his face. He is beautiful; he has always been beautiful, with that golden skin, that strong jaw, soft lips. But now he's beautiful because he looks…

Oh God, he looks like he's hurting. Strong, but hurting. If there's any guy who could take a punch at his weakest, it's Marcus Roma. But I don't want to hit him while he's down.

I just want to touch him. I want to go up to him, touch his face, find a way to make this all better for both of us. Find a way to erase the last five years, for both of us.

And I hate that I feel that way.

It's exhausting.

"Marcus…" I say, sitting down.

"We have a deal," he says quickly. Like he thinks I'm going to renege.

"We have a deal," I repeat. I just don't know how I'm going to survive it.

I'm worried about what he'll say next. If it will be the thing that finally cuts down my remaining defenses, that wears down my sense of danger, that gets through to me, and I'll just be bare to him. Too weak to hold off what I know isn't good for me. He won't even have earned it. He'll just have won forgiveness by attrition.

But I'm saved by a phone call.

Marcus doesn't immediately look away. He's still staring at me like he might never look away, and if it were anyone else it would unnerve me. Finally, his phone starts on the second cycle of the ring and fishes it out of his pocket, saying to me, "I'm sorry, it's work."

Meaning Alex Wolfe.

I take the opportunity to escape. I don't even say anything; I just head toward Shantha's office, shelter from the storm that is Marcus and all the memories that come with him. I almost get away.

"Lo, you working tonight?" he calls out after me.

I force myself to turn around and look at him one last time. I can handle that much.

"Nope," I say.

He smiles, brightening the room. "Good," he says, covering the phone with one hand. "I'll pick you up for a morning workout."

I swallow as I watch him walk out of the bar. Right. A morning workout. Just like old times.

Never mind that I am not nearly in the kind of shape that I was in five years ago. Suddenly that matters. Like it's all I have left to fight with — showing Marcus that I still have the heart to kick his ass in a workout. Of course, that's ridiculous. It's just because I need something, anything to defend myself with against the onslaught of emotion, lust, and pain that is Marcus Roma.

I stagger into Shantha's office, where she's not even pretending to go over invoices so much as watching through her cracked office door. We both hear the front door open and close, and as soon as it does, Shantha shouts:

"That's *the* Marcus? Holy shit! Why didn't you tell me?"

I wince. "Yeah. I know. I really don't even want to talk about it."

Shantha drops her reading glasses down the bridge of her nose and looks up at me like I know I'm being unreasonable.

"Not an option," she says.

"Fine," I sigh. "I will tell you all about this train wreck right after I tell you how we're going to save this bar and my house from those freaking developers."

8

MARCUS

I know what the call is about as soon as I see who's calling me. The last thing I want to do is leave Lo, but I can see she's got whiplash or fatigue or something just from being around me for a little while, and I don't want to push her too hard too fast.

So a phone call from Alex Wolfe it is.

I leave the bar, trying to keep myself under control, but I'm pissed off as soon as I pick up. And he knows why.

"What the fuck, Alex?" I bark into the phone, storming down Bedford Avenue. I don't even know where I'm going, I just need to walk.

"Brison said you were in a bad mood."

"This isn't a bad mood. This is me reacting to a threat."

"No one's made any threats, Marcus."

He is one condescending son of a bitch. But I know it won't do any good to argue, to try to make him admit what he's doing. The only thing that gets through to Alex Wolfe is consequences.

"Wrong, Alex," I say, stopping where I stand like a rock in the stream of pedestrians. I want to make sure he hears this clearly. "I'm making a threat. You do not mess with her, do you understand? No one messes with her. No one."

"Don't raise your voice to me," he says. I can hear him frown over the phone, and it almost makes me laugh.

"I'm not fucking joking, Alex."

"I can hear that," he says. "But I'm not seeing any progress, Marcus. We need her house. And approval from the zoning board will depend to some extent on whether the community objects. You know that."

And bribes. It will also depend on how many bribes he can spread around. Short of a public relations nightmare, he's not going to have a problem and we both know it.

"This is non-negotiable," I say. "This is a hard line. I don't want anyone messing with, approaching, or hassling Harlow Chase, and that includes Brison. And no goddamned dirty tricks, or I swear to God…"

"All right, all right." He sighs over the phone. "You've made your point, you don't have to get so upset. You know if you have concerns about things like this you only have to call. And I'd prefer that you and Brison try to get along for the sake of the business, at least."

I close my eyes and breathe. I should feel bad for Brison Wolfe. It would be hard to grow up an only son with only a sister who is totally uninterested in the business and then find out you suddenly had competition for the top spot. But Brison is just like his father, and I don't give a damn if I make him cry crocodile tears.

No. What really bothers me is how important it is to me that Alex Wolfe has put me next in line. That it still means so damn much to me that someone like him would believe in me. I'm still haunted by the fact that my dad didn't.

"You know, Marcus," Alex says. "You will have to make tough decisions if you are to head up the business. Keep that in mind."

Asshole.

I know he's an asshole. And he's the only real father I've ever had.

I hang up and start the walk back to my shiny hotel, brand new, right on the waterfront. I tell myself what I always tell myself: when Alex gives me a bigger slice of the pie, I can start to change how we do business. I'll have more control. I'll be able to protect people like Harlow.

The thing is, I need to protect Harlow now.

Man, I did not plan ahead. This one time, I did not plan ahead. I got one look at Harlow's face by the bridge and it became clear to me that all my previous plans were ashes. I don't even have a plan to win her back, to make it all right, without telling her the truth about why I left the way I did.

If I told her, she'd go ballistic. And Alex Wolfe would destroy her and Dill.

So that's right out. But how the hell do you show someone you always loved them, you always had them on your mind, if you can't tell them the reasons why you left?

It's while I'm staring at the clock by the side of my hotel bed, counting down the minutes until I can see Harlow again, that it comes to me.

***

I get a few hours sleep. Enough. I'm so bright-eyed and freaking bushytailed at the idea of working out with Lo again that I might as well have gotten the full eight. I end up jogging over to her house from the hotel in the murky gray light, smiling the whole way.

Walking up those stairs to ring her bell is a trip. She was always waiting for me back in high school, didn't want to wake anyone up. And then when she was living with the Mankowskis, well, that was more of a sneaking sort of situation for a while.

I don't know why this feels momentous, but it does. I ring and go back to wait for her on the sidewalk, bouncing up and down on my calves, happy as hell.

I have to remember she'll probably be pissed to see me. But I don't care. I'll take whatever time with her I can get.

She opens the door, wearing those tiny running shorts I remember, her hair tied back and her expression grim, like she's going to fight me the whole way. And then something amazing happens.

After her parents died, it was bad. It was bad for a long time. I did anything I could just to try to keep her going, and one of the first things I did was get her back out to train with me in the mornings. She wasn't sleeping much anyway, so it was at least something better to do. And just to mix it up, we started going to McCarren Park to run sprints on that track they have.

So this one morning, gray just like this one, we go over there, and the high school track team was setting up a bunch of hurdles. Or they were going to, because the hurdles were all just bunched together kind of close together right in the middle of the green. Lo sees them there and she just takes off in a sprint headed for that first hurdle.

You gotta understand, she had been so quiet those first few months. She didn't talk much to anyone but me. I could barely get her to eat, to work out with me, to go to school. She did all that stuff only when I asked her to. She was like a shadow of a person. And then all of a sudden she's in a dead sprint for a hurdle?

It took me by surprise, I will admit.

I wasn't the only one watching her, either. Bunch of sleepy track and field kids were just as confused.

So Lo tries to jump that first hurdle at an angle, kind of lengthwise, so she misses the rest of them, since they were all kind of bunched together. Don't ask me why. I doubt she even knew why. But she tried to clear that hurdle at a weird angle, and she clipped it.

And every single one of those hurdles fell, one by one. You know the kind that collapse when they fall? Some kind of safety thing? All of 'em, down, like collapsing dominos. Right in front of the entire confused track and field team.

And Lo takes the fall, rolling in that green grass, and just starts laughing at herself. I don't mean normal laughing. I mean, it was funny, but not, like, the funniest thing you've ever seen. But Lo had tears coming down her cheeks she was laughing so hard, and as soon as I figured it out, I was, too. Because she ran at the hurdle like she'd just decided to start feeling things again, and then she'd messed it up anyway and embarrassed herself, and the absurdity of it, like she finally got the courage to take a step, and tripped over her own feet anyway…

I don't know how to explain it. But that was the day that Harlow laughed again, and she did it laughing at herself. Believe me when I tell you that I've never been more relieved in my life.

So today, right now, as Lo starts to walk down those steps looking all proud and defiant, like spending time with me is going to be something difficult and terrible, something she has to conquer, she trips coming down the stairs and falls right into me.

She crashed into me.

Her body pressed against mine, her hands on my chest, her breath on my neck—damn. Instantly I feel myself start to get hard, and I have to put that on lockdown. Not easy when I can feel how breathless she is, too.

No matter how angry she is at me, no matter how much I deserve it, it won't change how we feel together.

Her hands linger on my chest just a second too long and her hips melt into me just enough to make me want to groan, and then she pushes off of me, and I can see her laughing at herself. Laughing at me, too, laughing at how dumb and awkward we are.

She looks at me, her eyes these dancing blue points in the morning gray, crinkling at the corners while she smiles.

"So," she says, exaggerating the word, "I won't do that again."

I raise an eyebrow. "Suit yourself."

But I am just so damn happy to see her laughing again. Smiling.

There's another one of those moments we have. When it's just electric between us, when I know she's looking at me just like I'm looking at her. Wanting it to be so much more. Except this time, when she looks back into my eyes, I see more than lust. I see hate. And hurt.

What did I expect?

I start to jog down the street, loping slow and easy, and find that she settles in with me just fine. Like old times. Like old times, except I'm carrying a secret, and I might be the worst thing to ever happen to her.

Because even with what I just saw, I can't bring myself to stay away.

9

HARLOW

Working out for the first time in months on no sleep sucks, believe me. But that is not the worst of it.

I was up practically all night. Restless. Mind churning, sifting through memories of Marcus, always shying away from the worst, the day that's at the core of so many of them. That's not unusual, though. The only thing I've ever remembered about the day my parents died is Marcus.

Days after that? Nothing, except Marcus being there. I mean, I must have done things. Talked to people, dealt with responsibilities, spoken to my bitchy Aunt Jill when she arrived to take Dill, even though she wouldn't take me. (I was "too much." Whatever. She just wanted control of the trust, and the house.)

I mean, I still existed during those days, but all I remember is the time I spent with Marcus. Weirdly—and I used to feel guilty about this, because I thought it meant I was incredibly shallow—I remember thinking how much it no longer mattered that he had gone and slept with Rosa right as I thought he was finally getting interested in me. I mean, of all the things to be preoccupied with when you've just been orphaned, right? But I think that was just the level my brain could handle. Strangely satisfied that he was hanging out with me instead.

Not just hanging out. I don't actually remember him leaving my side. The Mankowskis were super tolerant, come to think of it, maybe because Marcus was the only one who could get me to go to school. Or who could get me to sleep, eventually.

So my jerkwad brain is tossing these gems up all night while I'm thinking about what it's going to mean to spend all this time with Marcus again. And whenever I get too close to what happened later, to what Marcus became for me, I shut it down as much as I can. I can't deal. I can't deal, and I shouldn't be thinking about that, because he is not that anymore.

It's the emotional element that's pissing me off. It's the emotional element that makes me feel weak. I have to keep reminding myself: I don't want him to love me, or try to win me back, or any of that bullshit. I don't want to feel safe with him again. I mean, I can't want that. I want validation. I want an explanation of why he rejected and then abandoned me.

And God help me, I want him inside me.

This is the last place I find refuge. The only place I find refuge: thinking about Marcus taking me, turning it into something purely physical, rather than emotional. Taking me hard, taking me in the way he never quite did when we were sweet, relatively innocent teenagers in love. I want to hate fuck him. I want to put him in his place, and make sure that that is all he'll ever be to me again.

Or maybe I just want him. Maybe it's just chemical between us and I need to accept that.

Yeah, so this is everything that's going through my head as I walk down my front porch steps and trip into Marcus's arms.

Not even a little bit on purpose, I swear. Not consciously, anyway.

So of course I laugh. I mean, of course I laugh; I just made an ass out of myself, again, and there is nothing else you can do but laugh in that situation. Because the second he touches me, I'm wet, and my body comes roaring alive with wanting him. The second he puts his arms around me to steady me, I feel his strength, feel him holding me up the way he used to, and I remember how incredible it was to have Marcus Roma in my corner. And everything in me crumbles.

So when I look back at him, I remember to hate him. I remember to hate him for leaving me, for making me feel like nothing. I remember to hate him for making me weak.

And I remember to hate myself for not being able to get over any of it.

He sees it. I know he does by the look that passes across his face like a shadow. And that both elates me, in a sick way I'm not proud of, and breaks my heart, in a way that frightens me.

I am so, so relieved when he just starts running.

I don't even care when I catch myself falling into old rhythms, bantering with him, teasing him about how he's so out of shape. He's not out of shape, obviously; he's a Greek god. But I have to say something to cover up the fact that I haven't had a decent workout in months.

"McCarren Park?" he says, looking over his shoulder.

I smile and nod, and tell myself I'm not just playing it cool. I am cool. Because watching Marcus Roma build up a sweat is not going to get to me.

Or, rather, it will get to me, but only in one very specific way.

We hit the track and I start rehearsing the stuff I'd thought about yesterday. So, first of all, it's clear I'm not going to get answers from Marcus right away. He taught me all about this, after all. If you attack directly, your opponent instinctively blocks. You have to feint.

So I'll have to work my way around to explanations. It will probably involve lots of conversations about things I would rather forget, or at least not dwell on, but whatever. This was never going to be easy. But I've convinced myself I can handle it.

I have to. Besides the fact that this is an unconventional way to send Dill to the most emotionally expensive computer camp ever, I need to be sane and functioning when he gets back, not just a shapeless, emotional blob covered in chocolate and tears.

And, on top of all that, there's the project I outlined for Shantha yesterday. I've decided to go on the offensive where this development is concerned. I know they still need zoning approval, and I know they're trying to buy the building where The Alley has a lease and Shantha is totally on board to hold fundraisers for opposition at the bar. First step is that I need to canvass the neighborhood for support.

What's left of the neighborhood, anyway.

That is what's on my agenda for today, and I haven't decided if I can trust Marcus with the information. Well, that's not exactly true. I haven't decided if I want to trust him with the information before I have to. I mean, it's not like he won't figure it out when we start putting posters and stuff all over the place.

It's just pride. And spite.

I never knew spite could be such a motivating emotion, but hey, I'm keeping pace with Marcus Roma and I haven't passed out yet, so it obviously works pretty well.

I make the mistake of looking up at him, and just…Christ, he is gorgeous. The sun is higher in the sky, and that warm morning light is hitting him just right, setting off that golden skin and those light eyes. For once I'm thankful that he hasn't taken his shirt off.

He slows to a stop in front of me, running a hand through his hair, taking a deep breath and touching his toes once.

"Ok, warm up's over," he says.

I want to sit down and take a nap already. I can't believe I used to do this every morning.

"Tabata sprints?" he says.

I groan. Tabata intervals of anything are evil—it's twenty seconds of going all out, as hard as you can, then ten seconds of rest, and repeat until…well, if I remember correctly, until you pass out. At least that's the way Marcus used to do them. I think fighters who were less badass about it did a finite number.

But Tabata sprints? Today? Oh God.

"Did you turn wussy on me, Lo?" he says with that evil grin. He knows that he can get me to try any insane workout by telling me I can't do it. It's just straight up wrong.

"Oh, you are evil," I say. "Fine. Ten Tabata sprints."

Marcus looks slightly surprised. "We don't have to."

"You have a stopwatch?"

I'm determined now. I have to win at something out of all of this. I need one thing in my column.

"Yeah."

"Then call it," I say, and shake my legs out.

I'm suddenly determined to show Marcus Roma just how far I can push myself. Just how much I can fight. I bend one leg as if I've got a block behind me and zone in on his starting mark. I relish this moment, always have. I love the still, quiet fury of anticipation. Of knowing everything's about to…

Explode.

"Go!" he yells, and we both break into a full run, arms pumping, legs burning, throats scorched as we suck air into our aching lungs. I refuse to let him outpace me, even though it's impossible; he's so much bigger than I am. I resolve that I will not give in. I will keep pace with him on the last sprint. He might be bigger and stronger, but he will not have more heart than me.

It feels important on many levels.

On our ten-second break he stops, panting, waiting for me to catch up as I walk toward him. I don't say anything. If you can talk during a Tabata set, you're not doing it right.

By the fourth interval I can feel the heat coming off of my face and my legs starting to shake when I walk. Marcus looks the same, sweat pouring down his face. He peels his black t-shirt off and tosses it onto the green in the center of the track, and for a second I actually forget what I'm doing.

I watch his magnificent back shine with sweat in the morning sun on the next interval. It makes it easier.

I'm slowly catching his pace.

I feel like I'm about to throw up, I have a stitch, and I'm overheated, but I know I can catch him now.

By the last interval I think there's an actual, non-trivial possibility that I might die. I can feel my pulse like a jackhammer in every part of my body. My skin is red, and my body is covered in sweat. All I want is air, and there's not enough of it in the world.

But I catch him. I keep pace with him on that last interval, and at the end of it I look over to make sure he knows, as we're both pushing through those last seconds, and I see him smile briefly, through the pain.

We don't talk. We just collapse on the green grass beside the track. Marcus hands me his water bottle and I greedily suck half of it down.

I have no idea how long we lay there, side by side, silent and panting. But it occurs to me—sometime after I'm convinced that I will in fact live, but before I have the strength to get up—that we've just shared something again. There's no one else I've ever done this with. No one else who's ever seen me strip away all of the pretense and just get down to heart. No one else who's ever seen what I can do when I put my mind to it.

I don't even have the energy to be sad about it.

I turn my head, still lying on the grass, and see him lying next to me. He's put his hands behind his head, his eyes closed, soaking up the sun. My eyes trace a line down his strong, flexed arms to his pecs, his lats, and then every single one of those little muscles on his ribcage, like little scalloped waves, all the way down to his abs, and the edge of that unbelievably sexy V that disappears under the waistband of his shorts, and then…

God.

I can't—seriously cannot—look away.

I feel anxious now, too, and that's a terrible way to feel after a workout. I exhale a puff of air and try to identify where the terribleness is coming from; it's not hard. It's that I've had to work so hard to fight my feelings for Marcus—all my feelings for Marcus—and, as always, he seems so in control.

We could be feeling the same level of emotion, or want, or motivation, or whatever, but only I would be biting my lip, tense, constantly on the brink of exploding with whatever emotion it was. Marcus? That just wouldn't happen. He's quieter. Where I burn up, he smolders. But always, always a controlled burn. I've always wondered what on this planet could make him lose control. It's certainly not me.

And that is infuriating when I want him to want me more than I want him. When I want to be, for once, the one with the power. Because, once again, I want something from him and it's making me insane, and he just lies there, totally cool and relaxed. I want him to tell me everything. I want him to confess, and for that confession to answer all my questions, heal all my wounds. I want him to beg me forgiveness and more. I want him to beg me, and, crucially, I want it not to affect me when he does.

I want to know I can have him, but that I don't need him.

And I don't even care how awful that is.

I also, incidentally, really just freaking want him. God, watching him flex his ripped eight pack as he sits up pushes most coherent thoughts out of my mind. He's still sweaty. I love him when he's sweaty. When he smells most like himself, musky and male.

"Hey," he says, his voice low and rough. And those hypnotist eyes lock on me again.

I am suddenly incredibly aware of how long it's been since I've had sex. My entire body is aware. I'm wet again. Embarrassingly wet, from just his voice, his look, the sight of his body. He doesn't even have to touch me, and I can feel the pressure start to build between my legs. The physical response is almost overwhelming. Like he pushed a button and I'm his.

Damn it. That's not being in control.

"What?" I say.

"I've been thinking about it," he says. His breathing is already back to normal while mine is getting shallow and rapid all over again, and I can't help but watch his chest rise and fall. Watch all those very visible muscles work together. He is the perfect machine.

"Lo," he says again.

I look up. Damn him. He's smiling, but his eyes are burning, and I could swear he's feeling the sexual tension just as much as I am.

"I've been thinking, Lo. I know it's what you want, but I can't tell you the details about how and why I left like I did, not now. But I can show you what I did in the meantime. I never stopped thinking about you, Lo, not once. I can prove it."

I can't look away from Marcus's eyes, and when he says that—when he says he never stopped thinking about me, and he can prove it—the worst happens.

I give in. For a just a moment, I give in.

It's like there's this little version of me inside my heart, a version that never stopped believing that maybe Marcus really did love me, that there was some reason for the things that he did, for why he did the one thing he knew would hurt me the most—just leaving, no explanation—and she is growing. I've starved her over the years, shrunk her down to a manageable size and caged her up. And then Marcus says something like that and she grows.

For a second I'm her again. I'm feeling what she feels. I feel warm and happy and light, the grief peeling off of me in waves, leaving only relief behind. I feel happy, and I feel safe. Just for a second. It's like looking through a window on a beautiful day.

And it scares the shit out of me.

I revolt. I need to push myself as far away from that vulnerable place of emotion as possible. I need to show him that's not what this is about. What we're feeling when we're together, it's not emotion. It's not love. It can't be. It's just lust. And it can be satisfied.

I meet Marcus's gaze and say, "You want to just cut the bullshit and go back to my place?"

He doesn't say anything. Not at first. And then he just studies my face, frowning slightly.

He says, "What do you mean?"

"What do you think I mean?" I say. I smile at him, casually. Like none of this matters beyond the physical. Like none of it is important.

I see him grip the grass with his hands. I hear the low rumble in his chest. He knows exactly what I meant. He knows I meant sex.

"Why would you say that like that?" he says, his voice rough again.

For the first time I'm nervous that maybe he doesn't want me like I want him. That maybe I misread him. I mean, I can't know him all that well, right? As well as I always thought I did? Otherwise I wouldn't need answers from him in the first place.

"Why do you think?" I say.

I am feeling a lot less sexy. Marcus stares at me, dumbfounded. Then he shakes his head and says, "No, Harlow."

Well, that's it.

There's only so much humiliation I can stand. So much embarrassment. It's bad enough to spend time with the person who's hurt me the most, have to play his games about what he'll reveal to me and when, and have to do it all while fighting the memories he dredges up for me and the most profound attraction I've ever felt in my life.

But bald-faced rejection, too?

I just cannot.

I shake my head, unable to find the words, and push myself up off the grass, ready to just be anywhere else in the world. Anywhere, as long as it is far away from Marcus Roma.

"Lo," he says, but I'm not listening. I'm done. I'm gone.

I take two steps before my quads give out and my legs buckle. Maybe I have the willpower to fake being in shape for a single workout, but I didn't stretch or cool down, and my actual muscles don't know about pride or spite. They fail me.

Worse, they fail me just as I'm stepping onto the lip of the track, and my ankle sheers and twists under me as I go down, and I know right away that I'm not getting back up on my own. The pain is sharp and excruciating, the kind that literally takes your breath away, and all I can do is press my lips together and claw at the ground below me.

Marcus is there instantly.

"Lo!" he shouts, and his arms are around me almost before I hit the ground. I fight him. I don't want him to help me up. I don't want him to be the one who saves me, again. Especially not after that spectacular rejection.

"Leave me alone, Marcus!" I hiss. I'm grinding my teeth in pain, but I will not lose my composure.

"Let me see it, Lo."

"Fuck off!"

"No!"

I finally raise my head to glare at him through the tears gathering in my eyes, and that fierce concern on his face kills me. This was what I couldn't deal with. Marcus Roma playing at caring about me, even when he doesn't want me.

He glares right back at me anyway, and I know I'm screwed. He really is a pit bull when he wants to be. I know he's not going anywhere, and it's not like there's anyone else around to help me but some grandmas doing tai chi on the other side of the park.

God damn it.

"Give me your goddamn leg, Lo," Marcus orders.

I let out a string of curses and gingerly stretch out my leg for him. He puts those big, heavy boxer's hands on my flesh and I'm almost completely distracted from the growing mountain of pain that is my right ankle. Almost.

How can he not see how his touch affects me? He runs his hands down the length of my leg, easy, a light touch, for no discernible reason except that maybe he doesn't want to startle me when he gets to my ankle. Like I'm an injured deer or something, apt to jump and try to run away, hurting us both. He gets down to the rapidly swelling joint and touches it slightly with what looks like a feather touch but lances through me like a knife.

I gasp, and he grimaces.

"Just a little more," he says. And I close my eyes while he feels around the joint, looking for a break. Jesus God, but that hurts.

"It's a sprain," he says. "We should still go to the hospital."

I laugh, though at this point everything I do or say is just background noise to the cacophonous waves of pain emanating from my leg.

"You think I have health insurance?" I say.

He frowns. "I'll pay—"

"I swear to God, Marcus, do not finish that sentence."

Marcus looks at me and frowns, and I know he's actually contemplating physically taking me to the hospital anyway, and it's at that point that I try to get back up again on my own. I manage to launch myself off the grass, but I don't exactly have the one-legged launch balance thing down, and I fall right back down again—until Marcus catches me.

He has one arm around my back, and I think he just decides it'll be easier to deal with me if I'm not actually touching the ground because there's a pause, and then he just scoops me up entirely.

"Marcus—"

"Relax. I'm taking your stubborn ass home."

Marcus's voice rumbles in his chest again, this time next to my own. He's hugging me to him, holding me as easily as if I were weightless, lifting me up and down slightly as he walks so as not to bump my ankle. I have no choice but to throw my arms around his neck and hold on.

I'm pressed against his bare skin. I can feel his muscles working effortlessly, tirelessly.

He knows what it does to me when he carries me. He knows the effect it has on me. It's an immediate turn on for me, always has been. Damn it.

I'm actually kind of grateful for the pain in my ankle. One, the endorphins or opiates or whatever it is your brain doles out when you're in pain—those have started to kick in. I'm a little woozy. And two, the pulsing, throbbing ache is, in a way, displacing the pain I feel over Marcus. All that humiliation, the rejection, the reopened old wounds—my body doesn't have the energy to get worked up about all that when there's an actual physical injury to deal with.

Thank you, evolution.

Plus, I'm being carried around by a shirtless demigod. In my natural high, pain-crazy state, that doesn't seem half bad, so long as he doesn't open his mouth and remind me of all the reasons I have to hate him. It would make me almost delirious, turned on, and comforted all at once, the way it always did when he picked me up, if it didn't mean he was carrying me down the street to my own house like some demented mockery of a wedding.

Yeah, because it's not like I haven't had that fantasy before.

Wow, I am really losing it. That is most definitely something I would never allow myself to think about under normal circumstances.

"How you doing?" he asks me, looking down at me.

"Fine," I say, maybe too quickly. He holds me tighter.

When we get to my house, Marcus refuses to put me down. Completely refuses.

"How do you propose to get in the house, then?" I ask him.

"Get the key out of your shoe and unlock the door," he says. He says it like it's an order. Another one.

And he knows I still keep my key in my shoe.

I curse again and pretend not to see the smile curling at the corners of his mouth, and do as he says. He carries me into the living room and I suddenly think about how I haven't changed anything. It's almost exactly the same as it was when my parents were alive, except for a few lamps Dill and I have broken playing tag in the house (because I am still a cool big sister, even if I am also the grown up), and for the first time it occurs to me that this might be weird.

I look at Marcus closely to see his reaction. He does stop and take it in. But he's not weirded out. He looks…

He looks sad. Regretful.

"Is the right side of the couch still the good side?" he asks me.

"Yup."

Marcus doesn't move immediately, but I feel his fingers press into my flesh and it makes my breath hitch. Finally he takes a deep breath and walks across the living room, bending down and very slowly, very gently lowering me to the couch. Carefully he lifts my leg and stuffs a few pillows under it, then pulls me forward and puts one behind my back.

He straightens up and gives me a stern look. He looks about a hundred feet tall from where I am.

"Don't move," he says to me. "Do you hear me?"

"I'm not actually an idiot, Marcus."

"So what are you not going to do?"

I sigh. "Move."

There's no point in fighting this. I do occasionally manage to pick my battles, and this looks like one I'm going to have to strategically surrender. I lean back and listen to the bizarre sounds of Marcus Roma moving through my house. I never realized that I recognized the distinct pattern of his footsteps before, but I do. It couldn't be anyone else but him. I'd know them anywhere. And I can tell that he knows exactly where to go, that he's already gotten an ace bandage from the medicine cabinet upstairs, that now he's making an ice pack in the kitchen.

By the time he comes back with bandage, ice, water, and ibuprofen, I'm feeling even more out of it. This is just completely surreal to me.

It isn't until Marcus lifts my legs, sits down on the couch, and then elevates my leg on his lap before arranging the ice pack that I really come to.

"I can do all of this myself," I say.

He laughs. "Yeah, I can see you hopping up and down the stairs. Good idea."

Marcus puts one hand on my knee, not even sexually, but just because it's there and we're kind of in an awkward position. And it still sets me on fire, which is still disorienting and confusing. And because of that, a fresh wave of humiliation washes over me.

I asked him to come home and have sex with me. I propositioned him. And he said no. He looked at me like I was insane for even thinking it, and he said no.

I stiffen.

"You should leave," I say.

Marcus looks at me, shaking his head. Then he smiles. "Make me."

I bite my lip. I did not expect that. I didn't expect just blatant, arrogant refusal. It's shocking and offensive as hell, and I don't know why I find it so sexy. I don't want to find it so sexy.

Although, in some ways it's not so different from what he did after my parents died. He just refused to leave my side then, too. He'd sneak in through windows, show up in classes, whatever. But he was quiet about it, not forceful. Just always there. Now...it's different. He is forceful, and unapologetic, and aggressive.

Really aggressive.

And I really do find it incredibly hot. And that kind of disturbs me.

Which means I both want him to leave, since apparently every moment is going to be a turn on, only reminding me of how he's rejected me twice now, reminding me of how screwed up I've been since he left, and I also want him to stay right where he is. Maybe move that hand a little bit.

Nope, that's dangerous. He has to go.

"What are you doing?" I ask as he digs in his pocket. He's still not wearing a shirt. Just loose shorts. Thin, loose shorts.

He doesn't answer me, just pulls out his phone. It's already dialing.

"Get me the concierge," he says. And then a moment later, "I need you to get a special delivery to 232 Conselea Street. Can you do that? I need crutches. Female, five foot five and a half." He doesn't even need to look at me to remember how tall I am. "Great. Have someone bring the bag in my suite, same address. Keep my suite until I tell you not to."

I'm speechless. I didn't know hotel concierges did that kind of thing.

"You really need to leave," I say as he hangs up the phone.

"Not going anywhere," he says, not even looking at me. He's found the remote. "Not until you can walk on your own."

"Marcus, that could take days."

I can see a slow smile spreading across his face. "Yeah."

"You can't stay here. You can't. I can call Maria, she can—"

Marcus grumbles, turning to look me dead in the eye, and those eyes silence me. He is just achingly beautiful. And warm, and strong, and unyielding, in everything.

"Maria has a herniated disk and can't help you up those stairs," he says. "She can't carry you if you fall, and she doesn't know to watch you to make sure you don't do anything stupid, like trying to walk before the swelling's gone down. Lo, look at me."

I already am. I don't think I could look away.

He says, "Is there anyone else you want here day and night?"

I see the muscles in his neck tense, all the way down his traps, to his shoulders and arms. His jaw is clenched and he's staring at me, waiting on the next words to come out of my mouth.

Is there anyone else?

No. And there never has been.

"No," I say quietly.

"Then you're stuck with me," he says.

I guess I am.

10

MARCUS

I sleep like a baby in Harlow's house.

That Chase couch is known to be evil, always switching up its lumps and soft spots, so that just when you think you've got it figured out, nope—your back is screwed. And it kinda smells like an old couch. And it's at least ten years old.

But I sleep like a baby anyway. Right up until I hear something crash to the floor upstairs.

I get up those stairs so quickly I'm out of breath. Going from a deep sleep to what amounts to a long jump up a flight of stairs will do that to just about any athlete, I promise you. That, and I'm worried as hell. I throw open the door to Harlow's room, not even thinking to check any of the others—how did I know she's still in the same room?—and she looks up at me from the floor, grimacing.

"Ta-da," she says.

"What were you trying to do?" I say. "Break your foot off all the way?"

I let her wrap her arms around my neck and lift her carefully off the floor, trying hard to ignore that she still sleeps in a tank top and shorts. I'm just glad the hotel concierge was able to bring over some of my own things. Sweatpants are better than boxers right now, though not by much.

"If you must know," she says, "I was trying to go to the bathroom."

"Your crutches are right there."

"I didn't think I needed them."

I shake my head.

"Lo, you can't fight a sprain. It's a goddamn sprain. It's going to stay a sprain until it heals. You can't just beat it into submission."

She doesn't say anything as I help her get set up with her crutches, and it takes me a little too long to realize that maybe she didn't want my help. Or that maybe she wanted to see if it wasn't too bad, and I would have to leave if she could show me that she could walk. I wince at that. I know why she's feeling so raw. I'm not the most articulate guy in the world, not when I'm put on the spot, and believe me when I say that I did not expect Lo to ask me to take her back home and fuck her.

I was caught off guard, all right?

And the reason I said no, even though my dick screamed at me about it, was because it didn't feel right. It felt…defensive. Like it would have put more walls up than it knocked down. It would have been a short-term thrill that might have done more damage. And I'm playing the long game, here. Or at least I'm trying to, with all the self-control and discipline I can manage. I want this woman. I want her to be happy. At the very least, I want her to think about me and feel no pain.

I saw in her face that a quick hate fuck wasn't the way to do that.

Which seems reasonable, now that I've had time to think it out. But in the moment all I could say was "No," like it was this bad thing. And I do know Harlow Chase, and I know she has not been in the mood to talk about it. Lo's always preferred a cooling down period. She would have shut down if I'd brought it up and been totally unable to listen to reason.

Which is why I wait until I have a captive audience.

"You know why I said no, right?" I say right outside the bathroom door.

"Are you serious right now? While I'm peeing?"

I smile. "You wouldn't listen otherwise."

She doesn't say anything for a bit, just maybe curses under her breath. I can't quite catch what she calls me.

Finally she says, "It's not rocket surgery, Marcus. You said no because you didn't want to. It's not a big deal, just drop it."

"Rocket surgery?"

"Yes, it's very advanced surgery. On rockets. Stop being a dick."

"I wanted to, Lo," I say.

She gets quiet.

"I always want to," I say, shaking my head, thinking about how much I want her. "Always. Christ, if you only knew the things I think about doing to you."

I don't hear anything from the bathroom now, just dead quiet. I didn't tell her anything she shouldn't already know. But that doesn't mean she can handle it.

Finally the door opens and Lo is standing right there. She won't look me in the eye at first, but her chest moves up and down in a way I can't ignore. Her skin has this kind of glow in the low light, this shine to it, something I can follow along her delicate collar bones to her graceful shoulders, the tops of her soft breasts. I think back to when I would have been allowed to touch her, when I had that right, and it makes me crazy that I can't right now. It's insane that I can't just reach out and make her feel all the things she deserves to feel. But if I tried now it would just hurt her more.

"Well, thanks for the confidence boost," she says, adjusting her crutches. "But it was a terrible idea, so it's just as well. I'm going back to sleep."

I step aside and watch her make her way down the hall, seeing that she's already getting used to the crutches a little bit, even if she hates having to use them. She moves off like that, determinedly alone, but she looks at me, once, right before she goes back into her bedroom.

I don't know why I do what I do next. I don't really think about it. Don't need to. My feet are moving, and they seem to know where to go. I open the door to Lo's bedroom and take a second to look over her, lying there, looking away from me out the window, the way I looked over her so many times when things were bad. Just to see that she was ok. And then I do what I did for a little while back then, which is lie down on the floor next to her bed.

I hear her turn over, and I know she's looking at me. I know she's thinking about all those other nights I spent lying on her floor, or on the bed next to her, just so she could sleep. And I'll damn well do it every night she needs me to feel better. Just like I know she needs me now, even if she'd never admit it.

That couch is going to mess up my back, anyway.

After a while she says very softly, "Goodnight."

And that's that.

***

"Harlow, there's no way you can work tomorrow," Shantha says, looking at Harlow like Lo has been speaking in tongues. "And there's no way you can canvass the neighborhood. Have you lost your mind? Both of those things require ankles."

I smile and do a fist pump. "Who's right? This guy."

Lo rolls her eyes, but it's not in a hostile way. I know Shantha's watching the two of us, that she came over here to help her friend out and check up on the situation, and I swear Lo's been downright civil all day. Like she's accepted that she needs someone to help her, and I'm not evil incarnate anymore, so it might as well be me.

The key thing being that she no longer outright hates me. And she's stopped asking me direct questions about why I left.

I'm not sure what I did to earn that, since my plan to show her how I never forgot about her all this time hasn't come into place yet, but hell, I'm going to freaking enjoy it.

"Don't worry, Lo, it's a minor sprain," I say. "You'll be good to walk in a few days if you don't do anything dumb."

"Thank you for the vote of confidence," Lo says. "Shantha, can you put the flyers up, then? I can make a few phone calls, but…"

"Yeah, no worries," Shantha says, standing up with an air of having accomplished something. She looks me over again and says, "Take good care of her."

"What?" Lo says. "You're not staying for dinner?"

"I gotta get back to the bar, sweetie, you know that. We're shorthanded." Shantha smirks and then winks at me.

I get up to open the door for her, and as she's walking out Shantha's whole demeanor changes. She gives me the coldest side eye I've ever seen and says, "That is my best friend, Marcus. My family. The only family that accepts me as I am. Do not fuck with her. Understood?"

I blink. I'm a big guy, a fighter, and I work for Alex Wolfe. So it's not often that people threaten me, even implicitly. It's almost refreshing.

"Understood," I say, trying not to smile.

"Good. Thank you for taking care of her. Honey, I'll call you tomorrow!" she shouts out, and struts down the street.

Funny, right? That "accepts me" line. Seven years ago I might have been a dick to someone like Shantha. Now? I keep thinking about how I get what she means when she talks about the family that accepts her. You can't put a price on that. I should know.

So I like Shantha. I like that Harlow has her in her life. But I won't lie: I'm glad to have Lo to myself again, even if it's only because she injured herself when I said something dumb.

Messed up, right?

I don't care.

"What're the flyers for?" I ask Lo as I come back into the living room.

For the first time all day I see Lo stiffen. Get wary. Like she's remembered that I'm the bad guy, working for the enemy, here to mess with her. And with all that probably comes all the other stuff I've done.

I *am* the bad guy.

"The flyers are for how we're going to deal with the developers," Lo finally says.

I hold up hands. "None of my business," I say. The last thing I want her to think is that I'm…what? Doing my job?

That's the thing. It is my job to convince her to sell, and it's the best thing for her. But I put it out of my mind, just like I've ignored all of Alex's calls since I got here.

"Isn't it exactly your business?" she says quietly.

There's not much I can say to that. But I can look her in the eye.

Then I smile.

"Not right now. Right now, my business is dinner," I say, and haul her up from the couch, catch her in my arms. I just want the easiness we had back so badly, and we used to do this all the time. I help her get set up with her crutches and catch the look she's giving me.

"Wait, you think you're going to cook?" she asks.

"Yeah, and I'm gonna do it well," I say. "You heard the doorbell. I got groceries delivered."

"Yeah, I understand that the raw material for dinner is in the house. I'm questioning your ability to turn it into something edible."

I can't help it, I start to laugh. "I promise, Lo," I say, putting a hand over my heart, "I've changed."

Harlow tries to look serious, balanced over her crutches with her hair falling around her face, looking better than any other woman on the planet in just a tank top and sweat pants. But I know she's remembering, too. She's trying not to laugh.

I tried to cook her dinner once before. For her birthday. Her seventeenth birthday.

"I'll reserve judgment," she finally says, and follows me into the kitchen.

***

Harlow ends up helping me, sitting at the kitchen table, chopping up veggies for the ratatouille I'm going to make along with some pan-fried duck. Yeah, I'm trying to impress her, but so what? We settle into an easy rhythm, and I gotta wonder about it. Just yesterday she was ready to kill me every five minutes.

I don't know, I guess I can feel it, too. Part of it is how we're kind of reliving the past, in a way. It feels comfortable. Easy. This—cooking dinner for her? This is such a clear memory for me, one I've been thinking about a lot. One I thought about when I decided to cook dinner tonight.

Man, her seventeenth birthday.

It was her first birthday without her folks around. Can you imagine a heavier birthday? She's staying with this nice foster family, just kind of barely getting by, and then her birthday rolls around and no one knows what to do. And me, I was just as lost as anyone, but I wanted to make it the best birthday it could be. I was determined. If I could have trained for birthdays, I would have.

So I get this great big idea, I'm going to make her dinner and ask her what she wants, and then I'll figure out a way to get it for her. Easy, right?

I asked the Mankowskis if I could use their kitchen and if Harlow and I could have some time alone, and they seemed kind of relieved, like they didn't know what to do, either, but they trusted me. This wasn't some stupid seduction thing. I loved Harlow, and I was too damn careful to even think about trying anything physical on her until she was ready.

So there I was, pretending I knew what I was doing, Harlow sitting at a different kitchen table, watching me find a way to fuck up ravioli.

I still remember what she said to me. She said she felt bad about making everyone else feel bad.

"What are you talking about?" I said.

"Ok, example. Today, in English," she said, swirling the one glass of wine she was going to have. "You remember Lisa, right? My year?"

"Yeah, one of your friends. Used to come by the gym."

"Well, she's one of those people who remembers everyone's birthday, and makes a big thing about it. She gets everyone Valentine's Day cards and Christmas cards and Hanukkah chocolate and everything. She's Hallmark's dream. So today, in English, she comes up to me after class while I'm reading."

"You still read books you're not supposed to be reading during class?"

"Whatever, the Board of Ed should get better taste in books. But Lisa comes up to me, right, after I've just finished the chapter where Vronsky chases Anna Karenina to St. Petersburg—"

"I have no idea what you're talking about," I remember saying. The ravioli was exploding in the boiling water, little bits of cheese floating everywhere, and I had no idea why. Weird detail to remember.

Anyway, Lo went on.

"The point is, it's a big moment, and I was looking up and everything, but I was totally still in the book. And Lisa comes up to me and she asks me what I want for my birthday. And I just kind of stare at her, thinking about Vronsky and Anna Karenina, and I guess I looked…I don't know? Emotional? Or, like, pensive? And then Lisa gets this expression on her face…"

I turned around, forgetting about the ravioli. "Oh, shit," I said.

I remember Lo smiled, and covered her mouth like she felt kinda bad about smiling, but not really. "Yeah. She looked like she'd just accidentally killed a puppy, like her asking me what I want for my birthday was the only possible thing that could have reminded me that I can't have my parents back. Like I'd forgotten they were dead right up until she said something. I swear I could actually see the thought progression on her face. And I didn't even mean to, I just…wasn't paying attention."

We looked at each other for a beat before we both started laughing.

That was the thing about Lo. Her parents were dead, she only got to see her little brother once a week if she was lucky, she had to live in this house with strangers, and when she turned eighteen everything was going to get more complicated. She was working without a safety net, except for me.

So when she could, she found ways to laugh about it.

"Ok, don't give me the dead puppy dog face," I said, spooning the soggy ravioli onto plates. "But I want to know what you want."

I got the Harlow eye roll.

"I'm serious, Lo," I said, sitting down with her.

"I want Chinese," she said, looking at the plate.

See? Funny.

"We can get Chinese," I said, laughing. "Think about it if you have to. But tell me what you want more than anything else. Something real. I'll get it for you."

"I don't need to think about it," she said softly. I remember she poked at one ravioli, like she might wake it up. Then she looked up at me, her blue eyes big and wet. "But you can't get it for me. I want Dill."

I watched her pretend she wasn't on the verge of crying for a few seconds. I had to be careful. This was big.

"What do you mean?" I said.

"I want custody of Dill. As soon as I turn eighteen. I want my brother back." She looked back down again, moving the ravioli around aimlessly. "I can't believe I told you that. I know it's not possible, I just…you know how scared I get that something might happen, and he's going to grow up and not even know who I am at this rate, and—"

"Hey," I said to her. I reached across the table, grabbed her hand. And then I said, "Ok."

Lo snapped her head up. I guess she recognized my tone.

"What do you mean, 'ok?'"

"I mean we'll work on it. It's not impossible, right? You just have to grow up quicker. I'll help you train for that, too."

Man, what an idiot I was. I meant that one hundred percent, too. Totally ignorant of the process, having no idea about lawyers and the rest, but I sat there and told Harlow that I would help her get her brother back. She looked at me with this kind of dreamy expression, this half smile, like she couldn't believe what I was saying and was maybe humoring me.

Irony is a bitch.

But anyway, as I'm heating up the pan for the duck six years later, with Harlow right over there, slicing veggies like old times, this is what I'm thinking about. I'm thinking about how Harlow told me herself that she wanted Dill back more than anything else in the world, that she wanted her baby brother.

Or maybe I'm just thinking about all that because it's the only thing that makes me feel like less of an asshole. It's like a shield, the only thing that can protect me when I look at Harlow and see how much I hurt her by leaving the way I did. The only thing that can protect me from how much it hurts her now, that I can't tell her why I left. That I can't give her the answers she needs.

As if on freaking cue, Alex Wolfe calls me.

I hit the ignore button and throw the duck on.

"You hungry?" I ask.

"Starved."

"Good."

We sit down in silence, and I can't help but watch her, beautiful as always. Maybe it's all the thinking I've been doing, but I just can't take it anymore. I can't not give her something.

"I wasn't kidding, you know," I say to her. "About proving it. That I have proof that I never stopped thinking about you."

She looks up sharply, but doesn't say anything.

I say, "That proof, it's on the way."

"Big talk," she says, and takes a sip of wine.

"Lo, I know I'm not really out of the dog house," I say. "Why're you being so nice?"

Harlow looks up, grins. "I could say the same with this spread. When did you learn to cook?"

"I'm serious, Lo."

She looks down, and for a moment I see that it's all still there. The hurt, the anger, the confusion, the frustration. It hasn't gone away. Then she just shrugs and says, "I don't know. I think I'm just tired of being hurt, of all this stuff. It's tiring. And it's easier for right now to just…not. I know how to be around you like this."

Yeah, I know what she's talking about. There's something familiar about this. But that's not necessarily a good thing.

"For now," she says again.

I nod. That makes more sense to me. I smile at her and say, "I can wear you down slowly, no problem."

Lo pauses almost imperceptibly, cutting her meat. I know exactly what she's thinking about. I'm the only man on the planet who could know what she's thinking about. Her seventeenth birthday dinner didn't end when she told me what she wanted more than anything else in the world. We ordered out quick Chinese food and put it on fancy plates, eating and laughing, sitting across from each other exactly like this, stealing looks at each other, each of us wondering the same kinds of things. I know, because she told me later, that she'd been wondering what it would be like to kiss me.

And then, at the end of the night, she took my wrist in those delicate little fingers of hers. She tugged on me. I remember that still; it was such a gentle thing, but I just somehow…knew. I gathered her up in my arms and held her close to me, right against my body, and just held her. Breathed her in.

Christ, I wanted her so bad.

And I knew she wanted me, too. The way her hands slid up my back, the way she leaned into me, the way she buried her face in my neck. I could feel it.

But I also knew how fragile she was. Could feel that, too. How scared. She wanted me and was scared of it at the same time. I was safe to her, the only person in the world that was safe. So I kissed her softly on the neck, then on the cheek.

And I said, "I'll always be here."

"Thank you," she said.

Another thing I'll always remember, right there. Later she told me it was like we wore each other down slowly.

As it turned out, I didn't have to wait that long before she was ready. Before we both were. But I would have waited forever, and I would have done it with a smile on my face.

That's what she's thinking about now. What we're both thinking about as she looks up at me, her hair framing her beautiful face, her eyes big and open, her mouth so soft it's all I can do not to run my tongue along that bottom lip. I'm thinking about how that was the day we both knew it was going to happen. And then when it did…holy shit.

I've lived on the memory of her for five years.

My eyes trail down her long neck to those collarbones again, and then to her perfect breasts, and I'm thinking about how they used to peak just when I'd blow on them.

I'm thinking about how I could get her to come so sweetly with just my hand.

I'm thinking about what it felt like to bury myself inside Harlow Chase, look into her eyes, and feel her come all around me.

Yeah. I'm definitely ok with wearing her down slowly, if that's what I have to do.

Harlow recovers first, breaks the stare. She takes a sip of wine and clears her throat, trying to play it off like we weren't both just thinking about it.

"When did you get so ruthless?" she says, pretending to look shocked.

I don't even miss a beat.

"Five years without you," I say.

11

HARLOW

I feel like I'm slowly waking up from a dream. The better my ankle feels, the closer I get to full consciousness. These past few days with Marcus living in my house—sleeping right by my bed—have been utterly surreal. I haven't had the energy to stay constantly mad at him. It's almost just been easier to recede into a past that made sense, with him around like this, than it has been to deal with the present reality.

Except the facade is cracking. I can't pretend I don't want him. I can't pretend I don't spend every second in his presence in an amped up state of sexual frustration. I can't pretend that even while I'm so turned on, just by the way he gets up to clear dishes (seriously, what is that), there's this constant worry tearing at the edges of my perception, this reminder that there's ugliness coming. There's terrible things underneath all of this, things I don't want to feel.

It's not like my broken heart has been magically healed. It's more like I've drugged it into submission. And now it's coming down off that high.

It really doesn't help when he insists on inspecting my ankle.

"Have you tried putting weight on it?" he asks, holding my leg gently.

"I can kind of limp around," I say. I sound tense not because it hurts when he touches me, but because it sends shimmering heat up my leg, right to my core. "It's not so bad, actually."

Marcus is silent a moment, looking down at my ankle as though that's the most important thing in the world. He knows that as soon as I can walk around freely there's no more reason for him to stay here. And whatever it is he wants from me, he apparently hasn't it gotten it yet.

Was there ever a real reason for him to stay here? If I'd put my foot down, metaphorically speaking, Marcus would have left. But I didn't. I let him stay. I put myself through this.

I am at war with myself. I have needed something this easy for so long. For years. Nothing has been easy, not since Marcus left, and just being with him is so, so easy. So damn safe.

As long as I don't think too much about how badly he hurt me. And as long as I don't think about the future, when he'll inevitably choose something else over me again, when he'll hurt me all over again. If I let him.

I close my eyes and try not to think about how my skin feels electrically alive, just being in contact with his. I'm about to speak when he beats me to it.

"You heard from Dill?" he asks.

My eyes shoot open and I see him staring back at me as if this is actually important to him. We're sitting on the couch again, in the middle of a Die Hard movie marathon while it pours outside, another one of those summer storms. I'm waiting for Shantha to get back to me about how the initial publicity for the fundraising event at the bar is going. The idea is to get the neighborhood organized, raise enough money that we can attract some real press, put some pressure on the zoning board. Maybe if we make it too expensive and too annoying to continue the developers will go somewhere else. It's my only shot to save Dill's home.

And Dill doesn't even know what's going on. He's in love with his programming camp, totally oblivious to everything else. I didn't even understand half of his last email—it's like it was written in actual code—but I can tell when the kid is happy.

And I have Marcus to thank. Partially, anyway.

"Yeah," I answer him finally. "He's having a blast."

Marcus smiles like the freaking sun. "Good."

He still has his hand on my leg. I don't want to move it. I want to just continue to feel his hands on me without having to take responsibility for that particular decision or deal with any of the consequences involved.

It's not the sex that makes me uncomfortable. God no. It's the closeness. The real-but-fake intimacy. Like we're playing house. Like we're getting way too comfortable with each other, like I'm forgetting how he's capable of hurting me.

I figure someone who can ruthlessly leave you with no explanation once can do it twice. No explanation, no way to understand it. No guarantee he won't just do the same thing again. So no forgiveness. Definitely no forgetting.

"Hey, you ok?" Marcus asks me.

He's worried. He doesn't have the right to be worried about me. I take my leg back, move down to the other side of the couch.

"I'm fine," I say. It's a lie. I feel like the storm outside is just a mirror image of what's happening inside me, like my skin is just a thin layer preventing a freaking hurricane from ripping through my life, making all sorts of bad decisions, falling in love with ghosts all over the place.

That's how I have to think of him. The ghost that haunts my life. The ghost I need exorcised.

"You hungry yet?" he asks.

I can't believe he learned to cook. It's like he found his one flaw—besides the disappearing thing—and was like, oh, I'll just go take a class and become a world-class chef. No big deal.

Ok, for food made with his current skills, I can maybe let some things slide. Temporarily.

"Maybe," I say, narrowing my eyes.

He's grinning.

Then he gets up and lifts me up in his arms, totally inappropriate, totally crossing boundaries left and right, and it gets me to laugh anyway. Actually it gets me to scream and giggle, and I bat at his shoulders as he sets me down.

"Smile occasionally or I'm going to have to tickle you," he says.

I can't help but smile back at him. Whenever he smiles, it's absolutely infectious, and he's giving me the full Marcus smile now, trying to get me out of my funk. The thing is, he's beautiful. It take a real physical effort not to let my hands linger on his hard chest, not to feel the grain of his muscles through the thin material of his white t-shirt, not to press myself against him. He smells incredible.

"You're all talk," I say, and push him toward the kitchen.

Marcus stops, gives me the one-eyebrow raise. "Oh really?"

And now this feels dangerous again. Already. I put my hands on my hips, covering up how I have to put all that weight on one leg, and narrow my eyes.

"Then where's your super special proof, Marcus?"

The air changes. Sparks between us. Jesus. I've done it. I've brought up serious stuff. I think I've been avoiding it, even though I said I was going to ask him all these questions, just because I wasn't sure I could handle it. I'm still not. Like, really, really not. But he said he had proof that he never stopped thinking about me, that he never stopped caring. Of course I want to see it.

"That's fair," Marcus says. He looks at me seriously, imploringly. For all the world an honest guy trying to make good. I have to remind myself…what? Not to believe whatever he says next? Then why do I want to?

He says, "The guy who has the files that I need to prove to you what I've been doing the past five years was out in California on another job. He said he'd be back in town this week with all the files. He won't send that kind of thing over email, says it compromises him. He's kind of old school."

Wait. What the hell?

"What files? What are you talking about?"

Marcus frowns. "This is why I didn't bring it up. Think of it as a partial record of my activities and interests for the past five years."

"'Think of it as?' So then what is it really?"

Marcus stares at me. Silently.

"Were you checking up on me?" I ask. "Like, spying on me? And you have a record of this?"

"It's not that simple."

"What the hell is wrong with you?" I say softly.

I'm not even mad. I suppose eventually I'll be mad. Maybe if I saw what he'd actually done, I'd be mad. But right now I'm mostly just marveling at how incredibly weird it is that Marcus would have disappeared from my life like I didn't matter at all, and yet all this time he's had someone checking up on me.

Marcus runs a hand through his black hair, turning it into a disheveled, sexy mess, and looks at me with those mesmerizing, earnest eyes.

"I don't know," he says simply. "When it comes to you, everything is just… You're what's wrong with me, Lo. Simple as that."

"Marcus, I don't even know what to say to that."

"There's no reason you should. It's pretty weird."

I just stare at him for another moment. And this is where the fact that we know each other so well comes in. Because I watch him, and I can see everything he's feeling on his face, as if he was narrating it to me himself. I can see it in his body language, the way he leans against the doorframe, the way it looks like invisible rope is the only thing holding him back, like he wants to be where I am, close to me. He's in pain. This is what it looks like when Marcus Roma feels pain because he thinks I'm feeling pain.

I am just totally dumbfounded.

And I have to sit down, because of this freaking ankle.

"You ok?" he says, rushing forward while I hobble back to the couch, muttering under my breath.

"Just resting it," I say.

He stands there, silently. And then all of a sudden Marcus is down on his knees in front of me, and I'm trapped. Even if my ankle was healed, I don't think I could move. Just looking at him, looking at those eyes, that face—no woman could tear herself away. Even one who really, really should.

"Lo."

"Marcus, please don't."

That closeness, that dangerous closeness, the way he's almost touching me right now, the way I know he can look into my face and see what I'm feeling, too—I can't do that right now. Because the feelings I've been fighting are coming up to the surface. The fact that I never got over him, the fact that I still love with him, the fact that I can't look at him without wanting and hurting at the same time…he'll know it all.

And if he knows it, I might have to admit it. I might have to deal with it.

Am I ready for that?

What if the answer is that I still need him? That no matter what, I will never get over him? That I will have to feel this way forever? What if I finally allow myself to ask the question, and that's the answer?

I can't speak. Can't breathe. He looks into me—into me— and I know he sees it. I know he feels it. I'm on the cusp of breaking, of overflowing completely with five years' worth of emotion, when the doorbell rings.

Thank fucking God.

Well, that's my first reaction. My second reaction is, "Who the hell is that?"

Because it's raining outside, still. I mean, the weather is terrible. No one in their right mind would be out right now.

Unless it was an emergency.

Here's the thing: I am still a little nervous around police officers. Anyone official, really, anyone in a uniform, especially if they're coming to my door unexpectedly. Like if they have news? It's never going to be good news. It's a pretty reliable way to put me on a hair trigger for a panic attack.

I mean, it's understandable.

And I've been thinking about Dill. And this is the first time he's away from me since I got him back, and I haven't talked to him, and the only reason I haven't been out of my mind worrying about him is that Marcus has been making me crazy instead.

So my third reaction is to panic.

I push myself off the couch with all the force I can muster, needing to get to the door and see who's got something so important to tell me, and Marcus is there. He's holding me up, studying my face.

I fall back as soon as my ankle touches the ground, wincing.

"Just because you can walk doesn't mean you should," he says. And before I can yell at him, because, goddammit, I need to know who's at the door right now, Marcus picks me up—again—and starts to carry me to the door.

"This is ridiculous," I say, even as I'm starting to hyperventilate. It feels like a genuine panic attack coming on. It can't just be the doorbell. It has to be all the stress from the past few days, all the unresolved tension with Marcus, making my threshold lower.

"Dill is fine," Marcus says calmly. "They wouldn't come to your house if something had happened. They would call. Dill is fine. This is nothing. Probably just a neighbor whose power went out. Lo, look at me," he says.

We're just a few feet from the door, but he's looking at me with those calm, soothing eyes, and he's saying my name again. He's telling me the one thing anyone could tell me to get me to calm down right now, and it's working.

He is exactly what I need right now.

Why does it have to be him?

"Lo," he says again. "It's ok. Dill is fine."

"Ok," I say, feeling my heart rate slow down while my lungs start to work again. "Ok, you're right. Ok."

He puts me down right in front of the door and holds me up so I can balance on one leg. We look like we're about to compete in a three-legged race, except my face is also sweaty and red from the panic attack, and Marcus…Marcus still looks like a god.

The doorbell rings again. Whoever it is can see us. I take a deep breath and open the door.

"Maria!" I say, and practically try to drag her inside. She's wrapped up in a flimsy coat with a scarf around her head, all just to go next door. "What's wrong? What happened?"

"No, no, nothing's wrong," she's saying, slowly unwrapping herself from all those wet layers. She seems off, like there's something not quite right, but then she sees Marcus. I have never seen anyone's face light up like hers does.

"Marcus!" she screams, and grabs Marcus by his cheeks.

By his cheeks.

This might all be worth it for this single visual.

Maria is fussing over him like crazy, practically flapping her arms, and I realize it was kind of mean not to tell her he was back. I know she used to talk to him about me, that she used to ask him how I was doing, if I needed anything. She trusted him to know. She trusted him to take care of me.

Hurts to think about. Maybe that's why I didn't tell her.

I start to hop back to the living room, and Marcus immediately disentangles himself from Maria, giving her a kiss on the cheek as he does. In the next second he's by my side, insisting on holding me up again. I would brush him off, but he knows my balance is terrible and I probably would fall over.

"*Madre de dios*," Maria says. "What did you do?"

"We went running," I say. "I twisted it."

"She'll be ok," Marcus says, helping me onto the couch. "Just a mild sprain. I'm taking care of her."

Maria beams.

There is literally nothing she'd love in the world more than to see Marcus and me together again. Maria was probably the only other person heartbroken when he left.

She watches Marcus set me down, and I have literally never seen her happier.

"I'm gonna go make something to eat," Marcus says, looking between us. He seems to have figured out that Maria came here to tell me something.

And then Maria herself seems to remember.

And oh shit, whatever it is, it's not good. I have never, ever seen Maria Ruiz look nervous. Or…guilty?

What the hell?

"Maria," I say, and she silences me before I can even get going. She just shakes her head really quickly, looking down at her hands, her fingers pinching little knots in her dress. She looks miserable.

"What's wrong?" I ask. I'm genuinely worried now. The panic is coming back. "What happened?

"I'm so sorry, Lo," she says, and looks up. Her eyes are red. She's crying.

"Maria, please, tell me," I say, hearing the tension in my own voice, like I'm trying to choke back the panic, the stress, everything.

Maria takes my hand, rubbing her thumb across it too quickly, too hard. "They made such a good offer," she says. "I couldn't say no anymore."

"What?"

But of course I know what she means.

She sold her house to the developers. Alex Wolfe got to her.

"It means no more loans for college for John," Maria says quietly. "It means I can go to Texas, see my mother. It means I don't have to worry about retirement."

And this, right here, is where I feel both completely betrayed and at the same time realize that I am completely selfish.

Of course taking a million-dollar payoff will change Maria's life. Of course it will help her. John won't have to be in crippling debt when he gets out of med school, and that is huge. Maria won't have to work until she's doubled over in pain. Her life will be unequivocally better.

I know this. I would have known it before if I'd bothered to think about anyone other than Dill and myself. So why does it feel like the bottom of my world just fell out? Why do I feel like I can't breathe? Like no matter what I do, everything will fall away? That I'll lose everything?

I hate myself for this. I hate myself even more when I see how upset Maria is, when I remember that she's actually been crying because she didn't want to disappoint me for making a decision that will improve her life.

I force myself to smile at her, and it's a good thing I hug her, because I cannot keep that smile up for long.

"It's ok," I say. "Please don't be upset. I'm happy for you."

I squeeze her fiercely, because I love her. And because I love her, I can't let her see how broken up I really am. Even though it's horribly selfish, I can't control the way I feel.

Man, this isn't even top of the list of things that would be easier if I could control my feelings.

"It's ok," I say again, and I don't know if it's more for her or for me. Just when I'm not sure how much longer I can keep this up, Marcus comes to the rescue, like he somehow always does.

"What're you two up to?" he says, coming in with a bottle of wine. Maria turns around to look at him, but Marcus looks at me. He sees my face and he knows something's wrong. "Hey, Lo, how's your ankle?" he says.

He's already walking toward me, easy and confident in jeans and a t-shirt, his athleticism apparent in the slightest movement. He cocks his head at me, looking at me like he just needs me to play along.

Then he kneels down, takes my ankle gingerly in hand, and looks up at me.

"Be honest," he says, looking me in the eye. "You in pain?"

I can't even talk. I just nod. I feel like a terrible person, but I need Maria to leave. I can't hide how I feel from her and Marcus at the same time, I can't keep this up, I don't have the energy. I feel like I'm about to break.

"Maria," he says, "You think you could come back tomorrow?"

Maria jumps up, fluttering about, I think because now she thinks she might have been interrupting something. Whatever. It works. Marcus shows her out, smiling and laughing and promising to take good care of me, and in just a few minutes she's gone, and I'm free to lose my shit.

Except that I don't.

At least not in the way I expect to.

It does all come crashing down. Whatever walls and defenses I have left after living with Marcus—living with Marcus—for three days are just overrun in a flood of emotion, all of it swirling together, just one big muddy torrent of feels. Screw my ankle; I have to move around with this kind of thing happening inside me. I push myself up and manage to hobble into the kitchen, the pain not nearly as bad as I thought it would be. I stare at all the stuff Marcus has taken out for dinner and another wave hits me, because holy crap, this is absurd.

I haul myself up and kind of just sit there on the table and grip the edge of it, holding on while the wave rushes through me the way I learned to years ago. I'm also waiting to see what rises to the surface, to see how that incoherent mix of emotion clarifies.

When it does, the man who's the cause of all of this is standing right in front of me, the hard planes of his chest visible through that shirt, the intelligence of his eyes telling me I won't be able to hide any longer.

"Why are you doing this?" I ask him blankly.

Marcus's face is serious, too, like he knows this is big.

"What's wrong?" he says, moving toward me. "What happened?"

"Marcus, I really need an answer right now," I say. "Why are you doing this?"

I force myself to look up at him now that he's only inches away from me, and I know it registers on my face when he touches my wrist. Just the slightest touch, the pads of his fingers on my wrist, and it shudders through me.

I feel totally out of control, except when he touches me. Then I'm under his control.

"Because I want to make it up to you," he says softly.

I grip the table harder and will myself not to cry. "So this is all about you?" I ask. "Because you just don't want to feel guilty anymore? You'll just come back here, hang around for a while, and then bam, no more guilt for fucking up my life?"

Marcus's expression changes. His jaw clenches, his eyes burn. "I will never stop feeling guilty," he says.

The world stops. I'm aware of nothing except how close he is, and where he touches me.

"Good," I finally say. "You can't make it up to me. Do you know what you did to me? Do you have any idea what it was like for me, when you left like that?"

Marcus moves even closer, his legs coming between mine, pushing me farther up on the table. His hands circling around my wrists, moving up my arms. One hand, finally, underneath my chin, tilting it up to him. Giving me nowhere to run or hide, nothing to do but finally face this.

"Tell me," he says.

I didn't expect him to say that.

I open my mouth to speak, but no words will come. I don't know how to tell him, to tell anyone, what it was like. How bad I felt. How it was one of my greatest fears, the one I never told him about, all those times he asked me what I wanted most in the world, and I told him I wanted Dill, because that's what I was scared of losing most. But the other person I was terrified of losing was Marcus, because he was the person that gave me faith in the world again, and I never, ever told him that.

I thought he knew.

He must have known. My parents were taken, my only family didn't want me, my brother was taken, but Marcus was there. And then, suddenly, he wasn't, and it had all been a lie.

And even those words don't tell it. I don't know how to tell this story. I don't know how to show him what it did to me. How he broke me. What happened to me, in that bar, because of how broken I was.

He's looking at me, expecting me to say something, and instead my heart is breaking all over again.

"It hurts too much, Marcus," I manage. "It hurt too much then. I can't…"

Marcus leans his forehead against mine, his hands, his amazing hands, coming around to my back, holding me up.

"I'm sorry," he says.

"You were all I had left," I whisper. "And then you slept with me, after everything we went through, you were finally mine, and…you were everything to me. Everything. And then you left."

"I wasn't everything," he says, his voice rough, raw. "You needed Dill."

I feel something new boil up inside me and I put my hands on his chest and push him back so he has to look me in the eye for this.

"No," I say. "You do not get to talk about him. You don't get to talk about Dill and me, not anymore."

And then I break. I just start to cry in anger, and I'm hitting him on his chest, his arms. I'm not speaking coherently, just yelling at him, letting it all come out. He doesn't fight me. He just takes it, immoveable, not even reacting except for his face, which looks as close to tears as I've ever seen it. And when I start to lose steam, Marcus puts his arms around me and holds me while I cry, while the last of that rage and grief leaves my body in great, shuddering breaths.

When I'm finally breathing normally, resting against his chest, feeling his heartbeat in my bones and hating myself for taking comfort in it, he speaks.

"I loved you then, I love you now, and I did what I thought was best," he says fiercely. "And I would never hurt you deliberately, Lo, not ever."

I want to believe him so badly, and it confuses the shit out of me. Because that wasn't an explanation at all, and yet I want to accept it. Am I thinking clearly? Is this just because of this physical attraction? Is it because I'm afraid I'll never be over him?

I don't think a broken woman can make good decisions. I don't think I can make good decisions until I know whether I can get over him. It will always be about the place where I hurt, the place where he broke me, and not about what's best for me or for Dill.

I have to know. I have to know if this delirium is physical, if I can get it out of my system, finally exorcise the ghost of Marcus Roma from my life and just move the fuck on.

Or maybe the truth is that I can't fight it anymore.

Maybe him holding me like this, so close to him…maybe it's just my body overriding my brain.

I don't even fucking care.

He feels it, too, I can tell. Like a rising tide, something building in both of us, between us. Like on my seventeenth birthday, when I knew he really felt it for the first time. I feel my blood rushing inside me, the pressure that's been threatening me since I first saw him again pounding a demanding rhythm in my core, telling me to just go, just stop thinking, just do it.

"Lo," he rumbles.

"Fuck me," I say.

Marcus stops. His arms tighten around me and then they move, they uncoil, his hands sliding down to my waist. I breathe in when he touches me there and my abs flutter, and that stops him again. I hear his intake of breath. He pulls his head away from mine and looks down at me.

"Not like this," he says. He's almost pleading.

"Screw you, Marcus. I know you want me." I look down, finally, to see how hard he is beneath those jeans. God, so big. "We both know it. Pretending it's not…pretending this isn't happening isn't doing me any good. I don't care what it's doing to you, I care what it's doing to me. Believe me," I say, gripping hold of his shirt, "when I say that I don't think I owe you anything. But I am tired of being scared. I am tired of being scared that I'll lose what I have left of my ability to love, I'm tired of being scared that I'll lose my job, I'm tired of being scared…"

I stop here, have to gather myself, force myself to continue.

"I'm tired of being scared that I'll lose Dill," I say. "And, most of all, I am tired of being scared that I will never be over you."

I am so angry I can barely see, and I want him so badly it actually, physically hurts. Like the absence of him inside me aches.

I'm pulling at his shirt now, twisting it, and Marcus's fingers are digging into my waist, pushing under the waistband of my shorts, almost like they have a mind of their own. They must, because Marcus himself is rock solid and rigid, his body riddled with tension, his muscles working with restraint.

"Lo," he whispers, shaking his head.

"I don't want to have to think about this anymore," I say. "Please just help me to feel something else. Please."

His thumb sweeps along the inside of my waistband, coming around the front, dipping low so that I shudder, even while the muscles in his shoulders pop and it looks like he's struggling.

I want to scream.

I do.

I rip at his shirt; I go for the buttons on his jeans. I say, "I don't want to be scared of being broken forever because you fucking broke me…"

I think he's about to snap and finally take me when his hands move, lightning fast, and grab mine, pinning them to the table. Marcus is breathing heavy, his whole body hard and alive and pulsing between my legs as I sit on this stupid table, and when he looks at me, it's with a fierce hunger.

"Not until you tell the truth," he says. "Not until you say why."

I know exactly what he means. He can still see through me.

"Because I hate that it's you that does this to me," I say. "Why does it have to be you? I hate that it's you that makes me feel this. I hate you, Marcus, because I…"

Because I love him. But I can't say it.

He's leaning into me now, his head close to mine. He's smelling me. I can feel his lips move along my jaw, my ear, my neck…

"Please don't make me say the rest," I say. "You already know the truth, you bastard."

One hand moves to the back of my head, the other to my hip, and I can already feel the complete control he has over my body. Like he's just deciding. Feeling it out, the way he does.

I hate him so much for making me love him.

"Marcus, I need you to—"

He doesn't let me finish. With a growl, he threads his fingers through my hair and pulls my head back, his face hovering just above mine. For a beat his eyes pierce mine and I see what I feel echoed there: a wild need, a fierce, burning fever, the desperation of needing someone you can't have.

And then when it happens, it happens all at once: his mouth crushing mine, his hand pushing into my shorts, beneath my underwear, his fingers sliding between my wet folds, and then his hand gripping me there. He stops for a moment, as though just wanting to establish ownership, and his tongue parts my lips savagely. I moan into his mouth and grapple at his shoulders, trying to get him to move, to just do it already, because I feel like I might burst, but he's the one in control, and that drives me even higher. His other hand tightens its grip on my hair, and he takes what he wants, kissing me deeply until I yield to it, until I'm not thinking about anything at all.

My lips start to tingle, and it spreads downward. I move my hips against his hand and whimper, feeling how wet I am against him. I need him inside me, and he knows it. Slowly, too slowly—God, horribly slowly—he slips one finger inside me, drawing back to look at my face while he does it. I curl around him, biting my lip, my fingers digging into his shoulders.

"Please," I say again.

His face is dark, so dark, so hungry. This is all new even if it's not, even if my body responds to his as though we've always known each other like this. I remember what is was like the first time he was inside me, when he was so gentle and I was so nervous.

But now there's no gentleness, only hunger. I'm not scared of this. He's not scared of hurting me. He's only taking what he wants, and I'm giving him what I need him to take.

So he moves that finger inside me, and the younger me remembers what it was like the first time he made me come like this, looking into my eyes, all soft tenderness and not knowing how it would end, what would happen after, how it would feel. And now, today, looking into those green eyes and feeling him start to find the rhythm, my own hips guiding him, I know that tender man is under there, just like he was before, and I don't want that. I can't. I can't remember what it's like to let him love me, to trust him to love me, because I will fall apart.

I need something else from him. I need him to take me. I need him to posses me.

"I wish to God it wasn't you," I say again, panting while he watches me, while he's the picture of self-control as he's making me lose mine. "I wish I could want someone else the way… I've tried, with other guys…"

It's like I've slapped him. I have, in a way, telling him I've tried to love other men the way I love him. I've done it on purpose, and he knows it in the way that only he could. I'm goading him to get what I want.

Provoking him.

It works.

Marcus looks like he's just been hit, and I wonder if I will feel bad about hurting him later, and then I don't have time for that, because it's like he's been unleashed. He slams me down on the kitchen table with a growl, and his hand is ripping away my shorts, my underwear, leaving me completely bare. I moan as he pushes my shirt up to my neck, exposing my breasts, and I squeeze him with my thighs while he rips at the zipper of his jeans. I feel his big hands on my hips, hauling me back to the edge of the table, and then his thick, heavy cock nestles between my folds, moving up, down, taunting me.

"Oh God," I say. "Yes. Do it."

Marcus tightens his grip on my hip while I groan, and slips his other hand behind my head, forcing me to look directly at him while he's poised right at my entrance.

"You are *mine*," he says.

And he drives into me, filling me to the point where I scream in relief.

It hurts just right.

The shock of it dissipates, spreading outwards from deep inside me, until my nipples throb and my pussy aches. My body folds around him and it feels…oh God, it feels like I don't know how I lived without it, and like I'll die if I don't get more. I throw my arms out, trying to get a grip on something, anything, and I manage to clear the table, sending salt and pepper shakers, plates, whatever, all of it clattering to the floor. I'm looking around everywhere, wildly, crazed, and Marcus jerks my head up, making me look at him again.

And once those eyes have me, I can't look at anything else.

I. Can't. Speak.

"Mine," he says again, almost desperately, and thrusts into me again, hard, harder. Deeper.

Yes.

I cry out and try to wrap my legs around him. Marcus grabs one of them and pushes it up over his shoulder, withdrawing until he's almost out of me completely, and then he plunges back into me, hitting so deeply that I scream.

This isn't gentle. This isn't even healthy. This is brutal, animal, desperate claiming. This is Marcus giving in. This is me working out every conflicted thought, every troubled emotion I've had for the last five years.

And he knows it.

"Mine," he growls, reaching up to take hold of my breasts, pinching my nipples.

"Then fuck me like it," I say again. Damn the consequences.

"You know you're mine," he says, his voice ragged, sounding like he's coming apart, sounding more beast than man. He punctuates each word with a thrust, pumping into me again and again. "No one else. No one. You're mine, I'm yours."

He says that, and I know he's right, that no one else will ever make me feel like this, and, God help me, that's what starts to put me over the edge. It's already building. That pressure that's been gathering inside me is coalescing, drawing together, spinning me higher and higher until I float so high that I burst into nothingness, my body clenching around his while the rest of me shatters with a single, long scream.

I haven't come like that in years. I haven't come like that ever.

I'm not done.

Marcus isn't done.

I'm not really able to speak, and my senses are slowly coming back to me, almost piecemeal, but when Marcus starts to move inside me again I can tell he must have stopped. He waited. Now he's fucking me shallowly, sweat starting to gather on his brow, waiting for me to come back down to earth. He throws my arms up above my head and removes the rest of my clothing, so now I'm completely naked, letting him fuck me on my kitchen table. I don't even object. My limpid, liquid body is starting to heat again, and I know I'll do anything he wants.

He doesn't ask; he doesn't speak. He just picks me up off that table with a grunt while he's still inside me and starts walking.

I kind of laugh, a shocked giggle, because if I were to think about it, I know I wouldn't believe that this is really happening. I know where he's taking me. He's taking me upstairs to my bed.

We've never had sex in my bed.

It never worked out. I was in foster care, and my aunt lived here. It was always at his house. And then he left.

My legs are wrapped around him tight, but I can still feel him inside me, heavy and thick and moving slightly with every step. He fits me perfectly, so that the head of his cock presses up against this spot inside me that drives me wild. I'd forgotten about that. Maybe at the time I didn't know enough about my own body to know that that's what it was. I just knew Marcus felt amazing inside of me.

He still does.

I bury my face in his neck, because I need to scent him. I need to be completely covered in him. I don't even remember my reasons for this, how I got here, but having Marcus inside me puts me in a place beyond reasons, or sense, or any of that. There's just him and me.

And now he's lowering me onto my bed.

He pulls out of me and I whimper, not thinking much beyond the immediate. But then I see him strip his clothes off and I have to agree: This is better.

Oh God, this is better.

I don't know if I've ever seen him fully naked like this before. Erect. Huge. Just standing in front of me, his erection still slick from my juices, his chest heaving in big, deep breaths. We're not two teenagers figuring each other out anymore. This is different.

"Lie back and let me see you," he orders. His voice is different, too. Deep, rough.

I don't even question it. I just do it. Even the thought brings me back to the edge.

"Spread," he says, putting one massive hand around that beautiful cock.

My breath comes in tentative little gasps as I spread my legs for him. I watch him, watching me. I can feel his gaze on my body, can feel him linger, can feel his arousal. He pumps his erect cock once, twice, and his eyes are back on mine, and holy hell, I've never seen anything like it. I am on fire for him.

"Nothing will ever be as beautiful as you, like this," he says, his voice barely above a whisper.

And then he's on me, almost in one breath, pinning me to the bed, kissing me deeply, desperately, his mouth hungry and hot against mine. I try to run my hands along his body, to guide that magnificent erection inside me, but he takes my hands and pins them up above my head. Instead he kisses me senseless and stupid, his lips roving over mine, his tongue licking, probing, tasting. He sucks my bottom lip and I moan against his mouth, and I know this won't be the same. This won't be like downstairs.

This will be…

I don't have time to get scared, because Marcus is kissing me again. He's kissing me like he's dying, like he's been lost at sea and now by some miracle he's been found. He's kissing me like he might never get to do it again. He kisses away every last defense I have, until I am truly naked underneath him, raw and vulnerable and delirious with need.

"Please," I manage when he lets me breathe, but he just shakes his head, his mouth returning to my neck. He licks me, lets his tongue roam over my collarbone and down to my nipples. He takes my nipple in his hot, wet mouth and I shudder, my hips arching up to him, silently begging him. How can he stand it?

He sucks on one nipple, then the other, his hands moving up and down my legs, exploring every inch of me. This is torture.

This is worse than torture. This is tender.

"Marcus," I say, but it comes out a choked moan.

He kisses his way down my stomach like he wants to savor every part of me, dipping his tongue into my bellybutton, rubbing the scruff of his jaw against my soft skin. I know where he's going.

"Oh God," I say. "Marcus…"

But I can't tell him to stop, because I don't want him to stop. His mouth finds my inner thigh and his hands slip under my buttocks, lifting me ever so slightly. And maybe in the next second I might have found the strength to stop this before it becomes too intimate, before I'm truly lost, but I don't. His tongue enters me and I am undone.

He licks me from my entrance up to my clit, and I feel his fingers push into me again, and I lose it. This time my orgasm feels long and lingering, spreading slowly, making me feel light and airy. Making me see stars. Making me forget myself.

He's done it. As Marcus kisses his way back up my body, he must know. He must know he's worn me down, and now it's just me, stripped, exposed, true. Feeling safe in the world with him.

He kisses me, I taste myself on him, and I know.

His hands find my center again, and gently circle my clit, dragging me back to the point of arousal, and now I know my body really is his. I've never had three so quickly before, not in a row, and I don't know how my body can do it, not after what he's done to it already.

He positions the head of his cock at my entrance again, makes sure I can see it. I mewl at the sight, suddenly consumed all over again with desire for him. Then he pins me with those eyes, enters me briefly, and pulls out.

"Say it," he says. "Say you're mine, Lo."

I groan and thread my fingers into his thick black hair, trying to draw him to me, but he is immovable.

"No, baby," he says, and he nips at my neck, kissing me gently all the way up to my jaw, hovering just above my face. "Say it."

He is relentless.

He is gentle.

And he sees. Right. Through me.

Something about his eyes and this remembered, tender touch unlocks something inside me. I feel my own eyes water, and I know it's a lost cause. I know. Now I know. I am his. Not just my body. All of me. I have always been his. I will always be his.

No matter how badly it may hurt. No matter if I ever see him again.

"I'm yours," I whisper. And I know that it's true, and I'm helpless but to let Marcus Roma make love to me.

Marcus slides into me slowly, inch by delicious inch, letting me feel the full, thick weight of him, letting me feel him pulse inside me until we're feeling each beat together, breathing together, being together. He hasn't looked away. His eyes are locked with mine. This is closer than I've ever been to anyone in years, more than I've ever let anyone see. This is all of me. A soft noise escapes my throat and Marcus matches it, a ragged, rough cry as he begins to move inside me, but he doesn't look away. He holds my eyes with his the whole time, even when tears spill down to my temples, even as we both start to pant, even as I clench my teeth and arch my back with another glimpse of oblivion. When the contractions start deep within me I feel him shudder, I feel his cock twitch, and I feel him spill warmth deep, deep inside me.

And, God help me, it feels right.

And it continues to feel right, for a long time. While Marcus lies on top of me, his sweat cooling in the night air. While I listen to the last of the rain splutter against my window. It takes a while for the doubts, for the hurt, for the memories to claw their way back inside me, but they do. There was never any doubt that they would. Because those wounds never healed. Because being around Marcus, reminding myself of what we are, it hasn't fixed what's broken inside me. It's only strained it further.

Because now I have an answer. No, I won't ever be over him. There will always be this. There will always be Marcus Roma.

And he will always have broken my heart.

"Marcus," I say, my fingers tracing delicate patterns on his back while he lies across me.

"Yeah?" he says, turning his head. It's the first thing he's said since he made me admit I belonged to him.

"Lie to me. Tell me I won't have to love you for the rest of my life."

Marcus pushes himself up above me, but I can't see his expression anymore.

"Tell me I won't have to feel like this forever," I say.

"No," he says, and I feel his fingers on my face.

I close my eyes. Of course he won't. How could he? I wish more than anything I could stop loving him. I wish I could stop wanting him. I wish, most of all, that I could stop needing him.

Wishes don't really come true.

"I need to be alone," I say.

The saddest part is that when he does finally leave, I curl up with my sheets wrapped around me, searching for his scent on my bed so that I can fall asleep.

12

MARCUS

Yeah, I did not sleep, let me tell you. That couch went from comfortable to painful real quick. I wasn't going to sleep on Dill's bed. I wasn't going to even talk about the fact that it didn't look like she'd opened the door to her parents' bedroom in ages. It was definitely the couch for me.

Because Harlow really did need to be alone. The last thing I wanted to do was leave her, but I knew, looking at her face, that she needed me to leave. It killed me.

I lay awake for hours, going back and forth between replaying it all in my head, feeling the kind of joy I didn't think I'd ever get to feel again, and then thinking about how badly I must have fucked it up, and feeling like I deserved far worse than the pain of knowing I might lose Harlow forever.

Had it hurt her, what we did? She'd said she'd needed it. And she'd meant it—I could see it in her face. I kept telling myself I had to be sure that it wouldn't do even worse emotional damage than I'd already done, I had to be sure, but in the end, was I? Or did I just finally lose control and give in to what I wanted, what I've always wanted? And, in the process, did I screw this up beyond all repair?

I'm not used to questioning myself like this, and I don't fucking like it. Most things are simple. Harlow isn't.

I'm still lying here, trying to figure it out. It's morning now. Gray, still, the storm on its last legs. It's soggy and wet outside, and I couldn't give a damn. All I'm thinking about is Harlow.

The sight of her naked body. Jesus, the sight of her. The way her eyes get even bigger as she comes. The way she moves for me. The way I can feel it when she's about to lose control.

The way she tastes.

I said once before that I am not the strong one. I guess I proved that last night. And Harlow knew it. She knew what she was doing, knew I wouldn't be able to hold out forever. She'd already taken me, body and soul, and she made damn sure that I took her physically. And I don't regret a thing I said or did, because it was all true. Because she is mine, just like I'm hers.

But after that? Upstairs?

That was different.

I know that was different.

That might have been further than we should have gone. Because she let me make love to her, and she made love back, and I don't think either of us were entirely prepared for that. Even though I'd dreamed of exactly that, for five long years. In a million different ways. And it was better than anything I could have imagined.

I think I always knew this, even way back then, but now? Harlow Chase is the only one for me. As a man, I begin and end with her. I have become who I am because of her. She is everything.

Maybe it's a curse to meet the person who's meant for you when you're young, when you're stupid and reckless and think you know everything. Because look how badly I messed it up, even trying my best. And thinking about that makes me think about the pain I saw on Harlow's face when she asked me to leave. Not right afterward we made love, when she was happy, when I knew it was right, when I loved her as best as I knew how. Later. When she got to thinking, when she started to remember, when she realized she still had no reason to trust me.

I saw that look on her face, and I felt it. Just like I did before, I felt that aching, bloody hole open up in my chest, that place where I keep Harlow's pain like it was my own. Only this time it was poisoned, because I knew I had caused it all.

Yeah, so. No sleep for me. Since the sun came up I've been trying to make use of my time, trying to think of how I can make this up to her, make it better, at least until this development deal goes through and I can finally tell her the truth. And unfortunately there's approximately jack and shit that I can actually prove to her about about how I checked up on her and looked out for her all those years, until the private investigator that I hired to do it, Winslow, comes back into town with those files. And I know she'll need me to prove it, because I know better than anyone that my credibility is shot with her. Because I knew better than anyone how much it would hurt her when I left, and I did it anyway.

Anyway. Just like me to hire the one crazy dude who doesn't believe in Dropbox. I suppose I should cut him some slack, thinking everyone is spying on him all the time, since he's normally the guy doing the spying. But right now, with a possibly hurt and sad Harlow upstairs, I have no slack left in the line.

I'm thinking about what else I could do to help build her trust in me, to make her whole, to make us both whole—I could just tell her about some of that stuff, I guess, maybe about what I did for Dill's school, a few other things, even though all of that kind of makes me look like a crazed stalker—when I hear her start to move around up there.

I'm up like a damn rocket. All of me is up like a damn rocket. I'm cursing myself for getting hard just because I hear that Harlow continues to exist, especially under the circumstances, but it is what it is. I move to the bottom of the stairs, ready to go and help her down, when I see she's already there on the landing.

She just looks at me.

When she comes downstairs, walking so carefully on that ankle, I see that she's carrying the bag that the concierge brought me from the hotel.

Oh shit. Oh no.

"Lie to me," I say. My voice is hoarse. I can't even finish it.

Harlow just shakes her head, those beautiful lips pulled into a grim line, and brushes past me, walking toward the door. Fuck. No. I follow her, keeping calm, telling myself this is not the end. None of this is final.

Harlow opens the door, the watery sunlight streaming in from some damn ironic crack in the clouds, hitting her hair like a halo. She looks at me, puts out her hand. Hands me the bag.

"I'm mobile," she says, looking at her foot. "I can get around just fine. But I can't do this."

"Lo," I say. "Don't."

"I can't. I'm reneging on our deal. Take me to Judge Judy, I don't care. But I can't do this."

I take a deep breath and study her face. She's still hurting. Fuck, just looking at me hurts her. I don't know how to fix this, but I will. I will not leave it like this. I will not.

"Let me make good on my promise," I say.

I've made her so many promises. It almost doesn't matter which one I mean. They're all the same.

Make it right.

She doesn't say anything. She doesn't say no.

"I love you, Lo," I say as I'm stepping out the door. It's all I got.

"I know," she says, finally meeting my eyes.

The pain I see there rakes through me all the way back to the hotel, where I go right back up to my fancy suite and throw up until I'm too tired to feel anything else.

***

The worst hangover I've ever had in my life is from Harlow Chase.

Just like being inside her again is the happiest I've ever been, knowing that she's hurting now, again, because of me, is the closest to hell I hope to ever experience.

Normally I have an iron stomach. Even after a bottle of tequila, I'm not one to lose it. This? It's like my body itself is disgusted, and wants to punish me.

I'm fine with that.

The only other time I've ever felt like this was the first time Alex Wolfe had me do body work.

I don't mean on a car.

Isn't it fucked up that I don't even remember the details? It was right after I'd agreed to go out to California with Alex, right after I broke Harlow's heart to do it, and I was in a kind of all over haze. Not really thinking right. I didn't want to know too much, I know that, I didn't want to know anything about the guy's family, his life, any of that shit. I didn't want to see shades of gray. I wanted to take the guy into that warehouse knowing that I was about to do a bad thing to a bad man. Thought that would make it easier, somehow, but I don't know if it did.

I pulled up next to this guy's restaurant, some place he was running gambling in the back rooms, and waited. His name was Mikey, and he'd been skimming Alex's gambling business. I had a photo. I cornered him when he came out and when he saw me, standing there, next to that rented car,

I could see he knew why I was there. He looked at me like I was the angel of death.

He was quiet the whole way over. I guess I respected that, looking back. It would have been easier if he could have made me hate him in those few minutes. If he'd said something, anything, if someone had told me he beat his wife or something, it wouldn't have been so bad.

But Mikey was silent. Still. He didn't start to cry until he saw Alex, waiting for him.

Just the sight of Alex, and the man started crying. And then Alex looked at me.

I did refuse to tie him to a chair. I at least did that. Could not bring myself to hit a restrained man, like some kind of coward. But I still beat the shit out of him, and I did it because Alex told me to, because the guy was causing Alex problems. I covered my hands in this man's blood, chasing him around that damn warehouse until he begged, pleaded with me not to hit him anymore, while Alex Wolfe watched with cold, cold eyes. Seeing a grown man cry like that? It undoes something in you.

That was when I knew I was the bad guy. That I had turned into the bad guy.

I went home after that, to the nice place Alex had rented for me out in Santa Monica, and could feel the wrongness of it crawling over my skin until I wanted to rip it off, could feel myself turning into a damn monster until I knew the world would be better off without me in it. The scariest thing about that was that I finally understood how a man like me, someone who'd always been basically a decent guy, could turn into a something evil. I could see that path in front of me. It happened a little bit at a time, a response to every bad thing a man might have to do for himself or his family, like developing a callous. Every sin would make you worse, until after a while they stopped feeling like sins at all. Until maybe, after a very long while, you started to enjoy it.

Like Alex did.

The only way I was going to get through those years working for Alex and keep my soul was knowing I was doing it for Harlow.

The only thing that kept me even a little bit sane was Harlow.

The only thing that *ever* kept me sane was Harlow, but that night, it was crystal clear: I could only do this for her. I could become what I hate, I could commit every sin known to man, I could let myself turn into a monster, only if it was for her benefit, back in New York. Only if I knew it was buying her the life she needed. Only if I knew I was protecting her from Alex by doing it.

I could do damn near anything for her, I would give up anything for her, and that was the night I learned I would have to.

So that was also the night I called Matthias Winslow, a Private Investigator I found in the phone book, and told him I'd pay anything to keep tabs on a Harlow Chase living out in Brooklyn. So saying I spied on her to make sure she was ok is only half the story. I did it because I needed to know what I was fighting for. What was worth turning myself into this.

And every time, every damn time, the answer was the same: she was worth anything and everything I had to give. Including my soul.

That's what I'm thinking about while I sit in my hotel room, thinking about whether I'd just hurt Harlow Chase.

No wonder I feel like shit.

I finally manage to sleep, and when I finally wake up I don't remember. For a brief moment I think I'm still back at Harlow's. I can smell her on me, and I think she's next to me. So I get to experience that hell all over again.

That's about the time I get my shit together and man up. I make some calls. I get some real food in me. I make a few more calls.

And then I connect with the guy who's going to help me.

"Winslow," I say.

"Is this a landline?" he asks.

"Doesn't matter," I bark. "Get your ass over to the Wythe Hotel by tomorrow night or I will find you. Am I clear?"

"Mr. Roma, I'm still on a job—"

"If you want to keep working, you will be here. I'm tired of this shit. You get me the stuff I need or you're going to have problems, do you understand me?"

There's a frightened pause. I don't care. I am the bad guy. I've learned how to be the bad guy. And now I'm going to put it to a purpose.

"Yes, sir," he eventually says.

And then I prepare. Because I'm not giving up. I am going to make good on all those promises. I make a list of all the things I've done, good and bad, and all the things I've done for Harlow, good and bad, and I go through them one by one. Some of those things I am not proud of. Some of those things, I honestly wonder if, once she hears about them, she'll ever want to see me again. Some of those things I still can't tell her about, because I want to keep her safe.

And the reason why I can't tell her calls me again.

Alex Wolfe, blowing up my phone.

It annoys the hell out of me.

"What?" I say into the phone.

"You haven't answered my calls, you don't return my texts," he says. "I worry."

"Don't," I growl, and hang up.

But he should. The very next thing I do is make a list of things that need to happen for Harlow to be safe. She won't like this either. But it's time to stop pussyfooting around. She's already hurt, and that's the worst I can do to her. Now? My job is to protect her.

So the next evening I'm ready. I put on one of the suits I haven't bothered to wear since I've been here, liking the feel of it, knowing it represents a part of my life Harlow isn't familiar with. But it's the part she's going to need to get familiar with quickly. So I walk all the way from my hotel on the water back to her house, each step feeling better and better, like I'm closer to where I need to be.

Climbing the steps to her porch feels good.

Ringing that bell? Better.

And even when she answers and she's hesitant, and I can see how conflicted she is — I can see that she misses me, that she wants to know about this suit, that this is eating her up at least as much as it's eating me — I still know I'm on the right path.

"You ready to talk yet?" I ask her.

Lo leans her head against the doorframe and looks at me like she wants to let me in. Like she wants it badly. But she shakes her head.

"No," she says.

"I'll be back," I say.

And that's that. I leave her be. For now.

Next day, Winslow's at my suite, laying out a bunch of files. Old fashioned, like he's J. Edgar Hoover, all the stuff I've had him collect over the years. It's more than I thought, because it's not just stuff on Harlow. It's on me, too. In fact, it's mostly on me.

"You're thorough," I say.

Winslow smiles, his comb-over falling into his face. "These are just copies," he says. "Mind if I ask what you're going to do with all this?"

"I'm going to show it to her," I say.

Winslow, the guy who thinks the CIA has a satellite dedicated just to him, looks at me like I'm crazy. And I probably am, to show her any of this without giving her full context. Letting her know I had reasons to worry about her, that I had cause to want to make sure she was getting the things she deserved in life. But screw it, I never crossed a line. There aren't any photos, I didn't ever ask about who she was screwing. She'll see it for what it is.

"You want me to start a surveillance on her?" he says. "I could, maybe, for a few days, before I get back to that other job."

I think about Alex and his plans, and how Harlow is messing them up, and I think about it.

"No," I say. "But give me a heads-up if you happen to see anything funny, you know?"

Winslow nods. He knows what I'm talking about. I don't think Alex would go that far, but I'm looking out. This is my girl, after all. This is Harlow.

So when I go out that evening, I've got my briefcase with me for my walk back to Harlow's place. I'm starting to really enjoy it, even with all the ways the area's changed, just because I know where it ends. And when I finally get there and ring that bell and it's Shantha that answers, I'm not even upset.

"She home?" I ask.

Shantha eyes me narrowly. This is a good test: the best friend.

And the best friend still doesn't hate me. Just stands there, her hand on her hip, looking at me like I'm an idiot. I smile; I'll take that.

"Don't look so smug," Shantha warns me, like I'm not out of the woods yet. "I'll get her."

When Lo comes to the door she doesn't look as tired as she did, and she doesn't look as lost. She looks wary. But when she looks at me, I feel it. We both do.

That current. That thing between us.

"You can't keep doing this, Marcus," she says, leaning against that doorframe again. I want to kiss her against that door.

"Yes, I can," I say. "I keep my promises, Lo. Sometimes it just takes me a while."

Lo looks like she wants to believe. She still doesn't tell me no.

This time it's harder to walk away. Harder to leave her there, when I know the only place I should be is beside her. And behind her, and on top of her. I admit, I get carried away thinking about her by the time I'm back at the hotel. Thinking about all the things I'm going to do her, and all the things I'm going to do for her. Stuff I'm going to buy her. Things I'll surprise her with. It's random, but I remember that she always wanted to go to the opera, and I bet she never did. Like get real dressed up for no reason and go. That's something do for her easy. Hell, I'll take her to the opera in Vienna.

See? I let it get out of hand, like I'm little kid, giddy and in love for the first time, with no sense of proportion or timing.

So, I have to get a handle on it. Not so much because I think I should rein myself in, but because I can't let it be about me. This has got to be about her. About what she needs, what she deserves.

I do a shit ton of push-ups. Then sit-ups. I start in on the push-ups again, but it doesn't work. No matter what I do, I'm ready for her. I'm more alive, just thinking about her.

The next day it's raining. I wait until evening again, knowing she's still not working yet; Shantha won't let her until she's fully healed. My walk is later than it has been, and it's dark out, dark and wet, and no one's out on the street. I don't mind. Gives me time to think. Gives me time to start wondering about what my life is going to be like after all of this.

I pause. I haven't really thought about that, not once. What happens after. How I'm going to make all these pieces come together. Because the thing is, I can't go back to life without Harlow.

I'm stopped, just standing on the sidewalk underneath a tree, across the street from Harlow's house, letting the rain fall on me and thinking about this, when I see something.

Don't ask me how. These past five years have taught me a lot of things that normal people shouldn't know.

Maybe it's just a flicker. A shadow that doesn't fit. Maybe the thin, high sound of metal scraping against metal, standing out in all that soft rain. Maybe just instinct. But I walk to the side, deeper into the shadow of that tree, and then jog across the street, just behind a passing car so it will cover the noise.

I crouch.

The streetlight on my side is out. Down the block, the yellow-orange light pours over the glittering grass of her neighbor's yard, washes over the rain itself. It's bad visibility. Kind of a perfect night for what I think is happening.

I make my way silently down her driveway, to the path that leads to the kitchen door, and I see him. A man, crouched in front of that kitchen door, picking the lock.

Then I see red.

It's only because this isn't my first time that I don't go berserker on him. I stand perfectly still, holding myself to attention, my heart slamming into my chest while my blood rages for his blood. But this isn't some stupid neighborhood tough, this isn't some gang leader's asshole lackeys, this isn't some union shmuck—this is some guy breaking into Harlow's house.

This is a fucking home invasion.

I can only hold it for so long.

I keep myself under control just long enough to walk past the half flight of stairs that lead up to the little landing where he's crouched, trying to get to Harlow for whatever fucking purpose, though I can bet what. I keep it cool just long enough to get right next to that landing. And then I grab the iron railing, put one foot on the lip of the landing, and haul myself up in total silence. In one motion, I wrap my forearm around his neck from the back and swing back the way I came, flipping him backwards over that railing and down into the mud where he fucking belongs.

And then I'm on him.

I hit him a few times before I realize he's screaming. I can't blame him, I guess, since at this point, thinking about what might have happened if I hadn't been here, I'm close to killing him.

"Who's there?"

The light goes on over the kitchen door, and I know there's only one person it could be. I turn, and that's long enough for the guy under me to get some leverage. He twists out, throwing me off of him, and I jump back up, ready to fight him. He's better than I have any right to expect; he's trained. He dodges and I slip in the mud, and that's when he lands one punch.

Just one punch. I've taken much worse. It doesn't faze me, just breaks my momentum for a moment. But it's enough. Because this guy doesn't want to fight; he wants to run.

He goes straight over Harlow's fence, and then from there I know he could go into any number of yards, any number of streets. By the time I've got my balance, chasing him is pointless.

And besides, there's something more important to take care of.

"Marcus?" she says.

I turn around and look up and see her standing in the doorway, framed by light, like nothing is wrong.

Because nothing is wrong.

She's safe.

"What the hell happened to you?" she asks me.

I'm so relieved, I start to laugh.

***

I'm sitting in her kitchen again, at the very table where we had sex. We both thought about it when she told me to sit down, and we both knew the other person was thinking about it. There was that tell tale pause, you know, where you both just look at it then look at each other, and for a second you're right back there, feeling it all over again. I was right back inside her, putting her leg over my shoulder, telling her she's mine.

Made it kinda funny when she took my clothes. I tried not to smile.

My suit's in the laundry now, covered in mud, my briefcase dripping on a towel in the corner. I'm sitting here, drinking the tea she made me just because she made it, in my boxer briefs and an undershirt, and I can tell it's making her lose her concentration.

This time I do smile.

Hey, tonight's been a bad night, all around. I'll take what I can get.

"Are you going to tell me what happened?" she asks.

"I did."

"Why was someone trying to break into my house?" she says again.

This is the worst part, because she looks scared. And the truth is, I don't know for sure what happened because I let the guy get away, so I can't even reassure her with anything. All I can say is that, yeah, some scumbag tried to break into her house.

While she was inside.

The thought still makes me crazy. I feel my shoulders come forward and my back round and I curse under my breath, pissed off again that I didn't hold on to the guy.

I make myself look directly at Harlow, though. She's what's important. She's the only thing that matters.

And she's freaked out.

"I don't know," I say. "I'm telling the truth."

Harlow's lip shakes and her face flushes the way it does when she's upset, the way it does the few times I've ever really seen her cry, and she looks down at the table. I see her draw her eyebrows together, bite her lip. She's always so determined to be strong.

"That's worse, isn't it?" I say.

She nods.

"Lo."

She's gripping her own hands now, hard, digging her fingernails into the skin. I put my hand over hers; it's big enough to cover both of her little fists, my big, scarred, ugly boxer's hand over hers. The second I touch her, I feel it. She gasps at the contact. Looks up.

We stare at each other a second too long.

"Do you want me to take you somewhere else?" I ask her. "I'll take you anywhere you want to go. I'll put you up in a hotel if that'll help you feel safe."

She flashes that fierceness I love, shaking her head. Says, "No, I'm not leaving my home."

"Then I'm not leaving," I say.

Lo licks her lips. She looks like she wants to say something, but can't decide what. Her hands burn under mine.

"I will sleep on the goddamned porch if I have to," I say. "I'll camp out in the backyard—I don't care. But I'm not leaving."

I don't know how long the silence lasts between us. Could be a few seconds, could be minutes, but it feels like hours. Just hours of staring at her, breathing her in, looking at her and seeing everything I love: that strength, that intelligence, that fearlessness. She's the most beautiful woman in the world to me. And she's looking right back at me.

She hasn't moved her hands.

Finally, she says, "You don't have to sleep outside."

13

HARLOW

I look at Marcus's face, still wet from the rain outside, while he sits at the kitchen table where he gave me one of the best orgasms of my life, sitting there in barely any clothes at all, and I see the determination on that gorgeous face replaced by a sly smile.

I can't believe what I just said.

'You don't have to sleep outside?' Really? Could I have been any more suggestive if I'd tried?

The thing is, I'm not entirely sure it was an innocent mistake.

The past few days, since I kicked him out, I've missed him like an addict. I mean I've really felt it. Physically. An ache. A hole, an absence that needed to be filled, maybe something that was always there, but that I'd learned to ignore. Or that had been buried, after what happened with Dylan in the bathroom of the The Alley. Marcus unearthed it, woke it up, stoked it until it burned so hot I could barely think about anything else. I've looked forward to seeing him every day when he makes his daily pilgrimage to my house, and I've hated myself for it. Today he didn't come at the usual time, and it actually hurt me. It hurt, too, too much, that maybe a little rain drove him away; that, in the end, just like before, I wasn't that important to him. That he might just disappear all over again. Then I open my kitchen door to find Marcus beating the crap out of some guy who was trying to break into my home.

God, even the thought of that…some strange man, breaking in while I'm home? I was in the living room, reading with only one lamp on, so I tell myself that maybe it looked like my house was empty from the outside. Maybe he wasn't breaking in to get to me.

That's a big maybe.

But still, what would have happened if Marcus hadn't been here?

I shudder all over again, and forcibly shove all thoughts of that night at the bar and the man who tried to rape me out of my head. That is *not* what this was.

"You ok?" he asks me immediately.

His big, heavy hand still covers mine. It is comforting even if I don't want it to be. I look down and see that he broke the skin on his knuckles defending me, and I haven't even noticed until now.

"Jesus, Marcus, look at you," I murmur.

"You didn't answer the question."

"I don't know if I'm ok," I say, truthfully. "Please just…let me fix this."

Before he can say anything I've gotten up, my head spinning when I lose contact with him, and I'm headed for the bathroom. I get all the usual supplies—rubbing alcohol, bandages, Neosporin—and try not to think about how I'm not dealing with Dill's skinned knee, but instead cleaning the wounds of a man who just fought to protect me.

I don't want to need protection. I never have.

To bad you almost never get what you want.

When I come back Marcus is standing, still totally unable to remain seated while I'm up and about. He's searching my face, concerned, and when he finally sees the stuff I'm carrying he smiles slightly.

"You don't need to do all that," he says.

"Don't be ridiculous. Sit."

Marcus sits back down and obediently gives me his right hand, his green eyes studying me. I try to ignore that x-ray stare, try not to think too hard about what's happening here, or even what just happened outside, and instead pay attention to the job at hand. I still, after all these years, cannot get over his hands. They were always huge, just given his overall size, but somehow now they seem bigger. Definitely heavier. He must still hit the heavy bag, maybe even do knuckle push-ups, to keep that kind of bone density. I remember someone at one of his fights saying once that getting tagged with a Roma right cross was like getting hit in the face with a five-pound weight.

I believe it.

I think about how often the man trying to break into my home just got hit in the face with twin five-pound weights and I smile. I know I'm supposed to forgive and forget, but honestly, screw that. I'm glad Marcus hurt him.

Maybe he won't come back.

Marcus doesn't flinch when I rub the raw skin down with the alcohol, and I guess I shouldn't be surprised. No matter how tough I was in the gym, I would always, always be a huge baby about this kind of thing. Marcus, on the other hand, probably still eats nails for breakfast.

He's still studying me.

"What?" I say, squirming under that stare.

"I really will sleep on the floor," he says. "You don't even have to talk to me if you don't want to. But I'm not leaving you here alone."

I stop what I'm doing and I realize I'm holding my breath. He's giving me an out. He's giving me many outs. He's also making it clear that I have to make an active choice. That I have to decide what this will be.

And those words...

I'm not leaving you here alone.

Those are the words I've fantasized about him saying to me, over and over again, even though I knew it was pathetic. Those are the words that make me feel the weakest, because I want to hear them so badly. Those are the words I've wanted him to mean, for real, for everything, forever, and not just because he thinks someone is about to break into my house.

"You can't just move in here," I say quietly, trying not to think about the way his hands feel in mine. I'm almost done. Almost there. "I mean, until when? When will it be safe enough?"

It's not just a rhetorical question this time, but I mean it in so many different ways. And he knows that.

Marcus moves those big hands, moves the rubbing alcohol aside, moves the bandages, and takes my hand in his again. He grazes the back of my hand with the pad of his rough thumb, and I can't help but remember what it felt like to have that thumb on my clit, and heat pools between my legs.

Oh God, why am I thinking about that right now?

"Until this development deal is over and done with," he says, "I'm not going anywhere."

I look up.

Marcus Roma, big and strong in nothing but a thin undershirt and some boxer briefs, his hair wet, his jaw tense, is looking at me as though I am the most important thing on this Earth.

It's so intoxicating that I almost miss what he just said.

Almost.

"Is that what this was about?" I say, slowly. "Why that guy was trying to break in? Because I won't sell?"

Something flickers across his face. I don't know what, and it makes me uneasy. His hand is hot over mine, and now I know I should pull away—but I can't.

Damn it, I can't.

"Lo, look at me," he says. "I don't know if that's what it was. But it's possible."

"Jesus!" I say. I hadn't actually expected him to say that. I thought he'd laugh at me, reassure me that that kind of thing only happens in movies, that this was just some random bad luck that I'm not in any more danger than usual, living in New York.

I don't know if this is better, or worse.

I get up from the table, needing to just move around, to feel like I'm doing something rather than just sitting there, waiting for fate to come to me. Almost immediately I miss his touch. My body screams for it, wants to beg him to hold me, and it's just making me feel more confused and lost.

And then a few more pieces click into place, and I look at him again.

"That's why you're here," I say. "You didn't run into me accidentally. You're here, with me, specifically, for a reason."

The idea is just too horrible.

"No," he says loudly, getting up from the table, his brow furrowed. "No! Not like that, Lo. You know I work for Alex. He's invested in this, that's all. That's all."

"So he's big time, huh?" I say softly, leaning against the counter. This suddenly feels so overwhelming.

Somehow Marcus looks even worse than I feel. Like he's watching something bad happen and can't do anything about it. He used to look like that when he'd see me start to cry years ago, when something bad really had happened and there was nothing he could do but hold me.

He crosses the kitchen and comes close to me again, those big hands flexing, opening and closing in the air, until he's close enough to touch me. He puts them on my shoulders, keeps them light, comforting. I've never known another person with such a light touch when he wanted it.

"This thing, this development—it's going to happen," he says. "You can't stop him, Lo, no matter how hard you fight. There's too much money involved, and you don't know Alex."

I close my eyes and say it.

"Is that why you're here? To convince me to sell out?"

"No," he says. "Look at me, Lo."

I open my eyes. I look at him. It's one of the hardest things I've ever done, because I know that this time I'll be able to read him. I'll know if he means what he's about to say. And because I'm about to risk it, I can see that he has the power to break my heart all over again.

Marcus looks into me, deeply, one finger tracing the curve of my cheek. He says, "You don't have to trust me yet, Lo. But I'm here right now because I love you."

He means it. Something inside me flutters awake, like a flock of birds breaking into the air, and I find it hard to breathe. I can hear my own heartbeat, and I can feel my pulse between my legs.

Oh God.

"You have to sell," he says.

"What if I don't?"

"He'll make you."

I grip the edge of the kitchen counter. "No one can make me do anything."

"You don't know Alex like I do," Marcus says.

"So tell me about him," I say, and my voice is so urgent it surprises me. It surprises me realizing how much I want to know about this part of his life. About the part of his life that took him from me. "You work for him, you've been working for him, and more than that, he's your—"

"Don't say it," he says, putting a finger to my lips. "Don't tell me what he is to me. It's…it's fucking complicated."

His finger. On my lips.

It takes every ounce of self-control I have not to suck it into my mouth. Instead I bite my lip, and I can see what that does to him. He shifts his weight, and I can feel his erection against me. It's not even remotely fair.

"Don't touch me when you're trying to tell me what to do," I say.

He doesn't say anything. Just exhales powerfully. But he moves his finger.

"And what if I did sell?" I ask. Why am I bothering to pretend this is some kind of casual question? It's anything but casual. "What would happen then? You'd be gone, right? 'Thanks for the lay, see you later?'"

Marcus's face darkens. "No. I told you I'm not leaving. Not ever again."

"That doesn't work, Marcus. You can't have it both ways. You can't work for the man who's trying to destroy my home and be my…what? What do you even think you are?"

Marcus puts those big hands on either side of me on the kitchen counter, penning me in, and leans in until his mouth is only inches from mine.

"I'm the guy who's going to keep you safe," he says.

I shiver as I feel his breath on my neck, and my heart breaks as he says those words. "Oh. Is that all?" I ask.

His lips graze my ear, my cheek. He rubs his face against my neck, and then licks it, ever so lightly.

"No," he says in my ear. "That's not all."

Oh God. Oh God, oh God, oh God. The physicality of this man, and my attraction to him, removes all sense from my brain. I feel like a zombie, or like I'm hypnotized, like he could tell me to strip and my clothes would be half off before I even knew what was happening. Like I'm drunk on him, drunk and deranged and prone to making bad decisions.

This should be illegal. You should not be allowed to drive a human body while under this kind of influence.

"Marcus, I can't do a repeat of this," I say, and my breath is already ragged. "Please."

And I push against his chest, gently.

I can't look at him when he steps back because I know I'll be right back there, unable to think clearly through my desire for him. Not just for him, but for everything to be right between us. That was the worst part about sleeping with him again—seeing a glimpse of how it could be. Knowing I love him now more than I ever did, knowing that learning more about the world in the last five years has made me realize just how lucky I was to have him in my life at all. And then the hangover: remembering that it's not all right. That he still hasn't explained why he left, that he might do it again at any moment. Remembering what happened to me after he left the first time.

How could I bring him back into my life under those circumstances? How could I ever bring him into Dill's life under those circumstances?

That's why I kicked him out. Didn't seem to do any good, though. He's still in my life. Even if he weren't standing in my kitchen, looking down at me with such tender concern that it makes me weak, he'd still be in my life. Because I don't think he'll ever be out of my thoughts.

"Lo," he says.

"Goddammit," I say. I still can't look at him. I'm actually sweating, I'm so turned on, and I still have to say no. I still have to be responsible. And I am *furious*. "Why can't you just tell me? Why can't you just explain? Why can't you help me to understand so I can maybe, maybe, trust you again?"

He starts to speak, but he's got me going now. I have to get mad or I'll start to cry. I think about all those sleepless nights after he left, I think about all those men who treated me like crap, I think about Dylan in the bar. I think about how much I hated myself, how I thought I was just unloveable, if after all that Marcus Roma could leave me so easily.

I push him in the chest again, harder this time.

"Do you have any idea what it did to me when you left?" I ask him.

I can feel the anger roiling through my blood, twisting around the lust, the love, turning it all into something potent and powerful and destructive, and if I thought I was drunk on him before, I had no idea what that meant. I am no longer in the drivers seat. Something else is happening here. All those things I never said, all those things I felt: they're coming out.

I shove him, hard enough to surprise him.

"Do you know what *happened* to me?" I shout.

Marcus's eyes glitter softly, so softly, and when he speaks, his voice is gentle. "Tell me," he says.

It makes me so angry.

"Fuck you," I say. "Like you deserve to know? You want to know how badly you broke my heart? I drank for six months straight, Marcus, all the time. I hated myself. I hated everything about myself so much that I kept sleeping with guys who made me feel as shitty about myself as *you* did, just because it felt right. I went out with guys who treated me like crap, who made me feel worthless, and one of them tried to fucking *rape* me."

Time stops.

Oh God. I didn't mean to say that. I didn't. I look at Marcus, his face slowly collapsing in agony, and immediately I want to take it back. I never meant to tell him like this, in anger. I don't know if I ever meant to tell him at all. I want to somehow tell him it's not his fault, even though I just said it like it was, like I blame him, even though I don't. And I know he'll blame himself, no matter what I say, and that this is something I can never, ever take back.

"Harlow," he whispers.

I have never, ever seen him like this. Not when I'd have a panic attack, not after his father died. Never. He is ashen, his face slack, his mouth open in horror. He walks towards me and then collapses to his knees in front of me, putting his arms around my waist. He pulls me in tight, and when he presses his face into my stomach, I feel his tears soak through the thin material of my shirt.

I've never seen him cry before.

"I am so sorry," he says, his voice strangled, muffled. "I am so, so sorry."

"Stop," I say, and my own voice is thick with emotion. "Please, Marcus, it's not your fault. It wasn't anyone's fault but that asshole who... Marcus, *please.*"

He catches the tone in my voice and reacts, the way he always does, when I need something. He stands up, wiping his eyes so no one would ever be able to tell he'd shed a tear, and leans his head against mine. He puts his arms around me again, as though he can't bear to let go.

"Harlow, I—"

"Wait," I say. I'm struggling to find the words. I want to tell the truth, but this is one of those things that's so complicated that there are many parts to the truth. I don't know how to do all of them justice. "I've dealt with it, Marcus. I was so, so lucky, all things considered, and Shantha intervened, and...it didn't happen the way it could have. I'm over it, I think. I don't know. As much as anyone's ever over anything. I don't know the guy's last name, or where to find him, or anything, and I don't want to. It's just, it's something that happens to people, and I don't want it to have changed me, but it did, and now..."

I trail off. Do I tell him this? Do I let him in?

What's the point in denying the truth?

"What?" he asks me.

I take a deep breath, close my eyes, and feel his arms around me. It shouldn't help me feel better, it shouldn't make it feel safer to say what I'm about to say, but it does. Damn him, it does.

"I didn't want anybody, after that. Even before, I never really felt special about anyone, but afterwards, I couldn't…I couldn't feel that way about another person, not even physically. Not until you came back." I swallow, and force myself to look up at him. "It's always been you. I thought that part of my life was over. And now I want you so much…"

Marcus brushes against my cheek with the back of his hand while I blink back tears. The look of love on his face is so cosmically unfair, it just reminds me of what we *don't* have right now, just because I don't have any reason to trust him.

"Why does it have to be you? Why is it only you who makes me feel this way? You make me feel *alive* again, and you are such an asshole!"

I want to push away from him, but I can't. Instead I just watch my words hurt him.

"Why can't you tell me?" I ask again. "Why can't you just tell me so I know it wasn't my fault? Why can't you tell me so I know it wasn't that you stopped loving me, it wasn't that I didn't matter, that I wasn't…"

Right here, my heart just gives out. This whole night, this whole week, this whole conversation, it's just become too much. I start to cry, great, big, racking heaves, and Marcus holds me tight and I can't handle how good it feels. I can't handle that I want this, that I want him to hold me, to make me safe.

Now I really do push away from him, because I can't bear it, I can't bear anymore contact. I feel like if he keeps touching me I will lose all will, all discipline, and I will be lost. I will be head over heels in love, in *need*, with him, and then it will only be a matter of time before he breaks me all over again.

"Why can't you just *say something*?" I scream at him.

Marcus has looked as close to beaten down as I've ever seen him, right up until this moment. He's been in such obvious pain, and he's been looking at me like I'm the only thing in his universe, but he hasn't *done* anything—until now.

"Because you won't believe me!" he shouts back. He puts both hands on top of his head like he's going to rip his hair out, every large muscle in his huge body flexing, and he lets out a growl. His eyes still look like he's about to cry, like he wants to just pick me up and hold me for the rest of his life, but his body...

"Why won't you fucking *believe* me?" he asks again. "You think you're the only one who hurt? You don't know the things I've done, Lo, you don't know what I've become for you. You don't know..."

"What are you talking about?" I say. "Please just tell me what you're talking about!"

"Fuck!" he shouts, and turns around, slamming his fist down on the kitchen table. It rattles, and for a moment I think it will splinter down the middle, but it holds.

"I can't fucking tell you!" he shouts again, and he's angry, angrier than I've ever, ever seen him—but not at me. It's like he's just mad at the world, at life, looking around for something to take it out on.

"I can't fucking tell you, and you won't believe me no matter what I say, and I would have died," he says, turning back to look at me, those laser eyes spearing me, holding me in place, "I would have *died* to keep that from happening to you, Lo. I would have come back and killed him myself. I would have...Jesus, Lo, I would have done anything, anything..."

The worst part is that I do believe him. I believe that he would have died, rather than let Dylan follow me into that bathroom. I believe that he would have hunted Dylan down. That he still would, if I let him.

I don't want to believe him about this. It makes the rest too confusing.

"Why can't you tell me so I'll stop thinking it was my fault? That I just wasn't good enough? Why do you have to be so fucking cruel?"

Marcus catches my hand right as I'm about to shove him in the chest again, and his eyes flash at me. He's got a crease in his forehead, and the muscles in his jaw are pulsing. He looks like he's about to explode.

"Why can't you believe me when I say I'll tell you as soon as I can?" he rasps. "That the reason I can't is because I fucking love you?"

This stops me. He says it like that, and it sounds so simple.

I stop thinking about how much he hurt me, and think instead about all he did before that. Hasn't he earned that from me? The benefit of the doubt?

"Fuck!" he shouts, and releases me. He turns away from me, running a hand through his hair the way he does, and grabs his ruined briefcase from the corner, where it's been resting on a towel. He slams it on the kitchen table and flips it open, revealing a plain manila folder. He turns back to me and points at it.

"Here. Look at this. See what I've been doing with my miserable fucking life the past five years, and then tell me it was because you weren't good enough."

I look from him to the briefcase, not really comprehending. He'd said he would prove it, that he never forgot about me, but I kind of thought that wasn't meant to be taken literally. I mean, who has documented evidence of…whatever this is? I don't know where my driver's license is half the time. He has a briefcase of his life.

I look back at Marcus, and he's just this simmering tower of pent-up emotion. He's tense, his hands gripping the back of the chair I'd been sitting in, his arms flexing, his shoulders rolled forward. He's glowering ahead, almost like he's uncertain of what will happen next.

Marcus is almost never uncertain. Definitely not ever nervous.

I walk toward the folder he's put on the table, my curiosity overtaking my own apprehension. What I find seems inconsequential at first. A bunch of reports, typed out by an old fashioned typewriter, the kind of thing you never see anymore. They're styled like memos, written from some guy called M. Winslow to Mr. Roma. Then I see the fine print in the header: "Matthias Winslow, licensed Private Investigator."

Now I dig through the papers.

I finally manage to focus my eyes on one of these reports long enough to actually read a few lines. "Meanwhile, Dillinger continues to adjust to his new school, and their financial situation is stable. On a personal note, Harlow seems happier. Again, let me know if you'd like me to look further into her personal life; it's an easy add-on."

What.

I feel Marcus behind me, his abs to my back, his arms nearly around me. I can tell he wants to hold me. His breathing is fast, shallow.

"What is this?" I say.

"What it looks like."

"You really did spy on me?" I say, grabbing the folder and moving away from him, turning around, walking backwards into the living room. I need distance. "That wasn't an exaggeration? You paid someone else to spy on me?"

"No," he says, his voice catching. I watch his hands ball into fists, then release again. "Not like that. I didn't spy on you; I just needed to know that you were ok. That you had everything you needed."

I stare at him. That I had everything I needed? What kind of bullshit is that? He wanted to make sure providence somehow rained luck and money down upon me?

"What would you have done if I didn't have everything I need?" I ask, hardly believing this. My head is spinning.

"I would have made sure you did," he says, his expression changing. "I would have taken care of it."

I laugh. I can't help it. It's too absurd. "So you can leave—that's cool, right? You can just break my heart and leave, but God forbid I can't make the electric bill. That would have been the last straw. That's totally reasonable."

Marcus takes a deep breath. "It's not that simple."

"Oh, good. Because I was going to say that maybe you should have just asked me which thing I preferred. Having you around, or having you pay someone to tell you I wasn't starving to death."

He's just standing there, taking this from me, not offering up any more explanation. He's seething, like he has so much he wants to say but won't. Like why he would have to do this instead of actually stick around. I blow out the air in my lungs in an exasperated puff.

"Marcus, I don't even know where to begin with how screwed up this is," I say, and I rifle through the papers, pulling out another one at random. This one catches my eye because of the P.S. on the bottom. "I made the donation to Dillinger's school, as discussed, from an anonymous benefactor."

Oh, are you freaking kidding me?

Dill's school has only had one donation from an anonymous benefactor, and it was a big one. I wave the paper around. "*You*? You bought Dill's school a computer lab?"

I can't even look at him anymore. I collapse on the couch, put the folder down on the floor next to me, and rest my head in my hands.

He's taken away my ability to be mad at him and feel good about it, is the thing. It's not any more satisfying to know he was watching me, thinking about me, trying to find ways to provide for us the whole time. I thought it would help to know what he'd been up to, but it just makes me realize how much I really needed him. Just him.

Just. Him.

He comes and sits next to me, his weight dipping the couch, pulling me toward him. I don't fight it.

"Are you upset?" he asks. His own voice is still shaky. He's not making me talk about the attempted rape, but I can tell he's still thinking about it. That he doesn't want to let me out of his sight, his arms. It might take him awhile.

"Lo, are you ok?" he asks again.

I shake my head. I don't know. I don't know if I feel violated by his spying, just frustrated, or humiliated that Marcus knows these things about me. I'm thinking about all the dark times, the times when I really did struggle, when I was terrified, when I needed him most of all. I missed him and I was furious with him, and I was brokenhearted and betrayed, but at least I had the solace of knowing that all that suffering was in secret. At least I still had my pride.

And now I know he saw all of that. I mean, it's one thing to tell him. I still control that. It's another to know someone was watching.

"I don't know," I say.

He puts his hand on my back, and damn it, there it is again. That feeling, the longing for him—it swells right back up with no regard to what's happening. To the fact that my head is spinning, that I should be beyond freaked out to find out Marcus watched me all those years. To find that out on the same night he somehow happened to be here to protect me from a a freaking *home invasion*. His fingers burn a brand into me into me anyway, and his scent, the warmth of him, pulls me into the hollow underneath his arm.

I have so little self-control with him.

And for some reason, I like that.

"I wish I knew what to say to make it better," he says.

He doesn't finish. I wouldn't know what to fill in there, either. Instead I stand up, pulling myself away from his touch, like pulling against an elastic band, and make my way toward the stairs.

"You can have the couch," I say.

14

HARLOW

Sometimes all you need is time to put things in perspective. Sometimes a memory helps, too.

I'm lying awake in the relative dark of my bedroom, the only light coming in from the window by my bed and falling softly on me in a square of pale light against the darkness. It probably looks pretty, but it means I can't quite see into the shadows of my room. Shouldn't matter, right? I'm a grown up. I shouldn't be afraid of the dark.

Except once I get over the shock of Marcus's briefcase revelations and my own emotional meltdown, I'm right back to being in shock about the attempted home invasion. And those shadows are terrifying.

I start to think about whether I could have called 911 in time. I start to think about whether I could have used any of the skills Marcus taught me, whether I could have kicked the guy's ass before the cops got here, and it's horrible to have to admit that I couldn't. Even without the weak ankle, I'm out of shape, and I was never good enough to take on a fully grown man. I already have ample evidence of that, thanks to one horrible night in a bar.

Weirdly, the only thing that gives me some comfort is that, whether Marcus admits it or not, I'm convinced it had to do with this stupid real estate development. If it had been random, if it had been someone out to attack a woman alone in her house, that's a whole different order of scary. It can't be that.

Not that this isn't terrifying enough. Because that's what happens; the anxiety slowly grows, builds, takes on different shades, gathers weight, until it's full-blown terror. Until it's terror wrapped in anger that someone would do this to me, and for such a stupid, shallow reason.

The only other time in my life I've been this scared was right after my parents died, and I couldn't sleep because of it.

It's so strange to think back on how drastically grief and depression affected me. I've never really tried to explain it to anyone else, because every time I try to put it into words, it sounds so delusional, so truly ill, that I just give up. It's hard for me to understand it now, because even then I knew it was irrational, but it didn't matter. Only the fear mattered. I would lie awake, rigid with that fear, unable to move because I thought that if I did it might somehow disturb the order of the universe, that it might somehow anger fate, and the end result of this in my grief-crazed mind was always something terrible happening to Dill.

It really made no sense at all.

I couldn't move because Dill might choke in his sleep. I couldn't let myself fall asleep because Dill might fall down the stairs. I couldn't tell anyone because it might get back to my Aunt Jill, and she would take Dill away forever.

I couldn't even talk, couldn't explain what was happening to me. I was too afraid.

And it was Marcus who figured it out.

It was Marcus who realized I wasn't sleeping. I don't know, maybe other people noticed. But he was the only one who did something about it.

That's when he started sneaking into my bedroom at the Mankowskis at night, just a few days after the accident. The first time he tapped on my window, standing on a milk crate at the side of the house, I was actually relieved. I mean, I felt a jolt of terror at any kind of stimuli, any creak of the floorboards, any screech of tires, anything at all. But part of me was relieved that something was happening, that I had something—anything—to focus on besides the horrible scenarios that kept playing themselves out in my head.

Marcus climbing through my window was the only thing that got me to stop living those nightmares over and over again until my mind burned out on itself.

I think most people, myself included, would have taken one look at me and backed away slowly, because what was happening to me was overwhelming. I had bitten my fingernails until they bled; I had scratched holes in my sheets. I was sweaty with the effort of holding myself completely, rigidly still, my whole body one giant knot.

I haven't been able to remember what it actually *felt* like to be that scared in so long, like my body wouldn't let me. Like there was a block. I could talk about it, I knew the facts, but I couldn't feel it. Like it happened to someone else, some other version of me, and I was mostly grateful that I didn't have to be her anymore.

Until tonight. Tonight, it's coming back.

And the only thing that helped all those years ago was Marcus. He didn't say anything or do anything special, there wasn't some magic word or anything. He just climbed in through that window and stayed.

I remember him touching my cheek.

I remember him lying down next to me, so gently, trying not to disturb me.

I remember him taking my hands in his when I tried to scratch at them.

I remember the first time he held me when I cried like that, not about anything, just from the frustration of constantly being afraid. He was careful, leaning up on one elbow, gently lifting up my head until he could get his arm around me. And then he pulled me against his chest, which was the safest place I'd ever been.

I think it was his silence that allowed me to eventually speak. It wasn't the first night he came in through that window that I could talk about it. And I don't remember sleeping that night, though Marcus told me later that I did a little bit. I don't even know if it was the second night he was with me that I could talk about it. I just remember the terror slowly receding, the knowledge of Marcus lying next to me, calm, steady, certain, slowly replacing the looping visions of my little brother's death in my mind.

Until one night I just spoke out loud. I told him. I told him, and I wasn't afraid that saying it out loud would make it come true.

I just said, "I'm afraid that she won't watch him and Dill will smother in his sleep."

I think most people, in that situation, might try to get me to talk about it. Or they would try to reason with me, to convince me that nothing was going to happen to Dill, that it was a totally irrational fear. But I knew all of that already. I knew it was completely irrational, and I didn't want to talk about it anymore because I'd been thinking about it nonstop for hours already. The last thing in the world I needed to do was talk about it some more.

But Marcus was not most people. Marcus just kissed me on the temple and said, "I'll make sure he's ok."

And then he climbed back out of my window. I was paralyzed with fear until he came back, but the key is, he did come back. Marcus climbed back in, smiling at me.

He said, "I checked on him. I climbed that tree—you know the one next to that side of your house? He's not even sleeping with a blanket. He's all stretched out."

I actually smiled a little bit, my relief was so profound, but it was twinned with this sense of doom, like I couldn't see any way for it to get better. I said, "Marcus?"

"Yeah?"

"Lie to me. Tell me I won't always have to feel like this."

"Don't have to lie," he said, and pulled me back against his chest. "You're going to be ok."

It sounds so stupid, I know. Like such a simple thing. But that was the first time I remember letting go, even a little bit. I have tried and tried and tried to figure out why it worked. Why in the end that Marcus was the only thing to get between me and my fear of losing my brother, or between me and my fear of never getting better. Why I would believe it when Marcus said that Dill was safe, but wouldn't believe my own lying eyes, my own common sense.

I think, in the end, I just trusted Marcus more than I trusted anyone else. Even myself. He was always there. He was always in control.

And he did this, check on Dill for me, every night. He would check on Dill, and then he would lie next to me until I fell asleep, every night, for months. He'd have to wake up before the Mankowskis and sneak out, and he'd stay up late until I fell asleep. He couldn't have gotten more than a few hours of sleep a night the whole time. And he just kept doing it until slowly my fear began to recede, until slowly I began to regain some degree of control over my wildly terrified mind.

He made it seem like he wouldn't want to be anywhere else.

So since my parents died, lying next to Marcus Roma is the only way I've ever felt truly safe. It's the only time I haven't been afraid of what the world might do to me or the people I love.

So I'm thinking about all of this again because now, tonight, I finally remember the full body of terror of those nights when only Marcus could comfort me.

Lucky me.

I feel the ghost of it every time there's a sudden noise. Every time the neighbor's screen door bangs in the wind. Every time a leaf scuttles down the street.

It's not even that I'm afraid that the man will come back and break in. It's the old fear, the irrational one, only this time it's broadened in scope. It's no longer specific things happening to Dill; thank God I've managed to train myself to stop doing that. It's looser than that, amorphous, this thick, insidious black cloud of dread that I can feel closing in on me when I think about the house. About the developers. About everything that's happening.

Because I'm losing control of my life again.

Let me be clear: I think of myself as a rational person, albeit one sometimes beset by irrational feelings. And I know that I'm not actually in control of my own life, or at least not very much of it. But pretending that I have some say over what happens to Dill and me is what gets me through each day. And anything that shakes that illusion sends me right back on this path to sleeplessness.

Except. For. Marcus.

He is, to this day, the only person, thing, or whatever that can make me feel like I have no control and *like* it. The rules, for some unknown goddamn reason, simply do not apply to him. My attraction to Marcus, and the way it makes me lose control, the way it makes me feel like a mindless animal, the way it makes me lose my mind? Giving up control to Marcus? It's a relief.

And it's the only thing that can distract my mind from those self-destructive patterns of thought, from spinning around endlessly, thinking about all the ways that things can end badly.

I am too tired, lying here, torturing myself, to continue to question why.

I just want to feel safe again.

I force myself to get up and walk into the darkness of the rest of the house. I force myself to keep putting one foot in front of the other. I force myself down the stairs. And the truth is that with every step closer to him, I feel better. I wish it weren't like that. I wish I weren't like this.

But I am.

He's not asleep. I see him move as I come down the stairs; I see that he's heard me. By the time I walk through into the living room, he's sitting up on the couch, shirtless, his arms resting on those powerful legs, and he's looking up at me. Waiting.

All I have to do is put my hand out. By the time I manage to say, "Please," he's already stood up and taken it.

I lead him back up the stairs in silence, my body suddenly feeling the cold of the night. When I get frightened, truly anxious, on the constant verge of a panic attack, I get overheated. Afterwards, I'm freezing. Just holding Marcus's hand has brought me far enough back that I can feel the cold again. By the time we get back to my bed I'm shaking.

Marcus lets me lie down, and then, almost as if he's been in my mind, watching those memories with me, he lies down next to me, just the way he used to. Maybe it's just reflex for him, too. Maybe we just know how to be with each other. But he slides his arm underneath me and pulls me to his warm chest and holds me there until I stop shaking.

It takes me a few minutes to realize how tight he's holding me. Like he's scared. Like Marcus Roma is actually scared of something. And I realize the only thing that could scare him is what I said to him downstairs, what I threw in his face, like I wanted to hurt him: that someone hurt me, and it was his fault. Because as much as I don't trust him not to disappear on me again, I know him well enough to know that this is killing him inside.

Maybe Marcus needs to be close to me right now, too.

"It *wasn't* your fault," I whisper.

He doesn't say anything. Just holds me closer.

"Marcus, please, listen to me." I take another deep breath, and suddenly I'm glad I'm not looking into those eyes right now. I don't think I could say this if I were.

I say, "I always thought, because of how you taught me to fight, that I could defend myself, that I would always… I don't know. That I would always be safe in that way. It was terrifying to find out that I wasn't. I felt like I needed you, then, Marcus, I can't lie about that."

A strangled groan tears from his chest.

"But maybe something good came of it, too," I say quickly.

"Good?" he says. He doesn't believe me. He sounds tortured.

"Yeah, good. I needed to know I could deal with life without you. I think maybe I needed that more than anything, otherwise I would always wonder. I would always be afraid."

We start to talk about it, slowly. About what it was like for me when he left. And he lets slip a few more details about what it was like for him, haltingly, struggling with what to say. I'm mindful, the whole time, of what he said before: maybe I should believe him. Give him the benefit of the doubt.

It sounds so crazy, but then he says things like this:

"I did bad things while I was away from you," he says, his arms tightening around me. "I hurt people, because I had to. I turned into something evil."

I start in shock, and try to turn around in his arm, wanting to look at him. He won't let me.

"No," I say. "I don't care what you did. You could never be a bad person, Marcus. It's not in you."

And he couldn't. I know this like I know the sun will rise tomorrow: Marcus Roma is a good man. It's just that he might be a good man who doesn't love me quite as much as I love him. Who doesn't need me, the same way I need him.

Can I live with that?

"I left you," he says. "I let that happen to you."

"Marcus, the only time I've ever felt safe is when I'm yours."

I feel a shift in him. Those words—*when I'm yours*—they mean something different, to us.

"You are mine," he says softly.

His words make me clench. I can't help it. There's such a specific memory attached to it. The end of that summer, before he left, me telling him I liked it when he was forceful in bed. That it made me feel like I belonged to him. And it made me feel safe, too, safe and free to have him take me like that, in the weirdest freaking way. I have thought about this so much, especially since that night at the bar, and I don't pretend to understand it. But with Marcus, only with Marcus...it is right.

Heat is pooling between my legs.

It's like it's set off a switch. This driving need, this fire—I need him to put it out. I need Marcus to help me feel better tonight, in all the ways that only he can.

There is just no in between with him. With us. He doesn't just make me feel safe—he makes me feel wanted. And wanting.

It. Is. Insane.

And yet I can't trust him not to break me all over again.

On the other hand, if I'm already broken, what does it matter? If I can't be in control of my own life, I want to be in his control. Right here, in this bed.

"Marcus," I whisper.

He tightens the arm he has wrapped around me and nuzzles the back of my head. The best big spoon ever. My head is resting on his huge bicep, and I turn my face to kiss it.

I feel him stiffen.

"You remember how I told you what I liked, sometimes."

"Yes." His voice is gruff. I can tell he's still so careful, like he's afraid I might break.

But I need exactly the opposite from him right now.

I reach down and take the hand he has resting over my waist in this way that still manages to be chaste, to be so careful of me, and I squeeze it once. He kisses the back of my head and I smile, because he's still so considerate. I know he wants me; I can feel him harden against my butt. And I know he'd just suffer all night if that was what I needed him to do.

I take his giant hand and press it against my stomach. I let myself feel the thrill of it there, where my tank top has ridden up and it's just my bare skin. I don't think I will ever get over the feel of his skin against mine. There is nothing in the world like it, and I close my eyes and savor the little dancing lightning bolts that shoot out from the place where he touches me, traveling all over my body, bringing me to life.

I feel Marcus's muscles tense.

"I want to know how badly you want me," I whisper. "That I'm yours."

His hand is so heavy it's almost comically difficult to move it, even though I know he's helping me. He's letting me lead, for once. I'm tempted to tease him about it, but I don't think it will last.

Especially not when I put his hand on my breast.

I'm rewarded with a deliciously low rumble, deep in his chest. His hips move slightly, pressing the length of his hardness against my buttocks, and I don't even think he's aware of it. He's tight, tense, taut, like a line about to snap.

I will always admire his self-control.

"Lo," he says. "Are you sure?"

"I'm sure, now. I can do…I can handle sex with you. And I need it right now. I *need* to feel that." I lick my lips. Admitting that is somehow more of a turn on. "I don't know about anything else."

I have to be honest.

He shifts his weight, pushing himself up on the arm that I've been resting on, and I turn my head back to meet his eyes. They glitter in the dark, the only two points of light in the world.

"I want you," I whisper.

"Don't do this if we're not going to do this," he says, "because I can't take it."

I've never seen him look like this. Pleading. Almost like he's begging.

I wet my mouth, and remind myself that I've resolved to tell the truth.

"You know what I need. I need to be yours again," I say simply, my neck straining to look back at him. "*Yours*."

And he does know what I mean by that.

There's a pause.

Marcus looks at me like I'm the only thing that's ever existed for him. He looks at me like he will never look at anything else, ever again, in his life. He looks at me like he wants to love me, devour me, and own me all at once.

And then that giant hand squeezes my breast, hard, so hard I yelp and I think I almost come right there, and his hot mouth is over mine and kissing me, claiming me, while his other arm curls around and traps me where I am. He holds me prisoner like that while he kisses me, while he toys with my breasts, pulling my tank top down to get at the bare flesh. He has me on the edge already, panting when he lets me up for air, arching my back when he rolls my nipple in his fingers, pushing my butt into his lap just so I can feel him against me.

I don't even know how long he tortures me like this. I'm delirious from the outset, immediately soaking wet and moaning, immediately mindless from his kisses. He pulls back from kissing me, his arm tightening around my chest from underneath just long enough to rip at my shorts, pulling them down around my hips. His hand dips between my legs and into my slit, and I hear him groan when he feels how wet I am.

It sets him off.

I can feel the urgency as he rolls me partially onto my stomach, pulling my shorts down over my butt, down past my knees. I only just kick them off before he's pushing his leg between mine, spreading them. Not wide, just enough. He can't wait.

"Yes," I beg.

He's already there, hard as rock and thick and pushing past my entrance. I barely have time to moan, a strangled cry torn from my throat, and he's thrusting into me.

I gasp, eyes wide, face pushed down against my pillow. He's always big, but like this, with my legs not fully spread, he's so, so much bigger. It's mind-blowing.

He holds me down for leverage and drives in even deeper. I let out a wail, and I swear to God, I think I'm about to come before he's even fully inside me.

"I fucking love you, Lo," he says. "You are mine."

His knee pushes my legs farther apart, spreading me, and he plunges into me fully and I really do scream. I don't know how he's gotten me like this so quickly, facedown and on my forearms, his weight on top of me, his cock inside me, but it is exactly what I needed.

I'm wailing now, the noises coming from me punctuated by his thrusts as he pounds into me. He pauses, leans back slightly, his hands finding my hips. Then he hauls me back onto him, impaling me and spreading me farther, and I scream in pleasure.

I've lost control.

I feel free.

Marcus gathers my hair at the back of my neck, never missing a stroke, driving me higher with every movement, and pulls my head up just enough so that I can see him over my shoulder when he leans over me, his abs flexing as he fucks me from behind.

"You belong to me like this, Lo," he says.

"Yes," I stutter. Speech is leaving me.

Marcus falls on me, his mouth by my ear.

"And I'm yours," he says.

I feel his teeth close around my neck, holding me in this position, possessing me completely in this primal, animal way, and it sends me into a frenzy. I moan, I beg, I plead. Marcus growls into my neck and his hands cover mine, curling around the sheets, while he drives his cock into me over and over and over again.

I come screaming his name. It's the only word I can remember.

I'm still twitching from aftershocks when he pulls out of me and I whimper, not wanting him to leave. He's still hard. And when he rolls over so he's sitting back against the headboard and pulls me on top of him, I realize we're not done.

Marcus and his self-control.

"Can you sit up?" he asks me. He's holding me up like a rag doll, moving me around where he wants me. It makes me ready all over again.

"Yes," I say, only it sounds funny, because my lips have that pins and needles feeling and talking is weird.

Marcus moves me on top of him, straddling his lap, his erection pressed against my naked sex, reaching up my lower belly. I look down and stare at that for a second: his thick, swollen, magnificent cock, still shining with wetness, pressed hard against my fair skin. I feel the pressure of it, the promise of it, and I think I'm kind of transfixed.

"Lo," he says. "Look at me."

Ha.

I do. His hair is messed, and there's sweat on his brow, and his jaw is tense while he waits for me. But oh sweet Jesus, those eyes. They look at me and I see everything. I see our past together, I see every time he's wanted me, every time he's been there. Every time he's made me feel like this. I see his grief, his love, his regret. And I know that there's no one else who can see me like this, like I am right now, because there's no one else I can be like this with. I didn't even know this part of myself before Marcus. I didn't know what I liked, what I could be.

He helps me be all of me.

And he loves all of me.

I can see that love in his eyes. God, I can see it, and I can't protect myself from it, because I love him, too.

I am fucking doomed. And I'm not sure that I care anymore.

"Take this off," he orders. His hands are playing with the edges of my disheveled tank top, but I can tell from his voice: He wants to make me do it, because he told me to.

He's watching me.

Why does this feel more intimate than what we just did?

I lick my lips and try to hold my body still, my body that's still shaking from that last orgasm, still off-balance. I want to grind against his dick so badly, but somehow I know that's not how this will work. So I do what I'm told. I keep my eyes locked with his as my fingers find the bottom of my shirt and pull it up over my body. His hands follow, finding my naked breasts, grabbing them in two handfuls. He surveys them with a kind of satisfaction that turns me on even more, and I can't help but smile, sitting in front of him, naked for him.

His eyes come back up to mine while he plays with my breasts, picking up the tempo of the steady rhythm that's already pulsing between my legs, calling for him again. Needing him.

"Marcus," I pant. I'm quickly becoming desperate.

He pulls me down against him and kisses me while his hands move around to my back and down to my ass. He grips me there, firmly, his fingers digging in, and his kiss deepens.

Then he begins to lift me up, off of his legs, over his cock. To guide me.

Our wet mouths come apart, only inches away, and I'm breathing hard. I put my hands on his chest just to feel him, and his heart is beating as fast as mine. Marcus locks eyes with me again, not needing to say anything at all, and slowly lowers me onto his pulsing erection.

"I need to see you," he says.

I nod. I couldn't put a name to this, but I get it. I need him to see me, too. I need to see him. I need to know that I can make Marcus Roma lose control. I need to feel the ways we make each other whole. I need to feel the exact ways it will hurt when it comes to an end.

Marcus says, "Make yourself come for me."

And I know he loves me, just like I love him. If only that were enough.

Maybe we're both doomed.

15

MARCUS

Lo and I are driving up to see Dill for parents' weekend at his genius camp, and for the first time in years I'm feeling kinda worried.

I've been staying at Lo's since that night someone tried to break in. Since the night she told me some asshole tried to rape her. Since the night I learned that leaving her was so much worse than I thought it was.

She let me in that night and it's been touch and go since, but I'm still here. Neither of us knows what the hell she's doing. And I go back and forth between hating myself in ways I didn't know were possible because of what I let happen to her, to being so happy that she's let me back into her life, no matter how long it lasts.

At least I have the comfort of knowing what I want in the end: I want her. Simple. I'll figure out how that fits into the rest of my life later, and if it needs to, the rest of my life changes.

For her? It's more complicated. For one thing, there's Dill. For another, there's trust. And I can't even help her by telling her why I broke her heart other than to keep repeating, over and over again, like an idiot, that I did it because I loved her.

It's not fair to expect her to believe that and I don't think she does, not all the way. She knows I loved her, knows I still love her. I just don't think she can make that fit with how I left her.

But I think she's trying, which is more than I deserve.

That thought brings me a smile. The sex helps, too.

I can't keep my hands off of her. I can't get over how good she feels, how perfect she is. I would spend all day, every day, making her come if she'd let me. I look over at her, driving her sexy car in one of those tiny little tank tops, a skirt, and sunglasses, and I think about telling her to pull over, but I decide it's not the time. I had planned on coming with her to this parent's day thing just because I'm not comfortable with her going alone, not with the Alex Wolfe situation, and not with what she told me—hell, I never want her to be alone again—but it was nice to be asked. Makes me feel like I have a real shot.

As opposed to the aforementioned Alex Wolfe situation, which makes me feel fucking murderous.

Alex swore to me—swore—that he didn't have anything to do with the break-in. But I know him. I've seen him do worse. I've helped him do worse on other deals, in other places. Break into someone's house, mess it up just to scare the crap out of them, maybe throw them around a little? Par for the course with that man.

It makes me feel sick.

He's promised me this is different. He understands Harlow is different. I'm starting to understand that she isn't different, necessarily, she's just mine. I'm disgusted with the things I've done for Alex, even though I had damn good reasons for doing them, and I have no intention of doing them ever again. And that's something I'll have to deal with eventually.

I wish Alex wasn't like this.

And I wish I could believe him. What's worse is that I want to believe him, and I worry that this makes me weak. And I can't afford to be weak when Harlow is depending on me, even if she doesn't know it. Because the fundraiser and lobbying event she's set up at The Alley is coming up, and I'm maybe the only person in the neighborhood not surprised that Harlow's pulled it off. Harlow and Shantha have kicked ass, and I know there'll be members of the zoning board there, the ones Alex couldn't bribe, and they'll be receptive.

One of them is even thinking about running for City Council.

All of which means my girl has actually managed to fight the man no one else has been able to fight, and she's even shown that she might be able to hurt him. So she's a threat to Alex Wolfe. And that is fucking dangerous.

So yeah, I was going to tag along today even if she didn't ask. But it's nice to know she wants me here, nice to think about how she wants me to spend time with Dill. But a little scary for a man like me, too, because if there's one thing I don't know about, it's being a good father.

So. Like I said, worried.

But willing to overlook it while we purr up the highway in this fantastic ride. For some reason Harlow has a recent Challenger, black, tricked out, sexy as hell. And the woman has learned how to drive stick.

Yeah, I'm thinking about telling her to pull over again.

"Baby, where the hell did you get this car?" I ask her.

Funny, I'm not even expecting a real answer. You know, something like, "A dealership, same as anyone." I just didn't really think she had a thing for muscle cars.

But then she looks at me and gives me this flirtatious little smile with those beautiful red lips, and says, "A rock star gave it to me as a special thank you present."

What the actual fuck?

Look, I'm a man. I'm a certain kind of man. I hired a private investigator to check up on Harlow for years, and specifically told him not to tell me about any men in her life because I didn't want to commit any crimes and screw up her life any more than I already had. And I'm eventually going to find a way to track down the piece of garbage who hurt her, and hurt him right back. So she tells me she did something for a rock star to get this car as a goddamn thank you present, sitting there in that skirt with her thighs that I want so badly showing, and the words just bypass my rational mind and go straight to whatever the hell it is that makes men do stupid things.

"Pull over," I say.

She smiles wider. "No."

"Who gave it to you?"

"Declan Donovan."

"Why?"

Man, why do I even ask that question? What am I going to do if the answer is that they used to screw around? All it will accomplish is that I'll have an aneurysm, and then I'll have to buy her a new car, because she sure as hell won't be driving this one around anymore. And then I'll have to go hunt down a famous rock star, which sounds like a pain in the ass. But I still have to know.

Harlow actually holds out a few more seconds before she starts laughing. She looks at me kind of slyly, and I know she's been messing with me.

"Relax, caveman," she says. "I lent his girlfriend my parents' old car one night when she needed it, and this was his thank you."

Fun fact: The word 'relax' doesn't actually lower the levels of testosterone in my blood that are now sky high and telling me to do all kinds of dumb shit.

I say, "All you did was lend a friend your car, and he bought you this?"

"She wasn't a friend," Harlow says sharply. I know she'd kick my ass if was any more of a jerk, and I love that about her. "I'd only met her that night."

"And you lent her your car?"

Even through all my possessiveness I can feel Harlow's mood change a little bit, get a little somber, maybe. Now I'm worried about her.

"Tell me what happened," I say.

"No, it's nothing like that," she says, looking at me with this soft expression on her face, the kind of thing that makes me want to do things for her. "It's not anything bad. It's just… Your boss Mr. Wolfe did something incredible for me once for no reason. So I try to do that for other people when I can. That's all."

I turn to stone. I don't want her to say the rest even though I know what it's going to be, because when I hear it out loud, I don't know if I'll be able to keep quiet. And I have to keep my mouth shut, for Harlow's sake. This is exactly what I can't tell her about.

Harlow takes a deep breath and says, "Mr. Wolfe got me Dill. He was at the custody hearing, and I think… I mean, you know the kind of influence he has. He's the only reason I have custody. He did that for me."

Dear God, please let me hold this in.

I have to squeeze my hands into fists and concentrate on the road ahead, trying to let the anger and unfairness of the whole situation go. I have to remind myself that it's good that she has Dill, no matter how it happened. It's good that Alex saw to it himself. And of course Harlow would show gratitude; that's how she's built.

She's watching the road, but she steals a look at me. It's a love note and an apology all wrapped up in one. Like she's trying to tell me she understands about feeling indebted to Alex Wolfe. Like she thinks that's what's going on with me and she understands. I hate to see her feel guilty about anything.

She says, "I'm just saying, I know stuff with Alex Wolfe is complicated."

Lo doesn't know the half of it.

***

Going to see Dill, talking about Alex Wolfe, has me thinking about my family. About fathers. I lost one father and got a new one in the space of a week, and they were both pretty crappy at the job.

Let me explain.

My dad died. About a year and half after Harlow's parents were killed. I don't talk about him much, or at least not more than I have to, for reasons that will be obvious. His name was Juan Roma, and he hated me. I'd figured that much out by the time he passed, but I never knew why he hated me, and I figured I might never know. It was one of those things that just was, but that I would never stop trying to change. That was how I got into boxing in the first place, because Juan Roma loved it, and even as a little boy I knew things weren't quite right with him and me, but I thought that maybe, maybe if I learned to fight, he'd respect me like he respected the fighters on TV.

Didn't quite work out like that, but luckily I was a natural. I probably needed the outlet anyway.

Now, it wasn't just Juan that didn't like me. My moms wasn't such a big fan either. My mother was different about it, though. Juan actively hated me; you could see it in his face when he looked at me, this contempt, like he was look at something the dog dragged in. My moms? She would just prefer not to look at me at all, like it hurt her when she did.

I probably should have been more fucked up in the head than I was. Finding Harlow when I did saved my ass, made me into a real person. Gave me a purpose.

And by the time my dad died, Harlow wasn't over what happened to her parents or anything, not by a long shot, but she wasn't broken anymore, either. She'd come back alive, and now it wasn't the end of her, it was just something that hurt a whole hell of a lot. But Harlow was strong, Harlow could handle it by then. And Harlow had me.

And then Juan died, and I was confused as hell.

Weird, right? You watch someone go through what Harlow went through, and you can't help but think about what you would do in that situation. And I was so confident, like I'd learned from her or something, like I knew I'd be just fine.

Let me tell you, that is not how it works. I found out Juan died of a heart attack at work in the auto shop, just keeled over, dead before the ambulance even got there, and my reaction?

I was pissed off.

I was beyond pissed off. It was like all the anger at him over all those years finally ripened inside me, because now I was never going to get to tell him myself. He was never going to explain to me why he hated me. He was never going to give me a goddamned reason.

My mom couldn't look at me at all. She had family come in to help her with the arrangements, wouldn't even talk to me. They even sent my cousin Petey to tell me that the life insurance wouldn't cover the funeral and ask if I could I kick in.

Which is how I ended up fighting in an underground ring out in Queens for decent money. Seemed like killing two birds with one stone: fight, make the money, work off that anger. Get out of the house where I wasn't wanted.

Harlow wasn't at the first fight. And she got pissed when she found out where I'd been, like I didn't have a right to put my body at risk without her say-so, or at least without her being there. So after that I let her come. And knowing she was there, in the crowd, watching me?

That made me deadly.

So the day of the wake, I was set to fight later in the evening. I didn't let Harlow come to the wake with me, because I thought it would remind her too much of her parents. She put up a little argument, but in the end she agreed, which is how I knew I was right. Yeah, my dad dying wasn't a walk in the park, but it was nothing like what she went through. No sense in making it harder on her.

The wake was a total shitshow. You'd think the son would be welcome at his father's wake, but damn, I was like a leper. It had never been so obvious to me how much I wasn't wanted around these people. I don't know, maybe I just stopped covering up for them, or maybe I just stopped making excuses.

But none of it made sense until I talked to Alex Wolfe.

I thought I knew why he was there. He was my godfather, after all, even if I'd never understood why. He just waited in the back, not talking to anyone, which was weird for him, being the guy who knew everyone, the guy who was in business with everyone somehow. This time he just stood there, looking at me. Waiting for me.

So after I got tired of being the odd man out at my own father's funeral, I confronted Mr. Wolfe, as I still called him then. Remember, I was pissed off. Normal people, if they talked to Alex Wolfe like I talked to him, they'd have reason to be scared about what might happen to them after they got done talking.

Me? I was reckless. Alex just smiled.

I said, "What the fuck do you want today?"

I guess I hadn't forgotten he ran book against me on my Manny Dolan fight. That still pissed me off.

He said, "We should talk."

He took me to a bar, bought me whiskey. I still remember that. Don't know why. But now every time I smell whiskey, I think of Alex Wolfe calmly telling me that he was my natural father.

I think about the way that one piece of information made my entire life make sense.

I think about the way I wanted to beat Alex Wolfe until he was bloody and broken for not telling me sooner.

He just kept talking, like he didn't have a care in the world, while I sat there and slowly boiled over.

He said, "I've arranged for your mother to go down to Florida with her sister for a while, Marcus, and I've paid the rent on your apartment in the meantime. You'll have it to yourself. And I will pay for the funeral arrangements."

"Fuck no, you won't," I said to him, finally looking up from my glass of whiskey. I was going to pay to put that man in the ground.

I remember that Alex smiled.

"You've earned enough from your fights?" he asked me.

The man knew everything. And he told me more. Told me how my mother had been his side piece for twenty years, how my father—Juan, I mean—had known about it for fifteen. How my mother never wanted to have kids. How I was her guilt, and Juan's humiliation.

"Why didn't you tell me?" I asked him. I don't think I've ever been that close to real violence borne of anger before. I hope I never am again.

Alex just shrugged and said, "I made a promise to your mother. But Juan Roma is dead now, and you are my son, Marcus." Then he looked at me like this was real important. "You are my son."

With everything else that happened that day, with all the messed-up angles to this damn secret that had ruled my life, this was the thing that stood out to me the most: My mother was ashamed of me, the man I knew as my father hated me, and the only man who wanted to claim me as his son was Alex Wolfe.

But that came later, when I could think like a normal person. I left the bar not thinking much, just feeling. Everything too new, too jumbled for thoughts. I went and picked up Harlow and I took her to the illegal card room where I was going to fight.

Here's the thing: I don't remember much about that fight.

Normally I was a controlled fighter. The adrenaline spike never overwhelmed me; I never lost it, I just stayed calm and deadly. That night? All I remember is that I was aware of where Harlow was in the room at all times. Like my damn reference point, a north star, whatever. I remember that the guy I was fighting wore this bullshit armband with his club's logo on it, like something straight out of The Karate Kid. I remember getting up off his chest, my hands bloody, looking for Lo.

That's about it. I know I destroyed him. I won enough money to cover the funeral and then some.

But later? When Harlow took me home? I remember all of that in crystal clear detail. I remember how she patched up my hands, so careful with the rubbing alcohol that it made me smile. I remember how when I told her about Alex Wolfe, sitting on my bed, suddenly feeling dead tired, she got up from where she was sitting and stood right in front of me, threading one hand through my hair, stroking my forehead. I remember feeling bad about it, like I should be the one taking care of her, but also realizing that Harlow was the only person on the planet who could take care of me. She was the only person I would let get that close.

I didn't cry over it. I just hugged Harlow close to me, buried my face in her stomach, breathed her in. I remember that she was the one who pushed me back on my bed. I remember that she climbed on top of me, eyes shining like she was going to cry, but smiling softly at the same time.

And then I finally kissed her, because I understood that maybe I had been good enough the whole damn time.

***

I'm thinking about all this, and how because of all this crap I don't know how to be any kind of father, and how Alex Wolfe sure as hell hasn't shown me in the years I've been working for him, and how Harlow is sitting there, grateful to Alex for Dill, and it's a lot. It's a lot to take in. But I have Harlow next to me. We pull into this grassy lot in the back of this camp all the way up in the Catskills, and I have Harlow, and that makes most things all right.

I get out of the car before Harlow's even done parking it, and I walk around the front, keeping my eyes on her, until I get to her door. I open it for her, but I can't wait for her to get out on her own. I help her out and then I push her against that car and kiss her. I take her face in both of my hands and kiss her gently, kiss her hard, kiss her all the ways I know she likes to be kissed, until her arms are curling around my neck and my hands have found her waist.

I nip at her bottom lip and pull away, looking at her to let her know I'll finish this later. She's flushed and breathless.

"What did I do to deserve that?" she says.

"You're you."

I tug at the waist of her skirt, knowing we're late already, but she looks up at me, blushing.

"I think I need a minute," she says.

"We stay out here another minute and I'm going to take you in the backseat of that car," I tell her. She bites her lip and it makes my cock jump. "Jesus, I might do it anyway."

We stand there like that for too long, and I think about it. I do.

But damn it, I'm going to show her I can be good for Dill.

"C'mon," I say, and take her hand. "Dill is waiting."

16

HARLOW

It takes my brain more than a minute to start fully functioning again after that kiss.

I let Marcus lead me, in a kind of haze, through the parking lot to a tree-covered, sun-dappled lane leading up to the camp's main building. I don't know if it's the beauty of this place, the bliss of this past week with Marcus, or just that intoxication I've learned to expect whenever I'm with him, but I'm having trouble believing that any of this is real.

I mean, I do. I know it's really happening, and not just some fantasy I've cooked up for myself. But there's a part of me that won't trust my own senses. Not when it feels too good to be true.

Ever since that night someone tried to break in, and I let Marcus back in, things have been different, somehow. They've felt less chaotic, more settled. Like finally telling him how bad it was really did exorcise it from my life. Not entirely, obviously, but enough—I don't constantly vacillate between lust and anger anymore. I feel calmer. And I feel like I'm able to *see* Marcus better.

And it looks too good to be true.

I had that once before, after all, a life that was too good to be true. Twice, before, really, though I didn't fully appreciate how good I had it with my parents until they were gone. I have to tell myself no one appreciates what they have until it's gone, but I still feel guilty about it. The second time I had it so good was when I finally had Marcus. And then, of course, he left.

That's still the thing that haunts me, the thing that keeps me from falling fully for this, like every fiber of my being wants me to: he might do it again. He might leave me again. So that hasn't changed. I still have like this sober, rational Jiminy Cricket on my shoulder, warning me not to forget.

I just hate that little cricket.

Well, no, some things have changed. That's why Marcus is here today, I guess. Or I don't know, maybe that's a rationalization? When it comes down to it, I wanted him here.

I wanted to see him with Dill.

Which: sober Jiminy Cricket is freaking out about that, let me tell you.

So I decided to drive Marcus up here to see my little brother, to get an idea of What That Might Be Like, telling myself the whole time that I'm not falling for it, that I know it's not that serious, because it can't be. Because Marcus still hasn't told me what happened, still hasn't shown me that I can trust him not to just decide to leave again. But I asked him to come up here with me anyway, and naturally I'm thinking about Dill, and that starts to make me think about what Marcus would be like as a dad-type figure for Dill, and…

Well, then that kiss.

And that kiss makes me think of the first time Marcus kissed me.

And that makes me think about Marcus's dad and Marcus's father, who turned out not to be the same person at all.

***

In retrospect, it might have been a little messed up to finally let Marcus know how I felt about him on the same day as his dad's wake. I mean, if I had thought about it, probably even seventeen-year-old me would have recognized that to be inappropriate, and might have tried to respect a boundary I knew probably existed even if I didn't know exactly where it was.

I'm glad I didn't think about it too much. I'm glad that, at that point, it didn't seem like there were many boundaries between Marcus and me.

I'm glad that I recognized that he needed me as much as I needed him.

Marcus didn't let me go to the wake. At first I was pretty determined, because after all, Marcus had been right next to me at my parents' funeral. But I was approaching it as a point of principle, not as an actual experience that I was going to have in the real world, and Marcus knew me well enough to point this out. He zeroed in on the concrete details.

"There'll be a coffin."

"I know there'll be a coffin."

"Everyone will be in black, crying."

"I know."

He kept going like that, until I had to picture it in my mind, and I could feel the shape of what it would feel like to be in the middle of that. And, damn it, he was right: It would send me right back to where I was during my parents' funeral, which was, to put it lightly, not a good place. Marcus would have ended up taking care of me at his own dad's wake.

Is that fair? No. It just…it was what it was. I felt terrible about it, but Marcus didn't. He just kept telling me: it was different with his family. With his dad in particular.

"We weren't so close," he said.

The understatement to end all understatements, right there.

So I compromised. I said I wouldn't go to the wake, as long as he promised to come get me right afterwards, and then we'd go to the fight he had scheduled, and I wasn't going to leave his side after that.

About the fights—I mean, I'm not going to lie. I didn't think they were a great idea, but it was in that way that you know some things aren't great ideas, but you still find them exciting? Now, being older, having responsibilities, I'd probably be a lot more cautious. They weren't safe. I mean, I wasn't worried about Marcus's safety, because he was so damn good, but at the same time, of course I was worried about Marcus's safety. He was fighting. Illegally. Seeing him get hit—it was not a good feeling.

Good thing it didn't happen often.

What did happen often was that Marcus won. All the time, actually. He had a perfect record. And every time, here was the guy that I came with, the guy who at the time I thought would stand by me through anything, shirtless and ripped and sweating and owning the ring in front of a crowd of screaming strangers.

Call me crazy, but I did find it…exciting.

And frustrating. Because at that point, Marcus still hadn't touched me sexually. And I didn't know how to touch him. One day I'd be sure he wanted me as bad as I wanted him, the next I'd be sure he saw me as some kind of little sister, and crossing that line would irrevocably damage the most important relationship in my life. And the one thing I couldn't afford to lose, ever, was Marcus.

That was my greatest fear, actually, besides losing Dill. Losing Marcus. It was just easier to manage because Marcus was always there for me.

So he came by the Mankowskis' in his dad's car—I guessed now he'd inherited it—to pick me up for that fight, and I could tell immediately that something was different. I could tell that something had happened. I just assumed, maybe understandably, that it was about his dad's death, and the way that would bring up all of Marcus's feelings about his family. I knew better than anyone how grief can take you by surprise, how you'll never know what form it will take until it's upon you, and then you just have to figure out a way to deal with it.

So Marcus comes to pick me up with this expression on his face like I've never seen. He was usually so present with me, so attentive, and that day he wasn't even looking at me. It was like he was looking far ahead in the future, or far back in the past. His big hands gripped the steering wheel until his knuckles were white, boxer's knuckle evident on all of them, and I could see the corded muscles in his neck twist with tension.

"You ok?" I asked him.

"Don't know."

That was fair.

"You ok to fight?" I asked.

That's when he finally looked at me, and when he did it was like being in a spotlight. He looked at me and smiled, kind of slow, kind of sad, kind of sweet.

"Yeah," he said. He reached out one of those hands and cupped my face with it, his thumb brushing along my bottom lip.

I gasped so slightly, I'm not sure he heard. He just put the car in gear and drove on.

After that, I gripped the rough fabric of my seat the whole way to Queens, with my blood pulsing in my core, my skin heating under my shirt, my whole body extremely aware of the man next to me, and my mind telling it to shut up, his dad just died.

It was a confusing trip.

Truthfully, it was incredibly important to me to be there for Marcus like he'd been there for me. So I was going to support him no matter what he felt like he needed to do, underground fighting included. And I tried very, very hard to keep thinking about Marcus and what he actually needed, rather than what I wanted, every time he fought.

But that night, it was almost impossible.

I know Marcus doesn't remember much about that fight, but I do. First, the guy he was fighting was an ogre. I mean, I think they actually got him from some enchanted forest somewhere. He was huge. He was one of the only men I've ever seen who was actually bigger than Marcus, though he was softer, his muscle covered in a layer of fat. And he was bald, with scars all over his scalp, one on his cheek, and tattoos I couldn't decipher all over his body. They were the kind of unfinished, rough, messy tattoos that you know didn't happen in a tattoo parlor. And the one arm that wasn't tattooed was covered in this dumb red armband that had this black logo on it of a snarling wolf, something that I think was supposed to be super intimidating in a kind of racist way? I mean, the only places I'd ever seen armbands even remotely like that was in history books on the arms of Nazis. And Marcus was known as a Dominican fighter, even if nobody could ever place his ethnicity when they met him. I doubt the idiots with the armbands were unaware of the implications. Especially since I heard a few of them shout out "spic," which, really?

So I didn't feel great about all of that. Marcus, though, Marcus…when he walked out into that ring, quiet, the way he was, calm, totally confident, it felt different, for me. He looked at me and the look in his eyes…

Looking back, now I know what that look was. It was that same animal thing that happens when he's about to take me. The way he looks when we fuck, before we make love.

Back then? I wouldn't have known how to describe that look in those terms, but I knew vaguely what it meant. I knew it wasn't the kind of look a man gave a friend.

Or a little sister.

And I recognized my reaction. Purely physical. Purely carnal. I remember thinking it was getting harder and harder to remember to think only about what Marcus needed rather than what I wanted as those desires burned hotter and brighter. By the time they rang the bell I could have lit up that entire smoke filled room myself.

Everything else fell away except for Marcus.

The shouts of the people in the crowd, the smell of cigars and cigarettes and beer, the flashes of light as people took pictures — all of it muted while I picked up every little twitch of muscle in Marcus's chest, every bead of sweat on his brow, every movement of his eyes.

He looked at me again. And I don't know how, but it felt like he was just as conscious of me. Like whatever it was that tied us to each other, that way we were aware of each other, read each other, felt each other — it was just extra strong, like a sixth sense, drowning out all the noise around it.

I've never seen him fight like that.

Marcus was always a smart fighter, always totally unhurried, controlled. He'd play with his opponents a little, rope them in, see what they had, and then move in for a lethal blow. He had a lot of knock-outs, but all of them were technically proficient and beautiful to watch.

This was beautiful, too, but in a different way. Almost a frightening way. An animal way.

The bell rang and Marcus unleashed. He charged. Before anyone knew what had happened Marcus landed four, five, six punches, sending the ogre back on his heels and putting his hands up blindly. The big, possibly racist ogre got in a few swings, just desperate, unseeing punches that Marcus easily danced around. Then Marcus just hunted him around the ring, his eyes on fire, his body working in this terrible harmony, muscles flexing, contracting, releasing with explosive power.

The ogre tried to cheat in a way. I mean, in illegal fights there aren't a whole lot of rules, but generally you're not supposed to try to knee a guy in the balls. Bad form.

Which is why the crowd cheered when Marcus blocked the knee, knocked the ogre flat on his back, and then sat on his chest for a classic ground and pound.

The ref called it, tapped on Marcus's shoulder, and tried to haul him off the ogre. But Marcus wouldn't move. He stopped punching, his hands covered in blood, but he wouldn't let the man up, just hulking over him with sweat shining on the planes of his chest, his abs, his obliques, as he leaned over this much larger man that he'd just completely decimated.

I remember the ref actually trying to physically dislodge Marcus, and it was like watching a child try to push over a tree. I'm not sure Marcus even noticed.

Instead he reached down and ripped that armband right off the ogre's arm.

So when Marcus finally stood up, leaning back into the light, his chest heaving, he had that red armband in his hand. His eyes found me, like he knew where I'd been all along, like he didn't see anything else. And then he cut across that ring, pushing people aside until he got to me, and wordlessly offered it to me.

It was ridiculous. And it absolutely killed me.

I remember every detail of that. Every line in his striated shoulders, every shadow playing across his pecs, every drop of sweat and smear of blood on his skin. The exact shade of his gray-green eyes in that light, the way they burned through me, the way they saw nothing else.

I'm pretty sure that was the exact moment I stopped being able to think clearly around him. I'm not sure I ever started again.

He drove us back to his family's apartment, silent, brooding, and it wasn't until we got upstairs to that dark, empty place where he was now living all by himself that he told me what had happened with Alex Wolfe. There was still that tension, that sexual charge between us, that primal thing. It didn't go away. But Marcus told me that he'd found out Juan Roma wasn't his real father, and everything that meant for him, how it all came together, and it added to what we felt. It gave it depth.

When he let me in like that, told me how it all finally made sense to him, it somehow made me want him even more. I didn't just want him physically, I wanted to love him to the best of my ability. I'd never felt closer to anyone. I don't think I ever will, either.

It's always been Marcus.

I remember him sitting on his bed, saying, "That's why they hated me. It wasn't anything I did. It was never anything I did." Like it was this revelation, like he'd truly believed it was his fault, and I remember my heart breaking for him. I remember walking over to him, not being able to stand any distance between us any longer, and putting my hand through his hair until he looked up at me. I remember the expression of wonder on his face, eyes open, almost childlike. I remember pushing him back on his bed, just wanting to feel him, to hold him the way he'd held me so many times.

I remember saying, "Lie to me. Tell me you're ok."

"I don't have to lie," he said. "I have you."

And then he kissed me, and everything changed.

I felt...God. It felt like this door was opening to an entire world that I'd never seen before, and the ways of feeling, of being, that had been closed off to me now washed over me. All the ways I could love him flowed through me at once and it was overwhelming. I think I wanted all of him, right away, wanted to show him what had been building inside me for the past two years and change, wanted to show him every single thing I'd felt, every single thing that had made me love him.

Because I knew, even then. I knew I loved him. I knew it was special. I knew there would never be anyone else like him.

And I knew he felt it, too.

The way he kissed me, it was almost too much. Too sweet, too powerful, too charged. There was a part of me that shied away from it, like the first time I almost made myself come, and that feeling that came over me suddenly was so powerful that it frightened me. But Marcus made me brave. There were years of emotion distilled into that kiss, and it branded me for life.

We didn't go much further than that that night. We just kissed for hours and held each other close. We talked. We were both frightened of it, we both laughed at how long it had taken, we both couldn't wait to see what would happen next.

And the way he kissed me just now, in the freaking parking lot of Dill's camp, it was like that. Full of promise. Full of everything Marcus has to offer me, good and bad. Full of our history together.

Full of lust, too.

So maybe I shouldn't be so hard on myself for feeling unsteady on my feet as Marcus leads me into the mess hall, where all the parents are having juice and cookies or something while finding their kids. I won't be too hard on myself, but I have to be careful.

And not just for myself, and not just for Dill.

Because now, as I watch Dill give Marcus a high five, and the two of them start talking about video games like old friends (I got a hug, barely, in the way of eleven-year-old boys), I realize that maybe I should have been more careful for Marcus, too.

Maybe I should be thinking more about what it might have been like for Marcus, who'd been looking for a father his entire life, to have Alex Wolfe show up and claim him as a son. And what it might have been like to have Alex Wolfe ask him to come join his company, even if that meant being far away from me.

"Lo, come on, I wanna show Marcus the game!"

Dill's already scampering away, and Marcus puts his hand on the small of my back, guiding me through the mess of parents. We follow Dill to one of the computer labs and I'm grateful that Dill doesn't need much from me, because I am almost on another planet.

Watching the two of them.

Watching them tease each other, make each other laugh.

I realize I would kill for Dill to have another parent-type presence in his life. Maybe part of that is because I'm always afraid that I have no idea what I'm doing, that I am royally screwing it up and screwing Dill over in the process and I don't even know it. I mean, I'm making this up as I go along. Some people rock being single parents, or big sisters, or whatever, but I'm not sure I'm one of them. I constantly feel overwhelmed, even if I know that it's better for Dill to be with me, who loves him more than anything, than an aunt who only barely tolerates him. But it's not just that. I want Dill to think the whole world loves him, not just me. I want him to grow up knowing he's important to more than just me.

I realize how important that could be for him, and for the first time I really feel what the absence of that must have done to Marcus. I see it in how attentive he is with Dill, how he puts so much effort into this small interaction, how he treats Dill's every rambling, over-excited conversational offshoot like it's the most important thing anyone's ever said to him. How it all makes Dill shine even brighter than he usually does.

I want to say, "Lie to me. Tell me this isn't perfect."

And I wonder if Alex Wolfe promised Marcus something like this just by showing up and saying, "You're my son." I wonder if that was something that Marcus needed. Something I shouldn't begrudge him, even if he should have told me, if that's why he needed to leave.

I wonder if Marcus needed that more than he needed me. And it hurts.

God, does it hurt.

And it hurts to know that I'm really that selfish.

But I suck it up and do my best to join Dill and Marcus, who are already totally engrossed in Dill's game. Pretty soon I am, too, because Dill has punched it up a lot in a short time. Genius Boy has added some new puzzles to a few of the levels and is talking nonstop about commissioning artwork—oh God, how am I going to pay for that?—and having me do more music, and his excitement is absolutely infectious.

Marcus is smiling ear to ear. And I can tell when he looks at me that I must be, too.

"You are the most amazing kid," I say to Dill, punching him in the arm.

"I know." Dill shrugs, smiling, like he doesn't care. But he lets me ruffle his hair and kind of leans into me, and when we're about to leave he gives me this fierce little hug and says, "Thank you."

"This is what big sisters do," I say into the top of his head, and ruffle his hair again. I wonder what I'll do when he's bigger than me and I can't ruffle his hair or give him gentle noogies. The thought puts my stomach in knots.

And then the clever little man looks up at me, smiling. He says, "I like Marcus, Lo."

Seriously, what am I supposed to say to that? There's probably an appropriate response in some parenting handbook somewhere, but I'm pretty sure that, whatever it is, it's not getting flustered because your little brother is more perceptive than you gave him credit for.

I finally settle on this: "Me, too."

"So we'll hang out some more when I get home?"

Oh shit. Shit, shit, shit, shit, shit. This exactly what I don't know how to handle. So I flub it.

"Maybe," I say. "We'll see."

Thank God Dill is already on to other things. I can see his mind whirling around in there, probably thinking up other games he wants to make or stories he wants to tell.

"Ok," Dill says, already with that faraway look in his eyes. "I love you, Lo."

He's already off running to join a bunch of other little boys as I shout after him, "I love you, too, little man!"

Dill shoots me this horrified look over his shoulder, and Marcus laughs, walking back over to me. He was off talking to the camp director about I don't know what, giving me some time with Dill. Now he's shaking his head.

"Oh man, he is going to get it for that," Marcus says.

I cringe. He's right. I just made a serious mom-type mistake. I kind of can't believe I called Dill "little man" in front of all his new camp friends.

"Bad?" I ask.

Marcus is still smiling at me as we walk out to the parking lot, but now he shakes his head. "He's a tough kid. He'll be fine. Also, I call shotgun."

"Marcus, it's just the two of us. Where else were you going to sit, in the back?"

"I called shotgun for *you*. I have to drive this car, Lo."

I laugh, looking at his suddenly intense face, and then throw him the keys. Let the alpha male do whatever he needs to do with the car. I'm probably going to enjoy watching him drive it anyway.

And I do.

A lot.

But I also feel kind of pensive, thinking about all the stuff I saw between Marcus and Dill and the way it made me feel. The way it made me reevaluate how Marcus left. Don't get me wrong, I don't think there's an excuse for just up and leaving one night and sending me a freaking text message saying he's gone, then refusing to explain why. Even thinking about it now makes me angry, so I try to let it go, because, well, I'm already in deep.

But maybe he had a reason to leave.

Maybe he needed something I couldn't give him.

Maybe I wasn't enough family for him, even if he was enough for me.

"Baby, I need you to put those legs down," Marcus eventually says.

We're only about twenty minutes from home and I've been riding with my legs propped up on the dashboard because it's my car and it's comfortable, damn it. But they are my bare legs, and I am wearing a skirt. I grin.

"What are you talking about?" I say.

"If you don't want me to pull over and drag you into the backseat, I need you to put those legs down," he says. His voice is icy calm, which, for some reason, combined with the words he's saying to me, really does it for me.

Unfortunately, we're not on some isolated highway. There's other cars, people everywhere.

"I'm comfortable," I say. "And there are cops in speed traps all along this stretch."

He growls and flexes those arms. I smile, and decide to torture him a little bit. Might as well stretch those legs.

We get home a lot faster than twenty minutes.

He's out of the car practically before it's stopped moving, walking around to my side again, even more determined than he was before. I can't keep the smile off my face. Even with all the heavy stuff I've been thinking about today, Marcus Roma can still make me feel positively giddy about the things he's about to do to me.

He yanks open my door and immediately reaches in to undo my seatbelt, which makes me laugh as he hauls me out of the car.

"Marcus!"

He pays me no mind, dragging me up to the kitchen door and unlocking it in record time. "Stretching your legs out like that? No one rubs their legs together like that when they're stretching, Lo. That was straight up cruel," he says. "You're lucky I didn't just throw you down on the hood."

And then to prove the point, he picks me up and throws me over his shoulder as he walks inside, kicking the door closed behind him. I kind of squeal, though secretly I love it.

"Pick a room," he says.

"Oh my God, you're kidding."

"Living room it is," he says, slapping my ass before he sets me down on the arm of the couch. He towers over me as he turns my face up to his, and I love that, too. I love everything about this.

"I made a promise in that parking lot," he says, his hands starting to work up my bare thighs.

I shiver.

"You did?" I say.

His hands are already under my skirt, toying with the edge of my underwear.

"An implied promise," he says.

He's started stroking me along the length of me, through my underwear, where I'm already embarrassingly wet, and I feel my eyelids flutter.

"What's that?" I ask.

"I'm going to spend the rest of the day making you come," he says. Then with his free hand he tilts my chin up again, his pale eyes looking seriously into mine.

Oh God.

I have to say something. I can't not say something. I don't know where it comes from, and I don't know what it means, but I'm suddenly assaulted by a wave of guilt.

"Marcus," I say, and I put my hands on his arms, stopping him. "Marcus, I'm sorry for not understanding why you wanted to go work for Alex Wolfe."

Marcus stiffens, and for a moment I'm afraid I might have said the wrong thing. There's something in his face I can't quite read, and that feels so strange, so alienating and frightening to me. But then his eyes soften and it's the Marcus I know, the man who loves me, despite the ways he's hurt me.

"I love you, Lo," he says.

I'm breathless while he removes my clothes, item by item. I'm trying so hard not to think about how I might not be enough for him, how if I'm not enough for him he might leave again, but it's this persistent pain in the back of my mind, this worry.

And then, once he has me naked and panting for him, Marcus leans in and says, "Thank you for wanting me to be there today, Lo."

And it just about kills me.

I want him, even if I'm not enough for him, even if I'll never be enough for him. I want to believe in him. I want to believe he won't hurt me again.

"I want you to stay," I whisper back.

And I want him inside me, to push back the last of my doubts.

17

MARCUS

I don't know how I've let things get this far, this fast. The fundraiser that Harlow and Shantha dreamed up is scheduled for tomorrow night at Shantha's bar, and I haven't done jack shit about any of it yet. Still haven't talked to Alex. Still haven't figured out how to protect Harlow while the whole thing plays out.

Instead I've let myself get distracted by Lo. By Lo and Dill. I didn't expect to be that affected, I'll be honest. I didn't think that going to see Dill would be such a big deal. You think about those moments in your life, the ones that mark lines in the sand, where everything is fundamentally different afterwards, and some of them you can see coming. Death of a loved one is pretty obvious, I guess, for Lo and me, but there's also falling in love, having a kid—stuff like that. But some of them are stealth moments. Some of them just sneak up on you when you least expect it and change everything.

That's what happened to me when we went up to visit Dill.

I knew I was in love with Lo. I've known that for a long time. But I didn't know I had such a limited understanding of what being in love could mean.

That day? Jesus. It was like some giant reality show, This Could Be Your Life. Just a glimpse of what it would be like, and I fell even more in love with Harlow Chase, and I fell in love with the idea of being there for both her and Dill. Of being their family. Because it felt like this was the family I was supposed to have. Maybe the family I would have had, if I hadn't left.

Except I know it's not that simple.

That's what I have to keep reminding myself, when the guilt gets too bad. That I did what I had to do. That I took the only path available to me.

Except if my choice was all about noble sacrifice, I wouldn't feel this guilty, would I?

This is the kind of thing I've got swimming around in my head as I'm walking over to the bar to pick Harlow up after her shift. She's helping Shantha close a little bit early tonight, so they can get some sleep before they have to set up for the fundraiser tomorrow. Even so, I don't know how Harlow just pulled a bartending shift. I know I'm bone tired. I kept her in bed all night and then most of the day.

And I'd do it again in a heartbeat. In fact, I probably will. I can't help it. I'm getting worked up all over again just knowing I'm about to see her.

I got to keep it in check, though, because I know she needs to be on her game for this fundraiser. And so do I. Because if they pull this event off tomorrow, if they manage to convince some of the members of the zoning board who've said they'd come by, then they become a real problem for Alex. And Alex doesn't just let problems slide.

That's the other reason I'm going to pick up Harlow. I don't like how quiet it's been.

I don't like that Alex has stopped calling me, looking for updates.

I don't like how, when I get in sight of the bar, I can see a few men hanging around outside the bar even though it's just closed, the tips of their cigarettes glowing in the wet night air, bobbing up and down while they drunkenly pace. Drunks don't normally pace. They talk, they argue, they laugh, and they do it all a little too much, a little too emphatically, a little too loudly, but they don't goddamn pace.

And then the guys disappear around the corner all at once. Together.

I really don't like that.

That's when I start jogging. I don't know, maybe it's just that instinct again, maybe all the stuff I've seen working for Alex. But when I see Brison Wolfe across the street when I hit the corner, I know my instincts were right. I curse and head down the cross street, running now, and see the alley that gives the bar its name, where the back door opens and there's a dumpster. And I see at least three guys beating the shit out of a woman.

I flash all red for a second.

And then I bring it back down, because I need to keep my head on me. There are three of them. No, four. And Brison. But just one of me.

I will kill them all.

I charge in, my vision narrowed by all that adrenaline, and hit the first one hard, feeling his teeth crack under my fist. The next I pick up and throw against the wall, and by the time he hits the brick I'm already on the third, breaking his nose in three places with three straight rights.

I drop that one and turn, looking for the fourth, and that's when I see Brison again.

Brison, raining down body blows on the fourth guy, until the woman-beating piece of shit folds over himself and collapses to the floor, crying.

I did not expect that.

But I also don't have time for it. He's not on the wrong side, so he's not my problem. And the scumfuck bastards are already running away, scrambling down the alley, choking on their own blood. It's done. Only one thing left. I turn my head, looking for the woman they were beating on, more terrified than I've ever been or ever will be of what I'm about to see.

It's Shantha.

***

Shantha picks herself up off the dirty, wet pavement, stumbling only once before Brison steps in and puts a hand under her arm. She's got a cut lip, an eye that's already swelling up, and she's walking with a limp while she holds her ribs.

"You've got to go to the hospital," I say.

She shakes her head no, and Brison looks at me. Shantha just looks pissed.

"They'd call the police," she says. "I'm not dealing with that."

"Why the fuck not?" I shout.

Shantha just shakes her head, like there's something obvious I just don't get, and pounds on the back door to the bar. It must have closed in the scuffle. They got her while she was taking out the trash.

It's Harlow who opens the door, and as soon as she does her eyes go wide and she pulls Shantha inside.

"Oh Jesus, what happened?"

"Can you get the first aid kit in the office?" Shantha asks, and limps over to a table, taking a chair down so she can sit. Just steady as all hell. The rest of us are more shaken up than she is.

Harlow moves to go to the office, but I stop her. I have to. I put my arms around her and just feel her warmth against me, feel her heart beat, safe and sound, against mine. Harlow is surprised but lets me hold her, and I can feel her look up at me before she buries her face in my chest. I don't know if everyone actually goes quiet, but I know I don't hear anything else for a second or two.

Then I guess Brison goes to get the first aid kit while I keep hold of Lo, unable to let go of her while the adrenaline still flows through me, and things start to move again.

"Marcus," Lo whispers, and she pushes off my chest gently. I know she wants to go check on her best friend. I don't want to let her go, but I know I have to.

"Yeah," I say, forcing my arms to unwind. "Will you tell her to go get checked out?"

I think that's the first time Harlow gets a really, really good look at her friend without any distractions. Her eyes start to fill up.

"Oh my God," she says.

"Shantha," I say again. "You have to go to the hospital."

Shantha just shakes her head. "Haven't enjoyed myself when I've been there before," she says, and takes a napkin from where Harlow was rolling up the silverware for the next day to dab at her cut lip.

"This is dumb," I say. I'm frustrated. I know Shantha was the one to take care of Lo when she needed it. Shantha deserves the same.

"Marcus, leave it alone," Brison says, and I suddenly remember he's here.

And now I want to know why he's here.

I'm still jacked up from the adrenaline, from thinking that Brison was here with those thugs, that he'd come here to intimidate Harlow. I was going to kill him. I still might. Jesus Christ, he's my half-brother, and if he's here for Harlow, I will end him.

I turn on him fully, the roar in my ears blocking out what just happened outside.

"Why are you here?" I say. My voice is calm, low, while I rage inside. Brison knows me well enough to recognize it. He must see the look on my face.

"I was just here to talk, Marcus."

My half-brother looks at me, not cowed, not trying to lie. I know he was here to talk about the offer. To get Harlow to sell. To talk to her alone. What I don't know is what kind of conversation that would have been.

I growl. "Get the fuck out."

"Hey!" Shantha says. "My bar, my rules. That guy just beat the crap out of someone trying to hurt me. He gets a free drink, at least."

Brison and I stare at each other. It takes me way too long to realize Shantha is cracking a joke.

In fact, it takes Harlow's hand on my arm.

"You need to calm down," she whispers.

I look at her, and the worry, the disappointment in her eyes, and that does it. I stand down. She's right. I'm not going to bring Alex and Brison and what they may or not have planned for tomorrow into what happened tonight if it's not necessary. I shouldn't take the focus off of Shantha.

Even though Shantha is still more together than any of us, especially Harlow. Harlow is shaking like a leaf. All I want to do is wrap her up in my arms and not let go, ever, but I know she needs something else right now.

"Honey, what happened?" Lo says, pulling up a chair to her best friend. I've never seen Lo like this, like she's afraid to ask questions.

Shantha sighs, being dramatic on purpose, trying to defuse the tension for her friend, and pats Lo's hand. "I screwed up," she says. "I outed that guy."

Ok, at this point, I will admit, I'm confused. Brison is, too. Both of us are maybe not the most fashionable guys, but I have a head start, knowing that Shantha used to be a guy, and eventually even Brison picks up on what's going on. Actually, I can pinpoint the exact moment Brison picks up on it. It's about the same time she's explaining why those men attacked her.

"He kept telling me he recognized me and asking me where he knew me from, real flirtatious, getting really drunk with his boys," Shantha says to Harlow, wincing from the antiseptic. "And I knew, you know, but I wasn't saying anything, because I knew him from a gay bar. You know how I used to wait with my cab outside the gay bars back before I transitioned?"

Now I'm confused again. "What?" I say.

Shantha rolls her eyes. "Before this," she says, sweeping her hand down to indicate her whole body. Oh.

"I was a cab driver for my family's company back before they found out about me and kicked me out," Shantha says. "I used to wait outside gay clubs for the drunk gays and whoever so they had a safe way to get home late at night, right? You know, if I couldn't be out, I could at least drive people around. Whatever, it made sense at the time. That's how I knew him. I picked him up outside a club and brought him home to his nice suburban home."

Shantha's toying with that napkin now, tearing it up. Maybe she is shaken up.

"Anyway, I got stupid and told him exactly where he knew me from, and that didn't get the greatest reaction. And I would say he didn't approve of my personal choices since then, because he did *not* love that I'm a lady now. And one of his friends overheard, and then he had to go on about how he wasn't really gay, and I guess prove it to his boys…"

Shantha shrugs, but Harlow looks like she's about to cry.

"Jesus," Brison says.

"I should have been more careful," Shantha says quietly.

Now Harlow really does start to cry, and Shantha looks uncomfortable, like this is worse than what just happened to her. I kind of get it, in a way. Life can throw a bunch of crap at you, but there's nothing worse than other people pitying you for it. I know that's not what Harlow's doing, but damn,

Shantha clearly doesn't want to cry about it, and she doesn't want to be afraid.

And seeing Harlow cry about anything is like a knife to my heart. I kneel beside her, put hand over hers.

"Lo," I say.

"I know," she says. "I'm sorry. I'm just…emotional. Big week." Lo smiles up at Shantha.

"Tell me about it," Shantha says.

"Do you…?"

"Don't you dare ask me if we're going to cancel for tomorrow," Shantha says. "No way in hell we're canceling after all that work."

Harlow kind of frowns but doesn't say anything as she gets to work with that first aid kit, trying to bandage Shantha up. I look down at my fists; all that work Harlow did on me a few weeks ago is undone, my knuckles busted open, bleeding. It's only Harlow who can patch me up, and I get the feeling that Shantha wouldn't let anyone else near her right now, either. Harlow's her family, too.

It's even more obvious when I look at Brison, standing there, looking awkward as hell. I don't know what it's supposed to be like to have a brother, but I bet it's not this. I don't trust him.

And I know exactly who to blame for that.

***

So after my dad died and Alex Wolfe announced he was my natural father and my moms just checked out for Florida on Alex's dime, like she was just relieved to go, that's when Alex decided to take an interest in my affairs.

But that was when Harlow and I were finally starting to figure stuff out. And I was nineteen, with no real plan, working some shifts at the auto shop where my dad worked, so my affairs basically consisted of loving the hell out of my new girlfriend.

I guess it was a lot going on. If you've ever been in love, though, you know I was mostly thinking about Harlow. I mean I was just about crazy with happiness, like I finally understood what people got so worked up about, like it all finally made sense. I couldn't believe there'd been this huge slice of life that I'd been missing out on, and I couldn't imagine ever going back.

I just wanted her all the time. I wanted to be with her, to make her smile, to make her sigh, every damn second of every damn day.

And I pretty much did. I mean, I made that my mission.

The first time we saw each other after that first night we kissed had only maybe one second of awkwardness. A second of uncertainty, when I could see in her eyes and her body language that she was nervous, afraid that I'd say it was a mistake, that I wouldn't want her anymore, or that things would change somehow. I'd come to get her at the Mankowskis' back door the way I always did, and she stopped on that bottom step. Hesitated, tucking her blonde hair behind her ear, biting that bottom lip. And looked at me.

I just moved in and kissed her all over again, and that was that. No more room for doubt, for second-guessing. I was done with that. And after that, so was she.

Maybe what was most strange to me was how much things stayed the same after we admitted we were in love. Hanging out with Lo wasn't much different, except, obviously, when it was.

Jesus, the sounds she made when I touched her.

Those new parts of her, the things I hadn't seen before — the sounds, the smells, the way she felt against my hand — all of that made me fall even harder. I couldn't explore her enough, couldn't spend enough time getting to know what she liked, what she wanted. Harlow wasn't totally inexperienced, but she was still just barely eighteen and had never had sex. It was all new to her, and what I realized, one day, when I asked her if she'd let me just watch her make herself come? It was all new to me, too.

I'd never been this close to anyone I'd done anything with. It had never mattered this much. I felt like a freaking virgin.

And her face? She was lying back on my bed, her lips red and swollen from where I'd been kissing her, her eyes heavy and lidded—until I said that.

"I want to see you naked," I said. "I want to see you make yourself come, naked."

Then they opened wide, real wide, and she went from kind of shocked to scared to turned on.

I could see it in the way she got all red for me.

I could see it in the way she tried to contain a smile.

She didn't move at first. Neither did I.

"Only if you're naked with me," she finally said. Smiling at me.

Have you ever seen Superman change clothes? I could have beaten him. It got Lo laughing, giggling in my bed, and then she grabbed my hand and pulled me back over to her, on top of her clothed body. The second she felt my hard cock against her thigh I heard her gasp. I looked up, worried it was too much, but instead she looked...

She looked like she wanted me.

Now, in the end, it was Harlow who pushed for us to have sex when I was still worried that she wasn't ready. I still remember what she said to me: "I'm not going to break, Marcus." But there was nothing more precious to me than Lo, nothing, and I was damn careful with her.

So at the time my mind kind of blanked out. I froze, poised over her, ready to kiss her, but with everything on automatic lockdown while I got a handle on myself. Sex with Lo was like this burning, bright light somewhere on the horizon, this thing I wanted more than anything, but I wanted it the right way. If I had a fear, it was losing Lo, and a second one close behind was finally having sex with Lo and then finding out she regretted it because she wasn't ready. I'd screwed plenty of girls, and I wasn't going to screw her just because we were horny and impulsive. Eff that. I loved her.

Instead I grabbed two handfuls of sheets and twisted while I kissed her breathless again. Took all my strength not to move against her, knowing I could come from just her touching me, just her watching me.

Man, what I did before Lo wasn't even sex. It was just getting off. This? This was something different.

I remember her undressing for me, that day. I remember every detail, every gesture, every movement. I remember the way she shimmied out of her bra first, pulling it out from under her shirt, looking at me like she was embarrassed, having no idea that I thought the way a girl could do that was hot. Well, she didn't know until she saw my face. The way she started to blush as that shirt came off, the way her nipples were tiny, rosy little buds already, deep pink in the light of my bedroom. The way her breasts bounced slightly as she lay back down, her eyes on me the whole time.

It's not even the sexual element that gets to me when I think about it now. It's how brave she was, how willing to let me see. How much she trusted me.

How when she was finally naked, lifting her hips just slightly to let me help her get her panties off, she lay there, breathing hard, her chest shaking, gasping with nervousness and just the rawness of it. And me, I couldn't believe the gift I'd been given. Still don't.

I said, "I didn't know I could feel like this."

"Like what?"

"Happy like this." I lay down next to her and held her face in my hands, almost scared to move. "In love like this."

Those were the words that hit her. When I told her I was in love with her. Like it was a surprise to her, which to me seemed ridiculous. Of course I was in love with her. Anyway, I'd almost never seen Harlow look shy, but then?

She closed her eyes briefly, smiling big, and when she opened them again she had tears brimming on her eyelashes, and she said she loved me, too.

That's how perfect it was. No, it was even more perfect than that; the Mankowskis even approved. Had me over for dinner as her boyfriend, now that they knew, and now that things had changed. And Mr. Mankowski, when he made sure we weren't doing anything he wouldn't approve of in his house—and I wouldn't, I respected that man, taking Harlow in like that—he thanked me.

He said, "Thank you for being there for Harlow," clearing his throat and putting his hand out.

That man had known I'd been sneaking in to comfort Harlow for years.

It was that perfect.

And then Alex Wolfe came along.

Alex Wolfe would come by maybe once a week, sometimes more, taking me out to these dinners at restaurants he owned, drinks at clubs, wanting me to see how he did business. Asking about what my plans were, where I saw myself in five years, what I wanted to do with myself. Saying things like, "The auto shop is all right until you figure out what you want. Then we'll get you started."

That phrase echoed around inside my head a whole lot: We'll get you started.

There was a "we." Like my future, my life? It mattered to him. Alex Wolfe, my father, thought I could do something.

I have thought about this a lot. Because the only other person who believed in me like that was Harlow. So why did it matter more that my natural father did, too? I still don't know. Maybe Harlow had just been behind me for so long that I started to take it for granted, or maybe part of me still worried that the way she felt about me had more to do with what I'd done for her than the man I was—that if I hadn't been there for her after her parents died, I would have just been a teenage crush that she got over and she'd have been on to someone else. Or maybe I was just young and stupid. Whatever.

The point is that Alex Wolfe talking about all the things I could do with my life hit me like another kind of drug. I'd been dreaming about my dad, Juan Roma, telling me he was proud of me my whole damn life, and Alex Wolfe showed up and started talking like he already was proud of me. Like he had expectations for me because of it. It's hard to describe what that felt like even now. It was like this doubt I carried around with me all the time, this heavy feeling that nothing would ever be good enough—suddenly it was gone. I was light. I could do anything.

So maybe I didn't see the signs. Maybe I didn't pick up on what Alex was hinting at quick enough. But man, can you blame me?

And then right after I told Harlow I was in love with her, I'm eating lobster with Alex at this place he owned in Manhattan, real swank, and he's looking at me with this critical eye. The way he would get when he was asking one of his managers how business was, like he was evaluating everything.

"You getting pretty serious with that girl?" he asked.

Man, I was dumb. I smiled big. Proud of it. "Yeah," I said.

Alex sniffed and said, "Make sure you always use protection. You don't want to get tied to that now."

I lost my shit.

In retrospect, maybe I wouldn't have hulked out like that, getting up so quickly from the table that I knocked my chair over, leaning over my own father on my big boxer's hands, feeling the muscles in my back stretch the suit jacket they made me wear, if he hadn't called Harlow "that."

Nah. I would have lost it either way.

"Don't talk about her like that," I barked. "Ever."

I remember I felt the heat in my face. I hadn't been angry like that since I was a little boy and was still small enough to get pushed around.

And Alex just studied me. I remember that second when he was just taking my reaction in, his face unchanged. Then he put his hands up, smiled mildly, and said, "My mistake. I apologize."

And I was dumb enough to think that was the end of it.

***

So that's what I'm thinking about when I look at Brison, the brother I don't trust, while we're standing there in Shantha's bar while Harlow tries to take care of Shantha like she's family. I'm thinking about how Alex Wolfe started to show what he was right around the time Harlow and I were finally finding out what we were, and how much that screwed me up in such a short time. I'm thinking about how I wanted a father so badly it made me stupid.

And I'm thinking about the choices I made.

And the choices I'm going to make.

And, if I'm honest, I'm thinking about the fact that I still want it all. I still want Alex Wolfe to give me the keys to the kingdom and I still want to know that I'm his chosen son, and I still want to make Harlow happy.

A man can only make so many choices.

I try not to think so much as Harlow and Shantha are winding down. Brison left already, made his excuses, gave me a look as he was walking out the door, like he was saying this wasn't over. No shit it's not over. My hands curl into fists just thinking about it.

We wait around for a few more minutes until Shantha's roommate shows up, ready to take her home, Shantha still refusing to go to the hospital. There's no arguing with her, though, and honestly she's looking better already. Those drunks didn't get much time in before Brison and I were on them, and they were drunk, sloppy, not real fighters.

How she's handling the mental aspect—that's beyond my pay grade. You'd think someone would be in a puddle of tears after something like that, but Shantha is a soldier, like it's not the worst thing she's ever seen in the world. That almost seems worse to me, but Shantha's not going to let it break her, and I respect that.

It's not the night anyone wanted. But we all walk out, Shantha and her roommate Billy headed to a cab, me and Harlow walking. Lo insists.

"I need to clear my head," she says. But she puts her hand in mine and lets me hold her as close as I can. Whether that's for her or for me, I don't care. I'm not letting go.

By the time we get back to Lo's house, though, I'm practically buzzing with energy. Every shadow on the street, every car that comes by—all of it has me holding her closer, thinking about what I could have lost. She notices, too, so that when we get in the door and the first thing I do is put my arms around her, she finally says something.

"What is with you?" she asks. Her voice is muffled against my chest.

I take a deep breath and let her go long enough to speak. "I didn't know who it was," I say. "I didn't know who was on the ground."

Harlow props her chin up on my chest and looks up at me.

"Marcus, I'm fine," she says.

"Doesn't matter. Not letting go."

I smile down at her, not wanting her to get stressed out, or more stressed out than she already is. I know she can hear my heartbeat, how it speeds up whenever she touches me, how it's hammering now. Finally she giggles slightly and I laugh with her, both of us sounding kind of punch drunk.

"Ok, well, at least bring me upstairs," she says. "I need to get to bed."

I don't need to be told twice. I lift her up and let her bury her face in my neck, knowing she loves it when I pick her up like this. She told me once that getting lifted off the ground, knowing she's in my control—it's a comfort thing and a turn on all at once. And after that night of the break in, I'm not likely to forget about something like that.

"Don't worry," I say, walking up the stairs with her in my arms. "I'll let you sleep."

"Hmmm," she says.

I mean to let her sleep, I do. Just so long as I get to hold her while she does, that's fine with me. But we get up to her bedroom and she kicks her shoes off and I set her down on her own bed, and then it starts. Harlow kisses me. It starts small and sweet, but she feels the urgency in me. She takes my face in her hands and pulls back, looking at me, her face serious.

"I'm ok, Marcus," she says again.

"I know," I say. I sound like I'm choking on the words. I don't want to think about a world where she isn't ok.

So Harlow kisses me again, deeper, longer. And pretty soon I'm just ripping my clothes off and hers, too, just needing to feel her skin against mine, needing to cover her body with my own. It's not until we're both naked and Harlow's moaning into my neck, begging me to put it in, that this wave of desperation washes over me, this need to make it right—only I know I can't.

"What's wrong?" she asks me.

I shake my head, not knowing how to say it. Not knowing how to put all those years of missing her, of hurting her, of wishing it could be different into words. Of wishing that I had been different. That I had been better.

"Don't ever forgive me," I say. "I don't deserve it."

I see the tears well up in her eyes, and her lips part. She reaches up to touch my face, and damn it, damn it, I've made her sad.

"I love you," I tell her. "I love you more than I'll ever love anything. Do you know that?"

"Yes," she whispers.

I want that to be enough. I want so badly for that to be enough. But I wouldn't feel like this if it were.

LIE TO ME

"Love me," she says.
That's all I'll ever do.

18

HARLOW

The fundraiser and Community Action Night—its official name on the flyers Shantha and I put all over the neighborhood—is a huge success.

Even with Shantha's black eye and split lip, she's still swinging behind the bar, leaving me free to go out and, as she put it, "shmooze." I think under any other circumstances, with all these politicians and people in suits, I might feel out of place. Nervous about having to chat them up, impress them. But knowing this is about my home, this neighborhood, what I mostly feel is invigorated. I can do this. I am doing this.

And Marcus is right here with me.

He's in a suit, moving about, charming people. I forgot he could do that when he really wanted to. It's not normal for him and I know it tires him, but he can do it. And damn, does he clean up good.

It's almost enough to make me forget how uneasy I feel.

Ever since coming back from upstate, when we saw Dill, I've been trying to work on understanding. On moving through all the anger and abandonment I felt when he left, and trying to imagine why he must have done that. That sounds simple, or like something I should have done years ago, but I don't think I realized before how much Marcus just up and leaving like that triggered every single fault line in my still fragile psyche. I mean, losing people? Biggest fear, right there, for obvious reasons. And then I lost him.

It's not an excuse. I've been grappling with the idea, after watching him with Dill, and remembering all the ways he was there for me, that maybe I owe him a little bit of faith. Maybe I owed it to him, this whole time. I mean, granted, a five-year absence requires a whole lot of faith, but this is the man who went and checked on Dill and then crawled back up into my bedroom just to hold me until I fell asleep every night for three months. This is the man who refused to leave my side until I could eat on my own. This is the man who watched me crumple in grief and just said, nope, that's not happening, let me help you with that.

Talk about faith.

I just don't know. I love him, and I am terrified to lose him again. And part of me is sure I will, and so I'm holding back. I'm terrified to forgive him and be his again, his to hold, his to break. I can't help how I feel either way.

I'm a mess.

And none of these people can know it.

It looks like this might actually be working. There are so many more people here than I would have thought, and at least three members of the zoning board. Maria is here, too, even though she accepted the offer, just to be supportive. It makes me feel like we tapped into something, some resentment that was already there, like people had already had enough. It makes me feel like there's hope.

I stand up straight and smile and make myself walk over to Gus Finney, a portly little man with a big temper, a white beard, and a smiling red face who I think I remember from when I was a kid. He used to play the piano for the elementary school musicals. And now he has a reputation as being the firebrand on the zoning board, like this irritable little Santa Claus.

And he's thinking about running for City Council, which means he needs an issue, something to take a stand on. He's my best shot.

"Mr. Finney," I say. "I'm so glad you could make it."

"Have you seen the lady with the bacon wrapped shrimp?" he says. He seems really concerned about the shrimp. I don't entirely blame him; Shantha got a caterer friend to make some amazing appetizers.

Still, it's not exactly what I want to be talking about.

"I'll get you your own platter of shrimp if you stop this development," I say.

That gets his attention.

Finney looks at me, his red face round with surprise—round eyes, round cheeks, round mouth—and then he bursts out laughing.

"You favor subtlety, I see," he says. "I think if you want to start bribing people, young lady, you have a lot to learn."

My turn to grin. Until I realize he might not be joking—how can I ever compete with actual bribes?

And that's when I realize Gus Finny is looking pointedly at the front door. Across all those people, mingling, sipping their prosecco and red wines, eating their shrimp and crab rangoons, I suddenly see what Gus Finney sees.

Alex Wolfe. Alex and Brison Wolfe are crashing this event.

I immediately look for Marcus, and find him standing next to a wall, staring at his father and brother. And a coldness takes root in my heart.

***

Watching Marcus brood while he stares down his father makes me anxious in an immediate, reflexive way. There's a reason for that.

Looking back, I guess nothing is perfect forever, right? And Marcus was perfect. Once we admitted how we felt, once we started to get physical, it was just like this massive force with its own inexorable momentum, like we were both swept up in it. There wasn't much middle ground for either of us. We'd both been holding back for so long, for different reasons, that we had all this love, all this passion stored up.

It was…intense.

I wanted to have sex with him so badly I could feel it. I mean I could literally feel the desire radiating off of my skin, like heat. It made me insane. It felt like I was redlining my internal engine, like I needed some relief or I was going to spin apart at the seams, which is why it was good that Marcus was still the epitome of self-control.

I'm glad he made me wait. I'm glad he let me know how seriously he took it, how important it was to him, especially given what happened later. It would have crushed me to have to have to wonder, after he left, whether it meant as much to him as it did to me.

At least I had that.

That's not to say that everything outside of us was perfect. I learned to miss my parents in a whole new way as I was falling in love with Marcus. The first time I kissed him, the first time I stayed over, the first time I had sex—I couldn't help but wonder what it would have been like to have my mom to talk to. I had no one to talk to, though Mrs. Mankowski tried, because she was just that sweet. Standing there with her hair in curlers around her head, pretending it didn't make her uncomfortable. I just hugged her and thanked her, and said there was no need to worry.

She looked relieved.

But the truth was, I did need someone to talk to. Maybe if I'd had anyone in my life who could have done that, who could have been older, wiser, I wouldn't have let myself fall so far, so fast. I mean, I was imagining an entire life with Marcus already. It felt like the real thing, and we were different, and nothing could go wrong. We were invulnerable.

We were perfect.

The way I finally convinced Marcus I was ready to have sex with him was by asking him if he was ready—in all that time, it hadn't occurred to me that maybe it would be just as big a deal to him as it was to me, that maybe he wanted to make sure I was doing it for deeper reasons than just wanting him. I guess I'd gotten so used to Marcus thinking about me so much that I took it for granted. I owed him more than that, though.

Maybe I still do.

But nothing I do, nothing Marcus does or has done, nothing anyone does, can take the memory of our first time away from me. I don't know what anyone else's first time was like. I mean, I know, in the sense that people talk about it; I have an idea. There's awkward fumbling, and some people just want to get it over with, and some people actually get to be in love, though usually there's still some awkward fumbling going on.

Part of me wishes everyone could have a first time like the one Marcus gave me, but I don't think it would be possible without everything that came before it, and I don't wish that on anyone. Even we had a little bit of awkward fumbling in the beginning, Marcus being so careful with me, having to ease into me. I still remember his strong arms shaking on either side of me from the excitement, the set of his jaw as he controlled every movement, how is eyes never left mine. But it didn't take long for something to happen.

It crept up on me, slowly, filling me as Marcus filled me, until I was overcome. I remember the exact sensation. This storm ripped through me, this well of grief and gratitude and love, everything mixed together at once, all the weight and power of the last two and half years coming together in this moment when I could finally feel them all, when I could finally look at Marcus and let myself show him all the ways I felt about him. It was all there, the good and the bad, all the things that allowed me to know and love Marcus deeper, to know what it meant to appreciate him, to cherish him. To know that who I had become was inextricably tied to him, that we'd molded each other, shaped each other. I wouldn't have known something like that was actually possible. It felt like something that was happening to me, something that was changing me from the inside out, something I had no power to resist.

And I didn't want to resist it. I was happy. God, I was truly happy. I was so in love with Marcus Roma that he made me believe in happiness again. He made me believe in him, and that was all that mattered to me.

I'm also pretty sure most people don't get to have an orgasm the first time they have sex, either. But Marcus…well, he's Marcus. He made sure.

Anyway, I've heard it both ways, some people claiming that having sex changes you, others saying that there's no difference at all. Personally I think it's not sex that matters, it's whether or not the sex was emotionally significant. I know I was different afterwards. And Marcus was, too. I know this because he told me.

And I thank God that he told me, because if I had to piece together how he felt after what happened, I think it would have broken me beyond all repair.

So after sex, yes, we were more in love. This thing that we had shared together felt like ours alone, this thing that only we had experienced—I mean, we were young, of course we thought we were special. But it cemented us together even more, and convinced me that Marcus truly was mine.

But it was also around that time that Marcus started to seem distant sometimes, that he started to brood the way he's brooding now, standing in the shadows of the bar while he watches Alex Wolfe.

At the time, I told myself that I shouldn't take it personally. That whatever it was, I could trust Marcus. After all, he had just buried the man he'd grown up thinking was his father, and his mother had left town without even saying goodbye; I didn't think the fallout from that was going to disappear just because we were in love. I was determined to take care of him just like he'd taken care of me. So I told myself over and over again, Don't take it personally. Don't freak out.

Except, of course, obviously I was freaking out a little bit, because this was the first time Marcus had ever kept anything from me. Ever. I mean, Marcus not telling me about something important that was going on in his life? It didn't even occur to me as a possibility until it happened.

I don't know. Maybe we were too young to handle that kind of love. Maybe I just didn't handle it right. Maybe, in the same way that I'm starting to think I just wasn't enough for Marcus, I wasn't receptive enough, maybe I didn't listen enough.

But he started to brood, started to think heavily about things he wasn't telling me about, and he started to spend all that time with Alex Wolfe. And it wasn't too long after that that Marcus left me to go work for his father's company on the other side of the country. No, he didn't just leave. He disappeared. He didn't give me an explanation or a goodbye; all I got were some text messages, some vague promises, and, when I demanded more, even those stopped.

It was completely baffling. It still is baffling.

And here Marcus is again, brooding, as Alex Wolfe shows back up in my life. I can't help but wonder about what Marcus will do next.

I turn back to Gus Finney, who's telling me some story I'm sure I'm supposed to be laughing at, but I can barely see him. Instead I look again for Marcus, and this time I see him talking to Alex Wolfe, the two of them huddled away in a corner, and my stomach cramps. I feel cold. I feel lightheaded. I feel like I can't breathe at all, like my lungs are frozen in my chest, like my body doesn't want time to move forward, because it knows what happens next.

This is when Marcus leaves.

But no, dammit, this is exactly what I've been fighting against. This is exactly what I've been trying to figure out. Trying to find a way that Marcus leaving the way he did makes sense, a way to understand both how he loved me and how he left me. And all I've been able to come up with is that there's something I fundamentally don't understand. Watching Marcus talk to his father and his brother, the three of them standing there all looking alike, all with that same fierce expression, those same penetrating eyes, it occurs to me that maybe that sense of family belonging was just too important to him. That maybe I didn't have a right to deny him that. Because that was something I had that Marcus never got, and maybe he needed it.

I might never understand why he left me like that. But maybe I owe it to him—to the man who took care of me—to just believe him. To believe him that it mattered. That he did the best he could.

I want to trust him so badly.

And that's when Gus Finney leans in and says, "Pay attention, Ms. Chase. I think you'll like this."

Gus Finney grabs his shrimp fork and starts tapping away at his glass of prosecco, saying, "Excuse me, everyone! Excuse me!"

Slowly, the room falls silent. I feel myself start to blush under all that attention, because it feels like everyone can see what I'm really thinking about, which is, of course, Marcus. I know that's ridiculous, and I admonish myself to pay attention. Apparently something important is happening.

"I hope Ms. Chase here won't mind," Finney is saying, smiling at me with this patronizing Santa Claus thing he has going on, "but I want to take this opportunity to make what I think is a prescient announcement. Friends and neighbors, I'm going to run for City Council. I'm going to win. And we are going to stop these irresponsible developments right in their tracks!"

Finney raises his glass triumphantly amid some cheers and modest applause. I smile as hard as I can, clapping away, because I know I should be elated. This is the best-case scenario—someone else has taken up the fight, someone with the power to actually annoy the developers. Maybe they'll move on, even if it's only a couple of blocks over. Maybe I won't have to lose Dill's home.

So why don't I actually feel happy?

I let myself melt away into the crowd of movers and shakers coming forward to shake Finney's hand and do whatever it is these people do at moments like this—I don't know, make appointments for backroom deals? Trade secret handshakes?—because I'm just feeling disoriented. The truth is I can't get Marcus out of my mind. I turn and look for him again, and when I don't see him, my stomach drops even further.

He was just there. He was just talking to Alex Wolfe. And then Finney made his announcement, and now he's gone.

I spin around, totally oblivious to everything else now, desperately searching for any sign of Marcus. I'm so worked up that I miss him approach, and when I turn around again, he's right behind me.

I don't care if it makes me look crazy. I lean into him and try to burrow into his chest. I'm not thinking rationally; I'm just feeling the anxiety ebb away the more I touch him.

"Hey," Marcus says.

I'm almost afraid to look up at him. But I do. I do.

And he's smiling.

"You won," he whispers to me.

"Did I?"

"I think so," Marcus says. "For now. It means maybe we can come to a deal with Alex, and this will all be over."

I don't actually know what he means—a deal? But I nod blankly, not even feeling capable of thinking about it. The specter of Alex Wolfe looms too large in my mind.

Marcus touches my cheek with the back of his hand, his brows drawing together.

"Let's get you home," he says.

I couldn't agree more.

Marcus walks me home, going slow so that I can keep up in my ridiculous heels, holding my hand. The farther we get from the sight of Marcus and Alex Wolfe talking secretively in some corner, the better I start to feel, but I know it's not gone. I can't seem to shake it. Marcus can tell, but he's not prying.

I stumble on a broken slab of sidewalk, lost in all these stupid thoughts, and he catches me.

He says, "How are your feet?"

"Heels suck," I grumble. I never really figured out to how to walk in them, though I love the way they make my legs look in this slinky black thing that Shantha made me wear.

Marcus laughs, and his arm snakes around my waist. We're only a few feet from the house.

"You can't keep carrying me everywhere," I say, knowing what he's thinking.

"I can and you know it," he says, tightening that arm. We're stopped in the street now, and he's looking down at me. Gentle, smiling. Worried.

"It's ridiculous," I say.

"But you like it."

I smile. "Yeah."

I really, really do. He knows it. He knows it gives me a little thrill.

I'm just not sure that's enough right now.

"Lo," he says. I'm afraid to look at his eyes. I know he'll see exactly what it is I'm feeling, and I don't want him to. I don't want him to know how conflicted I am. I don't want him to know that I'm struggling.

And yet part of me rages against that, too, because it's so unfair. I have every right to struggle! He hasn't explained anything, and I'm still afraid of losing him.

"Lo, tell me," he says.

I sigh.

So he lifts me up off the ground, grinning as I gasp a little and grab at his neck while he walks to the front steps. God, this is such a weird physical reaction. The second my feet leave the ground, it's just…somehow easier.

"That is cheating," I mutter as he carries me inside.

"I'm a ruthless son of a bitch," he agrees.

He's not stopping. He's just walking us both up the stairs.

I can't help it. I have a physical reaction to that, too.

Marcus sets me down on my bed—the bed we've been sharing, like this is a normal thing, like this is something we do now, and I've just accepted that— on this bed, our bed, and then he kneels in front of me and gently takes my heels off.

God, that does feel good. Sometimes it's worth it to wear heels if you have the right person to help you take them off at the end of the night.

I sigh again, leaning back on my palms, and Marcus runs his hands up the front of my legs, making me give a little groan. He's still watching me. He still looks worried.

"Lo, tell me why you aren't happy," he says softly. "You got what you wanted tonight. What's wrong?"

"Can't get anything past you, huh?" I say.

"Nope."

And I can't do anything about those searching eyes. I pull myself back up and reach for his face, just wanting to hold it in front of me, while he puts his arms around my waist. I wish everything were simple. I wish I could just take the leap of faith and forgive and forget. I wish I could believe in him the way he believed in me back when everybody thought I had lost my mind, that I was irreparably damaged after my parents died. I hate myself for not having that faith, for not bothering to find a way to understand until five years later. I hate that I spent so much time hating him. I hate that I still have this physical fear that he'll leave, that I'll lose him, that this fear has taken root in my very core.

"I saw you talking to your father tonight," I say.

I call him "your father" for a reason. It has an effect.

He starts, "Lo, I was—"

"Wait, please," I say. "Just let me get it out."

Marcus falls silent, and now I can barely stand to look at him. He looks at me with so much love, and I don't know if I know what to do with it right now. I want to be able to accept it unconditionally. I want to feel as fearless as I did five years ago. I want to be brave. It feels like I'm on the edge of this cliff, trying to convince myself that jumping is an excellent idea, that jumping off of a damn cliff with Marcus Roma will heal what happened five years ago and makes us whole.

"I saw you talking to Alex," I say, trying not to choke up, "and it was like…right before you left—do you remember? You were spending so much time with him, and that was great, I was happy for you. But there was something you weren't telling me, I could tell, and it felt like…I just know you started talking to Alex Wolfe, and then you left to go work for him, and you didn't want me anymore."

I take a deep breath. I still can't look at him.

"And I'm not…I'm not trying to bring it up again," I say. "I do want you to tell me why, Marcus, but only when you're ready. I want to understand. I need to understand. But I want it to be because you're ready to tell me. I want it to be because you feel like you can tell me."

Shit, I feel like I'm about to cry. The words "I want to be good enough" almost pass my lips, but I cut them off, strangle them in my throat, because I know that's not fair.

It's not fair to make it about me. He has to tell me because he wants to, not because I blackmail him into it.

And I have to forgive him because it feels right, not because I feel compelled to by how much I need him.

"I don't know how to fix this," I say.

"Damn," he says.

I finally let myself look at him, and he looks heartbroken. It hurts.

"You should be happy right now," he says. "And instead, what I did, it's still making you sad. Still."

"Marcus, that's not exactly what I meant."

"I only ever tried to do the right thing, and I destroyed so much," he says, shaking his head. His hands move around my waist, his eyes look up. "Lo, listen. I promise you—"

"Shut up a second," I whisper, and I put one finger on his lips.

What he just said, right there? That he only ever tried to do the right thing? That's the part where I need to have faith. That's what I've been circling around, in my weird, broken, tortured way. And now I'm having one of those moments, where things fall into place, where all my previous thoughts arrange in a pattern that suddenly makes sense.

I think, in a way, I always kind of expected Marcus to be infallible. That if he did something, it was deliberate; it was because he chose exactly that, and not because he'd made an error in judgment or a mistake. But that's ridiculous. No one can live up to that standard, even if the reason I thought he could was because he always had.

So I have this choice. I don't know if I'm ready to make it. The fear pounds in my chest like a caged beast, just screaming to get out, to wreak havoc over my heart, to rule the rest of my life.

Screw that.

I lick my lips and say, "Marcus, I'm just scared you're going to leave again. That's it. I don't… I want you to be able to tell me what happened, but the truth is that's not what drives me. What drives me is that I'm terrified. I can't stop myself from loving you, I can't stop myself from needing you, I can't stop myself from wanting you. I'm yours, Marcus, even if it's not good for me. And then I see you talking to Alex, and I think, That's it, he's gone. And I can't take it again. So if that's what's happening, I have to find a way to—"

He doesn't let me finish. Marcus takes my hands in his and says, "I can't ever leave you again, Harlow. I'd be leaving my heart behind. It would kill me this time."

Full stop.

His face is steady. Serious. His eyes look straight into mine, and I know. It's so stupid, but I do, I know. I know he's telling the truth.

And that's when I jump off that cliff.

"I believe you," I say softly. "And I do forgive you, Marcus, even if you don't want me to. I hope you can forgive me, if I've ever failed you."

This look flashes across his face, like he's been stricken with something, and then he's standing over me, lifting me to my feet. He holds me so delicately, so carefully, I feel like he knows how hard that was for me. Like I've been broken for so long, and I've only just trusted him to catch me as I fall, and he knows it. He knows it.

"Thank you," he says. "Thank you for letting me love you."

I smile a little at that and shrug. "I do what I can."

Marcus grins back, his fingers tracing the edge of jaw, down to my neck.

"Keep doing it," he says.

His fingertips dance across my collarbone to the spaghetti straps of this slinky little dress and he starts to drag them down over my shoulders. Suddenly he stops, just as he's holding my dress up by the tips of his fingers.

"I don't deserve you, Lo," he says. "But I will."

Marcus kisses me, his lips warm and soft against mine, and lets my dress fall to the floor. He pulls away gently as he starts to touch me, softly, tenderly, his fingers feather light. He wants to watch me. I want to watch him.

This feels different, all over again.

Every time we've been together since he came back there's been this uncertainty in the background. This pain, this fear haunting me, this thing that would only be temporarily pushed to the corners of my mind by the way Marcus could make me feel when he touched me. But the fear would always come back. I always knew it would come back.

This time it's gone.

There's nothing here but us. Nothing between us, nothing hanging over us.

Marcus puts his hands on my naked body and I am truly bared to him. Not in the middle of sex, not in the middle of an orgasm, not because I need to feel something other than what I've been feeling. Just because it's him. He swallows, and for the first time in years I think he looks nervous.

The last time he looked at me like this was the first time we had sex.

"I love you," he says.

"I know," I say. I realize I'm smiling, and I can't stop. I push his suit jacket over his big shoulders and I loosen his tie. I have him out of his clothes in what feels like the longest minute of my life, and when he's finally naked in front of me, I start to tingle. It starts at my extremities and works it's way in, and in just a few seconds I'm actually bouncing up and down a little bit, just eager to touch him.

Marcus looks down, and I hear that telltale rumble in his chest.

I have about a second before he has me flat on my back, my legs wrapped around his waist, my arms around his neck. I'm laughing with just sheer joy, feeling free, lighter than I have in years, and by the time he looks up from playing with my breasts, I can see that he's just as giddy. Just as happy. And that fills me with happiness all over again.

"Jesus, I love you," he says. Like he's discovering a new species, or a new element. "So much."

"I know," I say again, and kiss his nose.

"No," he says, quietly. "But you will."

And it's changed again; it's shifted. Like it did years ago. He parts my thighs and enters me slowly, achingly slowly, watching my eyes every second. And this time I don't need to shy away from this tenderness, I don't need to be overwhelmed with sexual release to let it wash over me. I can just let him in. And when I do, it's like that first time again. All the things I've felt about Marcus, all the pain, all the loss, all the love, all of it comes to the surface, all of it comes together in one beautiful whole, and I realize that he's changed me again. I hadn't known how to forgive before. I'd never forgiven myself, or the world, or anyone for the pain that I'd felt or the people that I'd lost. But now, maybe I can.

He's helped me grow again. We've helped each other. We belong to each other even more.

"You belong to me," I tell him.

Then he shows me that I belong to him.

19

MARCUS

I wake up with Harlow next to me, the morning sun shining in on her beautiful face, and all I can think is that one man doesn't deserve to be this lucky.

I watch her sleep, her face so peaceful and pretty, and I can't believe how dumb I was. I've been having that thought in general about the past five years, but today it's specific, too. I should have figured that talking to Alex Wolfe would make her afraid that I might leave her again.

All I wanted to do when I saw him there was head off a disaster. I saw Alex walk in the door like he was coming to war, like he was there just to screw it up and intimidate people, and I knew that now was the time. Harlow and Shantha didn't know they were poking a hornets' nest when they decided to go up against Alex and actually be successful at it, but it was pretty much the only thing I was thinking about at that fundraiser. Just waiting for the other shoe to drop.

Feeling like a scumbag for not telling Lo all about it, too.

But I couldn't tell her. That's one of those threads where if I'd let her get at it and she had started to pull, the whole thing would start to unravel. She'd find out everything too soon, and she'd flip, and then she'd be a real threat to Alex Wolfe and he'd go after her. That's the thing I've been trying to prevent.

So I didn't tell her.

Again.

And she forgave me anyway.

I can't convey how much that blows my mind. Not knowing why I left, not knowing what choice I made, not knowing why I still refuse to tell her, not knowing about what Alex Wolfe is capable of — and still, she just decided to believe me. Decided to put her faith in me. Again.

I don't deserve her. I don't think there's a man on this Earth that deserves her, though I understand I might be biased in that assessment, but I know for damn sure that I don't deserve her.

So I'll work on it.

I'm still watching her sleep. I smile, thinking about how if she woke up to this, she'd laugh and call me creepy, but she'd still know that I'll always watch over her. And it's right then that I realize what my mistake has been all these years.

I hid things from Harlow in order to protect her. In order to give her the life she wanted. But that meant I made choices that I thought were best for her without even thinking about the fact that they weren't my goddamn choices. Or at least not only mine.

I don't know if it's because I got used to doing things for her, to looking out for her, when things got really bad after her parents passed. Or maybe that's just the best excuse that I can come up with. But I'm a grown man now, and I'm done making childish mistakes.

This is when I resolve to tell her everything.

And I'm perfectly happy just lying there, watching her sleep like a total sap, waiting for to her wake so I can tell her all this stuff, when my phone buzzes.

It takes me a second to figure out where it's coming from, but eventually I find my pants on the floor. I take just a moment to look back at Harlow, lying naked and gorgeous in the growing light, and smile just once more at my life.

And then I check my phone.

Brison.

I knew it. Alex wants a deal. I'm skeptical that he'll play fair, and just leave Harlow's neighborhood alone, but you never know. Redemption comes at the unlikeliest times. I should know.

"Brison," I say into my phone. I keep my voice down, even though there's no point. Lo sleeps like the dead, and needs her eight hours to feel human. Still, I don't want to disturb the scene. She looks so happy.

"We want to talk," Brison says.

"Good. When?"

"Now," Brison says. "Outside."

I frown. Pretty much the only thing that could get me to leave this bedroom right now is the prospect of coming back with something that will make Harlow happy, but that doesn't mean I have to enjoy it.

I hang up the phone and pull on the suit pants I had on the night before, throw on the jacket. I look ridiculous, but who cares? I'm about to get my girl everything she wants.

I'm actually smiling as I head down the stairs.

Brison's there, in a town car, across the street. Idling like he's some New Jersey mob guy, this serious expression on his face just barely visible through the tinted windows. I smile to myself because I think he must know they're beat.

I jog across the street, still happy, and rap on the window just to wake Brison up before I open the door and slip inside. Brison gives me a once over, taking in my shirtless suit style, and shakes his head.

"This is not Miami," he says.

I laugh. "Fuck off."

Brison pulls back into the street in silence.

"Where's Alex?" I ask him.

Brison shakes his head, and for the first time I notice he has that little muscle in his jaw that stands out when he gets pissed, just like I do. I can't resist goading him. I'm still pissed off that he came to the bar to talk to Harlow. That is a line that never should have been crossed.

"Still doing his errands, huh?" I say.

Brison's hands tighten on the wheel. I notice he's headed for the Brooklyn Queens Expressway, and I frown. That's farther than I thought we'd go, and I hadn't planned to be away from Harlow that long.

"I'm taking you where I'm supposed to take you," Brison says through clenched teeth.

"So you don't talk?" I say. "You don't have a say?"

Silence.

"I don't get you," Brison says finally.

"Why?" I ask him. "Because I don't come around to intimidate women? Or because I don't do everything Alex Wolfe tells me to?"

Brison shoots me a look that would be lethal if it wasn't like looking into a mirror. He says, "You're here now, aren't you?"

For some reason those words hit me hard. I ball my hands up, knowing they're itching for a fight, but it's only because those words reminded me of what Harlow told me last night. That the way she sees it, Alex Wolfe shows up, and I disappear. Alex Wolfe comes calling, and I leave.

That's not what this is. But I can't pretend it never happened.

***

Alex didn't let the subject of Harlow drop for long. It took me a while to figure out that Alex really did have plans for me, and that he must have had those plans for a while. He was never going to let me go on being Juan Roma's son forever, but Juan dying maybe got him to press fast forward a little bit. Or maybe it was Harlow who got him all panicky. Either way, he stepped up the pressure.

Those dinners out, they became more like interviews.

What were my interests in business? What were my strengths? All this stuff I'd only ever thought about in the abstract, figuring it would take me a lifetime of work to get to the point where anyone gave a crap about what I thought or what my interests were.

It's difficult to adjust to the idea of having a parent who cares about you. I guess a part of me didn't trust it. Seemed too good to be true, you know? But Alex, man, he was smart. He knew that. He started slow.

And he kept asking about Harlow.

Just poking around a little bit. Did I see a future with her? Hell yes. What other family did she have? None that cared. What were her prospects?

What the hell did that even mean? I didn't have prospects until Alex Wolfe showed up and told me I did.

One evening he came to pick me up at the gym, walked in in a three-piece suit, said hi to Pops. Looked at me like he was making a decision, the way a bookmaker might look over a horse, thinking, does he have what it takes. Then he says, "Ok, we'll talk."

What? Man, I'd just been working the speedbag. I had no idea what he meant.

"What are you talking about?" I asked him.

"Get dressed. I have an offer for you."

I won't deny I got a rush from that. As I said before, I am not proud of it, but I will admit to weakness when I have it, and knowing Alex Wolfe thought me capable of things made me feel important. Made me feel good. Like I said, I was young and dumb. Naïve.

So I went out with Alex. I watched him eat his steak and creamed spinach, getting more worked up by the second, thinking about all the things I could do for Lo and me with a real job, a real future. Thinking I could buy a house for us, maybe, if Harlow didn't want her parents', or thinking I could hire a lawyer and get custody of Dill. Thinking I could fix all the problems by myself.

"I have a job for you," Alex said, slicing into that steak, watching it bleed. Jesus, the things you remember. He looked over at me while he let that steak bleed all over the plate. "I want you to go California."

"California?"

Like I said, I was kind of dumb. I sat there thinking about how I was going to get Harlow out to California with me. I'd have to find a way to get Dill.

"California," Alex said again. "I have a project out there I could use your help on. Row houses, tracts of land, the city being a little bitch. I want you to learn the business."

I remember smiling. I didn't have a poker face at all back then.

"You'd be out there to learn, Marcus, at my expense," Alex says, eying me, taking a sip of his red wine. "No distractions. You'd be out there by yourself."

Slowly it fell into place. What he was really saying was "without Harlow."

"No," I said. "Can't do it."

Alex didn't hear no very often. You could see it on his face, working out whether or not I'd really just said that, figuring out how to respond to it. It was like a foreign language to him. In retrospect, kind of funny.

All he said in the end was, "I see."

But of course that wasn't the end of it.

It kind of took me a little while to get used to the idea that Alex thought of Harlow as a burden. As someone who wasn't going anywhere, who was trouble in any way, shape, or form. I didn't deal with it for a while as a legitimate problem beyond that first day when he talked about her in a disrespectful way and I just thought that was how he was with women, but only because I didn't really believe it. It was like he'd told me the sky was green. He was just wrong, and eventually he'd have to see that.

But slowly I realized that Alex wasn't kidding. He really didn't think Harlow was good enough for his son.

He saw her as a threat.

And once I figured that out I got pissed off all over again, no matter how much he tried to convince me to take that job in California. No matter how much money he offered me. No matter how much stock in his company he gave me.

"I stay with her, Alex," I said to him over another fancy dinner that tasted like ash in my mouth. He was starting to make me sick. "Or she comes with me, one or the other. I go where she goes. Don't pick a fight you're not going to win."

Hindsight is twenty-twenty, right? That was probably the worst thing I could have said to him. But I didn't know that until Alex Wolfe came back with his counter offer.

***

Brison and I have been driving in silence now for a good twenty minutes, getting farther and farther away from Harlow. Every exit we pass in the wrong direction is putting me more on edge, and I can see the vein in Brison's forehead pulsing, and I know this car is about to explode.

"You really prepared to tell the old man to go fuck himself?" Brison finally says.

"Yeah," I say. "I'm prepared to do a lot worse than that, depending on what he does next. Where are we going, Brison?"

"Jesus," Brison says, and pulls off the highway on some no-name exit surrounded by old warehouses and empty lots.

I tense up. This doesn't look right.

"Brison," I say. I'm ready to fight him in this car. I know I can take him; Brison's about my size, a strong guy, but he was never a fighter. I'd rather do it outside, though.

"He was going to pick you, you know," Brison says, still gripping the steering wheel hard, even though we're no longer moving. He's pulled into a parking lot next to a warehouse. No one's around.

"He still might pick you, even after all this, if you do what he wants," Brison says. He's getting angrier and angrier. I can't blame him. I know exactly what he's talking about.

Alex has put Brison and me in competition with one another ever since I went out to California. He let it be known that it was open season, that we'd have to fight for the right to be his heir. His daughter, the sister I don't know at all, a woman named Colette—she wanted none of that, got the hell out.

See, Colette is smart.

Brison and I aren't.

And I won. It kills him. I can see it in his white knuckles, his nostrils flaring like a damn bull's, that vein still pulsing away in his forehead like he's about to give himself a stroke.

"You have been fighting me for this for five years," Brison is saying. "I don't fucking believe you're giving it up."

"Brison, why'd you take me out here?" I say. "Where's Alex?"

My hand is on the door.

"Why?" Brison shouts. He hits the steering wheel with the palm of his hand and turns on me. "Why the hell would you give it all up for some woman?"

That's the moment when I go from hating my half-brother to pitying him.

"I hope you understand one day," I tell him. "For real, I do."

Brison blinks and looks at me with that vacant, 'no one's home' look, like I just popped him one. I don't think he's had a whole lot of experience with people wishing him well for no reason at all.

"I'll be damned," he finally says, sitting back in his seat and letting his hands drop.

"Where is Alex?" I ask him again.

"Marcus," Brison says, starting the car back up. "Alex was never coming. My job was just to get you out of the house."

Everything stops. Then:

There's my hand flying out to grab Brison's neck.

There's my pulse roaring in my head.

There are a million bad thoughts running through my mind.

"Let me take you back," Brison chokes out. I have him pinned back against the window, my right hand cocked, my left on his throat. "He's not going to hurt her, Marcus, he's not stupid. Just let me take you back. He thinks you're going to be gone for hours."

I curse. Brison doesn't know this, but Alex doesn't have to lay a finger on Harlow to hurt her.

"Go," I tell him. "You better hope you're right."

20

HARLOW

I wake up knowing something is wrong.

Well, the first thing that's wrong is that I'm awake at all. Marcus kept me up practically all night, and not that I'm complaining about that—not at all—but I am someone who needs her sleep. Or at least someone who needs more Marcus, as soon as I get up.

And that's the second thing that's wrong. I'm alone in my bed.

Our bed.

Thinking about it like that makes me smile. I turn over, blinking my eyes against the sun streaming in through my window, and listen intently for what he's doing downstairs. I would not put it past him to make breakfast, and I'll admit: I'm intrigued.

But no. Nothing.

So here is when the anxiety starts. Just a little twinge in my stomach, not a full-blown freak out or anything, nothing I can't handle. And I know it's unreasonable. It's just like a muscle that I used to use every day that I've put on bed rest, and it's threatening to cramp up in protest. But I remind myself of what I realized last night, of what I've been in the process of realizing ever since Marcus came back into my life: I don't have to be afraid like that.

He has *not* left me.

Having faith in Marcus proves not to be so hard. But having faith in the universe as a whole is an altogether different skill. That one might take me a while.

Ok, so I decide to deal with it. I'll just go find him. I force myself out of bed, my body aching in the best of ways, and wipe the sleep out of my eyes. I do a survey.

His clothes are gone.

Check that: Most of his clothes from last night are gone. His suitcase is still here, and his shirt is exactly where I dropped it last night, but his pants and jacket and shoes—gone.

So…that's weird.

I roll off my bed and dig up some boy shorts and a tank top, thinking Marcus will probably take them right off again when he sees me, and it's when I'm hopping around the room with my foot caught in the shorts that I hear someone knocking on the door. No, more like banging. Pounding.

He's locked out? How would that even…?

I pad toward the stairs, running a hand through my tangled hair, already smiling, thinking about what I'm going to ask him to do to me when I see him, when I hear the door open. So I hurry up, bouncing down the stairs, excited to see my man.

And I find Alex Wolfe standing in my foyer. Looking up at me.

Smiling.

***

I am no stranger to the extremities of emotion. Having your parents die unexpectedly at a relatively young age will familiarize you with a whole bunch of things you'd rather not know about, especially if you're already highly strung. But, once you've been through that ringer once, it's nice to be able recognize something bad when you can feel it coming. It helps you prepare when you know what it is.

Unfortunately, sometimes it also triggers a memory.

For me, it's physical at first. Seeing Alex Wolfe like that, smiling up at me like a predator, in my home… I don't know exactly why I get this feeling of being hunted, of being cornered, with the world about to fall down in flames around me, but I do. I recognize it as "impending doom."

I've only felt it a few times. When my parents died, when Marcus left, when Dylan had me cornered in a bathroom.

I mean, technically, Alex Wolfe should be no more than Marcus's father, to me. If anything, I should have a positive association with the man, considering his involvement, however shady, with helping me gain custody of Dill. I know I owe him everything.

But my body doesn't know that. My actual, physical body? It sees Alex Wolfe, and it says, "You're about to lose everything."

It takes everything I have to keep that under control. I feel it in my stomach first, this roiling nausea that heats me up from the inside until I can feel the anxiety start to burn through my skin, start to make me sweat. I grip the handrail of the stairs and try to ride it out.

But then comes the memory.

And the memory I most associate with this feeling of impending doom is what I can remember, however little, of the day I lost my parents.

It felt like dying.

I felt like this, sick, and like I was suffocating in the feeling, unable to catch my breath. It would slam into me and I'd fight, struggle for a while, trying to breathe in the thick, choking air, and I'd catch hold of Marcus, clinging to him like a piece of driftwood. I'd have a few moments like that, panting, heaving, crying, feeling grateful that that feeling had passed, and then I'd remember that it was true, that this was reality, that this was actually happening, and it would start all over again.

So basically a much gentler version of Hell, punctuated by brief moments of respite in Marcus's arms.

What I try to think about when this feeling comes back is how I am grateful that I haven't had to deal with anything else truly terrible happening in my life. I am so much luckier than many women, especially women in my situation, who end up in foster care, however briefly. I know I don't have it so bad in the scheme of things, and I know that I'm just wired for anxiety, and that it's something I have to deal with. So I try to think about how lucky I really am, and I try to remember that, whatever it is, I can deal with it.

Alex Wolfe, with that blood-curdling smile on his face, is making it very difficult to do that.

"How did you get in?" I ask him. I haven't moved since I first saw him.

"It's not a very secure door," Mr. Wolfe says, shaking his head in disapproval. "It just opened with barely any pressure at all."

I go from hot to cold in an instant.

"You broke in?" I say.

"No, I wouldn't say that," Mr. Wolfe says. He's wearing a three-piece suit again, very dapper, even though it's the end of summer. "The door opened, and I came in to make sure you were all right, Harlow. That's how I would put it."

I'm confused. That sounds a whole lot like the kind of breaking in that I would never be able to prosecute anyone for.

I feel a flash of fear, but I dismiss it as just my anxiety. As the ghost of fear from the last time I felt anxiety about losing everything like this. It's just my own issues, my own memories, messing with me again.

Or maybe it's just easier to think that I'm overreacting than it is deal with what's actually happening, which is that Alex Wolfe has broken into my house and he looks angry.

"Mr. Wolfe," I say, carefully making my way down the stairs. "I saw you at the fundraiser last night. I just want to say that I'm sorry if this causes you any inconvenience."

Mr. Wolfe raises his eyebrows, putting one hand to his chest in mock disbelief.

"Why should you be sorry, Harlow?" he says. "You won the battle."

This is his charming face. Suddenly I can see the family resemblance in that broad smile, the strong jaw, the light eyes, and I think of Marcus. And I tell myself that they must have more in common than just a great smile. After all, this is the man who stepped in and helped me get custody of my little brother. He can't be as scary as he seems right now.

"Thank you, Mr. Wolfe, but…" I hesitate. I've never spoken to him about this in explicit terms because I didn't want to jeopardize it, especially if Mr. Wolfe's influence on the custody case was less than aboveboard — which, let's be honest, of course it wasn't aboveboard.

But it's time.

"Mr. Wolfe, I know you got me Dill," I say. "I never understood why, but please believe me that I've always, always been grateful. I don't know, I guess I thought you took an interest because of Marcus, or… It doesn't matter. The point is, I know I owe you everything, and I can never repay that. And that's why I'm sorry."

I'm surprised to find I actually am starting to tear up. There's something cathartic about expressing gratitude, about apologizing. I've been carrying this debt around for so long, not knowing what I did to deserve such kindness, and therefore half-terrified that it would be taken away at any moment, that simply saying thank you has always felt impossible.

But I have to do it.

"Thank you," I say. I swallow back the tears, press my lips together. "Thank you," I say again.

And Alex Wolfe laughs.

"Don't thank me yet, little girl," he says, walking into my living room. "We're not done."

I'm starting to think my sense of danger isn't all that off. I'm starting to think maybe this isn't about memories after all.

"What do you mean?" I say, following him. Mr. Wolfe has sprawled out on my couch like he owns it.

"What I did to get you custody, Harlow, was bribe the judge," he says, putting both arms back on the couch. He looks comfortable. "It wasn't hard. It wasn't even very expensive, given the favors Judge McPhereson owed me at the time. Your brother cost me less than ten thousand dollars, Harlow, you know that?"

I'm speechless. I'm standing barefoot in front of the man who's responsible for giving me my family back, and he's telling me it was cheap. I don't know how to react.

Mr. Wolfe doesn't seem bothered. He spies a piece of lint on his pant leg and flicks it off, still talking.

"And what's more, Harlow—and this is probably the most pertinent point," he says, looking back up at me to make sure I'm paying attention, "but it would cost me about as much to take him away again."

Oh God.

I can feel his words begin to wind their way through my system, shutting my awareness of everything else down. Everything else becomes nonessential. Everything but what he's just said.

He could take Dill away.

"You really need a new couch," Mr. Wolfe says, shifting his weight.

"What are you talking about?" I whisper. "Taking Dill away? You can't take him away."

"Oh yes, I can," he says, standing up to his full, impressive height. He's not as tall as Marcus, but he's still over six feet, and he knows it. He makes me feel small. "I'm talking about the very many judges I happen to know very well. I'm talking about how easy it would be to have a social worker come around and make an unfavorable report about Dill's care."

Mr. Wolfe sneers at me and spreads his arm wide.

"This house, Harlow, it's falling apart. You just had to have the septic system replaced," he says, giving me a knowing, nasty look, "but who knows what else could go wrong? Who knows what Dill's exposed to? You work late hours for little pay in a trashy little bar with no hope of a future and you bring strange men around the house. Strange men with questionable ties to certain criminal elements."

Mr. Wolfe is getting angrier the more he talks. I'm having trouble following his words through my shock. I can't get past the mortal panic of having him tell me he could take Dill.

"You're the criminal element," I say when I can get my mouth working again.

Mr. Wolfe smiles again and shrugs. "Yes. So? The 'element' in that phrase is important. Means they can't prove anything. But they can take your brother away. Especially if I pay them enough. And Harlow, you're looking a little out of it right now, so let me be completely clear: You drop this little project of yours of saving a dying fucking neighborhood and you accept my offer for this shithole of house, you leave my son alone, or I make sure little Dillinger goes to foster care and you don't see him again until he's eighteen."

I stare at him. I'm numb. The world around me is still and unmoving, and I can't even feel the panic anymore.

"Harlow," Mr. Wolfe snarls at me, "do you understand?"

"You can't do that," I say flatly.

"I can, and I will. I'm done playing with you, little girl," he says, and he comes closer, looming over me with his face twisted up into this ugly mask of anger, and now the resemblance to Marcus is the thing I find scariest about this. It's a face that looks like Marcus, but with the expression of Dylan, when he pinned me in that bathroom.

I recoil in horror, my body jumping away, and Alex Wolfe pounces. He grabs my wrists and easily holds me motionless. At his mercy.

Alex Wolfe puts that face close to mine and says, "I indulged this little fantasy for the sake of my son, so that he could get it out of his system once and for all, but I can see now that I need to step in. This is over."

"Marcus won't let you do this."

Mr. Wolfe laughs. It's a different laugh, and some faraway, analytical part of my brain recognizes that this is his genuine laugh, not the one he uses to convince people he's a good person.

He laughs at me, and then he looks me up and down, and I can feel his cold eyes raking over my body, and it makes me feel dirty. Exposed.

"I can see why he keeps coming back, I'll give you that," he says. The feeling of his skin against mine makes me want to throw up. "But you're not good enough for him, Harlow. You're just some trash from the neighborhood, and Marcus is special. He's meant for more than this."

"You don't know anything about us," I say. My voice is coming back. So is my anger. "Marcus will not let you do this."

Alex Wolfe laughs again, a horrible sound. "Look around you. Do you see him here? I pulled him off this job, Harlow. Just like he did what I told him to five years ago, he did what I told him to today. He's gone."

Each word falls on my chest like a physical blow. Each word takes something out of me. I can't argue with him.

Marcus isn't here. Marcus is gone. Marcus did what I always feared, and left. The pressure of that old fear rising up inside me is unbearable, and I almost, almost give in. I can feel it wearing me down.

But damn it, Marcus deserves better.

"No," I say. My voice is so small. It sounds desperate. I don't know if I believe it.

"Yes," Alex sneers. He leans in like he's going to kiss me, holding me so I can't move, can't get away, and I turn my head away and close my eyes. I feel his hot breath on my cheek as he says, "Now sign the fucking papers or I will destroy your little life."

21

MARCUS

This car is too damn slow.

I'm gripping the door handles, the dashboard, anything, my whole body tense and primed to explode. Alex is alone with Harlow. I don't know that I believe Brison that Alex won't touch her. Five years ago I would have believed it, if only because I didn't know him.

Now?

I know what he's capable of.

I should have figured it out then. I shouldn't have made excuses for him. Shouldn't have thought that I'd be able to outsmart him.

Five years ago, after I'd told Alex Wolfe that Harlow and I were a package deal and I wasn't going anywhere without her, he came back at me with a new offer.

He didn't bother to take me out to dinner for this one. Just drove me around in a car like the one I'm in now. Said it all so matter-of-factly.

"You go out to California," he said to me, "And you forget about that girl, you stop all contact, and I'll make sure she gets custody of her little brother."

"What?" I said.

Like I didn't understand. Probably because I didn't. In a fundamental way, I didn't understand that people could be like this.

"You heard me," he said. "I'll talk to Judge McPhereson down at the club. I'll fix it. I'll pay for the lawyer. All she has to do is show up and she'll get her brother. But I fucking mean it, Marcus. You drop her completely," he said, looking at me with this intensity, like he'd let the mask fall. Then he leaned back and said, "You'll thank me later."

I wish I could say I had reacted all nobly and everything. That I'd fought him outright, told him to pull the car over, the whole thing. But I think that even then he'd started to rub off on me. Because I was thinking of the angles. Already, I was thinking I could find a way to play him.

Because if I could do this thing for Harlow? Man, that was the Holy Grail. Reuniting her family meant more to her than anything else in the world, so it meant more to me than anything else in the world. I really saw it like that, so damn simple. And I really thought I could play Alex Wolfe.

What I told him was, "I'll think about it."

And he smiled.

What I was thinking? I was thinking I'd do this, figure out a way to get what I wanted, get Dill in her custody, then go back to Harlow. What could he do, take Dill back? I figured I'd handle it. I figured maybe over time I could convince him that Harlow and I were the real deal, that he'd come to accept it, see that he was crazy for thinking she was a loser with no future. That he'd see that Harlow wasn't holding me back, but was the only thing that ever held me up.

I thought a lot of things. But mostly, I thought: I'll get her Dill. I'll get her Dill, and somehow it will all work out.

Like I said, I was dumb.

A few things I didn't figure on: finding out that my father, Alex Wolfe, was a ruthless, brutal, vindictive psychopath. He had legitimate businesses, too, plenty of them, but he ran all of them like a damn criminal. And he punished people who angered him, punished them violently, permanently. Sometimes he had me punish them. He liked to brag about how hard I could hit.

And he had an equal opportunity policy when it came to women.

I could handle him threatening me. And I fought back. I took out my anger on him routinely, let him know exactly what I thought. I think this is why Alex respects me more than the son he raised himself, because I'm willing to go toe to toe with him, unafraid. Willing to risk my neck.

But I could never risk Harlow.

I'd think about telling Alex I was done, I was gone, that I was going right back to her and being done with it—and then I'd think about what he might do to her. What he'd told me he did to the loved ones of people who betrayed him. And it was always enough to pull me back from the edge, to get me thinking that I had to plan, to make sure I had enough dough, enough leverage, enough juice to protect Harlow Chase from my father.

And then the arrogant son of a bitch decided to get involved with a development in the old neighborhood and took the opportunity to test my loyalty as it came. Put me in a position where I could choose him or Harlow.

This time, Alex was dumb. I was always going to choose Harlow. I had never chosen anything but Harlow. And the second I saw her again, it was over. It's been over. I've just been on borrowed time, trying to figure things out.

And now I'm racing down the B.Q.E. with Brison, trying not to lose my head, trying to stay one step ahead, trying to figure out what the vicious son of a bitch is going to do next.

I look over at Brison. I realize he didn't have to do this. I have no idea why he is helping me. But maybe he'll help some more.

"What chip is he going to play?" I say through clenched teeth.

"Something to do with the kid," Brison says.

I grind my teeth and feel my heart beating in my hands like a war drum. Dill. Of course he's going to go after Dill.

And Harlow will do anything for Dill.

Brison pulls onto Harlow's street and I'm already out the door, running toward her house. I'm furious. I'm furious at Alex, and I'm furious at myself for letting this happen. For letting it go on. For not being good enough to find another way.

When I see the front door hanging open, my sanity starts to shred, peeling away from me as I race toward the house. I keep thinking about how Harlow said she forgave me, how she said she believed in me. How I said I'd protect her.

It's not rational, but if he's hurt her, I'll kill him. I really will.

"Harlow!" I shout as I burst through the door.

I turn around and see them, see Harlow, crying, looking small and scared, and my father standing over her, his face twisted up.

He. Has. His. Hands. On her.

"Get the fuck away from her!" I yell.

I charge at my father, but he's already backing away, he's already let Harlow go, and so all I can see is her. All I can see is Lo, sad and confused, and looking up at me like she's just lost everything all over again.

"Did he hurt you?" I ask her.

Harlow blinks. I can see her hands are shaking, and I take them in my own. I kiss her hands, and then wordlessly I turn around, and find Alex cowering in the corner.

I take a step towards him.

"Marcus, I've tried to be reasonable. I'm just here to talk."

I take another step.

"Marcus," he says, softly. "You're my son."

One more.

"Damn it, you ungrateful fuck, I only want what's best for you!" Alex shouts. He sounds desperate, angry, upset, evil.

I hit him in the stomach.

I watch my father buckle, watch his face twist in disbelief, watch him feel the pain he had me dole out for five years for the first time. I feel the anger over all those years swelling inside me, I feel the monster Alex Wolfe turned me into start to take control, and I know I'll beat him to death for hurting Harlow, I'll do it right fucking here.

And then I feel Lo's hand on my arm, and the monster is gone. Just like that. I remember what's real, what's important.

I turn around and reach for her, just needing to feel her against me. I didn't know how panicked I was until I feel her arms around my neck, until I breathe her scent in, until I know she's still mine, she's breathing, she's ok.

Oh Jesus, what I've almost lost.

"Don't hurt him," Harlow says. "Marcus, promise me."

"I promise," I say. I can't deny her a goddamn thing.

And it's good she made me promise, because what she says next would have set me off.

"He says he's going to take Dill away," she says softly. "He says you were only ever here to get me to sell—"

Fuck that fucking scumbag fuck.

I pull back so I can look her in the eye, so she knows I'm not lying, so she knows the truth of what I feel. I have never felt this desperate in my damn life.

"I swear to you, Lo, that is not true—"

Harlow shakes her head, tears starting to spill onto her cheeks.

"I *know* that, Marcus, but he's going to take Dill!"

Part of me wants to laugh. I can't believe how amazing she is, that she didn't doubt my intentions, even given every damn reason in the world to think I was scum. But she's scared and panicked, and it's not the time. I squeeze her hands in mine.

"No, he's not," I say. "I promise you."

Our eyes meet, and for a second everything is calm. Everything is right. I know she loves me, and I know I'll do whatever I have to do be worthy of it, and I know she knows it.

"Lie to me," she says.

"Don't have to."

And that's when I turn on back on my father. He's only just now getting off the ground, his hand to his stomach, his face pale. He meets my gaze, and for the first time he looks like he doesn't know what to do, like he's not sure what's happening. Good. Let him squirm.

"Did you tell her?" I ask him.

He can't speak. Just looks at the floor. Pathetic.

I look back at Harlow, the only person in the room who matters, and I just lay it out, as simply as I should have years ago.

"You remember that birthday when I made that crappy ravioli? You remember what you told me?" I ask her.

I can see she remembers. She's just speechless for a second, her mind working a few steps ahead of mine, the way it always does. Finally she says, in this really tiny voice, "I told you I wanted Dill."

"Right. And I could see it on my own, Lo, the way you worried about him. You needed to have your family together. And then Alex kept coming by, trying to get me to go to California. And when I said I wouldn't go without you…"

She's stopped crying. I don't know if that's good or bad, if I'm about to get my ass kicked or what, but I can't stop now. I wipe the last tear off of her cheek and tell her.

"He said he'd get you custody of Dill if I left you behind. And if I didn't, you probably weren't ever going to get custody. I thought I'd figure out a way out of it, but..."

Shit. I might as well not beat around the bush. "I was dumb, and then I was a coward about it, and I never should have made those decisions for you."

"Marcus," she says. She's shaking her head rhythmically, back and forth, back and forth, her eyes bright and blue and wide. I can see her trying to find the words, but she doesn't have to. I already know.

I guess it's a lot to take in.

And I'm lost in her until I hear Alex's voice.

"Marcus, listen to me," he says, clearing his throat. He's sitting on the couch now, still looking like might throw up. He sounds different, not like I've heard him before. But I guess I've never seen him lose, either. And he knows he's beat if I've turned on him. I can hear it in his voice when speaks.

"Marcus, you can't throw it all away. Everything you've worked for the past five years. You can't. I won't give my company to a man who does this."

But when I turn around, I don't see what I expect. I don't see the conniving, vicious operator; I don't see an adversary. I see him looking panicked and crazy. I see what I know I looked like just minutes ago when I ran through that door.

My father, Alex Wofle, is begging.

I don't fall for it.

I choose Harlow.

"Listen carefully," I say. "I'm done. Harlow Chase is off-limits. Dill is off-limits. I don't give a shit what you do with the rest of your sorry ass life, but you do not touch them. You are done messing with this family, do you understand? Or I will burn you to the ground. Everything you've built, every crime you've committed—all of it. To the fucking ground."

Alex smiles weakly, like we're just negotiating, like this isn't deadly serious. I've got to make this crystal clear for him.

"Alex, look at me," I say. "*This* is my family. She is my family. Touch her, touch Dill, and it's over. I will go to the FBI. I will testify to every single damn thing I've seen you do, and everything I've done for you."

He looks at me, and smiles. He fucking smiles.

"Marcus, you're my son. Please. If you were going to do that, you would have done it years ago."

I freeze. I have to stop myself from hauling him up just so I can hit him again. The truth is, he's right—I could have done it, years ago. But he wouldn't have believed me. I wouldn't have believed me. Because I wasn't ruthless yet. I hadn't learned how to be vicious. I thought this is what I had to put up with for Lo and Dill. And I still believed there was a chance he'd one day give it up, that he'd change, that he wouldn't go after her, and I could be with Harlow.

I still believed that I could have it all. That Harlow could have Dill, and I could have her, and I could have a damn father, all at the same time.

I was dumb.

I look my father in the eye, and tell him the truth.

"It was always about Harlow, Alex. I was always doing this for Harlow. And I'll do worse than testify," I say. "If you go after them, I go after you."

And the next thing I see surprises me. I see Alex Wolfe looking at me, and understanding. I see him understand exactly what I mean, exactly how far I'll go. I see him understand that I belong, body and soul, to the woman standing behind me.

He doesn't know what to say.

I do.

"Get out," I say. "Before I throw you out."

"That won't be necessary," he finally says, getting up slowly. I don't think I hit him that hard. I think he's just shocked. Alex looks at me, and at Harlow, and he nods. He says, "You're my son, Marcus, whether you like it or not. That's why I believe you. So, all right. Hands off the Chases."

He smiles wryly at Harlow, and I ball my fists up, feel my back go up. I don't even want him to look at her.

"You won," Alex says to Lo. Then he looks at me and tells me, "And you're still my son."

I grit my teeth. I don't care what he says, what he thinks, how much pride he needs to save. As long as he walks out that door and never comes back. He looks at me. I look at him. This is my line in the sand.

I won't even give him the satisfaction of a goodbye.

He turns around, and for the last damn time, Alex Wolfe walks out of my life.

Out of our lives.

"Marcus," Harlow whispers.

It's not until he's out that door that I realize how hard I'm breathing, how my muscles ache to move, how much pure adrenaline is coursing through my veins. And it's not until he's gone that it's safe for me to feel anything but protective, but as soon as she speaks, as soon as I hear her voice and know she's safe, know she's mine, I see my future map out in front of me. For the first time, it's a good one.

I turn around and see her, my Harlow, standing there. Beautiful. Head up. Strong. And this look on her face, this look in her eyes, that I can't mistake for anything else. It's love, but it's also compassion.

The love of my life says, "Marcus, he's your father."

I cross the room, because I suddenly know that I won't breathe again until I can touch her. I put my hand up against her cheek and watch her lean into it, her eyes half-closed. She's the most beautiful thing on the planet. She's the best person I've ever known.

And there's something I need her to understand.

"You, Harlow, you're everything," I say. "You are my *everything*. You're the reason I learned how to laugh. You're the reason I learned how to be strong. You're the reason I learned how to be good. I am who I am because I found you. Because you let me love you."

Jesus, it feels good to say it.

Harlow's watching me, letting tears fall down her cheek and into my hand. She's smiling, but I can see, in those baby blues, she looks just how I feel. Like she can't believe she's living this moment. Like no one ever deserved to be this lucky. And I want her to know it's not luck, not for her. I'm the lucky one. I'm the luckiest man who ever lived, because I'm the one who gets to make sure she has the life she deserves.

"Lie to me," she whispers. "Tell me I'm dreaming."

"Don't have to," I say back. She smiles, and tries not to cry some more. I love her for that, too. "Everything I did, I did for you, Lo. Everything that I am, I am because I love you. And if you let me love you from now on, I will be better. I promise you. Every damn day, I will be better."

Harlow blinks back tears, shaking her head just so slightly. "Shut up," she says. "I love you just the way you are."

"That's good," I say. "Because you're mine."

"Yours," she says.

I look at Harlow's face, and see the best parts of who I want to be reflected there. I see the man she's made me. And I see the woman who holds my heart in her hands.

And I kiss her.

epilogue

HARLOW

Four months later...

I'm standing in my parents' old bedroom, by myself, and I have a decision to make.

When Marcus told me the truth about why he left, it changed everything. It didn't feel like it would, not at first. I mean, I'd already decided to forgive him, and I loved him, and honestly there wasn't anything he could have said that would have changed that. Obviously it hit me hard, right in the heart, to find out that he'd done all of this for me and Dill. That it had been about me and Dill, all the time. But there was so much going on that I don't think I fully felt it right away.

Some things take a while to grow, I guess.

It crept up on me at the weirdest moments. I'd be doing dishes or whatever, and I'd think of some random night back in high school when Marcus came by and surprised me while I was doing dishes, and instead of that memory leading inevitably to the end of Marcus leaving me—instead of reminding me that he'd crushed me, that he'd thrown me away—I thought about what he'd sacrificed for us, instead.

It changed everything.

Every memory, every feeling, every insecurity, every scar.

It took a while for that change to seep through me. That first week? There was a lot to take in. Alex Wolfe getting back in touch with Marcus, refusing to leave him alone, not wanting to let his son go. I guess that part is understandable. Marcus rejecting every offer Alex made, Marcus demanding the truth. Finding out that it really was Alex who had paid someone to break into my home to trash the place and scare me into selling. That it was Alex who had paid someone to sabotage my septic system, right after he came here and warned me that old houses like this always fall apart.

I should have been outraged—and wow, was Marcus furious—but all I remember thinking at the time was how much those stunts backfired. All they did was give me an excuse to let Marcus back into my life. As Marcus would say, I guess irony is a bitch.

So Marcus threw away his future with Alex Wolfe's company. Demanded that Alex buy out his equity, telling his father he wanted nothing to do with him. Telling him over and over again that if Alex ever did anything to threaten custody of Dill, Marcus would go to the police or the FBI or the SEC or whoever, and tell them everything he knew about everything Alex had ever done. That Marcus himself would take care of Alex. Etc. Etc.

That apparently hit home. Alex Wolfe looked like someone had knocked the life out of him, like he was about to shrivel up. If you'd told me that would happen, I might have thought I'd feel happy, but I didn't. All I felt was pity.

Slowly, though, the truth about what Marcus had done started to take hold within me, and I realized that I would have to change everything I thought or felt about the last five years. Every time I felt loss, or grief, or hurt because of

Marcus, now I know that he was feeling the same thing, on the other side of the country, completely alone—and he was doing it for me and Dill. He chose to go through that, knowing that I'd hate him, knowing that I wouldn't know why, and that he'd never get the credit for it.

And he did it because he loved me.

I like to think I would have been strong enough to do something like that for him. I hope I'll never have to find out.

Believe me when I say that I'm not holding it against him. He's right, that making a decision like that for me, without talking to me, wasn't fair. But it's hard for me to be mad at him for making a mistake about the exact way he planned to sacrifice for me. I mean, honestly. Only Marcus could continue to beat himself up for something like that.

Which: that is something I am working on with him. And he is getting better. He is starting to forgive himself for some of the things he's done. Every time I tell him how much I love him, and how proud I am of him, it seems to sink in a little bit more.

That's reason number one I'm standing in this empty bedroom that used to belong to my parents. I've pushed all the furniture out into the hall, except for the bed, which is in the middle, and covered with a painter's tarp. Then there's me, standing by myself with a couple of cans of red paint. I have no idea what I'm doing. Like, none at all. I don't even know what I was thinking. I was just speed-walking past the hardware store on my way home from the gym, not being used to the December cold yet, and I don't know what happened exactly, but some red decoration caught my eye.

I just knew something needed to change.

And now I'm second guessing myself, shaking. Wishing Marcus was here with me, and at the same time knowing I need to make this decision alone.

Marcus and Dill, by the way? Partners in crime. They're off together right now—when it snows heavily, Marcus has taken to doing these Rocky runs in McCarren park, where he tows Dill on this little plastic sled behind him. It always, always ends in a snowball fight, usually because Dill's been stockpiling snowballs the whole run and then mounts a sneak attack.

Watching the two of them together leaves me speechless, sometimes. Not just me, either. Maria has the same reaction. And she plans to stay in the area now that Marcus bought her house back from Alex at a steep discount, since the development plans were totally ruined, and basically gave it back to her for free. Anyway, the both of us are completely undone, watching Marcus with Dill. They already have their own private jokes, their own weird guy humor, and Marcus has been learning about video games, thinking seriously about investing. And what's more, I can see the happiness on Marcus' face. I can see him fall in love with us as a family, too.

It's like this whole new world has opened up for Dill just having another parent-type in his life. And as Shantha pointed out, pretty soon Dill's going to be dealing with girls, and my advice would have been crap. Marcus, on the other hand? Marcus is smooth, when he's not sacrificing five years of his life in secret.

"He got you back, didn't he?" Shantha said. "Took him what, a month?"

Yeah, can't argue with that.

Everything has come together. Shantha's bar, Maria's house, Marcus has even bought Pops' old gym. Marcus is grudgingly still talking to Alex, because I made him promise, even though he still won't let Alex anywhere near Dill and me. I can live with that for now, but I'm not going to let Marcus cut off contact with his father, not as long as Alex has a chance to change. And even though Marcus has rented an apartment nearby, he hasn't spent a single night there. Everything seems so perfect.

Which means I should be able to paint this damn room. And still my hand shakes.

It's just a coat of paint. I mean, it's not like I'm setting fire to the place or anything, but it feels...so permanent. And it's my parents' bedroom.

I kind of blame Dill for this. He came back from camp, not long after our showdown with Alex, and I told him all triumphantly that we wouldn't have to move and...his reaction could at best be described as indifference. I think he may have actually been a little disappointed.

It kind of took the wind out of my sails, a little bit. Had to think about it a bunch. Which was good, because I realized that I had just been treading water. Like, Dill? He doesn't have the same emotional connection this house, because he doesn't have the same emotional connection to the past in this house. Where for me, this place is...

It was full of ghosts, I guess. Full of the past. And so Dill being fairly indifferent made me realize two things: one, that I needed to start moving forward with my life. So I decided to go back to school, which Marcus is literally thrilled about—I've never seen anyone so excited about college. He keeps bringing me brochures.

And two, it made me realize that maybe this wasn't all about Dill. I mean, I don't think that eleven year old boys generally know what's best for them, and I do think it matters for Dill to be around people like Maria, but I had to confront the possibility that this was also about me. That I fought so hard and held on to this house so tight because I was fundamentally afraid of the future. I had been holding on for dear life for so long, trying not to let my past swallow me alive, that the past ended up holding me prisoner instead. I was afraid to let go of anything. It was like those nights I spent lying awake in my bed, too afraid to move or speak or even breathe, until Marcus lay down next to me.

I never even moved into the master bedroom. I still called it my parents' bedroom.

Which is why I am now standing here with a bucket of paint and some last minute nerves. Because I don't want this to be my parents' bedroom anymore. I want it to be our bedroom. I want it to belong to Marcus and me.

I want him to move in, for real.

If I'm honest, I want way more than that. I want him for the rest of my life. But there is a part of me that is still so anxious about pushing him too hard, about losing him again, even though I know it's crazy, I know in my heart that we fit together perfectly. So I know my anxieties and fears about this will fade with time, but for the moment, I can't even start painting. I definitely can't bring up marriage.

I keep standing motionless in the middle of the room even as I hear Marcus and Dill come in downstairs, unable to move. Even while I hear Dill tear through the kitchen, knowing he's going right for the Oreos and I should probably do something about that, even as I hear Marcus come up the stairs.

God, my heart is pounding.

I hear Marcus head to my bedroom — my old bedroom — and I hear the moment where he wonders why it's empty. Where he looks down the hall. And then I hear him walking towards me, and I'm starting to feel that surge of heat come over me.

"Baby, what're you doing?" he asks.

I turn around just as he comes up behind me, and I lean into his chest. He's sweaty from his Rocky run through the snow, but I love how he smells. I love how he feels against me, the way he wraps his arms around me, the way he nuzzles the top of my head. It's all perfect.

"You ok?" he says.

I nod into his chest and take a deep breath. Now or never.

"I'm painting this bedroom," I say.

"Yeah, that's what it looks like," he says. "Why?"

"Because I want it to be our bedroom." I look up to see this gentle smile on his face. A thought occurs to me. "You like red right? Oh man, I should have asked. I mean, 'ours', right? I should have asked. I can go back, get a different—"

"Shh," he says, and gives me a not so quick kiss. "I love red."

"Marcus," I say. I can hear the nervousness in my own voice. "It's not just about the paint."

"I know," he says. He's smiling, still. "Tell me."

Oh God, why is this so hard. I'm trembling. It's like I can feel this wonderful future just ahead of me, and all I have to do is not screw it up, and I am terrified I will choke. I'm terrified that I will say the wrong thing, do the wrong thing, and the universe will punish me for it and take him away again. It's so crazy. So I do the only thing that's ever helped when I feel like this: I look into Marcus' eyes.

And I see it all there. I see everything. I see how much he loves me.

"I want you to live here," I say. "I want this to be our home."

I can't quite say the rest. I can't quite say, please make me your wife. I'm not brave like he is, but oh man, I will take what I can get. And what I get is Marcus' smile, bright and big, and his strong arms squeezing me tight.

"I can do better than that," he says. He quickly kisses me on my bewildered forehead, and then shouts loud enough for Dill to hear, "Yo, Dillinger! It's time!"

It's what now?

"Be right there!" Dill yells back up.

Marcus must see my look of confused panic. He laughs.

"You know how I've been helping Dill with his homework?" Marcus asks.

I've always been skeptical of this. NASA couldn't help Dill with his homework, but Marcus and Dill have spent a lot of time at Dill's computer. I figured bonding is bonding.

"Yeah," I say. I'm wary.

"I haven't been helping him with his homework," Marcus confesses. I suppress a smile. "He's been helping me with something."

Oh, God, they've been plotting.

Just as my mind is spinning with all of the things these two could come up with together, Dill comes running in at that little boy speed, only this time he's carrying Marcus' laptop. I have to stop myself from lecturing Dill on running around with someone else's computer, but it's easy to do once I see how excited the little man is. Dill is actually bouncing up and down on the balls of his feet, grinning from ear to mischievous ear.

"What have you done?" I say. I almost don't want to know.

"C'mere," Marcus says, leading me over to the tarp covered bed. We all climb on top of it, Dill lugging the laptop along and setting it up in front of me.

"We made you a special game," Dill explains while he boots everything up.

"You did what?"

"You'll see," Marcus says.

"You have to play it to the end," Dill says, running the program. "I'll help if you want."

I open my mouth in mock shock. Like I'd need help. "Little booger," I say, and put him in a quick headlock before giving him a kiss on the top of his head.

Dill doesn't even complain about the kiss.

Something is definitely up.

I watch the computer screen while the game loads. It's got rudimentary graphics and music stolen from other famous videogames, which makes me smile. Dill did most of it himself then, and he did it quickly. But the puzzle is something different. My little character has to collect all these puzzle pieces with strange patterns on them and arrange them in a particular order, making what looks like a square with almost a barcode design on it. It's not too hard, but it's not easy, either.

Dill is smirking.

Finally I get the last piece, and then the music starts to change. Haltingly. Clumsily. But undeniably.

It's Mendelsshon's Wedding March.

I cover my mouth with my hands, afraid to speak.

The square has floated up off the ground in the little simulation, and now it's rotating around, like a rubiks cube, until the weird stripey patterns start to form letters.

It says, I LOVE YOU. MARRY ME.

"That's from Marcus," Dill says helpfully.

I look at Marcus, who's already looking at me. I can't look away from those eyes. I can't look away from the past that I see there, that past I wanted to run away from, and how, in Marcus' eyes, it's changing. It's all leading up to this. It's not something I need to run away from, or leave behind. It made me. It made him.

It made us.

"Dill, the ring," Marcus says. His eyes don't leave mine as Dill shoots out of the room, running at full speed. I can hear the little man rummaging around in his room, which, I'll be honest, has got to be the worst place to keep an engagement ring in the history of engagement ring hiding places.

But all I really see is Marcus.

Marcus, smiling. The corners of his beautiful, light green eyes crinkling, the dimple in his cheek deepening, the light shining on him. In him. He's happier than I've ever seen him. He pulls me toward him, his big hands gentle and strong, and then he touches the side of my face, so softly, so tenderly.

"I love you," he says, only this time it's a hoarse whisper.

I put my hand on his chest and grip his shirt, because I need something to hold on to. I feel like I'll blow away in the face of this, like I'll open my mouth and find my voice is gone, like I'm so happy that I'm afraid to speak.

"Lie to me," I finally say. "Lie to me, Marcus. I don't think I can handle this much happiness."

Marcus kisses me slowly, softly. I can always feel him in his kisses. It's reassuring, strong, loving.

"I'm not going to spend my life making you happy," he says, pulling away just enough that he can see my face. "I don't want to raise Dill as my own." He kisses me again, and I can feel the tears start to fall. "You don't make me a better man, every day, just because you let me love you." This time when he kisses me, I am crying, my tears wetting his face, his lips. "You aren't my whole heart."

"Marcus," I sob, burying my face in his neck. I can't help it. If I'm ever going to get over the feeling of being overwhelmed when good things happen, it will be because of him, but this is the best thing that's ever happened to me, and I'm falling apart.

"No, *you* are the best thing that's ever happened to me," I say, as though he's been reading my thoughts. He probably has.

"Is that a yes?" He's holding me now, comforting me, and I bet he's trying not to laugh at the same time. It grounds me, reminds me that I am kind of funny when I'm being serious. I love him for that, too.

"Oh my God, yes!" I say, clutching at his chest. "Please, yes."

I force myself to push off his chest, and hold his face with both hands, looking directly into his eyes. I want him to see what I saw. I want him to know.

I think he already does.

"Yes," I say again, and this time I kiss him.

The only thing that gets me to stop is Dill.

"Guys, that's gross," he says.

Marcus and I break apart laughing, and Marcus wipes the tears from my cheeks. Dill's standing right next to us now, fidgeting with a little blue box in his hands.

"You let him hold on to a Tiffany's ring?" I say, wide eyed.

"Were you going to look for it in his anime collection?" Marcus asks.

"It was my idea," Dill says, smiling again. He loves being right. "Can I do it?"

Marcus looks surprised, and then incredibly proud, looking at Dill. I feel it too, that swell in my heart. Dill wants us to be a family.

"What do you think, Lo?" Marcus asks.

I put my left hand out, grinning at both my boys. "I think somebody better ring me quick, before I lose my mind."

Dill grins and rips into the box, as eleven year old boys do, and I kind of laugh while I cringe, because, well, I should have seen that one coming. Marcus holds my hand. And just like that, Dill slips a giant freaking diamond onto my finger, Marcus holds me tight, and we have the beginnings of a family. Our own family.

"Are you going to cry?" Dill asks.

"Yes," I say, trying to keep the quiver out of my voice. "So?"

I expect Dill to roll his eyes, but instead he smiles, pushes his shaggy hair out of his eyes, and looks up at me kind of sheepishly.

"I guess it's ok this time," he says with a shrug.

"Oh yeah? C'mere, tough guy," Marcus says, and hauls Dill up for a one big monster hug, Marcus' giant arms encircling us both while Dill laughs and squirms away. And even though there's this slippery, mushiness-averse eleven year old telling us to stop being so lame, there is a moment when I know that I have something real. Something solid. Something that can't be taken from me.

I look at Marcus, and I know he's the one who's given this to me. He's given me this feeling, this sense that I'm connected to more than just Dill, that I really belong in this world. That what connects me to the people I love — to Marcus, to Dill, to Maria, to Shantha — is stronger than anything else this universe can hope to throw at me, and that

I don't need to live in fear that it will all be shattered at any moment. He's brought that back into my life.

He makes me safe. And I make him whole. And together, we're finally what we're meant to be.

THE END

A NOTE FROM THE AUTHOR

Thank you! I hope you loved Marcus and Harlow's story as much as I did. These two burrowed their way into my heart and just would not leave. I'm going to revisit them in the next book in this series, Brison's story, which will come out in 2014. If you want to get an email alerting you when my next book is available, you can sign up for my new releases list on my website, www.chloecoxbooks.com.

And I'd love to hear your thoughts on *Lie To Me*. You can connect with me on Facebook or email me at chloecoxwrites@gmail.com, or leave a review on Amazon or on Goodreads. I sincerely appreciate every review—I think they help other readers out, and I learn something with every review, too.

'Till the next book!

Chloe

CPSIA information can be obtained at www.ICGtesting.com
Printed in the USA
LVOW08s2343010915

452390LV00001B/169/P

Comparative Ethics Series /
Collection d'Éthique Comparée

Weaving Relationships
Canada-Guatemala Solidarity

Kathryn Anderson

*Donated by C. McPherson in
celebration of Susan DuMoulin's
Diploma of Christian Studies - V.S.T.
May 3, 2004*

With the hope that Canadian Memorial may continue in your vision of peace.
Kathryn Anderson
Aug. 2004

Published for the Canadian Corporation for Studies in Religion /
Corporation Canadienne des Sciences Religieuses
by Wilfrid Laurier University Press

2003

We acknowledge the financial support of the Government of Canada through the Book Publishing Industry Development Program for our publishing activities. We acknowledge the Government of Ontario through the Ontario Media Development Corporation's Ontario Book Initiative. We acknowledge a publication grant from The United Church of Canada.

National Library of Canada Cataloguing in Publication

Anderson, Kathryn, 1947–

    Weaving relationships : Canada-Guatemala solidarity / Kathryn Anderson.

(Comparative ethics series = Collection d'éthique comparée ; v. 7)
Includes bibliographical references and index.
ISBN 0-88920-428-4

    1. Church work with refugees—Guatemala. 2. Mayas—Crimes against—Guatemala. I. Canadian Corporation for Studies in Religion. II. Title. III. Series: Comparative ethics series ; v. 7.

BV4466.A53 2003   261.8'328'0897415207281   C2003-906449-2

© 2003 Canadian Corporation for Studies in Religion/
Corporation Canadienne des Science Religieuse.

Cover and text design by P.J. Woodland.

Every reasonable effort has been made to acquire permission for copyright material used in this text, and to acknowledge all such indebtedness accurately. Any errors and omissions called to the publisher's attention will be corrected in future printings.

∞
Printed in Canada

No part of this publication may be reproduced, stored in a retrieval system or transmitted, in any form or by any means, without the prior written consent of the publisher or a licence from The Canadian Copyright Licensing Agency (Access Copyright). For an Access Copyright licence, visit www.accesscopyright.ca or call toll free to 1-800-893-5777.

Order from:
WILFRID LAURIER UNIVERSITY PRESS
Waterloo, Ontario, Canada N2L 3C5
http://www.wlupress.wlu.ca

*To Josephina Inay vda. de Martínez,
who has served as mentor, inspiration, and guide
in my life journey and that of so many others.*

*To Wilf Bean,
my compañero, my life companion, whose love, support,
and wisdom has made this book possible.*

Photo by Valerie Mansour

Indian Tapestry

When I go up to the house of the Old Weaver
I watch in admiration
what comes forth from her mind:
a thousand designs being created
and not a single model from which to copy
the marvelous cloth
with which she will dress
the Companion of the True and Faithful One.

Men always ask me
to give the name of the label,
to specify the maker of the design,
But the Weaver cannot be pinned down
by designs,
nor patterns.
All of her weavings
are originals,
and there are no repeated patterns.
Her mind is beyond all foresight.
Her able hands do not accept patterns or models.
Whatever comes forth, comes forth,
but she Who Is will make it.
The colours of her threads
are firm:
blood,
sweat,
perseverance,
tears,
struggle,
and hope.
Colours that do not fade
with time.

The children of the children
of our children
will recognize the seal
of the Old Weaver.
Maybe then
it will be named,
But as a model,
it can never again
be repeated.

Each morning I have seen
how her agile fingers
choose the threads
one by one.
Her loom makes no noise,
and men
give it no importance,
and nevertheless,
the design
that emerges from Her Mind
hour after hour
will appear in threads
of many colours
in figures and symbols
which no one, ever again,
will be able to erase
or undo.

—Julia Esquivel, 1994

Contents

Prologue: Solidarity's Roots in a Refugee Camp ... xi
Preface ... xvii
Acknowledgments ... xxi
Introduction ... 1

I Setting Solidarity in Context
Map of Guatemala ... 8
1 A Brief Historical Overview ... 9
2 Maya Refugees—From Exodus to Return ... 21

II Weaving Threads of Solidarity
3 Project Accompaniment—A Canadian Response ... 37
   A: The Poor Accompany the Poor ... 37
   B: The Refugees Plan Their Return with Accompaniment ... 39
   C: Project Accompaniment Is Born ... 42

4 Accompaniment in War and Peace ... 57
   A: A Triumphant Return ... 57
   B: Crisis and Confrontation ... 73
   C: Life and Death in the Return Process ... 88
   D: Accompaniment after the Peace Accords ... 96

5 Project A Comes to a Close ... 101
   A: Making the Decision ... 101
   B: Unresolved Issues ... 104

6 The Christian Task Force on Central America in British Columbia ... 113
   A: Solidarity's Origins in Latin America and Canada ... 113
   B: Kindling the Vision in British Columbia ... 119
   C: The Christian Task Force Is Formed ... 123

7 Breaking the Silence in the Maritimes ... 131
   Phase 1: Network-Building 1988–1996 ... 131
   Phase 2: Strengthening Relationships 1997–1999 ... 141
   Phase 3: Forming a Covenant Relationship 1999– ... 147

x   Contents

III A Tapestry with Many Forms
8 New Forms of Solidarity ... 153
   - *A:* Building Public Awareness ... 153
   - *B:* Encounters with Guatemalans—Journeys North and South ... 156
   - *C:* Urgent Actions ... 161
   - *D:* Fairly Traded Crafts and Coffee ... 168
   - *E* Vigils ... 170
   - *F:* Advocacy and Lobbying ... 170
   - *G:* Security Accompaniment ... 175
   - *H:* Networking ... 179
   - *I:* Solidarity among Children ... 181
   - *J:* Solidarity among Youth ... 183
9 Solidarity's Creative Heart ... 189

IV The Spirituality of Solidarity and Its Challenges
10 Creating Relationships: The "Spirit" of Solidarity ... 199
   - *A:* Meaning and Spirituality ... 199
   - *B:* A Spirituality Forged through Relationships ... 200
   - *C:* Implications of a Spirituality of Relationship ... 206
11 Fresh Insights on Faith ... 229
   - *A:* Solidarity and Faith ... 229
   - *B:* Glimpses into Maya Spirituality ... 233
12 Four Challenges to the Church ... 241
   - *Challenge #1*: The Need to Create Justice-Seeking Communities ... 243
   - *Challenge #2*: The Need for a Fresh Vision of Mission ... 246
   - *Challenge #3*: Whole World Ecumenism ... 253
   - *Challenge #4*: Making Reparations ... 256

Epilogue: Keeping Vigil for an Elusive Peace ... 261
   - *Part 1:* What Shapes Solidarity Today? ... 263
   - *Part 2:* Where Do We Go from Here? ... 275

Abbreviations ... 289

Research Participants ... 291

Bibliography ... 293

Index ... 301

Prologue:
Solidarity's Roots in a Refugee Camp

> Nothing in my life or experience ever prepared me for this. It is 10:30 p.m. and the cries of hungry children pierce the stillness of the night in their clearing in the jungle in Chiapas, Mexico, three kilometres from the Guatemala border. Four thousand refugees are huddled together under thatched roofs and sheets of plastic. There are thousands more along the border—some with no shelter. No food has come for days because the truck couldn't make it over the muddy road. And even if it does, it takes two more days to get food up the river by boat. Two hundred thousand refugees in Mexico. The numbers boggle the mind. Back in Canada they're statistics. Here they all have names.
>
> —Journal of Wes Maultsaid, 1983

WES MAULTSAID, an Anglican priest and staff member with the British Columbia Interchurch Committee on World Development Education, and Marta Gloria de la Vega, a Guatemalan in exile, toured Guatemalan refugee camps in the Mexican state of Chiapas in January of 1983, invited by Hugh McCullum, then-Editor of the United Church *Observer*. Hugh first encountered the horror in Guatemala during a 1981 Inter-Church Committee on Human Rights in Latin America delegation. While the secular media showed virtually no interest in what many would now call "ethnic cleansing," McCullum worked to break down the wall of silence around "the quiet genocide" of the Maya people, alerting Canadians to the tragedy taking place.

Marta and Wes were representing the Guatemala Refugee Project, forerunner to the Christian Task Force on Central America in BC. They flew into Campamento Puerto Rico by small plane, while Hugh travelled elsewhere in the region. Soon they were sharing drawings, crayons, and toys from the Kamloops United Church Sunday School with refugee children, astonished that Canadian children knew of their plight. "You mean the children in Canada know we are here. How do they know? We are deep in the jungle and only a few people visit us" (Maultsaid, 1983). After electing Elena and Juan to be in charge of crayons and toys, the children decided to send drawings to the Canadian children. Wes captured some of the stories behind their drawings in his journal:

Children who fled their village. Photo by Valerie Mansour.

When I was a child I learned to work in the fields with my father. Our mothers also work hard and suffer but they keep their joy. Let us go to the Church and pray to Jesus that our sorrows come to an end. When the soldiers came everything changed in our village. They kill, burn, and destroy. The army killed my father. Because of him and many others who died I'll keep going...Now I am a refugee child and with solidarity from other nations I'll go back to my land. Thank you. My name is Eduardo and I am eleven years old.

I draw the houses that are on fire when the army came, because that is what happens. We had corn, beans, rice, and fruit. Because of that the army said we were guerrillas and because of that they kill us. I am ten years old. I walked two days. I had some roots with me.

I drew this thing because this is what the army did to us when the helicopter bombed us. They burned our fields, captured our people, and cut off their hands, feet, head, and arms. They capture families and shoot them in the stomachs and chest and hang them from trees. Because of that we cannot live in Guatemala. In any place they find us, they kill us. They do not kill us fast—they cut our eyes and our throat. If we run and they cannot catch us, they shoot us....I am from Huehuetenango and I am ten years old.

The children's drawings graphically represented a genocidal war.

"During the early eighties, a climate of terror spread out across much of the country, characterized by extreme violence against communities

Solidarity's Roots in a Refugee Camp

and organized movements, against which the people were completely defenceless. An atmosphere of constant danger totally disrupted the daily life of many families. Whether in the form of mass killings or the appearance of corpses bearing signs of torture, the horror was so massive and so flagrant that it defied the imagination" (REMHI, p. 9). That statement was based on testimonies by six thousand survivors, the vast majority Mayas, recorded by the Recovery of Historical Memory Project of the Archdiocese of Guatemala Human Rights Office. The description of a massacre of more than three hundred people in Cuarto Pueblo, Ixcán Grande Cooperative was typical of many testimonies. "What we have seen has been terrible: burned bodies, women with sticks stuck into them as if they were animals ready to be cooked as roast meat, children pierced with machetes. Women also murdered like Christ" (REMHI, p. 9).

Marta and Wes had read such testimonies, but did not truly comprehend the horror until they spent time with refugees, staying in the camp's makeshift health clinic. They were devastated. Marta Gloria wept as she remembered: "People were in far worse conditions than we had ever imagined. We were in the middle of people dying, children dying. I have never in my life seen or experienced such a harsh reality in such a massive way. I had never seen tuberculosis in kids. I saw this girl, nine years old. She was crying out in pain and we had nothing for her" (TI).

Wes wrote: "Seven years at University and Seminary cramming for exams in philosophy and theology. What a waste of time! God, I wish I knew something about health care. This man has an ugly rash all over his body. What to do? This child has been screaming for twenty minutes. What does he need?" (Maultsaid, 1983).

They were not alone in their response. Guatemalan priest and anthropologist Ricardo Falla used the term "conversion" to explain his experience of moving from disbelief to accepting that such horror actually occurred: "I too crossed the barrier of incredulity. In my case, this crossing took place in 1982, when I heard the firsthand account of the closest witness of the massacre in San Francisco, Nentón, Huehuetenango. There I put my fingers into the wound of the people's hands and put my hands into their sides to confirm that, as a people, they were mortally wounded but still alive. Before this experience, it was impossible for me to believe that human beings with hearts and flesh could be capable of reaching such mindless and merciless extremes of bestiality" (Falla, p. 3).

Yet in that clinic they also discovered amazing resilience, commitment and determination, not only to survive, but also to learn and to serve the community. Wes remarked on the young people chosen by the community to be trained as health care workers, learning the basics by whatever means they could. "Thank God for these four young health promoters. In their spare moments (rare) they pore over the book *Where There Is No Doctor*."

Solidarity's Roots in a Refugee Camp

Returned refugees remember the Cuarto Pueblo massacre. Photo by Brian Atkinson.

Marta and Wes attended eighteen-month-old Mario's funeral. The Maya lay church leader offered words of hope and spoke of Jesus' presence within the community: "That life and light is here with us, not only in each person, but in the community. We are in a time of darkness and death, but we cannot allow our light to be put out. For our children we must work together, strengthen each other and love one another so we can give them life" (Maultsaid, 1983).

The origins of much of Canadian solidarity with Guatemala can be traced to Wes and Martha's visit.

Preface

GUATEMALA UNEXPECTEDLY slipped into my life in July 1983. An adult educator and United Church of Canada diaconal minister, I was working at Dialogue Centre, a United Church ecumenical peace and justice program in Montreal. I was asked to be an official observer at the World Council of Churches (WCC) Assembly in Vancouver. No lover of bureaucratic meetings, church or otherwise, I reluctantly agreed to attend, more from a sense of duty and a desire to visit family and friends than from genuine enthusiasm.

Little did I know that the eloquence of a Guatemalan poet, journalist, and theologian, Julia Esquivel, would move me from reluctance to life-changing awareness. A diminutive woman in her fifties with short white hair, Julia had struggled against injustice all her adult life. A single-minded prophet, she was forced into exile, living among strangers in Switzerland, searching for ways to break the silence surrounding the brutal war in her homeland. Only a handful of the hundreds of people gathered from around the world knew the story that this courageous woman was about to share.

Her directness and passion were riveting as she told the story of thousands of Maya *campesinos* (rural farmers), church, cooperative and labour leaders, university students, and professors who were being tortured, disappeared, raped, and assassinated by the Guatemalan army. By the summer of 1983, over four hundred Maya villages had been burned to the ground; hundreds of horrific massacres of men, women, and children had taken place across the country; and more than a million Maya in a population of eight million had fled their homes to hide in the capital, the South Coast, and the mountains, or to seek refuge in Mexico.

Her story touched me deeply. I was enraged that lives could matter so little, that such horrendous terror could be perpetrated on thousands of social activists and entire communities of indigenous people without the world being aware. How was it that I, a fairly knowledgeable social activist, knew virtually nothing about this savage war being waged only a few hours' flight south? After all, Nicaragua and El Salvador appeared in the media regularly.

It never occurred to me that opening myself to her story would be only the first step in a lifelong journey that continues to renew and transform my faith, change my life choices and priorities, and challenge my world view. Nor did I know that many other Canadians would join the same journey. At first there seemed to be little I could do. I simply hoped Julia's testimony might influence those with influential positions in churches, labour unions, and political parties to take up the Guatemalan cause.

A few days later I attended a coffeehouse organized for WCC delegates by members of the Guatemala Refugee Project, an ecumenical group formed in British Columbia to sponsor labour lawyers Marta Gloria de la Vega and Enrique Torres and their five children. Julia Esquivel read her poetry, placing before us searing images of violence, dreams, and visions of hope. Exiled members of drama troupe Teatro Vivo and musical group Kin Lalat made us laugh and weep as they expressed in song and mime Guatemalans' suffering and determination.

Later both Teatro Vivo and Kin Lalat performed in Montreal. After the performances, I met refugees living in Montreal whose affirmation of life, resilience, hope, and commitment drew me to them. I joined a newly formed solidarity group, the Support Committee for the People of Guatemala. We met regularly, communicating in English, French, and Spanish with translation, often into two languages. We met over potluck suppers, with guacamole, beans, and corn tortillas as common fare. We had many differences—linguistic, cultural, political, personal—but we survived, worked together, and became friends. We kept alive the reality of those who had been "disappeared" by the Guatemalan army through monthly vigils in front of St. James United Church in downtown Montreal. We sent letters and petitions to the Canadian government urging Canada not to resume its aid to the Guatemalan government. We sent telegrams to the Guatemalan government and army protesting human rights violations. We spoke in churches, schools, universities and at Amnesty International meetings. We organized visits of Guatemalan political analysts, human rights workers, and another tour across Quebec of Kin Lalat. We held art displays and showed films. We fundraised for projects with displaced Mayas who were hiding in the mountains and jungles of Guatemala or had taken refuge in southern Mexico.

With solidarity work becoming increasingly significant in my life, I decided to visit Guatemala. Three months of studying Spanish and traveling in Guatemala and southern Mexico gave me a rudimentary understanding of the language and a greater understanding of Guatemala.

Preface

In 1988 I accepted a position at Tatamagouche Centre, a United Church adult education centre in Nova Scotia. This centre developed a relationship with a Maya church group, the Kaqchikel Presbytery, and marketed their handicrafts. We joined forces with Oxfam-Canada and the Atlantic Region Solidarity Network. Delegations to Guatemala and return visits to Canada by church and human rights partners took place. In 1991 the Maritimes-Guatemala Breaking the Silence Network (BTS) formed to coordinate and strengthen solidarity work. We activated a Maritimes section of Canada's human rights emergency response network, the Urgent Action Network (UAN). We became the Maritimes sponsor of Project Accompaniment, a network of Canadians who accompanied refugees returning from Mexico into Guatemala in the midst of war, including my own two-month participation. We also accompanied church leaders and their families whose lives were under threat. During 1996 my partner, Wilf Bean, and I served as United Church of Canada volunteers with the *Hermandad de Presbiterios Mayas* (the Fellowship of Maya Presbyteries).

Since returning to Canada, I have continued solidarity work at local, regional, and national levels. An encounter in Vancouver in 1983 has become a life journey, in which I have many companions. Telling their story has been one way for me to honour these friends. It has been a labour of love.

Acknowledgments

MY DEEPEST THANKS goes to the Guatemalans with whom I have been privileged to work in solidarity, first in Canada and then in Guatemala. Their lives are testimony to courage, hope, and an unextinguishable commitment to justice. This book does not begin to do justice to their passion for life nor to the profound influence they have had on the lives of so many Canadians. The privilege of walking alongside them, of hearing their stories, of watching their struggles and achievements led to this book.

I also want to give thanks to the many Canadians with whom I have shared the solidarity journey for the past two decades. Solidarity has given me a wonderful and unexpected gift of friendship with Canadians across the country, whose dedication, integrity, and compassion has inspired and sustained me. They too deserve to have their stories told.

I want to express my appreciation to the McGeachy Scholarship Committee of The United Church of Canada who agreed that a book about human rights solidarity was indeed a book about the mission of the church. I also want to thank the members of Project Accompaniment, the Christian Task Force on Central America, and the Maritimes-Guatemala Breaking the Silence Network for their openness to this project and their trust in me. Simone Carrodus, Ann Godderis, and Beth Abbott ensured that I found the documents, had the historical background, and made the contacts I needed. As I was planning my research, Faye Wakeling suggested that I first hear the voices of Guatemalans. This proved to be wise advice, enabling me to interpret Canadian perspectives in the light of the experiences of Guatemalans.

This book was written in collaboration with many Guatemalans and Canadians who gave me encouragement and support from the moment I proposed writing it. I am thankful for the generosity of all those who, without hesitation, gave their valuable time, their stories and their reflections, as well as constructive criticism, hospitality, personal documents, and more. I often felt humbled, as I listened to those individuals who live their lives with a rare depth of conviction and humanity. Readers will find the Canadian interviewees listed at the end of this book.

I obtained more rich material than I could possibly use, given constraints of time and book length. I was forced to make difficult choices about how many voices could appear in the text and about themes and sources. I want to especially thank those I interviewed who do not see your voices directly quoted in the text. I hope you will find your experiences and your views reflected nonetheless.

Rachel Holder deserves an award of merit for painstakingly transcribing, in record time, all the interviews done in Spanish. Thanks go, as well, to friends in Antigonish who did that same hard work with the interviews in English—including Diane Walsh, Heather Carson, and Lisa Burkett.

This book would not have come to fruition without my Advisory Committee in Nova Scotia, made up of Beth Abbott, Mary Corbett, Shelley Finson, Valerie Mansour, Don Murray, and Martin Rumscheidt. They spent hours reading chapter drafts and making specific suggestions about content, style, and organization. Thanks also go to members of the Christian Task Force in Central America: Bud Godderis, Ann Godderis, John Payne, and Marta Gloria de la Vega. What is more, this group of theologians, writers, and solidarity workers par excellence affirmed my efforts at times when I felt inadequate to the task. In addition, Valerie Mansour served as a most competent editor.

As a novice writer, I cannot begin to say how much I value the feedback from the Pictou County women writer's group, who got me started on the writing journey, from friends Janette Fecteau, Marion Kerans, Pat Kerans, and Jeanne Moffatt, and from writers Myrna Kostash and Joan Givner, who taught me the art and craft of writing. Comments from Professors Tom Faulkner and Paul Bowlby of the Comparative Ethics Committee of Wilfrid Laurier University Press helped me sharpen my manuscript. Brian Atkinson, Valerie Mansour, and Chap Haynes generously shared photos. Douglas Vaisey, reference librarian at St. Mary's University in Halifax, was an excellent guide to organizing the bibliography. Finally, thanks to Ruth Bradley-St-Cyr, Carroll Klein, Leslie Macredie, and Brian Henderson for skillfully guiding me through the final stages of my work.

Although the book could not have come into being without the collaboration of so many, I take personal responsibility for errors, omissions, or misinterpretations of the stories and materials people shared. My greatest hope is that this book serves to further the work of solidarity in the coming years.

Introduction

GUATEMALA'S CIVIL WAR formally ended on December 29, 1996, with the signing of peace accords. The end of war did not automatically bring peace, and the signing of peace accords did not mean the overnight establishment of democracy and justice. The call for solidarity from the Guatemalan popular movement (churches, trade unions, campesino, human rights, environmental, and women's groups) continued.

The Canadian solidarity movement began to reflect on how its work might change in the rapidly evolving context of globalization. Many thought it was time to document the solidarity relationship between Guatemalans and Canadians. We believed critical questions needed to be asked if solidarity were to grow in a mutually beneficial way:

- What has been solidarity's impact on the struggle of our Guatemalan friends?
- Does our involvement really matter?
- What solidarity responses have been most useful?
- What were our mistakes and shortcomings and what can we learn from them?
- What are the possibilities of solidarity across barriers of language, culture, and class?
- How have Canadians and Guatemalans changed their understanding of solidarity?
- What are the challenges of solidarity in a world of globalization and neo-liberalism?
- How has solidarity affected the spirituality of Canadians and Guatemalans?
- What are the implications for the church?

I was awarded The United Church of Canada's McGeachy Scholarship, given for research that inspires and challenges the church toward creative and faithful mission in contemporary society. I knew from my own story,

Author learning to make tortillas with Kaqchikel Presbytery friend. Photo by Valerie Monsour.

and the stories of countless others in Canada and in Guatemala, that exploring the solidarity experience would inevitably challenge, as well as inspire the church's understanding and practice of mission.

I decided to use a case-study approach, focusing on three Canadian networks: the Christian Task Force on Central America in British Columbia (CTF), the Maritimes-Guatemala Breaking the Silence Network (BTS), and Project Accompaniment Canada-Guatemala (Project A).

The CTF was formed by British Columbians engaged in solidarity with Central America, although my study focuses specifically on its work with Guatemala. BTS is a loose-knit network of individuals and groups in all three Maritime provinces. Project A was a coast-to-coast network of grassroots groups supporting the collective, organized return to Guatemala of Maya refugees who had fled to southern Mexico in the early 1980s. Project A accompaniers, by their physical presence and the support of local committees in Canada, offered security to the refugees as they returned to newly established communities in their homeland.

This book is a distillation of what I learned from interviews with Guatemalans and Canadians, from poring over books, articles, reports, and newsletters, and from reading diaries and poems generously shared by members of solidarity networks. My intention is to raise their voices, especially the experience and perspectives of Guatemalans, because I believe any congruent reflection on solidarity must give priority to voices from the South. I sought to discover the richness and diversity in approaches to solidarity as well as common threads in understanding and practice. I discovered the truth that social researcher Lillian Rubin had articulated: "The research seemed like a collaboration, since I learned from the people I spoke with what I had not known to ask and then incorporated it into the study, making it richer, more complex, and, I hope, more true to the fact and spirit of their lives" (Rubin, p. 25).

How the Book Is Organized

The book's organization corresponds to its two purposes. The first purpose is to tell the story of Canada-Guatemala solidarity from 1980–2000, through the eyes of members of the solidarity networks mentioned above and their Guatemalan partners. The second purpose is to reflect on the meaning of solidarity, as expressed by solidarity activists.

Section I, "Setting Solidarity in Context," provides basic background that will enable readers to understand the rest of the book. Chapter 1, "A Brief Historical Overview," introduces political, social, and cultural factors that led to the violence and repression of the 1980s and '90s. Chapter 2, "Maya Refugees—From Exodus to Return," focuses on the experience of Maya refugees who fled from Guatemala across the border into southern Mexico.

Section II, "Weaving Threads of Solidarity," tells the stories of three solidarity networks, Project Accompaniment, (Project A) the Christian Task Force on Central America in British Columbia (CTF) and the Maritimes-Guatemala Breaking the Silence Network (BTS). Chapter 3, "Project Accompaniment—A Canadian Response," places Project A within the context of the refugees' dogged determination to set their own conditions for a return to Guatemala in the context of war. Chapter 4, "Accompaniment in War and Peace," tells the story of Canadians who accompanied the refugee-led collective return process from 1993–1999. Chapter 5, "Project A Comes to a Close," describes how and why Project A came to an end and some of the tensions left unresolved. Chapter 6 outlines the development of the Christian Task Force in Central America in the larger context of Latin American solidarity in the 1970s and 80s. Chapter 7 tells the story of the Maritimes-Guatemala Breaking the Silence Network.

Section III, "A Tapestry with Many Forms," explains some of the ways solidarity has been expressed. Chapter 8, "New Forms of Solidarity," describes methods developed by the solidarity movement, such as public education, delegations to Guatemala and visitors to Canada, Urgent Actions, fair trade, vigils, advocacy and lobbying, security accompaniment, solidarity among children and youth, and regional, national, and international networking. Chapter 9, "Solidarity's Creative Heart," describes how integral music, art, poetry, and photography have been to the work of solidarity.

Section IV, "The Spirituality of Solidarity and Its Challenges," draws out the meaning of the solidarity experience for both Guatemalans and Canadians, using the optic of spirituality. Chapter 10, "Creating Relationships: The 'Spirit' of Solidarity" systematizes a spirituality of solidarity, based on the experience of both Guatemalans and Canadians. Chapter 11, "Fresh Insights on Faith," describes how the Guatemalan experience has transformed the faith of many Canadians. Chapter 12, "Four Challenges to the Church," points to the implications of solidarity experience for Canadian churches. The epilogue, "Keeping Vigil for an Elusive Peace," discusses the difficult challenges to solidarity since 2000, when a right-wing government, supported by the most hardline elements of the Guatemalan army, was elected.

Significant themes emerged that could not be addressed in any depth, if this book were ever to be completed. A theme deserving of more reflection is that of conflict within and among groups in Canada. This has been, and continues to be, a painful reality within the solidarity movement. Solidarity has also been affected by divisions within and among groups in Guatemala. Regretfully, I was not able to explore in any depth the causes of these conflicts and their impact on solidarity's effectiveness.

Another area worthy of research is the delicate and complex subject of international solidarity during an armed struggle. Solidarity was a response to massive injustice and horrific repression. In that context, some Canadians supported the armed resistance. Others, including pacifists, opposed such support. Still others believed solidarity's task was to support unarmed civilian groups working for justice and peace in Guatemala, while recognizing that some of these groups may have had connections with the armed resistance movement. Exploring this issue would take a book in itself. With continued repression in Guatemala, the time is not yet safe to discuss this important question.

※ Methodological and Technical Notes

I originally hoped to use a participatory research methodology in which both Guatemalans and Canadians would be involved in all stages of the research, that is, the development, carrying out, analysis, and interpretation of the research. However, I soon realized that such an approach was too ambitious, given the financial, geographical, language, and time constraints of research that included returned refugees living in remote areas of Guatemala, as well as solidarity groups from the Maritimes to British Columbia. However, from the beginning of the process, I sought collaboration wherever possible. Several network members contributed to shaping and narrowing research themes, developing the interview questions, providing me with a historical context, offering feedback on the manuscript, correcting errors and misunderstandings, and editing my writing.

This book is based to a large degree on interviews with Guatemalans and Canadians. Interviews in Guatemala took place in returned communities and with human rights workers in Guatemala City. Any quotes taken from these interviews are referred to in the text as TI (taped interviews). A list of Canadians interviewed appears at the end of the book. Because of continuing repression of human rights in Guatemala, I have not revealed the identities of Guatemalans interviewed, with the exception of those who are well-known public figures. Audio cassettes of interviews with Canadians are available from the United Church of Canada Archives, located in Victoria College, the University of Toronto.

The bibliography is divided into three sections: books and theses, articles and book chapters, and other resources, such as videos, Web sites, poems, prayers, and so on. The bibliography lists all documents referred to in the text that are available in the United Church Archives, such as newspaper articles, newsletters, reports, and unpublished poetry. Unless otherwise noted in the bibliography, the translation of interviews and quotes from materials in Spanish is my own.

1
Setting Solidarity in Context

Map of Guatemala

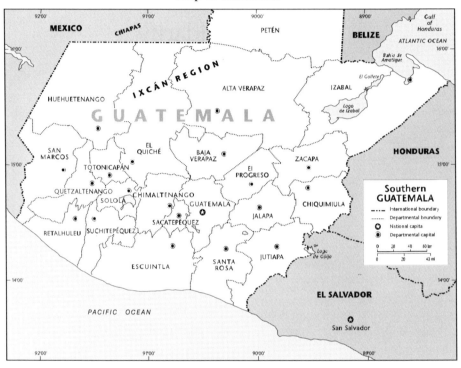

1   A Brief Historical Overview

> Brought by the wind they were mistaken for gods
> the bearded men who came from abroad
> they brought their rum, their guns, and their greed
> they ruled with terror for five centuries
> shrouded in mist, gun metal clouds overhead
> a teacher disappears and nothing is said
> and now the widow is considered a threat
> because they know she will never forget!
> —From *Land of the Maya* by Lennie Gallant

Roots of the Conflict

SINGER AND SONGWRITER Lennie Gallant, a Maritimes-Guatemala Breaking the Silence delegation member, connected the suffering he met with the ruthless colonial history that began with Pedro de Alvarado's conquest in 1524. Friar Bartolomé de las Casas accused the Spanish conquistador of "committing enormities, sufficient to fill a particular volume, so many were the slaughters, violences, injuries, butcheries, and beastly desolations" (cited in Montejo and Akab', p. 3).

Every era brought new forms of the same injustices, as landowners and the military continued to exploit and repress the Mayas. The regions of Guatemala with the highest concentration of indigenous people have always suffered the highest levels of political violence and repression.

Ricardo Falla compared the contemporary violence he painstakingly detailed to that of the Conquest (Falla, p. 5). The title and contents of *A Very Brief Testimonial Account of the Continued Destruction of Guatemala*, explicitly recall Las Casas's observations: "Five hundred years later, the atrocities related by the Bishop of Chiapas, Friar Bartolome de las Casas, were being repeated in the indigenous communities of Guatemala. We know that many people have tried to accuse the Bishop of Chiapas of exaggerating his accounts, but having lived in our own flesh the cruelties of the army in 1982, we can confirm that the accounts of the Bishop were not a product of his imagination, nor are those that we present here" (Montejo and Akab', p. 3).

Guatemala, the largest and most industrialized country in Central America, lies between the Caribbean Sea and the Pacific Ocean with a land area of 109,000 square kilometres (42,000 square miles). It is a country of breathtaking splendour: "The countryside exuded life—lush forested hillsides, volcanoes crowned by fluffy clowds and bathed in sunlight, the delicate bright patterns of indigenous clothing, expectant dogs on the roadside, and colourful stands of painted animals and masks" (*Network News*, King, 1991). Yet George Lovell entitled a recent book *Guatemala: A Beauty That Hurts* (Lovell, 2000). Ronald Wright describes "the cruel political landscape behind the scenery," adding: "Beauty cloaks Guatemala the way music hides screams" (Wright, p. 195).

Guatemala is a multi-ethnic, multilingual nation, with twenty-one Maya groups, heirs of a great ancient civilization. "Our grandfathers knew the stars, developed the calendar we still use today, and worked the land together" (cited by Nelson, p. 22). Today the women weave intricate, colourful designs passed on from generation to generation. Although Mayas are the majority of Guatemala's population overall and 80 percent of the rural population, their culture and community life have been continually denigrated. One refugee said: "Those who have been in power in Guatemala since the Spanish conquest have never appreciated or valued the richness of the Indian cultures. Instead they show contempt, because that's the only way they can subject us to exploitation and oppression. In order to dominate a people, they have to say: 'That culture is not worth anything; it is inferior'" (cited by Manz, 1988, p. 89).

Four out of five Mayas live in extreme poverty. Rich in human and natural resources, Guatemala is not a poor country, rather an impoverished one where wealth, land, and political power is concentrated in the hands of a non-Maya oligarchy. It has the most unequal land distribution in Latin America, with five hundred thousand rural families not meeting even subsistence conditions. According to Agriculture Ministry figures, 96 percent of agricultural producers share 20 percent of the country's farmland, while 70 percent of agricultural lands lie in the hands of only 0.15 percent of producers (*Central America Report*). In order to survive, men, women, and children have migrated to the coast for part of each year to work on immense sugar cane, banana, and coffee plantations at poverty wages in subhuman conditions. Even that work is disappearing, as technology displaces human labour.

A Brief Historical Overview

Throughout the last century a powerful army protected the interests of the wealthy. Over time it has become part of that elite. Senior officers, often illegally and by force, obtained vast tracts of land, forests, and mineral deposits. The military developed financial interests including the national airline and hydroelectric power company, a bank, insurance company, and publishing house. Military dictators ruled Guatemala for most of the twentieth century until 1985.

A notable exception was "the democratic spring" of 1944–54. Two democratically elected governments instituted reforms such as a labour code and social security system. Parties from across the political spectrum flourished. That watershed era ended when a CIA-backed mercenary army overthrew the Arbenz government as it attempted to implement agrarian reform, including the purchase of unused United Fruit Company land. Its president, Allan Dulles, was US Secretary of State John Foster Dulles's brother.

With McCarthyism at its peak, Canada did not dispute Washington's claim that Guatemala was a hotbed of communism. The government, the Co-operative Commonwealth Federation (CCF) and Conservative opposition, unions, and churches accepted Cold War rhetoric without question, although it was not based in fact. Canada supported the US position until 1985 (McFarlane, pp. 92–105).

The coup and further US intervention led to ex-military officers forming an armed resistance movement in 1961, the date often identified as the beginning of the civil war. The army became increasingly ruthless in efforts to eliminate the fledgling insurgent group. It relentlessly terrorized and silenced all forms of dissent by trade unions, political parties, peasant organizations, and indigenous groups.

In spite of deeply ingrained fear and widespread repression, an upsurge of community organization and popular unrest began in the late 1960s and early '70s. Maya communities, seeking to escape grinding poverty, chose local people to be trained as health and literacy promoters, formed cooperatives and developed organizations to fight for their rights. Catholic missionaries, transformed by their relationships with campesinos facing poverty and exploitation on a daily basis, offered support and training for these efforts.

In the late 1960s well-organized, aware, hard-working campesinos set out for the fertile, uninhabited Ixcán region in the northwest corner of Guatemala bordering on Mexico. The migration, barely noticed at the time, later became highly significant. Settlers carved cooperatives out of the rain forest to form the Ixcán Grande Agricultural Cooperative. They built community halls, churches, schools, and health clinics. They faced tropical heat, rains of almost six metres per year, mosquitoes and other insects, snakes, a lack of transportation and isolation. After a few years of backbreaking work, they became self-sufficient and began to enjoy the fruits of their labour. They marketed their crops with the help of Maryknoll priest William Woods, who airlifted their goods out of the Ixcán. A refugee told the story to a Canadian delegation: "The co-op sowed coffee and cardamom. Each member had the same size plot. Each member had to pay eighty quetzales for his land. A priest, William Woods, helped us with this work. We had some beef. Woods brought in some seeds for vanilla and we grew that. We got good prices for that. We were becoming successful" (PA Atlantic, p. 3).

A similar project was initiated in 1972 in nearby Santa María Tzejá, spurred on by Luis Gurriaran, a priest trained in cooperative development at the Coady International Institute in Antigonish, Nova Scotia. The government later established land-settlement schemes in the Ixcán and Petén regions of northern Guatemala.

An earthquake in 1976 levelled Maya communities across the Highlands, creating another impetus for organizing. With an international focus on Guatemala, the military government was forced to allow some space for the social movement to act. Strikes and demonstrations became more common. Community organizations began to flourish, such as the Committee of Peasant Unity, formed in 1978 by members of Catholic Action groups who had gained skills in social and economic analysis. They organized campesinos around issues of starvation wages (about $1US per day) and horrific living and working conditions on plantations.

Repression soon became commonplace in Maya communities, including torture, disappearances, massacres, and assassinations of peasant and community leaders, cooperative members, social promoters, priests, catechists, and Delegates of the Word (trained lay church leaders). Catholic Bishop Remi De Roo of the Diocese of Victoria described his 1979 encounter with Nobel Peace prizewinner Rigoberta Menchú's father, campesino leader and catechist Vicente Menchú. His son had recently been kidnapped, tortured, and murdered by the army and his wife would face the same fate a few months later: "The wrinkled, sunburned face of Vicente, a 75-year-old farmer, remains etched in my memory. After calmly describing the most horrendous tortures, the violation of men, women, and children, the wanton destruction of and burning of farms by army personnel, he concluded, 'There seems to be no promise or hope of life for us. If we

A Brief Historical Overview

Easter procession in the returned refugee community of Cuarto Pueblo. The cross bears the name of Father William (Guillermo) Woods. Photo by Brian Atkinson.

must die so our children can live, we are prepared to sacrifice our lives'" (De Roo, p. 17).

Two days later Menchú was one of thirty-six victims burned alive by the army, hours after they occupied the Spanish Embassy in a bid to focus attention on the plight of Maya communities.

Cooperatives were initiated as a moderate alternative to land reform and a way of providing limited economic progress without challenging the status quo. Even these attempts brought clergy and campesinos into conflict with landowners and the government. The army was likely responsible for William Woods's death in a 1976 plane crash as he was flying to an Ixcán Grande Cooperative community to celebrate Mass. Soon after, other priests in the region were forced to abandon their people.

When oil deposits were found, General Lucas García, president of Guatemala, and other officers grabbed vast tracts of land belonging to the Mayas. The army did not want aware, organized campesinos challenging its control. The Ixcán became known as the "Land of the Generals."

The Ixcán Cooperative communities were located close to the EGP (the Guerrilla Army of the Poor), a new armed resistance group that later joined forces with three other groups to form the URNG (Guatemalan National Revolutionary Unity). Although weak in numbers and military strength, the EGP gained allegiance from some members of Maya communities. The state's brutal reaction to any perceived threats to the status quo had pushed many campesinos towards support for more radical change. "Even modest proposals for social change met with a fierce response, making revolutionaries out of reformers" (Manz, 1988, p. 13). They provided support, such as food, first-aid, the evacuation of villages under army attack, roadblocks, and communication links. Many gave passive support by turning a blind eye.

Sister Noel O'Neill of the Sisters of Saint Joseph returned to Canada in 1981 after her convent was attacked with a grenade and the people she worked with received death threats. In an open letter to the people she had served, she described choices many were facing:

> I remember your inner struggles with the whole situation in the country and how some of you would share with me the painful decisions you were trying to make. Could you join an organized resistance group? Could you, in conscience, not? What about the question of taking up arms to defend your brothers and sisters on the other side of the country? What did it mean to be a Christian in such a situation? Some of you joined the resistance groups and became active in the "front line" of the struggle and this was an agonizing choice. Others chose to support the struggle in more indirect ways by keeping your communities united and working together or by teaching your people how to care for themselves in emergency situations. (cited in McFarlane, p. 180)

In 1979 the Sandinista revolutionary movement took power in Nicaragua in a popular uprising. Coupled with some support among Maya communities for the insurgency, Guatemala's elite felt threatened. The army reacted with unprecedented violence, despite the insurgency's military weakness. All sectors of society were cruelly persecuted, from trade unions and journalists to university students and professors, to the church. Virtually all social groups and political parties seeking change were destroyed. Death squads and the army killed one hundred to two hundred people each week.

Worse was yet to come. Maya campesinos became the army's key target in a ferocious eighteen-month-long scorched-earth campaign. Although members of some communities collaborated with the insurgency, they were an unarmed civilian population, massacred under a regime of State terror and violence intended to wipe out large groups of the indigenous population, in the name of "neutralizing the guerrilla." The great majority of campesinos had no relationship with the insurgency. Others were opposed to their existence or strategies, yet nonetheless became victims of the military. Anthropologist Beatriz Manz believes the army sought to destroy Maya communities and culture: "The particularly grisly nature and extensive scale of the campaign indicate a deeper purpose than combating the guerrilla forces or disrupting their social base. The purpose appeared to be eliminating future capacity for opposition, insuring that new seeds of revolution would not take root. As part of the campaign, the core of Indian community life was attacked by desecrating symbols and sacred places as well as destroying the milpas (cornfields) on which subsistence depended. In the process, the military disrupted traditional patterns of respect, authority and power" (Manz, 1988, p. 17).

A priest told Hugh McCullum the army terror was "racism at its deepest": "To destroy the indigenous you destroy the sacred things they believe in—life and land. When an indigenous baby is born, the parents bury the umbilical cord as a sign that the child is part of the land. The way to commit genocide is to destroy their links with the past by killing the old, to destroy their links with the future by killing the women, children and destroying fetuses, to destroy their love for the land by forcing them to flee from where the cord is buried and by burning their crops and villages" (McCullum, p. 54).

One-eighth of the population was displaced; thousands were massacred. More than four hundred villages were burnt to the ground. The UN-sponsored Commission for Historical Clarification identified 626 massacres systematically carried out by security forces (Comisión para el Esclarecimiento Histórico [Guatemala], p. 34). Rape, torture, forced disappearances, and assassinations were the norm. More than one hundred thousand children lost one or both parents.

US military advisors introduced the scorched-earth strategy of Vietnam. They trained Guatemalan officers at institutions such as the School of the Americas, now located in Fort Benning, Georgia (recently renamed the Western Hemisphere Institute for Security Cooperation). It was formed in 1946, ostensibly "to bring security to Latin America" (Delli Sante, pp. 60–79). Recently declassified CIA cables reveal US support for the massacres. In March 1999 then President Clinton visited Guatemala, where he apologized for US involvement: "It is important that I declare clearly that the support given to military and intelligence units implicated in acts of violence and extensive repression was an error we must not repeat."

Mutations

I keep thinking of the cardamom ovens
In the village of Momenlac
the hordes of bodies

>   shoved down latrines
>   the corpses strewn
>   on the path to Xoclac
>
>   I keep imagining entire villages
>   just like this one
>   erased
>   400 pueblos mute and smouldering
>   tongues cut out   of mouths
>   children's skulls smashed on the trunks
>
>   of trees that stood and watched
>   I keep looking around me thinking
>   these are the lucky ones
>   that weren't supposed to live
>   to tell these stories
>   tongues intact
>
>   I think about the soldiers
>   how they carry this around
>   an awful secret
>   tightly squeezed
>   in fists   or between teeth
>   a putrid taste
>   inside their mouths
>   that will not go away
>
>   The generals who concocted it
>   in boardrooms or from desks
>   in Washington
>   cut off
>   from their souls somehow
>   speaking without tongues.
>   —Liz Rees, 1997

Ricardo Falla documented ten massacres in the Ixcán region alone. In Cuarto Pueblo, 362 men, women, and children were murdered one Sunday in the Catholic and Evangelical churches and the marketplace. A witness described hearing the lieutenant exhort his soldiers to continue raping the women, mutilating the children, and torturing the men for four days preceding their immolation: "They are friends of the guerrillas, but they aren't saying so. We have to finish them all off, to put an end to the

Cross, atop monument in memory of massacre victims. Photo by Chap Haynes.

guerrillas. The women are preparing their food. If we finish them all off, things will soon calm down. The men are helping them. But when we ask them about that, they say they don't know anything. Lies!" (Falla, p. 89).

In a coup following a fraudulent election, General Efraín Ríos Montt replaced General Lucas García as president in early 1982. Also a product of US counter-insurgency training, he continued the scorched-earth campaign. He declared a state of siege and suspended the Constitution, including all human and civil rights. He imposed press censorship and created special courts with power to sentence to death, in secret hearings, people convicted of "political" crimes.

"Blood flowed like water," wrote Hugh McCullum. He described the regime as "barbarism with a Christian face," since many of Montt's advisers were proud members of the California-based fundamentalist Church of the Complete Word, known as *El Verbo* (McCullum, pp. 52–53). When Montt was asked how, as a Christian, he could justify the scorched-earth campaign, he is said to have replied: "I am doing everyone a favour. I kill the communist devils and send the Indian souls to heaven" (Wyatt, p. ix).

The Reagan administration restored military aid that had been suspended in 1978. It tried to portray the new president as a reformer who wanted to return Guatemala to democracy. Televangelist Pat Robertson urged viewers to pray "around the clock" for Ríos Montt. Evangelists Jerry Falwell and Billy Graham met with a Guatemalan aide to organize public relations and reconstruction funding for Guatemala. Much money came into the country through El Verbo's charity wing, Operation Lovelift, which many believe was CIA-backed (McCullum, p. 50). Canada's secretary of state for External Affairs, Mark McGuigan, quietly supported the US position. Canada's stance changed only after intense pressure by churches, solidarity groups, unions, and other groups (McFarlane, pp. 185, 190).

McCullum and Wes Maultsaid interviewed Jorge Serrano, President of the Council of State and a fundamentalist church elder. "We are in a spiritual battle in Guatemala and those of us in government are simply tools. The hand of the Lord guides our every action, so they cannot be wrong." They questioned him about the refugees without revealing their recent visit to the refugee camps. "There are fewer than three thousand in Mexico and they are forced there as hostages by the guerrillas," he replied. "They could come home. The Mexican press wants to embarrass us, so they say there are hundreds of thousands but we know better" (McCullum, p. 53). Serrano was elected President in 1990. In 1993 he tried to re-establish a dictatorship, then fled with millions of dollars from the state when his coup failed.

Over a million people were displaced (of a total population of eight million) from 1980–83, including 80 percent of the Highlands Maya population. Many were widows. Some fled to Guatemala City slums. Others eked out a living as farm workers on coastal plantations. Unemployed or working for starvation wages, without legal documentation, these "internal refugees" often assumed false identities, living a marginal existence with what remained of their brutalized and murdered families. Thousands of families hid from the military in the mountains or jungle, living a seminomadic life. Many families were captured while others, facing illness and starvation, emerged from hiding and turned themselves over to the army. Small, hidden pockets of displaced people gradually came together to form resistance communities (known as CPRs). They lived in privation and fear, often on the run, pursued and bombed by the military.

The story of Santa María Tzejá villagers was that of thousands of Maya campesinos: "A few villagers left fairly quickly for Mexico. But most fled to their cornfields, where they waited in isolated terror. Who could imagine the army would continue to threaten and kill indefinitely? Surely it would leave after a time. Gradually, however, it became clear that life was changed forever.

Most fled with only their clothes on their backs. They faced disease, especially malaria, with no medicine. Storms lashed at them. Babies were born and some died. Families constantly struggled to find food, and what they found could only be cooked during darkness, so the smoke would not give away their hiding places" (Taylor, 1998, p. 23).

2 Maya Refugees – From Exodus to Return

> From the Guatemalan Indians we have learned the philosophy of the perfect road. The perfect road has a way in and a way out; to go and to return. The Guatemalans here in Chiapas were pushed from the city to the field, to the jungle, to exile. They have a right to return. Theirs is a project to return; to return to their land; to return to freedom. —Guatemalan priest in Mexico, quoted in *Network News,* Gear and Golden

A MASS EXODUS from Guatemala into Mexico began. More than two hundred thousand campesinos fled with only the ragged clothes on their backs, traumatized by memories of rape, torture, and assassinations, as well as the loss of family members and neighbours who had become separated or died on the journey. Many hid in the jungle and mountains for months, even years, before crossing the border. A doctor listed their maladies: infections, pellagra, tuberculosis, parasites, extreme anxiety, malaria, amoebas, gastroenteritis, scabies, bronchitis, extreme anemia, pneumonia, and conjunctivitis. "We are recording hemoglobin counts of two (the normal is thirteen to fifteen), which means their blood is almost water. They have walked for hundreds of kilometres in this state. Their minds are so damaged, they regress daily.... We can stop it, even reverse it, but the disease is hunger" (McCullum, p. 49).

The first group fled cooperatives in the northern Petén region in April 1981. The Catholic Diocese of San Cristóbal de las Casas in Chiapas received them. Over the next three months more than three thousand campesinos fled after army massacres in several villages. When the scorched-earth counter-insurgency campaign spread throughout the Highlands and the Ixcán rain forest in 1982, the influx to Mexico surged dramatically.

Mexico was totally unprepared. Nearly two thousand Guatemalans were sent back across the border. After a barrage of national and international criticism Mexico agreed to grant the refugees temporary renewable visas and allowed the construction of refugee camps. They received basic food, including corn, beans, and rice, along with building supplies. By 1983, the UN High Commission on Refugees (UNHCR) had recognized forty-six thousand refugees in more than ninety refugee camps stretched out along the southern border of Chiapas.

At least twice that many refugees settled in coastal areas of Chiapas, where they lived dispersed and undocumented, without access to aid. Many were widows and children. They had fled from the more southern Departments of Guatemala alone, as individual families, or in small groups. "We were members of community groups, church-based groups or unions. The repression began against the leaders of these groups. The first killings were by death squads. We did not know who they were; they wore masks. Later it was the army who came into the communities. Things got worse; people were finding bodies everywhere. People became afraid and many started to leave the country.... We did not experience mass killings as in the Ixcán and Quiché. But things got worse and everyone started looking for ways to escape" (PA Atlantic, p. 5).

Without legal documents, they felt as if they were "living on the edge of a razor." They had to assume false identities. Fearful of deportation, they had little choice but to work at less than minimum wage. To avoid detection, they lived in small isolated groups throughout the region, abandoned their traditional dress, and spoke only Spanish.

※ Refugees Refuse Repatriation

Many refugees arrived politically aware and with a high level of organizational capacity. Many had been members of agricultural cooperatives. They immediately put to use skills learnt in Guatemala, first to survive and then to rebuild. They set about constructing camps near the border, as close to their homeland as possible. They built palm-thatched huts for each family, community buildings and roads to break their isolation from the world. Fifteen years later Wes Maultsaid marveled at their resilience and ability to organize themselves: "It was a real awakening to find these four thousand people in the jungle in Mexico after they had wandered through the mountains and to find how they were able to organize themselves very quickly in different ways, for health, for food, for shelter, for worship; how they were able to sustain that community even though they weren't all from the same individual village in Guatemala; how they were able to form something under this horrific sense of fleeing, of the fear of being pursued in the jungle" (TI).

Each camp elected community leaders and developed complex participatory decision-making processes. When possible, they produced their own corn and beans. Consumer cooperatives and community stores were established. They selected young people to study agronomy, livestock rearing, carpentry, mechanics, health, and education. Others were involved in activities to promote awareness of their rights, as well as the history and constitution of Guatemala. Women's groups formed, for many a first opportunity to participate in workshops and meetings. Pig and chicken projects and workshops in weaving, shoemaking, and carpentry were supported by the Diocese, Guatemalan non-governmental organizations (NGOs) in exile in Mexico, organizations such as the Jesuit Refugee Service, and agencies such as the UNHCR and the Mexican Commission to Aid Refugees. Canadian churches and NGOs funded several projects.

How Do We Sing to God in a Strange Land?

The lands that we will one day sow
we cannot forget
the cornfields that did not bear fruit
when life ceased
with the death of the fields
And we left very slowly
cradled by our mother
lulled to sleep by crickets
wanting to weep…
It is certain that we will return
running among the cucallo plants
that softly light our path
enabling us to walk.

With our bags full
with the seeds of justice
bursting with freedom,
with the warmth of your womb
we will return to caress you.

—Refugee song, "Como Cantar a Dios en Tierra Extraña?"

The refugees yearned to return to Guatemala. Many had thought they would stay a few days, at most a few months. But as the brutal war continued, only a small number of refugees repatriated. Instead they began to plan a collective return, making a clear distinction between "the Return" and "repatriation." The Return would be voluntary and collective, negotiated and organized by the refugees themselves in conditions of security and dignity. They saw repatriation as a government program to resettle families or small groups with conditions dictated by the army.

The refugees' commitment to return strengthened after yet another forced migration. Despite impassioned pleas and resistance, as well as church and international support, between 1984 and 1986 Mexico relocated 18,500 refugees to the Yucatan Peninsula. "The camp, Quetzal Edna, that we visited was a community that had no choice but to relocate. The people were taken by bus a thousand kilometres through a mountain range to the jungle. They were crammed in warehouses for three to four months. One hundred people, mostly small children, died and dysentery and TB were the primary problems" (Cooley, 1986).

Between 1981 and 1984, the Guatemalan army frequently raided refugee camps close to the border, sometimes kidnapping and assassinating residents. Guatemala wanted Mexico to send them back. Knowing it could not send them back, Mexico moved them instead. "On one level, Mexico wanted to stop the flow of refugees into its territory, and the relocation to distant and controlled camps would facilitate that. On another level, Chiapas is the poorest and in many ways the most neglected state in Mexico—therefore one of the most politically volatile. The government perceived that self-organized and politically conscious Guatemalan Indian peasant groups could provide an unwanted example of resistance to Chiapanecos. Moreover the ruling party was not anxious to make the most troublesome Diocese even stronger" (Manz, 1988, p. 150).

Mexico also had other interests. It wanted to be seen as a leader of the Contadora group of nations that had formed to promote peace in Central America. Guatemala insisted it would not participate in Contadora talks without refugee relocation. The US was pressuring Mexico to repatriate the refugees and even sent a representative to the camps to persuade the refugees to return. "The presence of a large refugee population along the border undermined Reagan's assertion that human rights were improving and therefore military and economic aid should be given to the Guatemalan government....The United States shared the Guatemalan military view of the refugees as pro-guerrilla or at least as anti-government and of the camps along the border aiding subversion. Easy communication with the refugees could foster resistance by other Guatemalans" (Manz, 1988, p. 150).

Their first years in the Yucatan were difficult. "Worsening conditions in the camps in Campeche and Quintana Roo due to lack of water and failing crops are feared to be tactics to force repatriation. In Campeche we learned that each family was allotted only three pints of water per day for drinking, cooking, bathing, and cleaning.... The crops planted by refugees in an effort to achieve self-sufficiency have not produced because of drought. The Mexican government, nevertheless, is continuing to reduce the amount of food provided to the camps according to the planned harvest" (*Network News,* Gear and Golden).

Refugees remaining in Chiapas in camps somewhat farther from the border feared the same fate. A refugee leader recalled that the pressure on those who stayed in Chiapas continued until 1986. "That was when we began to discuss the possibility of a return to Guatemala with international accompaniment, with guarantees and with observers of the return process" (TI).

General Mejía Víctores's military administration constantly appealed to refugees to repatriate through messages from government representatives, informers planted in the camps, radio messages, visits from civil defence patrol members, municipal authorities, the Guatemalan Red Cross (separate from the International Committee of the Red Cross), and missionaries from El Verbo, the church of former president Ríos Montt. It wanted to convey an image of Guatemala on the road to peace and democracy. It did not want the world to be reminded of refugees still in Mexico, a living testimony to ongoing repression.

Only about a thousand refugees had repatriated up to 1986, some because of harsh conditions in the Yucatan, others for fear of losing their land in Guatemala. Radio and press reports and personal contacts kept refugees aware of the continuing military repression. One man saw the irony in army pleas to repatriate. "They accused us of being a bunch of useless communists, yet now they are looking for a way to make us return" (Guatemalan Church in Exile, p. 45).

Indeed the army did not trust the refugees and was determined to keep them under its authority in "the war of reconstruction" that followed "the war of extermination" (AVANCSO, p. 122–27). The National Plan for Security and Development called for complete military control of rural communities while allowing a facade of democracy, including elections, to be presented to the outside world. The army established regional development poles, which they defined as "organized population centres...that guarantee the adherence of the population, and their support and participation with the Armed Institution against communist subversion" (Guatemalan Church in Exile, p. 28). These included model villages close to army bases or outposts, civil defence patrols, forced military recruitment of young men, ideological re-education centres, and reception centres. "The development poles are situated in the zones where the insurgency was strongest and generally serve as relocation sites for the displaced and will likely house the refugees returning from Mexico. In the Ixcán, where most of the former residents were either killed or are refugees in Mexico, many of the inhabitants are new settlers, lured by the promise of land...The residents of the model villages enjoy little freedom: the location of their homes is drawn from a hat, they often are prohibited from going to the land they once farmed or traveling freely in search of work or markets" (Manz, 1988, p. 43).

Model villages, like Vietnamese "strategic hamlets," enabled the army to control the population, "changing the cassettes" in the residents' heads (Nelson, p. 6). They were built by forced labour to house scorched-earth survivors, repatriated refugees, and displaced persons whom the army had captured in military offensives or who had turned themselves in, no longer able to survive in the mountains or jungle. An ecumenical delegation reported: "Many peasants have died since 1982 from starvation, or sickness aggravated by extreme malnutrition. Increasing numbers of others are driven by hunger into villages under the direct control of the military. Once there, they are forced to work on construction or agricultural projects in return for inadequate food rations and very low wages, if any. There are reports of deaths from starvation of peasants living in these villages which are inaccessible to visitors" (ICCHRLA, 1985).

All men not in the army were coerced into civil defence patrols (PACs), village paramilitary units forced to police their own communities, often for twenty-four to forty-eight hour shifts. "The PACs are extensions of the army, pervasive spies, used to control and inform on all elements of rural society even at the smallest community level. In fulfilling this function the PACs often act also as vigilantes, not only the eyes and the ears, but also the fist and gun of the army. There are scores of cases where assassinations of community leaders and militants in popular organizations have been attributed to members of the local PAC. If a man refuses to join a PAC he runs a terrible risk" (CAMG, 1987, p. 19).

Canadians saw first-hand evidence in a visit to a community with more than nine hundred widows: "The town itself is under constant repression with periodic disappearances still, and a great deal of forced recruitment of the young men. Every Thursday there is a meeting of the PAC leaders from all the surrounding villages with the military commander in the local detachment, where reports are received about the 'security' of the communities and the comings and goings of the local people" (CAMG, 1987, p. 14).

The women were terrorized:

> The effect of the terror and the present situation of displacement on rural women in particular has been hideous, and cannot be overemphasized. Hundreds of villages were razed to the ground during the massacres, and thousands of village women were raped and murdered by the military. Thousands more were widowed after public executions of their husbands, and the rape and murder of their children. As a result, displaced rural women live in fear and isolation in remote villages and urban slums, their native and family identity destroyed. Any attempts by the most courageous to begin to organize and rebuild their lives and communities have been met with further repression, brutal and deadly.
>
> We were told that the women are eating herbal abortives (which are very dangerous toxins, and often cause serious, even, fatal hemorrhage) due to the constant rape that they are exposed to by the soldiers who are based in the region. This is repeated in other parts of the country. (CAMG, 1987, p. 14)

The first stage of repatriation was a stay in a "re-education centre," where the army indoctrinated the returning refugees and captured internally displaced families, about their responsibilities to the military and the state. The army told them: "You are guilty in the face of the law of God; the army will save you, as the instrument of God; you must cooperate with the army in your salvation; this is the will of God" (CAMG, 1987, p. 15).

The army often harassed or killed repatriated refugees. They faced major obstacles in reclaiming their land. In some instances friends, relatives, or internally displaced people were farming their land and refused to return it. The military often prohibited access by owners to lands located in conflict areas. In other cases, members of the army and their allies (civil patrol leaders, military commissioners, civil authorities, and their family members) had taken possession of the land.

※ Pressure Intensifies

Civilian Vinicio Cerezo, elected president in late 1985, initiated a more intensive repatriation campaign. He claimed that democracy was making great strides in Guatemala. However he could not persuade most refugees that political, social, and economic conditions for secure repatriation existed. They were well aware that the government was under the army's thumb.

In July 1986 Mexican President Miguel de la Madrid invited Cerezo to Mexico to discuss the refugee issue. The refugees were not about to let their future be determined without their participation. They wrote open letters to the Mexican and Guatemalan presidents, the UNCHR, the Diocese of San Cristóbal, and other authorities. They stated their desire to return and the conditions they saw as essential. During Cerezo's visit, they made their situation and demands widely known in the Guatemalan and Mexican press. Cerezo responded by forming a repatriation commission—Special Commission for Attention to Repatriates (CEAR).

Guatemala's First Lady, Raquel Blandón de Cerezo, led a government commission that toured refugee camps in November 1986. Her tour was a turning point, although not the turning point the Government and the army had in mind. Blandón spoke for her husband: "We want to tell you that conditions exist for your return. There is democracy now. There is no more war….The guerrillas are out of style. Come and see for yourselves" (Guatemalan Church in Exile, p. 42).

Refugees protested: "When the President's wife appeared, she was greeted by the children of the camp carrying placards stating I WANT MY FATHER TO APPEAR, WHERE IS MY BROTHER?, etc. All the widows of the camp wore black sashes. They wrote a letter to their visitor which they insisted on reading aloud to her. In the letter they demanded the appearance of their loved ones and the punishment of the Guatemalan military who had caused their families so much suffering. During all this time the bells of the church were rung" (Godderis, 1988).

A refugee described Blandón's cultural ignorance and insensitivity. "She brought with her a young Indian 'princess.' Indian princesses, he explained, are not a part of Mayan tradition….This was an indication of how out of touch Cerezo was with the people. The refugees realized that this was a bit of theatre and noted that the young 'princess' said nothing during the visit" (Godderis, 1988).

Refugee mothers later wrote the First Lady: "Mrs. Raquel Blandón de Cerezo, woman and mother of a family, you know the pain we suffer when we have a child. We ask you, 'How would you feel if they killed your children?' For you and your friends, it is easy to say that we should forget what we have suffered, because you are happy with your children" (Guatemalan Church in Exile, p. 18).

CEAR lacked credibility. It denied incidents that were common knowledge and downplayed Guatemala's militarized control and the refugees' loss of lands. A founder of a refugee women's group recalled the aftermath of Blandón's visit: "We began to see that it was unjust for the government to bring the people back as nothing more than repatriated. They placed them where the government wanted, in development poles where they kept the people under control. They had no freedom. They gave them half an hour to go and collect their firewood. They forced them to grow flowers and they sent the flowers to sell in foreign countries. The goods they had to sell were rationed and they said that if they [the refugees] had a quintal [42 kg.] they must be planning to give a part to the guerrillas.... It was then that we began to organize and choose the Permanent Commissioners. We made a plan for what needed to be dealt with" (TI).

Other visitors were more truthful. The mayor of a Guatemalan town manipulated by the army into visiting the camps said in private: "I haven't come to pull the wool over your eyes. There are always threats and kidnappings. People are killed. If you return you will have to become patrolmen" (Guatemalan Church in Exile, p. 45). Refugees from one camp were invited to send representatives to see for themselves the conditions in Guatemala. After they returned the entire camp sent Cerezo a letter, denouncing the visit as orchestrated from start to finish.

In 1998 former accompanier Margie Loo returned to the Ixcán to do research for a video. She spoke with residents who had never left or had accepted repatriation. They recalled experiences of re-education, civil patrols, and forced labour for the army, making it clear how hard life had been. One man showed her scars he received as a civil patrol member in a battle with guerrilla troops. These stories coincide with what Guatemalan social scientist Myrna Mack heard in her groundbreaking research on the repatriated and internally displaced. As she was preparing to publish her findings, she was assassinated by military intelligence officers linked directly with the president's office.

Only 8,600 refugees accepted repatriation between 1986 and 1993. As the refugees in Mexico learned of the fate of those who had repatriated, they became even more convinced of the need to organize their own Return, with international accompaniment.

※ Refugees Forge Their Destiny

In August 1987 the Central American presidents signed the Esquipulas II Peace Accord that included an agreement to deal with each country's refugee situation. Guatemalan refugees immediately wrote an open letter asking that their thoughts be taken into account whenever potential solutions to their situation were discussed: "Without our participation no just solution is possible." After intense debate in every camp, the refugees agreed on and publicized internationally six conditions essential to their return:

- The right to return home, voluntarily, in a collective and organized fashion;
- The right to return to and take possession of their former lands;
- The right of organization and freedom of association;
- The right to life and integrity, both personal and of the community;
- The right to freedom of movement both within the country and internationally; and
- The right to be accompanied during the return by national and international groups.

The right to accompaniment specified "that we be allowed to have both international governmental and non-governmental organizations accompany us on our return to the country, and that they be allowed to stay with us as witnesses to the fulfillment of our petitions and as support for the achievement of our full economic, social, and political participation in the country" (Eguren and Mahony, p. 127). Another condition, stipulating verification and monitoring mechanisms, was added later.

This was a first step in what would turn out to be a long and arduous process. "It signified a decision by the refugees to re-enter the war in Guatemala—not in a military sense, but as active, campaigning citizens, willing to mobilize and join efforts with others working for democratic change in what was still a volatile and repressive political climate" (Cohen, p. 5). Each camp chose representatives to the Permanent Commissions of the Guatemalan Refugees (CCPP), responsible for negotiating and implementing the Return process. "The entire Return process was dogged by the hostile attitude of the Guatemalan authorities who dragged their feet and put obstacles in the way of the refugees at every opportunity. The members of the delegations to Guatemala were often charged with the main responsibility of solving these deadlocks to ensure that the process moved forward—a task that required a combination of campaigning and mobilizing, coupled with negotiation and diplomacy" (Cohen, p. 6).

Negotiations with the Cerezo administration failed. The refugees' legal adviser, Alfonso Bauer Paiz, described "the deliberate, constant, systematic unwillingness of the Cerezo government to dialogue" (Paiz and Alfaro, p. 311). Human rights violations increased massively after the army staged a series of attempted coups designed to ensure Cerezo's conformity with their agenda, which did not include negotiating with refugees.

In 1989 the CCPP was accepted as a member of the National Dialogue of Reconciliation, a process the Guatemalan government had reluctantly agreed to by signing the Esquipulas II Accords. It tried to block refugee participation, pressuring the UNHCR to declare that Permanent Commissioners returning to Guatemala for National Dialogue meetings would lose their refugee status and be subject to repatriation. The UNHCR also stated that they could not contact popular movement groups during their visit, calling this "meddling in internal politics." Although the government and UNHCR relented on both issues, the CCPP saw that the UNHCR, when pressured by the Guatemalan state, could not always be counted on to defend its interests. This reinforced its insistence on non-governmental accompaniment during the Return process. So did the positive experience of accompaniment by Peace Brigades International to National Dialogue meetings. Support for the refugees grew steadily throughout 1990 and 1991, with the National Dialogue final report strongly endorsing the refugees' conditions, a major step forward in gaining Guatemalan and international support.

The years 1991 and 1992 proved to be crucial in negotiations between the CCPP and the government. The CCPP was between a rock and a hard place as the government was insisting that the refugees return on its terms. Refugees were growing impatient. Many of their children had never set foot in Guatemala and were losing their language and cultural traditions. Those with land titles were afraid they would lose them, since the government was threatening to confiscate unoccupied land. Some began to plan an independent return.

In response to a campaign by solidarity groups and NGOs, the European Parliament had stated that its aid would depend on the government's just treatment of indigenous people and the civilian population in resistance communities hidden in the mountains and jungle. More than ever, the Guatemalan government wanted the international community to believe the situation had improved. It lobbied internationally for support for its plan. Mexico increased pressure on the refugees to repatriate by limiting their freedom of movement and reducing food aid.

Conditions were far from auspicious for repatriation. Assassinations, extrajudicial executions, and forced disappearances remained high. Development poles, model villages, and re-education centres were no longer part of government policy, but the army still controlled every village by locating small military bases throughout the countryside, along with maintaining military commissioners (civilians appointed by the military) and civil defence patrols. Peace negotiations between the government and the URNG were at an impasse.

In 1991 the refugees and government agreed to establish a Mediating Commission with representatives of the UN, the Guatemalan Bishops' Conference, the Government's Ombudsman for Human Rights, and the exiled Guatemalan Human Rights Commission. Nonetheless the government continued to block negotiations: "On May 24, 1991, in La Trinitaria, Chiapas, representatives of the Guatemalan government had agreed to negotiate with the Permanent Commissions the six conditions necessary in order to return to Guatemala. During the negotiations in early June, the Guatemalan government disregarded the agreement reached in La Trinitaria, rejected the six points presented by the refugees because those were political requests, and suggested that the Permanent Commissions were subversives" (CTF, 1991).

By June 1992 Guatemala had agreed to only two conditions: that the return be collective and voluntary, and that the returnees have the right to free association and organization. The army refused to agree to locating returned refugee communities in war zones, to eliminating forced military recruitment, or to disbanding civil defence patrols.

Negotiations dragged on. In 1992 the CCPP asked for assistance from supportive countries to facilitate dialogue and to monitor and verify agreements. The Canadian government, influenced by Ambassador Brian Dickson's pro-active stance toward the refugees, agreed to Embassy participation in GRICAR (International Support Group for the Return) along with diplomats from Mexico, France, and Sweden, and representatives of the International Council of Voluntary Agencies, the World Council of Churches, and the Lutheran World Federation. The role of GRICAR was critical. Patricia Fuller, Canada's first representative to GRICAR, said: "We were to be observers with a voice, witnesses with voices. We were present at all the negotiation stages and not just as silent observers. We came into play when things got difficult....We worked very closely with the Mediating Commission and tried to support their work. Often the partners would seek out assistance to try to resolve problems" (Bolan, p. A20).

Lajos Arendas, a later Canadian representative on GRICAR, saw its role as "helping the process by having an international presence during negotiations between Government and refugee representatives, so that if the Government promises something, just by the sheer presence of the international community witnesses there, they feel bound to keep the promise." He added: "We are not supposed to be active there, just passive, but in a way we have trespassed our original role because often we give advice to people on both sides" (TI). On several occasions the CCPP expressed appreciation for Canada's diplomatic efforts.

In early 1992 the Association of Dispersed Guatemalan Refugees (ARDIGUA) formed. They too wanted to participate in the Return process. "We know people who have returned to Guatemala on their own and have been disappeared. We want to organize so that we don't have to go alone and have greater security" (Project Counselling Services, p. 4). It was not easy to bring together those who had had to remain anonymous for a decade. Each individual or family had to be approached individually. Each contact provided other names. ARDIGUA grew, gained international support, and was recognized by the Guatemalan and Mexican governments and the UNHCR. However, its struggle to obtain land in the south of Guatemala, controlled by wealthy and powerful landowners, was long. Its first return did not take place until 1997.

Accords agreeing to the conditions the refugees had set out more than four years earlier were finally signed on October 8, 1992. The Guatemalan government at last officially recognized the peaceful nature of the Return and guaranteed the refugees access to land as well as security and the right to organize. Verification mechanisms by international and national organizations were established. After hard-fought debate, the government accepted the returnees' right to accompaniment by groups chosen by the refugees during the return, resettlement, and reintegration process.

Guatemalan returnees take pride in being the first group in the world to negotiate its own return. A returnee on the negotiating team commented: "At the global level this process had never happened before. It demonstrates to the world that it is possible to achieve things and establish foundations for the future" (TI). Another said: "We learned a lot in the school of refugees" (TI). No longer disempowered and terrorized, they were anxious to return. "We arrived in Mexico as humble people, afraid of people richer and 'better' than ourselves, afraid to speak to them as we were poor. But now we've taken courses and learned about human rights. We've overcome these attitudes" (Project A, 1993, p. 15).

II
Weaving Threads of Solidarity

3 Project Accompaniment – A Canadian Response

THIS CHAPTER EXPLAINS how and why Project Accompaniment (which came to be known as Project A), a network of Canadians who accompanied refugees returning from Mexico into Guatemala, originated. It sets Project A within the context of the refugees' dogged determination to set their own conditions for the Return to Guatemala in the context of war.

A : The Poor Accompany the Poor

When returned refugees recall their earliest memories of accompaniment, they name the poor campesinos in Chiapas, Mexico, who offered hospitality, shared what little they had, and protected them when they were still being deported to Guatemala. "For some time we had to wander hidden from Immigration, even in Mexican territory, seeking protection from our brother and sister campesinos" (TI). A Mexican campesino offered his testimony:

> On the afternoon of July 8, 1982, we realized that there were a lot of people, about 2,000 altogether, on the road. They were soaked to the skin and had no belongings. They were also carrying a dead person. They arrived late because they had buried two more in the mountains. Well, we went to them as Christians, and as Christians we had compassion for them. The suffering and the sadness we saw made it easy for us to extend our welcome to them. Then we had a meeting of all the communities. And all of us said: "It is good to accept them, because we are all Christians. Also we are of the same class: poor campesinos. Nothing makes them a different people. We are all the same."…We shared with them the little grain we had, such as beans, corn, and rice. Later we all ran out. (Guatemalan Church in Exile, p. 11)

Popular and courageous Bishop Samuel Ruiz of the Diocese of San Cristóbal, saw the unexpected arrival of the refugees on their doorstep as an opportunity: "We have learned what it means to be Christian with our brothers and sisters. We have learned the meaning of support in solidarity. While we were discussing the options for the poor, the urgency of responding here and now in very concrete terms to a given situation presented itself." He paid tribute to the Mexican campesinos in the Diocese: "It was a time when the demands and responses to those demands overwhelmed our capacity to deal with them. That is why I said: 'If our Mexican brothers and sisters hadn't been there, it all would have been impossible for us.' Their Christian example helped us gain an understanding of what the living faith of the poor, oppressed and despised means" (Guatemalan Church in Exile, p. 12).

Ruiz put into words the powerlessness many felt: "What word of comfort can we offer a mother who tumbled among the rocks in her flight, when that fall killed the baby on her back? Or another mother who inadvertently smothered her child to prevent it crying and betraying them to the pursuing soldiers? What word of comfort can we give to these people? Many of us have experienced this feeling of helplessness. We want to console and strengthen, say something meaningful to this person who bears this great sorrow, but the words die on our lips (Guatemalan Church in Exile, p. 12).

Refugees expressed deep appreciation for Diocesan accompaniment. "When we left Guatemala and took refuge in Mexico we felt alone. But the Catholic Church gave us spiritual and pastoral accompaniment. Because of this we said, 'We are no longer alone. The church is with us'" (TI).

Chiapas is the poorest state in Mexico. Nevertheless the Christian Solidarity Committee mobilized all the spiritual, medical, and financial resources it could muster. It developed emergency aid programs (shelter, food, and health); training programs for catechists and education and health promoters; and job creation projects (crafts, carpentry, tailoring, farming, etc.). Bishop Ruiz ensured that the refugees' cry for solidarity was heard by churches, ecumenical coalitions, solidarity groups, and NGOs.

The Mexican Diocese of Tapachula played a similar role, although more discreetly as most refugees in that region were dispersed and undocumented. Bishop Juvenal remarked: "Eight months have gone by in the experience of a work for which we were never prepared. But it is a rich experience which has taught us to serve selflessly" (Guatemalan Church in Exile, p. 18). Both Dioceses were stalwart in defending the refugees' rights with Mexican authorities.

B : The Refugees Plan Their Return with Accompaniment

By the time Marta de la Vega and Wes Maultsaid returned home in early 1983, their sense of helplessness had been transformed into a commitment to mobilize the solidarity community and churches. When the Christian Task Force on Central America (CTF) formed in 1984, refugee solidarity became a pillar of its work. Delegations returned to the camps yearly until the early 1990s, paving the way for national delegations that led to Project Accompaniment.

Guatemalan human rights, church, and women's organizations in Mexico City spoke with delegates. "Their information, stories, and analysis of the situation in Guatemala and of the refugees in exile were for me horrifying. Yet the people we talked with were careful and sensitive enough not to paralyze us," said Pam Cooley (TI).

Delegations then went to Chiapas and Campeche. They met with elected refugee leaders and refugees active in education, health, agricultural, and youth projects. Pam described the "overwhelming" welcome from the Christian Solidarity Committee. "It indicated to us the trusting relationship the Task Force has built over the years of consistent visiting and communication" (TI). Face-to-face encounters enabled delegates to return home with an in-depth understanding of the refugees' hopes, challenges, and plans, making them excellent advocates for the refugees in Canada. The delegates observed the refugees' programs and the organizing and popular education methods they used to involve community members, including youth and women.

Barbara Wood, still involved in human rights work today, was an early delegation member: "I was twenty-three years old. This was my first time being anywhere outside of Canada and the US. It was amazing. I was so taken with people's stories and their willingness to tell us their stories number one, but the horror of what they had lived through was burned into my brain and my heart....I remember thinking 'I can never let this go. This will always be with me, and I have to do something with this now that it's part of me.' I can remember standing in the camp and thinking that in my own mind....To be able to come back and put my energy into helping to create an organization or a base from which we could help the people there was really important" (TI).

All who spent time in the camps echoed her words. As visits became more regular, the refugees recognized that a friendship was forming. "Most of us have heard of Canada far away but now we have Canadian friends and that gives us strength and courage to keep on going. May God bless you in your lives and may we never be strangers to each other again" (Cooley, 1986).

Refugees began to envision a longer-term international presence. "The idea of accompaniment arose from the refugees themselves," recalled then-exiled lawyer Enrique Torres, leader of several delegations. He paraphrased their message: "It's good that you visit us. It's good that you bring us support. It brings joy to our hearts that you are here, but we would like you to be here longer" (TI). It was impossible to respond immediately to their call since Mexico did not allow internationals to stay in the camps, other than a few priests and Maryknoll sisters with whom the CTF made vital links.

NGOs staffed by Guatemalans exiled in Mexico supported refugee community development and training efforts. While they were in Canada seeking financial support, some of the initial thinking began that ultimately led to Project Accompaniment:

> We presented some projects to NGOs and churches who were supporting us. But we also discussed with many individuals and organizations how to move beyond the project support they were giving. How could we gain the Government's support? How could we have a greater Canadian involvement with the Guatemalan people? The idea emerged that support had to go beyond money, that it was also necessary to give support spiritually, politically, and also through human presence. This was perhaps what was new, since we were used to receiving economic support from many countries. We began to talk about the need for the presence of Canadians in these processes. We returned with what seemed to us to be a very good idea but we had to consult with the refugee groups. (TI)

They began a dialogue with refugees, who said they wanted to learn from the Salvadoran experience, where international accompaniment had been critical to the success of the refugee return from Honduras, despite government resistance. They invited Salvadoran returned refugees and Jesuits involved in accompaniment coordination to Mexico. "The Salvadoran experience helped us to recognize and understand above all the political importance of the presence of internationals in these processes because they are the eyes, they are the ears of the world in the face of such a situation" (TI).

The refugees decided that the right to accompaniment of their own choosing should be a condition for their return. Accompaniment was thoroughly explained and debated in each camp. Questions, doubts, and concerns were raised. Some refugees had heard that foreigners stole babies.

Others feared outside intervention in community affairs. However, when their leaders explained that accompaniers would be sent by groups who had demonstrated solidarity over many years and would be well trained, would speak Spanish, and would not intervene in internal decision-making, the refugees welcomed accompaniment.

Later events reinforced that desire. When seventy-seven refugee families returned from Honduras in 1991, they faced unfulfilled promises and deception. A health clinic was not built; wood for their houses never arrived; land they had been given was already occupied; young male returnees were told to present themselves for military duty; pressure was exerted to form civil patrols. "We said that we are going to return but not as they did, without accompaniment. Who took any account of what happened to them? We decided that we were not going to return unnoticed." (TI)

Having the government agree to accompaniment was a huge struggle. A refugee negotiator said: "International accompaniment was always a very controversial point because the government was very direct in signaling that the guerrilla's advisers would come by way of these foreigners" (TI). Patricia Fuller recalled her lobbying efforts through GRICAR:

> The presence of international accompaniers had been controversial in the numerous negotiating sessions leading up to the Return. The Guatemalan officials sitting at the table had voiced their concerns about foreigners stirring up trouble during the Return and in the camps. The Permanent Commissions representing the refugees were steadfast in their position—they were not coming home without accompaniers. The Mediating Commission, headed by De León Carpio and the Catholic bishop, Monsignor Avila, searched tirelessly for common ground. I sat with my Swedish, French, and Mexican embassy colleagues observing the talks, and in the corridors during the breaks I sought out the Guatemalan officials to offer my assurances. I had met the Canadian accompaniers on numerous occasions; the Project Accompaniment organizers had visited the embassy and explained their plans and preparations to us. They were highly responsible people, coming with a humanitarian agenda, not a political one, I said. They were well organized and trained for their role. They were going to be part of the solution, not part of the problem. (Fuller, p. 3)

Refugees believe fear of negative international publicity forced the government to agree to international accompaniment by members of solidarity networks. A refugee negotiator recalled the process: "They first said the Red Cross could provide accompaniment.... Later they had to accept accompaniment, that is to say politically they accepted it, because rejecting accompaniment might in some way have become known in the accompaniers' countries of origin" (TI). When the Permanent Commissions requested a letter-writing campaign, the Urgent Action Network inundated the Guatemalan and Canadian governments. In the following months and years, this lesson of the power of international pressure was not lost on the refugees or Canadians.

C : Project Accompaniment Is Born

In May 1988 the Permanent Commissions (CCPP) published an open letter to the people of Guatemala and international friends. For the first time they publicly declared their intention to return to Guatemala and requested international accompaniment. The CTF responded publicly: "We read with prayerful concern your call for international accompaniment....It will take much faith, however, for this concern to develop into a willingness to physically accompany your return. We hope now, however, to help prepare people in our community for this concrete way of walking with you, our brothers and sisters....We, as Christians, therefore join you in your effort to participate in the building of God's Kingdom where justice and peace reigns" (*Network News,* de la Vega).

In early 1989 an ad hoc group called the Guatemala Network Coordinating Committee formed with funding from Oxfam, CUSO, the Canadian Catholic Organization for Development and Peace, and the United Church of Canada in order to:

- Develop an education/action program in Canada focused on Guatemalan refugees in Mexico and displaced persons in Guatemala;
- Coordinate a Canadian response to the request for accompaniment; and
- Strengthen the network of Canadian organizations working in solidarity with the Guatemalan people by developing a structure for collaborative work between NGOs, churches, human rights groups, and solidarity committees.

Wes Maultsaid and Debbie Grisdale travelled to Mexico and Guatemala, receiving advice from refugees, human rights groups, and NGOs. They also consulted with Canadian groups. Wes and Debbie observed that the return process would be long and slow, controlled by the refugees. Believing that accompaniment should be long-term with moral, spiritual, and political dimensions, they urged that it become part of an integrated pro-

> **From 1989 Project Acompanante Report**
>
> *Positives*
> - The initiative came from Guatemala;
> - It will strengthen the relationships South and North and also across Canada;
> - It is good to be on the ground floor of program development and to be part of the thinking from the beginning. It will engage us in a continuing and deepening process regarding awareness, understanding, and respect for indigenous values;
> - The issue of "the Return" will expose the internal situation internationally; and
> - The refugees in southern Mexico and the Guatemalan NGOs in Mexico and Guatemala said that it is positive to have Canadians "present" in the process.
>
> *Cautions*
> - Regional groups or persons in Canada cannot just feed the "national" agenda;
> - We must take care not to "direct" the work from the "centre";
> - Local groups have to be faithful to their base;
> - Are we raising expectations with the refugees that we will maintain our work over the long haul? Do we have the resources and capacity to do it?
> - We have to be careful to set limits;
> - We have to take care that "refugees" and "widows" do not become fashionable and are not "used" to develop programs; and
> - We must take care to deepen our understanding of the situation inside Guatemala before we leap.

gram for NGOs, churches and community-based solidarity groups. They paraphrased messages the refugees had given them:

> "The Return" will be with people with whom we have been in exile—those who travelled and suffered with us. It will not only be a physical return but also a spiritual one, i.e., a liberation from exile to return to our earth and the land of our ancestors—an exodus through the desert of our sufferings. The timing is important because there must be a certain "conjuncture" in Guatemala. We do not want to be used as part of the military's counter-insurgency plan. We want good friends to accompany us throughout the process beginning now. We do not

Valerie Mansour and Pam Cooley with refugees in Chiapas. Photo by Pam Cooley.

want strangers to jump on board after our pilgrimage has begun. We want to discuss the Return face to face with people, not through a number of "intermediaries." (Grisdale and Maultsaid, 1989)

Debbie and Wes shared insights from encounters in Mexico and Guatemala.

Accompaniment means walking toward the new dawn. It means listening to each other, learning together, supporting each other on steep and rocky paths, rejoicing in community and mutual respect and commitment for a long journey.

Accompaniment demands a definition that is broad enough to include culture, religion, economics and social processes, but narrow enough so people can act now.

It means living with people and sharing their lives and dangerous times. It occurs on many levels, always moving toward stronger solidarity.

It means more than "we" (Canadians) accompanying "them" (Guatemalans) from Place A to Place B (although it does include that). There is a tremendous gap between us and them—we come from different social and cultural backgrounds and conditions and we have different roles, but we all choose to be on the same side against unjust policies and systems and for justice.

> It could take many forms such as giving financial support so people could return and build their homes and plant their crops, doing political advocacy work, monitoring the human rights situation, and organizing ways to help the CCPP in their international work.
> —Grisdale and Maultsaid, Project Acompanante, 1989.

The Guatemala Network Coordinating Committee organized a 1990 Canadian delegation that explored with Guatemalan refugees and NGOs in Mexico what the next steps should be. Delegates met with Guatemalan representatives of trade unions, the church, campesino organizations, and indigenous and human rights groups in Mexico City in order to understand the refugees' situation within the wider Guatemalan context. They then split into three groups to visit refugee camps in Chiapas and Campeche. A Guatemalan who had lived in exile in BC accompanied Caece Levo, Pam Cooley, and Valerie Mansour to a refugee camp on the Chiapas-Guatemala border. Interviewed in Guatemala, where he has returned to work on indigenous rights, he recalled the experience with enthusiasm: "That experience motivated them to put a great deal of effort into accompaniment work. Because of the need they saw at that time, it was much easier to create an accompaniment project. They knew the reality the refugees were living at that time....Never has there been a delegation as good as those three women. I will always remember them; a formal delegation, yet one with whom we never had any problems. We were never bored because we were always laughing and joking. I believe that characterized the delegation and created its real success."

Maritimes delegation member Valerie Mansour wrote: "After walking more than an hour in the scorching mid-day heat, we reach the top of a hill. We gape at a collection of wooden and clay brick huts bleakly nestled in the dry hill....'People don't actually live here,' I kept saying to myself. But in fact 1,700 people have been living in this camp for seven years....I remember staring in amazement at the steep Guatemalan mountains, trying to imagine how complete families, from children to grandparents, walked through the dense forests to Mexico....'We want to go home, but not until our safety and freedom are assured,' we're told time and again" (Mansour, 1990).

The delegation reported its findings:

> Despite some despair, resignation, and bitterness, we found that the people were well organized with immense dignity and hope in the face of such suffering, hardship, and Goliathic adversaries. What keeps these people going is their strong and clear vision for what is just, not only for themselves but for Guatemala, Central America, and indeed

the world community. They're building for a future, not only by developing their own skills—academic, work, social, and political—but by giving their children a sense of their roots and fostering in them a commitment to learn and to help their people. This is not easy in the face of so many struggles and temptations facing young people, but we found a maturity and a sense of purpose and belonging that is almost unthinkable in North American society. (*Project Acompañimento: A Visit to the Guatemalan People in Refuge in Mexico,* 1990, p. 5, 1990)

Delegates returned home, committed to ensuring Canadian accompaniment. Their first tasks were to increase public understanding of Guatemala's historical, political, and socio-economic situation and to create a community-based network across Canada, building on a decade of solidarity work. Pam Cooley and John Payne toured eleven communities in BC's Interior. "All of us have been doing the slide show routines, church conferences, Sunday morning sermons at local churches, church basement 'educationals,' trying to get Guatemala in the media; not an easy feat," wrote Pam (Cooley, 1990).

Atlantic Region Solidarity Network members sat in a rural Nova Scotia farmhouse one cold damp May weekend as delegation members shared their experience. They formed a small committee to encourage the development of what would become Project Accompaniment (Project A). In early 1991 Valerie Mansour took a short-term CUSO posting to develop linkages between Atlantic Canada and Central America. She spent three months in Mexico and Guatemala, including visits to refugee camps. Valerie reported: "The people need to know they haven't been forgotten. It would be an understatement to say they were impressed that someone would come from as far as Canada to see them. They set up meetings especially for me, went out of their way to explain things to me, and tolerated my beginner's Spanish. They know they need international support in order to return to Guatemala. They remembered the visit to Quetzal Edna made last year by three members of our group, Jeff, John, and Nadine, and were pleased that the same group was continuing its connection with them" (Mansour, 1991).

These experiences kept Canadians focused on the refugee return. They persisted in the work of letter-writing campaigns, educational events, media coverage, and lobbying of politicians. Commitment widened and deepened.

In the summer of 1991, Frances Arbour, then working with refugees through Project Counseling Services, a group supported by Canadian NGO

Project Accompaniment – A Canadian Response   47

Inter Pares, reported that pressures were intensifying for refugees to repatriate without waiting for the completion of the lengthy refugee-government negotiations. Canadian groups responded by better coordinating their activities, strengthening grassroots political support in Canada, and increasing NGO financial funding for the refugees.

A 1991 delegation deepened the relationship with the CCPP, who were hoping a first Return would occur in early 1992. In fact the Guatemalan government used delaying tactics to stall negotiations for almost another year. The delegation urged that a formal accompaniment network be created as soon as possible.

Susan Skaret, a mental health worker and volunteer in Comitancillo, Guatemala, was asked to represent Alberta on the delegation. She became Project A's first coordinator, supported by CUSO: "It was such an excellent educational experience with the wealth of information that was shared in sessions in Mexico City and then of course by the refugees in the camps. I'm sure that one thing that enhanced my commitment to PA was that the refugees were asking for this and it fit into a fairly neat package within the agreements. It was also really exciting to think of this happening on a national level—bringing everyone together for a common cause" (correspondence with author).

In December 1991 the CCPP invited international friends to Chiapas to share the refugees' vision, plans, and needs. The Central America Monitoring Group (CAMG), a consortium of Canadian NGOs, churches, and solidarity groups that monitored humanitarian and development assistance in Central America, sent three delegates. Pam Cooley, who represented solidarity groups, joined a Working Group with representatives of similar groups from other countries, including Peace Brigades International and Witness for Peace. They developed a model for security accompaniment and made a commitment to take direction from the CCPP concerning selection criteria and training requirements. Canadian representatives concluded: "Participants learned a great deal, deepening their understanding of the enormity, complexity and immediacy of the challenges which we share....Though the challenge is daunting and our preparedness insufficient, important steps forward were taken" (CAMG, 1992).

Pam came back committed to an integrated model of physical accompaniment: "Being from the community-based approach, solidarity approach, we thought, 'How do we do this? How do we have physical accompaniment, but really have an integrity around building community and learning all about how to work as groups in our own cities?' We didn't want to be paternalistic. We wanted to make sure that we were not doing *for* but doing *with*." She was determined to seize the moment: "I came back and not really knowing what the churches or the NGOs were going to do and respond, I felt it was the moment to put pressure on the NGO community and the church community to make sure that they responded not only at their level, but also supported a grassroots approach to this."

Solidarity groups across Canada received a draft proposal. In an accompanying letter seeking input and support, Pam wrote: "I know that there is support from individuals in the NGO and Church community who hold some purse strings and I want to show the others what a wonderful program we have here. Regardless of their encouragement or support we know the project will live on, but I can't help but think that it would be easier with some finances and as part of a larger strategy" (Cooley, 1991).

The Central America Monitoring Group approved the proposal in early 1992. Project A became part of a comprehensive support program for the Return through the Canadian Council for International Cooperation's Rehabilitation and Reconstruction Fund. Funded by CIDA and NGOs, it was part of an international project supported by such NGOs as Swedish Diakonia, Christian Aid in Britain, and Bread for the World in the US.

Anticipation was in the air from Victoria to St. John's. Tours by refugee representatives had a huge impact. In the spring of 1992 Pam Cooley became national coordinator and Western region staff person. Karen Kewell worked part-time in central Canada, based in Montreal. Beth Abbott of Halifax was responsible for Atlantic Canada. Administrative infrastructure was minimal. Project A shared offices, equipment, and phone lines with the Christian Task Force on Central America in Vancouver, the Social Justice Committee in Montreal, and Oxfam in Halifax.

The Network's shape became clear. It would consist of community-based groups across Canada, those with a long solidarity history as well as new groups formed expressly to support the Return. They would recruit accompaniers in their communities and fundraise to help cover accompaniers' costs, normally about $3,000 for a three-month stay in Mexico and Guatemala. Raising the Return's international profile required increasing Canadian awareness and support for the refugees, strengthening Urgent Action work and increasing lobbying efforts with the Canadian government. These groups became Project A's foundation and its strength.

The Kootenays solidarity group developed a model in which they asked potential accompaniers to be part of their group for at least six months. After the individual had successfully completed accompaniment training, he or she would go on a speaking tour with a returned accompanier to communities in the region. Through this tour and other activities such as fund-raising dinners the group raised the money the accompanier would need, at the same time building a strong base of understanding and support. While in Guatemala the accompanier wrote home regularly. Letters were printed in local newspapers and copies, along with updates, were sent out to a large mailing list. When the accompanier returned home, a debriefing session and speaking tour were planned. Ann Godderis commented: "The feedback we heard from the accompaniers we sent was that they really felt they were being accompanied themselves by literally hundreds of people back home, that they weren't doing the accompaniment on their own at all, and if there were a problem, there would be strong and organized support from Canada. With the personal connection established we could then talk to our communities, churches, etc., about the situation in Guatemala, offer analysis, encourage people to join the Urgent Action Network. When Guatemalan visitors then came, people had much more of an understanding of the country and the context."

Recruitment of accompaniers began. Project A was non-partisan, yet not neutral. It saw itself as an ally of the refugees and consciously supported their struggle for basic human rights, democracy, and peace in Guatemala. Potential volunteers were informed that Project A's purpose was not to offer "money, material aid, and technical know-how. Instead we were being asked to provide our presence, our visibility as foreigners, in the hopes that this would protect the refugees/returnees from their own government's military" (Abbott, p. 69). Accompaniers had to make a minimum commitment of six weeks (later changed to two months) and have ongoing involvement with their local support group.

Pam Cooley and Karen Ridd, a Canadian jailed while accompanying Salvadorans with Peace Brigades International (PBI), facilitated a first training that fall. The five-day "intense, challenging, highly personal experience" prepared participants to accompany refugees returning to areas where military operations and human rights violations could be expected. The training design and selection criteria were developed in consultation with Permanent Commissioners, the Central America Monitoring Group, Project A volunteers, and PBI, who initiated the first accompaniment program in Guatemala in 1983. Prospective accompaniers were informed in advance that they would participate in exercises that explore oppression, violence, and fears: "It is expected that the training will enable each participant to understand what s/he personally brings to conflict situations and will enhance their responses through the creation and use of a non-violence tool-kit. One transcendent goal of our work is to make accompaniers as cognizant as possible of the extreme situations that they may find themselves in as accompaniers so that they are fully aware of all the possible ramifications of being an accompanier" (PA, 1998).

A primary training objective was deepening the understanding and practice of non-violence. Through presentations, discussions, group exercises, and role-plays, participants deepened their comprehension of the accompanier's role and gained skills in human rights observing. They learned more about the goals, policies, structure, and operation of Project A, issues involved in the Return process, Guatemalan history, and the current context.

A key element of the training was a series of complex role-plays that simulated stressful situations such as military roadblocks, intimidation, interrogation, abusive language, pushing and shoving of refugees or accompaniers, kidnapping, and machismo sexism. The element of surprise played a significant part. Since accompaniment often required a high degree of fitness, some role-plays included physical exertion over an extended period. The facilitators designed and directed each scenario, assigning roles and preparing participants. Each person played different roles throughout the week, acting as a soldier, refugee, or accompanier.

Much of the learning took place in group reflections after each role-play. Participants shared their reactions to their roles. They were encouraged to consider other responses they might have made, rather than trying to figure out "the right response." They were asked to articulate and face their fears, since hard-earned experience by PBI and Witness for Peace had taught that only those who could name and deal with their fears were able to overcome them and accompany well in high-risk situations.

Only after struggling with issues raised by the role-play experience were participants given advice such as:

- When confronted by the army, stand with your hands open, not clenched; keep your arms open, not crossed over the chest, to non-verbally reduce the conflictive atmosphere;
- Walk at the side of the group, not in the centre, to help ensure refugees' safety; and
- Enter a vehicle last and exit first, to reduce the risk of abductions.

Most particpants shared Eva Manly's assessment: "The most valuable thing in the training from my point of view was role-playing, because I think it's a really good way of getting a sense of a potential situation. Having to play not only a person being accompanied but also playing the role of the accompanier and the worst one, playing the role of the Guatemalan heavy, is a really important experience because it puts people in touch with their own dark side" (TI).

The training methodology was not without criticism or controversy. Some trainers and participants questioned the need to act out violence in order to train accompaniers in non-violence. Although such simulations had been used in non-violence training since the US civil rights movement, critics were concerned about the unnecessary reproduction of violence and the impact on individuals who may have suffered previous abuse or trauma. After much debate, it was agreed role-plays would not include physical violence and participants would be told that they were free to withdraw at any time from a role-play.

As time went on, the training placed less emphasis on the possibility of physical violence and more on how to deal with threats of violence and psychological intimidation of both returnees and accompaniers. As the war came to an end, the situation became calmer. Accompaniers felt that training was creating expectations and anxieties that intimidation and violence would occur. The emphasis on responding to potential violence was downplayed even more.

Selection criteria were outlined at the beginning of the week: knowledge of Guatemala, self-awareness, knowledge of the theory and practice of non-violence, travel and work experience abroad, knowledge of group process and consensus, physical and psychological stamina, Spanish, and cultural sensitivity.

Participants were encouraged to discern their readiness to accompany. Although some decided to withdraw their applications, the trainers made the final decision. They felt a tremendous responsibility to select competent, trustworthy accompaniers. Sharing with a participant the decision that he or she was not suitable for accompaniment was a painful experience for all.

When accompaniers arrived in Mexico and Guatemala, they received a briefing on the current political context and the evolution of the refugees' situation. Security, communications, and emergency procedures were explained. Meetings were held with the CCPP. The orientation included a stay in a refugee camp. Accompaniers then received their assignments. On several occasions, at the end of the orientation, the Southern coordinators decided individuals were not ready to accompany, most often because they had not achieved sufficient Spanish fluency.

Excitement grew across Canada with the news that the October 8 Refugee Accords had been signed and the date of the first Return set for early January 1993. The Project A Steering Committee met face-to-face for the first time in Montreal that fall. They developed a participatory structure that functioned with some adaptations until 1999. Groups first discussed policy issues at the local and regional levels. Then the Steering Committee, made up of two representatives from each of the five regions (BC, the Prairies, Ontario, Quebec, the Atlantic), met annually along with staff members. Major or controversial recommendations were referred to the regions for consultation with local groups. Much of the decision-making was done through monthly or bi-monthly meetings of regional representatives by e-mail, with phone calls and faxes as needed. Susan Skaret and Randy Kohan later said: "We feel the success of Project Accompaniment is based on a strong national vision which its members embrace. Because they embrace Project Accompaniment as their own, they take ownership of it and dedicate themselves to it with passion and commitment" (correspondence with author).

Project A formed a Southern team who offered orientation and logistical support to accompaniers and delegations, helped develop accompaniment policy, and acted as a liaison among the refugees, the accompaniers, and Project A in Canada. They worked with the CCPP on accompaniers' placements in the refugee camps and the Returns; they developed communications, emergency, and security systems; they deepened relationships with refugee organizations and NGOs in southern Mexico and Guatemala, as well as with the Canadian Embassy; they collaborated with international partners; and they created a debriefing program for accompaniers before they left the South.

Gaby Labelle, long-time Latin America Working Group member and CUSO cooperant in Mexico, worked with Project A, as the liaison with refugee organizations and NGOs in Mexico City. Susan Skaret established Project A's presence in southern Mexico. The first accompanier, Vancouver community worker Frank Green, arrived soon after. They immediately set to work coordinating plans with the CCPP. Randy Kohan, Susan's partner, joined her some weeks later after language study in Guatemala. Susan said: "The challenge put to us by the refugees to work together in organizing a response to accompaniment was important. I regularly heard, upon joining PA, that the refugees were having to organize amongst three states, many refugee camps, and across two countries with limited resources (few phones, no e-mail, long journeys by bus, etc.) and so we should be able to work together with our unending resources. The challenge and commitment to their process pulled us together" (correspondence with author).

Project Accompaniment – A Canadian Response   53

To organize a mass return of refugees is a challenge in the best of situations. And this was not the best of situations, with the refugees returning to an isolated war zone. Logistical problems were massive. The CCPP and supporting groups had to find answers to everything from arranging for a supply of disposable diapers on each bus to ensuring the returnees' health and security. An accompanier put it this way: "Imagine the last time you moved. Now imagine that there are 2,000 people in your family, moving with you. Imagine that there is no house on the piece of land you are moving to. Imagine that you aren't sure if the land you are going to has been bought yet. And it takes two weeks to get there. And the road is deep mud. And there is a war going on" (unsigned report to Project A). Through constant communication with the CCPP and the network in Canada, Project A was ready with well-trained, flexible accompaniers when the Return caravan left Chiapas.

※ Refugees Forced Back to the Negotiation Table

After signing the October 8th accords, the Guatemalan government and the UNHCR agreed to the CCPP Operational Plan for the first Return, including the proposed route and date, January 13, 1993. In early January the returnees tore down their houses in the camps, taking everything they owned with them—tin roofing and wood from their homes, their dishes, clothing, machetes, and animals. Many carried all their worldly possessions on their backs down the mountainsides to main roads where trucks picked up their goods and buses transported them to Comitan, Chiapas.

The CCPP, however, was shocked and angry when CEAR, without notice, altered its agreement on January 5, insisting that only five hundred refugees a day could enter Guatemala and only through the isolated rain forest where they would be publicly invisible. The refugees insisted on traveling in one large caravan following the agreed-upon route, on the Inter-American Highway through the town of Huehuetenango to the capital, Guatemala City, before heading to Cobán and their final destination, the Ixcán. They were not about to return by the back door, hidden from the world. Rigoberta Menchú commented: "The people were afraid of silence. By that route, it would have been so easy for the Government to simply silence this Return, to lower its profile and its international dimension" (*Monitoring Update* #19).

CEAR underestimated refugee determination. They had survived overwhelming horror and had rebuilt their lives, fully intending to return home. CEAR was caught off guard when the CCPP, after consultation with the returning refugees, stated that the Return was going ahead January 13, with or without Guatemalan assent and UNHCR support. "They had a profoundly different understanding of the word 'impossible' than any Guatemalan government or UNHCR official. In their experience, the mere lack of a bus was hardly a major impediment....Walking to the border could hardly seem more difficult than what they had already survived.... The government's betrayal of the October 8 Accords was seen as a demand they crawl home submissively, contrary to everything they had struggled for" (Eguren and Mahony, p. 133).

The CCPP believe the immediate activation of international political support was critical in those tough negotiations: "There were a lot of problems. We fought with the government. I remember that, in the middle of one of our meetings with the government, the Director of CEAR told us that their house was full of faxes which had come from the international community pressuring for the Return to take place. But they weren't only there but in the vice-president of Guatemala's office and everywhere!" (TI).

On January 9, refugees and accompaniers in Quintana Roo set out on foot for Comitan, fourteen hundred kilometres away. Limited community funds were spent to charter buses from Campeche. Accompaniers, although fearful, were prepared to follow their lead and walk with them across the border. They had created bonds as they made final preparations for the journey home. Canadian accompanier Mary Ann Morris said: "I'm not so much afraid for myself because I have a sense that as foreigners we're protected. But just in this short period of time, you get to know people and you realize they already fled this violence once before. They are here because of violence in their community, because of family members being murdered. And they're going back to that. They're not nameless people. They are families and they are children I play with" (*When the People Lead,* 1993).

On the eve of January 12, faced with the returnees' unwavering determination and massive international pressure, both public and diplomatic (including that of the Canadian Embassy), the Guatemalan government agreed to the refugees' plan, with the departure postponed by a week.

Even those audacious enough to have signed up for this first Return were fearful of what lay ahead. The human rights situation continued to be alarming with no decrease in the number of murders, disappearances, and torture. It was impossible for campesinos to feel secure as army-controlled civil defence patrols carried out extra-judicial executions throughout the countryside. The minister of Defence was taking a hard line against the Return, accusing the CCPP of direct links with the guerrillas, thus implying that the army would be justified in any actions it might take against them. A permanent commissioner said that the minister was trying to frighten people in order to prevent them from returning to the country.

4   Accompaniment in War and Peace

> With much hard work and remarkable determination, the first group of twenty-five hundred refugees crossed the Mexican-Guatemalan border and settled in the northern Guatemalan Province of Quiché. The journey home was characterized by heavy rains, bitter cold, some military intimidation, inadequate supplies—and the birth of seven babies!   —Abbott, 1993

A : A Triumphant Return

ON JANUARY 20, 1993, returning refugees clambered aboard seventy-eight buses with one hundred and seven accompaniers from Canada, the US, Britain, and several European countries, notably Spain, Germany, and Holland. Canadians included retired teacher and writer Alison Acker, community development worker Frank Green, and geologist John Payne, from British Columbia; Manitoba rural outpost nurses Mary Ann Morris and Randy Janzen; and Robert Turcotte from Quebec. Victoria videographers Mike Simpson and Merran Smith had an additional task of filming the Return. *When the People Lead* was later shown several times on Vision TV, and widely distributed by Project A in both English and Spanish.

A newly formed Project A group in Victoria supported Merran and Mike; the Outreach Committee of his home congregation, West Vancouver United Church, sponsored John Payne; Frank Green and Mary Ann Morris were supported by the Christian Task Force on Central America, which Mary Ann had been active in before moving to Manitoba; Home Street Mennonite Church in Winnipeg supported Randy Janzen. Supporters were kept up-to-date on the Return, as well as related Urgent Action requests.

Hand-painted banners with messages such as "the Return is struggle, not resignation" hung from every bus. The refugees set off for the border, their fear turning to joy as the caravan entered Guatemala to a jubilant welcome. The sound of the beloved marimba melded with the applause

58 II – Weaving Threads of Solidarity

At the border. Photo by Brian Atkinson.

that rang out as campesinos, church leaders, and foreign diplomats greeted the refugees. A throng of Guatemalan and foreign journalists ensured extensive media coverage. High-level Guatemalan government officials were noticeably absent.

Nobel Peace Prize winner Rigoberta Menchú joined the refugees at the border. Her simple but moving speeches and poems, reported widely in the press, inspired refugees and accompaniers: "One feels like the volcanoes are speaking with you and that all the mountains are speaking to you. One feels a part of this, as if this is a rebirth of life" (cited by Kohan and Skaret, 1993). Canadian Ambassador Brian Dickson, with MPs Beryl Gaffney (Liberal) and Dan Heap (NDP), accompanied Menchú to the border, in another expression of Embassy support for the Return. Its proactive stance was a pleasant surprise to many in solidarity work. Susan Skaret and Randy Kohan wrote Project A: "They have been very supportive since we arrived here in Guatemala, and have been very present with the refugees in Huehuetenango, the Capital, and in Cobán....They are supporting Project A in many ways: each accompanier received a letter of support; they are willing to serve as an emergency contact for us; they are researching how to extend our visas and helping with the documentation....They gave us a ride to Coban; we attended a meeting with the Bishop of Alta Verapaz together with them and they strongly supported Project A" (Kohan and Skaret, 1993).

Accompanier John Payne was also appreciative: "The Ambassador was there, involved very much with what was going on....I'm sure Guatemalan government officials knew that Canada's policies were very much in favour of supporting the refugees" (TI).

Lajos Arendas, a Political Affairs officer at the Embassy from 1995–97, worked on the Guatemala desk in Ottawa during the first Returns. "Policies are made in Ottawa. But the orders given by Ottawa are clearly influenced by the Embassy itself, by the kind of reports we write. I strongly believe that there was some personal influence of Ambassador Dickson that made it happen that way, in a very positive way." He believes the Embassy valued accompaniment because the situation was still so precarious. "Nobody knew when it started how it would evolve and how the refugees would be accepted here. The Embassy was scared that something could go wrong. That's why it was so essential to have international presence" (TI).

The convoy travelled a few hours down the highway and stayed for two days at a temporary reception centre beside an army base in Huehuetenango. The refugees received temporary papers identifying them as returning refugees. The men received military exemption papers. CEAR had originally wanted the refugees to register at a military reception centre, as repatriated refugees had done: "This had a huge impact psychologically because not only did the army force us out of Guatemala but now they were going to put us through a military reception centre. The people were unhappy. We had to struggle so that they would dismantle these reception centres and construct civilian reception centres. We succeeded" (TI).

Canadian Embassy representative Patricia Fuller recalled that first evening in Guatemala: "The arrival this first night in Huehue [Huehuetenango] was quiet, almost hushed. Fear, uncertainty, hope, exhaustion, relief of a journey's end—all these emotions seemed evident in the eyes of the men, women, and children who stepped off the buses onto Guatemalan soil. What courage to be the first, what hope mixed with trepidation. What a leap of faith! No wonder they wanted to be accompanied in this voyage into their new future that could not help but also be a rendezvous with memories of a terrible past" (Fuller, p. 3).

Conflict soon erupted. After refugees identified soldiers in the reception centre, the Permanent Commissioners accused CEAR of allowing the army to infiltrate the documentation process. The Mediating Commission (an intermediary group with representatives from the UNHCR, the Catholic Church, the government's human rights office, and the exiled Guatemalan Human Rights Commission) later confirmed the accusation. The CCPP also criticized CEAR for insufficient beds, blankets, and food. The Diocese of Huehuetenango offered more beds and food but CEAR refused to allow the returnees to leave the reception centre.

CEAR, infuriated, stated that it would neither guarantee the convoy's security nor negotiate future returns. The CCPP replied that the Return would continue, relying for security on the momentum gained by international awareness and accompaniment. Stung by the criticisms, CEAR turned on the accompaniers, accusing them of taking the returnees' mattresses and food. A day later it accused accompaniers of being drug addicts. Such accusations recurred over and over in the next six years.

On the way to Quetzaltenango, an unforgettable scene unfolded. Despite temperatures below freezing, thousands of campesinos left mountain hamlets, villages, and towns, lining the Inter-American Highway for miles. Taking a considerable risk, they ignored army propaganda describing the returning refugees as "dangerous guerrillas." Instead they trusted Catholic and Protestant groups who had distributed booklets explaining why the refugees fled and were returning. John Payne commented: "The government had been spreading propaganda that these people were coming back basically to continue on the war. This was the guerrilla army that was coming back to rape your children, your wives and children, to kill. The refugees weren't sure what kind of reception they were going to get when they got back. It was overwhelmingly positive" (TI).

The buses were asked not to stop, but it was impossible to proceed. Throngs of people continually crossed the highway to shake hands and share gifts of food and money. "In towns and villages, crowds of happy

Guatemalans in their colourful traditional dress lined the road, waving huge signs of welcome to their brothers and sisters, letting off fireworks, making formal presentations and presenting simple gifts. From the buses, children threw thousands of leaflets into the wind, announcing the refugees' hope of a dignified and organized return as part of the overall reconstruction of the nation" (*Network News*, Carrodus and Payne).

The returnees were exuberant: "From inside the bus the power of the crowds on the road really was moving. I was sitting next to a man who seemed to feel impelled to affirm every show of welcome—he was literally waving his hand out the window nonstop for hours. He was tired, sick, and almost half asleep at times, but he wasn't going to let a single greeting of welcome go by without showing his gratitude"(Eguren and Mahony, p. 134).

The Catholic Church greeted the caravan with open arms when it reached Guatemala City, providing hospitality in three schools. A large crowd walked with the refugees to the Central Square in front of the National Palace and Cathedral for a "Celebration of National Re-encounter" organized by popular, labour, and religious groups. John Payne described the military surveillance: "As we were walking down the streets of Guatemala, Frank Green would be looking up and you could see a military person up in a balcony watching and keeping track of what was going on. You knew the situation was not completely free of risk for us. Then you looked at what it was for the people and you'd say: 'Wow, these people are really taking a big risk by doing this!'" (TI).

Mass was celebrated; food was shared; the crowd sang; Rigoberta Menchú spoke; leaders of popular groups welcomed the returnees. A refugee leader spoke in favour of the peace talks between the URNG and government: "The war of hunger also must end. This war does not end only with talks and signatures. Poverty and inequality must also be resolved. We want the repression and the human rights violations to end. We want land and peace" (Guatemalan Human Rights Commission, 1993).

As the caravan departed, a woman called Peace Brigades International with a death threat: "Are you listening? The communists protect the Guatemalan traitors. All the communists will die!" It was seen as an attempt to intimidate accompaniers and lower the number of international observers. Embassies were informed immediately. The Urgent Action Network asked Canadians to send faxes and letters to President Serrano with copies to Barbara McDougall, Secretary of State for External Affairs, and opposition MPs Lloyd Axworthy and Svend Robinson, demanding that the convoy's security be assured.

The most rugged part of the trip lay ahead. After a thirteen-hour journey, the returnees spent several days in shelters in the damp, cool mountainous community of Cobán. With insufficient warm clothing and blankets, many fell ill, particularly with respiratory problems. "The lack of support from the government provoked very high risks to the health of the returnees," said Bishop Gerardo Flores, adding that church and other agencies had done all they could. He noted local support: "The people here are with them, and they have expressed their joy at this Return. It has been such a spontaneous response that it shows how much suffering the war has brought" (*Monitoring Update* #18, 1993).

There were humorous moments. An accompanier told Ann Godderis about awaking in the church to the cheeping of baby chicks: "By the afternoon the church was overrun by baby chicks. The refugees had been told not to bring any of their animals, but they had tucked eggs into their clothing. The trip had taken longer than they had planned. So all the eggs were hatched" (TI).

The Government had made no effort to upgrade the unpaved road from Cobán to the Ixcán. With torrential downpours, the road had deteriorated into a sea of mud. It took three bone-crushing days for cattle trucks jam-packed with returnees and accompaniers to negotiate the last one hundred and twenty kilometres. They had to continually dig the trucks out of knee-deep mud. At one point tractors hauled the trucks through: "They made it only through their own determination to continue on, having only lukewarm support from the UNHCR, and without sufficient supplies. They pushed and pulled the trucks, shoulder to shoulder together, side by side with campesinos who came down nearby paths to help out and a half dozen volunteers from the Red Cross and personnel from the Dioceses of Quiché and the Verapaces" (*Monitoring Update* #19).

They walked the final four kilometres, as the last section of the thirty-kilometre road from Cantabal, the Ixcán's municipal centre, to their destination, Polígono 14, was impassable. The most vulnerable members of the group—pregnant mothers, the elderly, and small children—were airlifted from Cobán to Cantabal in planes contracted by the UNHCR, although the army had wanted to use its own planes. The CCPP, insisting that they were civilians, urged the government to "put its civilian institutions at the service of the returnees, and not the military" (*Monitoring Update* #17). Nonetheless the planes had to land at the nearby military base in Playa Grande, the largest in the region.

Residents of more than eighty indigenous communities travelled to the town of Chisec to offer the returnees a candle-lit welcome. A month later

Accompaniment in War and Peace

Starting over. Photo by Brian Atkinson.

local civil patrol members and military personnel would issue death threats, accusing participants of having "guerrilla sympathies." A few kilometres from Polígono 14, the tiny village of Santa Clara set off fireworks and played gentle marimba music as the first section of the caravan passed by. A few months later twenty-five Santa Clara families joined the new community.

※ Carving a Community out of the Jungle

On January 29, the first group of 362 refugees, including babies, pregnant women, and grandparents, crossed the hanging footbridge over the Gavilan River. They entered the 2,800-hectare former community of Polígono 14, which the army had burnt to the ground in February 1982, murdering thirteen inhabitants. Exhausted, they still found the energy to cry out, "Guatemala! A cry for life is a cry for peace! Long live freedom!"

CEAR, despite written agreements, had made virtually no preparations for their arrival. There was no food, only twenty latrines and three *galeras* (tin-roofed shelters with dirt floors and plastic walls held up by tree posts) that could house only three hundred people. Rain poured down incessantly.

The UNHCR contracted planes to bring in construction materials and food. The returnees set to work immediately, as they had done when they

Children at school in a returned community. Photo by Brian Atkinson.

settled the Ixcán twenty years before and again when they fled to Mexico. They cleared land, burning brush to scare away snakes and scorpions. The sound of machetes cutting wood to build huts echoed throughout the community. With a few tools and hundreds of metres of blue plastic, they constructed additional makeshift shelters. Polígono 14 became a sea of blue tents. Conditions improved steadily, especially after belongings and livestock arrived days later, delayed because of the incomplete road through the Chiapas rain forest to the nearby border crossing. Families planted their first gardens.

Polígono 14 was renamed Victoria 20 de enero (Victory, January 20) by the jubilant returnees. It soon became known as Victoria. "It is more difficult here," a resident told journalist Valerie Mansour when she visited the community on a grant from the International Centre for Human Rights and Democratic Development. Another agreed: "But the difference here is it's my country. I can plant corn here" (Mansour, 1993). Returnees, especially children, were often sick with respiratory infections, malaria, typhoid, and gastroenteritis. Five babies died in the first month, two from whooping cough. However, children were soon inoculated. Malnutrition lasted many months because families were often given rotting corn, full of insects and worms due to improper storage.

"At first sight, the crowded collection of tin roofs, palm branches, and brightly coloured tarp walls looks like a poor excuse for a community," Valerie wrote. However, she soon discovered a community in the mak-

Returned refugees await a baptism. Photo by Brian Atkinson.

ing. "The day begins with the loud sound of a grinder as the women line up to grind their corn to make tortillas. Until dusk, when they gather in community meetings, the residents work to make Victoria home" (Mansour, 1993). The first general assembly took place, where men and women elected community leaders, including health and education promoters. They named their priorities—construction of a school, health clinic, and roads.

The returnees started to clear more land to plant corn. As *hombres de maiz* ("people formed from corn," the sacred source of life), planting their land was a joy. They built offices in the town centre for groups such as the town council and the women's organization, "Mama Maquín." They set up a sawmill, a bakery with a homemade whitewashed clay oven, and small shops. Accompanier Colin Rowat wrote: "The word 'tienda' translates into English as a shop but something is lost. These tiendas are stores and houses rolled into the same makeshift shelter. Their frame of chopped wooden poles is skinned over with garbage bag plastic and roofed with corrugated sheet steel. The family's bed might lie in the shadows behind the table of goods, covered with bars of soap, bags of chips, avocados, and cigarettes" (Rowat, letter to support committee, 1994).

Despite ongoing fear and daily challenges, the returnees were content. A women's group leader said: "To return is to struggle. It is not giving up. We didn't come to sit down. We have to work, to clear the mountainsides, to start again. We're arriving in our beautiful land. It gives me a lot of pleasure" (*When the People Lead*).

When I visited Victoria in June 1993, community life was already well organized. The Saturday I arrived, the community held its six-hour-long monthly assembly. The committees on land, community development, security, Christian community, human rights, health, and youth presented their written reports orally. They had put tremendous effort into preparing them, no small achievement for people with little or no formal education. The reports reflected the astonishing progress made in less than five months. Some returnees were being formally trained as teachers and health workers. The children attended school every day, taught by their own people. Although malnutrition was still a serious problem, the community's health promoters were teaching people how to adapt to the climate and living conditions. In the community projects report, every penny was accounted for, including the contribution from The United Church of Canada through its partner, CIEDEG (the Guatemalan Protestant Conference of Churches for Development). Men freely participated in questions of health, the corn problems, and the misuse of alcohol in the supposedly dry community. Although many women attended and listened attentively, none spoke publicly.

After resolving more important issues, a lengthy, animated, sometimes hilarious discussion ensued about the pros and cons of capturing monkeys in the jungle to be kept as pets. One man pointed out that they had returned to Guatemala in search of freedom and therefore had no right to deny freedom to the animals around them. Apparently his logic could not be denied and discussion ended.

Early the next morning I went to Mass. The two-hour service, led entirely by lay catechists, began with reflection in small groups on biblical texts. We talked about the prophet Jeremiah's discouragement and his realization of his call. Unlike the assembly the day before, both women and men contributed fully. Guitars and marimba provided joyful music.

※ Accompaniment in Victoria

Most international accompaniers left in early February. A smaller group, including most of the Project A contingent, stayed on, sharing the joys and hardships of the early months. They helped build shelters and dug through hard clay to increase the number of latrines. They slept in hammocks over the damp dirt floors of their hut, known as *Casa Canadiense* (the Canadian House). They cooked over a fire, supplementing tortillas with pasta and a few vegetables or tinned mackerel purchased in the refugees' tiny shops.

They carried jugs home from the communal water taps, although, unlike the women they accompanied, they were never able to balance jugs full of water on their heads. The pure water, a rare and precious asset in Guatemala, was the result of a portable water purification system supplied by the NGO *Medicos del Mundo* (Doctors of the World). Accompaniers, not acclimatized to tropical heat and endless rains, suffered from gastroenteritis, typhoid, and pneumonia.

Returnees took responsibility for the accompaniers. They built them one-room huts with dirt floors throughout the community as well as an accompaniment office in the town centre. It contained a few rough log benches, a table, shelves, and an ancient typewriter. Families rotated the task of supplying food. At each mealtime, a family member would arrive at the door of Casa Canadiense with a huge pile of corn tortillas and, when they could afford it, beans, eggs, or *tamales* (corn pastries steamed in large leaves). "They bumped into each other bringing us tortillas. In the face of everything, their hospitality never stopped," recalled Terry O'Toole (TI).

When it became apparent how highly militarized and volatile the region was, the need for accompaniment became even clearer. The eyes of the world were no longer fixed on the refugees, as the massive media attention disappeared. Victoria was in a war zone where the military had been unable to control or defeat guerrilla forces. The UNHCR publicly expressed concern about the army's increased presence close to Victoria when the refugees arrived.

Victoria was only a few hours' walk from the resistance communities (CPRs) who had hidden in the rain forest for more than ten years to avoid military repression. As the first returnees arrived in Victoria, the CPRs issued a press release, noting that the army was deploying large numbers of troops to the Ixcán. A few weeks later military helicopters machine-gunned and bombed two CPR communities. While returned refugees were hoping to establish a peaceful existence, friends and relatives were fleeing to Mexico, accompanied by internationals including Karen Ridd, United Church of Canada representative on a delegation to the CPRs.

Returnees appreciated accompaniment: "We need accompaniers because we believe that if we arrived here alone, for sure the government would say, 'Where did they come from? They're guerrillas.' We don't want this to happen. We don't have weapons. We have come back openly, with our bags open and with all the accompaniers" (*When the People Lead*).

The army launched an offensive lasting several months. Bombing exercises were heard from Victoria. Military helicopters painted black with no

Mary Ann Morris documenting an incident. Photo by Valerie Mansour.

lights flew over the community most evenings. Mary Ann Morris reported: "Two days ago around 10:30 at night we started to hear helicopters and sure enough they came closer and closer. They just kept circling. I'd say they stayed for a good fifteen minutes. You could feel people looking up, wondering what was going on." She noted that soldiers often passed through or camped on Victoria lands: "Yesterday for example people were out cutting the forest, trying to clear land, when they encountered soldiers" (*When the People Lead*).

Residents felt deeply vulnerable as decade-old memories were aroused by military planes circling overhead, signaling the army's arrival. Although these actions did not technically violate the October 8 Accords, the returnees felt they violated its intent. They refused to be intimidated and decided to struggle for a demilitarized community. When soldiers were seen on their land, the community sent out a delegation, with accompaniers, to question them. The returnees then laid an official complaint with the government's human rights office located in the community. They also sent delegations, always with accompaniment, to register their opposition with the Playa Grande military base commander.

Accompaniers were not to intervene in community decisions. Their role was to listen to returnee concerns and fears and to be active observers. They detailed the refugees' concerns in a logbook, as well as the overflights and military presence, noting times, how long helicopters or soldiers stayed, manoeuvres, and type of equipment. This information was distributed to the CCPP, embassies, churches, GRICAR, the UNHCR, and NGOs. "We worked hard to deactivate the war in the Ixcán, to get rid of the military, denouncing what was happening in Victoria with the helicopter flights in the night. What helped us enormously was the political accompaniment of the international organizations who sent a huge number of messages to the government" (Permanent Commissioner).

A camera was essential accompaniment equipment. Mary Ann described her role when the police, directly linked with the army, entered the camp. The police were only supposed to come for a specific reason, since Victoria had organized its own system for dealing with offences. "As soon as we see police officers we're up, wandering around, taking pictures, so they know these people aren't isolated" (*When the People Lead*).

Informing the outside world as quickly as possible required coordination and caution. The only public phone was thirty kilometres away, next to the Playa Grande military base where the army monitored calls. Accompaniers used the Doctors of the World radiophone in Victoria for emergencies and that of the UNHCR in Cantabal when they could find a pickup or NGO vehicle making the trip to town. It was difficult to use radiophones to call Mexico or Canada, so carefully worded calls were made from the phone by the base. Less urgent information was sent out with accompaniers or agency staff leaving for Cobán by pickup or, weather permitting, small plane. Messages were passed on to Susan and Randy in Mexico who sent the information to Canada, asking people to inundate the Guatemalan government with letters demanding, for example, that military overflights be stopped. "It was most definitely a sign to the government and everyone watching the return process that the international world was standing beside the return process" (Susan Skaret, correspondence with author).

Relationships between accompaniers and refugees were established, an aspect of accompaniment emphasized time and again by both. "It is a rare privilege for people of different cultures to interact on a daily basis," said an accompanier. "We get to see, feel and hear the Guatemala that is a reality, not the usual tourist propaganda."

John Payne fondly recalled a heartwarming incident. "On the bus during the Return I had made friends with a family of two parents with four little girls and one boy. I had became seriously ill on the bus and had to return to Canada for a month. When I arrived for the first time in Victoria, the smallest girl in the family saw me walking down the path into town. Her eyes lit up and she greeted me with a huge smile and a shout, 'JUAN, YOU'RE ALIVE!' Somehow, she had thought that I had died from the illness" (TI).

Colin Rowat described a day when his stomach wasn't up to digesting tortillas and beans. When he bought a loaf of bread from an older woman, she invited him to eat it in her small shop:

> She clears a grandson from their bench to offer me a seat. Reluctant at first to impose, I then realize how ridiculous it would be to retreat back to my hammock, given the opportunity to get to know another member of this remarkable community....We chat. I am trying to understand how she has come to find herself here: Where did she live in Guatemala before coming here to the Cooperative? Where in Mexico had the family lived during the years of refuge?...She pours a cup and hands it to me. But it isn't the expected thin coffee. A cup of rich, hot, thick, healthy-smelling oatmeal. I was struck immediately by the feeling that she had done something special; my first sense was that she had broken some kind of rule. Reflecting later I realize that she had seen our relationship very differently than I had at first. I had entered her tienda as a client to financially support her in return for providing me with a desired product. The offer of the seat was friendly, but did not really alter this. The cup of oatmeal, however, meant that when I entered her tienda it had been as a guest in her home. (Rowat, letter to support committee, 1994)

I recall a moment of shared laughter while accompanying in Victoria with women who spoke little Spanish. Early each morning, just below Casa Canadiense, the women scrubbed their families' clothes clean on the slippery rocks of a shallow creek, crouching down to put water in their washtubs. When I attempted to do my wash, I usually left with my clothes only slightly cleaner than when I began! One morning I finished washing all my clothes and gathered them up. As I turned to leave, I slipped on the rocks, dropping all the clothes onto the dirt. I started to laugh and so did the women, who could scarcely believe a grown woman could be so incompetent in carrying out one of the basic tasks of a woman's life. I felt a camaraderie and start of a relationship, though I did not speak their languages.

Chance encounters became meaningful conversations. One day I saw my neighbour wearing a bright red *huipil* with embroidered designs of animals from Maya antiquity. I admired her traditional blouse, adding that some years before I had visited the Ixil region where the women wore that design. As we chatted, I dug from my backpack a small book I had stuck in the very bottom, hoping the soldiers at the military base where my flight had landed would not see it. Published by the Quiché Diocese, it recounts the lives of three priests assassinated by the army for their lead-

Children visiting Casa Canadiense. Photo by Valerie Mansour.

ership in developing cooperatives. She was attending literacy classes, so she could read a little of it. As we looked through the book, she told me stories of the visit of one of the priests to the hamlet where she lived. Not long after, he was murdered. This led to her describing her flight to Mexico with a small baby, the rain and the cold, her fright when she got lost in the mountains, worried that her baby would die of exposure, and how she managed to link up with another mother and children.

Children were ever-present around Casa Canadiense, finding accompaniers an entertaining diversion. The accompaniers learned to plan activities to keep the youngsters occupied, such as helping with homework or teaching them games. A deck of cards and Frisbee were invaluable. Showing photos of Canadian life was a great discussion starter.

Volunteers accompanied delegations to workshops and meetings in Cantabal, Cobán, and the Capital, on journeys to obtain legal identity papers in their communities of origin, or to search for additional land in the Ixcán and Alta Verapaz. One day a land delegation arrived in a distant community after an arduous hike through the mud, only to be turned away by the civil defence patrol, a warning signal of things to come.

In July, Edmonton students Reiko Cyr and Andrew Swan accompanied several returnees who wanted to verify that the army was checking out a marijuana field returnees had discovered on their land. The army must have tipped someone off, as it had been harvested by the time they arrived. They also accompanied a group searching for land mines. Although a claymore mine had previously exploded, injuring a returnee, none was found.

Accompaniers remained vigilant as the army questioned residents in an intimidating manner when they visited nearby villages. They attempted to discredit the returnees, handing out pamphlets in the villages accusing Victoria of being a guerrilla settlement.

Colin Rowat, who accompanied for eight months, in times of peace and of intense military conflict, wrote a letter to new volunteers. "Do not be misled if in your short stay here everything is quite peaceful, 'nothing happens,' or no one ever asks you to do any direct accompaniment task beyond just living in that community. If several months are calm and peaceful, that is in part attributable to the presence of accompaniment." He reminded supporters that "accompaniment of the refugees may sound glamourous or romantic from a distance but in fact it is hard work and very demanding. It requires a great deal of tolerance, patience, and understanding." He described qualities accompaniers needed to demonstrate. Flexibility, often known as the "F-word," was mentioned first. "We can never put enough emphasis on this characteristic. As it is often said, the best-laid plans can go astray. Therefore be ready for schedule changes which can be changed several times in the same day" (Rowat, letter to incoming accompaniers, 1994).

Health and physical fitness were important: "Even if you feel you are in good shape, it is very likely that you will fall ill in one form or another. During the Return itself, you will sleep on concrete floors in rooms with hundreds of people all with their coughs, colds, snoring, and a lot of children. Add to that long days and short nights (the majority of refugees like to get up at 5 a.m.). The more tired you get, the more vulnerable you will become to illnesses" (Rowat, letter to incoming accompaniers, 1994).

Tolerance of tough conditions was vital. "For example, the toilets can be rather 'perilous.' There is no privacy; the children love to play in your sleeping bags; and you may even find chickens inside!" (Rowat, letter to incoming accompaniers, 1994).

Project A fulfilled its mission. "We did what we had hoped to do, to stabilize a situation a certain amount so the people could get back and start out without a lot of interference. Obviously the government tried to make life as miserable as possible for them. But their hands were tied by the fact that they had to create a good international image," said John Payne (TI).

Accompaniment in War and Peace

The diplomatic risk Patricia Fuller took in lobbying for accompaniment was vindicated: "The Canadian accompaniers more than proved me right. Project Accompaniment provided the role model for all the accompaniers in that first return and in the camps I visited in the months that followed. It was a privilege to work with all of you; you made me very proud to be a representative of Canada" (Fuller, p. 3).

After a few months, life in Victoria was sometimes calmer than in many rural Guatemalan communities. Returnees had established what often appeared to be a haven of peace within a war zone. It was easy for accompaniers to forget they were in a conflict zone until an unexpected incident occurred.

B : Crisis and Confrontation

> We continue the struggle so as to be able to return. We return so as to be able to continue the struggle. —Refugee motto

The return to Victoria was the first step in a long and complex process that continued until April 1999. For the next few years accompaniment took place during war, army control of the government and the countryside, a major national crisis, and aggressive civil defence patrols.

※ An Attempted Coup and Its Aftermath

Forest ecologist Brian Egan from Victoria, BC, and Jean Claude Lauzon, school principal and father of five, from Sainte Sophie, Quebec, set out from Victoria 20 de enero at dawn on May 25, 1993, for an arduous thirty-hour trip to San Marcos with thirty returnees seeking birth certificates. The government had promised permanent documents at every step along the way—in Mexico, Huehuetenango, and Victoria—but they had not materialized. Without legal identity papers people were afraid to leave the community; UN documents identified them as refugees, making them easy targets for the military or civil defence patrols. So the group felt they had no choice but to hike for several hours in intense tropical heat, and then complete the journey in pickup trucks and rickety old Canadian-made Blue Bird school buses.

Unbeknownst to Brian and Jean-Claude, President Serrano, after weeks of protest over increased power rates, chose that morning to try to engineer a coup. With part of the army behind him, he suspended the constitution, dissolved Congress, and attempted to arrest public figures who might oppose his actions. After a few days of national chaos and massive popular resistance, Serrano fled Guatemala with the wealth he had amassed from the state while president. After several more days of confusion, the human rights ombudsman, Ramiro De León Carpio, was appointed president.

The instant Susan and Randy heard the news in Mexico they started calling the CCPP office in Guatemala City, trying to locate Brian and Jean Claude—without success! To everyone's relief Brian and Jean-Claude called two days later when they arrived exhausted in Huehuetenango, unaware of the crisis the country was undergoing. Susan told them to keep a low profile and stay calm.

Michelle Jay, a recent University of Prince Edward Island graduate, along with Tony Wringe, a school principal from Belleville, Ontario, and Terry O'Toole, a psychiatric nurse with four children from Antigonish, Nova Scotia, were with Susan and Randy in Campeche, following a ten-day stay in a refugee camp. They scoured newspapers, listened to shortwave radio, and communicated by phone and fax with the refugees' offices in Guatemala City and Mexico, the Canadian Embassy, and the UNHCR. Communication with Canada was essential, not least of all to inform anxious family members and supporters.

As the Campeche team kept Project A in Canada informed, Canadians asked their Members of Parliament to raise questions with Foreign Affairs Minister Barbara MacDougall. They asked that Canada censure Serrano's actions and offer assistance to Guatemalan organizations trying to restore democratic rule. The Project A committee in Victoria, BC, asked Canada to continue supporting "its 'peacekeepers'—the accompaniers who are standing between the unarmed returned refugees and the Guatemalan military forces" (Victoria, 1993).

Susan and Randy learned that the returnees were living in fear that the police and military might unleash a bloody campaign against them, given the army's ongoing operations in the Ixcán and its declarations linking the returnees with the guerrillas. There were few accompaniers in Victoria at that moment. After informing the Embassy, Michelle, Tony, and Terry crossed the Mexican border on May 29 with a detailed communications plan involving many phone calls to Susan and Randy and the Embassy. They met up with Brian and Jean-Claude in Huehuetenango. Jean-Claude and Michelle left for Victoria. A few days later Brian, Terry, and Tony accompanied the group of returnees from Huehuetenango back to Victoria.

The immediate aftermath of the failed coup served refugee interests. Civilian government was reaffirmed. De León Carpio, the new president, had been a member of the Mediating Commission, so he appointed a new

Accompaniment in War and Peace   75

director of CEAR and serious negotiations began again. The refugees pressed the new administration to ratify the October 8 Accords, negotiate specific returns, and most importantly, play an active role in facilitating arrangements for land purchases and credits. However, the new president soon acceded to army pressures.

※ A Canadian Accompanier Put to the Test

Project A often sent accompaniers with refugee delegations from Mexico seeking land in Guatemala for future Returns. In August 1993, Randy Kohan was with a delegation from ARDIGUA (the Association of Dispersed Guatemalan Refugees) when his accompaniment preparation was put to the test. His response likely saved the life of ARDIGUA leader Joaquín Jimenez Bautista.

Randy accompanied Joaquín to Todos Santos to obtain his baptismal and birth certificates, needed since he would frequently be travelling back and forth from Mexico to Guatemala. They set off on the six-hour journey from the capital to Huehuetenango and then along the rocky, windy road to Todos Santos in the back of a pickup supplied by the Catholic Church, along with a lawyer and driver. Joaquín received his papers from the municipal office without difficulty.

As they were about to leave, a few armed civil defence patrollers asked Joaquín to come with them. After a few words between the lawyer and the armed men, Joaquín went to the patrollers' one-room building. When he did not come out after about fifteen minutes, Randy entered the crowded office and saw Joaquín sitting at a table surrounded by armed men. For several hours, they accused him of having committed crimes as a member of the armed resistance in the early 1980s. The lawyer was no longer to be seen. Along with the driver, he had abandoned them and, Randy later learned, did not report what had happened to the authorities. (The lawyer, who may have been an army informer, was fired.)

Randy went to call for help. But there was no phone in Todos Santos. The post office where telegrams could be sent was closed for lunch. So Randy sent written messages with tourists waiting for the bus to Huehuetenango. He asked them to notify the Canadian Embassy, the UNHCR and the office in Guatemala City where the land delegation was staying. At 2 p.m. he sent the Embassy a telegram and then tried to find the local priest, but he was not in town.

Randy returned to the office where more people were entering, many with rifles. At least fifty armed men and over one hundred unarmed civilians were present. For the next five hours Randy stood inside the office or directly outside. The patrollers were carrying out a self-styled trial. Men arrived, watched, listened, or accused Joaquín of having been a guerrilla leader. As one group departed, another would enter. Some sought a lynching, while others wanted to delay the process until morning, when international groups could arrive and give the people of Todos Santos an opportunity to speak about Joaquín and their present social problems. Randy was asked several times to explain his presence, who Joaquín was, and why he had come to Todos Santos.

In the early evening four soldiers arrived from the Huehuetenango military base. Randy explained that he was accompanying Joaquín. They announced that they were taking him to Huehuetenango. The civil patrollers refused to hand him over. The military left and the situation worsened. A rope appeared. Some threatened to hang Joaquín. He was struck by hand and with whips. One hit Randy by chance.

Finally Randy decided to seek refuge in a Spanish language school for foreigners. Early the next morning, he approached the office with an international woman working at the school. By this time soldiers and the national police were there. Randy was told Joaquín had been taken to Huehuetenango. He left Todos Santos with the military, arriving at the Huehuetenango police station at 11 a.m. The police did not allow him to call the Canadian Embassy. Soon after, Joaquín arrived, bruised and battered, with a CEAR representative. Joaquín asked Randy to call the UNHCR and the Canadian Embassy. Randy was again refused permission but he did manage to speak to a CEAR representative by phone. An hour later he walked to the telephone company, where he placed calls to the Embassy, the UNHCR, and his accompaniment partner, Louise Sevigny, who had stayed with the rest of the ARDIGUA delegation. Still under surveillance, he was advised that the Embassy was sending a vehicle from the capital. At 3:30 p.m. he encountered a priest who gave him refuge until the Embassy car arrived that evening.

Minister of the Interior Ortiz Moscoso negotiated with the military, arguing that whether or not Joaquín had been a guerrilla the rule of law should reign. (A few months later Moscoso was removed from office following army pressure on the new president to replace reform-oriented officials.) Joaquín was freed and escorted to the Mexican border. His history never was revealed, but international humanitarian law maintains the right of ex-combatants to participate in civil society. Project A refused to comment on whether Joaquín had been a guerrilla, steadfastly maintaining its position of non-intervention in refugee decisions.

Randy's presence and actions may well have saved Joaquín's life. He reacted calmly and communicated as quickly and clearly as possible, two essentials of accompaniment in crisis situations. It is unlikely the government would have intervened if an accompanier had not been present. ARDIGUA leaders believe the civil defence patrollers would likely have killed Joaquín. Randy "ensured that the information got out when the others who were with them left them abandoned and returned without informing anyone." They were impressed when Randy arrived in the capital "a little frightened but still willing to continue accompanying us."

Although Randy finds it difficult to assess with certainty the impact of his presence, he believes it had deterrence value: "The fact that I was called upon more than once to identify myself and Joaquín to the hostile crowd may have dampened the desires of those eager to take drastic action…. There is no doubt that the civil patrols are capable of killing. In July of that year, another civil patrol massacred three members of CONAVIGUA (a Guatemalan women's organization). A protest the following month against the July massacre led to another civil patrol attack in which one person was killed and three others wounded" (Kohan, p. 8).

The Urgent Action Network was activated, prompting many Canadians to send letters of protest to Canadian and Guatemalan government officials. The Canadian Embassy added its voice in condemning the PAC action.

※ Conflict Intensifies

The Return to Victoria led to renewed discussion of an old issue. Several members of the nearby Ixcán Grande Cooperative, abandoned for over a decade after their forced exodus, were living in the overcrowded Victoria community. They reconnected with relatives and former neighbours living in the nearby resistance community, many of whom were also Cooperative members who had fled into the jungle. Together they began to wonder aloud about fulfilling their dream of resettling the Cooperative that had been such an extraordinary sign of hope in the 1970s and early '80s.

Almost five hundred members, including many who travelled to the Ixcán from refugee camps in Mexico, held a General Assembly in nearby Cantabal where they decided to work toward reconstructing the Cooperative. Linda Geggie, a student from Victoria, accompanied community representatives to negotiations over the following weeks. "It was an incredible process to witness. The representatives of the refugees have achieved such political development and empowerment in a short time. In view of this group's history, diversity, and lack of formal education, it was amazing to see the representatives sitting at the negotiation table, standing up to be heard, and insisting their demands be respected" (Geggie, 1993).

On October 26 the refugees and government agreed to a November 22 return. The army, however, refused the government's request to relocate their military bases outside the Cooperative's boundaries. The military had illegally taken over the five settlement areas within the Cooperative and had built outposts in each village centre. Cooperative members adamantly refused to re-enter as long as army posts remained. They were determined, nonetheless, to return from Mexico. "We are afraid, but if we wait until the army has moved, we will wait forever," said one member. The UNHCR suggested the returnees be temporarily located in the small crossroads settlement of Veracruz at the Cooperative's edge. The returning refugees agreed, but the government, under heavy army pressure, continued to stall, announcing a new Return date every few days.

The refugees threatened to start walking to Guatemala on November 26, whatever the consequences. Many had already torn down their houses and packed their bags. A Project A Atlantic delegation encountered families in Chiapas walking down the mountainsides with their possessions on their backs. Permanent Commissioners were dispatched to the camps to persuade people to wait just a few more days. The Project A delegates were told: "With the army involved, it is very dangerous. The refugees know very well what the army is capable of. But it is clear that they want to go and are ready to go. It is only with international support that they can return in a manner that will ensure their safety" (PA Atlantic).

I was accompanying in Victoria at that time. Cooperative members living in Victoria met most evenings around a campfire or by candlelight to prepare the arrival of their relatives and former neighbours. Excitement permeated the community as welcoming celebrations were planned for the caravan's arrival at the Ingenieros border crossing. Banners were painted; representatives of *Mama Maquín,* the youth group, and the CCPP wrote speeches; a country and western band wrote a song, while a marimba orchestra rehearsed traditional tunes. Cooperative members living in Victoria volunteered to go, with accompaniment, to Veracruz for several days to construct latrines and temporary shelter, funded by the Canadian NGO, CECI. Yet almost every day we heard the news that the Return was again postponed.

When it seemed the agreement was going to break down completely, the CCPP requested an international lobbying campaign. Susan and Randy contacted the Urgent Action Network. Beth Abbott, Atlantic Project A coordinator, in turn notified the Maritimes-Guatemala Breaking the Silence Network and the Project A Antigonish group. With interest generated by a Maritimes presence in the Ixcán, dozens of people from the Maritimes faxed the Guatemalan government to protest stalling tactics. They asked the Canadian government to use its diplomatic influence to pressure Guatemala to withdraw the bases. The Atlantic delegation expressed its concern personally to José Herran Lima, Canada's new GRICAR representative. The crisis was averted when the government finally agreed that twelve hundred refugees could return to Veracruz in December, despite army opposition.

It had rained heavily for several days. Gumboots were constant footwear. The mud was so slippery that it was difficult to climb even a slight incline. Early one morning I watched a little girl in her freshly washed dress skipping happily beside her father along a dirt road. She took a sudden tumble. She stood up, howling, covered from head to toe in mud. Everyone wondered whether the convoy could make it through the ill-maintained and treacherous roads on both sides of the border.

Luckily the day dawned with glorious sunshine. I joined a contingent of seventy people from Victoria and the resistance communities. We set out for the border crossing about forty-five kilometres away in rented trucks normally used for transporting cattle and cardamom. We soon saw a crowd of people standing beside buses, jeeps, and pickups. They were representatives of indigenous groups, NGOs, and churches who had travelled the day before all the way from Guatemala City, eager to greet this long-awaited return to the Cooperative. It had been a long and dangerous journey, as they travelled the same muddy potholed roads the refugees had traversed eleven months earlier. Now they were waiting for a tractor to haul an overturned truck through the mud. The convoy of vehicles followed, each slipping and sliding as they maneuvered up and down the hilly terrain.

Late that afternoon forty-three buses with almost thirteen hundred refugees rolled in, exhausted after their journey, but ecstatic to have finally arrived on Guatemalan soil. For three days they had sat on buses full of restless children from before dawn until late at night, sleeping on foam slabs in schools and churches with hundreds of families. As the band played, returnees, with their accompaniers, including two Canadians, poured off the buses, shouting, "We were refugees; we are Guatemalans" to cheers and embraces from the crowd. Welcoming speeches were made; songs were sung; photos were taken. It was near dusk as the buses set out for Cantabal where we were to stay for the night in the Catholic parish and the school. The muddy roads had turned into a quagmire. The short trip back to Cantabal took five to eight hours, as each bus was hauled through the muddiest area by tractor. As our truck, filled to the brim, slithered through the mud, I thought that perhaps driving in the freezing rain of Nova Scotia might be preferable! When we arrived, candles glimmered in the darkness. Hundreds of people had come out to welcome the refugees, a courageous act in this highly militarized town.

Early the next morning we sleepily awoke to sounds of babies crying and chicks cheeping, carried by families from Mexico. In a Mass of thanksgiving and celebration, the priest proclaimed that their Return was like the Israelites' return from exile. Nonetheless the returnees faced a sobering reality as they continued on to Veracruz, passing three military bases on the one and a half hour journey from Cantabal.

It was a joy and privilege to be present for this Return, to see the returnees' infectious hope and determination to create their lives anew. I was, however, anxious about what might occur in the coming months. Returning to Antigonish at Christmas, I wrote a letter to the local newspaper: "I am very aware of the Maya people, those still in Mexico hoping to return in the coming year and the returnees who will have celebrated in a simple and joyful way their first Christmas back in Guatemala. The return of these Maya families, including newborn babes, is a sign of peace and hope in a land where the dominating force is a powerful military. But the peace and hope is precarious, as it seems there is yet no room in the inn for the men, women, and children who fled the cruelty of a Herod of our time"(Anderson, 1994).

From the moment they crossed the border, the refugees shouted: "There will be no peace in our homes until the military has left." Accompanied by Canadians, over a thousand returnees marched peacefully to the Pueblo Nuevo base December 12 to deliver a letter to the commander demanding the outposts' removal: "We cannot accept that the constitutional right to private property is recognized and respected only for the powerful....We are ready to work without rest to construct the houses, schools, clinics, and churches, which you destroyed twelve years ago. Within a very short period we have to prepare the land for planting and we cannot wait long. We are sure that with the work and effort of all we can make the land, which you converted into ashes and rubble, grow and flourish again" (copy of letter sent to Project A, 1993).

Planes dropped leaflets on Veracruz on December 22, threatening anyone who they believed were linked to the guerrillas. A week later the army issued a press release, accusing the refugees of setting up roadblocks to recruit guerrilla members. The UNHCR and the government human rights office refuted the allegations, explaining that a temporary roadblock was set up after drunken drivers had passed through the community. In early January 1994 the army surrounded Veracruz. Children fled the school, their mothers ran from the river where they had been washing clothes, and their fathers rushed home from the fields. In February the army mobilized near Veracruz, destroying the returnees' recently sown corn and creating tremendous fear. Meanwhile the government Cooperatives Agency threatened to withdraw its support and recognition of the Cooperative as part of the national Cooperatives system if it continued its involvement in political issues.

With international pressure mounting, on January 25 the army finally agreed to relocate the Pueblo Nuevo base just outside Cooperative lands. The landmine situation, however, still had to be dealt with, so they had to wait until April before resettling the village they had fled in 1982. With continuous rain and cramped, harsh living conditions, the health of the population, especially of children, deteriorated. The temporary shelters were like ovens. With no floors and the structures too weak to hold enough hammocks, many families slept on the muddy damp ground. Amoebas and respiratory, eye, and skin infections were common. Beans and corn rations were insufficient and often of poor quality. The Cooperative president stated: "We have been uprooted more than once and we have survived. We had been transplanted to Mexico and had begun to put down roots. Now we are uprooted again. If no one cares for the plants, they will dry out; they will die. But with a little attention at this stage, we will prosper and grow" (Fox, p. 1).

On February 28 Colin Rowat and Marco Formicelli, from Quebec City, along with a Guatemala City architect, accompanied a delegation to Pueblo Nuevo to plan the resettlement. "The request to accompany the delegation came without warning, that very morning, so I grabbed my camera and notebook and crowded into the back of the Landcruiser. The two-hour walk took ten minutes by car, whisking us past the new military base, four minutes from our settlement in Veracruz—close enough to have heard the gunfire around it last week, far enough away not to know what really happened.... Marco and I step into one of the outpost's huts to escape the midday sun. We venture out occasionally to track the plane that has been floating back and forth overhead every twenty minutes" (Rowat, letter to support committee, 1994).

Marco and Colin discovered just how anxious the returnees were to eliminate any reminders of the army's presence. "It is confirmed that

Returned community of Cuarto Pueblo, Ixcán Grande Cooperative. Photo by Brian Atkinson.

tomorrow we will return to set fire to the old base so that new construction can begin. Just then we see the dense yellow smoke climbing from the fort's far end. Santiago has been there with his box of matches."

With the moves to Pueblo Nuevo in April and to Cuarto Pueblo in May, cornfields began to replace minefields. But the battle with the army was not yet over. More Cooperative members arrived from Mexico in early May. A military base still stood in Mayalán, their intended destination. In July over a thousand returnees marched to the base to demand its dismantlement. The army finally withdrew at the end of September and more families were able to return to their lands. The Ixcán Grande Cooperative was once again becoming a reality, although dangerous confrontations with the army continued throughout 1994 and 1995. Co-op members returned from Mexico in small groups until April 1996.

※ Accompaniment amidst Volatility

From the day the caravan arrived in Veracruz, the government launched a public offensive against accompaniers. They knew accompaniers were monitoring and publicizing the Ixcán Grande Cooperative Return, as daily Urgent Actions arrived from around the world supporting refugee demands. Computer programmer Larry Reid attended a meeting where the CEAR director accused accompaniers of being nothing but drunks and tourists. Reid vigorously refuted his comments.

The newspaper *Prensa Libre* attacked accompaniers on December 10: "They [the returnees] must put up with the presence of a group of foreigners, some of whom are well-intentioned. However this entails the bad habits of a culture far from that of the Maya, such as the consumption of drugs, especially marijuana and cocaine" (*Prensa Libre*, 1993).

During the December 12 protest at the Pueblo Nuevo military base, the refugees publicly declared their support for the accompaniment. "Our hearts are full of thankfulness towards all our brothers and sisters who are accompanying us on this difficult road. Their presence gives us courage to continue moving forward in spite of the accusations and threats against us" (Kohan and Skaret). A day later they issued a press release asking that accompaniment continue.

The army began its attack on accompaniers a day later, claiming returnees were irresponsible and manipulated by the guerrillas. It added, incorrectly, that foreigners had joined the protest. On December 14, a second newspaper reported that the president ordered an investigation of foreign participation "in acts of provocation." The foreign minister declared: "We're collecting information about who these foreigners are and what their motives are for participating in the repatriation process, since they have no right to be there.... If we can prove any anomalies, we will expel them" (*Siglo Veintiuno,* 1993). A few days later, a *Siglo Veintiuno* columnist demanded that accompaniers be thrown out of the country, stating that they were linked to the guerrillas, the Sandinistas, Basque separatists, the Shining Path revolutionaries in Peru, and the Palestinian Liberation Organization. Refugees and accompaniment groups feared an expulsion of accompaniers. Susan and Randy met with Embassy officials to express Project A's concern. Accusations died down after a chorus of international protests.

Robert Fox, then with Oxfam-Canada, made a visit to Veracruz in January 1994. The Cooperative president told him what happened when the military surrounded the community: "Some of the accompaniers began to take photos of the soldiers who disappeared like smoke. Without this accompaniment we would be much more fearful." Fox concluded: "In this battle of nerves—and M16s—the role of international accompaniment is key" (Fox, p. 2).

Accompaniers selected one of their members as coordinator. The Veracruz community also named a representative to welcome new accompaniers and act as liaison for sharing information. They met daily to exchange information and select people for assignments. These ranged from day trips to nearby fields to seven-day journeys with community members who wanted to clear land and plant corn closer to their intended destinations. Accompaniers always took cameras and tape recorders when they went with delegations to military outposts or the Playa Grande base. They kept a logbook and distributed regular reports.

No matter how basic the living situation, hospitality was fundamental. Josh Berson and Colin Rowat stayed with a group clearing lands in the jungle for planting:

> A lunch was quickly offered to us by two men, rice and coffee-flavoured tamales. This morning the eggs that had been found in the forest were added to our breakfasts. Hammocks appeared that afternoon and were strung for us. "You have to rest," we were told by these people who sweat out their days swinging machetes under the sun. Our efforts at constructing a bed for ourselves were halted by them and taken over as a pre-dinner project. Its completion was speeded by smiles and laughter. This genuine hospitality—not just a willingness but an ungrudging eagerness to help—constantly makes me pause. It lifts me out of darker moments here. And it makes me wonder how I can import this to Canada. (Rowat, letter to support committee, 1994)

The community knew Project A accompaniers were part of a network. Josh Berson said, "The refugees I lived with felt great solidarity knowing that a community in Vancouver, not just one person, is concerned enough about their safety and political process to send me as a representative" (Berson, 1994).

Project A had to make hard choices, such as the decision to accompany returnees in marches and demonstrations demanding the removal of military bases. Project A also sided with refugees in a dispute with the Guatemalan government and the UNHCR. In late April families temporarily housed in Veracruz could no longer accept deteriorating living conditions. They decided to move to Cuarto Pueblo without the agreement of the government and the UNHCR. Consequently there was no financial aid for their move, no verification of security in the zone, and no international assistance for infrastructure. The families carried their personal goods and construction materials on their backs. Project A accompanied them, committed to following the refugees' lead.

Bombing and machine-gun fire from nearby military skirmishes were often heard. Accompaniers were always present when Cooperative representatives met with the army in the struggle for relocation of the Mayalán base. By July the outpost still had not been moved. Eva Manly, video artist and mother of four adults, accompanied a delegation of returnees to inform the commander that over one thousand people were planning a march to the base: "They [the delegation] were pretty nervous approaching the military base. We waited out by the road while the head of the delegation and one or two people walked up to the gate of the military base. The commander came out and he called to us in perfect English. He seemed to be American-trained. Later the leader of our delegation took us around the community and showed us the ruins. He told us where they had had their power plant, where they had stored all the cardamom and coffee that their priest had airlifted out for them" (TI).

A few days later other accompaniers walked alongside the march. When they arrived at the base, they did not take part in the demonstration, but made themselves visible taking notes and photos.

At 4 a.m. on August 5, 1994, the community's security committee sounded an alarm to alert the community to the presence of troops near Veracruz. A nervous population walked out to meet two hundred soldiers with automatic weapons and bazookas. Cooperative leaders explained the community's policy of not permitting the entry of armed persons. The soldiers continued to move toward Veracruz. Residents moved closer to the soldiers, reminding them that the army had killed thousands of their family members and they had been forced to flee. The troops entered the community, forming columns, one beside the other, indicating that they were moving from the military outpost in Xalbal to the Mayalán base. The community formed a human barrier, letting about forty soldiers through. By this time another three hundred soldiers had arrived. The community insisted on talking with the troop commander, who asked that his battalion be allowed through to replace soldiers in Mayalán. The population refused, stating that the petition they had presented in July was being ignored. Shortly after the troops turned in the direction of Cantabal. The citizens accompanied them for a kilometre. Tensions mounted, especially when some of the soldiers took the safety off their guns and one soldier left his column and aimed his rifle at the group. Some heard soldiers say "we will be back" and "let them come as far as the bridge and we will capture them there." Montreal student François Meloche accompanied a delegation to the Playa Grande military base that afternoon. He videotaped the conversation with the commander in which the community made it clear they would not tolerate incursions onto their land.

Margie Loo, from Prince Edward Island, had been a volunteer for three years with a street-children's project in Quetzaltenango before joining Project A. She arrived in Veracruz shortly after Eva Manly left. "There were a lot of battles going on just then. At night we heard machine gun fire all the time. One day there was a battle and they were hauling bodies through Veracruz. We were counting the bodies we could see in the truck, and we could see the smoke from the bombs coming up. It was only a kilometre away. The military came through the town a lot. People really felt strongly the need for our presence there" (TI).

An incident remained vivid in Margie's mind:

> I accompanied a work brigade to just outside of Mayalán. They were people from Mayalán who hadn't returned yet but, they were working the land...a group of families who banded together to use that piece of land, which some of them owned. Some decided to go home earlier. The other accompanier was going to go with them and I was going to stay another two days. We decided we would walk part of the way together and then I'd come back. As we were walking out we started to hear a battle going on. It was really close to where the people were working. We couldn't tell if the battle was going on between us and the people or on the other side. I decided I had to go back right away because I knew that they were going to be nervous, but I was also very nervous. I was singing, at the top of my lungs, Rose Vaughan Trio songs so they would know that I was a gringa [North American] and I was there. The men were not so nervous but there was a woman who had gone along to do the cooking with her daughter. They had been

hiding under the bed. They were so happy to see me because they were so afraid. They obviously knew I couldn't do anything but my presence made a difference. So that for me was a real epiphany of what it meant to be accompanying. I wasn't doing anything. I was just there. (TI)

On August 31 the army finally moved the base three kilometres away. Thirty families immediately moved to Mayalán.

A few months later Margie Loo and Nathalie Brière replaced well-loved and respected Project A coordinators Susan Skaret and Randy Kohan. Their Ixcán experience enabled them to prepare accompaniers for an environment that continued to be explosive.

In October 1994 fierce battles took place just three kilometres west of Veracruz. On November 7 about one hundred and fifty soldiers arrived in Mayalán but the community impeded their entry to the village centre. In April 1995 a potentially dangerous confrontation between military troops and Cooperative members occurred in Mayalán. Marc Drouin and Nathalie Gauthier were wakened around midnight, and alerted to the presence of a battalion just outside the village, spotted during nightly rounds of the security committee. They grabbed their camera, notebooks, and flashlights and ran ahead of community members to where agitated refugees had surrounded the soldiers, many with their faces painted charcoal, ready for battle. Marc and Nathalie were a calming presence, continually assuring the soldiers that community members would not attack them, but were insisting on talking with them. They also reminded community members that acts of violence might only make matters worse. They took photos and precise notes. Eventually the battalion commander agreed to lead his troops into the village centre where they stayed until the next afternoon, when the Playa Grande base commander arrived by helicopter and promised that no further incursions would take place on Cooperative land.

What might have been a violent encounter became a victory in the returnees' ongoing struggle. A refugee leader suggested that the demilitarization of the Ixcán Grande Cooperatives was a major achievement of the Return process, accomplished through "the courage and organization of the refugees." He saw international accompaniment organizations as a significant support: "A huge number of messages were sent to the government. At a critical moment we could count on the strength of the accompaniers' presence in the Ixcán."

Arriving at the returned community of Los Angeles, Ixcan Grande Cooperative. Photo by Brian Atkinson.

C : Life and Death in the Return Process

> I could have stayed and died in Mexico. We had everything: water, electricity, schools, health clinics. But I didn't have my land.
> —elderly refugee to Brian Atkinson, 1995

The first Returns paved the way for many Returns that took place in a context of insecurity. The report of the UN Verification Mission stated: "The government has not adequately guaranteed the right of persons to their physical security and integrity, which is to say, to be free from torture, cruel and inhumane or degrading treatment" (UN Verification Mission, 1995). The desire to return increased following the New Year's Day 1994 Zapatista uprising in Mexico, which led to restrictions on refugees' freedom of movement. The search for land in several regions throughout Guatemala began. The process often bogged down when they encountered bureaucratic obstacles to land purchase and land credits. The government frequently refused to release funds donated by foreign governments and agencies, which they had likely diverted elsewhere. By May 1994 only six properties had been bought for resettlement while seventeen applications were pending. Refugees occupied land agency offices, as well as the Guatemalan consulate in Chetumal, Mexico. Soon after, the government agreed to a new land purchase.

Accompaniment in War and Peace   89

Many Returns were uneventful, and returnees began the long process of reconstructing their lives. Others proved challenging. Accompaniment groups struggled to respond to increased requests for accompaniers on Returns, in resettled communities, and on land delegations. A Permanent Commissioner said: "Every day the Return areas are more militarized. We want accompaniment, and if it is possible, we hope that it doubles" (PA, Report, 1994, p. 10). After the first flush of enthusiasm passed, numbers had decreased, at times resulting in a "drought" of accompaniers. Accompaniment groups were forced to prioritize communities in terms of the level of danger they might face. Project A redoubled its recruitment efforts with some success.

※ Huehuetenango

A second Return was scheduled for a week after the first one to Victoria. Refugees were ready to move to the Chaculá farm in the cool, mountainous Nentón region of Huehuetenango, just twenty kilometres across the border from their refugee camps. They requested accompaniment. "We know conditions do not exist in Guatemala for our Return but we need to return because of the difficult economic and labour situation here in Mexico. We can return and demand our constitutional rights but we will not survive alone" (PA Report, 1994, p. 16).

The journey to the rugged, forested Chaculá farm was put on hold when it seemed impossible to purchase land at a reasonable price. Refugees in one camp had already torn down their homes. The delay left the refugees understandably demoralized, but they refused to give up hope. "The people of the first Return have found their resurrection and now we are waiting in the sepulchre for our resurrection" (PA, April 1993, p. 7). Finally the government agreed to the selling price and to providing land credits. The Return was rescheduled for May 30, but was again postponed when CEAR became non-functional for a time after the failed coup.

In January 1994, 182 families finally set out for Chaculá. They formed a Cooperative named *Nueva Esperanza,* meaning New Hope, and became involved in a forestry project, agricultural production, and small enterprises. Located only sixteen kilometres from the San Francisco plantation where 483 people were massacred in 1982, memories were still vivid. A military post five kilometres away and civil defence patrols in the surrounding villages made fear a constant companion. The army justified its presence because banners and roadblocks appeared almost weekly on the access road into the community, supposedly guerrilla actions, more likely carried out by the army itself. Bus checks became a fact of life on the road between Nentón and Nueva Esperanza, as M16-wielding soldiers forced passengers to disembark from the buses. The returnees, with only UN documents, felt they could be army targets. They wanted constant accompaniment, often expressing fear of abandonment.

Victoria accompanier John Lydon watched the "vibrant" community establish itself: "This is home now and people are making it go with vigour and faith. Hope is something you *do* here as much as have. Clearing land, digging irrigation ditches, planting crops, reaching out to the surrounding communities, and knowing that all is not well in Guatemala. There is a wonderful audacity in this. They really have a lot of faith in each other and in their right to thrive, so it is a good experience for me in the power of the people" (Lydon, 1994).

※ **The Ixcán and Alta Verapaz**

With roads next to impassable, several Returns took place by air. When refugees returned to the Ixcán Grande Cooperative and the nearby Zona Reyna region in 1994, the only adequate landing strip was on the Playa Grande military base, the site of the prison and crematorium where family members and friends had been tortured and burned years before. The combination of flying for the first time, in mail planes without windows, and arriving at the military base created anxiety. The UNHCR and other agencies welcomed the refugees. Accompaniers' presence on the flights and at the base was reassuring, since soldiers were visible despite assurances to the contrary, and some returnees at first refused to disembark.

In May 1994 returnees originally from Santa Mariá Tzejá in the Zona Reyna returned to their lands. In their absence, the army had handed their lands over to other campesinos. In the October 8 Accords the government committed itself to finding a solution to this contentious issue. They offered money or land credits to sixty families, who agreed to relocate. Some families negotiated arrangements to purchase other land parcels. Others ended up crowded onto land on the edge of Cantabal. Villagers who had not fled warmly welcomed the refugees back. A complex, sometimes difficult, process of reintegration into their community began and still continues.

The return to nearby San Antonio Tzejá was not as successful. Thirty-eight families returned from Mexico in April 1995. They encountered massive resistance from those who had received their land from the army. They refused to give up the land, in part because they saw that people in Santa Mariá Tzejá had not yet received promised government land credits. A compromise became impossible when the army backed an organization fomenting resistance to the Return. Made up of civil defence patrols from four villages, including San Antonio Tzejá, it was led by Raúl Martínez, an employee of the oil company Basic Resources. The army could easily have ordered him to disband the organization. Instead he moved freely, despite a warrant out for his arrest because of a hostage-taking and other illegal actions. "The government's assurances to the returnees were worth nothing in the face of army resistance to the Return. The result was impunity for Martínez and lawlessness in the region" (Taylor, p. 95).

The returnees, frustrated by a two-month wait in the Catholic parish in Cantabal, decided to march to San Antonio Tzejá, accompanied by GRICAR, other international agencies, and a group of refugees returning to San Juan Ixcán. (That group re-entered their village without immediate problems, although they too later had to relocate because of land conflicts.) When they arrived near San Antonio Tzejá, armed civil patrollers blocked their entry. Five representatives of international agencies were taken hostage for twenty-four hours, including Canadian Grahame Russell. Ultimately the returnees were forced to establish themselves in a more isolated and difficult area, a two-hour walk further into the mountains. They named their new community *Cimiento de Esperanza* (Foundation of Hope). Canadian accompanier Erin Reid literally sang her way into the residents' hearts when she became the lead singer in a band started by young people in the community.

※ The Xamán Massacre

Two years after the October 8, 1992 Refugee Accords were signed, returnees founded the Aurora 8 de octubre (Dawn of October 8) community on the Xamán farm in Alta Verapaz. They joined residents who had worked for the previous owner. The most painful incident of the Return process occurred there on October 5, 1995. An army patrol opened fire, killing eleven and wounding over thirty, including several women and children. For the first time in a year, all accompaniers were temporarily absent.

Residents and visitors from other returned communities were happily preparing to celebrate the community's first anniversary and the third anniversary of the Return Accords when a patrol of twenty-six soldiers and an officer was spotted on Xamán's outskirts. Residents questioned why the patrol was on their land, in violation of the agreement made not to pass through returnees' lands. They asked the patrol to come to the village centre where villagers surrounded them. The patrol leader claimed they had come seeking an invitation to the celebration. Community members, offended by this response, insisted they remain until UN representatives arrived. The patrol started to leave and opened fire indiscriminately on the unarmed campesinos, using machine guns and grenades. The massacre may or may not have been premeditated, but the spontaneous and unrestrained use of arms indicated that the army still perceived the returnees as the enemy.

This episode was a painful reminder of the ongoing need for accompaniment. Xamán had been a quiet and peaceful community with seemingly little risk of confrontation. Accompaniers were away from the community at the time of the massacre. Refugees still in Mexico and returnees were frightened by this event. Montreal student Isabelle Gaudreau recounted her experience on a Return the day after the massacre and her assignment to accompany injured survivors receiving death threats while in a Guatemala City hospital: "We arrived at the border on October 6. It was there that we learned that eleven refugees who had returned less than a year earlier had been massacred by a military patrol the evening before in Xamán. The response was shock, disarray, terror. I left for the capital to be with the survivors who were hospitalized there. This was difficult in a climate where foreigners were being labeled as subversive, to be gotten rid of" (TI).

Project A and other accompaniment groups immediately ensured continous accompaniment of the Xamán community. Urgent Actions were sent out across Canada within twenty-four hours. Project A was active in the international campaign against impunity for those responsible. When witnesses from Xamán were in the courtroom in Cobán (a day's drive away), accompaniers provided security and monitored proceedings.

Throughout 1998 the judge consistently favoured the soldiers who claimed they shot in self-defence. They refused to answer questions of the prosecuting attorney and the joint plaintiff, the Rigoberta Menchú Tum Foundation. In November the prosecuting attorney was forced into exile after intimidation and death threats. When the trial resumed in January 1999 it was clear the new prosecutor was collaborating with the defence to ensure the soldiers received a sentence equal to time already served. The court lost evidence, including a military map, the state's main proof that the patrol was ordered to enter Xamán. The Foundation withdrew as joint plaintiffs in July, charging that their legal work was stymied. It said it would go to the Inter-American Human Rights Court instead. It continued to attend all proceedings. "We came to look for justice and we are not ready to make any concession that would signify that we validate a judicial farce. To stay in the process would have been a strike against the dignity of the victims, the dignity of the Xamán community, and our own dignity because we believe in a peace with justice and we believe that the Guatemalan people have a right to justice. We believe that in all of the cases where there are elements of the army involved, justice should be done" (cited by Long, 1999).

To the dismay of returnees and human rights groups, in December 1999 the Court of Appeal acquitted the patrol leader and fourteen soldiers for lack of sufficient proof. They had previously been found guilty of extra-judicial execution, attempted extra-judicial execution, trespassing, and inflicting bodily harm. The ten remaining soldiers were given nine years' imprisonment for simple homicide and a three-year commutable sentence for inflicting bodily harm. They were freed a few months later. "It seems that the victims of human rights violations are condemned to take the long road to justice," said Rigoberta Menchú (CERIGUA, 1999). In 2003 the case was still paralyzed.

The Xamán massacre deeply affected Canadians. Mary Ann Morris and Randy Janzen, accompaniers in Victoria 20 de enero, were close to a family who moved to Xamán. Their seven-year-old daughter, Maurilia Cox Max, was killed. Randy joined a Christian Task Force contingent who protested in Fort Benning, Georgia, in November 2000, as part of an ongoing campaign to shut down the School of the Americas (recently renamed the Western Hemisphere Institute for Security Cooperation). Risking arrest, Randy entered the base in a solemn funeral procession, holding high a sign with Maurilia's name and photo.

※ The South Coast

In the summer of 1994 ARDIGUA sent a nervous delegation to the South Coast. "Most of them had not been back to Guatemala since they fled and they were terrified, absolutely terrified on that bus ride home," Eva Manly recalled. They knew the powerful elite of coastal landowners was as resistant to refugee returns as the army in the Ixcán. They did not welcome a well-organized group of campesinos, aware of their rights as workers and planning to use a cooperative model of economic development. Because of the Joaquín Bautista incident the previous year, they asked Project A for two accompaniers.

The delegation not only initiated their long search for land but also used the visit to counter land-owners and army propaganda, and to gain campesino support for their future settlement. They used cultural activities to give campesinos in Quetzaltenango, Mazatenango, Retalhuleu, and San Marcos their own version of who they were:

> The last four days were like a travelling road show with the people from ARDIGUA, all ten of them, plus the entertainers. A guy from Mexico did a one-man show; there was a group of actors from a small theatre group in Guatemala City; there were musicians and a puppeteer from El Salvador. It was absolutely amazing. They rented a flatbed truck. In Xela [indigenous name for Quetzaltenango] they did their entertainment right in the central square with a PA system. It was very direct and political, giving the history of why people fled the country. Then a representative from ARDIGUA told about their personal experience, why the people wanted to come back to Guatemala, and what their dreams were. (TI)

The delegation returned to Mexico, having achieved its purpose without incident. However, ARDIGUA's efforts to purchase land were continually thwarted and they received no response to credit applications. No ARDIGUA Returns took place until late 1997.

Other refugees managed to resettle on the South Coast in 1995, a remarkable achievement given the resistance. The CCPP was repeatedly told that the government could only help them buy lands in conflict zones; that its credit agency had no money; that its land agency had no land. Refugees walked to the Mexican border when it became clear the government was blocking attempts to purchase land. New Brunswick accompanier and photojournalist Brian Atkinson, reported: "When I saw them they had made a highly visible, makeshift camp north of Chetumal, still in Mexico. The government said it would not negotiate under pressure—but within a month a farm in the south had been found for the refugees" (Atkinson, 1995).

The land was finally purchased after international pressure and GRICAR's lobbying. Sixty-seven families flew into Guatemala City on their way to the La Providencia farm near Escuintla. They were followed a few months later by a second group of thirty-five families who established a Cooperative in Suchitépequez. Several small Returns followed in 1996.

※ Petén

A lengthy, hard-fought battle to return to the northern Petén region bore fruit in April 1995 when 175 families flew into the airport in Santa Elena. Five days later, after two full days of celebrations and a Maya ceremony amidst the ancient pyramids of Tikal, they arrived at their destination, the El Quetzal farm of semi-tropical forest near the Mexican border.

Army opposition, along with lack of political will and coordination among land agencies in the Petén, had continually derailed negotiations.

Military officers had acquired large tracts of land for cattle production and were involved in widespread illegal trade in drugs and hardwood. The refugees ran into continuous roadblocks in attempts to clarify El Quetzal's status. Sixty percent of the land was located within a newly created protected area called the Maya Biosphere. Forty percent was in an adjoining buffer zone. The CCPP drew up plans for sustainable development, consistent with norms established for management of protected areas. They argued that, with adequate support, their needs and environmental conservation could be met in a mutually beneficial way. With illegal activities and mismanagement, the Maya Biosphere was being destroyed. Negotiations moved at a snail's pace. Government agencies did not produce needed information, stated frivolous objections, or did not turn up at meetings.

International pressure was once more a key element. The refugees produced an International Bulletin, aimed at securing moral, political, and financial support. They sent representatives to Europe, the US and Canada. As a result, many Canadians sent letters of support to the Canadian and Guatemalan governments and new accompaniers were recruited. With strong international pressure, the Mediating Commission and GRICAR took on an active lobbying and advocacy role in the fall of 1994, including a meeting with President De León Carpio. In January 1995 the president's private secretary instructed government institutions to do whatever was necessary for a return to El Quetzal within the framework of the Protected Areas laws. The final bureaucratic decision was taken in March.

The refugees took advantage of the wait to form the Union Maya Itzá Cooperative and to organize full community participation in the Return. Their aim was to ensure that everyone took part in decision making and contributed their own little bit, however small, to the preparations.

The returnees disembarked at the Flores airport, to find the reception area festooned with banners and decorations in the official colours of the Northern Branch of the Permanent Commissions. Red signified the blood of the martyrs, yellow the sun that strengthens the *hombres de maiz*, and green the colour of the forest and respect for nature. They celebrated a Maya rite in Tikal's main plaza, emphasizing their return as reclaiming their Maya heritage. They proclaimed the "Tikal Declaration," a statement of their purpose. The trip to Tikal required an extra day's stopover. When CEAR and the UNHCR refused to cover the additional costs, CONFREGUA (the Guatemalan Confederation of Catholic Religious) and United Church partner organization CIEDEG (the Guatemalan Protestant Conference of Churches for Development) stepped in.

The military reminded returnees of their presence. Uniformed armed soldiers showed up at their overnight lodging in Santa Elena, including a captain, two *kaibiles* (elite counter-insurgency forces, trained to carry out torture), a military specialist, and a member of the Military Police. En route to their second stop, two pickups with army personnel shadowed the convoy.

On Palm Sunday the returnees celebrated Jesus' entry into Jerusalem and their entry into El Quetzal. In July another 175 families returned to the Petén. The Guatemalan director of an NGO that worked with refugees wrote:

> Today in the Finca Esmeralda, the second return site of the northern sector, in the middle of the Petén jungle, I encountered Philippe, symbol of Canadian solidarity and fruit of the work that Project A began many years ago. I had the luck of being able to help develop Project A when the idea began to take shape, and today I have the satisfaction of seeing it realized. You are part of this historic happening that is the Return, which is a living project. You have accompanied the people in their exile, you continue now in their Return, and I am sure that you will accompany their reinsertion and future development. You are part of this history. At the same time, I believe, this strengthens your consciousness and prepares you for the future struggles that you may have, even those of your own country.
>
> The two-way solidarity is valuable. Later when our communities have constructed democracy and justice, and adults and children live in better conditions, you will be able to say, "We added our grain of sand."
>
> A strong embrace and continue forward; the path is long and you do it walking. The people of Guatemala and especially the returnees will remember you always and you will live in the heart of the nation.

D : Accompaniment after the Peace Accords

The civil war formally ended December 29, 1996, with the signing of the final Accord for a Firm and Lasting Peace. Guatemalans joyfully celebrated, but were anxious that international solidarity not disappear. The armed conflict had originally started because of poverty and extreme economic inequality. Not much had changed. The civil war left returnees with an ingrained fear that repression could reappear. Twelve-year-old Eligio Juan Pedro of the newly returned community Nueva Unión Maya shared his thoughts: "Accompaniers are important for us because of what would happen if the army entered again. The accompaniers are our witnesses" (Rees

Accompaniment in War and Peace 97

and Sevigny). However, concern about an immediate threat from the military lessened, since the army could no longer claim guerrilla activity as a justification. The final three years of accompaniment took place in a more peaceful context.

With threats of repression decreasing, the value of relationships became even clearer. In early 1998 the small, remote Ixcán village of Nueva Villa Hermosa, with both returnees and repatriated residents, requested accompaniment. The community sent a handwritten letter with signatures or thumbprints for those who couldn't write. They briefly mentioned security, but what was uppermost in their minds was their belief that accompaniers had brought a richness to communities simply by sharing their lives.

No Returns took place in the first six months of 1997, as bureaucratic obstacles to land purchases and credit approval increased significantly. The government wanted refugees to return to existing returned communities, which would often mean overcrowding.

ARDIGUA's first Return to the South Coast finally occurred in November 1997. Accompanier Godfrey Spragge, a retired urban planning professor (now deceased), described the departure scene: "People were disassembling houses built of wood, roofs of corrugated tin. Possessions, clothes, everything was bundled up with rope or stuffed in bags. One of us, looking at a small pile of possessions, remarked that that was all a family of perhaps eight owned. On the 26th of November all was ready. Trucks arrived and people's possession's were loaded to be taken to their new home in the province of San Marcos. We were taken with the refugees by bus to an assembly point, a large steel warehouse with a concrete floor where we stayed two nights. The whole refugee community turned out to see them off. It was a moment of transition, a moment of change, leaving a life they knew for the uncertainty of the future" (Spragge, 1997).

The returnees were still anxious to have accompaniment—with good reason! "The climate is warm, the land has produced good yields of coffee and the area produces much fruit. There is just one problem. Throughout the negotiations to purchase this farm, the local association of farm owners opposed the sale to a Maya community. Traditionally Mayas are brought from the Highlands in trucks to pick coffee or cotton or to cut sugar cane. In Guatemalan thinking, these people are at the bottom of the social scale. To have them as neighbours and equals is incomprehensible to many. Given these prejudices, it would not be out of character for farmers in the area to harass their new neighbours, perhaps even damage their property, in an effort to show them that they are not welcome" (Spragge, 1997).

The army's presence and the people's fear never entirely disappeared. In March 1999 Project A's final accompanier, Paul Williams, translated the returnees' report on military incursions:

> On Saturday, February 20, between 8 and 8:30 a.m., eighteen Guatemalan soldiers entered the community of Quetzal IV, Nentón, Huehuetenango. All carried full equipment, including rifle, grenades, and heavy backpack. While stopped in front of the school, one soldier asked a member of the community the following questions: Had they seen anyone strange? Was there an accompanier in the community? Were the people content? Was anyone bothering them? Where was the path to Quetzal I?
>
> Later the same day, it was learned that about fifty soldiers had congregated that afternoon in Quetzal I. The day before, a member of Quetzal IV had seen sixteen soldiers stopped in Quetzal I, at 2 and later at 5 p.m. This unsolicited "visit" has frightened a good many people in the community, especially the children. The discovery of a bullet on the soccer field after the soldiers' departure only reinforced the people's concern.
>
> The people of Quetzal IV are not opposed to the army's fulfillment of its duty to patrol the border. If for whatever reason the army deems it necessary to pass through our community, we request that the mayors be sent a written message to this effect, eight to ten days before such a visit. This will allow the mayors to notify the members of the community so that they not be frightened upon the arrival of soldiers. Furthermore, we demand that no soldiers pass through the community at night under any pretext. (Williams, 1998)

The community was greatly relieved that Paul had been present.

Paul was the last of 140 volunteers who accompanied returnees, delegations seeking land to purchase, work groups clearing lands for planting, groups coming to and from Mexico to attend cooperative meetings, two mass protests against military bases on cooperative lands, and two visits by refugee delegations to military bases. The average stay was three months, although several stayed six to eight months. The majority were in their twenties and thirties, although some were in their fifties and sixties. An older accompanier sometimes experienced ageism from other accompaniers: "The attitude that accompaniment and solidarity work are for young people only was not that uncommon." Couples who accompanied together found the refugees related well to them, since singleness is rare in Maya communities. When Permanent Commissioners expressed anxiety about the inadequate number of accompaniers, Eva Manly promptly recruited her son, Mark. He became an extremely knowledgeable accompanier during his six-month stint. A mother and daughter from Victoria also accompanied together.

5   Project A Comes to a Close

THIS CHAPTER FIRST DEALS with the challenging process of closing down a successful project. It then assesses some of the conflictual issues Project A faced during its existence.

A : Making the Decision

Should Project A continue or end? That quandary took almost two years to resolve, despite the fact that the organization was originally intended to last, at most, five years. In February 1998 Project A coordinator Lisa Roberts wrote: "These are tumultuous times, both on the ground in Guatemala and in the cyber-world of the cross-Canada network of Project Accompaniment. A little more than a year after the Peace Accords were signed, we find ourselves uncertain about our role in Guatemala. The Steering Committee, staff, and other members of the Network have written and read soul-searching epistles, proposals, and counter-proposals about the next step" (Roberts, #1).

Although the Return process took longer than five years, it became clear it would end in 1999. The Peace Accords were a turning point. Although military control was still a reality, many accompaniment groups felt security accompaniment was not essential. Returned refugees did not necessarily share that view. They had little confidence the Peace Accords would bring security. "It is not 100 percent sure that it [the army] is going to return, but what we think is that it has stopped for the time being. But if everyone leaves, MINUGUA, UNHCR, if you accompaniers leave because the government says there is nothing to worry about, that everything is calm, that is when violence will arrive. We don't have much trust in the peace" (TI).

The answer was obvious to some. Project A was never intended as a permanent institution but rather as another step in the evolution of solidarity work. It had responded to a need at a specific historical moment. It had fulfilled its mandate and should dissolve.

The choice was less clear for others. One hundred and forty Canadians had received training, gained experience in accompaniment, and been supported by a network of community-based groups across Canada. Accompaniers had a commitment to and understanding of Guatemala. Perhaps Project A should continue as Guatemala began post-war reconstruction. Paula Shaw, an accompanier who stayed in Guatemala to work in community development, wrote: "Security as a primary focus for Project A is not relevant now.... But does that mean we pat ourselves on the back and pack up our bags because Guatemala is no longer at war? I don't think so. In fact, perhaps Guatemala's hardest struggle is just beginning: to bring about real and lasting change to a country and people that have been truly screwed around by years of war and oppression, and to try not to disappear from the eyes of the world. Guatemala is still greatly in need of international support and solidarity, but we have to adapt and to fit the current needs" (Shaw, 1998).

In 1997 a research team explored the need for ongoing accompaniment. They found that returned communities wanted technical support, to learn how to plan and implement development projects. They wanted to gain skills in negotiating with municipal, national, and international agencies. Project A was not set up to recruit and place accompaniers with those skills.

In the summer of 1998 a second research team explored the possibility of accompanying the internally displaced, although Project A had no history of working with these groups. They discovered how difficult it would be to accompany a population with diverse experiences, circumstances, and needs. As well, many of these communities, like the returned communities, were seeking funding and training for community development. They were often living on lands they had occupied out of necessity, without legal documentation. Although they had strong moral and legal justification, the wealthy had power on their side. The role of accompaniers in such a volatile situation would be complex and dangerous. In 1991 Peace Brigades International had learned this when three accompaniers witnessed a police killing of a woman during a land occupation. The government expelled the witnesses and the entire organization was threatened with the same action. It seemed unlikely the Canadian Embassy would offer the same official support and documentation as they gave to Project A, whose role had been officially legitimized in the October 8 Accords.

Still, the decision was agonizing. Team members had seen first hand the challenges the internally uprooted faced when they had visited their communities. Inspired by their struggles to survive, the team wrestled with what they had found. Finally they concluded: "Sending accompaniers to internally displaced communities without considerable research into community history, internal conflicts, and organization would be irresponsible" (Roberts, #3). Gaining this knowledge, they felt, would be extremely difficult, if not impossible, for a small volunteer-based group. Even those who did not agree saw the problems. Nonetheless the need for continued solidarity was abundantly clear to the team. "What choice do we have but to fight for and celebrate the gift of life we share with the Guatemalans we have gotten to know?" (Rees, 1998).

The Steering Committee gathered on the 1998 Labour Day weekend, after regional discussions. They had sought advice from trusted "elders" who had supported Project A over the years. Their responses let the Committee see the issues through the eyes of others with a depth of experience in Guatemala, but without the same attachments as Project A members. Eleanor Douglas, then an Anglican Church staff member, e-mailed the Steering Committee: "It is quite acceptable for an organization to end. Maybe more should do so!!... It makes little sense to try and invent a role when the role clearly does not exist.... Project A played an important role efficiently in a particular situation and that situation has evolved. I agree that it does not make sense to create a new mandate for Project A that would make it similar to every other international development organization working in Guatemala" (Douglas, 1998).

The Steering Committee methodically analyzed pros and cons. Those for whom Project A had been a labour of love were being asked to dissolve the organization. The Guatemalan social movement still counted on Canadian solidarity. A few weeks before the meeting, Lisa Roberts wrote: "The increase in politically motivated threats and killing, beginning but not ending with the assassination of Bishop Juan Gerardi last April 26, is clear evidence of the attempt by military and other ultra-conservative sectors to roll back the gains made by human rights and popular groups" (Roberts, #3).

The Steering Committee recognized that Project A's focus on the Return process had resulted in a lack of connection to the larger solidarity movement. It would only agree to end Project A if an alternative national organization, linking Project A groups and individuals with the wider network across the country, took its place. Project A's ending became an impetus for creating the Guatemala-Canada Solidarity Network in March 1999.

B : Unresolved Issues

※ Friction among Accompaniers

Project A was built on the strong foundation of a decade of dialogue with refugees and Guatemalan NGOs. The accompaniment role was clear as were selection criteria and the need for thorough training and orientation. A Guatemalan active in planning the Return process said: "The presence of foreigners in our processes was something new, and we were a little fearful. So what we did was to define criteria: what kind of people could participate; those with a high level of awareness with a political clarity and a great deal of maturity to handle the situation. Later there were also criteria about what accompaniers should and shouldn't do; that their role was above all as observers, not participants, and that they were not to involve themselves in anything."

From the start, Project A accompaniers earned the respect and trust of refugees and their leaders as well as Guatemalan and international agencies. Most carried out their role well in a highly militarized situation. Policies were explained during the Canadian training and reviewed at the Southern orientation. Accompaniers signed an agreement with Project A, promising to abide by these policies and to comply with Mexican and Guatemalan laws, including laws against drug use and currency speculation. They agreed to follow Project A's direction with regard to placement, time off, and tasks, as well as behaviour in crises.

The Permanent Commissions (CCPP) and Project A signed a letter of agreement in January 1994. It stated that accompaniers would work in a non-confrontational manner with their primary role being that of observers who would keep Canadians informed. They would not make commitments to support development projects; these would be sent through NGO and church channels. Accompaniers would work in pairs for security and emotional support.

From the early days of the first Return, it was obvious that other international accompaniers did not have the same clarity about their role. The waiting period before the first Return was a time of confusion and uncertainty for accompaniers. During training in Canada, they had been told repeatedly that flexibility was an essential quality for accompaniers. This was soon tested:

> The Permanent Commissions, overwhelmed by the logistical needs of the refugees and the demands of the continuing negotiation process, left the foreigners to organize themselves....Some had experience, and some did not. Some spoke Spanish well; some did not. They did not

know one another, and no one had either the authority or the capacity at that moment to define or implement selection criteria for accompaniment. They were not sure if COMAR [the Mexican Refugee Commission] would let them onto the buses with the refugees. They were not sure if Guatemalan authorities would let them cross the border. No one was sure of anything. Urgency, chaos, and hope drove the process. (Eguren and Mahony, p. 133)

Cultural and political differences among accompaniers from groups with different training programs and policies were not easy to resolve in this intense situation. Little time was available to develop a coordination structure and behavioural norms. John Payne remarked: "I certainly felt that there was good vision amongst the Canadian accompaniers. I think our group pretty well held together. Some of the other groups that we worked with did not do so as much." Some accompaniers were not able to cooperate in close and difficult living conditions or to cope with having a lot of time on their hands, while others tried to insert themselves into the community inappropriately.

Tensions emerged between trained international accompaniers and *sueltos*, that is, accompaniers not affiliated with an accompaniment organization who were largely untrained. Project A accompaniers were told: "It is possible that you may encounter disorganized, badly prepared accompaniers who are often unknown to anyone." A UNHCR official assessed the presence of *sueltos* in this way: "They are really tourists or hippies joining the movement. I don't think they really represent a real protection, because you don't know who they represent, seriously, coming on their own," (Eguren and Mahony, p. 135).

Solutions were not easily found, since the individualistic *sueltos* felt little accountability to anyone and did not understand the reasons for behavioural norms. For example, returned communities discouraged the use of alcohol, although drinking did occur. A few accompaniers drank with community members. The behaviour of a few could have made it easy for the army, who saw accompaniers as troublemakers and "communists," to justify their expulsion.

Project A saw intervention in a community's internal affairs as highly inappropriate. An accompanier explained that "above all, we are not a part of the population or the organizations that we are accompanying. It is not *our* struggle, although at times we identify strongly with it." Colin Rowat wrote: "We are trying to help protect the space that the Guatemalan people have opened up for freedom; we are not here to tell them how to do it" (Rowat, letter to new accompaniers, 1994).

Not all accompaniers shared that view. Eva Manly recalled her disagreement with another accompanier's action: "There was a fight between two Guatemalans who had been drinking too much. An accompanier stepped in to resolve this. It was totally inappropriate for him to stick his neck out. It wasn't his business. He simply should have observed and let the local people deal with it. The people were able to handle it quite nicely themselves and too polite to say butt out."

The CCPP had little time to address these issues. However they affirmed the Canadian position, emphasizing to accompaniment groups the need for volunteers to have adequate preparation and to represent recognized groups. They stressed the value of Project A's training in non-violent responses to crises and requested better coordination among accompaniment groups and the accompaniers. However they also felt that restricting accompaniment to a few organizations would have meant fewer accompaniers and international contacts, as well as less international attention. Many accompaniment groups came to agree with Project A's approach. Tensions diminished with the creation of the Accompaniment Forum and dialogue among accompaniers. "The organization of accompaniers is a difficult task given the constant turnover of accompaniers, different working styles, and language barriers. Nevertheless, perhaps owing to the presence of accompaniers with a relatively long term commitment, this is developing" (Rowat, letter to support committee, 1994).

In early 1994 Colin Rowat, on behalf of longer-term accompaniers, composed a letter for incoming accompaniers. By this time more than a hundred internationals had stayed in the Ixcán from a few days to several weeks. "We have seen a lot of people suffer a lot of emotional turmoil because they were not adequately prepared for the difficult situation they had to face here in Guatemala" (Rowat, letter to new accompaniers, 1994).

Some accompaniers were culturally insensitive, appearing to treat the experience as a tourist adventure. Prospective accompaniers were asked to reflect on this: "Consider for a moment as you pull out your camera or ask someone probing questions, how many dozens of passing internationals have already taken returnees' photos or asked those questions, and passed out of their lives."

Some questions were dangerous: "Balancing curiosity with discretion is an art which many of us who come from countries where there are more freedoms and less risk simply do not have. We often have to satisfy our curiosity through passive observation while keeping our mouths shut.... The topic of the guerrilla movement is not appropriate conversation at any point. Keep in mind that Guatemala is famous for its spy networks and Victoria is not immune to this. Discussing the guerrillas could indirectly contribute to increasing someone's vulnerability" (Rowat, letter to new accompaniers, 1994).

※ The Accompanier's Role

Accompaniers and refugee leaders understood to varying degrees that the accompaniers' role was not that of development or technical assistance. However, Project A members were never able to agree on what was appropriate. Many accompaniers wanted to be active in the community, while not intervening in internal affairs or offering technical advice. Others felt accompaniers were there "*to be*," and that the need "*to do*" was a cultural need of Canadians, inappropriate to the accompaniment role. Still others felt the role should be restricted to human rights security work.

Paula Shaw was "quite furious" with two accompaniers, a Canadian and a Spaniard: "One time we were asked by one of the education promoters if we could give a little workshop to the kindergarten teachers, because they had very little skill at working with kids. And the two accompaniers I was with at that time were quite good with kids. All the kids were always in the galera [accompaniers' residence] playing with them. And they were absolutely against it: 'that's not what we do as accompaniers'" (TI).

Most resolved the issue individually, doing what they found appropriate. Nurses Mary Ann Morris and Randy Janzen worked informally with health promoters and assisted in a vaccination campaign. Linda Geggie participated in a Festival of Health in the Victoria community, enlisting fellow accompaniers to join her in a popular theatre skit about the importance of trees to a healthy environment. She recruited her neighbours to act in *El Mundo de la Composta*, a skit introducing "The World of Composting." John Payne offered his services as an experienced mapmaker when Victoria was ready to lay out its town plan and decide who would live where.

> Being a doer, I wanted to do something. So I said, "Well, I can make a map." I looked at the North Star one night and I said, "There's north." I started pacing, and wandering around the town, developing a little map by eyeball. Then one of the American accompaniers got out a small compass. Eventually I got the whole town put on a map. Several times, I enlisted the help of a curious young person to help me put his or her house on the map. At home in Vancouver, I printed it up as you would for a scientific report and made a bunch of copies and sent it back with the next accompaniers going down. A copy of the map was pinned up in the ccpp office and was proudly shown to visitors. It

gave the people a sense that their new home was really important because there it was on the map. (TI)

After a year-and-a-half's gestation the Accompaniment Forum held its first meeting in 1994, chaired by Susan Skaret. Sixteen accompaniment groups met regularly, sharing experiences and concerns, developing coherent policies and standards, and coordinating placements. Project A received frequent requests from international groups and solidarity organizations for training, selection, and placement information.

※ Language Fluency

Language fluency was a major source of conflict within Project A, which insisted on a good grasp of Spanish. "To do accompaniment you need to be able to understand what is going on around you in spite of tension and you may need to be able to communicate it by telephone in Spanish. It is very common that one's control of a language that is not one's native tongue diminishes greatly in times of stress and it is also common to be intimidated by telephones....Our own and others' lives may depend on your communication and we simply have no right to take on such a responsibility for which we may not be equipped linguistically" (PA, 1998).

Despite such clarity, this issue caused more strife between Southern coordinators and accompaniers than any other. After difficulties in the first year, Project A decided to give the orientation in Mexico and Guatemala in Spanish, which would quickly weed out those with insufficient fluency. Several accompaniers recognized their limitations and undertook further language study. Some, however, insisted their Spanish was acceptable, even though they had not understood critical issues in the orientation. Coordinators were then faced with having to tell them their Spanish was not yet adequate. Some accompaniers were reluctant to accept this news, causing considerable anguish to the coordinators. Others, like Paula Shaw, took it in stride: "I was one of the people who came who was very slow at learning languages. It was big trouble for me. Definitely, language is very, very important....The families that I'm friends with still laugh about some of the things I said when I was an accompanier. The story was that they were asking me how I could afford to be here. I said that I had a vaca (cow) instead of a beca (loan). And they said, 'Well who's taking care of my vaca?' And I was thinking 'My beca. Well, it's in the bank.' What? We still laugh about that" (TI).

※ Conflicts among the Refugees

Serious conflicts emerged in several returned communities, particularly Victoria 20 de enero and the Ixcán Grande Cooperative. Causes included long-standing issues unresolved before the 1980s violence began, differences about approaches to development, a desire by Permanent Commissioners to maintain power (although their mandate officially ended when communities returned), and disagreement as to whether or not to continue a strategic relationship with the armed resistance movement, the URNG. Most refugees, whether or not they had supported the URNG, acknowledged its influence, but also indicated that they did not control decision making in Mexico or in the returned communities. The Return to Victoria in January 1993, for example, reportedly took place without URNG support or agreement.

In Victoria, competing interests existed from the start. "At the time of the signing of the Peace Accords, that first Return community could hardly be described as a community at all. It was deeply divided, so riven, in fact, that there were two separate sets of schools and two town offices, serving the two main factions" (Taylor, p. 189).

Permanent Commissioners in the Ixcán Grande Cooperative tried to exclude the returnees' human rights group. They burned down the office of the women's organization, *Mama Maquín*. They claimed its members had no right to state their opinion publicly, since most were not legal members of the cooperative, as their husbands had the property rights and therefore the right to vote. In 1997 the CCPP tried, unsuccessfully, to illegally block the arrival of fifty-seven demobilized URNG combatants, claiming they were criminals. According to the Peace Accords they had a right to return to the community since they or their family owned plots of land.

These conflicts posed a dilemma. Accompaniers had chosen to walk alongside the returning refugees because they supported their desire to work towards a more just and democratic society. Project A had always supported the right of unarmed civilian groups to hold their own political preferences, while the CCPP appeared to be trying to impose their point of view on entire communities. The returnees seemed to be spending more time fighting among themselves than challenging injustice within Guatemalan society. Justice, democracy, and peace often appeared to be sorely lacking in dealing with conflict.

The CCPP's aggressive stance perturbed accompaniers. They were confused by various groups' positions on past and present guerrilla actions, attitudes, and structures. Some accompaniers were strong pacifists opposed to the use of force, while others were sympathetic to the URNG. Many accompaniers, with differing levels of awareness of the political history and complexity, had come to simply offer humanitarian support. Ironically pacifists sometimes found their sympathies lay with groups such as *Mama Maquín*, who maintained an alliance with the guerrillas, while those who were supportive of the URNG were disturbed by critical revelations of its structure and by the attitudes and behaviour of some leaders. Many female accompaniers had valued their relationship with *Mama Maquín*, and were distressed by attitudes of male refugee leaders. In the heat of discussion a long-time Project A member wrote: "The next time you meet, tell the Permanent Commissions that you are worried about their attitude. Tell them that you cannot promote support for a movement that does *not* respect the human rights of all their population, including women who have been the most discriminated against of all. What's this about the real members of the cooperative being the men? That's what the Guatemalan cooperative law says, but didn't they return to build a better society?"

How should Project A respond to a complex situation in which it was critical of the actions of the CCPP, the very group who had invited them to accompany the refugees? Should Project A withdraw? Should it publicly denounce the situation? Should it support one faction where there were no clear "good guys" and "bad guys?"

Project A developed its response after thorough analysis and dialogue with the CCPP, the Project A Network, and the Accompaniment Forum. Gaby Labelle encouraged Project A not to leave: "We've made a commitment to accompany this process of a people who may make a lot of errors but who have been the victim of such a horrible process of destruction of their humanity that they deserve support in the reconstruction. It will not be an easy task. For the time being, I think a prudent stand is to keep on doing accompaniment as 'observers,' not interfering but not absurdly neutral either.... Our solidarity actions cannot limit themselves to success stories. We must remain present in the difficult hours of trials and errors."

Project A decided to maintain accompaniment in these communities since its fundamental commitment was to the refugees. Accompaniers thought their presence might be constructive and took care not to align themselves with any one faction. It was, after all, not surprising that refugees were sorting out differences that had, of necessity during wartime, been suppressed. Accompaniers sent to the most conflictual communities were carefully chosen individuals with strong accompaniment experience and a good grasp of history. Accompaniment group representatives met with the CCPP to express their concerns. A respectful although somewhat more distant relationship was maintained with the CCPP who continued to request accompaniers and express appreciation for Project A's contribution.

6 The Christian Task Force on Central America in British Columbia

PROJECT ACCOMPANIMENT was rooted in solidarity relationships that began two decades earlier, particularly those built by the Christian Task Force on Central America (CTF), now called the Ecumenical Task Force for Justice in the Americas. Part A of this chapter summarizes Canada's early history of solidarity work, which had a major impact on CTF's formation. Part B describes the confluence of events leading to its founding. Part C describes its formation and functioning.

A : Solidarity's Origins in Latin America and Canada

> From the depths of the countries that make up Latin America a cry is rising to heaven, growing louder and more alarming all the time. It is the cry of a suffering people who demand justice, freedom, and respect for the basic rights of human beings and peoples.
> —Puebla #87, cited by Michael Czerny in *Compass*, 1997

Latin America was in upheaval throughout the 1960s and '70s. The poor emerged as an irreversible force in history, forming social movements throughout the continent to resist the exclusion and exploitation they faced daily. Juan de Dios Parra, secretary-general of the Latin American Human Rights Association, graphically summarized this reality:

- The poor were very poor and a few were very rich;
- Every day many children were starving to death;
- The peasants had no land, while the land-owners did not work on it; and
- Hundreds of thousands of people were dying month after month from preventable diseases.

They were struggling:

- To give everyone a life with dignity;
- To make human rights a shared minimum for all humankind;

- To ensure that no one would go to bed hungry;
- To conceive of development and its benefits as something which belonged to everyone; and
- To transform the "right to live" into the "right to live with dignity." (Parra, 2000)

Religious orders began to work in poor communities, inspired by the spirit of renewal emerging from the Second Vatican Council in the early 1960s. "Educated by the enormous suffering and hardened knowledge of the poor, they were led to radical conclusions about the extent of necessary reforms in the economic and social life of Latin America" (McFarlane, pp. 137–38). The Latin American Conference of Bishops' startling declaration of a preferential option for the poor arose out of this experience. "Instead of automatically blessing the status quo and standing by every dictator, the church began to assume a new optic, that of the poor in their millions who are poor not because God wills it but because of someone's choices and decisions" (Czerny, 1997, p. 9).

Young Christians volunteered in Latin America. Others met Latin Americans in delegations and meetings. They saw the implications for Canadians of the "preferential option." They called the church to see the world through the eyes of those on the margins of society. They recognized the need to accompany the impoverished in their struggles for justice and to analyze critically the economic and social structures causing poverty. "What is remarkable," observed theologian Gregory Baum at the time, "is that certain groups of Christians in these parts, along with their ecclesiastical leaders, have responded positively to this challenge" (Baum, p. 29).

Those were "heady years," wrote adult educator and community organizer Denise Nadeau:

> I learned that it was possible to bring together economics and theology, popular education and the Bible. I realized that the Bible meant something different when read with the eyes of the poor. Not only was it clear that throughout the Bible God was aligned with the poor, but also that "option for the poor" was central to the Church's ministry and mission.... Structural sin, the institutionalization of oppression in social and economic structures, was now named as an evil to be challenged and overcome in the struggle for God's Reign. Option for the poor meant a political commitment—our faith involved us in political struggle in solidarity with all marginalized and oppressed peoples. (*Network News,* Nadeau)

In 1973 the Central Intelligence Agency instigated the overthrow of Chile's democratically elected socialist government, replacing it with the

Pinochet military dictatorship. Ottawa had supported US policy a year earlier, voting to cut off all money to Chile from the International Monetary Fund. Unlike the overthrow of Guatemala's democratically elected government in 1954, this bloody coup and its aftermath were challenged by Canadian unions, the student movement, and churches. The government had to face the fact that many Canadians would no longer support its quiet affirmation of US policy.

A few Canadian Christians had developed relationships with Chilean groups struggling for justice. When their cry for solidarity demanded a response, they persuaded the churches to form the Inter-Church Committee on Chile. The churches' agenda now included networking, awareness-raising, and sending human rights delegations to Chile. Churches lobbied long and hard, pressuring Canada to condemn the coup and open its doors to Chilean refugees. When their campaign achieved success in late 1974, committees for ecumenical refugee sponsorship and resettlement formed across the country. By 1980 more than seven thousand Chileans had entered Canada.

Latin America solidarity work can, in many cases, be traced to Chileans' impact on Canadians. "One of the first really significant activities I was involved with was when we invited a Chilean group to come to Castlegar in 1976 or so and we put on a Peña (celebration)—great music, food, talk. Well over one hundred people came. The hall was jammed and we all had a fabulous time," recalled Ann Godderis (correspondence with author).

The Pinochet regime coupled the doctrine of "national security" with the imposition of neo-liberalism, promoted by University of Chicago economist Milton Friedman. Chile became a giant laboratory for this unregulated, free-market form of capitalism that included a structural adjustment package involving massive cuts in public expenditures. Neo-liberalism spread rapidly across the continent, and indeed throughout the world, enabling a few to become wealthy while the majority was pushed further and further into poverty. Massive human rights violations of those with the courage to resist began. In October 1976 several Central American theologians wrote an open letter to North American Christians: "Friends and fellow Christians, It is time that you realize that our continent is becoming one gigantic prison and, in some regions, one vast cemetery...that human rights, fundamental to the Gospel, are becoming a dead letter, without force. And all this is happening in order to maintain a structure of dependence that benefits those who have always held might and privilege, in your land and in our land, at the expense of the poor millions who are increasing throughout the width and breadth of the continent" (cited in Fairbairn, p. 172).

※ Inter-Church Committee on Human Rights in Latin America

Canadian churches heeded the plea. In 1976 the Inter-Church Committee on Chile became the Inter-Church Committee on Human Rights in Latin America (ICCHRLA), as a means for churches to defend victims of human rights violations and support Latin Americans in their struggles against the root causes of such violations. (No longer a separate entity, ICCHRLA has become part of a new ecumenical church coalition, Kairos.) "By participating with Latin American struggles for freedom and justice, Canadian Christians experience the work of the Gospel. The Committee should continue its active role in the defence of human rights and refugees from political oppression. It will assist Canadian churches in their relations with Latin America, particularly making present the moral and physical support of Canadian Christians in situations of oppression. It will seek the co-operation of other church and non-church groups who share the concerns with promoting human justice and who will stimulate widespread solidarity action when crucial issues arise" (cited in Fairbairn, p. 179).

ICCHRLA lobbied the Canadian government to take a stance independent of US Cold War policies in Latin America. After a positive response to its first presentation in 1978, it became convinced of the value of a regular presence at the UN Commission on Human Rights. It helped ecumenical partners in Latin America gain access to these meetings. It prepared annual human rights reports on priority countries, including Guatemala, for presentation to the UN and the Canadian government, as well as for public dissemination. Reinforced by a network of citizens who sent letters to Ottawa, it lobbied Canadian representatives at those meetings. Quaker Fred Franklin looked back admiringly: "Many visits to religious communities in Latin America, as well as return visits by some wonderful human beings, brought us face to face with the tremendous religious faith, buoyancy, and steadfastness of the Latin American people. Knowing of the daily terror and persecution in their homelands, this affected us profoundly. It was our constant inspiration as we tried to tell their story to the Canadian public and to influence our government's policies" (cited in Fairbairn, p. 179).

Soon after its founding, ICCHRLA received alarming reports of the deteriorating human rights situation in Central America. Frances Arbour, ICCHRLA executive director from 1977 to 1985, organized delegation after delegation, first to El Salvador and later to Guatemala. She developed relationships of trust with church and human rights groups throughout Central America and involved grassroots groups across Canada.

Bishop Remi De Roo travelled to Central America in 1980 on an ICCHRLA delegation. He met with Archbishop Oscar Romero in El Salvador just weeks before Romero's assassination by the army. He was in Guatemala when thirty-six Mayan campesinos were burned to death in the Spanish Embassy. He wrote: "Continued prayer for the suffering people of Guatemala, international solidarity with victims of repression, campaigns of protest against torture and assassination: these are some of the things in which we can participate while waiting for the day when the people can free themselves from decades of hunger and religious persecution" (De Roo, p. 19).

During Vatican II De Roo had been deeply influenced by Latin American bishops such as Samuel Ruiz from Chiapas, Mexico. His impassioned and insightful reflections inspired many to become involved in solidarity, like Deirdre Kelly and other CTF founders from Vancouver Island who heard him speak at an Easter retreat.

> I had never before heard of anything quite like that, where the Gospel was being lived out in the way the story was told about Nicaragua—the literacy campaigns with the young people going off in the summer and teaching people to read and write, the health crusades, the priests in the government who were involved in culture and education and the economy. All these kinds of things humanized the struggle to me at that time where I could see the Gospel that I had read being lived and acted out. That to me was deeply inspiring.
>
> We got busy right away. We visited every parish on the Island, talking to them about what was going on in Central America. We deeply felt the injustice that was occurring both in El Salvador and Guatemala. We also felt a contagious hope about what was happening in Nicaragua. (TI)

De Roo's impact went far beyond church walls. A presentation to trade unionists propelled Scotty Niesh, a life-long activist in the United Fisherman and Allied Workers' Union and his son, Kevin, also a trade unionist, into solidarity work.

※ Latin American Working Group

The Latin America Working Group (LAWG), a small, independent body with membership from churches, labour unions, and academia, was formed around the same time to do research, analysis, education, and lobbying. It was critical of the dominant influence of corporate interests on Canada's trade, aid, and diplomacy with Latin America. Because of its expertise, LAWG's analysis, research, and educational work became vital to the development of solidarity work. It developed links with activists across the country and groups such as the United Church, the Canadian Catholic Organization for Development and Peace, CUSO, and the Canadian Labour Congress. Members Louise Casselman and Gaby Labelle were based in Mexico City. Their analyses and contacts with social and political movements in Central America were invaluable to the emerging solidarity movement. Later, both Gaby and Louise had an ongoing relationship with CTF delegations and Gaby became a Project A staff member.

※ GATT-fly

Another church coalition, GATT-fly, founded in 1973, had a marked influence on many in the solidarity movement. Its name came from the General Agreement on Trade and Tariffs (GATT) combined with a pun on the word "gadfly." GATT-fly's role was to pester the government on trade and economic justice issues. (It later became the Ecumenical Coalition for Economic Justice. It is now part of the new Kairos ecumenical coalition.)

GATT-fly's mission was to do research and education on structural causes of economic injustice. Using popular education tools and methods, GATT-fly enabled church, community group, and trade union members to understand better the impact of Canada's foreign aid and trade policies. Although not specific to Latin America, it offered solidarity activists the analysis they needed to understand the root causes of poverty in Latin America.

※ Ten Days for World Development

In 1973 the Inter-Church Committee for World Development Education, formed by the Anglican, Lutheran, Presbyterian, Roman Catholic, and United Churches, created a program called Ten Days for World Development (later, Ten Days for Global Justice, which has also become part of Kairos). Each February, ten days were set aside for ecumenical groups to study a global justice issue and then take actions in their own lives, churches, and local communities. Many activities, including tours of Third World visitors, are held at that time. However, many local groups were active year-round. Ten Days became a network of community-based ecumenical groups, empowering people to build a more just world through a program of education and action.

Wes Maultsaid, a Ten Days field worker in the 1970s, believes the program enabled people "to break down some of the dogmatic barriers between the churches and find a way to work together around liberation concerns that wouldn't stifle them because of their particular denomina-

Marta Gloria de la Vega, a founder of the Christian Task Force on Central America. Photographer unknown.

tional barriers." He nurtured the growth of Ten Days groups and encouraged networking among far-flung communities. It became second nature to work together.

In 1980 Marta Gloria de la Vega, a labour lawyer in exile in Costa Rica, toured BC as a Ten Days visitor. Her openness, humility, and passion made an indelible impression on all who met her. She had fled Guatemala with Enrique Torres, also a labour lawyer, and their five children, after their names had appeared on a death list because of their work with those attempting to unionize at the large Coca-Cola plant in Guatemala City.

Central America became the Ten Days program focus from 1983–85, as Canadians recognized the need for strong and sustained solidarity action at that critical juncture in Central American history. Corina Dykstra noted: "This program brought significant growth to the church community, deepening the political and theological understanding of the Central American situation and increasing the number of people called to act on their faith on behalf of Central Americans" (Dykstra, p. 50).

B : Kindling the Vision in British Columbia

A 1981 solidarity tour by twenty trade unionists, church, and NGO delegates to Nicaragua had a huge influence on the formation of the Christian Task Force in 1984. Delegates returned with a passion to build a movement to resist US intervention. Their presentations generated wide public interest, leading to the formation of the BC-Nicaragua Solidarity Project and Tools for Peace. Tour member Scotty Niesh persuaded the United Fishermen and Allied Workers' Union to donate a huge amount of gear to a Nicaraguan fishers' cooperative, spearheading the formation of Tools for Peace. It became a national organization when the US blockaded Nicaragua. Canadians and Americans sought ways to send material support to Nicaragua.

Encountering Nicaragua's Base Christian Communities struck a deep chord. These small neighbourhood groups, full of life and dynamism, studied the Bible, prayed, offered members personal support, and carried out social action, from gaining access to water to participation in the Sandinista government's literacy campaign. They believed the God of the Bible was on the side of the poor and the oppressed. They attached great importance to the Exodus story of the liberation of the Israelites from oppression in the land of bondage. They believed that God's covenant with the people in the desert meant "never again Egypt, never again subservience to empire, never again subservience to oppression.... Even the worship of God was null and void unless people were dedicated to social justice" (Baum, p. 23).

The encounter with Base Christian Communities transformed Bud Godderis, says his partner, Ann. "I don't like using the words 'born again,' but he had been, before he left, a very disillusioned ex-priest who didn't really want anything to do with the organized church community" (TI). Bud says the encounter enabled him to rejoin the Christian community, finding kindred spirits who shared his vision of a justice-seeking faith community. With others, he began to envision how the Base Christian Community model might be adapted to nurture and empower Canadians: "Through our work in the South we were encouraged to bring the faith dimension to our work because it meant so much to the people we were working with. We found in the South that many of the people we worked with, including trade union people, were very strongly based in the church" (TI).

In 1982, six British Columbians visited Guatemalan and Salvadoran refugee camps in Honduras. With next to no media coverage, the stories they told were a first opportunity for many to become aware of the tragedy unfolding. "The group's return to BC and subsequent educational talks penetrated people's awareness and interest regarding the situation; the credibility of those who had first-hand experience in the region created a demand for more regular up-to-date information and opportunities for action" (Dykstra, p. 52).

With such powerful experiences, people from across BC felt the need to meet together. Week-long "Summer Justice-Making Institutes" were held at United and Anglican Church educational centres in Sorrento and Naramata. There, the vision that led to the CTF was kindled. The first event was held at Sorrento in August 1982. Over one hundred adults and their children gathered for encouragement and nourishment. Resource persons such as Bishop De Roo and Thomas Berger gave morning presentations. In the evening participants were involved in social analysis and biblical reflection. Ann Godderis said: "Morning worship in the beautiful Sorrento setting above the lake was really wonderful as was the late evening sharing around campfires. The children loved it" (TI).

A decision taken at the first Institute was fundamental to the CTF's creation. In 1982 word reached Wes Maultsaid that Marta, Enrique, and their children needed to leave Costa Rica. Threats to their lives had moved beyond Guatemala. Wes contacted individuals active in the Ten Days network, including Sandy and Don Robertson, then minister at Kamloops United Church. These individuals agreed to pledge enough money for Kamloops United Church to sponsor them officially as refugees. Project supporters demonstrated a remarkable degree of commitment. Marg Green said: "A number of people were putting in fifty and one hundred dollars a month for years, people with families that didn't have a lot of money" (TI). Families became deeply bonded as together they supported the project financially and personally. That level of commitment continued after the CTF's birth. The Guatemala Refugee Project was formed. The family arrived in July 1982.

At Sorrento, those who had pledged money agreed that the Guatemala Refugee Project would seek CIDA funding to match pledged funds on a three-to-one basis. This allowed Marta and Enrique to be hired as Project staff, thus moving the sponsorship from a charity model to a justice model. "They had the dignity of employment doing what they needed and wanted to do, that is, to educate and help mobilize Canadians to speak out around the gross and systematic violations of human rights in Guatemala," noted Ann Godderis (TI).

A year later, in collaboration with the BC CUSO office where Wes Maultsaid was then working, the Guatemala Refugee Project became the Central America Education and Action Project. Marta and Enrique continued as staff members. Churches, trade unions, educators, and youth worked together on projects they initiated, such as Canadian participation in a successful international campaign in support of Guatemalan Coca-Cola workers. Visits to Mexico and Central America took place. Leadership developed as delegates brought their experiences back home. Monimbo Crafts was formed to support refugees in Mexico through the sale of weavings made in refugee camps, and a communications project between BC children and children in refugee camps began.

In January of 1983 Marta and Wes travelled to refugee camps in Chiapas. This transformative experience led to further delegations to the camps at least once a year, and ultimately to the formation of Project Accompaniment. What was learned from the refugees had a major influence on the CTF's objectives and priorities (see also Prologue and chap. 3).

In 1983 the Justice-Making Institute was held in Sorrento just before the Sixth Assembly of the World Council of Churches (WCC) opened in Vancouver. This enabled a few Assembly participants to attend, including Hugh McCullum, Bob Carty, and Frances Arbour. Julia Esquivel, Guatemalan poet and theologian in exile, read her poetry of anguish and of unquenchable hope. Teatro Vivo, a popular theatre group comprised of gifted, highly trained young actors with no fixed country of refuge, used expressive mime and movement to draw participants into the daily injustice and repression Guatemalans faced. Musical group Kin Lalat, who had also been forced to flee Guatemala, used the marimba, flute, rainstick, drums, and other traditional instruments to convey its message. They sang in Spanish, with a short English introduction. Most songs were political; some were sad. They even sang a funny song about the fate of an activist chicken.

Ann Godderis described the experience:

> What a rich and powerful week it was! The whole approach changed. No longer were we sitting and listening. After worship and the introduction of a theme and some input, we worked together in groups—sharing and teaching each other. A much more empowering approach, for sure! We drew and role-played to help integrate and make sense of the structural analysis we were working on, and of course our Central American sisters and brothers contributed a lot to that process.
>
> The evenings were amazing—singing, storytelling, and poetry reading around a huge fire until very late into the night. Families took turns sharing their meals with Kin Lalat and Teatro Vivo. The worship was awesome. The final afternoon we had this liturgy where all of us, including the children, had a part in preparing different sections, summing up the week's learning and gifts. It started with a parade, singing and drumming, winding through the grounds of Sorrento, picking up people as it went and ending up at the circular worship site. Then we

ate together on the lawn outside the Centre, sharing our food and our love. (TI)

The WCC Assembly was another stimulus to the CTF's creation: "For many, a new vision was molded; that of peace with social justice" (Dykstra, p. 51). Mike Lewis, a community development worker and United Church delegate to the Assembly, had just returned to BC from a trip to Nicaragua, where US intervention had become overt and massive. He spoke to the Assembly and, along with others, influenced WCC policies on Nicaragua. Julia Esquivel spoke movingly, while Kin Lalat and Teatro Vivo offered powerful presentations to the Assembly coffeehouse, as well as the Vancouver Folk Festival. Most of the audience didn't understand Spanish, but mime, movement, and music transcended language. These groups later toured throughout BC and the rest of Canada, motivating new involvement in solidarity wherever they performed.

In 1984 Wes Maultsaid, Peter Bowles, Mary Ann Morris, and Deirdre Kelly drove from the Coast to the small town of Princeton to met Ann and Bud Godderis who had travelled from the Kootenays. In a tiny log motel unit by the banks of a river they prayed, reflected, and explored possibilities for accompanying Nicaraguan communities threatened by the Contra invasion. Inspired by Witness for Peace, a US group, they formed Witness for Justice and Peace. It sent delegations to conflict zones in Nicaragua where Contra forces had destroyed villages. Their presence served as a non-violent witness in the midst of the US-backed war, "a concrete attempt to show solidarity with the people in Nicaragua by sharing their life, with all its pain and tensions, and with its hope and vision of a new future" (Dykstra, p. 53). On their return, delegates shared their experiences wherever they could, thus mobilizing public opinion. Their discovery of the value of physical presence in conflict zones ultimately contributed to Project A's formation.

C : The Christian Task Force Is Formed

The Christian Task Force on Central America formed in 1984, culminating a decade-long process in which many people had forged strong bonds with one another. The hopes and struggles of Central Americans had caught the hearts and imaginations of many British Columbians. The Sandinista revolutionary movement victory in Nicaragua, followed by the US-backed "Contra" war; the assassination in El Salvador of Archbishop Oscar Romero and four US churchwomen; thousands of Guatemalans and Salvadorans seeking refuge from death squads and vicious armies—these events generated a groundswell.

The interest created by Central American visitors, work by people like Wes Maultsaid, Marta Gloria de la Vega, and Enrique Torres, information from national coalitions, and the passion of people newly involved in solidarity work converged. Many individuals recognized that the ongoing struggle in Central America needed a coordinated response. The Central America Education and Action Project was coming to a close. The Ten Days focus on Central America was to end in early 1985. Yet many in BC had made personal connections with the wartorn region and did not want to sever their links. Frank Green recalled: "A lot of people had this part in their heart that was very big. People at that point were saying: 'No, I know people down there personally.' That's where their energy wanted to stay. There was a brainstorming of people from around the province, from Ten Days, from Development and Peace, from the trips, asking, 'What's the best way to carry this forward if we can't depend on Ten Days putting the Central American agenda before everybody every year?'" (TI).

A core group from Vancouver Island, the Lower Mainland, and the Southern Interior met several times to start the planning for a network rooted in faith and community that would link the many committed individuals and groups under one umbrella. The founding meeting in September 1984 was "born of a shared experience and vision." Rooted in the Judeo-Christian prophetic tradition, an Old Testament verse became their theme: "This is what God asks of you, only this: to act justly, to love kindness, and to walk humbly with your God" (Micah 6:8). The Central American understanding of solidarity as a way of life was at the heart of their vision: "It implies taking risks, individually and collectively, to challenge the unjust structures of domination, to voice the 'truth' of injustice, and to work in concrete ways to further democracy" (Dykstra, p. 56). They formed a network that integrated faith, action, celebration, and reflection, which Mike Lewis saw as "inspired by people in quite desperate circumstances who seemed to have more capacity to celebrate life than we did" (TI).

The CTF established its objectives:

- To maintain and further evolve an educational program designed to build awareness, motivate, equip, and mobilize the Christian community in BC to active and effective solidarity with the struggle of Christians in Central America;
- To provide the coordination and organizational capacity to service the network as it evolves and to integrate new interest and leadership into ongoing education work; and

- To act as a vehicle through which the Christian community in BC can constructively collaborate with other constituencies interested in and/or committed to working for peace and justice in Central America. (CTF, 1984)

The CTF was "a flexible, nebulous, multi-dimensional organization, drawing members from twenty-six communities scattered throughout BC. The majority of its members were white and middle-class in ethos, if not in lifestyle or background" (Zarowny, p. 386). It had both active and supporting members. Supporting members participated in specific activities or public events, subscribed to the newsletter, or contributed financially. Active members entered into a covenant relationship, renewed at each Annual Meeting. They expressed their faith and hope through committing themselves to specific actions: "Our covenant links us with the people of Central America as they courageously struggle to live life in the midst of death. This covenant we take on is in response to their cry for justice—a step on the way to our liberation from the 'gods' of this world and to their liberation from the poverty and dictators of the two-thirds world. In celebration of this call to life, and with the hope shown to us through the lives of our Central American sisters and brothers, we walk forward, joined together in God's love, each one doing the tasks to which they feel called" (*Network News,* Lewis. p. 3).

Many offered leadership to groups in the Kootenays, Armstrong, Kamloops, Revelstoke/Salmon Arm, the Lower Mainland, and on Vancouver Island. Bud and Ann Godderis gave leadership to an informal network of church people, trade unionists, students, and other activists from several communities in the Kootenays. Although the group was independent of the CTF, several of its members were also CTF members. Ann Pellerine, a lay associate of the Congregation of Notre Dame, who later accompanied Marta Gloria to Guatemala, joined the local group because of her faith commitment, as well as links between the CTF and her union, the Health Sciences Association. Phil Molloy had worked in the North on justice issues, such as Aboriginal land claims, through the Canadian Catholic Organization for Development and Peace and the Steelworkers Union. When he returned to the Kootenays, he became aware of the CTF's work and decided to get involved.

The CTF offered groups visits by resource people, both Guatemalan and Canadian, and musical groups like Kin Lalat, as well as opportunities to join delegations to Central America and to participate in Urgent Action work, retreats, vigils, and the Annual Meeting. The CTF has been, says Bud Godderis, "an energy centre, a structure that allows contact with the

> **The Christian Task Force on Central America** calls us to membership within a covenant, to participate in the work of:
> - Enhancing opportunities for active expression of Christian solidarity between Christians in BC and Central America in accordance with the peace and justice policies and programmes of education and actions by the national churches; and
> - Contributing to the building, strengthening, and networking of communities struggling to integrate, activate, and celebrate their life of faith through concrete witness to the gospel's call to work for peace and justice.
>
> Our basic understanding of covenant is a commitment into which we enter together with God and with each other, as mutually responsible partners in the task to be living witnesses of God's love on earth. Our covenant links us with the people of Central America as they courageously struggle to live in the midst of death. This covenant we take on is in response to their cry for justice—a step on our way to liberation from the "gods" of the world and to their liberation from the poverty and dictators of the two-thirds world. In celebration of this call to life, and with the hope shown to us through the lives of our Central American sisters and brothers, we walk forward joined together in God's love, each one doing the tasks to which they feel called. Within this covenant, we commit ourselves to work in our communities, upholding the concerns of our sisters and brothers in Central America. I also commit myself to the following:
> - Regular prayer each Wednesday;
> - Fasting with prayer on first and third Wednesday;
> - Working with a task group of CTF (Communications, exposure/education tours, education/outreach, urgent action);
> - Pledge of Resistance; and
> - Financial pledge $_____ /month for ____ months

South that we really trust. It gives us information, it puts us in contact with people around the province, it feeds us, it is a mutual relationship to which we also contribute."

In many ways, the CTF has been less an organization than a community based on the quality and strength of relationships among people in Canada and in Central America. Ann Godderis believes "there was never, at least in my mind, the idea in the formation of the Task Force that we were empire-building or institution-building. Right from the beginning, we were going to try and do things differently. Our prime objective was not to build the CTF but to build solidarity" (TI).

However, an organizational structure was needed. It was not easy to find one appropriate to such varied and dispersed individuals and groups. "What was clear was that the members consciously needed and wanted a different organizational structure, which was rooted in the Gospel, was based on a covenant, reached decisions by consensus, and encouraged grassroots participation" (Zarowny, p. 386). Members did not want vertical, hierarchical structures that were typical of many churches.

A democratic, participatory model evolved, with involvement from across BC. "The central principle guiding the operation of the structure of the Task Force was that it be an instrument of coordination, not definition" (Dykstra, p. 59). Ann Godderis said: "The CTF really tried to be inclusive of people outside the Lower Mainland. When Wes, Barb Wood, Marta, and Enrique were initially involved in the formation stage and when the CTF was actually put together, we got a lot of early-morning phone calls. More recently we have received money to travel to Vancouver for executive meetings" (TI). Decisions are reached by consensus and grassroots participation encouraged.

Decisions on priorities and key policy directions are taken, after consultation with local groups, at the Annual Meeting, the one event each year where members gather from across the province. These meetings have often been filled with lively, sometimes conflictual debate. Since it is a time of renewal, creative liturgy and celebration are vital elements.

Volunteers have shaped the CTF's direction, in dialogue with Central American partners whose requests are at the heart of its work. Without their involvement in essential activities, including the executive, working groups, bookkeeping, administration, newsletter publication, and Urgent Actions, the CTF could never have grown and flourished. However, having paid staff working full or part-time in program development, coordination, and administration has allowed a consistent, ongoing range of activities. Marta Gloria de la Vega has been the anchor staff person, having worked with the CTF from its inception.

The CTF pioneered in developing forms of solidarity that have served the entire Canadian solidarity movement. Nonetheless, the road has not always been smooth. At times the group has faced severe financial problems, forcing painful choices in staffing and priorities. The tension between the need to ensure program implementation and the need to nurture the Task Force itself is ongoing. Given the level of need and frequent crises in Central America, it is easy to forget that, without constant communication, support, and networking among far-flung members and groups, the solidarity movement will not be as strong and vibrant as it might be. However Annual Meetings and special events, such as retreats with Julia Esquivel, continue to sustain the CTF.

Certain conflicts have recurred, centred on how the CTF should embody its recognition that solidarity needs to address injustice in both Guatemala and Canada. From its earliest days, some members wanted to expand the CTF mandate to include work in Canada. Others preferred to hold fast to a central focus on Central America, suggesting that one group cannot do everything. The conflict was often defined in terms of differing understandings of solidarity and of the CTF's mission. However, some saw it more as an organizational issue, since most groups outside the Lower Mainland had always had more direct linkages between Central American solidarity and work on local justice issues. For example, many folks in the Kootenays, especially those who were in a health workers' union, felt that they were making links between health issues in BC and groups struggling around health issues in Guatemala. This is a more challenging task in urban centres, where areas of focus often are compartmentalized. For some the question was not about the meaning of solidarity or the CTF mandate, but rather the role of the office and appropriate use of limited staff time.

The conflict deepened in 1995. Some members felt strongly that it was time to develop what they saw as a more congruent and integrated model in which the Christian Task Force would be rooted in struggles for justice in British Columbia and would then make links with groups struggling with those issues in Central America. Kathi Bentall said: "There were quite a few of us who wanted to be more inserted here, and from that place to make the links." For example, CTF members working in the inner city of Vancouver would make linkages with groups working on issues of homelessness in Guatemala.

Others felt, equally as strongly, that this strategy would divert CTF resources and staff from its ongoing commitment to Central American partners and from the support rurally based local groups needed. In an organization with strong, highly committed members, positions hardened, making it impossible to find common ground that might have led to experimentation, pilot projects, or other forms of compromise and innovation. Instead several members left the CTF and the staff's work stayed much the same.

A few years later, however, the CTF's work did shift, based on its original mandate that included work with Latin American refugees and immigrants. This had included assistance with translation, documentation, accompaniment to refugee hearings, or offering expert witness at hearings or in writing. The CTF supported family reunification and advocated for refugee claimants, offering expert witness, interpretation, and advocacy around immigration and refugee policies and laws. When the CTF was unable to assist, it made referrals to other organizations.

While continuing other areas of work, the CTF has refocused on this aspect of its mandate, prompted when Marta Gloria de la Vega became aware of culturally insensitive intervention by social workers, involving the apprehension of children from Latin American families by the BC Ministry for Children and Families. Marta first became an advocate for individual families. The CTF then decided to initiate meetings among representatives of several agencies, women's groups and advocacy groups. They formed the Task Group on Child Apprehensions to seek changes at the policy level, such as training in cultural sensitivity for social workers, and to encourage the Ministry to provide more support and preventative resources to families. That initiative has evolved into a CTF-sponsored project initially funded by the Legal Services Society, later by the Law Foundation of BC and the VanCity Credit Union's Partnership Fund. The CTF asks community groups and churches to sponsor workshops for Latin American family members that enable them to understand their rights and responsibilities under Canadian law, and to talk about issues from poverty to domestic violence.

In 2001 the CTF decided to continue the workshops for another three years and to train Latin Americans nominated by their church or community group as "family promoters" (based on the model of community promoters in Central America). Staff will accompany families to meetings or to court, provide information, and help them find needed resources. "The incredible benefit for the CTF is that this work puts us in much closer working contact with some incredible advocacy, anti-poverty, women's rights and other groups that are part of the Latin American community in the Lower Mainland," says Ann Godderis (correspondence with author).

After seventeen years, the CTF is very much alive, albeit with a new name, the Ecumenical Task Force for Justice in the Americas. Deirdre Kelly writes: "Always we are short of money, sometimes to the point of collapse. Yet the love for justice, for human rights, for peace, has outweighed the stress of managing to stay afloat" (*Network News,* Kelly). Over the years it has moved from a support model to a model of mutual solidarity and accompaniment. It continues its traditional work, while opening itself to new avenues of involvement. Chapter 8 describes the remarkable and extensive forms of solidarity it has developed.

7   Breaking the Silence in the Maritimes

> If you have come here to help me, you are wasting your time. But if you have come because your liberation is bound up with mine, then we can work together.

THE MARITIMES-GUATEMALA Breaking the Silence Network (BTS) mission statement begins with this quote, attributed to an Australian aboriginal woman. Like the Christian Task Force, it has come to see its purpose as seeking liberation in the North and the South, based on relationships of mutuality. The path has sometimes been rocky; we have sometimes been lost or confused along the way; our progress has been slow and sporadic. Yet much has been achieved.

BTS emerged a decade after solidarity work began in BC. It has developed an approach appropriate to the region, membership, and partner groups. Unlike the CTF, it is secular, rather than faith-based. However, many members are Christians and Tatamagouche Centre, a United Church of Canada adult education centre, offers active support. Our long-term partner, the Kaqchikel Presbytery, is also a United Church of Canada partner. BTS has relied more heavily than the CTF on volunteers, with staff support from organizations like Project Accompaniment, Oxfam-Canada, and Tatamagouche Centre.

Phase 1 : Network-Building 1988–1996

Founded in 1991, BTS now has four member groups (PEI, Fredericton, Antigonish, and South Shore/Halifax), as well as individuals from northern New Brunswick to Cape Breton. It grew out of Oxfam's efforts to develop support in the region for Central American struggles, in cooperation with groups like Development and Peace, and Ten Days for Global Justice. Oxfam had been a key organizer of a Maritimes tour by Kin Lalat in early 1988. Solidarity groups were active throughout the region, although El Salvador and Nicaragua were given greater priority. When government grants for development education were severely cut, Oxfam was forced to cut staff and therefore support to BTS.

A turning point for Guatemalan solidarity came in 1988 when Tatamagouche Centre decided to give a higher priority to social justice programming. I joined the staff, bringing solidarity experience with me, including a connection with the Kaqchikel Presbytery of the Presbyterian Church of Guatemala in the Chimaltenango region.

In the Protestant Reformed tradition, Presbyteries are regional decision-making bodies comprising lay and clergy representatives of local congregations. They are often staid and bureaucratic. This has been far from true for the Kaqchikel Presbytery. The Chimaltenango region was among those hardest hit by the violence of the 1980s. Pastor Vitalino Similox and his spouse, Margarita Valiente, ministered courageously to their Kaqchikel brothers and sisters. Working along with them were Pascual Serech, Manuel Saquic, and Lucio Martínez—all church leaders who would later die for their human rights work. They did not construct buildings or establish traditional worship services. Instead they created informal worshipping communities and community-based self-help groups, most often made up of women. They made no distinctions on the basis of religious affiliation. Those who had suffered from the violence, Protestant or Catholic, and were willing to work with their neighbours for survival and reconstruction, were welcome.

Encouraged by the United Church's Division of World Outreach, Tatamagouche Centre contacted the Kaqchikel Presbytery. I spent Easter 1989 in Guatemala, exploring the possibility of developing an ongoing relationship between the Kaqchikel Presbytery and the Centre. I was warmly received and returned home laden with colourful woven crafts, purchased from their women's groups, to be sold in the Maritimes. The Centre decided to develop an exchange program and established its goals:

- To develop a relationship between Tatamagouche Centre and the Kaqchikel Presbytery, as well as other groups such as CIEDEG (the Guatemalan Protestant Conference of Churches for Development), and groups, both religious and secular, working for human rights;
- To enable Maritimers to deepen their own faith and understanding of the meaning of social justice; and
- To have Tatamagouche Centre become a centre of solidarity and support for the Guatemalan people in their struggle for social justice.

We assumed Tatamagouche Centre would take the initiative by sending a delegation to Guatemala. The Kaqchikel Presbytery thought other-

First Breaking the Silence delegation with Canadian Ambassador Dickson. From the left: Lynn Caldwell, Cathie Crooks, Danielle Chiasson, Kathryn Anderson, Marian White, Susan Sellers, Ambassador Brian Dickson, Campbell Webster, Valerie Mansour, Hedy Koleszar, Lennie Gallant, Ernest Mutch. Photographer unknown.

wise. In early 1990 a letter arrived announcing that it was sending two skilled artisans to the Maritimes for a month. Although we felt quite unprepared for their arrival, we took up the challenge. A few weeks later, Josefina Inay and another Kaqchikel woman, both of whom had been displaced and had lost family members, stepped off the plane.

They had never travelled outside Guatemala nor had they spoken publicly about the Guatemalan conflict. Little did we know that Josefina, a Presbytery women's group organizer, would become our friend and companion, whom we have come to count on for practical advice and spiritual wisdom. Nor could we have foreseen the tragedy that would befall Josefina, her family, and her colleagues. Nor could we have imagined that in November 2001 we would be present for the ordination of Josefina Inay and Margarita, the first women ordained in the Presbyterian Church in Guatemala.

Both visitors were amazingly flexible and open to doing whatever we suggested, from public speaking, to demonstrating their extraordinary embroidery and weaving skills, to participating in a feast of lobster and wine. They shared personal stories of suffering, struggle, and courage with enormous dignity. This is how Josefina described it: "I talked with them about the strength of individuals, churches, and NGOs who were struggling in order that these *humiliations* (her emphasis) would no longer be permitted" (Inay, 2001). Their visit touched many individuals throughout the Maritimes. Guatemala began to become a reality for many people.

In 1991 Tatamagouche Centre, with financial support from the United Church, Oxfam, and CUSO, sent its first delegation to Guatemala. Its goal was to establish a base for the development of a network of Maritimers active in church and community groups, and committed to solidarity work. We spent several days with the Kaqchikel Presbytery, guided by Margarita and Josefina, staying for a night with displaced families in Chimaltenango.

Delegates were anguished as they slept on the floor in the same rooms with malnourished and ill children whose parents had no money for food and medicine. We saw the Presbytery sharing awareness, organization, education, health, and human rights with their people. Encouraged by Margarita and Josefina, along with Josefina's husband, Lucio, they had supported women in rural communities to form groups and undertake projects from literacy to crafts to agricultural ventures. We accompanied Josefina to a few groups, where she connected biblical reflection with awareness of their human rights as Mayas and as women. We also met with several human rights and community development groups, from a group of widows of the disappeared (CONAVIGUA) to groups working with street children in Guatemala City and Quetzaltenango.

We learned much from our first effort. Participants needed better preparation for the emotional and physical rigours of the trip. The encounter with people whose poverty and loss was so enormous left some in the group overwhelmed. We did not know the Kaqchikel Presbytery, our host group, very well, nor did they know us. Misunderstandings arose. They saw us as a typical North American church group and did not understand that we were a human rights delegation. They felt they should show us the more "churchy" aspects of their work and were reticent about explaining their work in communities and the depth of their commitment to the struggle for justice. Time to talk things through was a luxury during that period of great danger and suffering. We muddled through and recognized that, despite difficulties, errors, and question marks, we had been privileged to meet courageous, committed church and community leaders.

That first delegation sowed seeds that bore much fruit. Delegates wrote newspaper articles and spoke to countless churches, classes, and community groups, an activity that has continued with every Maritimes delegate and accompanier. The Maritimes-Guatemala Breaking the Silence Net-

Breaking the Silence in the Maritimes 135

Susan Sellers talks with shoeshine boy who studies while working. Photo by Ernest Mutch.

work was formed. Within months the Network had established the Atlantic Urgent Action Network, described in chapter 8. BTS helped prepare a delegation of Maritimes First Nations people to the Five Hundred Years of Indigenous, Black, and Popular Resistance Continental Conference held in Guatemala in October 1991. There indigenous and African-American peoples prepared their resistance to the celebration of Columbus's arrival in the Americas.

Campbell Webster convinced the Webster Family Foundation to support the work of Casa Alianza (Covenant House) with street children, Project Accompaniment, and a women's project in a returned community. Susan Sellers, who taught in River John, NS, initiated an educational project that lasted five years. Singer Lennie Gallant, moved by stories he heard of violence and yet of hope and resistance, wrote two powerful songs and has generously performed in solidarity fundraisers across the Maritimes.

Lennie became a good friend of delegation member Ernest Mutch, a retired Industrial Arts teacher. Ernest returned to PEI committed to supporting CEIPA, an NGO educating children forced to work as shoeshine boys or market workers. He wanted to establish a future for these youngsters. After digging up sufficient donations, Ernest and Campbell Webster drove a truckload of welding equipment from PEI to Quetzaltenango. Ernest stayed on for a few months to get the workshop up and running. The training has provided employment for many teens.

When then CBC radio host Vicki Gabereau was in PEI, Lennie introduced her to Ernest. In 1996, Ernest recruited volunteers to accompany him on another trip south to deliver a used school bus to CEIPA. Gerritt Loo, a retired school bus driver and father of BTS members Judy and Margie Loo, shared the driving. Gabereau travelled with the group through Mexico into Guatemala, later broadcasting a series of moving programs on her experience.

In 1992 new momentum arose when a second BTS delegation journeyed to Guatemala. Powerful meetings with the Archdiocese of Guatemala Human Rights Office (ODHAG) and representatives of the popular resistance communities (CPRs) brought home the ongoing struggle. A visit to Kaqchikel Presbytery women's groups in the villages of Bola de Oro and Cerro Alto made painfully clear the depth of poverty and all-pervasive fear. Delegates played with children with potbellies and dark hair tinged red, sure signs of parasites and malnutrition. Army trucks full of soldiers passed by as an elderly white-haired woman stood in her yard pointing to the spot where she had witnessed the murder of her husband and son in 1982. She told the group the army had woken them from their sleep, first shooting her husband who died immediately. Her son was bludgeoned to death and died slowly. When they were killed, she went to Chimaltenango and met Margarita Valiente who said, "Let's go back to Bola de Oro and start something together." Soon after the women's group in Bola de Oro started up. A pig-rearing project was their first effort. The women's determination to work together to survive, their love for their children, and their refusal to give in to fear challenged the delegation to reflect on the nature of hope, and the resiliency of the human spirit.

That same summer Project A was formally established. Unlike most regions where Project A groups developed apart from existing solidarity committees, refugee accompaniment became a BTS priority. The integration of Project A into the Maritimes network enabled accompaniers and local support committees to become active in ongoing solidarity work. This work grew more quickly during the years Beth Abbott was Atlantic region Project A coordinator. She helped local committees organize and recruit accompaniers, disseminate information on Guatemala to universities, churches, labour groups, and the media, and organize tours of the Maritimes by refugee leaders, as well as a delegation to Mexico and Guatemala.

Enthusiasm and support for the refugee Return mounted in 1993. Journalist Valerie Mansour received an International Centre for Human Rights

Breaking the Silence in the Maritimes

and Democratic Development award to cover the first refugee Return to Guatemala and the struggle of the resistance communities. Margarita Valiente and a Guatemalan refugee representative both toured the Maritimes that spring. Margarita's account of her visit to resistance communities and Yolanda's story of her community's flight across the border and determination to return touched many. In Antigonish, population five thousand, their presentations led to the formation of a Project A committee. With only about ten active members, the group has sponsored four accompaniers, recruited eight people for BTS delegations, spoken in public meetings, schools, and church gatherings on human rights and economic justice, written newspaper articles and letters to the editor, fundraised, supported sales of fairly traded coffee, and involved elementary, high school, and university students, as well as church members, in writing Urgent Actions.

When then President Serrano attempted a coup in May 1993, BTS was immediately mobilized to send faxes to the Canadian and Guatemalan governments. The Nova Scotia section of CUPE (the Canadian Union of Public Employees) and the Annual Meeting of the Maritime Conference of the United Church passed resolutions condemning Serrano's action and made the Canadian and Guatemalan governments aware of these resolutions. CUPE contributed a thousand dollars towards the costs of Terry O'Toole's accompaniment of refugees during this crisis. Terry was a nurse and union activist from Antigonish.

CIEDEG, of which the Kaqchikel Presbytery is an active member, was in danger because it had supported Nobel Peace Prize winner Rigoberta Menchú in her public resistance to Serrano's action. It requested United Church of Canada accompaniment. I responded, spending most of June in CIEDEG's offices, confident that, if anything should occur, BTS members would immediately exert pressure on the Canadian and Guatemalan governments.

An Atlantic delegation of church and community representatives spent two memorable weeks in southern Mexico and Guatemala in November 1993. They trekked into refugee camps in the Chiapas mountains to meet communities preparing their return to Guatemala. On a day still etched in their memories, they set out along a footpath for a camp high in the mountains, only to encounter entire families carrying their worldly possessions, from roofing to chickens, on their backs down the mountainside. The weary Maritimers continued trudging up the mountain. When they arrived, the remaining refugees explained that the families had set out for the Ixcán, fully aware that the army was adamantly refusing to vacate the returnees' cooperative lands that they had taken a decade earlier. Delegates could not have had a more graphic demonstration of the refugees' unequivocal determination to return to their homeland. They came home determined to increase support for the refugee Return process.

A four-member BTS delegation arrived in Guatemala City in late 1994 at a volatile moment. Bombs were exploding throughout the city. Refugees were still struggling to return to their communities. Delegates spoke with pastor and human rights worker Manuel Saquic in a town square. His life was under threat because of his very public efforts to bring to justice an army collaborator responsible for Presbytery leader Pascual Serech's murder a few months earlier. The encounter in the park sent a visible message to the ever-observant army that he had international support, although ultimately this finally did not deter them from murdering him.

In June 1995 BTS welcomed Antonio Otzoy, then Secretary of the Hermandad de Presbiterios Mayas (Fellowship of Maya Presbyteries), to the Maritimes. He travelled in the Maritimes for three weeks, inspiring many with his theological depth, Maya spirituality, and commitment to indigenous rights. He was accompanied by Mary Corbett, a Congregation of Notre Dame sister, who had returned to Canada in 1992, after living for twelve years in Guatemala. Her excellent translation skills and her grace and strength were instrumental in helping to build the bridges between Antonio and the communities he visited. In an evaluation at the end of his stay, Antonio reported that his objectives were more than met, as he was able to learn much about church and society in the Maritimes. The evaluation concluded:

> Until now, his experience had been a one-way street, with delegations such as ours from Canada, the US and Europe visiting Guatemala. The visit gave him an opportunity to come to know who we were and something of our reality, which then makes our visits to Guatemala a more mutual experience.... In a sense we are no longer strangers. It was very important for him to know us as individuals, but also to know our church and society, with all our strengths and weaknesses, problems and challenges. Antonio's visit deeply reinforced his understanding of the partnership between the Guatemalan church and the United Church as one of equals, where we have much to learn. (Anderson, 1995)

Antonio returned to Guatemala to find Presbytery and family members combing garbage dumps and ravines for fellow pastor Manuel Saquic, who had not returned home from his human rights work with the Presbytery. Having received many death threats over the past year, they suspected the worst. After days of desperate searching, his body turned up half-buried in a field of corn stalks, with thirty-three stab wounds. He had been kidnapped, tortured, and murdered. Lucio Martínez began to receive death threats immediately, and the United Church was asked to provide accompaniers. First Susan Skaret and Louise Sevigny responded, followed by Eva and Jim Manly. The power of this experience inspired Jim's book, *The Wounds of Manuel Saquic*.

His death forcibly reminded BTS that our solidarity is with those who risk their lives because of their commitment to their sisters and brothers and their determination to combat impunity. The army collaborator accused of the crime is still free, having received army sanctuary and protection since the day of the murder.

One rainy night that fall a BTS delegation trudged along a muddy jungle path to meet with residents of the returned community of Xamán, where witnesses told the story of the army's massacre just a few weeks earlier. A few days later we met with Margarita, Josefina, and Lucio, who shared their grief, horror, and anger at the loss of Manuel. With an American accompanier at his side, Lucio spoke of the continual death threats he and his family had received since Manuel's murder. Silence was our response, as all other responses seemed inadequate. Finally we gathered in a circle, said the Lord's Prayer together in Spanish and in English and returned silently to our hotel to ponder what he had said. The stress of death threats would take their toll within a year when Lucio died of a stroke. Many, including his family, say that he died of persecution.

The next day Lucio took us to meet the women's groups in Bola de Oro and Cerro Alto, a joyful contrast with the previous day's encounter. We witnessed Lucio's love for the land and his commitment to the welfare of the women and children of those villages. We shared in the women's joy and pride, as we ate together the chicken soup they had prepared, admired and purchased their weavings, and saw the recently born piglets they would later sell, a sign of the success of the pigs project the Presbytery had funded with United Church support. It was a graphic expression of the women's determined efforts to survive and ensure a future for their children. It reminded us how life-giving support from the United Church Mission and Service Fund and other churches and agencies can be.

Lucio, Josefina, and their daughters were not alone in receiving death threats. Manuel's widow, María, was also receiving threats, because she persisted in pressing charges against the man accused of his murder. Like countless others before them, the family had been forced to move from a village where they had deep roots to a poor, crowded, and violent section of Guatemala City. The five children were not allowed to play outside for fear of abduction. When the military started to harass María in the markets where she sold yard goods each day, accompaniment once again became an essential element of solidarity.

Mary Corbett accompanied the family for a few weeks, staying with them night and day. She accompanied María everywhere—at home, on the buses, in the markets, to Manuel's gravesite, to government offices where she told her story. My partner, Wilf Bean, and I lived in Guatemala that year and accompanied María and her family on several occasions, constantly astonished by their humour, their closeness and love for one another, their determination to pursue the case at whatever cost.

An evaluation at the end of 1995 stated:

> We are learning that solidarity means learning as we go. We are learning that there are tensions, weaknesses and contradictions in the Guatemalan church, just as there are here. We are learning that our solidarity goes beyond those contradictions, that it is not our place to judge or to intervene, and that God's Spirit continues to work, despite human weaknesses and mistakes. We are learning that trust and relationships are built slowly. Nevertheless we are developing a long-term relationship of trust, as we maintain our delegations to Guatemala and receive our partners here. Antonio Otzoy said in November 1995 to our delegation, "Your context and ours are very different, yet we can be bridge-builders. We need to continue learning how to build bridges with strong foundations." (Anderson, 1995)

In 1995 Breaking the Silence delegates visited a popular resistance community (CPR), the returned refugee community of Xamán a few weeks after an army massacre, and the Kaqchikel Presbytery a few months after Manuel Saquic's assassination, as well as the Myrna Mack Foundation, named after the assassinated Guatemalan anthropologist. Diane Walsh composed a song entitled REMHI, referring to the Archdiocese of Guatemala Human Rights Office process of truth-telling, known as the Recovery of Historical Memory.

Remhi

They came for a party, so they said
We'll help you to celebrate by shooting eleven dead
Eight-year-old boy out fishing, shot five times,
Soldiers try to blame their victims for this crime.

> *bring us your memories, bring us your pain*
> *expose their lies so you might live again*

Manuel was a pastor loved by his church
He told them to stand up against abuse
But mentioning Human Rights got him an unmarked grave
Tortured and battered he was found one day. (*Chorus*)

Myrna Mack came to study a people's way
Got too close to the facts so she had to pay
Twenty-five stab wounds screamed a message to all
"Don't talk to anyone, don't get involved..."

> *so many memories, stories of pain*
> *go tell the world so we might live again.*

Families in hiding fifteen years
Dodging bombs and fires...said "Enough of this fear."
Now they're living in the light of day and daring to hope
Guatemala will some day be a safe home.

> *bring us your memories, bring us your pain*
> *expose their lies so you might live again*
> *bring us your memories, bring us your pain*
> *we'll tell the world so you might live....*

Phase 2 : Strengthening Relationships 1997-1999

BTS met early in 1997 to assess the implications of the recently signed Peace Accords. It was tempting to walk away from the hard work of solidarity, knowing we had served a vital purpose. Many solidarity groups and individuals had departed after the Sandinista defeat in Nicaragua and the end of the war in El Salvador. However, those of us who had returned from extended stays in Guatemala paraphrased the message we received:

> Do not abandon us. The very structural problems that led to the war continue unresolved. Social and economic injustice remains. The unequal distribution of land and wealth has actually grown worse in recent years. The army remains powerful and is resistant to change. We are struggling to heal the wounds left from massacres, displacement, and fear. We are convinced the support and pressure of Canadian solidarity groups, together with counterparts in other areas of the world, could have a significant impact on the Guatemalan government.

BTS decided to continue its human rights work and strengthen its relationship with the Kaqchikel Presbytery. In a letter, followed up by a discussion with Margarita and Josefina, we stressed our desire to base the relationship on mutuality and friendship, although we would not exclude financial support, given the urgent need to reconstruct lives and communities.

In the meantime, BTS groups were involved in lengthy discussions around whether Project A should end. Maritimes representatives participated in 1997 and 1998 research teams. An attempt to organize a 1998 BTS delegation to Guatemala did not materialize. There seemed to be insufficient interest that in retrospect may simply have been a result of inadequate publicity. For a short time it seemed the solidarity movement in the Maritimes might be dying a slow death.

Those thoughts were erased by the news that Bishop Juan José Gerardi, founder of the Archdiocese of Guatemala Human Rights Office (ODHAG), had been bludgeoned to death April 26, 1998. Two days earlier, in the Guatemala City cathedral, he had presided over the presentation of *Guatemala: Never Again,* the landmark report of the Recovery of Historical Memory Project (REMHI) of the Human Rights Office of ODHAG. It held the army, civil defence patrols, military commissioners, and paramilitary groups responsible for most human rights violations during the thirty-four-year war. BTS delegations had visited ODHAG and understood the report's historical significance. We realized immediately that truth-telling was still an immense risk. If a highly respected Bishop could be murdered, what chance did campesinos have?

When a 1999 delegation was announced, the response was unexpectedly high. We formed two thirteen-person groups, one in March and one in November. The women's groups in Bola de Oro and Cerro Alto, as well as a group in nearby Labor de Falla, invited both delegations to stay in their homes overnight. In earlier years we were anxious that our presence in villages for longer than a few hours might bring unwanted attention to women and their families. We were aware of army *orejas* (spies, literally "ears") in every community and did not wish to put anyone at risk. The stay turned out to be a highlight of our journey, as the women and their families were able to share a little more of themselves with us and we with them.

We arrived at a home in Bola de Oro where two Maya women from a Guatemalan NGO were showing the women's groups how to make their own cough remedy, so that they would not have to spend scarce money on costly pharmaceuticals. They were also helping them grow vegetables hydroponically, that is, using water, because land is so scarce. The women used styrofoam, old rice bags, or old tires hung from the ceiling. Delegates were delighted to participate in the hands-on learning, to play games or sing and dance with the children, to share a meal of tortillas and corn soup. After lunch Miriam, a vibrant twenty-six-year-old mother of seven, explained that she had joined the women's group at age nine: "By then my father was already dead and I had to start to work….Now we are looking at small projects that will help our economic situation….We also receive training from the Presbytery about the value of women. We take part in a lot of marches for human rights and indigenous rights."

She described their battle against poverty as a struggle for water, land, health, and education, rather than a desire to obtain money or material goods. At the same time she expressed their gratitude for life. "We have great poverty here and many of us have dirt floors but what we have is the taste of life, great joy. In the morning the sun is there for us and the breeze in the day. We may have little in clothing or food but we have joy, and can't imagine what greater gift of God we could have." We responded by telling them that 20 percent of Canadian children live in poverty, homeless people die on the streets in winter, many First Nations communities are impoverished. The news seemed to perturb the women. "We need to know this," Miriam replied (MacDonald, March 24, 1999).

Later that afternoon part of the group set off for Miriam's home, while the rest of us stayed with Doña Francisca. After a supper of tortillas, eggs, and beans, we chatted with Josefina and Doña Francisca in the evening warmth, the full moon setting off the dark curves of the mountains surrounding us. Like most villagers, we were in bed by 8:30 p.m. We fell asleep to the snorts of pigs and shouts of a nearby evangelical pastor with a powerful sound system.

Earlier that day Miriam had spontaneously invited five group members to stay with her family:

> We pass several people, men, women, and children, with stacks of wood on their backs—part of the daily scavenging necessary to keep the fires burning in the kitchens of the villages. To our right, a barbed wire fence runs alongside the road and beyond it a wooded mountain. Miriam's hand sweeps the side of the mountain as she explains that it is privately owned. "We are not allowed to go in there." We are reminded of the sad fact that in Guatemala two percent of the population owns 90 percent of the land, and ten million other people, mostly Mayans, have to scrape a living from what's left to them. When we look across the range of mountains surrounding us, many of them wear the white scars of erosion and landslides. In their efforts to survive, to grow food, the indigenous people climb higher and higher up the sides of the mountains, deforesting it, creating patches of garden

until the erosion wrecks it all. It appears as if the mountains of Guatemala themselves are being brought crumbling to their knees under the weight of the demands being placed upon them.

We all found Miriam a remarkable person when she spoke to us of the troubles, hopes, and dreams that the women of the three villages nurse for their children and themselves. That evening, we discovered that Miriam shares her life with someone as impressive as herself. Her husband, Julio, is the mayor of Cerro Alto. It is a position of leadership without the political perks we normally associate with the role. He rises at 3 a.m., by 4 a.m. he is away to work in a steel fabrication plant in nearby Chimaltenango. He arrived home from work at seven in the evening. A man from the village comes to see him and Julio and they sit quietly talking about a village issue. At eight o'clock, Julio and Miriam, along with with six children, come into the bedroom to sit with us. It is obvious that it is Miriam and Julio's bedroom, surrendered in hospitality this night to the five guests who will share it and the floor. We visit, share pictures of families, landscapes, and the Inverness ice storm while the children curl around the visitors with a comfortable intimacy, and then Julio tells us that he has to go to bed, asking if it will be alright to pray with us first. Our host then leads us through prayers that include us, and we are struck again, as we have been before, by the faith woven into the lives of the people we meet. It is not a faith set aside for emergency miracles when required, or a faith that blames God for the poverty of their lives, but a faith that infuses their lives with an almost tangible joy. (MacDonald, March 24, 1999)

The sounds of roosters crowing and the scent of smoke from the open fire in the kitchen set apart from the house wakened us early. We heard the gentle, rhythmic "pit pat" of the women making tortillas—taking the corn dough in their hands and shaping it into perfectly round circles.

Three of the children, Axel, ten, Marino, eight, and Viki, six, disappeared for a while, and when they returned each was carrying on his or her head a large jar of water. Today, we follow our two guides along the dusty road to a mountain path where eventually we come to a water spout and concrete container. This, they tell us, is where the village gets its water. Only then, looking back up the side of the mountain, recalling the unmeasured but impressive distance we are from Miriam's house, do we come to appreciate the labour of the three children who had arrived laughing in their own yard the evening before carrying several gallons of water.... Our trek down the side of the mountain continues until we come to a laundry site, a place where the women wash their clothes. This is the dry season, but so far, they only have to go half way down the mountain. If it gets any drier, they will have to move their washing site down to the river at the foot of the mountain, another hour's walk. When we have huffed and puffed our way back up to the village, Margarita takes us to a well site. The village has been trying to bring water to itself for a long time. Finally, they were able to find the drilling apparatus and piping they needed, and the money to finance it. (MacDonald, March 24, 1999)

Josefina made a request: "When you get back to your communities, your churches, tell them what we have been able to accomplish here." Frank MacDonald remarked, "She is not a woman who looks at the distance that remains on this journey of the Mayan people of Bola de Oro, Cerro Alto, and Labor de Falla, but at the distance they have come."

The November delegation was present when right-wing Guatemalan Republican Front (FRG) presidential candidate Alfonso Portillo was elected. Rios Montt, was named president of Congress. Some voters in rural areas were frightened to vote against the FRG. Others, disillusioned by the previous government's failure to address the worsening situation of economic and personal security, were persuaded by FRG populist promises. The Left was divided and still rebuilding after the war.

Delegates served as official International Election Observers in Chimaltenango, as requested by the Kaqchikel Presbytery. The Observer Program was planned in collaboration with a Guatemalan coalition that carried out voter education and registration. We sent our observations to a team in the Capital, covering such topics as the presence of scrutineers from each party, irregularities in the voting process, attempts to influence voters, and the attitudes of voters, scrutineers, and authorities of the National Electoral Tribunal. The International Observers' report concluded that, although the election process was honest, structural flaws remained.

We came away feeling we had supported, in a small way, Guatemalans working hard to ensure fairer, more honest elections. We then travelled to the villages, where we were soon listening in on election conversations:

> After supper Doña Francisca's grandson [son of Felipe who the army had assassinated] and his wife and their two kids came over. Also one of the neighbour women came over with her two kids. The young couple supported the FRG, and the neighbour woman lit into them about how Portillo is a crook and a murderer. Mary [Corbett] says that it is the woman who has the more sophisticated analysis, probably thanks in part to education by the Presbytery. The young couple seems to be listening to her by the end of the discussion. She has told them stuff they hadn't heard before, but it's too late now—they have already cast their

votes. This to me is evidence of how powerful the FRG is—if they can convince the family of a murdered man to vote for the people who murdered him—YIKES! It also says that the election has not been discussed too openly here in the village—this discussion should have taken place before. (Brazier diary, 1999)

Marta

I watch her as she retrieves
one by one
each little grain
that slips out of her basket
into the dust
between her small bare feet:
not one is left behind.

I watch her as she gathers
scraps of wood,
quickly, efficiently,
—just enough
to make this morning's tortillas—
then hurries her bundle across
hard-packed earth
to the kitchen house.

Suddenly, she turns
to flash me
a glorious smile.
How different, her life,
from that of the carefree
pampered children
where I live,
who will never understand
the way she does
that every
morsel
of life
is a precious
gift.

—*Pat Loucks, November 1999*

Phase 3 : Forming a Covenant Relationship 1999–

Breaking the Silence, at its 1999 gathering at Tatamagouche Centre, decided to send a Special Commission to Guatemala to explore how to strengthen its relationship with the Kaqchikel Presbytery and the women's groups in Bola de Oro, Cerro Alto, and Labor de Falla. Ideas included twinning of schools, support for small community projects, and learning skills, such as weaving and herbal medicine, from the women. On New Year's Day 2000 a few of us met to plan the trip. We could not help but feel this was an auspicious way to begin a new century!

Five of us arrived in Chimaltenango in April. We spent our first few days informally visiting the villages, as well as meeting with Josefina and Margarita and the elected leaders of the women's groups. The women met in small groups to discuss our proposal to deepen and formalize our relationship with them. When we asked them to name what they could offer us, they struggled with their responses. They had never consciously considered the possibility that they had gifts to share. However, ideas soon emerged, as they recognized the wealth of knowledge they had about natural medicine, agriculture, cultural traditions, weaving, and embroidery.

We spent our last morning with teachers and students in the two-room Labor de Falla school. Late that afternoon we strolled back to Bola de Oro to a celebration culminating ten years of a growing friendship with the Kaqchikel Presbytery. We had understood the women were going to invite their spouses and children to a short covenant-signing ceremony, followed by a meal of tamales.

To our surprise, as we walked toward Doña Francisca's home, we saw men, women, teens, and children streaming in through the gate. It was chaotic and noisy as the crowd gathered. Quiet descended when representatives of Breaking the Silence, the Presbytery, and the women's groups signed a covenant. We promised to continue building relationships of friendship and mutuality for the benefit of both groups, which would include exchanges between the groups and support by BTS for small projects developed and implemented by the women's groups.

Celebrating began in earnest. In just two days, the women had pulled together a cultural event with music, dances, and hilarious skits, organized by one of the teachers we had met earlier. We were asked on the spot to contribute a Canadian cultural dance. Somehow we pulled off a circle dance in which Creighton Brown, the only male in our group, danced with each of us in turn. Josefina joined in. The crowd went wild with applause and laughter at our crazy, impromptu dance. Needless to say, we left Bola de Oro the next morning rejoicing at a celebration far surpassing our hopes and expectations! Susan Sellers commented: "All of us renewed our own personal connections and commitments to this ravaged country; these dignified, hopeful people" (Sellers, 2000).

A month later Vilma, a twenty-year-old woman from Labor de Falla, and Josefina, who had visited us a decade earlier, flew into Halifax. After an orientation at Tatamagouche Centre, they toured the Maritimes, accompanied by their translator and guide, Mary Corbett. Josefina shared the history, vision, and programs of the Presbytery while Vilma spoke about her work experience in a *maquila* (sweatshop), a food-processing plant where vegetables are prepared for export. She described the abusive working conditions and low pay. As happens repeatedly once young workers start to stand up for their rights, she was illegally fired.

They attended the Maritime Conference of the United Church. Vilma participated in a three-day Youth Forum with 120 teens. You could have heard a pin drop as she told them of the war's impact on her family and her struggle to get grade six schooling. She told them about picking coffee at age nine to make enough money to buy exercise books, earning two dollars for a hundred pounds of beans. The teens made connections with their lives as coffee drinkers and as consumers of brand-name clothing assembled in *maquilas*.

Vilma and Josefina were honoured to participate in a Mi'kmaq spiritual ceremony at Esgenoopetitj (Burnt Church), a First Nations community struggling mightily to claim its right to manage its natural resources. They visited a transition house, a food bank, and an inner-city ministry. They walked on beaches and shared their stories at a community crafts fair. They were resource persons for the BTS Young Adult delegation orientation. At Tatamagouche Centre's Annual Meeting, we again celebrated our relationship through a second signing of the covenant between the Kaqchikel Presbytery and Breaking the Silence. Vilma and Josefina expressed how empowering it had been to share their personal stories, as well as the vision, hopes, and struggles of the Presbytery and the women's groups, with their Maritimes *compañeros* (companions).

Since signing the covenant, Breaking the Silence has funded pigs projects in all three communities and has sent two delegations. The itinerary for the BTS young adult delegation in August 2001 included a day-long exchange with a Kaqchikel Presbytery youth group and visits to the Labor de Falla and Cerro Alto schools. The Labor de Falla students prepared a cultural event in which they sang, danced, and acted out a traditional wedding ceremony. The event was videotaped for the River John school, who in turn sent a videotape back to Labor de Falla. The November 2001 delegation spent two full days in Bola de Oro, Cerro Alto, and Labor de Falla, making jam with the Bola de Oro women's group (a fund-raising project for the women's group), visiting the pig projects, and spending time with the families of the women's group members.

Tatamagouche Centre has sent twenty-one CIDA-funded youth interns to Guatemala. They have worked with BTS partner groups on human rights, forest conservation, community development, fair trade coffee, gender, organic agriculture, and a water project. Their in-depth preparation and on-the-ground experience is offering new life to Breaking the Silence.

Renewing the covenant, February 2003. Mary Corbett, Josefina Inay, Kathryn Anderson, Carole Woodhall, and a young friend. Photo by Chap Haynes.

Solidarity work is ongoing. Members send Urgent Actions, support fair trade coffee initiatives, protest the Free Trade Area of the Americas agreement, and educate the public in churches, union meetings, schools, and universities. The work is challenging, at times disheartening, yet the courage, strength, and determination of the Guatemalan people inspire us to continue.

III
A Tapestry with Many Forms

8   New Forms of Solidarity

THIS CHAPTER DESCRIBES the many forms of solidarity that have emerged from the Christian Task Force on Central America (CTF) in British Columbia and Breaking the Silence (BTS) in the Maritimes. Based on "building bridges, connections, experience, and education," they have been creative, flexible responses to unprecedented repression in Guatemala.

※ Guiding Principles

Two principles are woven into the fabric of the work of the Christian Task Force and Breaking the Silence, whatever the forms solidarity may take.

- Inspiration and leadership for solidarity comes from Guatemalan partners. They offer the vision and example as they struggle with hope against insurmountable odds, risking their lives for even the simplest of activities that promote the dignity and interests of the poor. They are a key source of knowledge, enabling Canadians to understand their daily reality of injustice and its root causes. They give direction to the work—they make the requests and define the kind of support needed.
- Learning and action are intimately related. Adult learning is understood as a process of reflection leading to commitment and action. It is neither passive nor separate from political action. It happens through a circular process of taking action on repression and the systematic violation of human rights, reflecting critically on the action, and then acting again with a deeper understanding and commitment (Dykstra, p. 58).

A : Building Public Awareness

Without constant efforts to move beyond preaching to the converted, the solidarity movement would not exist. Reaching out to new people is a task that must be done over and over again in order to strengthen solidarity's support base. Breaking the Silence and the Christian Task Force believe the greatest possibility for change lies in building the solidarity movement in local communities. Most solidarity workers first ventured out to a meeting in a church basement, university auditorium, or union hall. Drawn by a poster, newspaper article, or personal invitation, a public event became the first step in an involvement that deepened into a relationship and commitment. (As I explain in the preface, that is what happened to me.)

Gaining an audience for solidarity events is not easy. How do you persuade Canadians to become interested in the reality of people in a distant country with a different culture? How do you persuade them to attend an event on genocide, torture, or human rights abuse, when they would prefer not to hear, especially if they have a sneaking suspicion that it might have something to do with their own lives?

By far the most effective means of involving new people is "personal testimony," through which family, friends, colleagues, community, and church groups are touched and challenged to new understandings and to action. Few are drawn into solidarity work through political analysis alone, no matter how relevant and articulate it may be. Analysis is utterly essential to effective solidarity work, but is rarely the best way to get new people involved.

Slide shows and presentations by a visiting Guatemalan or a recently returned Canadian in the local church, community hall, or university campus have had a remarkable impact. A dozen people gathered around a kitchen table with cups of coffee (fairly traded!) has often had more influence and potential for long-term involvement than a large meeting where individuals make no personal contact with the speaker or sponsoring group.

Guatemalans who have journeyed to Canada to share stories of their struggle have deeply moved Canadians. These visits, however, are few and far between. Often the testimony of a recently returned Canadian allows the listener to identify with the speaker. A degree of credibility exists that may not be there when the "expert" or outsider comes to speak. "It is not some leftist telling them what reality is but their daughter or a member of their church who they have seen grow up," said a CTF member. Trade unionists who have described to fellow workers their encounters with *maquila* (sweatshop) workers, determined to form a union in spite of death threats and firings, have done more to build support for a union's international solidarity fund or human rights work than any number of brochures or leaders' exhortations. Bob Smith, former United Church Moderator and now retired minister, tells of neighbours who had dis-

New Forms of Solidarity

missed stories from Central America as "left-wing propaganda." When he returned from Guatemala after Bishop Gerardi's assassination, they saw him on TV and heard him on the CBC. "They knew me as an ordinary neighbour. They had to take it seriously" (TI).

Popular education tools and methodology have been the basis of public education. Ann Godderis saw the change when the CTF moved from a passive model of education to active participation:

> I can still remember the excitement when some of the concepts started to sink in—the difference in learning when people participate rather than just sit and listen; what happens when one uses drawing, music, role playing, etc. So ever since then, at an absolute minimum, we make sure at any event that people at least introduce themselves and talk about why they've come before we start whatever it is we do. Usually we break into pairs before we have questions, just so people have spoken and in that way have some more involvement in what's happening. We try and sit in as close to a circle as we can. It now seems so wrong when we go to a more traditional format, not much of a chance for any commitment or building a relationship. (TI)

Solidarity groups often carry out their educational efforts with existent groups. Bud Godderis noted: "We did a lot of our work through the churches. In spite of all their failures, they have always had some presence in solidarity work. We were glad to work with anyone who was willing to work with us—churches, trade unions, the NDP. We tried to do education work through the NDP Club. We worked closely with the Carpenters' Union" (TI).

For many years the CTF carried out intensive programming during Central America Week. The US Religious Task Force on Central America originated the idea as a way to commemorate Archbishop Romero's assassination March 24, 1980, through prayer, study, and action. Well-publicized events were held throughout BC, with speakers, audio-visual materials, and print materials. CTF members often spoke during or after church services. It became an integral part of the year's calendar in many churches and communities.

But touching people's hearts is insufficient. Without offering concrete actions, cynicism and hopelessness may be the results. Therefore most presentations include time for questions and comments. Rare is the event where someone does not ask the obvious question, "Why did this happen?" Other questions soon follow: Why didn't the media cover this? Why do we rarely hear about Guatemala? Was the US involved? What is our government's position?

The critical moment comes when someone asks: What can we do? Not to offer a concrete action is to foster despair, social paralysis, and the sense of powerlessness so prevalent in Canadian society. The answer is always: Each of us can do something. Many people's first response is to donate money. While not discouraging donations, audience members are also challenged to respond more personally and critically to issues raised. For example, individuals may be asked to sign a petition that is carefully explained and supplemented with background material to take home. Or they might be asked to send Urgent Actions to the Guatemalan and Canadian governments.

Once people have made a personal connection with an issue they become hungry for information and analysis the mass media do not provide. The CTF has responded to this need through publishing a regular newsletter, *Network News*. BTS circulates news updates, analyses, and Urgent Actions by e-mail to an extensive Maritimes network.

B : Encounters with Guatemalans – Journeys North and South

> The responsibility that comes from that encounter with other human beings who are in such desperate circumstances and who live with graciousness and hope is something that inspires one to deal with the grind of continuing the work over the long term in the Canadian context. We knew right from the beginning of the Task Force that personal experience had to be the foundation for building the core leadership and extending the networks.
>
> —Mike Lewis (TI)

Similar comments were made repeatedly. "If you analyze the people in our region who are the people who do the work, the connecting, the organizing, almost without exception they have had an experience with people somewhere in Central America," noted Ann Godderis (TI).

Canadians have learned how significant it is for Guatemalans to share their stories. Marta Gloria de la Vega described one such experience:

> That evening the volcano was a friend and silent witness, listening with us as we shared the suffering and hope that exist today in Guatemala. A silent witness, comforting us with its presence outside our hotel, while inside the widows and children of the disappeared tearfully spoke to us of their loved ones who had been murdered and disappeared fourteen years before. For the women especially, it was necessary to speak. Some of them had never spoken in front of a group, and after what they had lived through, they were afraid. For fourteen

years they had carried their pain in silence. Those of us attending the Trade Union conference this summer were the first to hear them tell their histories in public. It was important for these women and children to share with others their tears, their struggle for survival, and the love they felt for their disappeared husbands and fathers. For us, it was a privilege to hear their words and hold their grief as they shared such painful memories. Their loved ones are not forgotten. (*Network News*, de la Vega, 1994)

※ Going South

Visits vary, from groups of three or four people to exposure tours with up to twenty participants. Delegations have an amazing impact on groups' capacity to do solidarity work in the Kootenays, says Ann Godderis: "We are constantly making it possible to go South. It moves people to a different level of understanding of what the realities are in the South and what the connections are between the South and here. It breaks them out of the little cocoon they are in here. If they have gone on delegations, they understand too that people in the South are very able to look after themselves if these structures we are a part of would get off their backs. It moves people from an inclination to do charity to an inclination to do justice work" (TI).

- *Introductory Exposure Tours*

The CTF and BTS give high priority to introducing youth and adults to Central America. The BTS offers tours with Tatamagouche Centre leadership. The CTF decided that organizing and leading exposure tours would place an enormous demand on already overtaxed staff and volunteers. They asked GATE, a US-based ecumenical program that offers ten-day exposure tours to those who want "a better understanding of the lives and struggles of people in the two-thirds world," to lead its tours. These tours first took place in Nicaragua or Mexico and more recently in Guatemala. Sandy Robertson recalled her encounter with refugees: "Their stories of repression and torture and of their struggle to survive in a new land moved us deeply. We also were impressed by their vitality and capacity to keep going in such horrendous situations. From a visit to a small, very bare house that temporarily shelters thirty-seven refugees, I carry in my mind the picture of a blackboard on which was written a list of plans for a party. The previous night the refugees had had a party in that barren room. Imagine—a celebration of life in the midst of distress and in the midst of what we might consider to be so meagre!" (*Network News*, Robertson and White).

Orientation is critical to a delegation's success. CTF orientations range from a series of programs offered over several weeks to a weekend session with a previous GATE participant. BTS participants attend a minimum of two overnight gatherings at Tatamagouche Centre. Sessions on history, culture, and the current situation are given, along with attention to security and health concerns, group norms, and finances. Several articles and books are required reading.

A re-entry event is equally important. Each day of a tour is packed full with emotionally, intellectually, and physically demanding experiences. Although the group meets most evenings for reflection, much of the integration of the experience can only occur back home. Without debriefing, there is a risk that much of the tour's value may be lost, as delegates are reimmersed into Canadian life and isolated from others who understand their experience. Participants have the chance to share what they've learned, support each other, evaluate the experience, compile information gathered, and plan future involvement. They discover what the experience has taught them not only about Central America but also about Canadian society. They are encouraged to contact the media, write articles for church and community newspapers, and speak publicly, as well as to join a local solidarity or social justice group.

A tour is a brief experience that, as Mary Corbett points out, "does not necessarily ensure an accurate, never mind complete, understanding of what the reality of a country like Guatemala is. Participants could still tend to come away with a romanticized notion. Like it or not, I think that's an easy possibility on a delegation, especially if they perhaps don't have a lot of background knowledge" (TI). Nonetheless she and others conclude that the value of delegations far outweighs the limitations.

- *Deeper Encounters*

Every year or so, four to six CTF members spent time with partner church and popular organizations in order to strengthen relationships. Staff and active volunteers were chosen, thus building a depth of understanding and analysis among the leadership. Delegates strove for a mutual dialogue with representatives of campesino, church, human rights, and women's groups.

> Several days were spent sharing analysis of both the global and North American economic situation and the Guatemalan reality. In a country where only one percent of women workers belong to unions, and where trade unionists continue to be repressed, threatened, and killed, the work to improve working conditions, including those in the maquiladoras or assembly plants, is monumental. But each night after

a long day of sessions, we would laugh and sing together until the early morning hours. As Canadians we were more often than not spectators, but at the same time incredibly warmed by their spirit, particularly by their laughter in the midst of struggle. (*Network News,* King, 1994)

Delegations have been schools where Guatemalans are the teachers, posing hard questions and sharing their experience and analysis. They challenge delegates to question critically the CTF's work and adapt it to the evolving situation. They call for a response that necessarily requires mutual collaboration in the process of change. Through these delegations, trusting relationships between Canadians and Guatemalans have been established and existing bonds strengthened. Their findings have shaped the CTF program, including its advocacy work with the Canadian government.

Delegates participate in an intensive orientation process in Canada. They read current Guatemalan analyses and Canadian NGO and government policy documents, as well as gaining background knowledge of groups to be visited. After returning, delegates gather to develop a common analysis and recommendations.

- *National and International Delegations*

Through participating in organizations such as the Central America Monitoring Group and the Guatemala-Canada Solidarity Network, the CTF and BTS have supported national and international delegations. In February 1991, Bob Smith flew by helicopter with the Guatemalan deputy ombudsman for human rights and two Guatemalan bishops to two resistance communities (CPRs) in the high, cold, heavily forested Sierra Madres. This was the first public visit since the campesinos had gone into hiding in the early 1980s. Bob wrote: "Dawn is breaking, and as I burrow down into the warmth of my borrowed sleeping bag, I suddenly realize something is missing. Unlike every other place I have travelled in the tropics there are no roosters crowing. And then I remember. The peasants of Caba in the high Sierra of the province of Quiché in Guatemala have tied the vocal chords of their roosters to prevent this. They don't want to draw the attention of the army patrols that arrive without warning to destroy crops, slaughter animals, burn houses, and kidnap the members" (*Network News,* Smith).

The Sierra CPRs had only a few months earlier made their existence known to the world. They placed a paid announcement in the Guatemalan press: "We are civilian non-combatants. We are tired of being hunted like animals, cut off from our families, denied all contact with our priests and pastors. We demand an end to the oppression." The army accused them of being nothing more than a guerrilla front, so they held a press conference to explain that they had always been non-combatant unarmed civilian populations. They attributed their ten years of relentless persecution and bombing to their refusal to return to army-controlled model villages.

Religious and human rights organizations, supported by the Canadian and Swedish embassies, pressured the Guatemalan government to allow national and international groups into the CPRs to assess the validity of their claims. Bob was a witness: "The roosters of Caba have been silenced, but the people's voice is strong and clear....Someone said that 'statistics are human faces with the tears wiped off.' We saw the faces, and we saw the tears, but we also heard their voices, strong, clear, well informed, articulate" (*Network News,* Smith).

※ Coming North

Since many Canadians have neither the time nor financial, physical, and emotional resources needed to travel, representatives of Guatemalan NGOs, churches, and unions, as well as refugee and internally displaced groups, are invited to Canada. Ann Godderis observes: "People who come are incredibly generous with their time and energy, very skilled, with good analysis" (TI). Since this is a costly venture, groups often collaborate with NGOs, churches, universities, and unions.

Canadians who hear first-hand testimonies and analyses gain new insights and often move to a deeper level of involvement:

> **Ann Godderis:** I can give you a long list of people who say they got involved because of who they met. They can still remember a particular event, who spoke, and what they said. They help people more than anything move from their local reality in Canada to the Southern reality and understand the linkages between what is happening here and what is happening there.
>
> **Bud Godderis:** What we have seen in the South, the terrible exploitation and callous disregard for human suffering, is starting to happen here more and more. It is a new experience for us to face that callousness. We need to learn to carry on, to keep our hope up. It is even more important for them to come and teach us about that. They teach us how to struggle in adverse conditions. (TI)

A human rights worker's tour of the Kootenays had many outcomes. A school twinned with a school in a marginalized community near Guatemala City. A teacher joined young people on a YouthGATE tour. The Labour Council sent Urgent Actions and supported the YouthGATE tour financially. They invited another Guatemalan to speak at a Labour Day picnic of five thousand people.

Refugees visited Canada in 1992 and 1993 to share their story of empowered community organization and their hope for the future. In a public meeting attended by about forty people in Antigonish, NS, a refugee recounted her community's flight from army massacres to a refugee camp. News items about refugees turned into a story with a human face that inspired the formation of the local Project A group.

Mary Corbett shared her learning in accompanying Antonio Otzoy, representative of the *Hermandad de Presbiterios Mayas* (the Fellowship of Maya Presbyteries), during a three-week visit to the Maritimes:

> It gave me the strongest indication of the importance of the partner coming here to know our story. I had a strong impression of his profound disturbance and perhaps even anger (although not at Canadians) as he gained a more complete and accurate truth about Canada. I will never forget his dismay when I took him to the Food Bank. As he began to hear about the present economic reality here, I think it was truly a shock for him that such a situation of need existed here in Canada and I was deeply moved by that. His openness and depth of reflection were such that, by the end of his visit, I heard him telling small communities here that he would never want them to have to go through what his people had endured. In some way I believe he was saying: "The same reality is beginning to unfold here, to a much lesser degree, it is true. You still have time, but you must address this." (TI)

C : Urgent Actions

> This is the very human face of our work—when appeals come into the office telling of a person with a name, a family, a place of work, an age, and why they have been targeted for terrible unimaginable attacks on themselves or their loved ones. The reports are terrible things to read, often sent by human rights organizations which don't believe in watering down the facts to make for easier reading.　　　　　　　　　　　—*Network News*, Kranabetter

※ History

In 1986 the CTF set up the Central America Urgent Action Network (UAN) to mobilize an immediate response when crises occurred. Writing Urgent Actions is the solidarity activity that has involved the most Canadians, both the newly aware and those with long-term involvement. Most appeals concern abuses arising from political repression and militarization or violations of humanitarian law. An Urgent Action often asks that a letter be sent the government and/or Armed Forces of the country in question. Individuals may also be asked to urge Canadian and occasionally UN or US government officials to monitor and pressure the government involved or make changes in their own policy toward that country. For example, members have been encouraged to question Canada's aid policy, its support for the Central American peace process or refugee policy. Many letters have been sent asking Canada to take a stronger stance on human rights in Guatemala, as well as at UN and other international meetings.

In 1990 Jon Carrodus, math teacher and volunteer UAN coordinator, wrote:

> A human rights worker has been kidnapped by the military and is being held and tortured without charges being laid; the life of a vocal critic of government is being threatened; villages are being bombed or burned. Over the past four years, we have developed a strong and committed network of people willing to write letters or send telegrams quickly on reception of information from us about such urgent situations. I am pleased to report that now over one hundred people are direct contacts, and many of these have their own networks in their communities. Unfortunately, the number of distressing situations to which we are asked to respond is also increasing. Two years ago we sent out about twenty appeals in one year. Now we send twenty every two months! (*Network News,* Carrodus)

In 1990, with Canadian Council for International Cooperation support, the CTF united efforts with two Montreal groups, the Social Justice Committee and the *Comite Chretien pour les Droits Humaines en Amerique Latine* (Christian Committee for Human Rights in Latin America) to develop a Canada-wide Urgent Action Network. The CTF was responsible for Western Canada and the Montreal groups for Eastern Canada. When the first Maritimes-Guatemala BTS delegation returned from Guatemala in 1991, they decided to establish an Atlantic Network. Supported by Evelyn Riggs of the Halifax Oxfam office, a brochure was produced and members recruited. For several years artist Pat Loucks sent out a mailing from the Oxfam office whenever Urgent Actions arrived from Montreal.

In 1991 the International Centre for Human Rights and Democratic Development (now called Rights and Democracy) began to fund the UAN, paying a part-time coordinator's salary for each of the three organizations and modest office, communications, and travel expenses. By the summer of 1992 Network members included 385 individuals and organizations (church, solidarity, trade union, student, indigenous, and women's groups),

New Forms of Solidarity 163

many of whom acted as a point of contact for others. More recently CECI, a Quebec-based NGO, supported the UAN through the Canadian government's Democracy and Development Fund. However, its funding was cut from Phase 3 of the Democracy and Development fund in 2001, to the consternation of letter writers who were once again receiving growing numbers of Urgent Actions.

※ Impact

> **Trade unionist:** When I was working in a union federation, many of my companions were threatened. Their lives were saved because of Urgent Actions. The attention also gave them the strength not to flee Guatemala. (TI)
>
> **Human rights worker:** The Urgent Action Network was very important for us. It is difficult for people to understand how much pressure and importance is contained in a letter filled with concern for the safety of a person who we assumed had been "disappeared." Even if the person disappeared, the fact that the government understood that there was a political consequence to what they were doing was very important in reducing the violence. (TI)

Many Guatemalans see Urgent Actions as the most important form of Canadian solidarity. For the letter writers, human rights abuses are no longer statistics. They are about flesh and blood individuals with families, histories, deep faith, and social commitments.

Not all Urgent Actions have an immediate impact. Nonetheless Guatemalans testify to lives saved and abuses stopped. "The people we met in Guatemala could see a value for themselves in worldwide exposure, so the government and military know people are watching them and the things they do can't be hidden," said Ann Pellerine. She met a human rights worker who had been kidnapped and sexually assaulted. "To hear from her the value of having letters from people, the value of letters from northern BC and the Kootenays, you just understand that it is really valuable to do that, that there is a value for their protection" (TI). The human rights worker said: "Urgent Actions truly gave me support and security, along with the accompaniment of Peter Golden, Deirdre Kelly, and Marta Gloria when I went to the Public Ministry to make a declaration, because I didn't have the courage to go alone. I no longer felt alone. The laws here in Guatemala are very good, it is true, but they are not enforced. But if there is international pressure and statements, they are more attentive" (TI).

When the army intelligence unit assassinated Myrna Mack because of her research on the internally displaced, the UAN participated in an international campaign to bring the intellectual and material authors of the crime to justice. Her family thanked letter writers: "'You shall know the truth and the truth shall set you free' (John 8:32). With an academic rigour for justice, she brought to light this piece of reality that many of us had been unable to perceive before. On September 11, 1990, her assassins sought to extinguish this light, reflected in her eyes, and the strength of her heart. But your solidarity, and that of many others, is helping to prevent despair from prevailing in our country. Thank you for being part of forging a new era of justice and fraternity among Guatemalans. This will be the new dawn where Myrna awaits us with her faith and her smile" (*Network News*, Mack).

Solidarity has helped Myrna's sister, Helen, find the courage and strength to establish the Myrna Mack Foundation to work against impunity and carry out human rights education. International pressure has supported her persistent efforts to bring before the courts those responsible for the murder. Overcoming the tremendous blocks of impunity and judicial corruption, the material author was tried and jailed. The even more difficult task of bringing to justice the intellectual authors continues more than a decade later.

Letter-writing campaigns have brought about policy and funding changes in CIDA and DFAIT (Department of Foreign Affairs and International Trade). When Canada cut funding to the legal advocacy program of *Casa Alianza* (Covenant House), an NGO working with street children, an Urgent Action was sent out including information about children's rights, violence perpetrated on street children, often by the police, and the impunity that protects the guilty. Lyn Kerans, a primary school teacher in Halifax, responded: "We had visited Covenant House. I was so angry. I wrote off a letter. I could say in that letter that I had seen the work that they had done and it really affected me. I got a letter back finally from the Government. Enough Canadians had written that they didn't cut the funding" (TI).

After a major campaign, Canada changed its policy at the UN High Commission on Human Rights, voting to name Guatemala one of the worst offenders. This enabled the appointment of special UN observers whose reports, publicized in Guatemala and internationally, succeeded in pressuring the army to reduce its human rights violations.

Former Canadian Embassy political affairs officer Lajos Arendas commented on the impact of letters: "In general I think they are very useful because they put the Ministry on its toes all the time. I think it's good for them [citizens] to know what the Canadian position is." He recalled the importance of letters when the Guatemalan government was refusing to honour its land credit obligations to the refugees: "There was a major deadlock. It lasted a long time. In that case I think the letter campaign was instrumental because it put more pressure on. It became an irritant to all the people getting letters in the Guatemalan government" (TI).

※ The Process

When a Central American group, Amnesty International, or the Inter-Church Committee on Human Rights in Latin America sends an appeal by e-mail or fax, the Christian Task Force and the Social Justice Committee immediately prepare an Urgent Action. It includes an incident description, the likely cause of the violation, who may be responsible, and suggested actions. Necessary mailing and e-mail addresses and fax and phone numbers are listed.

Education and action go hand in hand. The Urgent Action often includes information not readily accessible through the media, such as a brief analysis from a MINUGUA or ICCHRLA report. It places the incident in the context of themes or patterns in the country and may provide historical background, socio-economic trends, updates from human rights groups, or reports on Canada's stance. Excerpts from the Universal Declaration of Human Rights, Standard Minimum Rules for Treatment of Prisoners, the UN Convention on Children's Rights, or Central American Peace and Refugee Accords have been included. For several years the UAN distributed a Human Rights Profile of Guatemala, giving a brief history of Guatemala, explaining the human rights situation, including the violation of economic and social rights, and describing Guatemalan human rights groups.

Many individuals receive Urgent Actions directly. Others are contact people, fanning the requests out to members of solidarity, church, and union groups. The advent of computer databases and e-mail has speeded up the work. Specific sectors may be approached. For example, student organizations were asked to respond when Guatemalan student leaders were assassinated. Churches were mobilized after Bishop Gerardi's murder.

Writers are asked to send personal rather than form letters. Lajos Arendas was irritated when he received copies of a letter someone had distributed: "Clearly the person is not doing the writing. It looks fake and then it doesn't look good somehow. That gives somehow a lack of authenticity to the letter and that bothers me, to be honest" (TI). Letter writing becomes part of an educational process when individuals compose their own letters. They must think about the issues, which leads to a deepened understanding and often a discovery of the links between specific abuses and the violation of economic, social, and cultural rights.

Letter writers are asked to be succinct and polite, refraining from attacking or blaming individuals while still clearly naming their concern. Project A learned this lesson the hard way when it named a Canadian government official in an Urgent Action. The letter created anger and defensiveness on the part of the Embassy. Project A spent time and energy explaining that its concern was with the government's stance on this issue, rather than criticism of an individual. Fortunately the official then became open to hearing the real concern and the government's position changed.

※ Urgent Actions—Valuable, Yet Problematic

Urgent Actions often empower individuals who might otherwise feel powerless about human rights violations. Tara Scurr says, "By responding to Urgent Actions, you are reminding yourself that you are part of democracy. I have to write to my MP. Who is my MP?" (TI). In September 2001 Fatina Elkurdi, a BTS young adult delegation member, wrote the minister of Foreign Affairs and International Trade, urging the Canadian government to be more responsive to the deteriorating human rights situation: "I am a Canadian who by virtue of my nationality can write this letter freely, a freedom the social movement in Guatemala is not afforded. My life is not at risk by writing this. Since as Canadians we have this privilege, we also have the serious responsibility for paying attention to and actively working against those international parties who are responsible for such injustice." Solidarity activists agree with Tara and Fatina and respond frequently to Urgent Actions. A remarkable example is a small group in the tiny Nova Scotia hamlet of West Branch whose members for many years responded to every Urgent Action they received.

Not all Urgent Actions get equal attention, especially if several arrive in the same week. There tends to be a lesser response to situations people know less about, even if the situation is just as serious. Ann Godderis noted: "If it is someone I know personally, I am really moved to work. People need to feel a part of something, engaged to then have the energy to sit down and write a letter." When a human rights worker who had visited the Kootenays was kidnapped, it was easy to mobilize letter writers: "We knew her and felt like part of her life." Canadians felt connected to refugees and responded in huge numbers to crises during the Return process.

New Forms of Solidarity

During a 1996 Embassy visit, an official told Ann and Bud Godderis that the volume of letters and therefore Canadian interest in Guatemala seemed to be dropping. Letter writers argued that the government often did not even acknowledge their letters, much less address their concerns. Bud mentioned "a certain callousness" in the government that he had not found previously. However Ann contends that not writing gives the government "permission to be more concerned with trade and economic issues than human rights. As citizens we still have an obligation, even if we don't think it will have an effect, to speak up and demand that they listen" (TI).

Urgent Actions can feel burdensome and generate guilt. Tara Scurr reports that letter writers sometimes feel "bogged down" and say: "Oh no, not another one!" Project A Antigonish members' reactions to the mention of Urgent Actions are not atypical:

Heather Carson: I'm terrible at it!

Sandra O'Toole: I'm worse.

Diane Walsh: I'm worse.

Heather Carson: We get the letters kind of late. By the time I find the time it seems almost crazy to write the letter. I know the importance of it. I know the value of it. I'm terrible at it. (TI)

Janette Fecteau challenged them: "Sure, you have all these doubts and I do, too. The Urgent Action comes late, and I send letters by mail, so I know that's going to take another week. But I feel like it's worth it. I guess it's faith. I believe that it's such a small thing. It's easy to get discouraged, but it might be the only thing that I can do. So I just do it. I take courage by the doggedness of the people, up against something so huge, just quietly and courageously keeping on" (TI). Letter writing is not for everyone, remarked one person: "What you do should be in the line of the gifts you have. I don't have time and have to accept that I'm not called to that. But there are people who like to do that kind of work" (TI). Ann Godderis acknowledges, "it sometimes seems overwhelming. We have had to search for ways to do it creatively so it doesn't wear people down" (TI).

Some groups ensure members receive only one request per month. In Victoria and Fredericton people gather over lunch to write Urgent Actions. Project A Antigonish had a potluck supper near Christmas to write greeting cards to corporations concerning sweatshop labour. Churches have encouraged worshippers to stay after church to write Urgent Actions. They provide paper, pens, and stamped envelopes, as well as coffee.

A lack of feedback about results of Urgent Actions discourages people, noted Tara Scurr. Some groups in Guatemala now try to keep writers informed about the impact of their letters. Ann Godderis remarked, "People do care when we get back to them about the results" (TI).

The sense of urgency to respond to Urgent Actions has at times meant that insufficient time has been given to analyzing the nature and number of Urgent Actions, and what other kinds of responses may be needed. As Kathi Bentall said, "We need to slow down and say to ourselves: 'We just received a phone call. What does that mean?'" (TI).

D : Fairly Traded Crafts and Coffee

Marketing Guatemalan crafts to support poor women and their families was an early solidarity effort. Monimbo Crafts began in BC in 1982. Weavings were purchased from those directly affected by the violence, including refugees in Mexico and internally displaced widows in Guatemala. Mike Lewis recounted its beginnings:

> I wrote a letter to a bunch of people and raised some money to get a little capital pool which was, as I recall, $25,000. We looked at what we might do in terms of moving refugee products, clothing, table cloths, into some kind of marketing effort, which really became a marketing company. We really didn't move it into the regular distribution outlets one would in a normal business enterprise. It became a way of linking the marketing and selling of goods into an educational strategy. It was really classic solidarity work with an economic aspect to it. We probably sold in two to two and a half years $150,000 to $175,000 worth of goods. We linked it to conferences. We linked it to all kinds of things. (TI)

However, it became impossible to maintain other solidarity work and at the same time sustain Monimbo Crafts as a business needing a great deal of voluntary energy.

Some groups now integrate a lower volume of sales into their work. After Kootenay group members returned from visiting refugee camps, the group formed Teardrop Crafts. Volunteers sell the crafts, along with fairly traded coffee, at solidarity and social justice events. Similarly Tatamagouche Centre sells weavings purchased from Kaqchikel Presbytery women's groups, with sales of up to $5,000 a year.

Along with the women obtaining better prices for their weavings than they would by selling to tourists in Guatemala, these projects encourage the weaving tradition's preservation. Crafts have a flyer or tag attached,

New Forms of Solidarity

explaining a little about the current situation in Guatemala and the artisans themselves. This can begin the educational process and for some is an entry point into solidarity work.

Still many who sell crafts see its limitations. Tara Scurr said, "It is important to do direct monetary solidarity. But sometimes it can be an easy out for people, to appease their guilt. It can also be a really good opening. 'Where did you get that lovely shirt?'" (TI).

Solidarity groups also support the fair trade movement, with a particular focus on coffee. Fair trade organizations in Canada, the US, and Europe purchase coffee beans directly from small producers, formed into cooperatives, often doubling or tripling the rate paid on national and international markets.

After oil, coffee is the world's most valuable trading commodity. Because of a glut on the world market, the international price for coffee beans has been at its lowest in thirty years. Most Guatemala coffee is grown on large plantations, where workers pick coffee under brutal conditions. Pesticides, fungicides, herbicides, and fertilizers, dangerous to workers, wildlife, and soil, are used for faster production. Men earn less than $3 US a day for picking a hundred pounds of coffee or more, and women and children often earn less for the same work.

BC groups, led by BC CASA and Co-Development Canada (Co-Dev), market *Café Justicia,* purchasing coffee beans from members of the Campesino Committee of the Highlands (CCDA), an organization that struggles for land and labour rights. Supported by the CCDA, campesinos are forming small coffee cooperatives to achieve better working and living conditions for their communities. These cooperatives are making the transition to growing coffee organically. Grown without chemicals, the beans ripen slowly under a protective canopy of diverse trees, enhancing the coffee's flavour, as well as providing shelter and nesting places for birds. Organic growing also reduces dependence on a single crop, as fruits can be harvested from the shade trees.

BTS has also supported fair trade coffee through its link with Just Us! Coffee Roasters, a Nova Scotia workers' cooperative that has imported fairly traded and organically grown coffee since 1996. BTS supported educational programs promoting fairly traded coffee. Members participated in a Ten Days for Global Justice campaign to have stores across Canada stock fairly traded coffees. Churches and community groups throughout the Maritimes now serve Just Us! Coffee, and all grocery chains sell their coffee.

In 2001 Just Us! And BTS placed Caren Weisbart, a CIDA-funded Tatamagouche Centre intern, with CCDA to explore the feasibility of purchasing coffee from CCDA members. In the spring of 2002, after Jeff Moore of Just Us! visited the CCDA, they agreed to purchase 6,000 pounds of coffee beans, with the proviso that BTS take an active role in marketing the coffee. When Caren returned to the Maritimes, she initiated a marketing and educational campaign for the coffee, labeled *Breaking the Silence Coffee*. She then returned to the CCDA, this time as a BTS volunteer, supporting CCDA efforts to achieve fair trade and organic certification. In the spring of 2003, CCDA shipped a second order to Just Us!, who hired Beth Abbott to develop a follow-up campaign focused on churches and labour groups.

E : Vigils

From 1984–89 the CTF held vigils on the second Friday of each month in front of the Guatemalan consulate in Vancouver, an opportunity for new members to join long-standing members in a public witness. The vigils signaled to the Guatemalan and Canadian governments that Canadians and refugees in Canada were determined to make citizens aware of human rights violations in Guatemala. Large banners with names of the disappeared were created; participants handed out leaflets describing human rights abuse and what Canadians could do; they asked passers-by to sign petitions; they performed street theatre; they hosted high-profile speakers such as church leaders and MPs; newspapers, radio, and TV were alerted, ensuring wide coverage. The Vancouver vigil spilled over into other cities, such as Montreal. Since that time, many vigils have been held across the country in response to emergency situations or to mark important dates, such as the anniversary of Bishop Gerardi's assassination.

F : Advocacy and Lobbying

Analysis from the perspective of the poor has led to action strategies that enable citizens to analyze critically and oppose government policies. Former cabinet ministers Lloyd Axworthy and Paul Martin have acknowledged that churches and solidarity groups have developed a citizenry that asks articulate and probing questions about Canada's social, economic, and international policies. That was certainly true when the CTF participated in a successful cross-Canada campaign in the 1980s with the goal of establishing a just peace in Central America.

New Forms of Solidarity

Canada was continuing what Conservative MP Flora MacDonald called the Liberals' "quiet acquiescence" to US Cold War actions relentlessly inflicted on Latin America. In the House of Commons, she asked, "What is Canada prepared to do in an area close to home, within this hemisphere, where we have very serious obligations to help maintain peace?" External Affairs Minister Mark McGuigan replied, "I am not aware that we have any serious obligation in that part of the world, in Central America, which is not an area of traditional Canadian interest." He supported the Reagan administration's approval of Ríos Montt, the fundamentalist president of Guatemala who was maintaining and defending the army's campaign of mass terror. Ottawa recognized the regime a few days after the 1982 military coup, praising it for "making the right sounds about reform" (McFarlane, p. 185).

In 1982, at the urging of Central American partners, a national action campaign emerged, with a two-pronged strategy, face-to-face lobbying of government officials combined with public pressure. Coalitions and denominational staff collaborated with Ten Days representatives from across Canada. Jeanne Moffatt, at that time Ten Days program coordinator, called the experience "an outstanding example of dynamic interaction" between volunteers whose contributions to policy-making were honoured and staff who shared strategic experience and analysis. "It was an exciting time and the BC network of Ten Days committees, who were the foundation of what was to become to the Christian Task Force, played an important role in all of this" (correspondence with author).

CTF members pressed Ottawa to denounce human rights abuses and urge Central American countries to agree to the Contadora and Esquipulas II Peace Accords. Staff and volunteers monitored Parliamentary Commissions, responding to their reports through letters, phone calls, and visits to political leaders. They kept MPs and opposition critics up-to-date on issues. They corresponded with the minister and External Affairs officials, questioning new developments or policy changes. Meetings were arranged with journalists and editorial boards to encourage press coverage.

Lobbying efforts at first seemed fruitless. Canada's support for American policy seemed unwavering. However, people persisted, continuing to write letters and meet with their MPs from 1982–85. The Department of External Affairs was receiving up to two hundred letters a week, each one individually written and almost all opposing Canada's support for US policy. The Prime Minister's Office received more letters on Central America than on any other issue, many resulting from the ICCHRLA/Ten Days campaign. MPs inundated the Parliamentary Library, requesting background information. The new minister of External Affairs, Allan MacEachen, visited Central America. Canada began to take a more independent stance, giving greater support to the Central American peace process and the UN Commission on Human Rights. "Having a large number of people in Canada aware of what was going on and demanding that the Canadian government do something about the human rights violations forced the government not to follow so tightly in the footsteps of Reagan," Ann Godderis observed (TI).

Members of grassroots groups gained confidence in their lobbying and letter-writing skills, as well as knowledge of the issues. They were no longer easily deterred by government "experts." Many had been on delegations to Central America: "Stories abound of people whose level of self-confidence grew in the course of a brief encounter with an MP. They learned that their MPs were not all-knowing, and they discovered that their sources of information (partners who represented the poor in each of the Central American countries) often offered a totally different perspective from that of their MPs" (Moffatt, p. 164).

Government official David Bickford acknowledged this: "It used to be that we could say in External Affairs that we are the people with the expertise. We could say: 'We've got a man down there on the spot who can tell you the way it is.' Now the churches come back and say, 'No, we had a team down there last week, and this is the way it is'" (cited in McFarlane, p. 166).

In 1986 Ten Days for World Development cited an External Affairs official impressed by letter writers' sophistication. He acknowledged that letters on human rights issues were the fastest-growing source of public pressure. The 1986 Special Joint Parliamentary Committee on Canada's International Relations Report states:

> Our experience on this Committee revealed that the foreign policy constituency in our country is larger, better organized, and far more active than before. Hundreds of Canadians took the time and trouble to make submissions to the Committee.... Over three-quarters of all the written submissions and letters we received from the public dealt with three broad concerns: human rights in South Africa and Central America, peace and arms control, and development assistance. Whatever the previously perceived national interest in these matters, the government must take careful note of such indications of intense and pervasive public interest because its effect is to place these concerns on the national agenda. (pp. 5, 7)

New Forms of Solidarity

In 1986 the CTF initiated a campaign against resuming bilateral aid to the Guatemalan government. Canada had suspended assistance in 1981 when it co-sponsored a UN resolution condemning Guatemalan human rights violations: "It is impossible for Canada to meet its stated objective of helping those most in need of humanitarian assistance by means of a bilateral aid program. By its very public and official nature, government to government aid would subject all involved to army scrutiny and further control. Any increased assistance should therefore go to credible Canadian NGOs able to work away from army control and observation; to the 200,000 or more refugees unable to return safely to Guatemala; and to a more responsive and humane refugee program within Canada itself" (*Networking... Action Newsletter*, 1986, p. 6).

Guatemalans were concerned about a possible shift in Canada's policy when civilian Vinicio Cerezo was elected at the end of 1985. They feared that offering bilateral aid to the Cerezo administration would be seen as a message of approval to a government still controlled by the army. They wanted aid tied to demonstrated improvements in human rights. They shared their views with United Church Moderator Bob Smith during his first visit to Guatemala and with CTF delegations visiting refugee camps.

Their concerns were amply justified. The Guatemalan government succumbed to military pressures and did nothing to reduce, much less end human rights violations. It refused to negotiate seriously a peace settlement or refugee return. It was clear, as well, that international aid was allowing the government to invest more of its resources in the military.

Canadian officials were lobbied to stop the renewal of aid. The CTF prepared a flyer as well as a more in-depth booklet, "Aid to Guatemala: What Canadians Must Know," containing background materials. Articles and updates appeared in CTF's newsletter, *Network News*. Public educational events took place with Guatemalans sharing their perspectives on Canadian aid. The BC Conference of the United Church passed a resolution urging the government to maintain its freeze on bilateral aid. Those involved in public education were given additional analytical material. Other groups across Canada became involved. In Montreal both the Social Justice Committee and the Support Committee for the People of Guatemala supported the campaign.

When External Affairs indicated they were considering the resumption of aid, writers were asked to send a second letter questioning that response. For example, External Affairs stated that Guatemalan exile groups supported this policy. Letter writers were encouraged to ask which groups had expressed such support. Ann Godderis's letter noted that those most in need of humanitarian aid—the displaced, widows, and orphans—were seen by the army as potential subversives and targets of control. She pointed to the ample proof that the army was freely continuing to use selective killings, torture, and disappearances as control strategies.

Canada resumed bilateral aid in November 1987, despite widespread opposition. Lobbying increased. A new brochure suggested aid be offered only when the Guatemalan government had made progress in fulfilling conditions for a "firm and lasting peace":

- The ending of systematic human rights violations and the investigation of the fate of the 38,000 disappeared, with those responsible brought to trial;
- Dismantlement of the structure of military control in all areas of civilian life;
- The safe return and resettlement of refugees and the internally displaced; and
- Fundamental reforms to move Guatemala in the direction of justice in land distribution, the distribution of wealth, and taxation.

The education and action campaign continued into the 1990s. With an increasingly vocal constituency, the government became more cautious in its approach to bilateral aid, changing how aid was distributed and to whom. Many Canadians became sufficiently knowledgeable to question the nature of the bilateral aid program and its impact on the Guatemalan government. A CTF activist observed: "Ottawa knows that there is a large, well-informed, and well-organized body of voters from many sectors right across the country who are paying attention to External Affairs and CIDA policies and actions." As individuals developed lobbying skills, another purpose was being served as well, that of building an authentic democracy in Canada, through well-informed citizen participation.

However, weaknesses have been noted both in the work of advocacy and Urgent Actions, such as insufficient follow-up and support of volunteers, especially new people. Corina Dykstra saw a need for workshops to develop volunteers' skills, as well as feedback and encouragement about the value of their efforts. This work, she suggested, should not be ad hoc, but a strategic, integral part of solidarity practice. She also saw a need for more regular monitoring of media coverage and media misinformation and disinformation (Dykstra, p. 110).

Several people I spoke with believe it is harder to influence government policy now than in the past. They echo Tara Scurr's words: "It is getting

New Forms of Solidarity 175

harder and harder to get our voices heard, as our government becomes more and more trade-oriented. But we still have that space, and it is still important to keep that opening" (TI).

G : Security Accompaniment

Accompaniment of individuals and organizations whose lives are threatened is another form of solidarity. Guatemalans are convinced accompaniers' presence, combined with their capacity to mobilize international publicity and pressure immediately, has protected them. Project A accompanied an entire Return process over many years. However, Canadians have also accompanied individuals and small groups for short periods of time.

In April 1988 Marta Gloria de la Vega set foot on Guatemalan soil for the first time since fleeing her homeland a decade earlier. She and her colleagues from RUOG (United Representation of the Guatemalan Opposition)—including Rigoberta Menchú—were responding to an invitation from Guatemala's ambassador to the UN. During the 1988 session of the UN Human Rights Commission, he challenged RUOG representatives to assess the Guatemalan situation for themselves, never dreaming they would accept. They had come to test the government's good faith in proclaiming democracy and to challenge publicly the government's attempt to impose a requirement on returnees that they sign an amnesty statement. Anyone who signed this statement was put in the position of admitting they were criminals. They hoped to exchange views with participants in the National Dialogue getting underway as a result of the 1987 Esquipulas II Accord for the Establishment of a Firm and Lasting Peace, signed by the Guatemalan government.

RUOG knew it was far too risky to return without protective witnesses. Bob Smith and another United Church minister, Chris Ferguson, who was working in Costa Rica at the time, joined European and British Parliament members, a Mexican congressman, five assistants to US congressmen, an International Indian Treaty Council representative, a representative of US Catholic religious orders, and journalists. Ann and Bud Godderis flew into Guatemala City minutes before RUOG's arrival from Costa Rica. It was an armed camp, said Ann: "There were tanks around the periphery and soldiers on the roof. It was terrifying, wondering what might happen. I'm not sure Rigoberta would have survived without international accompaniment" (TI).

When the group stepped off the plane, a phalanx of heavily armed policemen in buses and on motorcycles met them. Rigoberta Menchú, later awarded the Nobel Peace Prize, and Dr. Rolando Castillo, former dean of the Medical School, were immediately detained. They were asked to sign the amnesty but refused and were taken to a police station. Marta Gloria's passport was seized. Marta Gloria and Frank LaRue were held in their hotel where three thousand supporters gathered outside.

Accompaniers wasted no time in mobilizing international pressure. Menchú and Castillo were released within five hours without criminal charges, after an avalanche of Urgent Actions flooded the Guatemalan government. Publicity around their detention focused international attention on the delegation's security. Jim Manly, United Church minister and NDP Member of Parliament, raised the issue of their safety in the House of Commons.

Marta Gloria wrote: "The fear that we felt on Monday night on arrival was evident, that sensation in the skin that comes out of knowing that anything can happen at any moment in Guatemala" (*Network News*, de la Vega, 1988). RUOG believed the dangers they had faced were worth the risk at that critical juncture. By refusing to sign the amnesty, they set an extremely important precedent, a signal to the refugees that they too could refuse to admit to any wrongdoing. They met with the National Reconciliation Commission, as well as the Archbishop, a UN representative, the International Red Cross, and several union, peasant, and student organizations. Campesinos travelled to the city to meet with them. Quiché residents travelled from their villages to larger towns to watch the evening news on television where Rigoberta spoke in Quiché. RUOG valued accompaniment combined with Urgent Actions.

> It was meaningful to see that borders, distance, and languages are not obstacles but positive elements in the search for peace. The letters, telegrams, and phone calls that arrived from church people, trade unions, women, and humanitarian organizations from different countries made a difference in terms of the protection of the group and the fulfillment of the objectives of the trip....It was not possible to make the visit without the international delegation who were giving their time, risking their lives, and contributing to the search for peace in Guatemala and Central America. (*Network News*, de la Vega, 1988)

Late one night, a year later, Marta Gloria called trade unionist Kevin Niesh in Victoria, asking him to be her companion on a second RUOG delegation. In a hastily called family conference, his wife and daughter gave their approval to what they saw as a "worthy and honoured task." Knowing media and political contacts would be their only protection, he spent the next two weeks making contact with the Labour Council and his

New Forms of Solidarity

union, the BC Government Employees' Union, along with MPs and members of the BC Legislature, the CBC, and a local radio station and newspaper. He formed a support network that included an Amnesty International local unit, the Victoria Central America Support Committee, and the Trade Union Solidarity Group.

Mid-flight, the plane suddenly turned back to Mexico City due to a "problem" at the Guatemala City airport. They turned back towards Guatemala a half-hour later:

> We moved smoothly through customs and were one of the first ones out of the strangely deserted airport....There was no one to meet us, and the city streets were empty; then downtown we saw the first gun emplacements and the squads of heavily armed soldiers on the corners. It was only after we got to the hotel that we were told a right-wing coup attempt had been in progress since 5:00 a.m., and had only just been put down...everything had changed as death squads decided that the government's instability meant that it was now open season on the ruog leaders. By noon, five death threats had been made ordering us out of the country within forty-eight hours or we would die. (Niesh, 1989)

They carried on with their plans. Kevin's first task was to ensure Canadian support. He maintained daily contact with his network, who mobilized a cross-Canada response. The Guatemalan government was inundated with phone calls, telegrams, and faxes. His long-distance media interviews and press releases issued by the Victoria unit of Amnesty International calling on President Cerezo to ensure the group's security, generating widespread media coverage in Canada, were no doubt noted by Guatemalan diplomats in Vancouver and Ottawa.

Kevin accompanied group members to and from meetings where he stood guard. Intimidation continued, but the delegation was able to carry out most of its agenda:

> What with meetings happening all week with unions, churches, NGOs, political parties, and student groups, I ended up spending much of my time in the back of a speeding car or standing guard on corners, not knowing where I was. The death squads kept things tense with numerous phone threats and on Wednesday (Mother's Day) flowers were delivered to our apartment with a lovely card from the death squads warning us to leave, "or else." The mothers of Frank LaRue and Raúl Molina both received Mothers' Day flowers and death threats as well. Thursday things heated up with us being chased by a Toyota truck with polarized windshields. Our Guatemalan driver did some

fancy driving (running a red light) and managed to lose them, although the Toyota was persistent enough to jump a curb and cross a median to try to catch us. That same evening, following a very successful meeting at the University, we were all settling down for bed when we were told there was a bomb outside our apartment building. We were evacuated while a bomb disposal squad defused three bombs in our car. (Niesh, 1989)

They left Guatemala ahead of schedule, when it became clear that groups with whom they were meeting immediately became targets of disappearances and bombings. The government and army were far from ready to allow free exchange between the Guatemalan popular movement and exiled Guatemalans working internationally for human rights and a just peace settlement. However, several large meetings were held, a great deal of networking took place, and numerous political contacts were established.

In an open letter Marta Gloria expressed RUOG's thanks for accompaniment and the numerous messages sent to Guatemala, the Canadian government, and their families. "They gave us the certainty of not being alone and how relatively small distance is when you are together in a work for justice. The love and needs of our people and your beautiful solidarity gave us the strength we needed." She ended the letter with these words: "Well, my friends, we will go back to Guatemala. We don't know the date yet, and it is not because we are unaware of the situation or that we are a little crazy but because the work for social justice in our country requires that we respond to the call" (*Network News,* de la Vega, 1989).

On his return to Canada Kevin challenged trade unionists:

> This trip has helped me to draw into focus all my beliefs and concerns about Third World workers and Canadian workers' lack of support for their struggle. A union motto that I live by, "An Injury to One is an Injury to All," is often used by trade unions, but I don't see it being applied with much vigour to help the injured workers of the Third World. I have a hard time being a union activist, fighting for wages and benefits in Canada, when brothers and sisters are suffering and dying in huge numbers overseas with often little or no support for their struggle from us....Whether it's cheap Korean cars, Guatemalan bananas, Hong Kong car parts, Mexican toys, Taiwanese clothing, Brazilian beef, or the huge profits of our major banks, it's all made with the blood and sweat of Third World workers. (Niesh, 1989)

Such accompaniment is not easy for those being accompanied, points out Eva Manly: "There's a lot of pressure for people in having strangers live

New Forms of Solidarity

with them. I think that must create a real strain for the people who are on the receiving end, quite apart from all the pressure they're under because of the stress. I can't imagine having a whole series of strangers coming to live in our house" (TI).

Accompaniment requires patience, humility, and a willingness to be in the background. Bud Godderis, who accompanied a later RUOG delegation, cited Bob Smith's counsel:

> Remember when you go down South that you are the servant of the servants of God. As a servant you are not going to be expecting people to be waiting on you or looking after your interest. You're going to find that you don't count for very much and you don't understand anything because you don't speak Spanish. Don't get uptight about it. You're not there for them to look after you. That was the most valuable thing I could have learned, because I did get worn out after the first hour listening to Spanish and I did want someone to translate for me. That was out and I knew it. So I didn't get all uptight about it and give Marta a lot of problems. A lot of Canadians forget that and think they are the ones who should be served. It is hard to grasp that in effect you're giving authority to these people as teachers. You're giving them space to do their work. You can't allow yourself to get in the way. (TI)

H : Networking

Not all solidarity challenges have to do with working North-South. Regional and national collaboration in Canada is an ongoing issue. Both the CTF and BTS have tried to collaborate with solidarity groups, unions, church-related organizations, and NGOs regionally and nationally. However the movement has faced many obstacles.

Language poses a problem. Translating letters, e-mail, and documents is time-consuming, and conference calls are next to impossible, so the level of coordination between francophone and anglophone groups is not what it should be. Canadian geography is another challenge. Face-to-face meetings are rare in a country where it costs less to travel to Guatemala than from Halifax to Vancouver. Without such gatherings, it is difficult to build trust and share ideas and resources that could increase solidarity's impact. At times tensions between solidarity groups and NGOs have arisen around roles, relationships with government, and control of the content and strategies of programs and advocacy campaigns. With most NGOs in Ottawa, Toronto, and Montreal, and solidarity groups scattered across the country, geography makes it harder to work through these issues.

In spite of these challenges, solidarity groups have developed fruitful relationships with one another, with related groups, and with NGOs. The Christian Task Force was instrumental in establishing Project Accompaniment. It was a member of the BC Inter-Agency Committee on Central America, working together with Tools for Peace, student groups, CUSO, Oxfam, Development and Peace, and the Trade Union Group on tours, educational events, and common actions. It has worked with several unions on *maquila* solidarity, education, and delegations to Guatemala. For many years the BC Conference of the United Church gave a substantial grant to the CTF and looked to it for direction in its Central American work. However, after recent restructuring, the BC Conference no longer has a Division of Global Concern. As a result, the CTF lost both its strong link with the United Church and its funding. The national office of the United Church still funds the CTF, support that is much appreciated. The CTF continues to have a strong relationship with the Anglican and Lutheran churches and with several religious orders. At different times the CTF has worked closely with ICCHRLA, Ten Days, the Central America Monitoring Group and the Inter-Agency Working Group on Latin America. Marta Gloria continues to be a resource person for Ten Days events, church gatherings, and university classes. The CTF particularly values participation in the Canada-Central America Urgent Action Network, despite the challenges:

> The cross-fertilization of ideas, strategies, and educational resources and expertise has been rich and rewarding. The three partner organizations have been able to complement each others' strengths, and the work of all three has been deepened, especially in areas of education, communication, and exchange with Central American human rights groups....The distance between Vancouver and Montreal provided a challenge in decision-making and information sharing, which was answered by more frequent telephone communication. The increased cost is more than offset by the value of the increased contact, which allowed for more efficient coordination at both national and regional levels. (*Network News* #10)

In the Atlantic region Breaking the Silence has strong ties with NGOs, churches, and union groups such as Oxfam, Tatamagouche Centre, the United Church, Catholic religious communities, and the Canadian Union of Postal Workers. Both BTS and the CTF helped found and maintain the Guatemala-Canada Solidarity Network. Churches and NGOs gave strong moral and financial support to the GCSN's founding meeting in 1999. A GCSN-organized tour across Canada in 2000 by Claudia Agreda of the Archdiocese of Guatemala Office on Human Rights was funded to a large extent by churches and religious communities.

New Forms of Solidarity

International networking is a vital part of solidarity. The CTF and HIJOS (BC Chapter) are campaigning to shut down the School of the Americas (SOA) on the military base in Fort Benning, Georgia. It trained members of the Guatemalan military in counter-insurgency in the 1980s and still does so today under a new name, the Defense Institute for Hemispheric Security Cooperation. For the past three years, CTF members have protested with more than ten thousand others.

In 2000, risking arrest, they entered the military base in a solemn funeral procession to express outrage at the SOA's deadly impact:

> As we crossed the line into Fort Benning, the names of Eva, Paula, and Veronika's families and friends were called out. We sang out "Presente!" [They are here!] Randy carried the name and spirit of his little friend Maurilia Cox Max, a little seven-year-old killed along with ten others by soldiers in the October 1995 massacre in Xamán. Natalie carried a cross bearing the name of Oscar Romero—a person she deeply admires. Jennifer's cross honoured Stanley Rother, a priest who was murdered in his home in Santiago Atitlán because of his community work. He became part of her life when she went on a GATE tour to Guatemala. My cross was marked Mario Alioto López Sánchez, who was a young student martyred in Guatemala. (*Network News,* Godderis)

This cross-border networking fuels CTF energies: "It was heartwarming and liberating to feel part of this non-violent protest and to be with so many diverse people who care about and believe in making a difference—people who have the courage to say that change *will* come and believe that we have to be present, as our friends in the South are present to us in our memories and in our hearts" (Godderis, 2000).

I : Solidarity among Children

Solidarity is not an adults-only affair. Gen Creighton, now in her late 20s, said, "I grew up in the Christian Task Force. It was quite an important experience in community for me" (TI). Marg Green highlighted the significance of community for families: "There were people like us raising children within the CTF. It was a really big part of bringing up children in a context of community. We'd meet each other through Task Force meetings, potlucks, summer justice-making weeks, and all that kind of thing. Brian, our third child, just got married this summer. He wanted some people who were formative through his life there. They were people from those networks, even though he hadn't been involved for ages" (TI).

Gen says a CTF project shaped her world view and influenced her commitment to social justice as a young adult, including a decision to spend several months volunteering with young people in a marginalized zone of Guatemala City. Sunday schools sent cards and drawings to youngsters in the camps, who sent back pictures of the devastation they had survived, of military helicopters and planes or of their communities burning to the ground. However, refugee children were encouraged to recall happy memories from their past, as well. They drew flowers, animals, and birds to help them release their feelings, move beyond the recurring nightmares many still had, and express the hope they had deep within themselves.

The pictures were also displayed in churches and at public events. "Those drawings were a powerful testimony," recalled Wes Maultsaid (TI). Some were included in a booklet and National Film Board short film, produced by Linda Dale.

Teacher Susan Sellers, member of the first BTS delegation, met street educators with CEIPA, a Guatemalan NGO that offers education to children who must work for a living. When she returned to rural River John, Nova Scotia, she initiated an in-depth program in her school. Students corresponded with street educators, raised money for a street kids program for several years running, and prepared scrapbooks about their community and school life. In return the street kids school sent information. Geography, history, and culture came alive. Susan invited speakers, both Guatemalan and Canadian, to her classes. Students learned about Maritimes connections to Guatemala through multinational corporations, solidarity groups, imported foods such as coffee and snow peas, refugees living in Atlantic Canada, and the North American Free Trade Agrement. The entire school, parents, and the community were invited to see a play about the five hundredth anniversary of European contact with the New World, written, produced, acted, and videotaped by her class. Several students wrote letters protesting human rights abuses. Former students and their parents still recall how important Susan's efforts were in raising awareness of injustice. Almost a decade later Susan, with financial support from the Nova Scotia Teachers' Union, joined a BTS Special Commission to strengthen links between BTS and the Kaqchikel Presbytery. She wanted to explore the possibility of twinning her school with the Labor de Falla school, built by parents in collaboration with the Kaqchikel Presbytery and US Presbyterian Church volunteers. She wanted her students to learn that "many Guatemalan children their ages lead rich lives despite grinding poverty" and "that Guatemalans can probably teach them more about living than the other way around." She went with questions: How can I facilitate a positive, viable, non-condescending exchange between the Labor de Falla and River John schools? How can I show that they have much to offer us, not as specimens, but rather as equal partners in a valid learning experience? (Sellers, 2001).

The two teachers, themselves Kaqchikel, had impressed BTS delegations with their dedication to and affection for their students. They teach three or four grades at a time, without any books, and often receive their salaries several months late. They responded to Susan's suggestion of twinning with enthusiasm, proposing a cultural exchange.

When Susan returned home she displayed photographs, artwork, and weavings from Guatemala in her classroom. Some weeks later Guatemalan visitors Josefina and Vilma visited the school. Her students wrote journals and essays and created art projects, stemming from discussions on Guatemala as a country representative of the developing world. The grade 9 class learned about NGOs and human rights organizations and then wrote letters of concern to government officials in Canada and Guatemala. As a result, many students came to Susan wanting to know more. Susan commented: "This marks the beginning stage of the cross-cultural understandings and service learning I aim to accomplish" (Sellers, 2000).

A few months later a BTS young adult delegation videotaped a cultural presentation by the Labor de Falla students. Both schools received copies. The Labor de Falla students also sent a cassette of songs to the River John students, who have reciprocated with their own cassette and video. When Susan met with the teachers, they expressed a deep desire for the children to have the opportunity to read, yet the school had no books. So the River John students fund-raised, enabling the teachers to purchase a variety of books for their students.

J : Solidarity among Youth

"Where are the young people? How do we involve youth?" was the constant refrain of a movement dominated by baby boomers, now middle-aged. Louise Casselman said, "We all talk about the need to rejuvenate the work. But very few of us, I include myself, have been involved in working with youth and looking at programs that would bring youth along, because some of the ways to bring youth along of course go against the grain of the old-stage work." Louise added: "Some people are challenging themselves and the work in such a way that they're developing programs with youth. Hopefully they are going to let those programs not be just to develop youth but also to have the youth take over these programs" (TI). The CTF took up that challenge early on, enabling fresh, vibrant voices to emerge.

"I learned that the Guatemalan people have a true heart for life, whether they are just struggling to get by or if they are working at a human rights organization," said a young woman whose life direction was fundamentally changed through a CTF-sponsored YouthGATE tour (Miskell and Scurr, p.6). The YouthGATE study tours began in 1991. Gen Creighton helped organize the first of many such tours:

> We were tired of looking through an adult perspective only. Bronwyn [Carrodus] and I decided to start up a youth group. It was really important to get an alternative perspective. The experience in Mexico was a really good time of learning and community. It was also a really important time when we put together what we would do for follow-up. We put together an extravaganza. People were really interested. It had a huge impact on our involvement in the church.
>
> It was there that I really switched from charity work, from sending clothes to seeing people actively struggling for change. It was connected to a liberation theology context. People that were rich and poor were working together. I saw my own position not as a benefactor, but as a co-struggler. Some people in the group continued direct action, some brought their experience into how they look at their lives. Several people are involved with Amnesty and with Urgent Actions. (TI)

In 1998 nine Kootenay youth and four adults travelled to Guatemala. Preparation started months before the tour, with meetings, educational sessions, and fundraising. These events built community among the group and created an "amazing" base of support in their communities. Ann Godderis describes the long-term impact:

> They just kept going—meeting with the local Catholic bishop to ask for Canadian bishops' solidarity with the call for a proper investigation of Bishop Gerardi's murder and an end to impunity, making dramatic presentations to schools and youth groups about their experiences, going to Washington, DC, and Fort Benning, where they called for the closure of the School of the Americas, linking up with HIJOS [an organization founded by children of the disappeared, which has a BC chapter]. All in their own ways are making a difference. Some are much more involved than others in social justice work, but they have all been changed by the experience. They will continue to contribute many good things to this world because of the breaking open that happened in Guatemala. (TI)

The CTF has worked with youth in other ways. It has been a frequent resource to the BC Central America Student Alliance (BC CASA), a collec-

New Forms of Solidarity

tive formed in 1989 to support Guatemala's State University Student Association, which was then receiving constant death threats. Before a delegation could be sent, fourteen student leaders had been "disappeared" or murdered. A year later, BC CASA members went to Guatemala to document the human rights situation students were confronting. Since that time, it has maintained contact with Guatemalan grassroots groups. In yearly visits members meet with student associations, women's groups, unions, human rights organizations, and marginalized communities. On their return they make presentations in schools, colleges, and universities, send Urgent Actions, and sell fair-trade coffee.

Public postering by HIJOS in Guatemala City warns: "Danger. Police in the area." Photo by Chap Haynes.

Tara Scurr is a former CASA member and now a Council of Canadians organizer. She attended a high school conference on Latin America but had no place to put her energies until she travelled with BC CASA to Guatemala in 1993. When she returned, she wrote Urgent Actions and volunteered with the CTF. She organized YouthGATE tours and worked with youth energized by the anti-globalization movement.

Eventually the CTF hired her and made youth work a high priority. Determined not to ghettoize youth, she built bridges between younger and older people. She tells the story of travelling in the Okanagan Valley and the Kootenays. CTF members would say to her: "Young people aren't interested in anything." At the same time, younger people were saying to her: "We have all these problems, we have all these worries, we have all these concerns—and nowhere to go with them." She decided to bring older and younger people together to share experiences and work. Tara is a testament to the importance of building bridges, as she tells how significant it has been for her to "get to know people like Marta, Bud, and Ann, people who have made solidarity a part of their lives—something to learn from, to make it a part of my life. It helps me deepen my own commitment, to question, to challenge, to love" (TI).

Though the CTF pioneered solidarity work with youth, Gen and Tara say that YouthGATE participants did not integrate easily into the CTF. "There were limited opportunities for young people except YouthGATE," said Gen (TI). She and Tara caution against making young people fit into adult structures. For example, efforts to involve youth through participation on the executive did not work. Class, exam, and work schedules meant that they often had to miss executive meetings. The solidarity movement has to be more intentional about including youth, they say. Tara calls on the solidarity movement to take the time to learn what young people want and respect their political knowledge and perspectives. She adds, "young people bring freshness, new ideas and new energy. They are angry, but they are also acting out of a place of love" (TI). Tara emphasizes the power of Canadian and Guatemalan youth relating to one another. For example, she wants to see Canadian youth making links with young people working in Guatemalan *maquilas*.

Breaking the Silence was conscious of the need to focus on the hopes and struggles of Guatemalan youth, with more than half of Guatemala's population under age fifteen. On the first BTS Young Adult delegation in August 2000, fifteen young adults, ages eighteen to twenty-six, learned from Guatemalan counterparts about human rights, economic justice, and mutual support.

Wendy Méndez of HIJOS Guatemala told her story. (HIJOS is an international organization founded by children whose parents were disappeared in Argentina. The acronym, which means children in Spanish, stands for "children for truth and justice, against forgetting and silence.") She came to Canada as a child after the army "disappeared" her mother. As a young adult she joined the HIJOS BC chapter. Wendy returned to her birthplace in 1999. She and thirty others, some as young as sixteen, formed a new HIJOS chapter.

When HIJOS used street theatre and demonstrations to demand that those who tortured and murdered their families be brought to justice, they received death threats, first by phone and later in person. They were followed by cars with darkened windows. Although terrorized, the group refused to stop its work. They set up a Web site and launched an Urgent Action campaign. Letter writers urged the Canadian and Guatemalan governments to protect HIJOS members. Wendy told the delegation how harassment and death threats stopped "from one day to the next," after the government was flooded by faxes and e-mails. When HIJOS members saw a huge pile of copies of messages sent by Canadians, some said it felt like the protection they had never known as children.

However, a few weeks after the BTS delegation returned home, HIJOS received new threats and, this time, assaults. However, they continued their protests against impunity. During a demonstration against Ríos Montt, individuals were hired to shout obscenities at them. Delegation members wrote to the Guatemalan and Canadian governments and had their friends write as well. They copied their letters to HIJOS. Wendy responded: "They tried to bring our spirits down but everyone united and didn't let up the protest. In fact they were forced to leave. The protest went well and no one was hurt, so while you are supporting us we feel safer to take these kinds of actions. We can't thank you enough" (e-mail correspondence with delegation). Two HIJOS representatives toured Maritimes universities and high schools in 2002.

Letter to President Portillo from a Young Adult Delegation Member

I personally feel greatly concerned that this incident, and other recent events including death threats to other human rights activists, suggest that Guatemalan activists are not free to speak out and fight against abuse, injustice, and impunity. I am concerned that the peace process is nothing more than words on paper, and that there is perhaps no actual commitment from the government to create a more just, peaceful, and free country.

I would very much like to be proven wrong, of course. In order to be convinced that the Guatemalan government is committed to justice, peace, and freedom, I believe that a number of things must happen:

1. That there be no further attacks, threats, and robberies towards those who are working towards making Guatemala a safer and more just country.

2. That attacks such as the one which occurred in the FAMDEGUA office on September 4 be dealt with promptly and thoroughly. This would involve an investigation into who was responsible, both materially and intellectually, and would also involve prosecution of all of those people involved in the attack in any way.

3. That the government make a serious commitment to healing those who were affected by the war, to bringing those responsible for deaths, disappearances, and massacres to justice, and to assisting materially those who were displaced or otherwise disadvantaged materially during the war.

—Chris Chapman, September, 2000

Delegates asked Tatamagouche Centre to seek funding from the CIDA International Youth Internship Program, to enable young adults to have a more in-depth experience in Guatemala. We received approval for six internships with Guatemalan partners in 2001, nine interships in 2002, and six internships in 2003. After a six-week training program in adult education and community development at Tatamagouche Centre, the interns travel to Guatemala for a seven-month period of Spanish study and work in community development and human rights with Guatemalan NGOs. Having gained profound learnings about solidarity, community development, and human rights, they are infusing the solidarity movement with fresh leadership and energy.

9 Solidarity's Creative Heart

> Every totalitarian regime dreads the poet.
> —Source unknown

GUATEMALANS DO NOT SEPARATE artistic expression from political action. Tito Medina of Kin Lalat said: "Connecting song and music with solidarity was a way of keeping hope alive, because we had lost so much" (TI). A refugee told Wes Maultsaid: "We took the community's marimba apart. Everyone had to carry a piece. We carried it all the way because if we don't have our music and our marimba to keep our memory and our hope alive, then we will die here" (TI).

Without the arts, argues Wes Maultsaid, solidarity becomes "too intellectual, not emotional or passionate enough" (TI). Julia Esquivel agrees. "Socio-political analyses are often forgotten. They have an impact on a certain group of people, intellectuals, academics, and those already aware, allowing them to deepen their knowledge. But songs, theatre, and poetry have a more permanent impact" (TI). Ann Godderis says: "The expression of who people are, what their hopes and dreams are, through a medium other than one's intellect, is very important. Poetry, music, religious expression, touch another part of a human being. It is part of the richness of the Christian Task Force that we are learning to be much more than a head walking around" (TI).

Many were drawn into the solidarity movement as they glimpsed Guatemalans' costly hope and struggle through songs of the exiled musical group Kin Lalat (a Quiché word meaning sound), mime and movement of the theatre troupe Teatro Vivo (which means living theatre), and the poetry of Julia Esquivel. Wes Maultsaid still thinks about the power of the coffeehouse held during the World Council of Churches Assembly. "I'll always remember that evening. Events like that were transforming events because they really brought people together around a cultural event which also had a lot of politics in it" (TI).

Marimba players. Photo by Valerie Mansour.

That night I sat on the floor of the University of British Columbia Graduate Student Centre. The last rays of sun shone through the windows as poet and theologian Julia Esquivel invited the audience into her life and the lives of her people. She read poetry of crucifixion and resurrection, of holy rage barely contained, of the struggle to hope in the midst of the deepest suffering. Christ was present for Julia in the horror and the hope of the Guatemalan people. It was a moment of conversion, of knowing that the truth of faith and of life had to do with struggle and suffering, resistance and resurrection. I realized that intellectual struggles with Christian belief were far less important than a willingness to choose life, to resist evil, to live with hope and to be open to God's grace even in the places of deepest despair.

Later that evening the crowd laughed and wept with the youthful actors of Teatro Vivo and musicians of Kin Lalat who had fled their beloved homeland after losing countless family members and friends. Their performances opened hearts and minds to life amidst death, hope born of despair, resistance in the face of suffering, and new life arising from the crucifixion of a people. By the end of the evening, I knew I could not walk away from this new-found knowledge and leave the struggle to others with more influence and power. I had no idea what that might mean, other than perhaps signing a petition or writing a letter to the Canadian government about the urgency of accepting Guatemalan refugees. The political, spiritual, and personal implications unfolded gradually and continue to unfold to this day.

An exiled Guatemalan found the use of theatre and music, with their capacity to use humour along with pathos, a gentler way to tell a painful story. "Not only was it very sad and painful to talk about the massacres, torture, persecution, kidnappings, and everything going on at that time, but it was also very wearing. Each time we gave a talk describing the realities, we began to relive the Guatemalan reality. It was extremely difficult for us. The presence of groups like Teatro Vivo and Kin Lalat was a major turning point in solidarity with Guatemala. Through culture, through music and theatre, they could deliver the same message but not in as cruel a way as we did when we gave talks" (TI).

Former CTF staff member Tara Scurr believes theatre, music, and poetry resonate with youth. "They don't want to hear about the yoke of oppression." She described how Kin Lalat's concerts at Langara College contributed to the growth of the Central America Student Alliance (CASA). Their lively, passionate music would be accompanied by Tito Medina's interpretation of the songs. Moved by the music, students would often stay long after the concert ended to browse through materials at the CASA table, ask questions, and ultimately get involved (TI).

Maritimes singer Lennie Gallant, whose evocative images of social reality have won him many songwriting awards, was a 1991 BTS delegation

Lennie Gallant with Canadian Ambassador Dickson. Photo by Valerie Mansour.

member. "It was a very powerful experience for me to see people who were working under such amazing adversity, working with such courage and absolute faith in what they were doing. It was the first time I had ever spent so much time meeting so many people who, in many cases, put their lives on the line for what they believe in" (TI).

Since the delegation, Lennie has contributed greatly to Guatemalan solidarity work, giving benefit concerts throughout the Maritimes. He wrote *Land of the Maya* in Guatemala and recorded it in the Halifax CBC studio, with profits from its sale going to Oxfam projects.

> It was written after we had met so many different people of Maya descent who were being persecuted by the elite. That coincided with the five hundred years' celebration of Columbus' discovering of America. I remember sitting in a van and this melody started coming to me. The whole idea of the song spilled out onto paper. My usual response to something that affects me deeply is to try and capture it in song, if I can. I felt a lot of anger, sorrow, pain, and joy all wrapped up into one—anger at the situation, anger at the injustice, and sorrow at the situation, but also being able to experience people who had such great spirit for life despite all the adversity they had to deal with. (TI)

He says a good entertainer "can make you aware of something you didn't know about that perhaps is very dark, but at the same time you were able to enjoy the whole experience because it was tempered with something else that made you laugh." Music is essential to solidarity, he adds: "A song can go a long way towards changing your perception of an issue because songs affect you the way that a speech or an article or a document never could. Songs are meant to touch your heart. A really good song is going to do it in a way that explains the situation to you without being preachy or without trying to hit you over the head."

Land of the Maya

Brought by the wind they were mistaken for gods
the bearded men who came from abroad
they brought their rum, their guns and their greed
they ruled with terror for five centuries
shrouded in mist, gun metal clouds overhead
a teacher disappears and nothing is said
and now the widow is considered a threat
because they know she will never forget!

> In the land of the Maya, the stories are told
> Of five hundred years in search of gold
> five hundred years of murder and hate
> something to celebrate

Photos of faces on the activist's wall
they tell him he may be the next to fall
oh he can hear them calling out his name
he's got to try so they've not died in vain
he stood on a church spire, looked o'er the land
he saw the preacher and the slaughtered lambs
bullet holes in the mission doors
he saw the street children and their garbage sores

> chorus

ooh Guatemala, a sleeping volcano, a beauty in chains
ooh Guatemala, there's too much pain, you've got to change

In Chichicastenango there's a stone on a hill
It's broken but the Maya honour it still

> they pray for peace, they pray for rain
> they pray for justice for a people in pain
>
> chorus 2x
>
> brought by the wind they were mistaken for gods.
>
> —Lennie Gallant, 1991

Breaking the Silence member and Project A accompanier Brian Atkinson is a photojournalist whose photos and articles on Guatemala have appeared in numerous newspapers and magazines. Photography and writing document significant historical processes, he says, quickly adding that they offer much more:

> By writing, interviewing, photographing, and the like, you are telling the people you are working in solidarity with that you think their struggle is important and that others should know of it. Writing and photography are two of the most powerful weapons we have when returning to our home countries, when we try and engage the media, and through it, other Canadians in the struggle.
>
> Photography captures the imagination and emotions of people and can make what seems so far away and distant, more immediate and real. It can also tell the people who the struggle is directed against, or who oppose the changes that our solidarity work hopes to help facilitate, that a document of the struggle and opposition is being carried beyond the borders of the home country. In my experience in Guatemala and the Ixcán in particular, and on a much lighter note, it is such a gift to be able to pass out photos to the people you have met in the communities. (TI)

Julia Esquivel compiled *Threatened with Resurrection: Prayers and Poems from an Exiled Guatemalan,* "a confession of agony and hope, of pain and struggle out of the Christian faith" as "a small offering to the Guatemalan people" (Esquivel, 1994, p. 7). "Poetry served as oxygen for me, preventing me from exploding with pain. I had a constant pain in my chest that has now disappeared, thank God. I had constant nightmares about what was happening in Guatemala. Poetry was a timely channel for healing at least a part of the pain that was overwhelming me. But it was precisely because of this overwhelming pain that the poems had an impact, because they transmitted the terrible suffering of the people, especially the indigenous people of the Highlands" (TI).

Her poetry "brings the tears, the spilled blood, the agony of Guatemala into our own experience....These pictures haunt Julia Esquivel's thoughts. She wants to burn these images into our minds as well, so we will know

Solidarity's Creative Heart

Three women in the returned community of Los Angeles, where Brian was a Project A accompanier. Photo by Brian Atkinson.

and not forget," suggests theologian Rosemary Radford Reuther. Julia's poems have been read in countless liturgies, retreats, meditations, and prayer vigils. "Because I did not abandon Guatemala nor my faith, my poetry is infused with biblical language. It has been useful because many Christian people around the world pray for Guatemala and are present with us through their prayer and solidarity." Reuther points out that Julia directly connects Jesus with Guatemala's suffering, citing chapter 25 of the Gospel of Matthew:

> "I was hungry; I was thirsty; I was in prison; I was tortured; I was murdered and you ignored me." Or, "I was hungry, thirsty, in prison, tortured, murdered, and you ministered to me." "When did we see you thus, Lord?" "When I was the hungry Guatemalan child; the imprisoned social worker; the tortured and massacred priest." Here, concretely, in the sufferings and death of her people, is Jesus. Jesus dies a thousand times in the deaths of peasants and Indians and their friends. (Reuther, p. 11)

Suffering is not her final word. "But more than the pain, more than the deaths, the message of Julia Esquivel is one of life and hope. Hers is a hope for life so indomitable, so improbable in the face of the reign of evil that one can only name it resurrection hope" (Reuther, p. 9).

I Am Not Afraid of Death

I am no longer afraid of death,
I know well
its dark, cold corridors
leading to life.

I am afraid rather of that life
which does not come out of death,
which cramps our hands
and slows our march.

I am afraid of my fear
and even more of the fear of others,
who do not know where they are going,
who continue clinging
to what they think is life
which we know to be death!

I live each day to kill death;
I die each day to give birth to life,
And in this death of death,
I die a thousand times
And am reborn another thousand
Through that love
From my People,
Which nourishes hope!

—Julia Esquivel
Threatened with Resurrection, p. 67

IV
The Spirituality of Solidarity and Its Challenges

10   Creating Relationships: The "Spirit" of Solidarity

> To not make an option with the poor is to make an option for the rich. This is not just a political option; it is a spiritual option, an option for life in the face of death. It is a choice to find the experience of God in our daily lives. —*Network News,* Nadeau

SOLIDARITY IS "REVOLUTIONARY," claims Marta Gloria de la Vega, adding that it is "of the heart, of faith," not simply an intellectual response. Tito Medina speaks of "the mysticism of solidarity," a movement for political action yet something that goes to the very heart of what it means to be human. This chapter describes the spirituality of solidarity, "a way of being in the world at this time of great suffering and desperate hope" (Henry, p. 1). Based on the bond of mutual relationship, this spirituality insists that our human calling to be makers of peace and justice is not done apart from or "for" those who are marginalized, excluded, and impoverished in this world. It differs radically from the spirituality of those who close their eyes and hearts to the gulf between those with material wealth and the economically impoverished. Part A explains the understanding of spirituality used in this chapter. Part B describes a spirituality of solidarity. Part C discusses the implications of this spirituality.

A : Meaning and Spirituality

I had intended to write a separate chapter on solidarity's meaning. I planned to use "secular" language, since the term "spirituality" can be problematic. It can evoke the irrelevance or negativity of traditional religious upbringing for some or the image of "self-absorbed spirituality" where one "is turned in toward oneself and one's own family, property, race, class, gender, religion, etc. as the Alpha and Omega, the beginning and the end, of whatever really matters" (Heyward, p. 5).

However, I found it impossible to separate meaning and spirituality since those I interviewed often linked solidarity, meaning, and spirituality together. Frameworks for defining spirituality varied. Some spoke from within the Christian tradition, while pushing the boundaries of its institutional expression. Others saw themselves on the margins of Christian faith, seeking a wider spirituality than they had found within that tradition. Still others do not identify their spirituality with a faith tradition. Yet in the solidarity movement all have experienced meaning, depth, and life that many name as "spiritual." I am therefore using an integrative approach that articulates the rich meaning that has emerged from twenty years of solidarity experience.

※ Defining Spirituality

Spirituality does not refer to dogmas, rites, denominational membership, or religious practices. Rather, suggest Casaldáliga and Vigil, it derives from the word "spirit." In Western tradition, influenced by Greek philosophy, spirit has often been opposed to matter. People are seen as "spiritual" when they live without concern for material reality. In the Hebrew tradition, however, spirit inhabits reality. It gives life, fills with power, moves, and impels people, propelling them into growth and creativity. Spirituality therefore consists first and foremost in living with spirit. It is an ethos, an attitude, an energy, an inspiration. It includes the values that give depth, strength, and consistency to our lives—those we place at the centre of our lives, our purpose, our relationship to the mystery of life. The more consciously we live and act, the more we cultivate our values, our ideals, our basic choices, and our utopias, the deeper and richer our spirituality. Solidarity is a particular expression of spirituality, of living with spirit (Casaldáliga and Vigil, pp. 2–6).

B : A Spirituality Forged through Relationships

> We have much to learn from our compañeros. May we have the courage and vision to receive the gifts they offer us, created out of their own experience of suffering and persistent hope.
> —Maureen Curle, *Networking Action Newsletter*
> Spring Issue, 1986, Vol. 5

The spirituality of solidarity emerges from the devastating and urgent reality of our world where 80 percent of human beings live in poverty. "Many men and women in Central America and elsewhere are dying the slow death of oppression or the quick death of repression. This is the most basic fact in the world today—and it is a fact utterly in defiance of God's will" (Sobrino, p. 9). Yet middle-class Canadians tend, as theologian Gregory Baum says, "to reconcile ourselves fairly easily to the unjust distribution of power and justice in the world" (Baum, p. 39).

However, the ease of some Canadians was disturbed in the late 1970s and early '80s when the media spotlight focused on the assassination of priests, an archbishop, and four Catholic women in El Salvador. "Thousands of people had already been butchered in this poor, bloodsoaked country....The death of four American women finally broke through the media screen that diverts us from unknowing. We began to understand the deep, wide destruction of human lives in Central America" (Manly, p. 11). Lay missionary Jean Donovan was in her twenties when Salvadoran security forces assaulted, raped, and murdered her. Donovan's willingness to risk her life changed Project A founder Pam Cooley's life irrevocably: "That to me is love. That's what people are looking for in their lives—to give and to receive. Her death is what got so many thousands of people involved with Central America, including me" (TI). Similarly the news of the murder of priests and catechists that led to the departure of all clergy and religious from the Quiché Diocese, in order to protect the lives of campesinos, awakened Canadians to assassinations, disappearances, torture, and massacres throughout Guatemala.

Many journeyed to Central America to learn first-hand what was happening and why. Others wrote countless letters, made official statements denouncing the repression, sent material aid, organized solidarity groups, raised funds, pressured their governments, celebrated liturgies, and held demonstrations. Theologian Jon Sobrino saw it as a contemporary expression of the biblical story of the Good Samaritan. "Many individuals and institutions have made the church of El Salvador their 'neighbour' in the gospel meaning of the term: they have not taken a detour in order to avoid seeing the wounded on the road, but instead have come closer to examine the situation and to help" (Sobrino, p. 2). Startled by the unanticipated response from the North, he decided to analyze that response. Because his analysis resonates with the responses of those I interviewed, his framework guides these reflections, along with other Latin Americans and North Americans who have pondered solidarity's meaning.

※ A Spirituality of Relationship

> Solidarity is mutual support, where we carry the weight of a problem between us and this lightens the burden.
>
> —Refugee leader (TI)

Feminist theologian Carter Heyward sees mutual relationship as the very purpose and meaning of our existence. She understands mutuality as being interpersonal, social, and political.

> Mutuality is much more than right relations between friends, lovers, or colleagues. Mutuality is the creative basis of our lives, the world, and God. It is the dynamic of our life together in the world insofar as we are fostering justice and compassion. Moreover it is the constant wellspring of our power to make justice-love.
>
> By relation I am speaking of the radical connectedness of all reality, in which all parts are mutually interactive. The term mutual has a double meaning, both metaphysical and ethical, both mystical and moral….We need to help one another learn how to participate in building a world in which the radically mutual basis of our life together will be noticed and desired, struggled for, and celebrated. Ethically, the struggle for mutual relation becomes our life-commitment. (Heyward, p. 62)

Her understanding is akin to the spirit underlying solidarity expressed by those I interviewed. I anticipated that most individuals would describe solidarity in terms of political action. After all, these were activists for whom solidarity actions were of the highest priority, given Guatemala's life-and-death struggle. However, without negating the critical importance of action, they focus time and again on solidarity as dissolving the isolation of two solitudes, the affluent and the impoverished, through relationship, mutuality, and reciprocity.

When I had completed my interviews with Guatemalans, I observed: "Virtually every single person has said to me that the human relationship has been incredibly valuable to them. To put a face to something, to know that there are people who really care, that they're not alone in the struggle—that's something that's been communicated to me over and over again, in the most surprising places, by the most political people. They'll say that the political is very important, but it's related to a deeper question of being human" (Anderson, 1998, p. 7).

Jim and Eva Manly accompanied Kaqchikel Presbytery pastor Lucio Martínez and his family after another pastor, Manuel Saquic, was assassinated for his human rights work. For Jim, solidarity is a response to a spiritual yearning within human beings, "a deep longing for justice, fairness, and harmony. This longing begins with the needs of our own lives and gradually extends to other members of our family, tribe, and nation. In today's world we have begun to see all people everywhere as our brothers and sisters. The indignity done to one person degrades the image of God in all of us" (Manly, 1997, p. 60).

Creating Relationships: The "Spirit" of Solidarity

Canadians speak passionately of the need for "direct and vital" relationships. Michael Czerny says: "We are saturated with information on injustice and suffering....TV images are pornographic. They do not bring us closer to the poor; they distance us and only show us their most frightening face. We are ignorant of their hopes, their real difficulties, their real suffering" (Czerny, 1998, p. 55).

The Guatemala-Canada Solidarity Network's vision statement enunciates this spirit clearly. "There are strengths on both sides of the bridge and there are links that bind us together across the bridge. We have learned and are continuing to learn to work together by walking across the bridge and sharing with one another" (GCSN, www.gcsn.org).

Heather Carson says that her solidarity involvement has shaped her spirituality: "There's a real deep, deep place, but not conventional and not what you think of when you first hear the word. I've developed a much broader definition of the word spirituality. The phrase that keeps coming back to me all the time is 'breaking the silence.' To me the spiritual is linked to the personal as well as the social and the cosmic. It's all connected. There's a connection between my own life and the lives of people in Guatemala" (TI).

Daniele Hart, a lawyer in Halifax, expresses a similar sense of interconnectedness: "Solidarity has deepened my understanding that everyone and everything are connected to each other, and that we're all part of one reality. It has consolidated or reinforced and made more profound the understanding that we all share the same spiritual space. That's been the evolution for me. When I'm more involved and have more commitment to this work, I always feel more connected to other people, including my own family, my friends, and all of life generally, because of the [Maya] culture's appreciation for life of any type" (TI).

A worker in a Guatemalan NGO that focuses on women and youth offers her viewpoint:

> Delegations are important for two reasons. One is human sharing, the human relationship that gives life. The accompaniment relationship gives a lot of energy to both them and us—it is lived, touched, felt equally. The participants in delegations help us to charge our batteries. It is also a sharing that is not based just on an economic relationship. Rather, it is a very direct, very human relationship...not just a relationship on paper. Rather, delegations are effective because we here learn a lot and so do the Canadians. As well it allows us to know what problems solidarity is facing, what problems Canadians are facing, how they live, what they think, while they learn about the conditions we face here. (TI)

When solidarity is envisioned as reciprocity, Guatemalans have a depth of experience to offer, says a Guatemalan who lived for several years in Canada. "Canadians have opened themselves, have widened their expectations, vision, and commitment to a deeper relationship which is not just giving a certain amount of money to a project. Through a more human and deeper relationship with one another, a relationship has been built between citizens in one context and citizens in another. Perhaps we have different types of needs, but together we can find alternatives for improving our conditions of life. I'm talking not only about material and physical life, but also conditions of spiritual life, of relationships" (TI).

The work of the Christian Task Force on Central America (CTF), Project Accompaniment (Project A), and the Maritimes-Guatemala Breaking the Silence Network (BTS) has been based on a vision of solidarity as a two-way process of building respectful relationships of trust, collaboration, cooperation, and exchange. Gaby Labelle, a liaison in Mexico between the Guatemalan social movement and Canadian solidarity groups and NGOs for two decades, expresses appreciation for "the two-way solidarity option and the long-term solidarity option, not just solidarity in a moment of crisis, but the building of relationships between Canadians and Guatemalans, the people-to-people relationships" (TI).

The CTF approach, "We're not just here to help. We're here to learn," has broken through stereotypes, claims Marta Gloria de la Vega: "The people were very open to respect who we were, we others. That is essential in a work of solidarity—mutuality, learning to fall, to rise, but also a mutual respect. For example, we in the South don't have to fit into how someone sees us in the North, nor do the people in the North have to fit into the stereotypes we create in the South" (TI).

CTF delegates to a Chiapas refugee camp demonstrated the friendship that had developed over a decade. They presented cassettes of refugee children's songs and poems recorded by an earlier delegation and played in churches and schools throughout BC. They also showed them delegations' reports that, although in English, showed how the CTF had shared their story. They said: "These reports are part of our response which, although small for the magnitude of the situation in which you are living, has been made with lots of love and solidarity" (*Network News,* Marchal).

Finally they presented five *huipils,* the colourful and intricately woven blouses of the Maya women. These *huipils* had special significance. An early delegation met refugee women selling their deeply valued blouses to feed and buy medicine for their children. Delegates were reluctant to purchase them, since they knew these blouses represented their identity and

Creating Relationships: The "Spirit" of Solidarity 205

culture, as well as months of labour. The women insisted. So the delegates bought them, but decided not to sell them back home. Rather they would seek an opportunity to return them to the refugee women as a symbol of their solidarity: "We return these *huipils* to the groups of women who with sacrifice, dignity, and love maintain their faith in God and in humanity....We trust that your struggle and sacrifice will be crowned by the establishment of a society in which the love for life and peace as the fruit of justice will prevail" (*Network News,* Marchal).

Linda Geggie's account of the relationship between three accompaniers and a family in a refugee camp reflects Project A's experience: "Mateo took us to his house. They have so little and gave so much. This touched us very deeply. He and his wife and three girls live in a small two-room hut made of wood with a corrugated tin roof, no electricity, only a cooking fire, a dirt floor. Their youngest child, nearly a month old, Maria, was really sick and they hadn't slept for two or three nights. Yet they fed us dinner and offered us their home....When we departed, Mateo asked that we send a message to Canadians. 'The road we are taking is very difficult but it is the hand of our brothers and sisters that lifts up our hearts and hopes and give us the strength to go on. Many, many thanks'" (Geggie, 1993).

Eva Manly described her experience accompanying an elderly returnee: "We arrived at the crossroads to catch a pick-up truck back to Veracruz. Suddenly soldiers encircled us. They had been hiding in the ditches as part of a military simulation in which they were practising the non-verbal giving and receiving of commands. I would have been absolutely terrified if I had been alone. I felt very much accompanied by José. I know that he also felt accompanied by me" (TI).

Bev Brazier's prayer expresses the BTS vision of solidarity: "God, let this change me—let me not be a consumer of their pain so that I'm always thinking, 'Wow, this will really impress people back home to give to the Mission and Service Fund.' Let me not leech off of their hope for my own purposes, but somehow let us stand, each where we are, strengthened by the knowledge of the others' working and being. Amen" (Brazier, 1999).

Pam Cooley describes the most vital learning from her solidarity experience: "Relationship is the essence of being a part of any kind of social action. I attempt to develop the same kind of deep relationship with any project that I'm in now" (TI). Ann Godderis sees solidarity work in Canada as a community development process based far more on friendships than on highly organized groups or structures. "The work is based on personal friendships and relationships with people. I can go through a map of the Kootenays [pointing to where people live], all of whom contributed to the CTF Urgent Actions, received visitors, supported Project Accompaniment. We have a network of really strong relationships built up over the years." She notes: "The basis of all this work in building solidarity is encouraging people to break away from this individualistic culture into a sense of being part of something bigger than themselves" (TI).

From the earliest days, Wes Maultsaid saw that embodying this vision of solidarity required a transformation in attitude and practice:

> It was a time of rethinking a lot of issues. What were these development programs that we were doing? We were often talking about the poor of the world and how we in our part of the world could assist them in some way—a mentality that it was our Christian responsibility to respond to their needs. Then we heard a lot more about liberation, that the people themselves were beginning to look at the Scriptures in another way. It wasn't that they wanted to receive from us a kind of charity. What they wanted was to develop another kind of relationship with us at a deeper level. I think that really awakened in us a different way of trying to work. What made a real difference to us was the theology in Latin America. (TI)

C : Implications of a Spirituality of Relationship
※ Mutuality, Not Aid

"Solidarity is definitely not perpetuating inequality through charity," asserts Lisa Bamford, who works with refugees and immigrants in Fredericton (TI). She confirms Sobrino's conviction that solidarity is not uni-directional aid flowing from the North to the South, from the "haves" to the "have-nots": "Solidarity of this sort is not mere humanitarian aid, of the kind that often is prompted by natural disasters, for example. That kind of aid is obviously good and necessary and is a correct response to an ethical imperative. But if solidarity were no more than material aid, it would not be anything more than a magnified kind of almsgiving where givers offer something they own without thereby feeling a deep-down personal commitment or without feeling any need to continue this aid. In authentic solidarity the first effort to give aid commits a person at a deeper level than that of mere giving and becomes an ongoing process, not a contribution" (Sobrino, p. 3).

Enrique Torres has a unique vantage point, having lived in Vancouver for fifteen years before returning to Guatemala. He believes Canadians need to develop a spirit of humility and respect: "They must say to themselves: 'I enter this relationship searching, not from the perspective of "I'm on top of the hill and I'm going to give to someone who has nothing." Rather I go with the attitude that I am going to be present to this situation. I will offer what I have but I will also be open to what they offer me'" (TI).

For Antonio Otzoy, Presbyterian pastor and Maya priest, a willingness to open oneself to the suffering of others is at the heart of solidarity. "Suffering, pain, and hunger are nothing more than a lack of solidarity. The elders have a saying: 'The spirit does not accumulate wealth. The spirit shares. Only human beings who lack spirit accumulate wealth.' But we who do not have this spirit of solidarity, we want wealth for ourselves....And there is no way out for the poor, except for the way of human solidarity, where my pain becomes the pain of many, where my troubles become the troubles of many, where my weeping becomes the weeping of many" (TI).

He contrasts this understanding of solidarity with the more facile and common usage of the term, using Hurricane Mitch as an example: "If someone was physically present, many will say: 'Good, he is showing solidarity.' But to what extent was that person supposedly in solidarity genuinely opening himself to the suffering of the other?...It was said that there was a great deal of solidarity because many people came, a lot of food was sent. But in reality this was in no way an expression of the deeper aspects of solidarity."

Returned refugees also understand solidarity as a willingness to suffer with them: "Canadians don't have to come and live in this country. They have the option of living peacefully in their own country. But thanks to the conscience of Canadians, they came to suffer here with us. They suffered the heat, the cold, the lack of water, since there was sometimes no water to bathe, mosquitoes. We need to recognize the efforts of our companions who did not leave us abandoned. Those companions will always be present to us. We will always remember them because they came to be with us for months or years and we never paid them even five quetzals" (TI).

Accompaniers, however, are reticent to characterize their experience as suffering. Eva Manly said: "Some of the physical difficulties of accompaniment we can live with quite easily. It's like going camping. You know you are going to go home to the comforts of home later. We know the realities, like bathing in very shallow water, getting parasites, sleeping on bamboo poles or the ground or whatever; will end" (TI).

Yet they do recognize that at times their experience was costly. Liz Rees accompanied returned communities after the signing of the Peace Accords:

> What does it mean to be a witness in communities like Santa Marta, San Jorge, Salinas? There is such a startling sense of injustice here, now, when all is supposedly at peace in Guatemala. There is a weight to these experiences that one does not know quite how to put down. The thought of shedding it all is tempting yet terrifying. At a presentation we attended one night a couple of weeks ago, we saw [pictures of] the exhumation of four mass graves. There were images of skulls, bones, rubber boots—the unearthed horrors of a not-so-distant past. What makes it all bearable is a deep sense of privilege and joy in simply being here, participating at some level in the life of these communities. (Rees, 1998)

Accompaniers were fearful at times, yet their desire to be present to their neighbours enabled them to transcend fear. Bob Smith recalls his feelings accompanying Marta Gloria de la Vega.

> It was the first time I felt like I was really in great danger. I remember waking in Costa Rica the morning we were to fly into Guatemala, watching the dawn with the knowledge that the death squad had said they would get us. I remember saying to myself, "Now I begin to become a disciple," which some second-century martyr had said. I can remember walking out of the hotel and seeing the guys in the blistering hot sun with their heavy leather jackets, knowing they were probably plainclothes military or police. I remember making damn sure that I was between them and Marta and being surprised that I had done it....I remember Marta and I going to see Nineth de Garcia [a founder of GAM, the Group of Families of the Disappeared]. I suddenly realized that the great fear Marta was obviously experiencing that week in Guatemala was what people like Nineth de Garcia were living with every day of their lives. (TI)

Guatemalans contrast aid with solidarity. A human rights worker in marginalized communities sees aid as giving "something from your excess. Solidarity is sharing what matters to you, what sustains you" (TI). A trade unionist says: "Aid is always conditioned in some form and, practically speaking, tends to make groups very dependent and deny their own purpose and spirit....Solidarity is a form of pressure that unites people, a demonstration of the love between peoples. It is not something that is conditioned; it is not something that one gives and then withdraws; it serves no personal or individual end or self-interest. Rather its purpose is the community's development" (TI).

The director of a Guatemalan NGO worked with Canadians in refugee camps in Mexico and returned communities in Guatemala. In the 1980s,

Creating Relationships: The "Spirit" of Solidarity

he had travelled to Canada, seeking economic and political support. He outlines the evolution in understanding solidarity.

> Our idea of solidarity at that time was solely one-way, as if we were only going to receive because our needs were so great. We first realized that solidarity was not only economic; rather there was a moral support, a spiritual support that we very badly needed at that time, as well as a type of political support from the Canadian people to make the situation in Guatemala known. Then we gradually learned that solidarity is not simply one-way, but two-way. As you give to us and support us, we also contribute our experience to you. It is human solidarity, in which we must encounter one another. If you give me $50,000 for a project, it's good. But if you offer me spiritual and moral support and we encounter one another as human beings, it is far more than the $50,000. If we don't have this kind of solidarity, we are going to destroy the world. (TI)

He is not denying the value of material support. However, such support, when based on mutuality, openness, respect, and humility, is seen differently.

A Maya refugee who lived in Vancouver before returning to Mexico and then to Guatemala to work for indigenous rights places a high value on what to Canadians may appear to be small and insignificant tasks, such as writing letters or selling cups of coffee and cookies to raise money for Guatemalan projects. "When we speak of support in material terms, we are distorting it, because what they did was not just material. What they did was a great spiritual work that we must remember and tell to our children and grandchildren in the future. It would take two or three books to tell what they have contributed, not so much economically but in political solidarity, so that the people of Guatemala would not feel alone....The contribution they have given is a contribution that, from my point of view, they gave without self-interest. They gave because not only are they believers but they live their Christian faith" (TI).

A refugee leader sees material solidarity as only a part of the process. "Solidarity is a two-way process. We are in solidarity with you as much as you are in solidarity with us. You have supported us not only by your physical presence but on some occasions by your economic presence, material presence, providing clothing and other things the community needed. When we help you in your spiritual life through our culture and through sharing with you the value of struggle, that too is solidarity" (TI).

Three widows and the adolescent daughter of "disappeared" trade unionists described the excruciating fear, isolation, and poverty they suffered. They badly needed and received material support. Yet for them solidarity implies far more: "We want more communication directly with you. At the very minimum you should come to our homes and eat with us, even if we only have beans to offer you" (TI).

Gaby Labelle believes it has sometimes been easier for the solidarity movement than for NGOs to develop mutual relationships, since they have little money to offer. NGOs must focus more on project development and funding. When solidarity workers met with Guatemalan popular organizations, "they were aware there was no money there. So it was a different type of discussion" (TI).

At the Guatemala-Canada Solidarity Network founding meeting, a representative of the Archdiocese of Guatemala Office of Human Rights reminded delegates that when Canadians plan and carry out projects without Guatemalan participation all along the way we diminish their dignity. Partners must always be asked what they can give. "If you do all the giving, what have you left for us to give?"

Moving from a "helping" relationship to a mutual relationship takes time. CTF member Simone Carrodus shares her evolution: "My involvement is not about help. It may have started off as help but it's not about help" (TI). But Canadians still have a long way to go, says Wes Maultsaid: "I don't think we found a way to bring people from Central America into the decision making in our organizations. They were not involved in making the decisions about our work and so even though we talk about solidarity, it was still one-way. It wasn't reciprocal. We brought people from Central America to visit in BC on tours. But during the time they were in Canada what we expected of them was to give us an analysis of their own country, tell us the stories of their own country. We very seldom had them sit down and help us analyze our country" (TI).

※ The Impoverished Are Teachers and Leaders

> I expected to see material poverty; I did not expect to see such an intense richness in their emotional and spiritual lives. I expected to see, or hear of, suffering; I was not prepared for their joy or the profundity of their hope. I expected dirt and poor food and ragged clothing; I did not expect the beauty of the faces, of the smiles. I expected suspicion and fear; I received open welcome and genuine love. I went to the camps hoping to discover the humanity of the people behind the facts. I came back from the camps having discovered something new and profound about my own humanity.
>
> —Lynn Wytenbroek, Project Accompaniment 1993 report

Creating Relationships: The "Spirit" of Solidarity

Lynn's experience is typical of those who enter into a relationship of mutuality with the poor, claims Jon Sobrino: "Those who do so recover in their own life the deep meaning they thought they had lost; they recover their human dignity by becoming integrated into the pain and the suffering of the poor. From the poor they receive, in a way they hardly expected, new eyes for seeing the ultimate truth of things and new energies for exploring unknown and dangerous paths....They undergo the experience of being sent to others only to find their own truth. At the very moment of giving they find themselves expressing gratitude for something new and better that they have been given" (Sobrino, p. 11).

A refugee described accompaniment as a school in which Canadians are the students. Julia Esquivel agrees: "When solidarity is true, when it is authentic, it is not only an activity but it is a process of learning, a process of conversion which does not end but continues to deepen, clarify, and purify. It is a road of learning." She adds: "It frees them from their material comforts, their conformity, their ease. It moves them and sets them on the road of brotherhood and sisterhood in the encounter with the other. It has changed the vision of life for many people....It is a mystery how the suffering of some awakens and gives life to others, but it appears to me to be something beautiful in spite of all the pain and all the suffering it signifies" (TI).

Luis Gurriaran is a priest who has accompanied Maya people for over forty years, often in the most arduous circumstances. He lived amongst a community carving out a new life in the rain forest, and later joined the resistance communities hiding in the mountains. He has become convinced that the oppressed and exploited are "bearers of the good news of hope." This is a contradiction in terms for many Canadians. How is it that impoverished, violated, and exploited people offer good news? Surely poverty, violence, and exploitation are not good news.

Gurriaran is suggesting that solidarity is a spiritual journey in which the impoverished share their lives, hopes, and struggles with the affluent, who thus begin to understand the problems of the poor. They take up the challenge of working for structural and lifestyle changes in the North that are needed if life is to change in the South. It is a difficult, complex, often costly process. Yet those who respond to the call move from the bondage of consumerism, individualism, financial success, and cynicism to freedom and a sense of meaning in life.

A Guatemalan alludes to the biblical story of "the widow's mite," where Jesus contrasts the meagre giving of the wealthy with the generous offering of the widow with few resources—Mark 12:44: "For all of them have contributed out of their abundance, but she out of her poverty has put in everything she had, all she had to live on." He says, "Sharing, when you have little and you share the little you have and when someone has a great deal and shares nothing—this is the lesson that comes from the solidarity of the poor, from the people....The government can give five or ten million and it's clear that for them it is very little. But when the people share the little they have, they share it with love" (TI).

Another Guatemalan speaks passionately of the hope his wounded people offer: "When we succeed in creating a relationship of sisters and brothers with you and we begin to share our suffering, it is not because we want you to feel the suffering in your own flesh. Rather we want you to know that there is a hope that we have and can share with you who don't have hope. This learning and this experience which we give to you is incredibly important in order not to lose the human spirit which really is being lost in the Western world....This spirit of humanity is the greatest contribution which we as Guatemalans, as Mayas, as Ladinos, as the poor can give to our friends, our brothers and sisters, our companions in Canadian solidarity" (TI).

Generosity in the face of extreme poverty and suffering seems normal to refugees. Yet their stories make it easy to understand why Canadians were astonished by their generosity. A refugee woman leader laughs as she recalls her family's first meal with accompaniers. She had gone out of her way to add black beans to their usual diet of tortillas and chiles: "When the first accompaniers arrived, it was really hard for them. We even had to teach them how to eat! I remember very well when three accompaniers arrived at my house to have a meal with me and my two girls. I made some beans for them to eat. But first they ate the beans separately and then they ate the tortillas without any beans. That isn't our custom, and it was really funny. So my girls took their own plates and said that they were going to make tacos. They put their food in the tortillas and began to eat" (TI).

The coordinator of a returnee women's bee-keeping project states simply: "They learned what our situation is like, how it is to be poor" (TI). Another returnee believes the awareness of the extreme poverty of most Guatemalans was "a good lesson" for accompaniers. "They came to understand the reality of our lives, what our suffering is, what our sacrifices are, that the government of Guatemala does not give us any support. We have to put pressure on the government to get even a little attention, a little help" (TI).

- *From the Vantage Point of Canadians*

Accompaniment involves a willingness to be led by the refugees, says Lisa Bamford. "It is more of a secondary or childlike role. That's hard for a lot of us who have a model that is very different, because being there like a child and being led or not being the person with the information or not taking control of the situation is countercultural to us" (TI).

Yet when Canadians are open to being led, they are offered the gift of seeing life differently, says Eva Manly. "I always end up feeling like I have received a lot more than I have contributed, because it stretches your world view. Sometimes it turns your world view on end" (TI). Jim Manly writes: "The lightning flashes of Central America have illuminated our world; we have seen not only greed, sadism, and violence, but also people who speak the truth to power, who stand up for one another, who organize and sacrifice for rights and freedom.... In the lightning flash of these events we can see and understand our world more clearly, get our bearings so that we can participate in creating something better" (Manly, p. 92).

This passionate spirituality emerges from the roots of our being. It is grounded in "the reality that the injustice unleashed on the oppressed is so serious that it merits our unavoidable attention, our perception that life itself would lose its meaning if we were to live with our backs turned on the poor, the irreversible decision to consecrate our lives in one way or another to the service of the people, in order to eradicate the injustice of which they are the victims" (Casaldáliga and Vigil, p. 38).

Many Canadians are convinced such a spirituality can only be a burden, with overwhelming problems and issues too complex and remote to understand. Others associate "justice" with demoralizing powerlessness and guilt. To be sure, solidarity workers are brought up against the harsh realities of poverty, suffering, and oppression and therefore the tough questions about the meaning of life and their lives, and the realities of structural economic and social injustice. They are confronted with an ethical imperative.

However, solidarity activists seldom speak of paralyzing despair or overwhelming guilt. Rather they speak of the gift and the joy of community, liberation, and mutuality in relationships. They tell of hope and laughter as well as deep suffering. Guilt is replaced by empowerment and energy that lead to personal and collective action. "Contact with the poor touches the most authentic within us, opens life possibilities we could not even imagine, even inexplicable delight. The face of the other who is vulnerable calls me, moves me, invites me and helps me to enter into the solidarity process" (Czerny, 1998, p. 56).

Biodiversity researcher Judy Loo says: "I've met wonderful people. I have a strong purpose in my life that I think some people don't have, and there are things that are much more important to me than owning a house or many of the things that preoccupy us" (TI). Paraphrasing Sobrino, Mary Corbett remarks that the impoverished offer gifts that have a tremendous humanizing potential in a "structurally selfish world": "Those on the 'underside' offer us their poverty and violation as the opportunity for conversion to cooperation instead of competition, community instead of individualism, hope, faith, creativity; to demonstrating resistance, love, 'the certainty of meaning that we usually lack' and the embrace of forgiveness demonstrated in the acceptance and the relationship they extend to us" (TI).

Refugee legal advisor Alfonso Bauer Paiz said: "No matter how bad things are, change is still possible, and worth struggling for" (cited in Gronau, 1997). This inextinguishable hope against hope is, for many Canadians, the greatest gift they receive from Guatemalans. In a letter to her support committee, accompanier Tamara MacKenzie wrote: "I sometimes feel a sense of helplessness when I see the injustices in the world around me. Meeting these refugees and learning about their experiences, seeing how they have struggled and their continued hope and determination has inspired me. Their hope has given me hope." Bev Brazier wrote in her diary: "Mary [Corbett] talked about despair as a North American luxury. We expect *results* immediately. What we need to do is do what is right. Period. Whether or not we have a hope of succeeding. That reminded me of something Beverly Wildung Harrison said about social justice. She no longer believes we are going to 'win' this—that she does what she does simply because she has to look at herself in the mirror every morning. I never forgot that. Walking humble, knowing that I am not God *but I am me* and I have to be true to that. I can't do everything but I can do something."

The courage of Guatemalans sustained Heather Carson during a difficult period. "In the past year I lost my job because of a desire to speak what for me is truth. But when I listen to people's stories and what they live in Guatemala and when I think of what I've learned, what I've lost is nothing. And they're still part of the struggle. So it's sometimes a spark of courage" (TI).

After completing university, Margie Loo volunteered with a street children's project, then became an accompanier and Southern coordinator of Project A.

Creating Relationships: The "Spirit" of Solidarity 215

> From the time I was a kid I wanted to have an experience with poverty and a different culture. I always thought I wanted to go to Africa. At first I didn't want to go to Guatemala because it seemed too close. But I realized when I got there that it was a totally different world that was very close to us. It changed everything. Part of it was the reality of living in a different culture. It gave me a completely different understanding of my place in the world, what I have a right to and what other people have a right to. Look at how many resources we have in Canada. It is not that Guatemala is a less wealthy country. It's just that the resources are not shared with many people. You see things more critically. It's important to go outside your own culture and be educated and live in another culture in order to be able to see clearly. It has given me a deep understanding of the dignity and spirit of Guatemalans in the face of incredible odds, but it has also given me insight into my own land and culture. (TI)

Geologist John Payne was in his late forties when he accompanied the first refugee Return. Coming from a society where achieving "my goals," "my fulfillment," "my growth," is the prime purpose in life for many, he was greatly affected by a community where people work together to create a future for their community and their children. "It was a very meaningful, deep experience for everyone; being thrown into an environment that was completely foreign to us, quite a strange environment, a difficult environment. Through it there were so many positive things in terms of relationships with different people, and just seeing how people with nothing basically give you everything and struggle so hard for goals that are beyond themselves, for their children, for the future of their community" (TI).

Generosity, acceptance, and inclusion are even more startling in light of history, says Mary Corbett: "Simply by being a 'foreigner' from a place of greater wealth and power, I felt I was part of a presence that kept alive the hard memory of the colonization experience. To have been gifted with relationships, then—from deep friendship, to intimacy, to having a 'second home' experience, to becoming 'sister' to the Latin American women in my congregation—meant that, once again, Guatemala was giving away its wealth.... It was very precious, especially when it was offered to me by Guatemalans who are Maya and have been impoverished" (TI).

※ Critical Thinking Is Nurtured

> Social illiteracy means being unable to read—to interpret the events that are going on in society. Unfortunately, many institutions do

> not teach Canadians to read social reality. A good percentage of the population remains unaware of how society works or where it is headed. —Czerny and Swift, p. 56

Many Canadians have become socially literate through solidarity involvement. Sobrino observes that, when faced with the terrible reality of "the slow death of oppression or the quick death of repression," Northerners cannot help but ask the fundamental question—why? (Sobrino, p. 9). That was what Canadians asked when they learned of widespread massacres and the refugees' desperate situation. A few years later, as the massive violence lessened, more Canadians were able to see Guatemala for themselves and to question the unjust distribution of wealth.

Margarita Valiente and Josefina Inay were shocked as they experienced the chasm between the daily life of Guatemalans and that of North American church members whom they visited.

> **Josefina:** You have everything—televisions, fridges, and you can even choose what you want to eat, since everything is available! But our communities have nothing!
>
> **Margarita:** When we were in the United States, the table was full of food—potatoes, chicken, and everything! It was not that we didn't want to eat it, but we asked ourselves why don't we have this?

When groups visit women's groups, they are disturbed that people have so little to eat, only tortillas with chiles, observes Margarita. They begin to question the unjust distribution of wealth: "We have so much food. This is an injustice. It shouldn't be this way. When they become aware of this reality, they share exactly the same feelings that we have." Josefina adds: "They really see what the people suffer. They start to talk and reflect on what this means for them."

After Canadians meet workers on coffee plantations and in sweatshops that export clothing to North America, they pose questions that challenge consumerism and corporations' ethical practices. Who makes these clothes; who picks this coffee; why are they paid so little and have such horrendous working conditions; why does the Canadian government permit companies to purchase goods assembled in these conditions? In seeking answers to these questions, Canadians are beginning to do social analysis. In attempting to understand root causes, they unearth the historical and structural causes of persecution and exploitation. They learn that there is much more than a gap between North and South; there is a cause-and-effect relationship "between affluent societies where life and the most basic rights of the human person are safeguarded and societies where misery, blatant violation of human rights, and death prevail" (Sobrino, p. 9).

Creating Relationships: The "Spirit" of Solidarity

Analysis has been a crucial element of solidarity and is the first step in responding lovingly to injustice. It moves us beyond uncritically and passively accepting injustice. It refuses to give a charity response when justice is due. It goes to root causes, rather than responding to symptoms. It requires discipline and rigour. Jeanne Moffatt wrote: "Awareness-raising and action went hand-in-hand, creating that education-action-analysis-education circle. This means to say that we were all learning *while* acting and the action created in us a desire for more information and learning, leading to more action" (correspondence with author).

Gaby Labelle values the linking of action and analysis: "They [the CTF] were all trying to analyze the situation too—not just doing campaigns and support things but also trying to understand what the Guatemalan situation was about. I felt they were all trying to stay on top of what was happening and not draw conclusions but trying to analyze the different actors. I learned a lot from the way they worked, the way they looked at the situation and tried to understand before they did anything." (TI)

Solidarity workers question the attitude held by many Canadians that economic, social, and political analysis is the province of "the experts":

> **Eva Manly:** We don't have any excuse for not doing political and economic analysis in Canada. When you see people who are barely literate doing analysis of their situation in the global context, then it makes you realize that we are just either lazy or our sense of helplessness is so great. (TI)
>
> **Bob Smith:** It was the time of the Gulf War. I remember this person who was probably illiterate giving us the latest news out of the Gulf and using the experience of the suffering people in Iraq as a metaphor for what they were going through. Obviously they were listening on short-wave radios—keeping up, well informed, and very perceptive about systems that do those kinds of things to people whether in Guatemala or in the Middle East. (TI)

Economic analysis, combined with experience, leads to new visions and insights. After meeting locked-out *maquila* workers and analyzing the causes of their situation, Keith Hagerman and Carol Kell preached a sermon: "Economic justice should not be a luxury that few can afford, but should be the basic rights extended to all people. Only then will we realize that vision of God's *shalom,* the Kingdom of God, where the wolf shall lie down with the lamb, and the calf, and the lion and the sheep together, and none shall be afraid" (Hagerman and Kell, 1999).

IV – The Spirituality of Solidarity and Its Challenges

※ We Are Called to a Spirituality of Action, of Seeking Justice and Peace

The people I interviewed often refer to solidarity as a spirituality of action. Many find regular spiritual practices such as prayer, meditation, and participation in guided retreats a vital necessity, but do not see these practices as an end in themselves. Essential to their spirituality is both a transformation of their personal lifestyle and participation in struggle for more just, respectful relationships and more equitable economic systems.

Sobrino says shared responsibility with the poor for social transformation becomes urgent as the poor share their joys and struggles, their hopes and fears, and Northerners learn that our way of life depends on the exploitation and death of others. Jim Manly suggests we need to hear the voices of "the nameless ones" who died in massacres and assassinations. "What does our death mean to you? How have you incorporated our struggle, our death into your struggle, your life?" (Manly, p. 28). For Terry O'Toole, solidarity is a continual invitation to personal conversion. "It's never over. As comfortable as my life might be, the situation of other people doesn't allow it to remain comfortable" (TI). Judy Loo says: "When I began to understand what was really happening in Central America, I remember the realization that I had learned too much to ever go back. I couldn't turn my back on this and walk away from it. I just had to try to do something about it. That feeling has never gone away" (TI).

Diane Walsh, an adult educator, is still challenged by her 1995 delegation experience: "It was such a deep earthquake. I still haven't figured out the fault lines and where they go. The delegation for me was a faith experience, a spiritual experience. It was like: 'Here is the Gospel, right here. Here is a test of what it is to be a person of faith. Here you are faced with a colossal evil. What are you going to do about it?' The response of the people we were talking to was not a violent response. It was a real faith response: 'We're just going to keep building and constructing as opposed to destroying.' I still think of them now as inspirational. When I think of how people need to react in the face of evil, that's my benchmark" (TI).

A CPR member spoke very directly to Bob Smith: "You will be our Moses." Taken aback, Bob replied, "What do you mean?" He answered: "You are going to go out and tell the people of the world so that we may leave the place of the wilderness and return to the Promised Land" (TI).

※ Solidarity Is for the Long Haul

Archbishop Romero said: "We may never see the end results, but that is the difference between the master builder and the worker. We are workers, not master builders; ministers, not messiahs. We are prophets of a future that is not our own" (cited in Henry, p. 12). Beth Abbott, who has steadfastly staffed both Project A and the Guatemala-Canada Solidarity Network, often going without pay for months at a time, is sustained by "the approach of many Guatemalans that participation in the struggle should not depend on seeing immediate results. The idea that the generations to come behind us will benefit from the work we do today is an important one for all of us. Of course it means even more in Guatemala or other places where the work we do today can bring on untold suffering and hardship for those involved" (TI).

Solidarity is about committed relationships. As the war ended, Guatemalans were fearful that Canadians would forget about them. Solidarity had lost ground in El Salvador and Nicaragua when the crisis ended. I was reminded of this when I stood up to leave an interview with a Guatemalan woman who works with women in marginalized zones. She asked me to sit down and turn on the cassette recorder again. "It is incredibly important in the present political context that not only human solidarity but political solidarity continue. I believe it is becoming even more important because the Peace Accords were signed on behalf of all the people of Guatemala. The war ended and the violations of human rights continue—at the trade union level, at the political level, at the social level. Instead of solidarity lessening, I think it must be strengthened because of this same political context, because of the great importance of pressure in the implementation of the Peace Accords" (TI).

A union leader delivers the same message:

> We are still not able to see justice and peace. Repression continues in a more sophisticated, more psychological form. There is no real freedom of expression; there are still limitations. But even in this situation we are trying to re-weave the social fabric. It is necessary for the people to have the security of international accompaniment in these new efforts.... We are in a new political space where we have to put into practice what we could not practise for a long period of time, that is, we have to stimulate the real democratization of the country, because during thirty years of war, people could not express themselves. We have to build democracy. That is why it is important that the world's population, and particularly Canada, be present in Guatemala, so that they know what is happening, that they come and participate with the people and accompany them in this new stage. (TI)

Vitalino Similox, a Presbyterian pastor and 1999 vice-presidential candidate of the left-wing Alliance for a New Nation, says: "Solidarity has no end. It is permanent. You have to be there in good times and bad. It is constantly changing but we must carry on until we build this new world for which Jesus came. Until we see the Reign of God expressed in its fullness, we will need solidarity because I understand that what solidarity is seeking is the construction of a Reign where God truly lives among us because there is no disparity" (TI).

Aware that long-term commitment is challenging for Canadians, Gaby Labelle asks: "How do we make solidarity something that is naturally part of people's lives and not some momentary enthusiasm for a given cause? Do we stop at Calvary or do we try to accompany until the day of the Resurrection? I do not mean we as individuals but we as a group, no matter who leaves and who stays" (TI). Paula Shaw, an accompanier who stayed to work as a CUSO cooperant with Guatemalan NGOs, sees the danger of "trendiness"—"first Nicaragua, then El Salvador. Now it's Guatemala. Where is it going to be next? Once the war is over, then the real war on poverty and all those other things continue. Those are the wars that are much more difficult because they're very, very long-term" (TI).

A woman who returned to Guatemala from exile in Canada to work with marginalized women says: "There are people who left saying that, since the Peace had been signed, they were no longer needed. They went off to Chiapas or Eastern Europe or other places." Ending on a hopeful note, she says that those who have deeply invested themselves "have fallen in love with Guatemala. They are not going to leave Guatemala. I believe it is from this base that we can maintain the relationship, since in any case it is a human relationship among people, and it is with these people that we will continue working" (TI).

One Afternoon in Nueva Union

Eligio looks at me intently.
Swallows
says he's still afraid
the government wants to kill him

His hand makes a fist
in front of his mouth
he's only 12 years old
I want to tell him
they'll never return

> that he'll grow old
> and swing in a hammock
>
> I want to tell him
> that people in Canada
> really care about this
>
> I draw my knees into my chest
> look into his eyes
> realize that I'm scared too
> scared I will forget.
> —Liz Rees, 1997

※ Solidarity Is Circular

> It is essential living in North America to be in touch with people who are on the margins, on the edge. Solidarity has moved me to being in solidarity with people in the Inner City, on the margins here. —Kathi Bentall (TI)

Canadians who open themselves to the impoverished of Central America receive deeply. In turn, says Sobrino, the poor commission them to look afresh at their own societies. Yvonne Zarowny describes this "sobering and intimidating" process as "a loss of naivete":

> As the veils were lifted from our eyes so that we could truly see the carnage and multilevel violence that is Central America, we turned with "new eyes" to Canadian society. What were we challenged to see? Beside Canadian complicity in the violence of Central America, we were challenged to go beneath the veneer of our polite society to see the oppression and marginalization of aboriginal peoples. We were challenged to see the increasing concentration of power and wealth in the hands of a few; to see the growth of real, material poverty in Canada; and to see the diminishing hope for positive social change. We were challenged to relearn Canadian history to become familiar with our own popular movements for social justice, which were violently suppressed. We were challenged to realize the parallels between the Canadian economy and those of "dependent" countries. (Zarowny, p. 388)

Breaking the Silence members made similar links:

> **Heather Carson:** Solidarity is recognizing that the struggles the people in Guatemala are facing are the same as the struggles we in Canada

are facing. Sometimes it's easier to see it in another place first. It helps us recognize things in our own situation and learn from what they've done.

Wilf Bean: For me, part of the significance is that as we see the capacity of Guatemalans to keep faith that their lives can be transformed, we share our sense of feeling quite powerless in Canadian politics. We ask ourselves: "How do we learn from them to keep faith that this can be transformed?"

Diane Walsh: Antonio's big point was: "You have to try to transform your own reality wherever you are, or why talk to us? Don't just be interested in our thing down here. You have to be interested in addressing these same root evils in your own culture, in your own context."

Terry O'Toole: I see it as being involved in each other's history. That becomes inescapable. We can no more hope for justice in their society if we also don't have a focus on justice on this one. Their understanding of our structures is what helped me see that. (TI)

It is often said: Think globally and act locally. However, Guatemalan and Canadian responses suggest we must now think and act globally and locally. BTS members have identified numerous common issues needing work—human security, economic justice, environmental sustainability, race and gender equality, community solidarity, cultural diversity, and respect for sexual orientation. Sister of Charity Gerry Lancaster speaks passionately of the similarities she saw during a Project A Atlantic delegation: "I step out of my own country and then begin to critique what is really happening in my own country. More and more we discover that the same things that have happened in Central America are now happening in our own countries: deforestation, the fishery, our own natural resources, even to the point of selling our water" (TI).

The CTF has deepened its understanding of the need "to see the fundamental issues as the same everywhere—the neo-liberal, corporate agenda breaking down everything in its path in both Canada and elsewhere," says Ann Godderis. "In our newsletter, for example, we more frequently tend to include both Canada and Central America in the discussion of an issue" (TI).

Kootenays solidarity network members make links between Guatemalan solidarity and local issues such as environmental, forestry, and land rights issues. Some members collaborate with others to resist the health care system's deterioration. They march in protests, and undertook a successful campaign to retain the local hospital's social worker position. Some have strong connections with End Legislated Poverty (ELP) campaigns and work locally with low-income people. Most are involved with groups such as the Council of Canadians in order to challenge the corporate agenda.

CTF members Ken and Kathy English were poignantly reminded of links between the powerless and abused in Canada and in Guatemala when they led an Advent service on refugees. A woman who had spent months in a shelter for abused women shared with them her deep identification with the refugees' homelessness and struggle to find hope.

A Guatemalan leader values visits to Canada where she saw Canadians struggling with similar issues:

> Canadians have forgotten how they had come to achieve a good standard of living. It was the result of the struggle of many people who came before. I have seen, unfortunately, how the situation was different the first time I was in Canada, economically, politically, and socially. Each time I have had the opportunity to travel to Canada I have seen how the quality of life you had earlier has been lessening.... Sometimes we have the false idea that people in other countries, and especially the people of Canada, live very well, without problems, since everything is available to them. The truth, I now believe, is that problems exist in all countries.
>
> Above all, the opportunity to share a little of the situation of women was very important because one thinks that in other countries which are "developed," as they say, violence against women is not so deep. But nonetheless violence does exist there and sometimes one sees cases of women beaten, mistreated, or simply psychological violence. One realizes that it is the same as what happens here. (TI)

A refugee leader suggests Canadians think in terms of long-term reciprocity: "Perhaps later we can serve as accompaniers when you have a political problem and need accompaniment and observers. Perhaps one day we can offer our opinion on how to resolve problems in your country" (TI). Canadians are now thinking it may be useful, and challenging, to invite Maya people to observe Aboriginal rights conflicts in Canada.

Aboriginal rights are an area where many find similarities and links. Lillian Howard was a First Nations representative to the Five Hundred Years of Indigenous, Black, and Popular Resistance Continental Conference in 1991.

> When I saw the conditions of the people in Guatemala, I was shocked that in the '80s thousands of indigenous people in Guatemala were being massacred. I couldn't believe the horror stories of peoples and towns being wiped out completely.... At the same time, I was so struck

by the strength and determination of Guatemalan women, their will to survive. They were risking their life on a daily basis....I was shocked when I returned home, but also realized that I couldn't belittle the struggle of our First Nations' peoples, because we too are facing constant psychological genocide as we battle assimilation policies of the government....I realize that the injustices are happening still, and that history has to be written from the Indigenous perspective. The women of Guatemala gave me the strength to address this issue. (*Network News*, Howard)

After BTS member Judy Loo returned from Guatemala, she joined the Aboriginal Rights Coalition (ARC). During an ARC event at Tatamagouche Centre in the fall of 1999, she proposed that a witness/observer project similar to Project Accompaniment be initiated. A few weeks earlier 150 non-native lobster fishers had descended on Esgenoopetitij (Burnt Church). They cut the community's lobster traps that had been set soon after the Supreme Court, in the Marshall Decision, recognized Aboriginal peoples' right to fish for a moderate living. Within a few months a team of Maritimers who had been active in Project A implemented a training program for an ARC/Tatamagouche Centre human rights observer team.

Such perceptions led the Guatemala-Canada Solidarity Network to define its mission as working together to achieve societies of peace, justice, and equality, in both Guatemala and Canada:

We Canadians must learn to do a better job of sharing our struggles and needs with our Guatemalan partners. Our role is one of support and our relationship of solidarity means:
- working together to awaken social awareness in our respective countries;
- being profoundly aware of the rights of indigenous people and working consistently for the respect of these rights; and
- pursuing the goal of gender equality (GCSN, www.gcsn.org).

However, in the face of economic globalization, it is not just a question of identifying and collaborating on similar issues. "We should understand that a similar process of social erosion is at work, beyond variations in rhythm and contexts, in both North and South. Thus a distinction between solidarity with the marginalized here and there is outdated," writes Michael Czerny. "The more clear our awareness of a common corporate agenda for Canada and the Americas, the more evident became the necessity for mutual solidarity" (Czerny, p. 1).

Wilf Bean, Tatamagouche Centre program director, sees solidarity as "coming together to transform something you're both involved in. It's

Creating Relationships: The "Spirit" of Solidarity 225

not just helping someone out with their problem. It's doing something together that is affecting both of us" (TI). A Guatemalan woman differentiates between solidarity now and solidarity when saving lives was the immediate concern:

> Now we are experiencing common processes at a global level which have similar effects on us, although in different forms depending on who we are and what type of economy we have....So solidarity is uniting ourselves for common struggle. In the face of globalization, we need to be in a common front to find alternative forms of survival which can neutralize the effects globalization can have. To achieve this, peoples have to work together. Instead of investing energy in stopping globalization, I believe it is better to put our energy into alternatives that neutralize its effects so that we strengthen ourselves, because it is weakening us.
>
> For women it is even more the case, because the problems of women are the same all over the world. For some they are more intense, for others less. Some women in other countries have already gained much more space, much more right to be recognized and have the conditions for taking positive actions toward equality of opportunities. Others like ourselves are still searching and have to do a lot to achieve that. (TI)

Denise Nadeau also refers to our common participation in a global economic system dominated by a network of powerful economic interests. "We are all in the same sea, though not necessarily in the same boat. Neo-liberalism impacts us here in Canada as workers, homemakers, parents. Because our standard of living has been partly based on exploitation of the South, the impact on us is less; but the dynamic of neo-liberalism is the same—the rich are getting wealthier, the poor are getting poorer....Our solidarity can now be more of an equal exchange; in fact we are the ones who can benefit most from the organizing, the analysis, the skills, and the hopes of oppressed groups who are resisting both here in Canada and in the South. The realization that we have the most to learn is part of the dynamic of learning to be friends" (Nadeau, *Network News*).

Making connections creates dilemmas, however. Individuals and groups struggle with how to deal with the urgent issues they now see more clearly. Many have found the solution in collective work, forming or joining ecumenical and secular networks and coalitions. In discussing the need for solidarity to face injustice in Canadian society, Tara Scurr observes: "We don't have to do it all. We can share the work. We don't have all of the responsibility, all of the burden. We don't have enough time or money. We will do ourselves in if we don't use our connections" (TI). Many struggle to put into practice Archbishop Romero's counsel: "We cannot do everything, and there is a sense of liberation in realizing that. This enables us to do something, and to do it very well" (Henry, p. 12).

※ Activist Burnout

Solidarity often makes urgent demands that can bring individuals and groups to the brink of burnout. Solidarity activists mentioned that words by Thomas Merton serve to remind them that true solidarity must be lifegiving. Charlie Kennedy carries this quote from Merton in his wallet as a constant reminder not to give in to the temptation to feel that he can save the world by himself:

> To allow oneself to be carried away by a multitude of conflicting concerns, to surrender to too many demands, to commit oneself to too many projects, to want to help everyone in everything is to succumb to violence. The frenzy of the activist neutralizes his work for peace. It destroys his own inner capacity for peace. It destroys the fruitfulness of his own work, because it kills the root of inner wisdom which makes life fruitful. (Merton, p. 86)

The solidarity journey starts with a call to respond from the depths of our being. It continues as we confront solidarity's dilemmas and challenges. Many identify with Denise Nadeau's "constant journey" to struggle for the ideal and yet accept "where I am now":

> I have felt a need for a deeper spiritual engagement—a conversion of heart, that moves the option with the poor from an intellectual or merely political option to a way one lives and experiences daily life and relationships. I have felt the hollowness of frenzied activism as well as the distancing that happens in doing solidarity work with those miles away. I have felt a split between how I talk and what I actually do; or rather I've felt more a hardness of heart which has belied what I say. I have realized the need for a spiritual practice that helps me in my own way of being.
>
> I also live with major contradictions in my life, a white middle-class woman living comfortably in my own home in rural BC, while much of my political and paid work is solidarity with women of colour and poor women internationally. I still struggle with what making an option for the poor means for me in the long term—is it moving to live with poor people and shedding all my material trappings or is it working with the gifts and privileges I have to affect changes where I am now? How can I avoid paternalism and the old missionary pattern in

the first (not to mention learning to trust God enough to take the risk) and self-deception and cooption in the second? (*Network News*, Nadeau, p. 8)

11   Fresh Insights on Faith

THE SOLIDARITY EXPERIENCE has changed the faith of Canadian Christians. Part A of this chapter highlights some of the insights they have gained. Part B describes discoveries Canadians have begun to make about Maya spirituality's significance.

A : Solidarity and Faith

Faith is transformed and deepened by solidarity with Guatemalans. It is literacy training in faith, humanization, and politics for Northerners, says Julia Esquivel. "It marks them forever, touches their conscience, the core of their being, and makes them different persons. An encounter at this level of human depth does not leave them indifferent, does not leave them the same" (TI).

Mary Corbett says: "The impoverished, excluded, and violated of Guatemala turned me around full circle in terms of even my own understanding and way of living my faith, what I would tend to call my spirituality. The starting point for everything would now need to be from the place of the most victimized" (TI).

Ann Godderis's social commitment brought her into solidarity work: "It's important for me to be really clear that at that time I was not a Christian. I had never been really involved in a church. I was nominally United Church but it was only in name. I had such an overload of bad images about what the word 'God' meant, what the word 'Christian' meant and all the other vocabulary associated with the church. I had some images that I certainly wasn't comfortable with and I just didn't understand a lot of the deeper meaning behind those images. I was certainly one that you could say in a sense learned a lot or was converted by this whole encounter with people from the South" (TI).

While hosting visitors, Ann had in-depth discussions with people who lived their faith with a zest, depth, and commitment to justice she had not encountered before. Meetings, Bible studies, and liturgies she had begun to take part in began to make sense. She now participates in a weekly prayer group with social justice activists. She has served on United Church and ecumenical social justice committees and the Christian Task Force executive.

Bob Smith was an articulate, compassionate pastor of upper-middle-class congregations and a creative liberal theologian. His encounters in Guatemala changed his life, ministry, and theology. While United Church Moderator he travelled with ICCHRLA executive director Frances Arbour and Hugh McCullum, then *United Church Observer* editor, on a 1985 clandestine visit to Guatemalan church leaders. Ostensibly tourists, their real purpose was to make contact with "a beleaguered group of priests, religious, Protestant pastors, and laypeople" (TI). Bob accompanied Marta Gloria de la Vega on her first high-risk visit to Guatemala in 1988 when her colleagues Rigoberta Menchú and Dr. Rolando Castillo were arrested as they stepped off the plane. In 1991 he joined the first ecumenical team to visit the resistance communities (CPRs) publicly. In 1998 he represented the Canadian Council of Churches when Bishop Juan Jose Gerardi publicly presented *Guatemala: Never Again*, the report that led to his murder two days later.

Bob says, "I'd led a pretty sheltered life. I'd not travelled at all in the Third World and so all of these experiences were late changes." He believes his first journeys to Guatemala not only touched him deeply but also moved him "to a new place," to the inner city of Vancouver where he completed his pastoral ministry: "Solidarity cannot mean that I become a poor person any more than I can become a Guatemalan. Solidarity means that I learn to see the view from below.... I received a new way of viewing the world, an optic that I think is the authentic way. The phrase that I use to describe this is Margaret Atwood's 'the facts of this world seen clearly are seen through tears; why tell me then there is something wrong with my eyes?'" (TI).

Biblical texts have taken on surprising and powerful new meanings for Bob Smith: "I had always thought the biblical injunction to care for the widow and the fatherless was about as innocuous a directive as it was possible to find. Not in the Quiché though. It is a subversive act to care for the widows and orphans, one pastor told us. He has 150 widows, each with an average of five children, in his three rural congregations. He risks his life to find food and care for them, or to encourage them to develop small cooperative projects" (TI).

Bob continues: "It's so easy for people to get caught up in what is peripheral theologically and miss the focus on justice." He finds many theological discussions irrelevant, since he now believes that meeting

Fresh Insights on Faith

"Jesus incognito" is the only authentic encounter with Jesus. "The only Jesus that is real for me is the Jesus hidden in the face of the suffering sister or brother" (TI).

Since retiring, Bob has worked tirelessly to ensure that the United Church fulfill its moral and financial responsibilities to Aboriginal people concerning residential school abuses, however unpopular and costly that position may be.

Deirdre Kelly, who works for the Catholic Diocese of Victoria, has been on several delegations to southern Mexico and Guatemala. Relationships with Guatemalans have transformed her biblical reading. Texts reverberate with new meaning: "The stories lived in Guatemala are biblical stories to me. They can be put in that very context of what it was like in Jesus' time. It occurred to me that when Jesus was a young man, before he even began his journey, he was in the synagogue and he was handed a scroll. He unravelled it and found this one part of this huge scroll to read out. He said, 'The Spirit of God has anointed me. He sent me to bring good news to the poor and to release the captives,' etc. I thought: This is the central message. Why would Jesus do that at the very beginning of his journey? Why would he zero right in on that? Well! What a reflection! When you read the Gospel, read the Bible with that in mind, it becomes alive" (TI).

In a similar vein, Mary Corbett says:

> With the Gospel imperative from Philippians chapter 2 to "let the same mind be in you that was in Christ Jesus," I cannot go very far without recognizing the startling similarities between the reality and people who engaged Jesus in his time, and the reality and people I see today in Guatemala. Solidarity is what I see the Jesus experience as being about—making present the dream of God in the life of a people. Jesus did this by focusing more on the compassion of God than on the holiness of God, and that became a strongly social and political framework in his life. It was expressed in his anger towards the sources of suffering and exclusion—whether individual or systemic, religious or social. It pointed to an alternative social vision—of justice, inclusion, peace, liberation, and abundant life for all. (TI)

During a CTF retreat at a rustic church camp in BC's Interior, Julia Esquivel offered an interpretation of the Beatitudes that Ann Godderis still recalls:

> We did most of our sharing around a big fire under some huge trees within hearing of a little stream. Julia said it reminded her in many ways of Guatemala. She shared with us the interpretation/translation by a French theologian who interpreted "Blessed are" or "Happy are"

as "on the march." The poor, those who mourn, the peacemakers, and so on are so filled up with the spirit that they have to move, they are "on the march" and nothing will stop them. The usual use of the words "Blessed" or "Happy" are like we are patting people on the head and saying: "That's okay. You can stay where you are; you can be still and inactive; you can be satisfied because you are 'blessed.'" Instead there is this marvellous energy, this movement which is exactly what is present when we are with the people named in the Beatitudes and have the grace to listen and be open to what is present. (TI)

On the March!

Titanic task,
a divine task, ours:
to make ourselves human!
On the march!
knocking down idols
breaking chains
tearing free!

On the march!
Relinquishing ourselves,
advancing, stumbling, falling,
and rising again!
Moving on!

Fix your eyes always on utopia,
on that lost paradise
always present and always distant.
Powerful magnet,
unrecognized strength, denied, attacked
by the anti-humans.
Vocation first
and final,
a thousand times lost
a thousand times found.

Sole possibility
to live with meaning,
to know Life
to fuse with her intimately,
illuminated!

—Julia Esquivel, Managua, November 4, 1988,
from *The Certainty of Spring*

Eva Manly gained a new appreciation of the Old Testament while accompanying refugees: "On two or three different occasions, once with a priest and then a couple of times with a catechist, I heard people using the story of Noah's Ark as a parallel between their experience and the Old Testament. They talked about the period of massacres as the flood, and the CPRs in the jungles and the mountains, as the Ark, and at that time they were preparing for being in the Promised Land. They used drawings and illustrations" (TI).

Terry O'Toole makes connections between the refugees' return and the Exodus from Egypt: "What the people are trying to do is actually an Exodus thing….The most important move people can make is from servitude, slavery, and violence into a new kind of living or a living where they don't have to worry about violence and hunger.…It's that image of people moving out of that unlivable situation into one where they could be themselves, have their culture thrive, and not have to worry about literally being blown away. It was that kind of freedom" (TI).

Growing in faith is a two-way process. Guatemalans say the presence of Canadian accompaniers and delegations strengthens their faith and offers them hope. A widow of a disappeared union leader shared how God sustained her in the midst of painful loss and constant fear: "God gave me strength and courage to move forward, but also when Martita [Marta Gloria] comes to see us and talk things over with us, we feel encouraged. As human beings, we need a lot of spiritual and moral support. One person can help another. When we receive new people and share our story, it enables us to move forward" (TI).

A Guatemalan woman who has suffered serious illness and assaults because of her work with marginalized women, stresses the significance of learning from Canadians about a faith "where you think for yourself and don't go along with everything the Bible says. You have to analyze it." She has gained a greater sense of women's equality. "God does not privilege men in decision making. Women have hearts, they have brains." Encounters with Canadian women empower Guatemalan women to challenge the church hierarchy: "That is no longer the way it is. Each of us is capable of understanding and analyzing the word of God with you" (TI).

B : Glimpses into Maya Spirituality

> Our enormous capacity as North Americans to feel superior comes, in part, I suspect from our failure to give ourselves the opportunity to know and appreciate the culture and the history, and hence to

> recognize the genuine personhood of people from Central America....We must not continue the destruction and obliteration of the heritage that they bring. We must join, or at least not further impede their struggle not only to preserve, not only their lives, but their customs, cultures and values. —Chilcote, p. 146

A few Canadians have begun to open themselves to the Maya spiritual tradition and to support the post-war struggle by Mayas to reclaim their heritage. In Maya spirituality all dimensions of existence are sacred. "Nothing escapes from our theological reflection: our work, our planting and harvesting, rain and drought, human rights and popular struggles, our persecutions, martyrs and exiles, our dreams, our traditions, etc., since at every moment we try to respond to the current reality we are living" (Similox, p. 2).

A few BTS delegation members received a hint of Maya spirituality's vitality when asked to accompany Josefina Inay to pray for a young man with serious abdominal pains. She asked the family for a sip of water, herbs, and an egg. After using these symbols like a blessing, she began to pray intensely. She explained later that she grew up with the spirituality of her ancestors, along with her childhood Catholic faith. She later became Pentecostal, then Presbyterian. "She sees no reason why she should have to abandon any of those paths to God. Her openness to all the possibilities of God was something we would encounter more than once among the indigenous people of Guatemala" (MacDonald, March 31, 1999).

The next day Antonio Otzoy, a Maya priest and Christian pastor, met us at Iximché, the ancient Kaqchikel capital: "In the name of grandparents, both past and present, I welcome you to this sacred place." He believes passionately in dialogue and mutual respect between Maya and Christian spiritualities. "The exchange of religious experience is a way to mutually nourish one another" (Otzoy p. 8). Dialogue was never a possibility in the past, he points out, since Western expressions of Christianity condemned Maya spiritual expressions and imposed Christianity, negating Maya experiences of God. Dialogue and mutual respect are badly needed at this time in Guatemala's history, he says, in order to create a culture of peace, mutual respect, and tolerance in the context of death and social breakdown. "Spiritual and social development demands an exchange between two religious expressions based on life, justice, and peace" (Otzoy, p. 1).

We walked with Antonio through the ancient Maya site and silently entered a grove of trees. We saw a mound of smoke-blackened rocks, with melted wax at the bottom and a series of ash-covered circles. We were on consecrated ground. "This was the place where our grandparents came to refresh their souls and renew their thoughts," said Antonio. He prayed to the Creator and Former of Life, the Heart of Heaven and Earth, for permission for what he was about to do. He then led us back to the ruins. We sat in a circle. He laid out a woven Maya cross, a central Maya symbol, and explained the significance of the colours and the meaning of the four points of the cross, representing the cardinal directions, north, south, east, and west.

Asked if being a Christian pastor and a Maya priest was an oxymoron, Antonio replied: "If our mental framework is narrow, we will have difficulty making those connections, but the more open we try to be to the possibility of God moving within us, it is astounding how easy it is." He unfolded the bundle he had been carrying in a kerchief. It contained raw sugar, incense, tree bark, candles, kindling full of sap, water, and copal, a kind of tree resin. Each item was passed around the group for us to savour the taste, the smell, the feel and to share our sensory response. "I want to smell the fragrance of God," he says, a sentiment that struck a chord for many in the group. After explaining the meaning of each symbol in Maya rites, he led us back to the grove.

> On the ground made sacred by centuries and generations of Maya people bringing their finest aspirations, their most beautiful hopes, their clearest vision before their God, Antonio unfolds his bundle again and begins making a circle of sugar within which the contents of the bundle are arranged. While he prays, Antonio lights the kindling and the flames begin to consume the sacrifice.
>
> There is not one of our group who is not aware that we are being given a special trust through Antonio Otzoy, a fleeting glimpse of an ancient and hidden spirituality. While the fire burns and the fragrance of God is moved by the breeze to touch each of us, we enter into the spirit of this generous gift. (MacDonald, March 31, 1999)

Ceremony

The sound of the trees and the sound of his voice
intertwined, inseparable
The trees are our brothers with living spirits
enfolding us as we smell the fragrance of God
rising from the sacred fire.
    God is all around us.
God, the Creator, the Spirit of Life, Goddess
    Life's power through the ages, over death, over evil
The mystery of antiquity seeps into our souls.

> Our brothers the trees, the black ancient rocks,
>   the fragrant smoke
> but most of all, the voice
>   Soft—now Kakchiquel, now Spanish
> Gentle—rising and falling
>   like soft wind in the pine needles above.
>   But strong—so strong. Binding us here and now
> to this people
> Binding us to the mystery of the Creator
> through antiquity
> Binding us to the light that defies destruction
> Through the profound darkness of 500 years.
>
> —Judy Loo, March 1999

Jim Manly was inspired to write *The Wounds of Manuel Saquic* during a Maya rite at Iximché while accompanying Lucio Martínez after Manuel's assassination: "Lucio sat with his head in his hands. Someone asked if he was well. 'I felt the presence of Manuel and the others.' The time at Iximché, the ceremony and the prayers had worked together to bring Lucio to a direct experience of what we call 'The Communion of Saints.'...For a brief moment, the power of prayer broke through the iron curtain of reality separating our world of experience from those whom we think of as dead (p. 23).

Returning refugees have placed great importance on reclaiming spiritual traditions: "We had to hide all of our Maya culture because of the repression we were living under. We were left with a fragmented culture. So when we were in Mexico we didn't say anything about our traditions. But then when we were preparing to come back we said: "Look, we want to begin to rescue our culture because the young people are growing up" (TI).

Accompaniers caught glimpses of how prayer and ritual have enabled the Maya to sustain their spirits and dignity in the face of continual suffering and exploitation over five hundred years. When eight hundred refugees returned to the northern Petén region they took an extra day to visit Tikal. They celebrated a special rite in the main plaza of the ancient temples, a public sign of their intention to reclaim their heritage and reconnect with the ancestors they had left behind.

Returnees often identified sacred spaces upon arrival. In LaEsmeralda, a returned community in Petén, they chose a tree-covered hill, naming it Moisés (Moses). A Catholic catechist shared how much the community valued accompaniers' respectful interest in and attendance at Maya spir-

Fresh Insights on Faith 237

itual gatherings. Returnees felt affirmed by accompaniers' participation in the ritual: "We Mayas have Maya rites, where we burn candles and incense. It is so lovely, so pleasant. For you who do not have this where you come from, it has an impact on you. Solidarity becomes stronger when we share with one another" (TI).

Maya spirituality's deep sense of interconnectedness often strikes Canadians. Two active United Church members, Daniele Hart and Pat Loucks, describe how it has influenced their world view. "It's become more and more of a coming together," says Pat. "I think about the importance of the connection to the earth, the circle, the cycle of life, and how they [Mayas] live with life and death as a day-to-day thing. There's not a separation. It's like the one flows into the other and flows out of the other." This spirituality speaks to Daniele in a way that Christianity often has not. "At a deeper level the Christian tradition has a very similar way of understanding things. But in the way most of us have been brought up, there's been a more separating understanding of God up there, and us down here" (TI).

Ross White, a CTF member and United Church minister, summarized a lecture given by José Serech, executive secretary of the Maya Centre for Research and Documentation, to a GATE delegation. He described Maya spirituality's repression when a supposedly superior theology arrived with the Conquest. He then told the creation story from the Popul Vuh, a Maya sacred book that traces human existence to the sacred elements of water, air, land, and especially corn. He noted that Mayas often feel blocked by the traditional interpretation of the doctrine of the Trinity, which has no female elements and places men above women and humans above animals. In Maya belief every creature has a special relationship with God. Ross concludes the time has come to find common ground with indigenous belief systems like that of the Maya, lest Christ's commission to preach the Gospel throughout the world is misinterpreted as giving without receiving from other cultures whose teachings might help mend a broken and suffering earth (*Network News*, White).

Gaby Labelle believes the Maya cosmovision, especially its sense of the interconnectedness of the human community, is a gift to solidarity: "When you talk with them about solidarity, you are talking with them about something that is part of their spiritual life, a mutual solidarity. It's not just giving, it's not just receiving and giving. It's sharing a vision. We're more used to an individualistic religion where everybody saves their own soul or you try to save the other soul. But for them there is this dimension of a community of humanity, a spiritual community" (TI).

238 IV – The Spirituality of Solidarity and Its Challenges

Returned refugee girl carries corn sheaves with joy. Photo by Brian Atkinson.

Lennie Gallant's 1991 song *Land of the Maya* tells of a BTS delegation's encounter with Maya spirituality.

> In Chichicastenango there's a stone on a hill
> It's broken but the Maya honour it still
> they pray for peace, they pray for rain
> they pray for justice for a people in pain

Delegates had stopped for a day in Chichicastenango, a town popular with tourists because of its large and colourful crafts market, on our way to visit a human rights group in Santa Cruz del Quiché. Men and women were carrying out Maya rituals on the steep stone steps of the Santo Tomás Catholic church and within the church itself, using flowers, candles, alcohol, and incense, seemingly oblivious to the tourists surrounding them and the Mass being celebrated. Although we did not understand what we were seeing, we sensed that we were glimpsing a reverence toward life and an expression of a deeply rooted tradition.

A shoeshine boy offered to lead us to a sacred site for a few quetzals. We agreed, yet wondered whether we were going to see a show created for tourists. However, when we walked through a pine forest, having clambered up a steep path to an open space similar to that of Iximché, we knew immediately we were in a holy place. We quieted, as we listened to a Maya priest murmur prayers and watched him light candles, burn incense, and sprinkle alcohol. The youngster, whose father was a Maya priest, was knowledgeable and articulate. He translated some of the prayers from Quiché into Spanish for us.

Lennie's description of the meaning of that experience summarizes the value Canadians have found in opening themselves, albeit in small ways, to Maya spirituality. "It encapsulated so much of the spirit of the people there. No matter what they had endured, no matter how oppressed they were, they still believed there was a brighter future and a hope for them and for the country" (TI).

A BTS delegation spent November 1, 1999, in Sumpango, a Maya town that celebrates All Saints Day through flying homemade kites as prayer offerings to the ancestors.

All Souls Day, Sumpango

On this day, every year,
joyful throngs of kite-fliers
climb to the hilltop,
dwarfed beneath their huge creations
—nothing more than tissue paper, and glue—
but weighted with
dizzying impossible
colours, throbbing patterns
that carry
an ancient tale of
the fiery heart and soul
of a people.

And when
they release these gifts to
the sky
there is a kind of rising,
—an uprising—
an act of faith
that leaves me
awestruck,
humbled
by this passion for life
offering itself
in all its intensity
all its being
to the universe.

—Pat Loucks

12 Four Challenges to the Church

> The faith and hope of the popular church provides a different understanding of an active faith—one that involves risk and the cost of life in the struggle for social justice. The Central America experience challenges the work that North American churches might be able to play in the struggle for change.
> —Dykstra, p. 112

SOLIDARITY RELATIONSHIPS transform and deepen Canadians' faith. Yet when they return to their home churches, solidarity activists often become frustrated, saddened, and disenchanted. They do not readily find a passion for justice in the life of most local churches. They discover that "the notion of a spirituality that relates to politics seems foreign to both clergy and laity" (cited in Moffatt, p. 162). Their experience offers a challenge to the church to transform itself, re-vision its mission, and create a new lifestyle based on justice and community.

Many individuals faced hostility and rejection in solidarity's early days: "We found ourselves labeled communists because of our attempts to be truly Christian. Often the most venomous attacks came from within our own congregations. This was not the response for which most of us were prepared by our Sunday-School teachers or by catechism" (Zarowny, p. 389). In the mid-1990s Denise Nadeau described the church's lack of support for her struggle to live faithfully. "It is abandoning any pretense of making an option for the poor and is retreating to promoting privatized personal spirituality as a way of coping with the sweeping global changes people are experiencing" (*Network News,* Nadeau).

Michelle Jay, who works with immigrants on PEI, believes her accompaniment experience strengthened her spiritually. Yet she is no longer very active in the church. "It's been more difficult to somehow come back and be a part of a faith community that doesn't regularly, in my mind, address unjust situations of people in Guatemala or other parts of the world. Some people are very closed to that and especially closed to the challenge beyond the charity model.... Solidarity is a very small part of organized religion and not just solidarity with other countries or other people but solidarity within the community. It [the church] can get very closed" (TI).

Accompanier Terry O'Toole attends Mass with an extra five-dollar bill in his pocket. If the homily includes a concern for justice, he adds it to his offering. Most Sundays he returns home with the bill in his pocket. It is ironic, says Mary Corbett, a Congregation of Notre Dame member, to often feel that she is "on the margins of the church which planted the seeds of faith that led her to solidarity." Much of what happens in the church can also feel irrelevant, she adds. "If the way I ritualize, celebrate my faith, and focus my commitment is not based in the reality of the starting-place of the Judeo-Christian God, that is, the place of the most dispossessed, then it's neither real nor authentic" (TI).

Many Christians feel they no longer "fit" within the church that first nurtured their faith. Eva Manly dropped out of the church for almost a decade, frustrated with its lack of desire to seek justice. "It was the people of Central America who kept me from giving up on the institutional church completely" (TI). Jim Manly thinks those who leave the local church do so with good reason. "They don't feel nurtured; they experience the hangover from the nineteenth century of denominationalism; they find that the local church will just carry on regardless of what kind of involvement they have had with other people of faith and commitment" (TI). Margie Loo returned to PEI after almost six years in Guatemala. At one time she saw the church as an avenue for doing work on justice and poverty and considered ordination. Two years after returning from Guatemala, she said: "I have so much respect for people of faith in the church, but at the same time I have a real conflict with the church, with the institution. I'm really having a hard time finding a faith community like I had in Guatemala." She now participates in a Quaker community: "I've been searching through different kinds of churches to find one. I know that for me the community has to be people who are concerned about things like what's happening in Guatemala. That is a very fundamental part of it. If that is not there, then I can't relate to the spirituality. It comes back to the whole thing of the church as an institution....The church was saying: 'No, you can't do this because it is too political and we want to save souls. We don't want to save lives.' I found it devastating in the beginning because it flew totally in the face of what I understood Christianity to be about" (TI).

Ann Godderis is frustrated by responses to workshops she and her partner, Bud, have offered to help people work on the structural roots of poverty: "I've come to the conclusion that Canadian prejudice towards people living in poverty is deeper and more entrenched than racism, gender bias, sexism, even homophobia. It is such a contradiction that the Christian faith is all about a man who was born into poverty, walked with, and loved poor people. Our churches are so far from truly accepting that, never mind trying to live it out. When you think about it, the gulf between practice and ideal is so enormous I despair of it being bridged" (correspondence with author). Her despair is not complete. She ends her comments by saying: "This spirituality of solidarity might make a small difference."

Challenge #1 : The Need to Create Justice-Seeking Communities

Many solidarity workers believe that faith, though profoundly personal, does not grow in isolation. Like Sobrino, they believe community is essential for faith to flourish. "We must be actively open to the faith of others if we are to continually grasp the mystery of God and allow it to be revealed in all its richness.... Each person's personal commitment is something that challenges, stimulates, and opens possibilities for the commitment of others" (Sobrino, p. 34).

However they often find life-giving, justice-seeking community more readily in solidarity groups than in churches. For some that has meant exile from the institutional church. Others remain, committed to working for justice from within and to transforming the institution itself. Some who stay find the church a lonely place. "I meet individuals working in complete isolation who are not getting the support they deserve and need," says Deirdre Kelly. "That's devastating!" (TI).

The majority of those who have stayed have found or created a community of support within their local church. Simone and Jon Carrodus belong to Highlands United Church, a suburban church where small groups offer sustenance for their solidarity involvement. Simone quotes her friend Jeanie MacDonald: "You can come on Sunday morning and worship with four hundred other people but you need a much smaller group to give you community." Others find support "on the edges" of the church. For example, Mary Corbett and Gerry Lancaster participated in the Atlantic Ecumenical Justice Network and the Atlantic Inter-Congregational Social Justice Network.

Whether or not they are active church members, the solidarity community offers many the spiritual sustenance and challenge they seek. In reflecting on over twenty years of solidarity work, Louise Casselman says: "Solidarity is rooted in community" (TI). She sees solidarity groups as "ethically based communities," what theologian Barbara Rumscheidt called "sorely needed antidotes to the dehumanizing impacts of globalization" (Rumscheidt, p. 106). There they find a deep spiritual affinity with others from different denominations or with those without a faith framework. Michelle Jay says: "In some ways my spiritual community is the solidarity community" (TI). Jon Carrodus observes: "Those involved in the solidarity movement from different denominations seem to have more in common with people in solidarity than with other members of their church who do not see social action as being appropriate" (TI).

The Christian Task Force (CTF) developed in part because Christians in the solidarity movement were deeply dissatisfied with their churches. Wes Maultsaid remarked: "The churches had been captivated by the dominant culture and were in many ways reflecting the dominant culture, so that our theology was not liberating" (TI). They glimpsed in the Base Christian Communities of Central America the justice-seeking communities they longed for. "Members experienced working models of community that supported people while encouraging them to transform their society into one that was socially just" (Zarowny, p. 386).

Mike Lewis recalls the "fire in the belly," the passion to integrate solidarity with authentic community:

> So many people were struggling for meaning, for a way of being authentic in their faith by integrating action, reflection, celebration, and worship, which so often in institutional church life becomes a disjointed set of activities. Thus we experienced in part what we imagined would be experienced in a Base Community. Even if it was episodic, it nevertheless had the same kind of dynamic and quality of experience and a way of experiencing grace, if you will, that connected us with suffering, connected us with hope, and connected us with a sense of being part of something larger than ourselves.
>
> We created a model that made the linkage between faith and action, between, if you will, personal prayer and political solidarity, between issues in our own backyard and issues remote from the Canadian context in Central America. It offered a way of staying connected with the church, but it was not the church in the institutional way which had in a sense already driven them from it. It rekindled and provided another avenue for people who were already alienated to have a way of expressing their faith. (TI)

For Bob Smith CTF gatherings were experiences of "authentic church," exemplifying what the church should be: People came from a number of different faith backgrounds. They had identified a need and had brought their various gifts humbly to address that need and then discovered that when they came together they needed to say some words or they needed to do something. They needed to pray. So, out of their primary commitment to serve the world in that small part of the world, they developed ad hoc liturgies and life in the spirit. Nobody said, 'Well, what are the rules around admission to the Eucharist. Or what does ordination mean? Or could you please explicate the third article of the Nicene Constantinople Creed?'" (TI).

Ken English, a teacher in BC's Interior, affirmed the CTF model of community: "All those meetings and retreats and visits have strengthened the bonds among ourselves. Perhaps we have developed a model for a community of people who do not live together but nevertheless share an unbreakable bond. Our visits and contacts with communities in Central America have strengthened our own community. Setting apart large amounts of time in our meetings for community building keeps us going and strengthens our commitment.... For some of us living in isolated towns and seeing each other infrequently, the model of community that we have built is essential to our faith, work, and commitment to one another" (*Network News,* English).

Ken emphasized "Spirit": "Spirit glues us together whether 'churched' or 'unchurched.' We are not afraid to call upon the Spirit of God, to let it move us, to let it join us together. The time set aside for prayer, worship, reflection, and sharing is essential to us as community. The Spirit teaches us to be respectful of one another, allows us to share on a deeper level, indeed allows us to love one another" (*Network News,* English).

Solidarity groups have provided a badly needed alternative community for Christians committed to social justice. Jim Manly wishes, however, that local churches were more open to the experience and challenge of justice-seeking Christians, since he believes solidarity groups, with their specific focus, cannot fully express all aspects of Christian life and faith.

In looking back, Wes Maultsaid believes the prophetic and pastoral often became separated in the model of community he helped form. The CTF enabled Christians to be "on the cutting edge," but it did not affect the ongoing life of local churches.

> They didn't connect with the life of people in parish churches who also had a lot of other things to worry about, whether their kids were on drugs or whether they could pay the mortgage or have a job next week. You didn't have to go back to your parish and try to convince people who were serving coffee or making muffins that this was an issue that the church should participate in. So you could have your high moments by being an event person. That's what I often worry about because I used to do that myself. I went to a lot of events which were

usually high energy events but then I never went to a parish church for years. I wasn't part of a parish, worshipping where I had to struggle with the regular parish issues that people have to struggle with all the time. So I felt myself that I got isolated from parish life. (TI)

Although some did form ongoing spiritually sustaining groups locally, he believes too many, including himself, were dependent for spiritual nurture on CTF events such as Annual General Meetings, Justice-Making Institutes, and retreats. He does not deny the power of such events where individuals who often felt isolated in their far-flung local communities worked, played, and worshipped, together. "However, when we went our own ways, I don't ever remember being involved in a regular reflection group that was sustaining for the people that were in it" (TI).

Wes thinks ecumenical justice groups have a tendency to become communities of exclusion where a few people become close friends and become more and more knowledgeable. He quotes Father Bill Smith, whose solidarity with Central Americans inspired many before his untimely death in 1988. "We don't want to keep sending the same people to learn more and more, when we need to send more people and spread it out more." However Wes recognizes the need for community. "The formation of Christian community is not going to be so much denominational as it has been in the past. People go where they find life and challenge and commitment and hope. They're going to go there no matter what it's called" (TI).

In earlier years Bud and Ann Godderis say that they, along with many others, sought community through the CTF network, "but on reflection our roots are really here." They now belong to a small local prayer group with other justice seekers. "We wanted to pray and to have that base for our work, so we started a reflection group. I personally feel it is the most important part of our work, that all the rest springs from that. It provides the elements of reflective prayer and Scripture. It has become my church, in effect" (TI). Ann Pellerine, also a member of the prayer group, added: "Solidarity is not done in solitude. I don't think anyone can do solidarity without being in community with people convinced of the same truths. I couldn't conceive of myself only having the Christian Task Force. Without the local group I wouldn't be able to do anything. I need the affirmation, the strength I get from group members" (TI).

Challenge #2 : The Need for a Fresh Vision of Mission

The term "mission," like the term "spirituality," is fraught with difficulties. Many equate the term with going to other places to announce Christian faith to non-Christians and establish new churches. Latin Americans call the church to a new understanding of mission as taking common action with the impoverished of the world for life and against the forces of death. "The name of God is blasphemed when churches of any confession ignore the problems of humankind or relativize them in God's name or actually stand on the side of those who oppress the poor. The greater the solidarity of the churches with the poor, the purer will be their faith and the truer it will be in practice" (Sobrino, p. 27).

Guatemalans have much to teach us about mission, declares a Guatemalan leader: "The church takes as its mission to promote justice in this world in order for there to be favourable conditions for all. The church cannot begin to construct a political system but yes, it must promote justice. When it is promoting justice, it necessarily has to face injustice. It has to announce injustice. That is its mission. If it fails, it is falling into sin" (TI). This vision is intimately related to Jesus' life, death, and resurrection and his unswerving focus on God's Reign. Casaldáliga and Vigil suggest that Jesus' purpose was not to found a church but to serve the Reign of *Shalom*, a Hebrew word meaning right relationships with God and one another that result in harmony, wholeness, peace, well-being, joy, and justice. (The Spanish word *reino* is translated here as Reign. It may also be translated as Kingdom. However, I believe the word Reign is a more inclusive, less patriarchal term that more accurately translates the meaning of theologians cited here.) Whenever the church works for justice, love, forgiveness, freedom, and reconciliation with the impoverished, the dispossessed, and the excluded, it is working for Jesus' cause.

Maya pastor and human rights leader Vitalino Similox contrasts "helping the poor" with solidarity, which he understands as constructing the *Shalom* Reign. "Solidarity is building God's Reign where we are all equal, different, yes, by virtue of our situations, but where we don't see ourselves as superior or inferior. When we share in this way, taking decisions together with each person offering what he or she is able to offer, we are constructing God's Reign" (TI).

Canadians have formed a similar vision of mission. "Solidarity is a really big part of what I am called to do in order to live my baptismal promises, to live the Gospel," says Ann Pellerine (TI). "We are all called to be God's partners in working for *shalom*. To me that is the essential component of the Central America work I do. So those partners are all just as important as I am," says Simone Carrodus. Her partner, Jon, adds: "What we are called to do is to work for justice rather than just to worship God. Working for justice is working for God" (TI).

Deirdre Kelly grew up understanding mission as "proselytizing and then coming home and telling about it." Her view of mission is now based on the Hebrew Testament Jubilee vision in which debt is cancelled, land restored to the landless, and slaves released. It offers "a new dream for ourselves and for those in Central America" through working *with* the poor, in an attitude of respect and understanding (TI).

Theologian Juan Pico suggests that solidarity acts are similar to Jesus' responses to hunger, social segregation, illness as both suffering and social stigma, the commercialization of religion, and religious oppression (Pico, 1985). For Vitalino Similox, Jesus' life and teachings are the primary source for understanding solidarity: "You have to start from the solidarity of Jesus Christ who made himself equal with us, experienced the most painful suffering a human being could undergo, lived a difficult life, having renounced a series of human privileges, including wealth and power. Instead he opted for the poor, identified with their cause, and lived for this cause until his death at the hands of the politicians, religious leaders, and military officers of his time" (TI).

Julia Esquivel says: "When Jesus began his ministry on earth, he moved among poor people, the marginalized, the condemned of the earth....That was why he was called a wine drinker and a friend of innkeepers. He moved about in that environment, showing solidarity. They didn't call it that in the Gospels, but the healings, the cures, the multiplication of the loaves, the teaching to give a drink to those who are thirsty, visit the prisoner, give food to the hungry, clothe the naked—that is the language of solidarity....He was a brother to people from very far away, very different, very poor people. He transcended differences in language, culture, and social and economic levels" (TI).

Jesus' teaching of "love of neighbour" is basic to this vision of mission. Marta Gloria de la Vega began her reflections on faith and solidarity by emphasizing how Jesus' teaching about the relationship with "my neighbour" is fundamental. Faith is not just about "my individual relationship with God." It is about the relationship with "my sister, my brother." Margarita Valiente puts it this way: "If we weep with those who weep, if we laugh with those who laugh, if we suffer with those who suffer, that has Christian meaning. I therefore believe that what you and we are doing has Christian meaning because we are fulfilling the Bible, not only with words but with acts" (TI).

A woman refugee leader believes the Gospel calls for relationship to be at the very heart of the church's life: "Holy Scripture teaches us we can't live alone in this world without the love and friendship of sisters and brothers who live in solidarity. We can say that the spirit of Christianity is to be in solidarity with one another, to understand our neighbour's need. That is why Jesus Christ came." In her mind the historical Jesus, the human calling to be in solidarity, and the experience as refugees in Mexico are deeply related. She compares the Mexican peasants who, motivated by Christian faith, offered the refugees "a hand of solidarity" with the shepherds, "the humble people" who were the first to accompany Jesus (TI).

Only a few years earlier most refugees had never encountered foreigners. They welcomed accompaniers into their midst who were different from themselves in every way—race, culture, class, language. To quote a catechist in a returned community, "Jesus said that solidarity is love for one another. With that teaching we feel as a brother and sister to everyone. We have one God and one faith. When we are accompanied, we feel like we are one family" (TI).

The response of a couple in a returned refugee community makes the generous, even sacrificial, nature of love of neighbour even clearer.

> **AP:** The accompanier is not one of our people but is different. I think that here we're practising our Christian faith since we don't reject them because they are from another country or for their skin colour, their height. I believe this is very important.
>
> **MS:** On the contrary, we were worried about what they were going to eat. Sometimes we had no beans, so we looked for eggs. (TI)

> *Para ti* (*For you*)
>
> Maria places eggs
> in my hands
> two smooth ovals
> fragile gifts
> I cup in the nest
> of my palms
>
> I look up at her eyes
> feel my shell
> begin to crack
> I open slowly
> to what's inside
> her worn hands
> connecting
> with mine
>
> —Liz Rees, 1997

Having decided to deepen its relationship with the Kaqchikel Presbytery, BTS struggled with how best to develop a mutual relationship. We had met deeply compassionate individuals who had participated in short-term service projects in Guatemala, such as medical teams and construction projects (schools, churches, health clinics). Yet it often seemed that the principal and sometimes only relationship was of donor to recipient. There was little opportunity for those being helped to share their lives, culture, knowledge, and skills, much less any time given to help the visitors understand the root causes of the poverty of those whom they were serving.

Comparing two approaches to mission by US churches helped BTS clarify what it was seeking. It may also offer congregations an understanding of how they might approach mission. These examples are not offered in order to judge committed volunteers who want to express their love of neighbour in concrete ways. Rather the intent is to encourage project and program development that is mutual and enriching for all.

The first example involves an American health workers' team who volunteered a week of their time to offer health clinics in two locales. The clinics were sorely needed by families with little access to health services and ongoing medical concerns, especially parasites and respiratory problems. In the Presbyterian Church of Guatemala's seminary, the team offered a workshop for Presbyterian laypeople being trained as health promoters in their local communities, then worked alongside a few of them in a one-day clinic. The workshop and clinic were lively and interactive, but in the evening, each group went its separate way, losing an opportunity to evaluate, plan for the future, and build an ongoing relationship.

The team then set out early one morning for a Maya community. Upon arrival, they immediately plunged into their work and worked all day, not even stopping to eat. Villagers arrived in large numbers and expressed their gratitude for the health care, although aware it was a temporary solution. The team spent little time getting to know the people. Community members were not able to offer hospitality to their guests, a fundamental aspect of their culture; photos and stories were not exchanged; no ongoing relationship was developed.

The team departed without discovering a major cause of their health problems, lack of food. Corn and beans had run out. It was not yet harvest time. Many, in order to earn some money, were about to migrate to the tropical south coast to work in exploitative conditions. Villagers had no time to express their concern about a lack of a health clinic or their desire to train community members as health promoters. The community had suffered enormously from army violence, yet the volunteers were not aware of this, nor did they reflect on the culpability of their own government and their responsibility to influence US policies. The health team offered a much-needed service, but they restricted themselves to a donor-recipient relationship. They lost an opportunity to develop the mutuality essential to solidarity.

The Needham Congregational Church, "the establishment church" in an affluent Boston suburb, has taken another approach. The friendship that has grown between the village of Santa María Tzejá in the Ixcán rain forest and the Needham Church shows the possibilities of an intentional, long-term, people-to-people approach (Taylor with Rhoads, 1996).

Ironically, the relationship with this village, slowly rebuilding after the ravages of the army's violence, began when the church refused to offer sanctuary to refugees facing deportation. It did agree, however, to form a committee to investigate how it might become more involved in justice and peace work. After Clark Taylor had described a recent journey to Santa María Tzejá, the committee agreed to explore forming a partnership with the village.

Moved by the scars of violence they encountered, the first delegation in 1986 undertook a deeper analysis of Guatemala and recommended that the congregation develop an ongoing relationship with the village. "Throughout this process the villagers of Santa María Tzejá have been our partners. They have told us their stories—shared their suffering, their faith, their needs, their hopes" (Taylor with Rhoads).

They recruited committee members with varying perspectives in order to convince the congregation that this was not a project of a few "radicals" but rather a moral commitment. After an educational process, many in the congregation committed themselves to continue the relationship and to work for peace and justice in Guatemala. The church now sends twice-yearly delegations whose primary commitment is to "listen carefully and try to absorb everything." They have a few "ironclad" principles:

- Accompany the people at their request in their work toward a strong and secure community;
- Work with the people and respond to their priorities;
- Do only that which will promote unity in the community;
- Give no gifts of material value to individuals; and
- Keep development subordinate to people-to-people interaction.

The relationship has nourished both communities:

Santa María Tzejá: While the villagers have been grateful for this support in the face of their own government's neglect of them (for some it has been the primary, if not only, reward of the relationship), many individuals have expressed their views that the partnership carries more important, less tangible benefits. First among these is the perception that Needham's twice-yearly visits to the village provide a measure of security against a repeat of the violence that earlier destroyed it. Moreover, some villagers have expressed the hope and desire that the relationship will continue into future generations.

Needham: In addition to providing an outlet for social action, the partnership we enjoy with the village of Santa María Tzejá has altered the lives of a number of individuals in Needham in more dramatic ways. Some have changed or redirected their careers, and several of our young people have been motivated to pursue study and activism related to Latin American issues. Indeed, the intertwined issues of poverty and affluence remain constantly before the Needham Congregational Church in large measure because of our involvement with Santa María Tzejá. We who have so much are discovering, as our relationship with Santa María Tzejá deepens, that we bear a certain responsibility for the community's deprivations and that political justice cannot be divorced from economic justice. Such realizations in turn bear upon our understanding of American domestic and foreign policy. (Taylor with Rhoads)

The church has funded projects such as construction of a health clinic and school, and training for health and education promoters. They struggle continually with the "nettlesome" issue of paternalism. "It never goes away. It is, in fact, unavoidable for those who seek to work responsibly across distance, culture, gender, race, and class. Minimizing paternalism demands constant reflection in the midst of action and the best mentoring available to sharpen reflection." However, they believe financial support is valid, when there is a commitment to friendship and to mutual planning and decision making, along with "a relentless commitment for structural change and social justice, both in Guatemala and the US" (Taylor with Rhoads).

In 1980, the congregation saw itself as "a caring community," with caring focused inward. A decade later, it defined itself as a church in mission and worship, with each activity reinforcing the other. Not only has it maintained links with Guatemala but it has begun a relationship with an inner-city school, using many of the same principles. The authors conclude that the church offers "a faith context which, however conservative and inwardly directed it may be, contains within it a moral framework for action....The church is still far from committing itself to the liberation of the oppressed in the Third, or even the First World. It is still a suburban, establishment church in an affluent town. But it has clearly moved away

Challenge #3 : Whole World Ecumenism

> I have been learning a beautiful and harsh truth, that the Christian faith does not separate us from the world but immerses us in it: that the Church, therefore, is not a fortress set apart from the city, but a follower of the Jesus who loved, worked, struggled, and died in the midst of the city.
> —Archbishop Romero, cited in *Mending the World*, p. 19

A radically new ecumenism is needed, argues Sobrino, suggesting that the most scandalous division the church must face is not disunity among denominations or between Christians and those of no faith. It is the division between life and death, between those who die because of oppression and those who live because of it. Solidarity does not arise because the struggle for justice is defined as Christian, claims Juan Pico. "It arises because the project is understood as human and humanizing; it does not need any supplemental religious legitimation above and beyond its inherent legitimacy....Where there is a thrust for life and a human struggle for that thrust, the force of life in Jesus Christ is at work (John 3: 20–21)....The task of Christians is to share the insights they receive from their faith to humanity's task of creating shalom" (Pico, pp. 61–63).

Mending the World: An Ecumenical Vision for Healing and Reconciliation, a United Church of Canada report on interfaith relations, offers a similar view. Human life is life in relationship with one another and with nature, "not just our kinfolk, or our kind." Whereas traditional ecumenical activity has been church-centred, placing emphasis on the churches as they relate to one another both in matters of faith and service, the broader ecumenism is world-centred, placing emphasis on churches relating to the world beyond themselves, to persons involved in other religious traditions, ideologies, and secular agencies. In this understanding of 'whole world ecumenism,' the churches are called to make common cause with individuals and institutions of good will who are committed to compassion, peace, and justice in the world" (*Mending the World*, p. 2).

Solidarity has taught Deirdre Kelly the absolute necessity of whole world ecumenism: "When Bob Smith goes down to Bishop Gerardi's announcement of *Nunca Mas* (*Guatemala: Never Again*, the Catholic Church's human rights report) and Gerardi a few days later is assassinated, Bob brings that message to all of us, not just to Protestants or to Christians" (TI).

Many Christians assume their commitment to justice should be expressed primarily through involvement in church groups of their denomination. Solidarity challenges that notion. "Anybody was accepted in the CTF—United Church, Anglican, Mennonite, Lutherans, Presbyterians, even some people who were not Christians," recalls Enrique Torres. "There were no constraints from any denomination. The key was the Christian mandate of charity. It was a commitment. We were bound together by Christ's message to love our brethren" (TI).

Collaboration with non-Christians and participation in secular groups are equally expressions of whole world ecumenism. Deirdre says: "We can't work all by ourselves.... There is no other way that it's going to work. In order to move forward, strategically we have to. But I don't think it's just strategic. We're called to live with differences and work with differences" (TI).

Tara Scurr goes further: "I don't think the CTF is ecumenical enough." She believes alternative kinds of spirituality are being left out and points to the Kootenays YouthGATE trip as a model, where Baha'i, evangelical, and Catholic youth were involved (TI).

Jim Manly comments: "Central American solidarity movements are very important for the church because often some of the really important work has been done by groups that aren't related to the church. Indeed some of them have had a traditional antipathy to the church, but as we share common objectives in solidarity, we develop new respect for each other, so that we learn through solidarity" (TI).

Canadians who want to work overseas in support of the church's mission often believe this implies serving with the church. The solidarity experience challenges that notion. For many Christians, work with secular solidarity groups has been a valued means of expressing their faith. Mennonite Randy Janzen saw accompaniment as "a calling...to hear the words of Christ and to make a difference in this world through acts of love and faith." Project A allowed United Church member John Payne to live out his faith beyond the church walls: "I hadn't done this kind of thing before. I had worked in the church, put my money in the plate, and then done music with the kids and a lot of things fairly close to home. But I never actually had gone out, in a sense on the mission field, you might say, getting out and involved with people in a struggle, particularly a struggle for justice" (TI).

Some Christians feel more at home in church groups. However, with good will and openness, that need not be a huge problem, as Deirdre Kelly discovered: "When I first started to work in the Central America Support

Committee, I think I was the only one coming from a Christian base. Again, all I had to do was learn. I didn't know my history as well as they did. They had things they taught me and I hope I had something to teach them, as well" (TI).

Simone Carrodus views collaborative work with unions as a highlight of her CTF. As she worked with trade unionists on the issue of *maquilas*, discussing educational and action strategies and planning major events such as a *maquila* fashion show, stereotypes broke down. They came to see each other as partners working for a common goal: "What I might call *shalom*, he might call workers' rights, with an understanding being that we can work together, that we need to address each other as sisters and brothers" (TI).

Project A was a secular organization supported by both NGOs and churches, but strongly influenced by Christian faith perspectives to solidarity and accompaniment. Guatemalans valued this model of cooperation. "We understood there were joint efforts by churches, other groups, and individuals with excellent results," says a refugee leader (TI).

Wes Maultsaid believes Project A demonstrates the value of moving beyond denominational boundaries to support secular organizations where Christians find a place. Daniele Hart summarizes the attitude of many who supported Project A: "If Project Accompaniment is meeting the goals, the larger vision of the church in terms of what we are trying to accomplish, what the mission is trying to accomplish, then who cares if it's with the church?" Beth Abbott remarks, "I have appreciated how Project A has managed to mean so much to so many people with and without the church component." She recalls that a draft application form included a question about accompaniment in the context of faith. It was deleted, so as not to scare off applicants who did not use "churchy language." Mary Corbett values Breaking the Silence as a group that welcomes both those with and without a faith orientation: "I don't want my participation in the Network to be experienced as trying to "bring religion" into the group. My concern is that nobody in the group feels constrained to fit into a religious framework. That being said, BTS is a very privileged place for the mission of God, as I understand it. To be working in collaboration with others who have experienced a motivation that draws them to a response like this transcends for me any denominational or religious boundaries or structures. I believe it comes from our deepest and most commonly held motivations, dreams, and values." (TI)

BTS leadership has tried to foster an atmosphere of openness and respect in delegations and gatherings that allows people to speak from their experience and convictions. Some members have at times felt tension between those who come into BTS from a faith base and those who do not. There are always some who feel uneasy in a group not based on Christian faith. Michelle Jay sees the other side of the coin: "There have been a few times when there have been people involved in certain solidarity meetings or gatherings who felt that there were too many assumptions about everyone being a spiritual person in a religious or church sense." (TI)

As with Project A, the passionate desire to work together in the face of injustice has enabled members to live with these tensions and build deep and lasting friendships that transcend faith boundaries. Mary Corbett cherishes friendships she has made: "I'm racing to catch up to the depth of commitment of other people who identify themselves as not having a religious or faith context. I often experience them as being miles ahead of me in terms of quality and depth of commitment. I've had so many experiences of knowing that I am part of a church which, with its own acknowledged mistakes and injustice, can still be so restrictive, exclusionary, and even condemnatory of some people it sees as 'outside the lines' that I feel grateful and privileged that they will even offer me the possibility of relationship" (TI).

Mission as solidarity means that Canadian churches must develop relationships with non-church partners. Church-to-church partnerships are natural, notes a Guatemalan, but churches "must strengthen other groups working for justice as well…although they are not of the church. To share with those who are lacking means not only with my brothers and sisters in the church but to all in need, whether or not they are members of my church" (TI). Lyn Kerans is encouraged by United Church support for solidarity work. "It's very affirming of the Spirit moving through and transforming the United Church that it is letting go of just church-to-church work and doing very deep solidarity work with a place like Guatemala. I see it as really lifegiving" (TI).

Challenge #4 : Making Reparations

Solidarity workers have had to come to terms with the truth of our mission inheritance. Deirdre Kelly is blunt: "We screwed up a lot of the world. We have trodden over people economically, culturally, and with our religion, shoving it down people's throats in an imperialistic manner" (TI). Marta Gloria de la Vega says that until recently relationships in the Americas have been "relationships of power in which the North has profited from the resources, both natural and human, of the South" (TI).

When the church shows solidarity with the impoverished, it breaks with this history. It affirms the poor as agents of their own destiny and accompanies them as friends and companions in a communion of struggle and hope, no longer treating them as aid beneficiaries. Furthermore, claims Sobrino, the church is fulfilling its duty to make reparations for the wrongs it has wrought through past mission work.

Paradoxically this obligation becomes an opportunity to create small, utopian expressions of what relationships between South and North might be like if they were based on the interests of the poor rather than those of the powerful. Solidarity offers the possibility of abandoning an order that contradicts life, opposing an economic system that normalizes anti-solidarity. Marta Gloria contrasts today's solidarity movement with the church's history of violence:

> We, the people who were in the Christian Task Force and in other places of solidarity, did not say that we have come to evangelize, we have come to convert. No, there was a different attitude. "Sisters, brothers, what is happening to you? In what way can we help? How can we respond?" Those questions, that openness would open an incredible road. If we had arrived to preach, to say this is what you should do, we would never have had solidarity, there would never have been a change in what I feel has happened again and again for many centuries. That also required a change in the people of the South after the experiences, many of them good but many very negative, of a process of violent christianization which was very costly, which was disrespectful of cultures, of the human being. (TI)

A United Church of Canada report articulates the perspective of many of those I interviewed:

> To think of ourselves as full "partners" in the life and work of the churches with whom we are associated overseas is presumptuous. It is our partners in Africa, Asia, the Caribbean, and Latin America who make the witness, suffer the persecution, absorb the defeats, and celebrate the victories of being faithful to Christ in those places. Our level of participation makes us junior partners at best. Partnership means becoming involved with others in God's mission for wholeness of life, especially on behalf of the poor and powerless. Partnership brings people together in community for mutual empowerment through the sharing of gifts, recognized as gifts freely given by God for the benefit of all, not possessions which some may control. We need the gifts our partners can share with us. They have gifts of spiritual and theological insight, of faithfulness in witness, the experience of costly discipleship. We acknowledge that these gifts carry a higher value in

kingdom terms than some we offer. (United Church of Canada, 1988, pp. 615–16)

"I always thought of accompaniment as the call from Jesus for people to be present with other people," says Wes Maultsaid. "What it is to be a Christian is to be *with* people. You have to think that you're not the person who is the senior partner in this kind of relationship." He adds that we still have a long way to go in creating a mission based on mutuality and reciprocity: "We never really asked them if they could help us to look at our churches and Christian communities, our spirituality. We mostly brought them to talk about their own. We failed to allow them to be the people who could critique our work. We didn't actually have them sit down for an extended reflection on what the Scripture has to say about our common faith" (TI).

For Enrique Torres, following Jesus means moving away from a "charity" or "donor/recipient" mentality that carries with it a sense of superiority: "Jesus' commandment to love your neighbour must be the motivation for solidarity for the Christian. It is not the love of a superior to an inferior, it is not the love of a greater to a lesser, it is the love for another who is equal.... He also said that the proof of love for God is in your love for your neighbour. There are people who think: 'We'll give to the poor what we have that is left over, that is extra, that we don't need, to those who are lesser than ourselves.' This type of thinking is piety, but it's not solidarity. It is not true charity. It is not love for your neighbour" (TI).

Jim Manly says: "Christians speak of themselves as a people of the way. It's a way we share with one another, a lot we share with Christ. As Christ has shown the solidarity of God with us, then we're ready to share that solidarity with other people, and to accompany other people in their walk." He draws out what this means for the church. "We can share workers, we can share resources when they're asked for, but equally we have to be willing to see our needs for some of the resources other people can share with us, that we don't have. It's a total mission of the whole people of God, not a mission of one part of the church to other parts of the world" (TI).

Friendship is perhaps the best way of understanding this approach to mission. Denise Nadeau writes:

> Option "for" the poor still carries a note of mission "for"; a doing for others that is paternalistic and disempowers others. Option "with" the poor is to be with people with our common frailties in the spirit of our common struggle for our common humanity. This removes the struggle from the framework of a success-failure agenda and also raises

the possibility of being friends, not servants (John 15:15). It is our long-term commitment to friends that carries Life and Spirit in these dark times. To be friends with those we are in solidarity with we must truly be ourselves, revealing our own vulnerabilities and weaknesses, dispelling any myth that we are superior because of our privilege. (*Network News,* Nadeau)

Epilogue:
Keeping Vigil for an Elusive Peace

> Peace is possible—a peace that is born from the truth that comes from each one of us and from all of us. It is a painful truth, full of memories of the country's deep and bloody wounds. It is a liberating and humanizing truth that makes it possible for all men and women to come to terms with themselves and their life stories. It is a truth that challenges each one of us to recognize our individual and collective responsibility and to commit ourselves to action so that those abominable acts never happen again.
> —Bishop Juan José Gerardi, April 24, 1998. REMHI, p. xxv

BISHOP GERARDI SPOKE THESE WORDS during the presentation of the Recovery of Historical Memory Report (REMHI) in the Guatemala City Cathedral. Two days later he was assassinated by military guards linked to the president's office. His words continue to inspire and guide both Guatemalans and the international solidarity movement.

Sixteen months before Gerardi's murder, the solidarity movement celebrated the December 29, 1996, signing of the final Accord for a Firm and Lasting Peace, which culminated UN-brokered peace negotiations that began in 1990. "You don't sign peace, you build peace," was an oft-heard phrase. At first the construction of peace seemed to be progressing, slowly but surely. His assassination was a strong signal that the military's grip on the country remained intact.

In 2000, FRG right-wing candidate Alfonso Portillo was elected president and General Ríos Montt became the head of Congress. It became even clearer that the vigil for peace with justice was far from over. Shortly after the events of September 11, 2001, Samantha Sams, then coordinator of the Guatemala-Canada Solidarity Network, wrote: "While much of the world trembles in the face of war, Guatemala still struggles to piece together some peace. Nearly five years since the signing of yet-to-be-implemented

262　Epilogue – Keeping Vigil for an Elusive Peace

Returned refugee child carries sign calling for peace. Photo by Brian Atkinson.

Peace Accords and almost halfway through the right wing FRG's disastrous administration, Guatemalan Civil Society remains as insistent as ever upon finding its way out of a labyrinth of impoverishment and impunity" (Sams, 2001).

This chapter names factors shaping Canadian solidarity with Guatemala since 1996. It also points to priority areas where solidarity is maintaining and deepening its work.

Epilogue – Keeping Vigil for an Elusive Peace

Part 1 : What Shapes Solidarity Today?

※ The Guatemalan Context

One morning in early November 2000, I was forcibly reminded of the gravity of Guatemala's situation. I was preoccupied by a deadline looming for submission of a proposal for young adults to work as interns with human rights groups and NGOs in Guatemala. I was also anxious to complete this book. While my focus was Guatemala, I had set aside the grim reality of a deteriorating human rights situation in which defenders and promoters of human rights had once again become targets of intimidation and repression.

"Not a single torture more." Poster for the International Day of support for torture victims, sponsored by a coalition of Guatemalan human rights groups. Photo by Chap Haynes.

Mid-morning I checked my e-mail. My careful compartmentalization disintegrated, as I was reminded of the urgent need for ongoing solidarity. A few days earlier I had read the good news that thousands of women had marched in several Guatemalan cities during the International Women's March 2000 Against Violence and Poverty. Now I was reading a disturbing message from an Oxfam-Canada partner group in Guatemala: "I seem to be the bird who delivers bad omens, but something has occurred and the worst thing would be not to denounce it. Yesterday at almost 11 a.m. the office of the women's association, *Mujer Vamos Adelante* [Women Let Us Go Forward], was invaded. AMVA, an organization that struggles with great determination for the development and welfare of women and against violence toward women, has done tremendous work" (e-mail sent by Oxfam Canada to members of the Americas Policy Group, Canadian Council for International Cooperation).

The e-mail described how five armed men attacked fifteen members of AMVA. They stole computers with irreplaceable files and the women's purses containing wallets, documents, agendas, keys, and address books, leaving them feeling very insecure. They committed vulgarities in front of the women and raped a young woman. As soon as the assailants left, the women called police headquarters, only two blocks away, as well as other government officials. All were extremely slow to respond. The writer explained that she had not given details of the attack in order to satisfy morbid curiosity, but rather to contribute to the healing process through speaking publicly.

This was no isolated incident. Human rights groups had been targeted in recent months, as they sought to bring charges before domestic and international courts against those responsible for gross and systematic human rights violations during the war, including General Riós Montt. Peasant and indigenous leaders seeking to address the country's enormous economic and land gap were also being targeted. They had suffered death threats, intimidation, kidnapping, torture, disappearance, and summary executions. Now women were being attacked:

> It has been a year of great aggression against the women's movement and women in general. We faced the situation in April of the forced disappearance of Professor Mayra Gutiérrez (who was researching the profitable business of adoptions). This year about fifty women, whose bodies show signs of rape, shots in the forehead [indicating a premeditated political act], and other indignities, have been tossed into abandoned sites in the Capital (similar to what occurred in the era of the dictatorships). The authorities say this is the act of a serial killer, but the method used corresponds more closely to that of extra-judicial executions. Some months ago, when the press agency CERIGUA was being continually harassed, one of its reporters was the object of a sexual aggression "so that you don't get involved in any more nonsense." (e-mail from Oxfam Canada)

Soon after an Urgent Action, entitled "Members of Womens' Organisations Assaulted," appeared on the computer screen. That same week heavily armed men had entered the offices of a CTF partner, Women in Solidarity (AMES), threatening and kicking two women. They stole cash, computer equipment, a television and video recorder, sound equipment, and medicine from their clinic. AMES works with people excluded from land, education, and health care, especially women working in sweatshops and living in marginal areas, many of whom are victims of the war. In early November, a group working to reduce violence against women in the Department of Izabal was also attacked. The Christian Task Force backgrounder stated: "Women, in particular, have suffered greatly as victims of violence themselves or as survivors of acts of violence against their family members and loved ones. When a husband or partner is killed, the woman often must take on the added responsibilities of sole breadwinner, family counsellor, caregiver for elderly parents and in-laws, and single parent. The effect on women's mental and physical health has been substantial."

Epilogue – Keeping Vigil for an Elusive Peace

It suggested the military were reacting to such acts as Rigoberta Menchú's laying of charges in Spain against Riós Montt for genocide and an Open Letter to the president by more than thirty Guatemalan groups, protesting Byron Barrientos's appointment as minister of the Interior. He had been a member of the G-2 (military intelligence) during the years of the worst persecution, abductions, torture, and genocide. Barrientos, together with the Congressional vice-president and the National Civil Police director, later charged human rights activists with creating instability and causing confrontations.

The Urgent Action included excerpts from a United Nations Verification Mission to Guatemala (MINUGUA) Special Report, produced after a rapid increase in intimidations, disappearances, violent deaths, and threats to NGOs, journalists, human rights defenders, and those working in the justice system. "MINUGUA reiterates the unavoidable obligation of the State to guarantee that there is respect for human rights and protection to all citizens. We are especially concerned with the fulfillment of the commitment contained in the Global Accord on Human Rights, to adopt special protective measures for the organizations and individuals that work promoting and defending human rights" (United Nations, July 2000).

Urgent Action Network members were urged to write President Portillo, with copies to Canada's minister of Foreign Affairs and ambassador in Guatemala:

- Expressing concern at these acts of intimidation;
- Requesting an objective and complete investigation into the attacks on womens' groups and the robbery of valuable office equipment and files;
- Asking that those responsible be brought to justice in order to break the cycle of impunity;
- Requesting that the climate of insecurity and impunity caused by the lack of respect for human rights or the rule of law be brought to an end; and
- Asking that the Guatemalan government, following the UN-sponsored Truth Commission's recommendations, remove and do not appoint to positions of power those accused of gross human rights violations.

By 2003, six years after the signing of the Peace Accords, the government had failed to implement the Peace Accords and recommendations of the Historical Clarification Commission, and to ensure the strengthening of the rule of law. The human rights situations had deteriorated with ever-increasing levels of human rights violations and escalating violence. This was especially the case for indigenous people, women, journalists, land activists, members of the legal community, and all those who confront impunity and work for human rights. In a special report, Amnesty International indicated that virtually all human rights groups had suffered serious abuses. Incidents included office raids during which records on human rights cases were taken, monitoring of communications and interference in electronic data storage and threats and attacks on staff, including rape, torture, and extrajudicial executions. The report observed that the wave of violations against human rights defenders resembled patterns during the armed conflict.

Amnesty International attributed the gravity of the situation to the government's lack of will to improved the human rights situation and the policies it had adopted. "The political strategies of the current Guatemalan government are, if anything, reinforcing certain patterns of violations which were being committed before the signing of the Peace Accords and their policies are aggravating rather than improving the human rights situation. The present wave of violence and intimidation seriously threatens the rule of law" (http://web.amnesty.org/library/index AI INDEX: AMR 34/022/200, April 1, 2003).

President Portillo had become little more than a mouthpiece for President of Congress Riós Montt and his backers, many of whom were responsible for the genocide of the early 1980s. The repressive military and intelligence apparatus of the State had not been eliminated, and the military budget had increased dramatically. One corruption scandal within government followed another, as massive sums of money disappeared from health and education ministries.

A key agreement in the Peace Accords was demilitarization of the country and redefining the army's role in a democratic society. By June of 2003, the commitment to abolish one of the most notorious intelligence agencies, the Estado Mayor Presidencial (EMP) translated as the Presidential High Command, had not been implemented. Ample evidence shows that this unit, often working in collaboration with criminal gangs, carried out surveillance and intimidation of human rights leaders as well as acts of violence, including extrajudicial executions. In fact the government increased the EMP's budget. It transferred funds from the Peace Secretariate (established to oversee implementation of the Peace Accords) and from the Ministries of Energy and Mines and of Agriculture, Livestock, and Nutrition at a time when rural people were suffering from an economic crisis caused by falling coffee prices, drought, widespread hunger, and in many areas, famine.

Epilogue – Keeping Vigil for an Elusive Peace

The re-emergence of the Civil Defence Patrol (PACs) in mid-2002 created more turmoil, fear, and frustration. Ex-civil patrollers remobilized to demand compensation for forced participation in the PACs. To achieve their goal, they demonstrated and blocked roads. In areas where PAC members had perpetrated massacres and mass rapes, they threatened human rights groups and staff of the ombudsperson's office, blaming them for the fact that they had not received payments. Partial compensation began in April 2003, with the promise by the FRG of further payments after the elections at the end of 2003, if the party is re-elected.

※ The Peace Accords and Canada's Response

The Peace Accords are substantive agreements that address human rights, resettlement, the Truth Commission, indigenous rights, socioeconomic issues, and demilitarization. They lay the groundwork for an end to the political violence that reached genocidal proportions. If implemented, they have the potential to change economic policies that perpetuate an ever-widening gap between a wealthy minority and an impoverished majority. "Beyond correcting the distortions from the decades of repression and war (that is, making Guatemala a normal country), they attempt to turn a society that was racist and exclusionary to the core into a fully democratic and multicultural/intercultural society" (Jonas, p. 244). In particular, the Global Accord on Human Rights, along with recommendations of the Catholic Church's Recuperation of Historical Memory Project and the UN-mandated Historical Clarification Commission, provide a framework for addressing past abuses and ensuring they never occur again.

Jim Gronau, a CUSO cooperant who worked with a network of NGOs and cooperatives, saw the Accords as a guide for the solidarity movement: "They are probably the best basis Guatemala has at the moment in the struggle to achieve social justice. International solidarity should work closely with groups inside the country to make of the accords a real beginning for correcting social injustice and for trying to heal the wounds inflicted by the war" (Gronau, *Reunion*, p. 1).

Canadians heeded such urgings, forming the Guatemala-Canada Solidarity Network (GCSN) to support the peace process. Informal collaboration in the 1980s and early '90s had enabled the formation of Project A and the Urgent Action Network, as well as several solidarity campaigns. However, networking had weakened, in good part because government funding to solidarity groups, learners' centres, and NGOs for public education in Canada had been severely cut. In many cases local Project A committees had concentrated only on refugee accompaniment. Many returned accompaniers, as well as the local Project A groups, had not become part of the wider informal network. With Project A coming to an end, it was time to rebuild.

Forty delegates representing groups from BC to the Maritimes met in Montreal in March 1999 to renew and strengthen Canada's solidarity movement. They formed the GCSN "to motivate the Canadian government and peoples to deepen and strengthen their support of peace building, justice, and equality in Guatemala through supporting Guatemalan civil society initiatives." Its role is to strengthen member groups through effective communication among groups within Canada and with Guatemalan partners. The GCSN shares information and analysis, sustains and strengthens the Urgent Action Network, and supports tours of Guatemalans to Canada and national delegations there.

Since that time, the Peace Accords have faced major setbacks. Constitutional reforms needed to change the role of the army and judicial system and to fully realize indigenous rights were defeated in a mid-1999 referendum, in which only 18.5 percent of potential voters participated. The "No" side carried out a massive television and press campaign, while the "Yes" side was not well organized enough to combat the lack of information and understanding that led to the high rate of abstention. The "Yes" won in most rural, indigenous areas but numerically the result was decided in Guatemala City.

Nonetheless, many groups, especially indigenous groups, still strive to implement the Accords. Commissions, such as those set up under the Accord on the Rights and Identity of Indigenous Peoples, continually face obstacles and delays. The MINUGUA Report on the Verification of the Peace Accords cites "notable delays," "lack of sufficient funds," "no registered advances," "paralyzed proposals," "numerous difficulties," "the exclusion of fundamental themes," and "lack of compliance" (United Nations, Sept. 2000).

Not a single peace-related law was passed in the Portillo administration's first year. More than thirty-five thousand families had requested land from the Land Fund; it had funding to buy property for fifteen hundred. MINUGUA pointed to the new police force created by the Peace Accords as the principal author of extrajudicial executions. It expressed "deep concern" at decrees passed that mandate the Military Police and Armed Forces to collaborate with the police in public security operations. These decrees violate the Peace Accords that call for demilitarization, limiting the military's mandate to defending the country against external threats, and strengthening the civil power of the State.

At the beginning of 2002, the Portillo administration declared that they are not bound by the Peace Accords, since they were signed by a previous government. These setbacks are profound and discouraging. Nonetheless Guatemalan partners still believe that the Accords remain the ground on which solidarity should base its work. They also believe international support is needed to support the strengthening of grassroots participation in the peace process.

※ Setbacks and "A Reason for Joy"

Solidarity is guided by the vision and hopes expressed in the Peace Accords. Yet solidarity in its present form continues precisely because of the obstacles in bringing to fruition the goals embedded in the Peace Accords. Many think the peace process is stalled or even moving backwards. Human rights, non-governmental, indigenous, and women's groups see this time as a period of "armed peace" with increased personal and economic insecurity.

In 1997 Jim Gronau wrote: "Social and economic injustice remain; the army, one of the worst human rights violators in the hemisphere, is unrepentant and resistant to change; and the Guatemalan people struggle to heal the wounds left from massacres, displacement, and fear." He cited a statement by the Archdiocesan Office on Human Rights. "After thirty-six years of savagery, Guatemala needs perhaps another seventy-two of tender, loving care, of demonstrations of forgiveness, security, generosity, mutual support, and openness." Jim went on to say that "absolutely none of this will be forthcoming, though, unless the underlying causes of the armed conflict are dealt with seriously. The unjust and inefficient taxation structure must be changed, social services must be made reliable and significant, and so on" (Gronau, *Reunion,* p. 1). His comments are truer than ever today.

After a period of relative calm, the elite's stubborn resistance to change became clear in the April 1998 "peace-time" assassination of seventy-five-year-old Bishop Juan José Gerardi. His skull was crushed by a cement block. His murder galvanized the solidarity movement. When Mary Corbett addressed a commemorative event in Guatemala City's Central Plaza on behalf of the Guatemala-Canada Solidarity Network a year later, she recalled: "When some of us were hoping that things could be changing, Bishop Gerardi was assassinated. His death confirmed what others among us suspected: that violence and injustice are not eliminated by the mere signing of a peace accord. Therefore, the time has not yet come to end our solidarity" (Corbett, 1999).

"The truth in our country has been twisted and silenced. We wanted to show the human drama and to share with others the sorrow and the anguish of the thousands of dead, disappeared, and tortured," Gerardi said of the report *Guatemala: Never Again,* which he presented two days before his murder (REMHI, p. xxiv). The presentation symbolized returning to the people their own truth. Trusted, well-trained community members had conducted more than six thousand interviews, 61 percent in indigenous languages and 39 percent in Spanish. Two hundred thousand Guatemalan civilians were killed, including fifty thousand who were "disappeared," the vast majority by the army and its paramilitary allies, says the Report. It describes military structures tied to the terror and names generals Lucas García, Riós Montt, and Mejía Víctores, army commanders-in-chief in the 1980s.

Many believe the military killed Gerardi, not only for fingering them as the chief human rights abuser but also because of the Report's bold recommendations. It urged the State to acknowledge responsibility for massive and systematic human rights violations, pay reparations, fire officers and soldiers who committed atrocities, and shake up the clandestine security and intelligence services. It also called for continued international monitoring.

A year later, in 1999, the case remained unsolved. Suspects within military intelligence had not been pursued; evidence had been destroyed, and innocent people, even a dog, jailed as an absurd chain of accusations unfolded. Several witnesses and Judge Henry Monroy fled to Canada after threats and intimidations.

Who Killed the Bishop?

Who killed the Bishop?
We all want to know.
Was it the homeless man
Who laid him low?
Was it the Priest?
Or was it the dog?
Or some passerby
Just out for a jog?
Was it the gang girl
The niece of his friend
Who brought him to this
Untimely end?

Epilogue – Keeping Vigil for an Elusive Peace

Each strange hypothesis
Is treated as true.
Police take suspects
And jail them on cue.
Watch the ancient dog
Stiff with arthritis
Arrest him quick
Before he can bite us.

What's that you say
About a report?
He talked too much
Wouldn't cut it short?
And what of the shirtless man
Who left in a car
With license plates
Telling who they are?

It's impossible
The soldiers claim.
Talk about that brings
The wrong kind of fame.
They'll name a new suspect
On and on it goes.
Who killed the Bishop?
No one says, but everyone knows.

—Judy Loo, March 1999

The GCSN, at its 1999 founding meeting, decided to participate in an international campaign against impunity. "We can only hope that, yet again, concerted pressure from the international community will contribute positively to the tireless efforts of the Guatemalan people seeking to end impunity in the Gerardi and other such cases and to ensure the implementation of the Peace Accords" (Lemieux, 1999).

The GCSN invited organizations, churches, and individuals to honour Bishop Gerardi and all the victims of violence by participating in commemorative events, such as vigils, church services, and public presentations, by asking the Canadian government to support the Truth Commission's recommendations actively, and by signing an Open Letter. It was broadcast on community radio stations across Guatemala and published in a major newspaper. It urged the Guatemalan government to:

- End impunity and seek justice in the Gerardi and similar cases;
- Act immediately on Truth Commission recommendations; and
- Establish a National Foundation of Peace and Harmony to aid, promote, and monitor the implementation of these recommendations.

Commemorative events were held in small towns and large cities from Nova Scotia to Vancouver Island. In Antigonish more than forty people came to a Good Friday evening reflection while in Fredericton a noon-hour public vigil took place. There was wide media coverage, both national and local.

At the beginning of 2000 the murder remained unsolved. The GCSN invited a representative of the Archdiocesan Office on Human Rights to travel across Canada in early April. From Newfoundland to Calgary she raised the profile of the struggle against impunity.

Winnipeg's experience shows what a small group can achieve. After an interview with a *Winnipeg Free Press* reporter, along with a Guatemalan refugee living in Winnipeg, she attended a lunch at a church:

> We had Central American food made by some Salvadoran friends, and the biggest problem of the day was that we were overwhelmed by people and had to stretch the food very thinly. She spoke very eloquently about her work, with some very meaningful words about Holy Week. It was very powerful to hear her equate Jesus' death and resurrection with what the people were going through with the exhumation process. She showed her slides. We had managed to acquire many carnations, thinking that she wanted to hand them out, as she had done in Montreal for a special service. One of our members had set up a shrine of sorts around a picture of Bishop Gerardi. She was moved to see him there. She got out her book of names of the people killed, tortured, and disappeared, and passed it around. She asked everyone to read a name and to take a flower in that person's honour and to remember them. We had fifty copies of our handouts and every single thing went. We counted sixty people present at the talk who had come from Catholic, United, Unitarian, Mennonite, and Lutheran churches and from the theological schools and a couple of other organizations. The CBC Radio afternoon host attended this event and did an interview. (White, 2000)

That evening she spoke to more than 115 people, including refugees, students, church people, and representatives of Aboriginal organizations: "She showed the video about the exhumations, and she did an impromptu slide show collage along with the song 'Todo Cambia' by Mercedes Sosa,

Epilogue – Keeping Vigil for an Elusive Peace

sung by Omar Velásquez and Rafael Reyes, two local Salvadoran-Canadian musicians who played and sang that night. That part was the highlight for her for sure, and much appreciated by the crowd. There was an extensive question period and much interest. People stayed for food and a chance to talk.... Between the two events, $850 in profit was donated for the paid ad campaign. Petitions were circulated at both events" (White, 2000).

She met with the head of the Manitoba Chiefs. Aboriginal elders shared a pipe ceremony with her. The Grand Chief and the elders gave her gifts of sweet grass, tobacco, wild rice, and four-directions candles. The Aboriginal People's TV Network aired her meeting with the elders, along with an excerpt from a video on ODHAG's involvement in the exhumation of mass graves.

Ten days later a GCSN delegation participated in the second Gerardi commemoration in Guatemala City. They met with human rights groups in the countryside and the Capital. Mary Corbett spoke to the crowd gathered in the Central Plaza. "We have come from Canada to offer you our greetings of solidarity in this moment of your journey between the darkness of death and the light brought by truth.... The time has not yet come to end our solidarity. And, indeed, we will feel very privileged if we may accompany you in your journey to peace" (Corbett, 1999).

A historic breakthrough in the struggle against impunity came on June 8, 2001, when three army officers were found guilty of participating in the Gerardi murder. ODHAG sent a message far and wide: "'Grace and truth have met, justice and peace have embraced. Truth is breaking forth from the earth, and justice is coming down from the heavens' (Psalm 85:10–11). We wish to thank each and every demonstration of solidarity, support, prayers, and fraternity that, throughout this process, we received from diverse sectors of the Guatemalan people, the Catholic community, as well as the international community."

The Guatemala-Canada Solidarity Network (GCSN) southern coordinator wrote: "This verdict was emitted despite systematic intimidations, threats, and attacks on justice workers, members of the ODHAG team, and witnesses. These acts of intimidation appeared to be planned and carried out with the aid of extensive human, logistical, and operative capacity, significant infrastructure and ample access to intelligence units. For so many people to have had the courage and conviction to continue their labours related to this case, in the struggle against impunity and the strengthening of the rule of law, is an important step forward for Guatemala" (e-mail to the GCSN).

A lawyer who had worked with ODHAG reflected on the personal impact of the verdict and paid tribute to his friend and teacher: "That justice was done provoked in me a feeling—distinct from joy—that now I can perceive without rage, as profound sadness caused by having lost a friend and teacher. The Friend that gave me his life, asking for nothing in return. The Teacher that gave me his wisdom, so that I might learn.... And so on the day of the sentence I was able for the first time to cry with sorrow for his death" (cited in e-mail sent by Susanne Rumsey, August 2001).

Since Judge Henry Monroy's arrival in Canada in 1999, he has spoken to large numbers of people throughout Canada, often in gatherings sponsored by Guatemala-Canada Solidarity Network groups. He called the verdict "a reason for joy," but also cautioned that the repressive apparatus of the State had not been dismantled, not even the Presidential Guard, responsible for large numbers of killings.

Judge Monroy's caution proved prophetic. By mid-2003 little progress had been made in the battle against impunity. Appeals of the convictions of the army officers responsible for Bishop Gerardi's murder continued, while human rights abuses escalated.

※ Relationships Continue to Inspire

In the present context many Canadians might have lost heart if it were not for relationships that continue to grow and deepen with Guatemalans in human rights groups, churches, and the social movement. Solidarity receives its energy and spirit from the hope, resilience, generosity, and commitment of so many Guatemalans in the face of continued repression and suffering .

A Breaking the Silence delegation of young adults, ages eighteen to twenty-six, travelled in Guatemala in the summer of 2000. They never failed to be inspired by the determination of those they met, such as Wendy Meńdez, a representative of HIJOS, a group of young people whose parents had been disappeared, tortured, and murdered and were now themselves under threat; Iqui Bal'aan, a youth theatre group from a marginalized zone of the Capital; or Maya women carrying out small community projects in order to send their children to school. They adamantly refuse to give the economic and military elite the last word.

Epilogue – Keeping Vigil for an Elusive Peace

Part 2 : Where Do We Go from Here?

※ Strengthening the Justice System, Ending Impunity

At the end of 2001, a UN report on the independence of judges and lawyers pointed to the "social cancer" of impunity as a key source of the human rights crisis in the country. It was highly critical of government inaction and an incompetent justice system and warned that if impunity were not addressed, it would slowly destroy Guatemalan society.

As earlier chapters have shown, effective solidarity actions can increase the political cost of attacks and intimidation against social activists. Many means are being used—Urgent Actions, paid announcements in the Guatemalan media enumerating violations, letters of support to affected groups, pressure on the Canadian government. Along with these ongoing actions, the GCSN has initiated security accompaniment and an advocacy campaign with the Canadian government.

※ Security Accompaniment

In the spring of 2000 the GCSN, along with other international solidarity groups and networks, agreed to accompany witnesses from remote Maya villages who are pressing charges against the army high command responsible for the violence in 1981–82. Accompaniment is a way to support those fighting against impunity, struggling for justice, truth telling, and reconciliation, and pressuring for the justice system's reform.

The decision to lay charges came after a three-year process of research on war crimes in regions the UN-sponsored Truth Commission classified as having suffered genocide. Those involved decided to speak out about the atrocities and to push for justice through laying hundreds of charges, thus hoping to force a criminal investigation that would lead to trials for genocide, crimes against humanity, and war crimes. The process is led by the people themselves, with support from CALDH (the Centre for Legal Action in Human Rights) but without manipulation by NGOs, political parties, or other groups. The emphasis is on justice, not revenge, based on the belief that a truer, more just path to reconciliation requires that those who orchestrated genocidal crimes be brought to justice.

The request, passed on by the GCSN coordinator, stated: "The people asking for accompaniment are aware of the great risk that they are taking by speaking out about the truth—no longer as anonymous victims or witnesses...but as public actors with names and faces. They are conscious of the fact that an international presence can (a) ensure that information about their situation reaches the outside world, (b) diffuse a certain amount of tension, and even (c) save lives.... Building on past experience, they can offer moral and political support to Guatemalans struggling for justice in this new step towards peace and reconciliation" (e-mail to the GCSN). A later clarification added: "No one can be exactly certain as to how the current government, never mind all of the parallel underground forces related to ex-army officials, may react. There will certainly be threats and intimidations. Whether or not there will be anything more is impossible to know, but we cannot forget how important accompaniment has been in preventing these things—just as we cannot forget that the day the Xamán massacre took place, there were no accompaniers in the community" (e-mail to the GCSN).

She noted that a young man, known to many Canadians, had suffered a string of intimidations and even a kidnapping when no internationals could meet his request for accompaniment during a trial in which he himself was accompanying widows who had charged an ex-military commissioner with murder, rape, and theft. (He and his family were forced to leave Guatemala in January 2002, after death threats and intimidation resumed, this time also directed to his wife and children. They are active members of and resource persons for Breaking the Silence.) Their case is "small potatoes" in comparison to trials that might take place for genocide and crimes against humanity, she added. "The scale and implications are magnified three hundred times over."

Canada's first accompanier this time, Finola Shankar, from the Kingston solidarity group, wrote: "This is a very big thing in Guatemala as it is the first genocide case (not to be the last) and it is the first one against the intellectual authors. Rigoberta Menchú has brought similar charges to the Spanish courts but these ones will go through the Guatemalan 'justice' system. I am not sure that many people think that justice will actually be done, but it is still an important and necessary step.... Perhaps it will bring international attention back to impunity in Guatemala and you never know, we might be surprised!" (Shankar, May 2000).

Finola's experience confirmed the need for accompaniment. She felt frustrated at the start. "We ended up doing a lot of waiting around as we waited to introduce ourselves to witnesses, communities, and community leaders." Soon, however, people started to come by the office to chat and to share their concerns. She accompanied widows who laid a complaint against a man who had threatened them during the exhumation of a mass grave. "It is amazing how just your presence can make someone feel so much better. I think now too with uncertainties about the new Portillo/Riós Montt government it is really important that people are

Epilogue – Keeping Vigil for an Elusive Peace

accompanied and feel that there are things like Urgent Action Networks behind international observers."

Finola did not want to leave: "Staying in the communities, despite the fleas and stomach sicknesses, was always my favorite. I haven't spent such a lot of time playing with children and sipping tepid, sweet coffee since I worked in a day camp (minus the coffee I guess!). Many of the witnesses who I was dealing with are widows so for me it was interesting to see how the women organized and interacted amongst themselves. In one *aldea* [village] they had a sleep-over for both nights. (The women decided they would visit me because, despite my rubber boots, they thought the mud along the paths would be too difficult for me to deal with!!). I was there with all the women who were participating. They made me traditional vegetarian treats. I was their first accompanier and their first non-family visitor. As women they chatted and joked and told secrets with me" (Shankar, July 2000).

Although Finola's accompaniment was reminiscent of earlier experiences, new aspects emerged. One Friday the Maya-Achi Widows' Organization asked her to accompany them to the *Ministerio Público* (the attorney-general's office) to arrange the release of fifteen family members' remains, unearthed during a recent exhumation: "All the preparations were ready for a wake that night with a Mass and a little procession. The arrangements were also made for the burial the next day. The marimba was paid for, the food was cooking, people had been notified (no small task in rural Guatemala), and candles and flowers had been bought, not to mention that these people had been waiting for months for the return of their dead" (Shankar, July 2000).

A government official told the women the Foundation responsible for the exhumation had not met the bureaucratic requirements and he could not hand over the remains until Monday. He then left for the Capital. "It wasn't the guy's fault, but the attitude was what bothered me (this in a public office where regular people aren't allowed to use the toilet, exceptions are made for foreigners and certain *ladinos,* and where he was dealing with me rather than the president of the Widows' Organization who was also there)."

Soon after his departure, the Foundation representative, along with a human rights worker and an American anthropologist, arrived. When they made a fuss, a lower-level inspector relented:

> Bending the rules a little and cutting some corners they had us out of there by just before 4 p.m. The sad thing was that we all knew that if it had just been Carlos and the family members waiting for the remains

they would have got them on Monday and not on Friday. I was constantly saddened by how used to poor treatment and disrespect everyone seems to be.

In the end the wake and the burial turned out well. So many people came, even just from neighbouring *aldeas* to pay their respects. I was also surprised at how honest and political the priests were in their sermons, acknowledging the offences that the church too has committed. I was happy to see that there was a Maya ceremony in the church after the Mass and that the Maya priests were given a space to speak within the Mass. (Shankar, July 10, 2000)

※ Advocacy with the Canadian Government

Concerned by the gravity of the human rights situation, the GCSN is convinced that Canada must use its leverage strategically and proactively, as it did in supporting refugee negotiations with the government and the peace process. The GCSN believes that Canada should support the United Nations' Verification Mission to Guatemala (MINUGUA) until the Peace Accords are fulfilled, through financial, personnel, and political support, and should encourage other countries to do the same. Canada should take every opportunity, both bilaterally and multilaterally, to push for full compliance with recommendations of the Historical Clarification Commission and the Recovery of Historical Memory Project.

In September 2000 Prime Minister Chretien flew to Guatemala for a day to discuss trade issues with the Central American presidents in advance of the Summit of the Americas in Quebec City in April 2001. Given Canada's earlier support for the peace process and human rights, as well as the rapidly deteriorating human rights situation, both Guatemalans and Canadians were upset that the prime minister did not find an hour in the day to meet with human rights groups nor did he speak publicly about human rights. Canada lost a historic opportunity to send a message to the Guatemalan government. Many felt the Portillo administration saw this omission as a lack of interest by Canada in human rights and impunity. That same night, human rights groups were threatened. The prime minister's response or lack thereof reinforced impressions that trade and investment were higher on Canada's agenda than human rights, impunity, and the rule of law.

※ A Letter to Minister Minna

A few months after the prime minister visited Guatemala, the GCSN learned that Maria Minna, at that time Canada's minister for International Cooperation, was going to visit to Guatemala. Once again no plans had

Epilogue – Keeping Vigil for an Elusive Peace

been made for her to meet human rights groups. With only two days' notice, the GCSN mobilized members across the country, who sent letters and e-mails to Minister Minna via the Canadian Embassy in Guatemala, asking that her agenda include human rights groups. The pressure worked, and she did meet with representatives of human rights groups.

> January 11th, 2001
>
> Dear Minister Minna,
>
> I am writing you concerning your trip to Guatemala. I received the press release concerning your trip to Guatemala yesterday through the Canadian Council for International Cooperation. At the same time, I received an Urgent Action from the Office of Human Rights of the Archdiocese of Guatemala, concerning death threats to Mynor Melgar, a lawyer with the ODHAG. The Maritimes-Guatemala Breaking the Silence Network, with members throughout the Maritimes, has had a relationship with the Office of Human Rights since its founding a decade ago, have had tours visiting their office many times, and hosted a representative of ODHAG's Historical Memory Project last April.
>
> Naturally, we are pleased that you are going to Guatemala. At the same time, we want to urge you to meet with human rights leaders at the ODHAG and other human rights groups and ask that you make a public statement while in Guatemala concerning human rights. It is of paramount importance that high-level foreign leaders, such as yourself, meet with human rights leaders and speak publicly in Guatemala at this time of deteriorating human rights. I am aware that CIDA's stated priority for Guatemala is in the area of human rights, so I would hope that you would visit the representatives of human rights groups under threat.
>
> As I write this, I recall how proud I was to be a Canadian at the time that Canada, through its Embassy staff, supported the refugees' negotiations with the Guatemalan government and supported Canadians accompanying refugees returning to Guatemala, through Project Accompaniment. I hope that such leadership in the area of human rights can once again be expressed during your visit to Guatemala.
>
> Yours sincerely,
> Kathryn Anderson

Most solidarity activists valued the Embassy's openness to dialogue and active support for Project Accompaniment in the first half of the 1990s. More recently many have felt that that their expressions of concern about human rights and economic justice and their questions about Canada's policies and actions were not welcomed by the Embassy. This was disturbing to many Canadians who believe critical, questioning citizens are a sign of a flourishing democracy. However, a more positive and welcoming attitude has been noted recently, creating a sense of hope that a more constructive, yet critical, relationship is again developing.

Guatemalans continue to insist that international pressure, when coordinated with their efforts, can tip the balance in favour of justice. On every occasion they tell Canadians to insist that the Canadian government's relationship with Guatemala be based on its human rights record. The Canadian government's position on free trade challenges the solidarity movement to focus on the free trade agenda in the coming years insisting that trade agreements must promote human rights and economic justice.

※ Economic Injustice

Economic exploitation was a root cause of the violence in the 1980s. Since that time poverty has actually worsened. Eighty-five percent of Guatemalans live in poverty and 70 percent in extreme poverty. Eighty percent lack adequate housing. The official unemployment figure is 46 percent, while many think the real figure is closer to 60 percent. The basic cost of living comes to about $300 US per family per month, while the minimum legal wage is about $100.

The Christian Task Force and Breaking the Silence, along with other GCSN member groups, are addressing economic injustice in the rapidly evolving context of globalization. Groups are focusing on negative impacts of World Bank and International Monetary Fund policies on Guatemalan communities such as Rió Negro, whose refusal to give up its land for a World Bank-financed hydroelectric project led to massive repression. Solidarity networks are deeply concerned about harmful consequences for Guatemalans of the Free Trade Area of the Americas Agreement (FTAA) and the related Central American Plan Puebla-Panama. In April 2001 a dozen BTS members drove to Quebec City to join in the protests against the FTAA, and in the process became aware that harsh repression of dissent was the Canadian government response.

A particular focus of both CTF and BTS is the *maquila* industry, a major expression of the new global economic order. About 280 textile factories in Guatemala, often owned by Korean and other Pacific Rim companies, produce blue jeans, tennis shoes, knitwear, sweatshirts, and other garments. Canadian and US companies purchase these items for the North American consumer market. Guatemala is an ideal location for these factories, with its cheap and competent labour force, mainly young Maya

Epilogue – Keeping Vigil for an Elusive Peace

women desperate for work. Working conditions are harsh—low wages, abusive bosses, forced overtime, little regard for health and safety.

Recent BTS delegations who set out to learn about the *maquila* industry came up with strikingly similar findings. Carol Kell and Keith Hagerman shared their discoveries in a sermon preached in Antigonish:

> The feeling in a *maquila* is one of choking dust from the material used and poor ventilation, the feeling of confinement because you can't leave your station for a drink of water or a breath of fresh air. The feeling of physical and psychological abuse from supervisors who feel they are above the laws of the country and know they won't be prosecuted. The feeling of frustration of the workers at Ace International who have been keeping a vigil outside the *maquila* ever since they were locked out for organizing a union. The feeling of fear when we went to talk to them and the manager came out to see what was going on. These workers will not give up until they know the feeling of freedom to work without fear of ruining their health or safety. (Hagerman and Kell, 1999)

On a side street in an industrial zone of Guatemala City, the March 1999 delegation met women, children, and a few men camped out in a crude hut beside a factory. Just before Christmas, the Philips-Van Heusen *maquila*, where the workers had won a hard-fought battle to unionize, had closed without warning. Workers simply received a flyer saying the company had lost a client.

UNITE (the Union of Needletrade, Industrial and Textile Employees), an international union with Canadian affiliates, had offered union leaders its experience in 1996. A leader was secretly recruited for every ten workers. Trainers went to their homes, often located down the sides of ravines in marginalized communities, where they washed clothes, played with children, or helped with other chores until the women were free to meet with them. After intensive training, the new leaders began to sign up workers. The leaders and those who signed up were placed on the worst machines. Mechanics were never available for repairs. Management offered workers bribes. Non-unionists were always favoured. Keeping the workers supportive required constant work. "Someone was always about to crack," said Teresa Caertano, UNITE staffer. The union never let management forget about them. They did "the turtle," working as slowly as possible for an hour, then resuming their normal pace. Periodically someone stood up and shouted: "What do we want?" The workers replied: "Justice!" "When do we want it?" "Now!"

Company CEO Bruce Klatsky sat on a White House anti-sweatshop task force and on the board of Human Rights Watch. When UNITE threatened to demonstrate at a fundraising dinner in Washington, DC, he agreed to send Human Rights Watch investigators to the plant. They corroborated virtually everything the workers had said. Klatsky finally agreed to negotiate. A collective agreement was signed. Wages and working conditions for the five hundred workers improved, meeting Labour Code laws concerning hours, minimum wage, and minimum worker age. They won some benefits, such as a small amount of money to offset childcare costs. Management could not fire anyone without meeting with the union. For the first time workers could buy their children nutritious food and pay bills on time.

The fired workers showed us faxed letters of protest solidarity groups had sent the company. They said: "We can't let the seed die now." They told us the struggle was for all workers and their children. Judy Loo wrote: "It is hard for us to imagine that they will win, but we know that, regardless of the outcome, this is one struggle that must continue" (Loo, "Textile"). Indeed they did lose that battle when economic need forced them to seek other work.

One windy, raw, gray morning, the November 1999 delegation travelled down an isolated side road outside Guatemala City to meet young women who had been locked out of the Korean-owned *maquila*, Ace International, in late August. They had organized a union when they could no longer tolerate abusive working conditions, including beatings, emotional abuse, and a refusal to allow workers to get medical help they had paid for through payroll deductions. The company stated that the US buyer was unwilling to buy from a unionized plant, a claim the women refuted, saying it was the owners who refused to allow a union. Seven hundred workers were let go, starting with the union executive. They were owed for six weeks' work, which was never paid. The plant has likely opened again under a new name but with the same owners, a frequent practice by owners to avoid Guatemalan law. Bev Brazier, a delegation member, remembers: "While we were outside talking to the workers, we noticed the look of the place: like something from an old World War II movie—concrete walls, barbed wire, and a tower at the gate where guards with guns keep watch. One was watching us. Then a boss approached us. Even though I knew he would not hurt us—there would be too much international attention if he did—still when he began to approach I felt real fear. What must it be like for these women who have no power and no way to protect themselves? They must feel that fear every time" (Brazier, 1999).

Epilogue – Keeping Vigil for an Elusive Peace   283

Equally sobering were stories of long hours, low pay, and verbal abuse, told by Maya *maquila* domestic and agricultural workers, some as young as twelve years old, to BTS Young Adults delegation members. Still delegates found hope in the work of Conrado de La Cruz, an NGO that brings young women and girls together on Sundays, their only day off, to learn about their rights. They also accompanied a human rights worker to a *maquila* where she chatted with young women about their rights as they sat on the curb eating lunch. They were impressed by the pioneering work of the Commission for the Verification of Corporate Codes of Conduct (COVERCO), an independent monitoring group that verifies whether companies such as Starbucks and Liz Claiborne are complying with Guatemalan law and their own codes of conduct.

The delegations caught glimpses into globalization's impact on Guatemalan youth and women. But the workers and organizers' courage, determination, and creativity did not allow despair: "All is not hopeless. We met with union organizers and with other human rights workers who are involved in a process of education, telling workers about their rights under national and international labour codes. Workers in these sweatshops are often uneducated and have little understanding of their rights. Educating workers and helping workers to organize together has brought pressure on the offending companies. These organizations are working with issues of minimum age requirements, security and sanitation, wages and health, and abuse of workers, with the aim of restoring dignity to workers and providing workers with a living wage" (sermon by Hagerman and Kell).

Delegates meeting with an Embassy official questioned Canada's policy regarding Canadian companies purchasing from companies that flagrantly disregard international and Guatemalan labour codes. The Embassy representative suggested the government had no desire to regulate trade as a means to ensure human rights. As we had just met those who were suffering because of this hands-off approach, we left feeling frustrated and ashamed by Canada's stance.

The Embassy's response reinforced the need to support the long-term struggle, in a globalized economy, for just working conditions and wages in *maquilas* and on plantations. BTS members are convinced the battle will only be won when organizing in the South is supported by pressure on government and industry from consumers, unions, churches, and students in the North: "We asked: 'What can we do?' We were told that letters do have an influence on the Ministry of Labour, on the government of Guatemala, and indeed on the role of our own government. We are not helpless. We can be part of transforming the working situation of people in other parts of the world, alongside those working face to face helping people to organize and demand their rights" (Hagerman and Kell, 1999).

BTS joined the Canada-wide Maquila Solidarity Network (MSN). Members were active in a 1999 holiday season MSN campaign. After delegates described their meetings with *maquila* workers, the Antigonish Project A group wrote greeting cards during a Christmas potluck. They asked that, as citizens and consumers, Hudson's Bay (the Bay and Zellers) and Sears Canada give them verifiable assurances that clothes, shoes, and toys are manufactured in workplaces that follow internationally recognized labour standards and local laws. They pointed out that retailers and manufacturers in the UK, Europe, and the US had agreed to labour codes that include minimum labour standards and mechanisms for independent verification. They asked the CEOs to press Retail Council members to adopt similar codes of conduct.

However, the Retail Council opted out of negotiations, instead drafting its own very weak code. "This is particularly disturbing," said Canadian Labour Congress president Ken Georgetti, "because recognizing the fundamental rights of workers to associate freely and bargain collectively is the key to ending sweatshop abuses." He accused the Bay and Sears, who had seemed committed to developing a meaningful code, of allowing Wal-Mart, which controls 40 percent of the Canadian department store trade, to dictate policy. "The Retail Council adopted a lowest common denominator approach to code negotiations in order to appease its most anti-labour members. Wal-Mart sat on the committee that drafted the Retail Council's proposal, which we now fear will become their code of conduct. A company that sells clothes made in Burma, where forced labour is a well-documented reality, is not serious about labour or other human rights." Solidarity activists were not surprised to learn that government support for the negotiation process had not materialized. "The government did not come through with needed funding for the process. More importantly it was not willing to put pressure on the associations and companies in support of ILO core labour rights" (www.web.net/~msn, Nov. 2000).

However, the struggle to have companies adopt credible, effective, transparent, and accountable codes of conduct is far from over. The *maquila* sector continues to pay few taxes, a payoff for providing jobs, even if it is cheap labour. Taking its cue from the determination of the youth and women Canadians have met in Guatemala, the solidarity movement has maintained its involvement in this and other struggles for economic justice. Long-overdue fiscal reform, especially a more egalitarian tax system, is an area needing solidarity pressure. A promised Fiscal Pact that would include taxing the wealthy, who pay virtually no taxes, has never been enacted, due to resistance by the wealthy. "The bottom line of the dallying around the Fiscal Pact is that without it development in the country will remain on hold" (Sams and Taylor, p. 8).

The solidarity movement also needs to focus on the economic system itself, researching and challenging economic policies, as the Latin America Working Group did in an earlier period. Canadian scholars Liisa North and Alan Simmons argue: "Links between choice of economic policy, social equity, and possibilities of democratization cannot be ignored." They recognize that international neo-liberal economic policies have supported "tangible, but limited, improvements" in human rights. "Egregious human rights abuses, after all, do not ensure a secure investment climate." But they note that neo-liberalism supports changes that sustain or increase socioeconomic inequality, "thereby incubating the potential for the return to violent repression and armed resistance." They add: "Neo-liberal rhetoric promises that increased foreign investment and trade expansion will lead to economic growth that will benefit all; that structural adjustment policies (SAPS) will make the state more efficient and the public more self-reliant." North and Simmons note that outcomes have been rather different, pointing to increased insecurity of the landless, the poor, and women, and the lack of land reform, while the military "continues to threaten and intimidate but stops short of massacres and widespread killings" (North and Simmonds, p. 279–81).

In spite of grievous losses and setbacks, the visions and the hope, the yearning for peace and justice, have not been extinguished. Relationships continue to nourish and inspire. In the fall of 2001 Deirdre Kelly wrote:

> As the journey progresses, small yet constant steps of solidarity keep brothers and sisters in Latin America close to our spirits and hearts... some dead, some still living.... I recall the energy generated as we sat with unionists drinking Coke at the *Jornadas*, aching with the fatal acts of privatization. Those pictures of young martyrs on the walls. Memories of riding horses into the refugee camp while beside us walked members of *La Quetzal* in knee-deep mud. Images of sweat glistening on the backs of the seasonal cane-cutters, the shy smile of women cooking tortillas. The small child holding an even smaller child. We

286 Epilogue – Keeping Vigil for an Elusive Peace

Guatemala children call Canadians to solidarity. Photo by Chap Haynes.

continue to recognize the costs of those who have suffered and continue to suffer. In an ultimate way, isn't it really us who have been accompanied? (*Network News*, Kelly, p. 2)

Epilogue – Keeping Vigil for an Elusive Peace

The final words of Julia Esquivel's poem, "Threatened With Resurrection," written in 1980, still beckon Canadians (Esquivel, 1994, p. 63).

> Join us in this vigil
> and you will know what it is to dream!
> Then you will know how marvelous it is
> to live threatened with Resurrection!
>
> To dream awake,
> to keep watch asleep
> to live while dying
> And to know ourselves already
> Resurrected!

Abbreviations

ARC	Aboriginal Rights Coalition
AMES	Association of Women in Solidarity
AMVA	Women Let Us Go Forward
ARDIGUA	Association of Dispersed Guatemalan Refugees
AVANSCO	Association for the Advance of the Social Sciences in Guatemala
BC	British Columbia
BTS	Maritimes-Guatemala Breaking the Silence Network
CALDH	Centre for Legal Action in Human Rights
CAMG	Central America Monitoring Group
CASA	Central America Student Alliance
CCDA	Campesino Committee of the Highlands
CCPP	Permanent Commissions of the Guatemalan Refugees
CEAR	Special Commission for Attention to Repatriates
CECI	Canadian Centre for International Studies and Cooperation
CEIPA	Ecumenical Centre for Pastoral Integration
CIA	Central Intelligence Agency
CIDA	Canadian International Development Agency
CIEDEG	Guatemalan Protestant Conference of Churches for Development
COMAR	Mexican Refugee Commission
CONAVIGUA	National Council of Guatemalan Widows
CONFREGUA	Guatemalan Conference of Catholic Religious
COVERCO	Commission for the Verification of Codes of Conduct
CPR	Communities of Population in Resistance
CTF	Christian Task Force on Central America
DFAIT	Department of Foreign Affairs and International Trade
EGP	Guerrilla Army of the Poor
EMP	Presidential High Command
FAMDEGUA	Families of the Disappeared of Guatemala

FTAA	Free Trade Area of the Americas
FRG	Guatemalan Republican Front
GATE	Global Awareness through Experience
GCSN	Guatemala-Canada Solidarity Network
GRICAR	International Group for Consulting and Supporting the Return
HIJOS	Children For Truth and Justice, against Forgetting and Silence
ICCHRLA	Inter-Church Committee on Human Rights in Latin America
MINUGUA	United Nations Verification Mission to Guatemala
MSN	Maquila Solidarity Network
NDP	New Democratic Party of Canada
NGO	Non-Governmental Organization
ODHAG	Archdiocese of Guatemala Human Rights Office
PA	Project Accompaniment
PAC	Civil Defence Patrol
PBI	Peace Brigades International
Project A	Project Accompaniment
REMHI	Recovery of Historical Memory Project
RUOG	United Representation of the Guatemalan Opposition
SOA	School of the Americas
TI	Taped Interview
UAN	Urgent Action Network
UNHCR	United Nations High Commission on Refugees
URNG	Guatemalan National Revolutionary Unity
WCC	World Council of Churches

Research Participants

THIS LIST DOES NOT INCLUDE most Guatemalans interviewed. Because of ongoing security concerns in Guatemala, only those Guatemalans whose names are already well known in the public domain have been used. Those who are identified by name are individuals whose names appear frequently in the print and electronic media in Guatemala.

Beth Abbott	Bud Godderis	Phil Molloy
Frances Arbour	Marg Green	Eric Mooers
Lajos Arendas	Frank Green	Denise Nadeau
Brian Atkinson	Luis Gurriaran	Sandra O'Toole
Lisa Bamford	Daniele Hart	Terry O'Toole
Wilf Bean	Randy Kohan	John Payne
Kathi Bentall	Gaby Labelle	Ann Pellerine
Nathalie Brière	Frank LaRue	Don Robertson
Jon Carrodus	Mike Lewis	Tara Scurr
Simone Carrodus	Judy Loo	Susan Sellers
Heather Carson	Margie Loo	Susan Skaret
Louise Casselman	Pat Loucks	Robert Smith
Pam Cooley	Lyn Kerans	Enrique Torres
Mary Corbett	Eva Manly	Marta Gloria de la Vega
Gen Creighton	Jim Manly	Diane Walsh
Janette Fecteau	Mark Manly	Brenda Wemp
Ann Godderis	Wes Maultsaid	Barbara Wood

Bibliography

Books and Theses

Associación para el Avance de las Ciencias Sociales en Guatemala (AVANSCO). *Donde Esta El Futuro: Procesos de reintegration en comunidades de retornados* [Where Is the Future?—Processes of reintegration in communities of those who have returned]. Cuaderno de Investigacion No. 8. Guatemala: Inforpress Centroamericana, 1992.

Baum, Gregory. *Compassion and Solidarity: The Church for Others*. Montreal: CBC Enterprises/les Entreprises Radio Canada, 1987.

Casaldáliga, Pedro, and Jose-María Vigil. *Political Holiness: A Spirituality of Liberation*. Maryknoll, NY: Orbis Books, 1994.

Commission for Historical Clarification. *Guatemala, Memory of Silence: Report of the Commission for Historical Clarification, Conclusions and Recommendations*. Guatemala: Commission for Historical Clarification, 1999.

Czerny, Michael, SJ, and Jamie Swift. *Getting Started on Social Analysis in Canada*. 1st ed. Toronto: Between the Lines, 1984.

De Roo, Remi J. *Of Justice, Revolutions and Human Rights: Notes on a Trip to Central America*. Victoria, BC: Diocese of Victoria, 1980.

Delli Sante, Angela. *Nightmare or Reality: Guatemala in the 1980s*. Amsterdam: Thela Publishers, 1996.

Dykstra, Corina Maria. *Education for Social Transformation: A Quest for the Practice of Democracy*. Unpublished Masters thesis, University of British Columbia, 1990.

Eguren, Luis Enrique, and Liam Mahony. *Unarmed Bodyguards: International Accompaniment for the Protection of Human Rights*. West Hartford: Kumerian Press, 1997.

Esquivel, Julia. *The Certainty of Spring: Poems by a Guatemalan in Exile*. Washington: Ecumenical Program on Central America and the Caribbean (EPICA), 1993 section on solidarity, n.p.

———. *Threatened with Resurrection—Amenazado de resurrección: Prayers and Poems from an Exiled Guatemalan*. 2nd ed. Elgin, IL: Brethren Press, 1994.

Falla, Ricardo. *Massacres in the Jungle: Ixcán, Guatemala (1975–1982)*. Trans. Julia Howland. Boulder: Westview Press, 1994.

Gómez, Emilio Abreu. *The Popal Vuh*. Trans. Regina Patrón. Merida, Mexico: Producción Editorial Dunte, 1992.

Henry, Jennifer. *Jubilee! A Justice Spirituality*. Toronto: Ecumenical Coalition for Economic Justice, 1999.

Heyward, Carter. *Saving Jesus from Those Who Are Right: Rethinking What It Means to Be Christian.* Minneapolis: Fortress Press, 1999.
Inay, Josefina Vda. de Martínez. *El Proceso de Ordenación Pastoral de Una Mujer Indigena y la Organisación de Una Iglesia Local Multietnica.* Guatemala City: Imprenta UNESAT, 2001.
Jonas, Susanne. *Of Centaurs and Doves: Guatemala's Peace Process.* Boulder: Westview Press, 2000.
Lovell, George. *A Beauty That Hurts: Life and Death in Guatemala.* 2nd ed. Toronto: Between the Lines, 2000.
Manly, James Douglas. *The Wounds of Manuel Saquic: Biblical Reflections from Guatemala.* Etobicoke: United Church Publishing House, 1997.
Manz, Beatrice. *Refugees of a Hidden War: The Aftermath of Counterinsurgency in Guatemala.* Albany, NY: State University of New York Press, 1988.
McFarlane, Peter. *Northern Shadows: Canadians and Central America.* Toronto: Between the Lines, 1989.
Merton, Thomas. *Conjectures of a Guilty Bystander.* NY: Doubleday, 1968.
Miskell, Tyron, and Tara Scurr. *The YouthGATE to Guatemala Handbook.* Vancouver: Christian Task Force on Central America, 1999 (a thorough guide to preparing and debriefing young participants in study tours to Guatemala, available from CTF).
Montejo, Victor, and Akab' Kanil. *Brevisima Relacion Testimonial de la Continua Destruccion del Mayab' (Guatemala).* Providence: Guatemala Scholars' Network, 1992.
Nelson, Diane. *A Finger in the Wound: Body Politics in Quincentennial Guatemala.* Berkeley: University of California Press, 1999.
Paiz, Alfonso Bauer, and Ivan Carpio Alfaro. *Memorias de Alfonso Bauer Paiz, Historia No Oficial de Guatemala.* Guatemala: Rusticatio Ediciones, 1996.
REMHI (Recovery of Historical Memory Project). *Guatemala, Never Again!/ REMHI, Recovery of Historical Memory Project; the Official Report of the Human Rights Office, Archdiocese of Guatemala.* (English version). Maryknoll, NY: Orbis Books, 1999.
Rubin, Lillian. *Families on the Faultline: America's Working Class Speaks about the Family, the Economy, Race and Ethnicity.* New York: Harper Collins, 1985.
Rumscheidt, Barbara. *No Room for Grace: Pastoral Theology and Dehumanization in the Global Economy.* Grand Rapids, MI: William B. Eerdmans, 1998.
Taylor, Clark. *Return of Guatemala's Refugees: Reweaving the Torn.* Philadelphia: Temple University Press, 1998.
United Church of Canada. *Mending the World: An Ecumenical Vision for Healing and Reconciliation.* Toronto: United Church of Canada, 1999.
Wright, Ronald. *Time among the Maya: Travels in Belize, Guatemala, and Mexico.* Markham: Penguin, 1989.

Articles and Book Chapters

Abbott, Beth. "Project Accompaniment: A Canadian Response" in *Nonviolent Intervention across Borders: A Recurrent Vision*. Ed. Yeshua Moser-Puang-suwan and Thomas Weber. Honolulu: University of Hawaii Press, 2000, 163–74.

Atkinson, Brian. "Coming Home: Refugees Return to Guatemala" in *New Brunswick Reader*. June 24, 1995, 10–13.

Bolan, Kim. *Vancouver Sun*. Feb. 20, 1993, A2 [contains quotation for Patricia Fuller].

Canada, Special Joint Committee on Canada's International Relations. *Independence and Internationalism: Report of the Special Joint Committee of the Senate and the House of Commons on Canada's International Relations*. Ottawa: Queen's Printer, 1986.

Chilcote, Marilyn. "Response to Felip Ixcot Jalpen's chapter, 'The Traditions and Culture of the Mayan-Quiché People'" in *Sanctuary: A Resource Guide for Understanding and Participating in the Central American Refugees' Struggle*. Ed. Gary MacEoin. San Francisco: Harper & Row, 1985. 146–47.

Cohen, Naomi. "El Retorno: Preparing the Return of Guatemalan Refugees" in *Convergence* 31, 3 (1998): 4–10.

Czerny, Michael, SJ. "Christians Made Justice a Vital Concern" in *Compass*. Mar./Apr. 1997.

———. "La dimension personal de la solidaridad" in *Hacia Una Sociedad Mas Solidaria*. Bilbao: Ediciones Mensajero, 1998. 51–64.

Fairbairn, Bill. "The Inter-Church Committee on Human Rights in Latin America" in *Coalitions for Justice: The Story of Canada's Interchurch Coalitions*. Ed. Christopher Lind and Joe Mihevc. Ottawa: Novalis Press, 1994. 169–84.

Guatemalan Church in Exile. "Guatemala: Refugees and Repatriation" in *Quarterly Bulletin of the Guatemalan Church in Exile* 7, 2 (1997).

Mansour, Valerie. "Refugees Cry Freedom—Guatemalans Speak Out for Change in Homeland" in *Halifax Chronicle-Herald*, June 30, 1990, B1.

———. "Guatemalan Refugees Endure Hardship, Fear" and "Guatemalans' Welcome Touches Antigonish Nurse" in *Halifax Chronicle-Herald*, July 31, 1993, C1.

Manz, Beatrice. "The Transformation of La Esperanza" in *Harvest of Violence: The Maya Indians and the Guatemalan Crisis*. Ed. Robert M. Carmack. Norman: University of Oklahoma Press, 1988. 70–89.

McCullum, Hugh. "Guatemala's New Gospel" in *The United Church Observer*, New Series 46, 10 (Apr. 1983): 49–54.

Moffatt, Jeanne. "Ten days for World Development" in *Coalitions for Justice: The Story of Canada's Interchurch Coalitions*. Ed. Christopher Lind and Joe Mihevc. Ottawa: Novalis Press, 1994. 151–68.

North, Liisa B., and Alan B. Simmonds. "Concluding Reflections: Refugee Return, National Transformation, and Neoliberal Restructuring" in *Journeys of Fear: Refugee Return and National Transformation in Guate-*

mala. Ed. Liisa North and Alan Simmonds. Montreal: McGill-Queen's University Press, 1999. 272–300.

Pico, Juan Hernandez, SJ. "Solidarity with the Poor and the Unity of the Church" in *A Theology of Christian Solidarity*. Ed. Jon Sobrino and Juan Hernandez Pico, Maryknoll. NY: Orbis Books, 1985. 43–69.

Reuther, Rosemary Radford. "Introduction" to *Threatened with Resurrection—Amenazado de resurrección*. 2nd ed. Elgin, IL: Brethren Press, 1994.

Similox, Vitalino Salazar. "Algunas Propuestas de la Religiosidad Maya, hacia un Pluralismo Religioso, en el Marco de los Acuerdos de Paz." Pamphlet printed by Conferencia de Iglesias Evangelicas de Guatemala (CIEDEG), 1999.

Sobrino, Jon, SJ. "Bearing with One Another in Faith" in *A Theology of Christian Solidarity*. Ed. Jon Sobrino and Juan Hernandez Pico. Maryknoll, NY: Orbis Books, 1985. 1–42.

Wyatt, Peter. "Foreword" in *The Wounds of Manuel Saquic: Biblical Reflections from Guatemala*, by James Douglas Manly. Etobicoke: United Church Publishing House, 1997.

Zarowny, Yvonne. "Liberation Theology in a Canadian Context: A Case Study" in *Liberation Theology and Sociopolitical Liberation: A Reader*. Ed. Jorge García Antezana. Burnaby: Institute for the Humanities, Simon Fraser University, 1992.

Other Resources
(Videos, Web sites, Poems, Prayers and Songs, Unpublished Reports, Diaries)

Abbott, Beth. Cited in report to Project Accompaniment Atlantic, 1993.

Amnesty International. http://www.web.amnesty.org/library/index/AI Apr. 1, 2003.

Anderson, Kathryn. "Letter to the Editor," *The Antigonish Casket*, Jan. 1994.

———. *Reflections on Guatemala-Breaking the Silence: Tatamagouche Centre's Relationship with the Guatemalan People, 1988–1995*. Unpublished report (in Archives).

———. "Listening to the Guatemalan Experience of Solidarity" in *Proyecto A, Newsletter of Canadian Accompaniment in Guatemala* 1, 2 (1998): 4 (in Archives).

Archbishop's Office on Human Rights in Guatemala. E-mail—Letter of thanks, June 2001.

Berson, Josh. Letter to Vancouver support committee, 1994 (in Archives).

Briere, Natalie, and Margie Loo. Project Accompaniment: Pre-training package (in Archives).

Brazier, Bev. Personal diary. November 1999, e-mail to delegation members.

Canada/Central America Urgent Action Network. *Guatemala: A Human Rights Profile: 1991*.

Central America Monitoring Group. Unpublished 1987 report on human rights in Guatemala, 1987 (in Archives).

Bibliography

———. Report by delegates to a meeting with the Permanent Commissions, 1992 (in Archives).
Central America Report. "Guategate: a barrage of accusations and investigations" in 27, 23 (2000).
CERIGUA. *Xamán Massacre: 15 Soldiers Freed*, in Weekly Briefs #40, Dec. 17, 1999. http://www.tulane.edu/~libweb/RESTRICTED/CERIGUA/1999_1217.txt.
Chapman, Chris. E-mail copy of Urgent Action, Sept. 2000.
Christian Task Force on Central America Formation Document. 1984 (in Archives).
———. "Canada—Bilateral Aid to Guatemala" in *Networking...Action Newsletter.* 5, 1 (1986): 6.
———. *Summary of Negotiations Meeting between the Refugees in Mexico and the Guatemalan Government.* June 1991 (in Archives).
"Como Cantar a Dios en Tierra Extrana?" in *Voces del Tiempo: Revista de Religion y Sociedad Guatemala* 7 (July–Sept. 1993): 20.
Cooley, Pamela. "About the Trip: A Report from Pamela Cooley" in *Networking...Action Newsletter, Christian Task Force on Central America* 5, 1 (1986).
———. Letter, Apr. 1990 (in Archives).
———. Letter, Dec. 1991 (in Archives).
Corbett, Mary. Address commemorating the murder of Bishop Gerardi, Guatemala City, Apr. 26, 1999. Shared with author (in Archives).
Curle, Maureen. "Editorial." *Networking...Action Newsletter, Christian Task Force on Central America* 5, 4 (1986): 2.
Douglas, Eleanor. E-mail to Steering Committee, August 1998.
Fox, Robert. Unpublished Report to Central America Monitoring Group, 1994 (in Archives).
Fuller, Patricia. *Proyecto A, Project A: Commemorative Issue* June 1999, 3 (in Archives).
Gallant, Lennie. *Land of the Maya*, on cassette, produced for Oxfam Canada. Copyright: Revenant Records (SOCAN) 1991.
Geggie, Linda. Report to Project A, 1993 (in Archives).
Godderis, Bud. Christian Task Force on Central America Delegation Report, 1988 (in Archives).
Grisdale, Debbie, and Wes Maultsaid. *Project Acompanante*, Report to Guatemala Network Coordinating Committee, 1989 (in Archives).
Gronau, Jim. *Reunion* 4, 1 (1997).
Guatemala-Canada Solidarity Network. http://www.gcsn.org, Nov. 2000.
Guatemala Human Rights Commission Refugee Return Report #4. Feb. 1993.
Guatemala Human Rights Commission/USA. Update #4. Jan. 1993.
Hagerman, Keith, and Carol Kell. "ALREADY and NOT YET: Sensing the Kingdom." Sermon preached at St. James United Church, Antigonish, Nova Scotia, Nov. 1999.
Inter-Church Committee on Human Rights in Latin America (ACCHRLA). 1985 delegation report.
Kohan, Randy. "*International Presence—A Personal Recollection*" in Project Accompaniment Pre-Training Package, Appendix 1 (in Archives).

Kohan, Randy, and Susan Skaret. Report to Project Accompaniment, Jan. 1993 (in Archives).
Lemieux, Paul. Guatemala-Canada Solidarity Network Solidarity Campaign, 1999 (circulated by e-mail).
Lewis, Mike. "Evolving Our Covenant: Toward a More Participatory, Accountable Community." *Networking...ACTION Newsletter* 5, 3 (1985): 3-4.
Long, Dan. *Situation Report #56,* World Council of Churches, May 1995. E-mailed to organizations supporting Guatemalan refugees.
Loo, Judy. "Ceremony," unpublished poem. Apr. 1999.
———. "Textile Maquilas and Workers Rights." *Inverness Oran News,* Apr. 14, 1999.
———. "Who Killed the Bishop?" *Inverness Oran News,* Apr. 14, 1999.
Loucks, Pat. "All Souls Day," "Sumpango," and "Marta," unpublished poems. Nov. 1999.
Lydon, John. Letter to Victoria Project Accompaniment Committee, 1994 (in Archives).
MacDonald, Frank. Series of five articles in *Inverness Oran News,* Mar.-Apr. 1999 (in Archives).
MacKenzie,Tamara. Letter to support committee, 1995 (in Archives).
Manly, Eva. Report to Project Accompaniment, 1994 (in Archives).
Mansour, Valerie. Unpublished report to CUSO, 1991 (in Archives).
Maquila Solidarity Network. http://www.web.net/~msn Nov. 2000.
Maultsaid, Wes. Personal diary, Jan. 1983.
Monitoring Update: The First Return of the Guatemalan Refugees. Updates #17, 18, 19, Jesuit Refugee Service (in Archives).
Network News. Christian Task Force on Central America Newsletter, Vancouver:
  Carrodus, Jon, "Urgent Action Network Swamped by Requests," 5, 1 (1990): 6.
  Carrodus, Simone, and John Payne. "The Return—An Update: Guatemala" 8, 1 (1993): 2.
  de la Vega, Marta Gloria. "Mission of Peace Takes Guatemalan Exiles Home" 3, 2 (1988): 3.
  ———. "Support from Canadians Crucial for Trip to Guatemala: A Letter of Thanks" 4, 2 (1989): 5.
  ———. "When the Silence Is Broken" 10, 1 (1994): 2.
  English, Ken. "My Precious Community" 10, 1 (1994): 11.
  Gear, Janet, and Peter Golden. "A Trip to the Refugee Camps" 2, 2 (1987): 1-2.
  Godderis, Bud. "School of the Americas Watch Update" Spring 2001: 4-5.
  Howard, Lillian. "First Nations in Canada Respond to Challenge of '500 Years'" 7, 1 (1992).
  Kelly, Deirdre. "A Letter to Our Sustaining Members" Fall 2001: 2.
  King, Kathi. "Images of Beauty, Strength, and Suffering" 6, 1 (1991): 4-6.
  ———. "Laugh with Tears and Cry with Laughter" 10, 1 (1994): 4-5.
  Kranabetter, Rita. "When the Gifts Feel Like Stones" 10, 1 (1994): 7.

Marchal, Martha. "Huipiles Return Home" 7, 1 (1992): 3.
Nadeau, Denise. "Option *with* the Poor" 9, 3 (1994): 8–10.
Robertson, Sandi, and Jeannie White. "GATE Way to Mexico" 5, 2: 7.
Smith, Robert. "Communities of Resistance Seek End to Repression" 6, 1 (1991): 1.
White, Ross. "Clandestine Theology No More" 8, 1 (1993): 6.
Niesh, Kevin. "Visit Colourful and Friendly Guatemala" in *La Voz* (Vancouver) 4, 2 (1989): 8.
Otzoy, Antonio. "El Dialogo Entre Las Espiritualidades" (Dialogue among Spiritualities), unpublished article, 2000.
Parliamentary Relations Secretariat, Parliament of Canada, Ottawa Report on the 79th Inter-Parliamentary Conference: Guatemala City, Guatemala, Apr. 11–16, 1998, 10.
Parra, Juan de Dios (Secretary-General of the Latin American Human Rights Association). From a paper given to the Norwegian Peoples Aid 60th anniversary conference, January 2000. E-mail distributed to members of the Americas Policy Group, Canadian Council for International Cooperation.
Prensa Libre (Newspaper). Guatemala City, Dec. 10, 1993.
Project Accompaniment (reports in Archives). Apr. 1993 Delegation report.
———. Atlantic Delegation report, *Is Corn Subversive?* 1994.
———. Pre-Training Package, 1998.
———. Report, June 1993–May 1994.
———. Report to the Inter-American Commission on Human Rights of the Organization of American States and the Canadian Embassy in Guatemala, Sept. 2, 1993.
Project Acompañimiento: A Visit to the Guatemalan People in Refuge in Mexico. 1990.
Project Counselling Services for Latin America Report. 1991 (in Archives).
Rees, Liz. "Mutations," "One Afternoon in Nueva Union," and "Para Ti (For you)," unpublished poems, 1997.
———. "Special Team: A Personal Reflection" in *Proyecto A: Newsletter of Canadian Accompaniment in Guatemala,* 1, 3 (1998): 3 (in Archives).
Rees, Liz, and Louise Sevigny. *Edmonton Journal,* June 1, 1997.
Roberts, Lisa. "New Directions for Project Accompaniment" in *Proyecto A: Newsletter of Canadian Accompaniment in Guatemala,* 1, 1 (1998): 2 (in Archives).
———. "Transitioning" in *Proyecto A: Newsletter of Canadian Accompaniment in Guatemala* 1, 3 (1998): 2 (in Archives).
Rowat, Colin. Letter to support committee, 1994 (in Archives).
———. Letter to new accompaniers, 1994 (in Archives).
Sams, Samantha. *Guatemalan Peace Building: Between Dignity and Demise.* Guatemala-Canada Solidarity Network, Sept. 2001. http://www.gcsn.org/situ/situ.html.
———. *Informe Sobre el Acompañamiento Para Las Denuncias por Genocidio y Otros Casos.* Guatemala-Canada Solidarity Network, Sept. 2002. http://www.gcsn.org/situ/situ.html.

Sams, Samantha, and Ruth Taylor. *Almost a Year in Power: Promises, Pacts and Political In-Fighting*. Guatemala-Canada Solidarity Network, Nov. 2000. http://www.gcsn.org/situ/situ.html

Shankar, Finola. E-mails, May 1 and July 10, 2000.

Sellers, Susan. Personal diary, 2000, shared with author.

Shaw, Paula. "Where Should PA Go? Saber" in *Proyecto A: Newsletter of Canadian Accompaniment in Guatemala*, 2, 8 (1998) (in Archives).

Siglo Veintiuno (Guatemalan newspaper). Dec. 14, Dec. 16, 1993.

Spragge, Godfrey. Report to Project Accompaniment, 1997 (in Archives).

Taylor, Clark with Lynn Rhoads. "Partners across Borders: Santa María Tzejá, Guatemala, and the Congregational Church of Needham, Massachusetts, 1996 Revision." http://www.tiac.net/users/robd/guatemala/ Apr. 2002.

Ten Days for World Development (Canadian ecumenical coalition) 1983 materials.

United Church of Canada. 1988 General Council, Division of World Outreach Report, pp. 615–16.

United Nations Verification Mission in Guatemala (MINUGUA). March 1995 Report. Spanish versions of these reports are available at http://www.minugua.guate.net/

———. July 2000 Special Report.

———. Sept. 2000 Report.

Victoria Project Accompaniment Committee. Letter to Canadian government, May 1993.

Walsh, Diane. *REMHI*, unpublished lyrics of song, 1995.

When the People Lead [videorecording]. Produced by Variations on a Wave in co-production with Canadian International Development Agency; produced and directed by Merran Smith, Michael Simpson; written by Merran Smith, Richmond, BC: Imagemedia Services, 1993.

White, Melanie. Winnipeg evaluation of ODHAG Visit, Apr. 2000. Sent as e-mail attachment to Guatemala-Canada Solidarity Network Steering Committee.

Williams, Paul. Report to Project Accompaniment, Apr. 1998 (in Archives).

Index

Abbott, Beth, 48, 57, 78, 136, 170, 219, 255
Aboriginal People's TV Network, 273
Aboriginal Rights Coalition (ARC), 224
accompaniment, 25, 29; by Canadians, 46-49, 57, 73, 102, 105-106, 123; by church, 37-38, 139; communication by, 69; controlled by refugees, 40, 42, 47, 213, 251; definition of, 44, 211, 254; difficulties of, 207-208; discussion about, 40-41; equipment for, 69, 84, 86, 87; funding for, 137; government response to, 41-42, 60, 83-84, 105; health concerns for, 67, 72; need for, 41, 46, 67, 84, 89, 96-98; ongoing, 66-73, 96, 102, 141; recruitment for, 49, 89, 95, 99, 136; and relationships with refugees, 69-71, 84-85, 97, 110, 203, 205, 212, 236-37, 249, 285-86; requests for, 137, 223; right to, 30, 31, 33, 40; role of, 47-48, 68-69, 72, 77, 85-87, 104-108, 110, 179, 233, 258; and security, 47, 61, 78, 90, 91-92, 101-102, 140, 175-79, 219, 252, 275-78; selection for, 47, 51, 84, 98-99, 108; training for, 47, 48-51, 75, 104-105. *See also* Project Accompaniment
Accompaniment Forum, 106, 108, 110
Ace International, 281, 282
Acker, Alison, 57
Africa, 215
Agreda, Claudia, 180
aid, 206-207, 208-210, 257; food aid, xi, 31
"Aid to Guatemala: What Canadians Must Know" (CTF), 173
"All Souls Day, Sumpango" (Loucks), 239-40

Alliance for a New Nation, 219
Alta Verapaz, 91
Amnesty International, xviii, 165, 177, 184, 266
Anderson, Kathryn, 2, 149, 279; accompaniment by, 78-80, 137, 140; as delegate, 66, 147, 133; recruitment to solidarity work, xvii-xix, 154, 189-91; on relationships, 70, 219; staff involvement by, 132, 263
Anglican Church, 118, 180
Arbour, Frances, 46-47, 116, 122, 230
Archdiocese of Guatemala Human Rights Office (ODHAG), xiv, 136, 140, 142, 180, 210, 269, 272-74, 279
Arendas, Lajos, 32, 59, 164-65
Argentina, 186
army. *See* military
assassinations, 54-55, 136, 145, 264; of church workers, 70-71, 181, 201, 202; of Gerardi, 103, 142, 155, 165, 170, 184, 230, 253, 261, 269-74; of Mack, 29, 140, 163-64; of Romero, 117, 123, 155, 181; of Saquic, 138, 236; threats of, 119, 139
Association of Dispersed Guatemalan Refugees (ARDIGUA), 32-33, 75, 76, 77, 93-94, 97
Atkinson, Brian, 88, 94, 194, 195
Atlantic Ecumenical Justice Network, 243
Atlantic Inter-Congregational Social Justice Network, 243
Atlantic Region Solidarity Network, xix, 46
Atlantic Urgent Action Network, 135 *See also* Urgent Action Network
Atwood, Margaret, 230
Aurora 8 de octubre, 91

301

302 Index

Avila, Monsignor, 41
Axworthy, Lloyd, 61, 170

Bamford, Lisa, 206, 213
Barrientos, Byron, 265
Base Christian Communities (Nicaragua), 120, 244
Basic Resources, 91
Bauer Paiz, Alfonso, 30, 214
Baum, Gregory, 114, 201
Bautista, Joaquín Jimenez, 75-77, 93
BC-Nicaragua Solidarity Project, 119
Bean, Wilf, xix, 140, 222, 224-25
Bentall, Kathi, 128, 168
Berger, Thomas, 121
Berson, Josh, 84-85
Bible, 134, 195; on justice, 124, 217, 273; on poverty, 114, 120, 211-12; relevance to Guatemala of, 201, 218, 230-33; solidarity in, 248-49, 259
Bickford, David, 172
Blandón de Cerezo, Raquel, 28-29
Bola de Oro, 136, 139, 142, 145, 147-49
Bowles, Peter, 123
Brazier, Bev, 205, 214, 282
Bread for the World, 48
Breaking the Silence Coffee, 170
Breaking the Silence Network. *See* Maritimes-Guatemala Breaking the Silence Network
Brière, Nathalie, 87
Britain, 57
British Columbia Government Employees' Union, 177
British Columbia Inter-Agency Committee on Central America, 180
British Columbia Interchurch Committee on World Development Education, xi
British Columbia Ministry for Children and Families, 129
Brooks, Cathie, 133
Brown, Creighton, 147

Caba, 159-60
Caertano, Teresa, 281
Café Justicia, 169
Caldwell, Lynn, 133
cameras, 69, 81, 84, 86, 194

Campeche (Mexico), 24-25, 39, 45, 54, 74
Campesino Committee of the Highlands (CCDA), 169-70
campesinos, xvii; organization of, 11-14, 93, 169; refugee movement of, 21-22; security of, 54, 159-60, 201; solidarity among, 37-38, 62, 90, 93-94; targeted in scorched-earth campaign, 14-17, 18-19, 21; violence against, 117. *See also* Maya people; refugees
Canada, 239; attitude to poverty in, 201, 221-23, 242-43; awareness in, xi-xii, 46, 48-49, 120-21, 134, 170, 212, 214-17, 221-26; commitment to accompaniment in, 46-49, 57, 73, 102, 105-106, 220; Department of Foreign Affairs and International Trade, 164, 265; and diplomacy, 32, 73, 79, 117, 278-79; Embassy of, 52, 54, 59-60, 74, 75-76, 77, 84, 102, 160, 279-80, 283-84; foreign aid by, xviii, 115, 118, 162, 173-74; funding in, 163, 267; government policy of, 155, 159, 162, 170-72, 271, 283-84; group conflict in, 4, 128; injustices in, 224, 225; lobbying in, 42, 48, 73, 74, 116, 171-75, 275; mission in, 247-48; refugees in, xviii, 39, 115, 121; similarity of issues in, 160, 221-25; solidarity with Chileans, 115; solidarity with Guatemalans, xvi, xviii, 1, 39-40, 42, 79, 95, 96, 103, 132, 163, 166-67, 204, 206-207, 212, 268, 278; solidarity with Nicaraguans, 120, 131; solidarity with Salvadorans, 131; and support for US policies in, 11, 18, 115, 116, 155, 171-72
Canadian Catholic Organization for Development and Peace, 42, 118, 124, 125, 131, 180
Canadian Centre for International Studies and Cooperation (CECI), 78, 163
Canadian Council for International Cooperation, 48, 162, 263, 279
Canadian Council of Churches, 230
Canadian International Development Agency (CIDA), 48, 121, 149, 164, 170, 174, 188

Canadian Labour Congress, 118, 284
Canadian Union of Postal Workers, 180
Canadian Union of Public Employees, 137
Cantabal, 62, 71, 77, 79-80, 86, 90-91
capitalism, 115
Carpenter's Union, 155
Carrodus, Bronwyn, 184
Carrodus, Jon, 162, 243, 244, 247
Carrodus, Simone, 210, 243, 247, 255
Carson, Heather, 167, 203, 214, 221-22
Carty, Bob, 122
Casa Alianza, 135, 164
Casa Canadiense, 66-67, 71
Casaldáliga, Pedro, 200, 247
Casselman, Louise, 118, 183, 243
Castillo, Rolando, 176, 230
Catholic Action, 12
Catholic Church, 60, 61, 118
CBC radio, 136, 177
censorship, 17
Central America, 116, 118, 119, 122, 124-25, 157, 162, 171-72, 213. *See also* Latin America; specific countries
Central America Education and Action Project, 121-22, 124. *See also* Guatemala Refugee Project
Central America Monitoring Group (CAMG), 47, 48, 49, 159, 180
Central America Student Alliance (CASA), 169, 184-85, 191
Central America Support Committee, 254-55
Central America Week, 155
Central American Plan Puebla-Panama, 280
Central Intelligence Agency, 11, 15, 18, 114
"Ceremony" (Loo), 234-35
Cerezo, Vinicio, 27-28, 173, 177
Cerro Alto (Guatemala), 136, 139, 142, 144-45, 147, 148-49
Chaculá, 89-90
Chapman, Chris, 187
Chiapas (Mexico), 44, 47, 117; refugee camps in, xi, 24-25, 45, 122, 137, 204; refugees in, 21-22, 37-39; routes through, 53, 78
Chiasson, Danielle, 133

Chichicastenango, 238-39
children, 12-13, 71; and culture, 31, 46, 129, 236; education of, 135-36, 182; health of, 15, 64, 134, 136; and hunger, xi, 113-14, 134, 136; labour by, 135-36, 144, 148, 182; rapport with, 71, 107, 122, 148-49; rights of, 164; and solidarity, 182-83; street, 135-36, 186-87; and testimony, xi-xii, 182
Children for Truth and Justice, against Forgetting and Silence (HIJOS), 181, 184, 186-87, 274
Chile, 114-15
Chimaltenango, 132, 134, 136, 144, 145, 147
Chisec, 62
Chretien, Jean, 278
Christian Aid (Britain), 48
Christian Solidarity Committee, 38, 39
Christian Task Force on Central America (CTF), xi, 2, 93, 117; agenda of, 122, 124-25, 128-29, 153-54, 159; difficulties of, 127-28; domestic awareness in, 222; and education, 157, 173; formation of, 39, 113, 119-20, 121, 123, 171, 244-46; and government policy, 170; mutuality in, 204; role of, 42, 165, 257, 280; spirituality in, 189, 245-46, 254; staffing in, 118, 230, 237; structure of, 127, 131, 162, 179-81, 185, 264; support from, 48, 57; youth in, 183-86
Christianity, 17-18; and church, 66, 229, 241-42, 244-46; and justice, 253-54; and Mayan spirituality, 234-35, 237; and mission, 246-47, 253; and solidarity, 14, 37-38, 42, 114-16, 229-30, 241-42, 254-56, 258-59; and spirituality, 200
Church of the Complete Word. *See* El Verbo
Cimiento de Esperanza, 91
civil defence patrols (PAC), 26, 31, 54, 63, 71, 75-77, 89, 91, 267
Clinton, William, 15
Coady International Institute (NS), 12
Cobán, 59, 62, 71, 92
Coca Cola, 119, 122

Co-Development Canada (Co-Dev), 169
coffee, 169-70, 216
Cold War, 11, 116, 171
Comite Chretien pour les Droits Humaines en Amerique Latine, 162
Commission for Historical Clarification (UN), 15
Commission for the Verification of Corporate Codes of Conduct (COVERCO), 283
Committee of Peasant Unity, 12
communities, 90, 109-11; Christian, 120, 246; development of, 102, 145, 184, 205, 208, 215, 251; faith, 241-43; Jesus in, xv-xvi; organization of, 11-13, 47-48, 66, 95, 161; solidarity, 243-46; violence against, xii-xiv, 12-13
Communities of Population in Resistance (CPR), 67, 18, 67, 77, 79, 136, 137, 140, 159-60, 211, 230
"Como Cantar a Dios en Tierra Extraña?", 23
Congregation of Notre Dame, 125, 138, 242
Conquest, 9-10, 237
Conrado de La Cruz, 283
Contadora Peace Accords. *See* Peace Accords
Contras, 123
Cooley, Pam, 39, 44, 45, 46, 47-48, 49, 201, 205
Co-operative Commonwealth Federation (CCF), 11
Cooperatives Agency, 81
Corbett, Mary, 145, 149; accompaniment by, 138, 140, 148, 161; on churches, 242, 243; on justice, 269; on relationships, 256; on solidarity, 214, 215, 273; on spirituality, 229, 231, 255; on understanding, 158
Costa Rica, 119, 208
Council of Canadians, 185, 223
Cox Max, Maurilia, 93, 181
Creighton, Gen, 181-82, 184, 186
Cuarto Pueblo, xiv, 16, 82, 83, 85
CUSO, 42, 46, 47, 52, 118, 121, 134, 180, 267
Cyr, Reiko, 71
Czerny, Michael, 113, 203, 224

Dale, Linda, 182
de Alvarado, Pedro, 9
de Dios Parra, Juan, 113
de Garcia, Nineth, 208
de la Madrid, Miguel, 28
de la Vega, Marta Gloria, 185; and accompaniment, 125, 175-78, 163, 179, 208, 230; on faith, 248; on mission, 256, 257; on story-telling, 156-57; as refugee, xviii, 121; refugee work by, xi, xiv-xvi, 39, 119, 124, 129, 233; on solidarity, 199, 204; as staff, 121, 127; as resource person, 180
de las Casas, Bartolomé, 9
De León Carpio, Ramiro, 41, 74-75, 95
De Roo, Bishop Remi, 12-13, 117, 121
democracy, 11, 266; establishment of, 1, 109, 280, 285; facade of, 17, 25, 27; reality of, 96, 166, 174, 175, 219
Dialogue Centre, xvii
Dickson, Brian, 32, 59, 133, 192
Doctors of the World, 67, 69
Doña Francisca (Guatemalan activist), 143, 145, 147
Donovan, Jean, 201
Drouin, Marc, 87
drugs, 60, 71-72, 83, 95, 104
Dulles, Allan, 11
Dulles, John Foster, 11
Dykstra, Corina, 119, 174

Ecumenical Centre for Pastoral Integration (CEIPA), 135, 182
Ecumenical Coalition for Economic Justice. *See* GATT-fly
Ecumenical Task Force for Justice in the Americas. *See* Christian Task Force on Central America
ecumenism, 253-56
Egan, Brian, 73-74
El Quetzal, 94-95, 96
El Salvador, xvii, 40, 116-17, 123, 131, 141, 201, 219, 220
El Verbo, 17-18, 25
elections, 145-46
Elkurdi, Fatina, 166
End Legislated Poverty (ELP), 222
English, Kathy, 223
English, Ken, 223, 245
Escuintla, 94

Index

Esgenoopetitj (NS), 148, 224
Esquipulas II Peace Accords. *See* Peace Accords
Esquivel, Julia, xvii-xviii, 122, 123, 128, 189; on biblical interpretation, 190-91, 194-96, 231-32, 248; "Indian Tapestry," vii-viii; "Threatened with Resurrection," 287; on solidarity, 211, 229, 287
Estado Mayor Presidencial (EMP), 266
ethnic cleansing. *See* genocide
exile, xvii, 21, 23, 45, 119
exposure tours, 157-58

faith, 167, 233; active, 241, 244, 248, 254; and community, 241-43; as response, 90, 144, 218, 240; transformation of, 229-30, 241
Falla, Ricardo, xiv, 9
Falwell, Jerry, 17
fear, 57; and accompaniment, 49-50, 54; as part of life, 89, 98, 209, 220-21, 281, 282; transcendence of, 136, 196, 205, 208
Fecteau, Janette, 167
Felipe (son of Doña Francisca), 145
Ferguson, Chris, 175
First Nations, 135, 143, 148, 223-24, 231, 273
Five Hundred Years of Indigenous, Black, and Popular Resistance Continental Conference, 135, 223
Flores, Bishop Gerardo, 62
Free Trade of the Americas Agreement (FTAA), 280
Formicelli, Marco, 81
Fox, Robert, 84
Franklin, Fred, 116
Free Trade Area of the Americas, 149
Friedman, Milton, 115
Fuller, Patricia, 32, 41, 60, 73
funding, 88; for accompaniment, 57, 137; cuts to, 131-32, 163, 164, 284; for delegations, 134, 160-61, 188; for organizations, 162-63, 170, 180, 267; for projects, 23, 129, 135, 148-49, 156; for Returns, 46-49, 78, 95

Gabereau, Vicki, 136
Gaffney, Beryl, 59
Gallant, Lennie, 9, 133, 135, 136, 191-94, 238-39
Garciá, Lucas, 13, 270
GATE, 157-58, 181, 237; Youth, 160-61, 184-86, 254
GATT-fly, 118
Gaudreau, Isabelle, 92
Gauthier, Nathalie, 87
Geggie, Linda, 77-78, 107, 205
gender equality, 224
genocide, xii, 224; charges of, 265, 275-76; responsibility for, 14-15, 21, 266; and silence, xi, xvii
Georgetti, Ken, 284
Gerardi, Bishop Juan José, 103, 142, 155, 165, 170, 184, 230, 253, 261, 269-74
Germany, 57
Global Accord on Human Rights, 265
globalization, 1, 185, 224-25, 244, 280, 283
Godderis, Ann, 125, 185; on accompaniment, 49, 62; on arts, 189; on Canada, 222, 242-43; on education through delegations, 157, 184; experiences of, 115, 122-23, 175, 229-30, 231-32; on dignity, 121; on involvement, 120, 126, 127, 155, 167; on policy, 172, 174; on relationships, 129, 156, 160, 166, 205-206; on spirituality, 246
Godderis, Bud, 120, 123, 125-26, 155, 160, 167, 175, 179, 185, 242, 246
Golden, Peter, 163
Graham, Billy, 17
Green, Frank, 52, 57, 61
Green, Marg, 121, 181
Grisdale, Debbie, 42-45
Gronau, Jim, 267, 269
Group of Families of the Disappeared (GAM), 208
Guatemala, 52; Canadian aid in, xviii; Canadian delegations to, 45, 116-17, 132, 134-36, 137-38, 142, 147, 157-60, 175-78, 184-85, 203, 218, 273-74; Canadian solidarity with, 262; Canadian solidarity with refugees in, xvi, xviii, 1, 39-40, 42, 79, 95, 96, 103, 132, 163, 166-67, 204, 206-207, 212, 229; civil war in, 1, 11, 96, 219;

colonial history of, 9-10, 215; coup in, 73-75, 89, 137, 177; delegations to Canada from, 132-34, 137, 138, 148, 154, 160-61, 187-88, 272-73; international image of, 31, 41-42, 53-54, 60, 72, 163-65, 173; negotiations with government of, 30-33, 41, 47, 53-55, 74-75, 78, 85, 165, 208; political power in, 10-11, 13-14, 17-18, 27-28, 145, 261-62, 265-66, 268, 276-77; repression in, 4-5, 10, 13-14, 25, 106-107, 121, 122, 153. *See also* military
Guatemala-Canada Solidarity Network, 269, 271-80; creation of, 103, 180, 210, 267-68, 271; links with other organizations, 159; mission of, 203, 224; staffing of, 219, 261
Guatemala City, 59, 61, 71, 94, 119, 134, 138, 139, 181, 268, 273, 281
Guatemala: Never Again. See *Nunca Mas*
Guatemala Refugee Project, xi-xii, xviii, 121. *See also* Christian Task Force on Central America in BC
Guatemalan Bishops' Conference, 31
Guatemalan Confederation of Catholic Religious (CONFREGUA), 95
Guatemalan Human Rights Commission, 32, 60
Guatemalan National Revolutionary Unity (URNG), 13, 61, 109
Guatemalan Network Coordinating Committee, 42, 45
Guatemalan Protestant Conference of Churches for Development (CIEDEG), 66, 95, 132, 137
Guatemalan Red Cross, 25, 41
Guatemalan Republican Front (FRG), 145-46, 261-62, 267
Guerrilla Army of the Poor (EGP), 13-14
guerrillas, 14, 89, 97; alleged links with refugees, 29, 63, 80-81, 83, 107; involvement with, 109-10; refugees accused of being, xii, 55, 60, 72; resistance by, 67, 106-107
Gurriaran, Luis, 12, 211
Gutiérrez, Mayra, 264

Hagerman, Keith, 217, 281
Harrison, Beverly Wildung, 214
Hart, Daniele, 203, 237, 255
health care, xiv, 250-51
Health Sciences Association, 125
Heap, Dan, 59
Hermandad de Presbiterios Mayas, xix, 138, 161
Heyward, Carter, 202
Highlands United Church, 243
Historical Clarification Commission, 265, 278
Holland, 57
Home Street Mennonite Church (Winnipeg), 57
Honduras, 40, 41, 120
hope, 90, 196; despite suffering, 153, 156, 191, 195, 213, 239, 285; for future, 12-13, 144, 161; inextinguishable, 136, 189, 214; signs of, 77; and solidarity, 212, 233
Howard, Lillian, 223-24
Hudson's Bay, 284
Huehuetenango (Guatemala), xii, xiv, 53, 59-60, 74, 75, 89-90, 98
Huehuetenango, Diocese of, 60
huipils, 204-205
human rights, 17, 134; advocates for, 103, 107, 109, 115-17, 132, 143, 264-65; concern for, 110, 113, 167, 172, 224, 265, 278-80; death for, 132, 201, 202; deterioration in, 263, 265-66, 274; improvements in, 173, 283; knowledge of, 33, 134, 164; violations of, 30, 49, 54, 61, 115-16, 121, 142, 153, 164, 166, 170, 219, 270
Human Rights Watch, 282

"I Am Not Afraid of Death" (Esquivel), 196
impunity, 184, 187, 265, 271-72, 273, 275, 278. *See also* military: and lawlessness
Inay, Josefina, 139, 142, 143, 149; delegations with, 133-34, 147, 148, 183; on Guatemalan life, 145, 216; on spirituality, 234
injustice, xvii, 9, 118, 122, 128, 208, 213, 217, 224, 247. *See also* justice
Inter-Agency Working Group on Latin America, 180

Index

Inter-American Human Rights Court, 92
Inter-Church Committee for World Development Education, 118
Inter-Church Committee on Chile. *See* Inter-Church Committee on Human Rights in Latin America
Inter-Church Committee on Human Rights in Latin America (ICCHRLA), xi, 116, 165, 171, 180, 230
Inter Pares, 47
International Centre for Human Rights and Democratic Development, 64, 136-37, 162
International Committee of the Red Cross, 25
International Council of Voluntary Agencies, 32
International Election Observers, 145
International Indian Treaty Council, 175
International Monetary Fund, 115, 280
International Support Group for the Return (GRICAR), 32, 41, 69, 79, 91, 94, 95
International Women's March 2000 Against Violence and Poverty, 263
Iqui Bal'aan, 274
Ixcán region, 12-13, 16, 21, 251; accompaniment in, 97, 106, 194; military in, 67-69, 74, 85-87, 93; return to, 26, 62, 64, 79, 137
Ixcán Grande Agricultural Cooperative, xiv, 12-13, 77-88, 90, 109
Ixmiché, 234-36, 239
Izabal, Department of, 264

Janzen, Randy, 57, 93, 107, 181, 254
Jay, Michelle, 74, 241, 244, 256
Jesuit Refugee Service, 23
Jesus Christ, 220, 272; exemplifies solidarity, 247, 248, 253, 258; presence of, xv-xvi, 191; on poverty, 211; and suffering, 195, 231
joy, 57, 143-44, 210, 274
Juan Pedro, Eligio, 96
Julio (mayor of Cerro Alto), 144
Just Us!, 169-70

justice, 109, 125; and Christianity, 242; commitment to, 120, 134, 138, 164, 244, 247, 254; economic, 269, 280-85; and empowerment, 213-14; establishment of, 1, 42, 96; importance of, 230, 274; responsibility for, 252; struggle for, 92-93, 113-14, 253, 261; system of, 275-76. *See also* injustice
Juvenal, Bishop, 38

Kairos, 116, 118
Kamloops United Church, xi-xii, 121
Kaqchikel Presbytery, 2, 137, 140, 145, 182, 234; accompaniment in, 139-40, 202; fair trade with, xix, 132, 168-69; links with Tatamagouche Centre, 131, 132-34, 141-42, 147-48, 250; women's groups of, 132, 136, 147-48, 168
Kell, Carol, 217, 281
Kelly, Deirdre, 117, 123, 129; accompaniment by, 163, 231, 285-86; on Bible, 231; on ecumenism, 243, 253, 254-55; on mission, 248, 256
Kennedy, Charlie, 226
Kerans, Lyn, 164, 256
Kewell, Karen, 48
Kin Lalat, xviii, 122-23, 125, 131, 189, 191
Klatsky, Bruce, 282
Kohan, Randy, 52, 59, 69, 74, 75-77, 78, 84, 87
Koleszar, Hedy, 133

La Providencia, 94
Labelle, Gaby, 52, 118, 204, 210, 217, 220, 237
Labor de Falla (Guatemala), 142, 145, 147, 148-49, 182-83
labour, 10
Labour Council, 160-61, 176
LaEsmeralda, 236
Lancaster, Gerry, 222, 243
land: distribution of, 10-11, 13, 27, 90, 113, 141, 143; refugee purchase of, 33, 71, 75, 88-89, 93-94, 97-98, 165, 268; right to, 80, 143; seized by army, 31, 137
Land of the Maya (Gallant), 9, 192-94, 238-39

308 Index

Langara College (BC), 191
language, 46, 51, 70, 108, 123, 179
LaRue, Frank, 176, 177
Latin America, 113-18, 171, 206. *See also* specific countries
Latin America Working Group, 52, 117-18, 285
Latin American Conference of Bishops, 114
Latin American Human Rights Association, 113
Lauzon, Jean Claude, 73-74
Law Foundation of British Columbia, 129
Legal Services Society, 129
letter-writing campaigns, 46; and education, 165-66, 182-83; as evidence of concern, 77, 95, 167, 271-72; and policy change, 116, 164, 171-74, 265, 283-84; requests for, 42, 69; and security, 61, 186
Lewis, Mike, 123, 124, 156, 168, 244
Levo, Caece, 45
Lima, José Herran, 79
Liz Claiborne, 283
Loo, Gerritt, 136
Loo, Judy, 136, 214, 218, 224, 234-35, 270-71, 282
Loo, Margie, 29, 86-87, 214-15, 242
López Sánchez, Mario Alioto, 181
Los Angeles (Guatemala), 195
Loucks, Pat, 146, 162, 237, 239-40
love, 249, 258
Lovell, George, 10
Lutheran Church, 118, 180
Lutheran World Federation, 32
Lydon, John, 90

MacDonald, Flora, 171
MacDonald, Frank, 145
MacDonald, Jeanie, 243
MacEachen, Allan, 172
Mack, Myrna, 29, 140, 163-64
MacKenzie, Tamara, 214
Mama Maquín, 78, 109, 110
Manitoba Chiefs, 273
Manly, Eva, 86, 99, 217; accompaniment by, 85, 93, 139, 202, 205, 233; on accompaniment, 50-51, 106, 178-79, 207, 213; on church involvement, 242
Manly, Jim, 139, 202, 213, 218, 236, 242, 245, 254, 258

Mansour, Valerie, 44, 45-46, 64-65, 133, 136-37
Manz, Beatriz, 14-15
Maquila Solidarity Network (MSN), 284
maquilas, 148, 154, 158, 167, 180, 186, 216, 217, 255, 264, 280-84
Maritimes-Guatemala Breaking the Silence Network (BTN), 2, 79, 157, 186, 221-22, 276, 279; delegations by, 9, 136-37, 148-49, 159, 162, 191-92, 239, 274, 281; and fair trade, 169; mission of, xix, 131, 134-36, 141-42, 148-49, 153-54, 204, 250, 255-56, 280; structure of, 131, 179-81
"Marta" (Loucks), 146
Martin, Paul, 170
Martínez, Lucio, 132, 134, 139, 202, 236
Martínez, Raúl, 91
massacres, xiv, 14-17, 21, 77, 89, 223; in Xamán, 91-93, 139, 140, 181, 276
Mateo (accompanied Guatemalan), 205
Maultsaid, Wes, 123, 124; journals of, xi-xii, 42-45; on organizations, 118-19, 210, 244, 245-46, 255; refugee camp experience of, xiv-xvi, 18, 22, 39, 121-22, 182; on solidarity, 189, 206
Maya-Achi Widows' Organization, 277-78
Maya Biosphere, 95
Maya Centre for Research and Documentation, 237
Maya people, 145; culture of, 10, 28, 31, 70, 95, 203, 233-34, 236; genocide of, xi, xiv, xvii, 14-17, 223-24; persecution of, 191919192, 215; repression of, 9, 97-98, 236; rights of, 134; spirituality of, 138, 229-40. *See also* campesinos; refugees
Mayalán, 83, 85-87
Mazatenango, 93
McCullum, Hugh, xi, 15, 17, 18, 122, 230
McDougall, Barbara, 61, 74
McGuigan, Mark, 18, 171
media: coverage in, 46, 49, 58-59, 67, 80, 137, 174, 194, 272-73; and

Index

influence of publicity, 41-42, 176-77, 201, 275; silence in, xi, xvii, 120, 155-56, 165
Mediating Commission, 31-32, 41, 60, 74, 95
Medina, Tito, 189, 191, 199
Melgar, Mynor, 279
Meloche, François, 86
Menchú, Rigoberta, 12, 137; arrest of, 175-76, 230; human rights lawsuit by, 13, 93, 265, 276; refugee solidarity by, 53, 58-59, 61
Menchú, Vicente, 12-13
Méndez, Wendy, 186-87, 274
Mending the World: An Ecumenical Vision for Healing and Reconciliation (United Church report), 253
Mennonites, 254
Merton, Thomas, 226
Mexican Commission to Aid Refugees, 23
Mexican Refugee Commission (COMAR), 105
Mexico, 88, 122; delegations to, 136, 137-38, 157; as refugee destination, xvii, 21-22; treatment of refugees in, 24, 28, 31, 38, 52, 88, 89
Mexico City, 118
military: control by, 25-27, 30, 32, 59, 75, 76, 101, 141, 159-60, 171, 173-74, 261, 266, 268-70; destruction by, xii, xvii, 63, 80; disappearances by, xviii, 54, 186, 270; intimidation by, 63, 72, 75-76, 80-81, 177, 273, 285; and lawlessness, 90-93, 95, 138-39, 164, 269, 270-71; presence of, 67, 74, 81-83, 89-90, 96, 98; propaganda by, 60, 72, 97; relocation of, 78-79, 81, 85-87, 137; spies for, 75, 142; status of, 11; surveillance by, 61; torture by, xii, xvii, 12-13, 90. *See also* assassinations; impunity
Minna, Maria, 278-79
Miriam (Guatemalan activist), 143-44
mission, 1-2, 241, 246-48, 250-53, 255-59
missionaries, 11
model villages, 25-26, 160
Moffat, Jeanne, 171, 217
Moisés, 236

Molina, Rául, 177
Molloy, Phil, 125
Monimbo Crafts, 122, 168
Monroy, Henry, 270, 274
Moore, Jeff, 170
Morris, Mary Ann, 54, 57, 68-69, 93, 107, 123
Moscoso, Ortiz, 76
Mujer Vamos Adelante, 263-64
music, 10, 23, 57, 66, 78, 189, 192-93, 272-73
"Mutations" (Rees), 15-16
Mutch, Ernest, 133, 135-36
Myrna Mack Foundation, 140, 164

Nadeau, Denise, 114, 225, 226-27, 241, 258-59
National Council of Guatemalan Widows (CONAVIGUA), 77, 134
National Dialogue of Reconciliation, 30-31
National Electoral Tribunal, 145
National Film Board, 182
National Plan for Security and Development, 25
Needham Congregational Church (MA), 251-53
Nentón, 90, 98
neo-liberalism, 1, 115, 222, 225, 285
Network News, 156, 173
New Democratic Party, 155
Nicaragua, xvii, 14, 117, 131, 141, 219, 220; delegations to, 119-20, 123, 157
Niesh, Kevin, 117, 176-78
Niesh, Scotty, 117, 120
non-governmental organizations (NGOs), 45, 52, 173; communication with, 42-43, 69, 104; funding by, 23, 40, 46-48, 78, 163, 210; projects by, 135, 142-43, 283
North, Liisa, 285
North American Free Trade Agreement, 182
Nova Scotia Teachers' Union, 182
Nueva Esperanza, 89-90
Nueva Unión Maya, 96
Nunca Mas, 142, 230, 253, 270

October 8 Accords. *See* Peace Accords
Ombudsman for Human Rights, 31
"On the March!" (Esquivel), 232

"One Afternoon in Nueva Union" (Rees), 220-21
O'Neill, Sister Noel, 14
Operation Lovelift, 18
O'Toole, Sandra, 167
O'Toole, Terry, 67, 74, 137, 218, 222, 233, 242
Otzoy, Antonio, 138, 140, 161, 207, 222, 234-35
Oxfam, xix, 42, 48, 84, 131-32, 134, 162, 180, 192, 263-64

pacifism, 4, 110
"Para ti (For you)" (Rees), 249
paternalism, 226, 252, 258
Payne, John, 46, 60; accompaniment by, 57, 59, 61, 69, 215; on accompaniment, 72, 105, 107-108, 254
peace, 1, 42, 61, 261, 269
Peace Accords, 24; and solidarity work, 141, 267, 269; implementation of, 219, 261-62, 265, 268-69, 271, 278; ratification of, 75, 171; results of, 30, 90, 102, 175; signing of, 1, 29, 51, 91, 109, 265; violation of, 68
Peace Brigades International (PBI), 31, 47, 49, 50, 61, 102
Pellerine, Ann, 125, 163, 246, 247
Permanent Commissions of the Guatemalan Refugees (CCPP), 95; communication with, 51, 69, 74; confronts military, 60, 62; requests accompaniment, 47, 49, 99, 104-106, 110; and returns, 30-32, 42, 53-55, 78-79, 94, 109
Petén, 12, 21, 94-96, 236
Philips-Van Heusen, 281-82
Pico, Juan, 248, 253
Pinochet, Augusto, 115
Playa Grande, 84, 87, 90
poetry, vii-viii, xviii, 122, 189-91, 194-96
Poligono 14. *See* Victoria 20 de enero
Popul Vuh, 237
Portillo, Alfonso, 145, 187, 261, 265, 266, 268, 276, 278
poverty, 37-38; and awareness, 221; biblical concern with, 114, 120, 247; extent of, 136, 200-201; fight against, 12, 61, 143, 220; life despite, 143-44, 182; origins of, 10-11, 113-14, 115, 118, 242-43, 280; and sharing, 212; and solidarity, 199, 207, 218, 226-27, 241, 247, 257, 258-59; and spiritual renewal, 210-12, 213-14
Presbyterian Church, 118, 132, 133, 182, 250
Project Accompaniment Canada-Guatemala (Project A), xix, 2, 37, 96, 110, 175, 219; agenda of, 41, 204, 205; communication with, 78-79; Embassy support for, 59-60, 84, 166, 279; end of, 101, 142, 268; foundation of, 39, 40, 46, 104, 113, 122, 123, 136, 161, 180, 267; and ongoing accompaniment, 66; productions by, 57; reports of, 43; role of, 74, 85, 109-11; and spirituality, 254, 255; Steering Committee, 52, 101, 103; structure of, 47, 48-49, 52, 84, 118, 131, 136-37, 255; success of, 72-73
Project Counseling Services, 46
Pueblo Nuevo, 80-81, 83

Quetzal I, 98
Quetzal IV, 98
Quetzal Edna, 24, 46
Quetzaltenango, 60, 93, 134, 135
Quiché, 57, 159, 189, 230
Quiché, Diocese of, 62, 70, 201
Quintana Roo, 24, 54

racism, 15
Reagan, Ronald, 17, 24, 171, 172
Recovery of Historical Memory Project (REMHI), xiv, 140, 142, 261, 278
Reid, Erin, 91
Reid, Larry, 83
Rees, Liz, 15-16, 207-208, 220-21, 249
refugee camps; conditions in, xi, xiv, 24-25, 88; delegations to, 28-29, 39-40, 45-46, 120, 122, 137-38, 173, 204, 285-86; in Mexico, 22, 24, 94; organization in, 23, 45-46; stays at, 51, 52, 74
refugees, 38-39, 128, 223; accused of links to guerrillas, xii, 14, 55, 60, 63, 67, 72, 74, 75, 80-81, 83, 160; in Canada, xviii, 121, 128; and culture, 57, 189, 191;

determination of, 53-54, 57, 78, 137-38, 157; health problems of, 21, 24; individuality of, xi, xiv, xvii, 54, 117, 160, 202; internal, 18, 27, 29, 102-103, 139-40, 159-60, 163, 168; legal identities of, 59, 71, 73, 75; to Mexico, 21-22, 168; organization of, 22-24, 28-29, 52, 77-78; political status of, 18, 22, 31, 37-38, 45; repatriation of, 23, 24, 25, 27-29, 31, 47, 59; rights of, 21, 38; Salvadoran, 40-41, 49, 123; sponsorship of, 115, 121; tours by, 48, 136, 148, 160-61, 210. *See also* Returns

"REMHI" (Walsh), 140-41

resistance, 4, 13-14, 75, 109, 135. *See also* Communities of Population in Resistance

Retail Council of Canada, 284

Retalhuleu, 93

Returns, 2, 23–25; accompaniment with, 29-30, 33, 37-38, 40, 42-44, 48, 67, 136-37; conditions of, 28-30, 32, 37, 40, 53; dangers of, 32-33, 91-92; and demilitarization, 78, 81-82, 85-87; Embassy support for, 59-60; end of, 101; health conditions during, 62, 64; military opposition to, 80-88, 89, 90-96; negotiations for, 30-33, 47, 53-55, 78, 94-95; reality of, 51-54, 57, 79-80, 104-105; and rebuilding, 63-66, 82, 107-108; reception during, 57-61, 62-63, 78, 79, 90, 95; and security, 60, 88

Reuther, Rosemary Radford, 195

Reyes, Rafael, 273

Ridd, Karen, 49

Riggs, Evelyn, 162

rights: to accompaniment, 30, 33; children's, 164; civil, 17, 51; indigenous, 138, 143, 223–24; property, 109; of refugees, 38; to return, 21, 29-30, 109. *See also* human rights

Rigoberta Menchú Tum Foundation, 92-93

Rió Negro, 280

Ríos Montt, Efráin, 17, 171, 187, 261, 264, 265, 266, 270, 276

River John School (NS), 148-49, 182-83

Roberts, Lisa, 101, 103

Robertson, Don, 121

Robertson, Pat, 17

Robertson, Sandy, 121, 157

Robinson, Svend, 61

role-playing, 50-51, 155

Roman Catholic Church. *See* Catholic Church

Romero, Archbishop Oscar, 117, 123, 155, 181, 226, 253

Rother, Stanley, 181

Rowat, Colin, 65, 70, 72, 81, 84, 105, 106

Rubin, Lillian, 3

Ruiz, Bishop Samuel, 37-38, 117

Rumscheidt, Barbara, 244

Rumsey, Susanne, 274

Russell, Grahame, 91

Salinas, 208

Sams, Samantha, 261-62

San Antonio Tzejá, 90-91

San Cristóbal de las Casas, Diocese of, 21, 37-38

San Francisco (Guatemala), 89

San Jorge, 208

San Juan Ixcán, 91

San Marcos, 73, 93

Sandanistas, 14, 123, 141

Santa Clara, 63

Santa Cruz del Quiché, 239

Santa Elena, 94

Santa María Tzejá, 12, 18, 90, 251-53

Santa Marta, 208

Santiago Atitlán, 181

Santo Thomás Catholic church, 239

Saquic, Manuel, 132, 138-40, 202, 236

Saquic, María, 139-40

School of the Americas (GA), 15, 93, 181, 184

Scurr, Tara, 166, 167, 168, 169, 174-75, 185, 191, 225-26, 254

Sears Canada, 284

Sellers, Susan, 133, 148, 182-83

Serech, José, 237

Serech, Pascual, 132, 138

Serrano, Jorge, 18, 61, 73-75, 137

Sevigny, Louise, 76, 139

Shalom, 247, 253, 255

Shankar, Finola, 276-78

Shaw, Paula, 102, 107, 108, 220

Sierra Madres, 159

Similox, Vitalino, 132, 219-20, 247, 248
Simmons, Alan, 285
Simpson, Mike, 57
Skaret, Susan, 47, 52, 59, 69, 74, 78, 84, 87, 108, 139
Smith, Bob, 154-55, 173, 217, 253; accompaniments by, 159-60, 175, 208, 230; on faith, 218, 230-31, 244-45; on solidarity, 179, 246
Smith, Merran, 57
Sobrino, Jon, 216, 243; on churches, 253, 257; on poor, 211, 214, 218, 221; on solidarity, 206, 201
social activism, xvii-xix. *See also* accompaniment; solidarity
social justice, 132, 157–58, 178, 184, 214, 241, 245
Social Justice Committee, 48, 162, 165, 173
social literacy, 215-16
solidarity movement, xviii-xix, 131; and analysis, 217, 251; conflict in, 4, 140; and children, 181-82; and church groups, 114, 118-19, 155, 254, 257; and collaboration, 179-81; and community, 243-46; development of, 118, 132, 155-56; and education, 117, 120, 122, 124, 129, 133-35, 153, 168-69, 204, 211; and fair trade, xix, 168-170; and faith, 229-30, 241; leadership for, 153; and meaning, 199-200, 201, 205-206, 208-209, 211, 214, 248; and music, 189, 193; and mutuality, 138, 140, 142, 143, 147-49, 158, 182-83, 199, 200, 201-204, 206-207, 209-213, 224-25, 237, 247, 250-53, 257-59, 285-86; recruitment to, 117, 123, 153-56, 158, 183-84, 189; and refugees, 38-39, 42-44, 47; and relationships, 102-103, 113, 123-26, 131, 155-56, 166, 202-206, 210-11, 219-20, 248-49, 256, 274; results of, 214, 218-19, 275; role played by, 48, 84-85, 128, 178; and shared responsibility, 225-26, 254; and spirituality, 199-201, 202-203, 211, 218, 226-27, 237, 243; and suffering, 207, 211-12; and trade unions, 117, 120, 154, 158-59, 176-78, 219, 255, 281-82; within Canada, 221-25
Sosa, Mercedes, 272
South Coast, 33, 93-94, 97
Spain, 13, 57, 117, 265, 276
Special Commission for Attention to Repatriates (CEAR), 28-29, 75, 76, 95, 89; accusations by, 60, 83-84; renegations by, 53-54, 59-60, 63
Special Joint Parliamentary Committee on Canada's International Relations Report, 172
Spirit, 200, 245
spirituality, 1; definitions of, 200, 203, 229; Maya, 229-40; and politics, 241, 242; and solidarity, 199-201, 202-203, 211-14, 218, 226-27, 237, 243; source of, 213
Spragge, Godfrey, 97
Starbucks, 283
State University Student Association (Guatemala), 185
Steelworkers Union, 125
Suchitépequez, 94
sueltos, 105
"Summer Justice-Making Institutes," 121-23, 246
Summit of the Americas, 278
Sumpango, 239-40
Support Committee for the People of Guatemala, xviii, 173
Swan, Andrew
sweatshops. *See maquilas*
Sweden, 160
Swedish Diakonia, 48

Tapachula, Diocese of, 38
Task Group on Child Apprehensions, 129
Tatamagouche Centre (NS), xix, 131-32, 134, 147-49, 157-58, 168, 180, 188, 224
Taylor, Clark, 251
Teardrop Crafts, 168
Teatro Vivo, xviii, 122-23, 189, 191
Ten Days for Global Justice. *See* Ten Days for World Development
Ten Days for World Development, 118-19, 121, 124, 131, 169, 171-72, 180
testimonies, xi-xii, xiv, 16-17, 45, 154

Index

"Threatened with Resurrection" (Esquivel), 287
Threatened with Resurrection: Prayers and Poems from an Exiled Guatemalan (Esquivel), 194, 196
Tikal, 94, 95, 236
"Todo Cambia" (Sosa), 272-73
Todos Santos, 75–76
Tools for Peace, 119, 180
Torres, Enrique, xviii, 40, 119, 121, 124, 206-207, 254, 258
torture, xii-xiv, 263
Trade Union Solidarity Group, 177, 180
truth, 261, 270, 273
Truth Commission, 271, 275
Turcotte, Robert, 57

Union of Needletrade, Industrial and Textile Employees (UNITE), 281-82
Union Maya Itzá Coooperative, 95
United Church of Canada, 5, 231, 254; funding by, 1, 42, 66, 134, 139, 180; links with other organizations of, 66, 118, 131, 180; meetings of, 137, 148; organizations of, xvii, xix, 132; reports of, 253, 257-58; resolutions by, 173; support by, 256
United Church Observer, xi, 230
United Fisherman and Allied Workers' Union, 117, 120
United Fruit Company, 11
United Nations Commission on Human Rights, 116, 164, 172, 175
United Nations Commission on Refugees (UNHCR), 22, 60, 105; communication with, 69, 74, 75-76; negotiations by, 30-31, 53-54, 78, 85; support from, 23, 62, 63, 67, 90, 95
United Nations Verification Mission (MINUGUA), 88, 165, 265, 268, 278
United Representation of the Guatemalan Opposition (RUOG), 175-76, 178, 179
United States, 51, 57, 207; aid by, 250-53; military intervention by, 11, 17-18; military training by, 15, 17; policy of, 251, 252; political intervention by, 24, 114-15, 119-20, 123, 155, 171

United States Religious Task Force on Central America, 155
Urgent Action Network (UAN), 127, 267; activation of, 78, 92; and awareness, 48, 83, 277; and education, 165-66; importance of, 42, 163-65; involvement in, 49, 125, 137, 149, 160, 161, 180, 184, 268; and policy change, 164; requests by, 57, 77, 156, 161-62, 167, 264-65; responses to, 166-68; results of, 176; and security, 61, 279; structure of, xix, 162-63, 165

VanCity Credit Union, 129
Vancouver Folk Festival, 123
Valiente, Margarita, 136, 139, 216, 248; delegations with, 134, 137, 142, 145, 147; ministry by, 132, 133
Vatican II, 114, 117
Velásquez, Omar, 273
Veracruz, 78-81, 83, 84, 85, 87, 205
Verapaces, Diocese of, 62
Very Brief Testimonial Account of the Continued Destruction of Guatemala (Montejo and Akab'), 9-10
Víctores, Mejía, 25, 270
Victoria, Diocese of, 231
Victoria 20 de enero, 62-73, 74, 77-78, 93, 107, 109
Victoria Central America Support Committee, 177
Vigil, Jose-María, 200, 247
vigils, xviii, 170, 261
Vilma (Guatemalan delegate), 148, 183
violence, xii-xiv, 9-10, 13–14, 51; comprehension of, xiv, 39; non-, 49-51, 106, 123, 181
Vision TV, 57
voices, 2-3, 32

Wal-Mart, 284
Walsh, Diane, 140–41, 167, 218, 222
water, 67, 143, 144–45, 222
wealth, 10–11, 141, 207, 216
Webster, Campbell, 133, 135
Webster Family Foundation, 135
Weisbart, Caren, 170
West Vancouver United Church, 57
Western Hemisphere Institute for Security Cooperation. *See* School of the Americas

When the People Lead, 57
Where There Is No Doctor (Werner, Thuman, Maxwell), xiv
White, Marian, 133
White, Ross, 237
"Who Killed the Bishop?" (Loo), 270-71
Williams, Paul, 98
Winnipeg Free Press, 272
Witness for Justice and Peace, 123
Witness for Peace, 47, 50, 123
women: and economic support, 132, 149, 168-69, 204-205, 274, 281; equality of, 233; ordination of, 133; organizations for, 23, 136, 139, 142, 147-49, 263-64, 277-78; on relationships, 220, 226, 277; and rights, 134, 143, 225; suffering of, 156-57, 223-24; violence against, 223, 263-64
Women in Solidarity (AMES), 264
Wood, Barbara, 39
Woodhall, Carole, 149
Woods, William, 12, 13
World Bank, 280
World Council of Churches, 32; Assembly, xvii, 122-23, 189-91
Wounds of Manuel Saquic, The (Manly), 139, 236
Wright, Ronald, 10
Wringe, Tony, 74
Wytenbroek, Lynn, 210-211

Xalbal, 86
Xamán, 91-93, 139, 140, 181, 276

Yolanda (refugee delegate), 137
youth, 183-88; and arts, 191, 274; interns, 149, 188; involvement of
Yucatan Peninsula (Mexico), 24-25

Zapatista, 88
Zarowny, Yvonne, 221
Zona Reyna, 90

6. *The Rhetoric of the Babylonian Talmud, Its Social Meaning and Context*
   Jack N. Lightstone / 1994 / xiv + 317 pp.
7. *Whose Historical Jesus?*
   Edited by William E. Arnal and Michel Desjardins / 1997 / vi + 337 pp.
8. *Religious Rivalries and the Struggle for Success in Caesarea Maritima*
   Edited by Terence L. Donaldson / 2000 / xiv + 402 pp.
9. *Text and Artifact in the Religions of Mediterranean Antiquity*
   Edited by Stephen G. Wilson and Michel Desjardins / 2000 / xvi + 616 pp.
10. *Parables of War: Reading John's Jewish Apocalypse*
    by John W. Marshall / 2001 / viii + 262 pp.
11. *Mishnah and the Social Formation of the Early Rabbinic Guild:
    A Socio-Rhetorical Approach*
    by Jack N. Lightstone / 2002 / xii + 240 pp.
12. *The Social Setting of the Ministry as Reflected in the Writings of Hermas,
    Clement and Ignatius*
    Harry O. Maier / 1991, second impression 2002 / x + 234 pp.

The Study of Religion in Canada / Sciences Religieuses au Canada

1. *Religious Studies in Alberta: A State-of-the-Art Review*
   Ronald W. Neufeldt / 1983 / xiv + 145 pp.
2. *Les sciences religieuses au Québec depuis 1972*
   Louis Rousseau et Michel Despland / 1988 / 158 p.
3. *Religious Studies in Ontario: A State-of-the-Art Review*
   Harold Remus, William Closson James and Daniel Fraikin / 1992 / xviii + 422 pp.
4. *Religious Studies in Manitoba and Saskatchewan: A State-of-the-Art Review*
   John M. Badertscher, Gordon Harland and Roland E. Miller / 1993 / vi + 166 pp.
5. *The Study of Religion in British Columbia: A State-of-the-Art Review*
   Brian J. Fraser / 1995 / x + 127 pp.
6. *Religious Studies in Atlantic Canada: A State-of-the-Art Review*
   Paul W. R. Bowlby with Tom Faulkner / 2001 / xii + 208 pp.

Studies in Women and Religion / Études sur les femmes et la religion

1. *Femmes et religions**
   Sous la direction de Denise Veillette / 1995 / xviii + 466 p.
2. *The Work of Their Hands: Mennonite Women's Societies in Canada*
   Gloria Neufeld Redekop / 1996 / xvi + 172 pp.
3. *Profiles of Anabaptist Women: Sixteenth-Century Reforming Pioneers*
   Edited by C. Arnold Snyder and Linda A. Huebert Hecht / 1996 / xxii + 438 pp.
4. *Voices and Echoes: Canadian Women's Spirituality*
   Edited by Jo-Anne Elder and Colin O'Connell / 1997 / xxviii + 237 pp.
5. *Obedience, Suspicion and the Gospel of Mark: A Mennonite-Feminist Exploration
   of Biblical Authority*
   Lydia Neufeld Harder / 1998 / xiv + 168 pp.
6. *Clothed in Integrity: Weaving Just Cultural Relations and the Garment Industry*
   Barbara Paleczny / 2000 / xxxiv + 352 pp.
7. *Women in God's Army: Gender and Equality in the Early Salvation Army*
   Andrew Mark Eason / 2003 / xiv + 246 pp.
8. *Pour libérer la théologie.* Variations autour de la pensée féministe d'Ivone
   Gebara Pierrette Daviau, dir. / 2002 / 212 pp.
9. *Linking Sexuality and Gender: Naming Violence against Women in The United
   Church of Canada*
   Tracy J. Trothen / 2003 / x + 166 pp.

*Only available from Les Presses de l'Université Laval

SR Supplements

1. *Footnotes to a Theology: The Karl Barth Colloquium of 1972*
   Edited and Introduced by Martin Rumscheidt / 1974 / viii + 151 pp. / OUT OF PRINT
2. *Martin Heidegger's Philosophy of Religion*
   John R. Williams / 1977 / x + 190 pp. / OUT OF PRINT
3. *Mystics and Scholars: The Calgary Conference on Mysticism 1976*
   Edited by Harold Coward and Terence Penelhum / 1977 / viii + 121 pp. / OUT OF PRINT
4. *God's Intention for Man: Essays in Christian Anthropology*
   William O. Fennell / 1977 / xii + 56 pp. / OUT OF PRINT
5. *"Language" in Indian Philosophy and Religion*
   Edited and Introduced by Harold G. Coward / 1978 / x + 98 pp. / OUT OF PRINT
6. *Beyond Mysticism*
   James R. Horne / 1978 / vi + 158 pp. / OUT OF PRINT
7. *The Religious Dimension of Socrates' Thought*
   James Beckman / 1979 / xii + 276 pp. / OUT OF PRINT
8. *Native Religious Traditions*
   Edited by Earle H. Waugh and K. Dad Prithipaul / 1979 / xii + 244 pp. / OUT OF PRINT
9. *Developments in Buddhist Thought: Canadian Contributions to Buddhist Studies*
   Edited by Roy C. Amore / 1979 / iv + 196 pp.
10. *The Bodhisattva Doctrine in Buddhism*
    Edited and Introduced by Leslie S. Kawamura / 1981 / xxii + 274 pp. / OUT OF PRINT
11. *Political Theology in the Canadian Context*
    Edited by Benjamin G. Smillie / 1982 / xii + 260 pp.
12. *Truth and Compassion: Essays on Judaism and Religion in Memory of Rabbi Dr. Solomon Frank*
    Edited by Howard Joseph, Jack N. Lightstone and Michael D. Oppenheim / 1983 / vi + 217 pp. / OUT OF PRINT
13. *Craving and Salvation: A Study in Buddhist Soteriology*
    Bruce Matthews / 1983 / xiv + 138 pp. / OUT OF PRINT
14. *The Moral Mystic*
    James R. Horne / 1983 / x + 134 pp.
15. *Ignatian Spirituality in a Secular Age*
    Edited by George P. Schner / 1984 / viii + 128 pp. / OUT OF PRINT
16. *Studies in the Book of Job*
    Edited by Walter E. Aufrecht / 1985 / xii + 76 pp.
17. *Christ and Modernity: Christian Self-Understanding in a Technological Age*
    David J. Hawkin / 1985 / x + 181 pp.
18. *Young Man Shinran: A Reappraisal of Shinran's Life*
    Takamichi Takahatake / 1987 / xvi + 228 pp. / OUT OF PRINT
19. *Modernity and Religion*
    Edited by William Nicholls / 1987 / vi + 191 pp.
20. *The Social Uplifters: Presbyterian Progressives and the Social Gospel in Canada, 1875-1915*
    Brian J. Fraser / 1988 / xvi + 212 pp. / OUT OF PRINT

Series discontinued

Available from:

Wilfrid Laurier University Press

Waterloo, Ontario, Canada N2L 3C5
Telephone: (519) 884-0710, ext. 6124
Fax: (519) 725-1399
E-mail: press@wlu.ca
World Wide Web: http://www.wlupress.wlu.ca

21. *The Call of Conscience: French Protestant Responses to the Algerian War, 1954-1962*
    Geoffrey Adams / 1998 / xxii + 270 pp.
22. *Clinical Pastoral Supervision and the Theology of Charles Gerkin*
    Thomas St. James O'Connor / 1998 / x + 152 pp.
23. *Faith and Fiction: A Theological Critique of the Narrative Strategies of Hugh MacLennan and Morley Callaghan*
    Barbara Pell / 1998 / v + 141 pp.
24. *God and the Chip: Religion and the Culture of Technology*
    William A. Stahl / 1999 / vi + 186 pp.
25. *The Religious Dreamworld of Apuleius' Metamorphoses: Recovering a Forgotten Hermeneutic*
    James Gollnick / 1999 / xiv + 178 pp.
26. *Edward Schillebeeckx and Hans Frei: A Conversation on Method and Christology*
    Marguerite Abdul-Masih / 2001 / vi + 194 pp.
27. *Radical Difference: A Defence of Hendrik Kraemer's Theology of Religions*
    Tim S. Perry / 2001 / x + 170 pp.
28. *Hindu Iconoclasts: Rammohun Roy, Dayananda Sarasvati and Nineteenth-Century Polemics against Idolatry*
    Noel Salmond / 2003 / x + 182 pp.

Comparative Ethics Series / Collection d'Éthique Comparée

1. *Muslim Ethics and Modernity: A Comparative Study of the Ethical Thought of Sayyid Ahmad Khan and Mawlana Mawdudi*
   Sheila McDonough / 1984 / x + 130 pp. / OUT OF PRINT
2. *Methodist Education in Peru: Social Gospel, Politics, and American Ideological and Economic Penetration, 1888-1930*
   Rosa del Carmen Bruno-Jofré / 1988 / xiv + 223 pp.
3. *Prophets, Pastors and Public Choices: Canadian Churches and the Mackenzie Valley Pipeline Debate*
   Roger Hutchinson / 1992 / xiv + 142 pp. / OUT OF PRINT
4. *In Good Faith: Canadian Churches Against Apartheid*
   Renate Pratt / 1997 / xii + 366 pp.
5. *Towards an Ethics of Community: Negotiations of Difference in a Pluralist Society*
   James H. Olthuis, editor / 2000 / x + 230 pp.
6. *Doing Ethics in a Pluralistic World: Essays in Honour of Roger C. Hutchinson*
   Phyllis J. Airhart, Marilyn J. Legge and Gary L. Redcliffe, editors / 2002 / viii + 264 pp.
7. *Weaving Relationships: Canada-Guatamala Solidarity*
   Kathryn Anderson / 2003 / xxii + 322 pp.

Studies in Christianity and Judaism / Études sur le christianisme et le judaïsme

1. *A Study in Anti-Gnostic Polemics: Irenaeus, Hippolytus, and Epiphanius*
   Gérard Vallée / 1981 / xii + 114 pp. / OUT OF PRINT
2. *Anti-Judaism in Early Christianity Vol. 1, Paul and the Gospels*
   Edited by Peter Richardson with David Granskou / 1986 / x + 232 pp.
   Vol. 2, *Separation and Polemic*
   Edited by Stephen G. Wilson / 1986 / xii + 185 pp.
3. *Society, the Sacred, and Scripture in Ancient Judaism: A Sociology of Knowledge*
   Jack N. Lightstone / 1988 / xiv + 126 pp.
4. *Law in Religious Communities in the Roman Period: The Debate Over* Torah *and* Nomos *in Post-Biblical Judaism and Early Christianity*
   Peter Richardson and Stephen Westerholm with A. I. Baumgarten, Michael Pettem and Cecilia Wassén / 1991 / x + 164 pp.
5. *Dangerous Food: 1 Corinthians 8-10 in Its Context*
   Peter D. Gooch / 1993 / xviii + 178 pp.

Series Published by Wilfrid Laurier University Press for the Canadian Corporation for Studies in Religion / Corporation Canadienne des Sciences Religieuses

Editions SR

1. *La langue de Ya'udi : description et classement de l'ancien parler de Zencircli dans le cadre des langues sémitiques du nord-ouest*
   Paul-Eugène Dion, O.P. / 1974 / viii + 511 p. / OUT OF PRINT
2. *The Conception of Punishment in Early Indian Literature*
   Terence P. Day / 1982 / iv + 328 pp.
3. *Traditions in Contact and Change: Selected Proceedings of the XIVth Congress of the International Association for the History of Religions*
   Edited by Peter Slater and Donald Wiebe with Maurice Boutin and Harold Coward / 1983 / x + 758 pp. / OUT OF PRINT
4. *Le messianisme de Louis Riel*
   Gilles Martel / 1984 / xviii + 483 p.
5. *Mythologies and Philosophies of Salvation in the Theistic Traditions of India*
   Klaus K. Klostermaier / 1984 / xvi + 549 pp. / OUT OF PRINT
6. *Averroes' Doctrine of Immortality: A Matter of Controversy*
   Ovey N. Mohammed / 1984 / vi + 202 pp. / OUT OF PRINT
7. *L'étude des religions dans les écoles : l'expérience américaine, anglaise et canadienne*
   Fernand Ouellet / 1985 / xvi + 666 p.
8. *Of God and Maxim Guns: Presbyterianism in Nigeria, 1846-1966*
   Geoffrey Johnston / 1988 / iv + 322 pp.
9. *A Victorian Missionary and Canadian Indian Policy: Cultural Synthesis vs Cultural Replacement*
   David A. Nock / 1988 / x + 194 pp. / OUT OF PRINT
10. *Prometheus Rebound: The Irony of Atheism*
    Joseph C. McLelland / 1988 / xvi + 366 pp.
11. *Competition in Religious Life*
    Jay Newman / 1989 / viii + 237 pp.
12. *The Huguenots and French Opinion, 1685-1787: The Enlightenment Debate on Toleration*
    Geoffrey Adams / 1991 / xiv + 335 pp.
13. *Religion in History: The Word, the Idea, the Reality / La religion dans l'histoire : le mot, l'idée, la réalité*
    Edited by/Sous la direction de Michel Despland and/et Gérard Vallée
    1992 / x + 252 pp.
14. *Sharing Without Reckoning: Imperfect Right and the Norms of Reciprocity*
    Millard Schumaker / 1992 / xiv + 112 pp.
15. *Love and the Soul: Psychological Interpretations of the Eros and Psyche Myth*
    James Gollnick / 1992 / viii + 174 pp.
16. *The Promise of Critical Theology: Essays in Honour of Charles Davis*
    Edited by Marc P. Lalonde / 1995 / xii + 146 pp.
17. *The Five Aggregates: Understanding Theravāda Psychology and Soteriology*
    Mathieu Boisvert / 1995 / xii + 166 pp.
18. *Mysticism and Vocation*
    James R. Horne / 1996 / vi + 110 pp.
19. *Memory and Hope: Strands of Canadian Baptist History*
    Edited by David T. Priestley / 1996 / viii + 211 pp.
20. *The Concept of Equity in Calvin's Ethics**
    Guenther H. Haas / 1997 / xii + 205 pp.

*Available in the United Kingdom and Europe from Paternoster Press.